THE BEST OF
ARCHIE COMICS
STARRING Betty & Veronica

THE BEST OF
ARCHIE COMICS

STARRING

Betty & Veronica

Published by Archie Comic Publications, Inc.
325 Fayette Avenue, Mamaroneck, New York 10543-2318.

ArchieComics.com

ISBN: 978-1-936975-88-4

Publisher / Co-CEO: Jon Goldwater
Co-CEO: Nancy Silberkleit
President: Mike Pellerito
Co-President / Editor-In-Chief: Victor Gorelick
Senior Vice President – Sales and Business Development: Jim Sokolowski
Senior Vice President – Publishing and Operations: Harold Buchholz
Senior Vice President – Publicity & Marketing: Alex Segura
Executive Director of Editorial: Paul Kaminski
Production Manager: Stephen Oswald
Project Coordinator & Book Design: Joe Morciglio
Archivist/Lead Researcher: Jack Copley
Lead Production Artist: Carlos Antunes
Editorial Assistant / Proofreader: Jamie Lee Rotante
Production: Jonathan Betancourt, Steve Golebiewski, Jon Gray, Duncan McLachlan, Steven Scott, Patrick Woodruff

Stories written by:

Frank Doyle, George Gladir, George Frese, Mike Pellowski, Rod Ollerenshaw, Bill Golliher, Paul Kupperberg, Dan Parent

Artwork by:

Bob Montana, Harry Sahle, Bill Vigoda, Bill Woggon, Irv Novick, George Frese, Dan DeCarlo, Bob Bolling, Samm Schwartz, Harry Lucey, Doug Crane, Jeff Shultz, Dan Parent, Pat Kennedy, Stan Goldberg, Dan DeCarlo Jr., Eleanor Woik, Janice Valleau (Ginger), Rudy Lapick, Alison Flood, Jimmy DeCarlo, Jim Amash, Jon D'Agostino, Joe Edwards, Rich Koslowski, Bob Smith, Al Milgrom, Al McLean, Terry Szenics, Bill Yoshida, Jack Morelli, Janice Chiang, Vince DeCarlo, Barry Grossman, Tom Chu, Sheldon Brodsky, Rosario "Tito" Peña, Digikore Studios

Welcome to *The Best of Archie Comics Starring Betty & Veronica*

This is it: the very first compilation of all-time favorite Betty & Veronica stories! Selected from seventy years of warm and witty tales by Archie editors, writers, artists, and fans, you'll find here a decade-by-decade guided tour of comics' most beloved best friends and rivals. We hope you'll enjoy experiencing the changes in Betty and Veronica's art styles, fashions, fads and themes through the years, and that you'll also get some entertaining insight, both from the people who love these characters dearly, as well as some of the wonderful artists and writers who have brought B&V to life. We've worked with the best available materials to reproduce these stories for you. In some cases that is from high-quality line art and color files. In other cases, because some of these classic hand-picked stories haven't seen print in years and the original art is no longer available, we've worked from scans of the original printed comics. As you read along, we hope you'll discover some new favorite stories of your own as we celebrate all things Betty & Veronica!

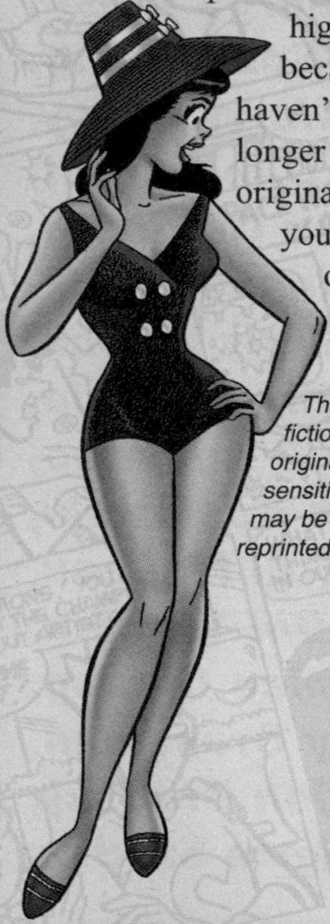

The stories, characters and incidents in this collection are entirely fictional. This book contains some material that was originally created in a less racially and socially sensitive time in our society and reflects attitudes that may be interpreted as offensive today. The stories are reprinted here without alteration for historical reference.

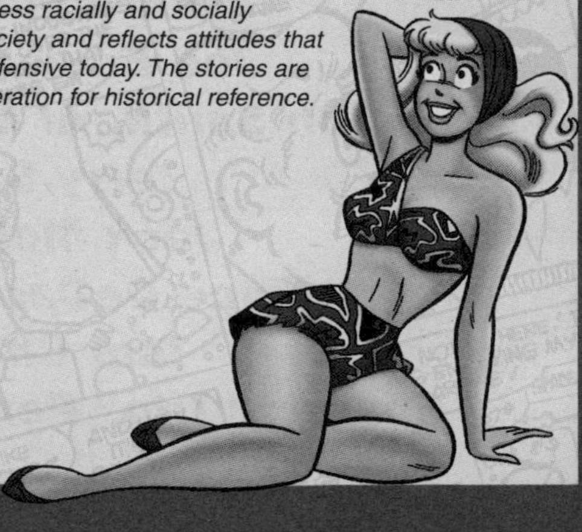

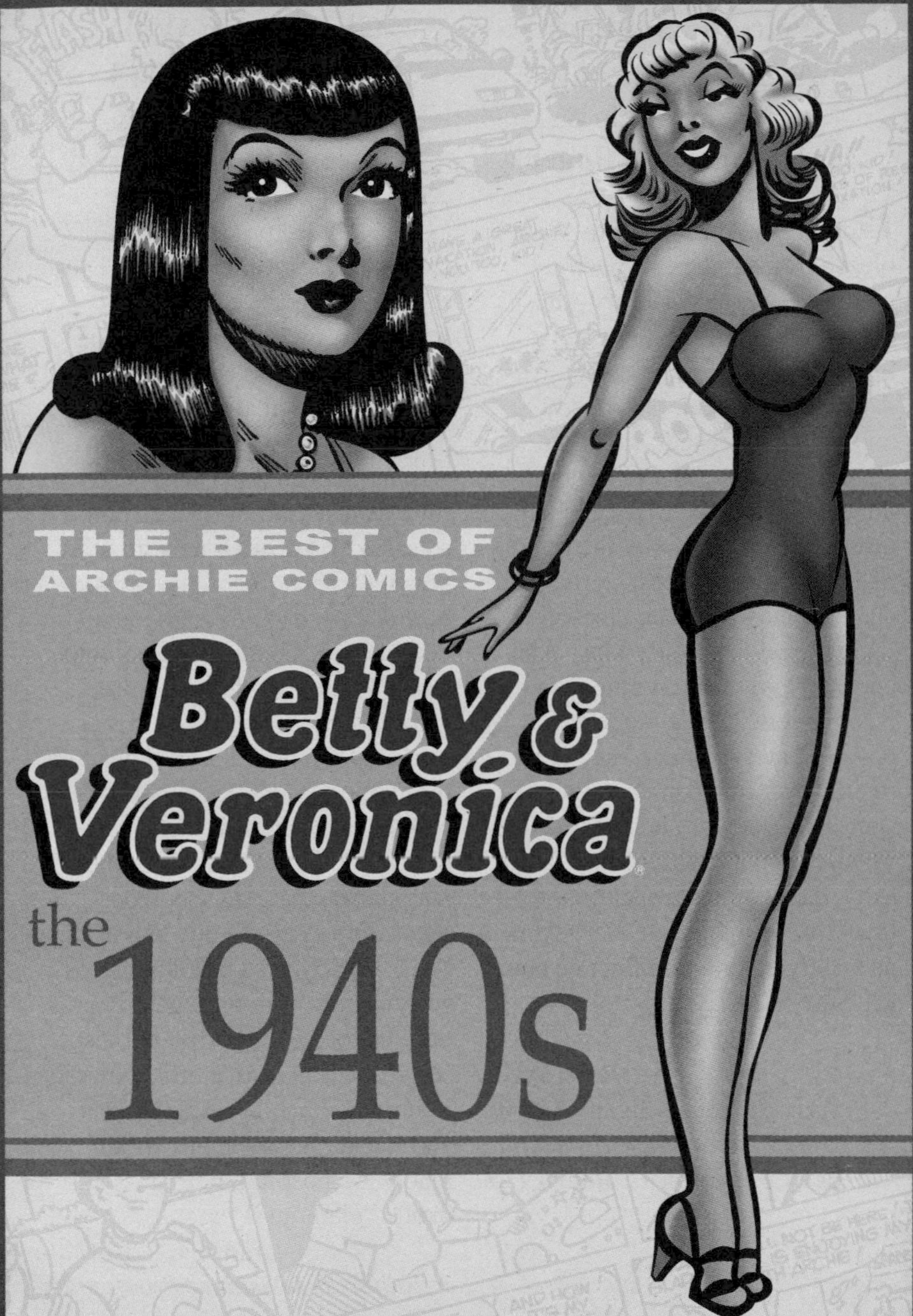
THE BEST OF
ARCHIE COMICS
Betty & Veronica®
the 1940s

Welcome Soldiers
Archie #3, 1943
by Harry Sahle &
Janice Valleau (Ginger)

Both Mary Ann and Betty Cooper blazed trails in their respective mediums. I consider Mary Ann to be among the first "women's lib" characters on television. As an independent, fair, handy and organized leader, she often showed the men how to get things done. Likewise, it is Betty who is most likely to get under the hood of Archie's car to get it started again so they continue their date! Sadly, I feel that while Mary Ann and Betty were among the first positive female role models in popular entertainment, they are rapidly becoming an endangered species in popular entertainment. There is still a place for the "good girl" in entertainment and I am thankful the images of Mary Ann and Betty endure to influence new generations today.

-- **Dawn Wells**
Mary Ann on Gilligan's Island,
Excerpted from her foreword to
Betty & Veronica Summer Fun

Glamour in White
Archie #4, 1943
by Harry Sahle &
Janice Valleau (Ginger)

The early Betty & Veronica stories are very interesting because the dynamic between the girls was so drastically different. The two girls, though from different backgrounds, treated each other as equals who weren't afraid to step up to each other when the time came—and they were both so sassy! How often now do you see Betty spending all day in a beauty parlor to get ready then complaining about doing volunteer work? Actually, I have to admit... I think of the two girls of this era, I prefer Veronica! Even if her motivations were occasionally self-serving, she still went out of her way to help others. Plus, her fashion was fab and she had a great Bettie Page-esque hairstyle! What I really love best about this story is how both girls get to not only be the "eye candy," but also serve as the slapstick and comedic relief! Even while being klutzes and wreaking havoc in—of all places—a hospital, both girls still exude "glamour"!

-- **Jamie Lee Rotante**
Editorial Assistant / Proofreader,
Archie Comics

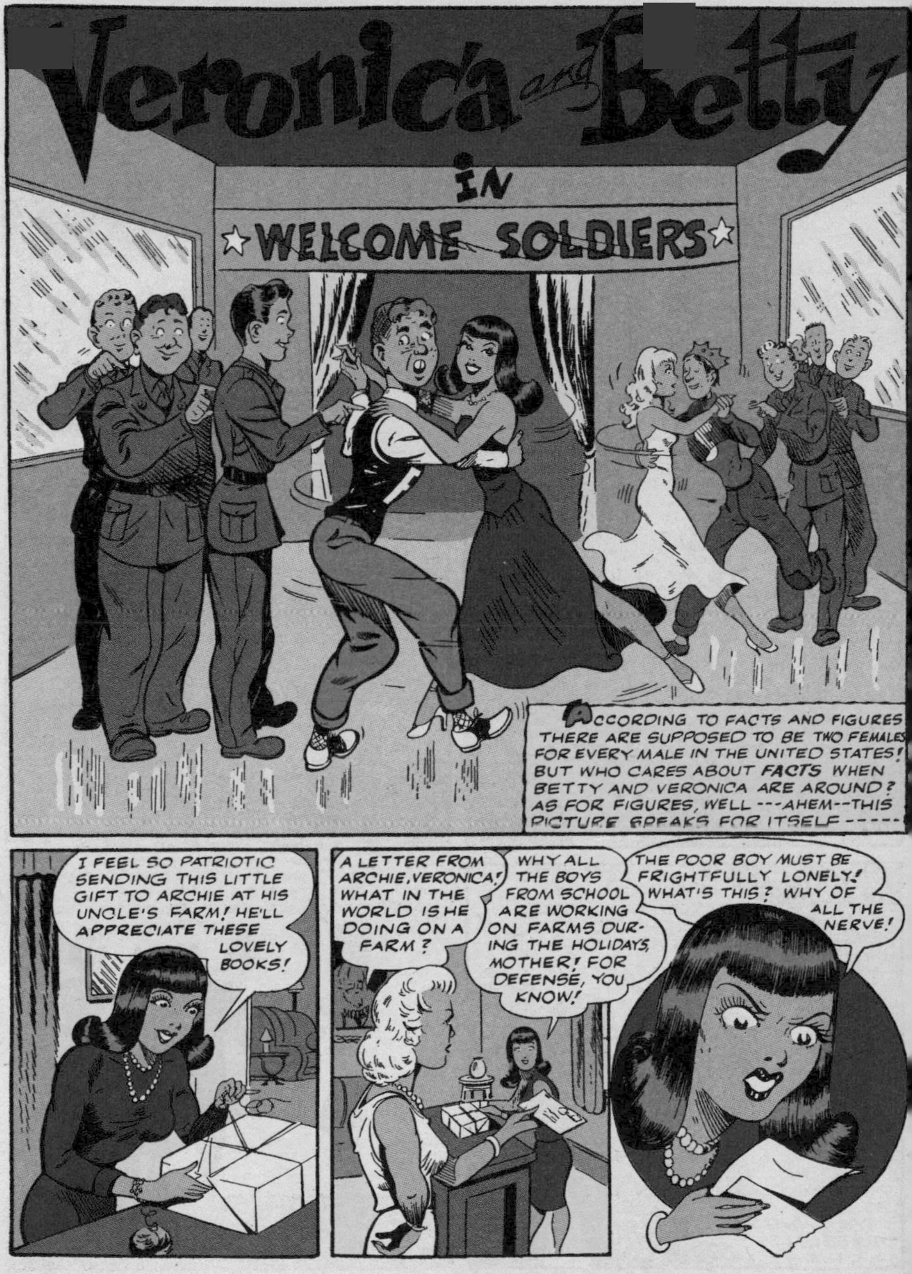
[redacted] Veronica and [redacted] Betty
IN
WELCOME SOLDIERS
ACCORDING TO FACTS AND FIGURES THERE ARE SUPPOSED TO BE TWO FEMALES FOR EVERY MALE IN THE UNITED STATES! BUT WHO CARES ABOUT FACTS WHEN BETTY AND VERONICA ARE AROUND? AS FOR FIGURES, WELL ---AHEM--THIS PICTURE SPEAKS FOR ITSELF -----
I FEEL SO PATRIOTIC SENDING THIS LITTLE GIFT TO ARCHIE AT HIS UNCLE'S FARM! HE'LL APPRECIATE THESE LOVELY BOOKS!
A LETTER FROM ARCHIE, VERONICA! WHAT IN THE WORLD IS HE DOING ON A FARM?
WHY ALL THE BOYS FROM SCHOOL ARE WORKING ON FARMS DURING THE HOLIDAYS, MOTHER! FOR DEFENSE, YOU KNOW!
THE POOR BOY MUST BE FRIGHTFULLY LONELY! WHAT'S THIS? WHY OF ALL THE NERVE!

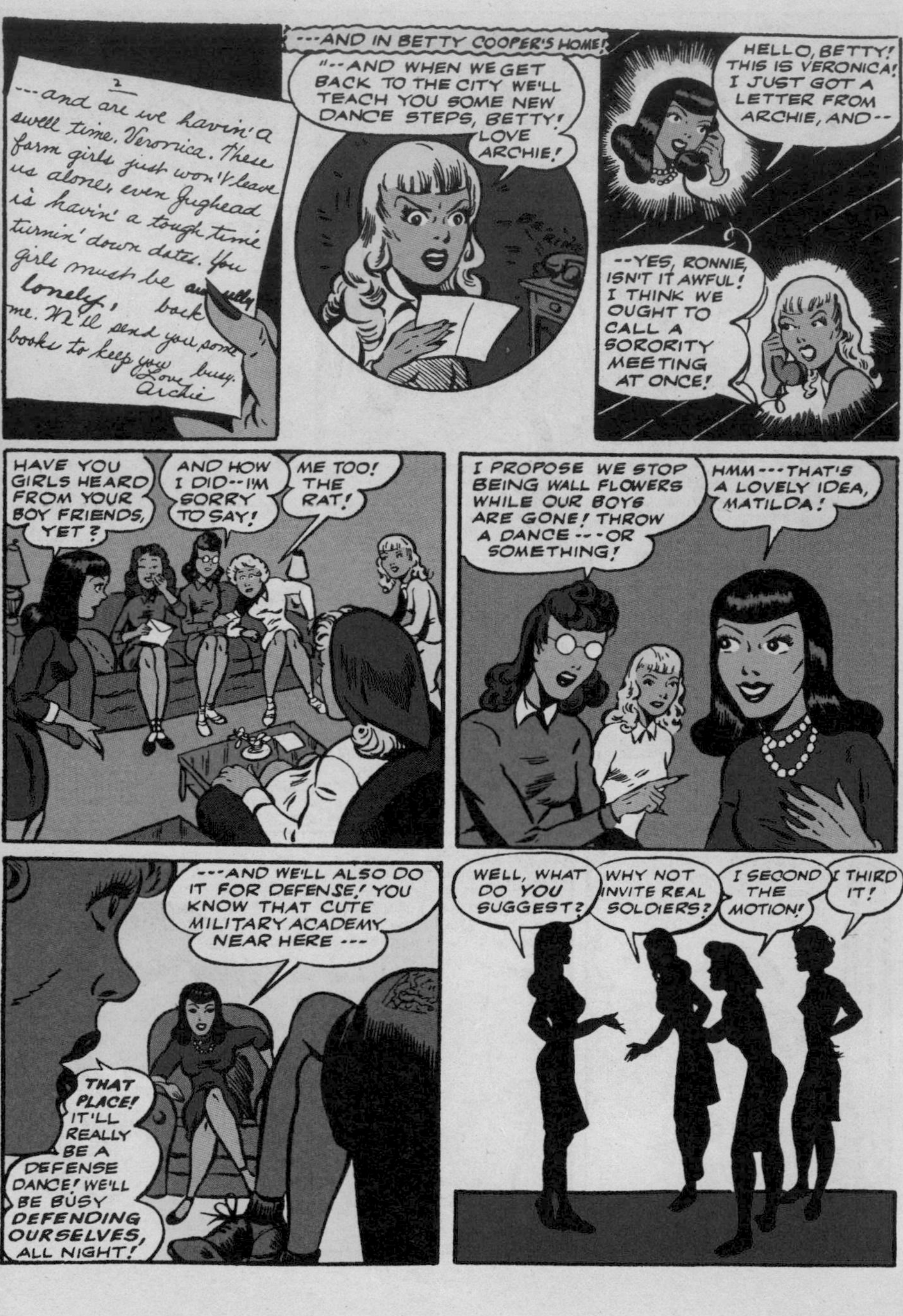
2
---and are we havin' a swell time, Veronica. These farm girls just won't leave us alone, even Jughead is havin' a tough time turnin' down dates. You girls must be awfully lonely, back me. We'll send you some books to keep you busy.
Love
Archie
---AND IN BETTY COOPER'S HOME!
"--AND WHEN WE GET BACK TO THE CITY WE'LL TEACH YOU SOME NEW DANCE STEPS, BETTY! LOVE ARCHIE!
HELLO, BETTY! THIS IS VERONICA! I JUST GOT A LETTER FROM ARCHIE, AND--
--YES, RONNIE, ISN'T IT AWFUL! I THINK WE OUGHT TO CALL A SORORITY MEETING AT ONCE!
HAVE YOU GIRLS HEARD FROM YOUR BOY FRIENDS, YET?
AND HOW I DID--I'M SORRY TO SAY!
ME TOO! THE RAT!
I PROPOSE WE STOP BEING WALL FLOWERS WHILE OUR BOYS ARE GONE! THROW A DANCE ---OR SOMETHING!
HMM---THAT'S A LOVELY IDEA, MATILDA!
---AND WE'LL ALSO DO IT FOR DEFENSE! YOU KNOW THAT CUTE MILITARY ACADEMY NEAR HERE ---
THAT PLACE! IT'LL REALLY BE A DEFENSE DANCE! WE'LL BE BUSY DEFENDING OURSELVES, ALL NIGHT!
WELL, WHAT DO YOU SUGGEST?
WHY NOT INVITE REAL SOLDIERS?
I SECOND THE MOTION!
I THIRD IT!

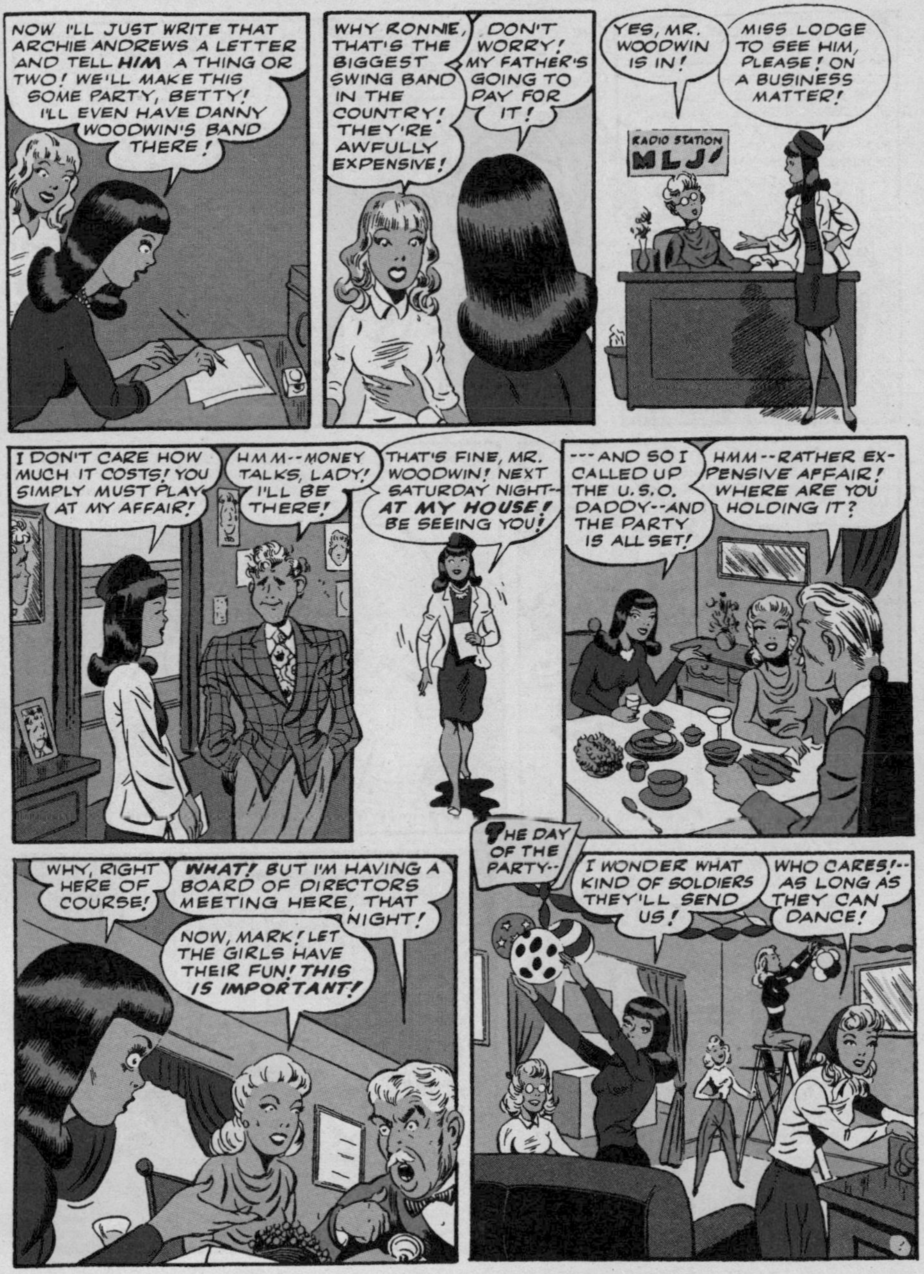
NOW I'LL JUST WRITE THAT ARCHIE ANDREWS A LETTER AND TELL HIM A THING OR TWO! WE'LL MAKE THIS SOME PARTY, BETTY! I'LL EVEN HAVE DANNY WOODWIN'S BAND THERE!
WHY RONNIE, THAT'S THE BIGGEST SWING BAND IN THE COUNTRY! THEY'RE AWFULLY EXPENSIVE!
DON'T WORRY! MY FATHER'S GOING TO PAY FOR IT!
YES, MR. WOODWIN IS IN!
MISS LODGE TO SEE HIM, PLEASE! ON A BUSINESS MATTER!
RADIO STATION MLJ!
I DON'T CARE HOW MUCH IT COSTS! YOU SIMPLY MUST PLAY AT MY AFFAIR!
HMM--MONEY TALKS, LADY! I'LL BE THERE!
THAT'S FINE, MR. WOODWIN! NEXT SATURDAY NIGHT--AT MY HOUSE! BE SEEING YOU!
---AND SO I CALLED UP THE U.S.O. DADDY--AND THE PARTY IS ALL SET!
HMM--RATHER EXPENSIVE AFFAIR! WHERE ARE YOU HOLDING IT?
WHY, RIGHT HERE OF COURSE!
WHAT! BUT I'M HAVING A BOARD OF DIRECTORS MEETING HERE, THAT NIGHT!
NOW, MARK! LET THE GIRLS HAVE THEIR FUN! THIS IS IMPORTANT!
THE DAY OF THE PARTY--
I WONDER WHAT KIND OF SOLDIERS THEY'LL SEND US!
WHO CARES!--AS LONG AS THEY CAN DANCE!

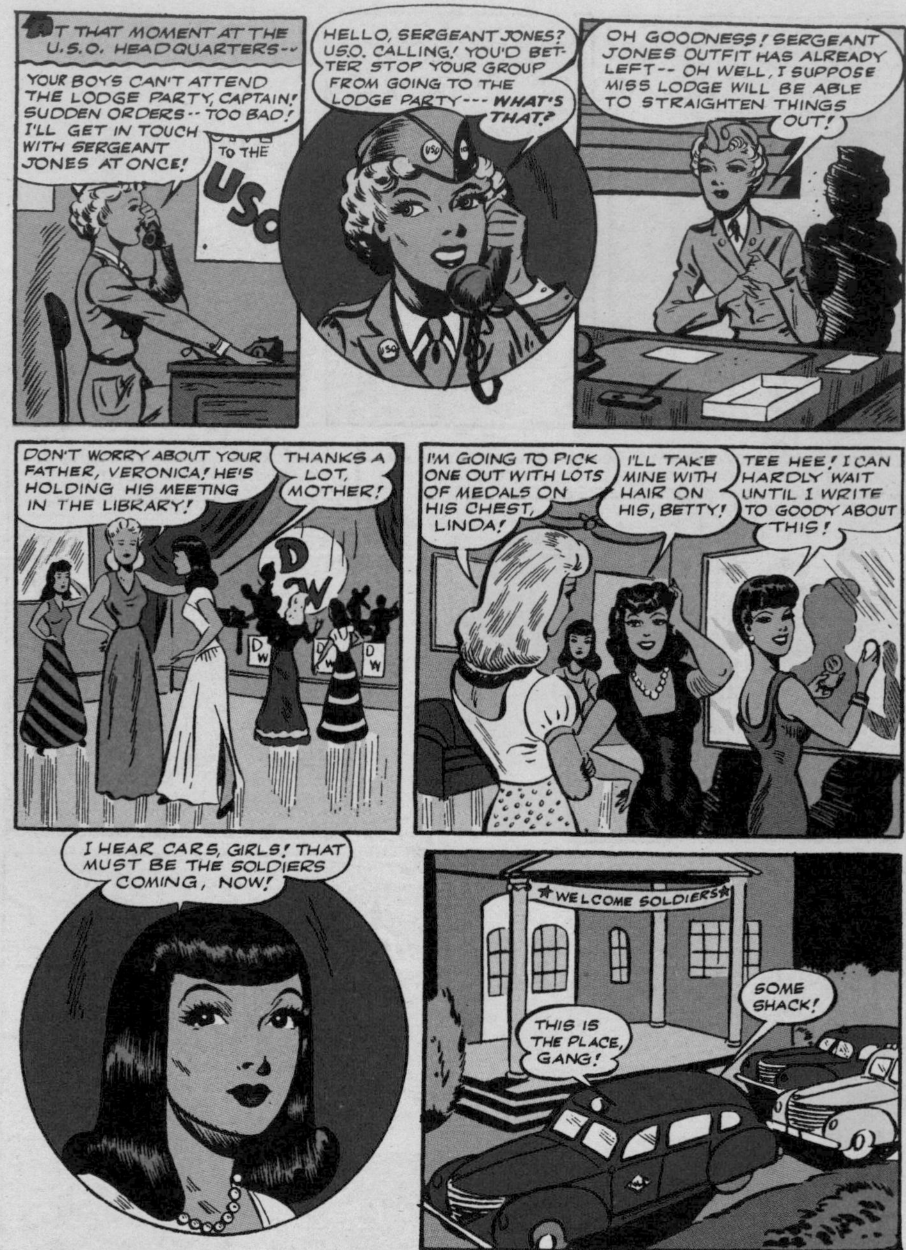
AT THAT MOMENT AT THE U.S.O. HEADQUARTERS--
YOUR BOYS CAN'T ATTEND THE LODGE PARTY, CAPTAIN! SUDDEN ORDERS -- TOO BAD! I'LL GET IN TOUCH WITH SERGEANT JONES AT ONCE!
TO THE
USO
HELLO, SERGEANT JONES? USO. CALLING! YOU'D BETTER STOP YOUR GROUP FROM GOING TO THE LODGE PARTY--- WHAT'S THAT?
OH GOODNESS! SERGEANT JONES OUTFIT HAS ALREADY LEFT -- OH WELL, I SUPPOSE MISS LODGE WILL BE ABLE TO STRAIGHTEN THINGS OUT!
DON'T WORRY ABOUT YOUR FATHER, VERONICA! HE'S HOLDING HIS MEETING IN THE LIBRARY!
THANKS A LOT, MOTHER!
I'M GOING TO PICK ONE OUT WITH LOTS OF MEDALS ON HIS CHEST, LINDA!
I'LL TAKE MINE WITH HAIR ON HIS, BETTY!
TEE HEE! I CAN HARDLY WAIT UNTIL I WRITE TO GOODY ABOUT THIS!
I HEAR CARS, GIRLS! THAT MUST BE THE SOLDIERS COMING, NOW!
WELCOME SOLDIERS
THIS IS THE PLACE, GANG!
SOME SHACK!

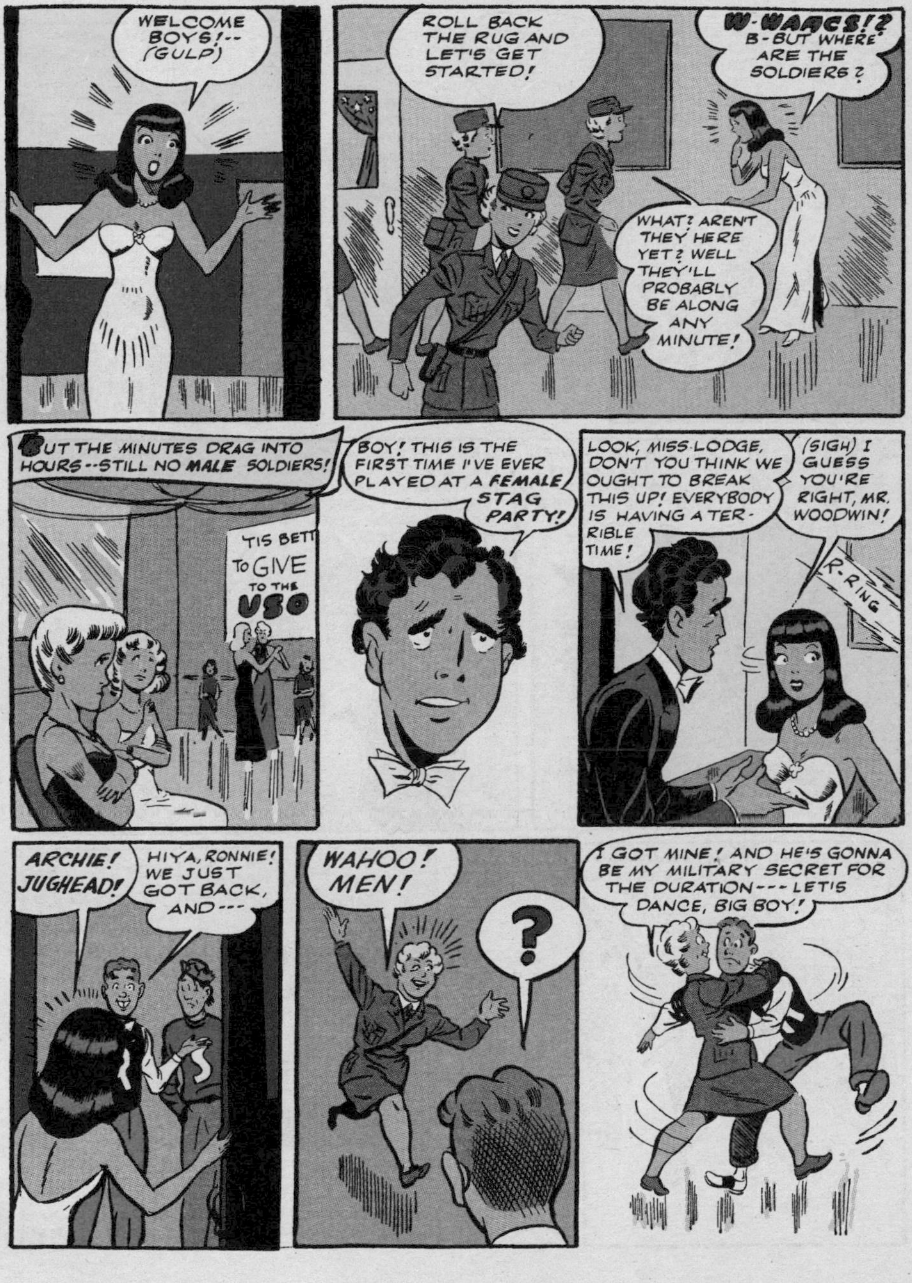
WELCOME BOYS!-- (GULP)
ROLL BACK THE RUG AND LET'S GET STARTED!
W-WAACS!? B-BUT WHERE ARE THE SOLDIERS?
WHAT? AREN'T THEY HERE YET? WELL THEY'LL PROBABLY BE ALONG ANY MINUTE!
BUT THE MINUTES DRAG INTO HOURS--STILL NO MALE SOLDIERS!
'TIS BETT TO GIVE TO THE USO
BOY! THIS IS THE FIRST TIME I'VE EVER PLAYED AT A FEMALE STAG PARTY!
LOOK, MISS LODGE, DON'T YOU THINK WE OUGHT TO BREAK THIS UP! EVERYBODY IS HAVING A TERRIBLE TIME!
(SIGH) I GUESS YOU'RE RIGHT, MR. WOODWIN!
R-RING
ARCHIE! JUGHEAD!
HIYA, RONNIE! WE JUST GOT BACK, AND---
WAHOO! MEN!
?
I GOT MINE! AND HE'S GONNA BE MY MILITARY SECRET FOR THE DURATION--- LET'S DANCE, BIG BOY!

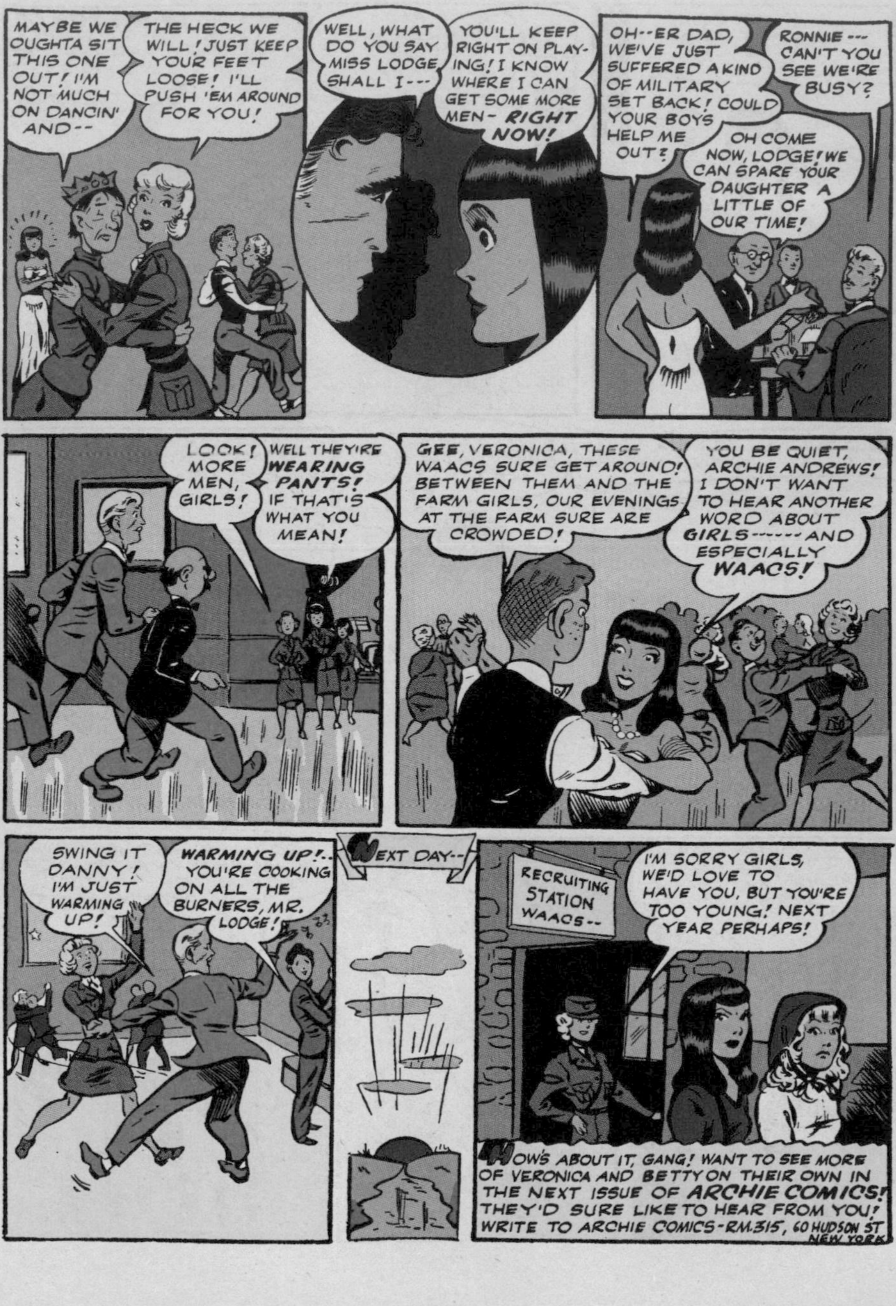
MAYBE WE OUGHTA SIT THIS ONE OUT! I'M NOT MUCH ON DANCIN' AND--
THE HECK WE WILL! JUST KEEP YOUR FEET LOOSE! I'LL PUSH 'EM AROUND FOR YOU!
WELL, WHAT DO YOU SAY MISS LODGE, SHALL I---
YOU'LL KEEP RIGHT ON PLAYING! I KNOW WHERE I CAN GET SOME MORE MEN- RIGHT NOW!
OH--ER DAD, WE'VE JUST SUFFERED A KIND OF MILITARY SET BACK! COULD YOUR BOYS HELP ME OUT?
RONNIE --- CAN'T YOU SEE WE'RE BUSY?
OH COME NOW, LODGE! WE CAN SPARE YOUR DAUGHTER A LITTLE OF OUR TIME!
LOOK! MORE MEN, GIRLS!
WELL THEY'RE WEARING PANTS! IF THAT'S WHAT YOU MEAN!
GEE, VERONICA, THESE WAACS SURE GET AROUND! BETWEEN THEM AND THE FARM GIRLS, OUR EVENINGS AT THE FARM SURE ARE CROWDED!
YOU BE QUIET, ARCHIE ANDREWS! I DON'T WANT TO HEAR ANOTHER WORD ABOUT GIRLS------AND ESPECIALLY WAACS!
SWING IT DANNY! I'M JUST WARMING UP!
WARMING UP!.. YOU'RE COOKING ON ALL THE BURNERS, MR. LODGE!
NEXT DAY--
RECRUITING STATION WAACS--
I'M SORRY GIRLS, WE'D LOVE TO HAVE YOU, BUT YOU'RE TOO YOUNG! NEXT YEAR PERHAPS!
HOW'S ABOUT IT, GANG! WANT TO SEE MORE OF VERONICA AND BETTY ON THEIR OWN IN THE NEXT ISSUE OF ARCHIE COMICS! THEY'D SURE LIKE TO HEAR FROM YOU! WRITE TO ARCHIE COMICS-RM.315, 60 HUDSON ST NEW YORK

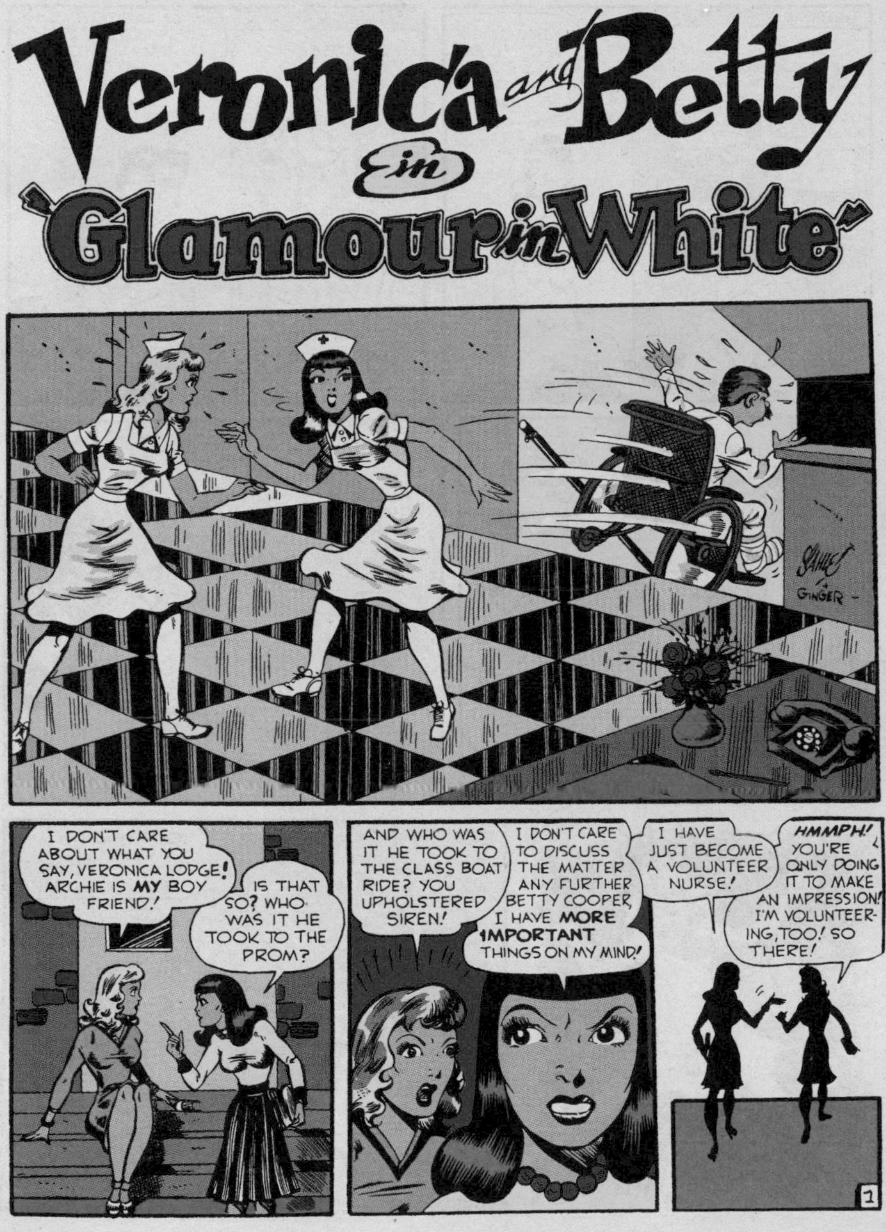
Veronica and Betty
in
"Glamour in White"
SAHLE / GINGER
I DON'T CARE ABOUT WHAT YOU SAY, VERONICA LODGE! ARCHIE IS MY BOY FRIEND!
IS THAT SO? WHO WAS IT HE TOOK TO THE PROM?
AND WHO WAS IT HE TOOK TO THE CLASS BOAT RIDE? YOU UPHOLSTERED SIREN!
I DON'T CARE TO DISCUSS THE MATTER ANY FURTHER BETTY COOPER, I HAVE MORE IMPORTANT THINGS ON MY MIND!
I HAVE JUST BECOME A VOLUNTEER NURSE!
HMMPH! YOU'RE ONLY DOING IT TO MAKE AN IMPRESSION! I'M VOLUNTEERING, TOO! SO THERE!
1

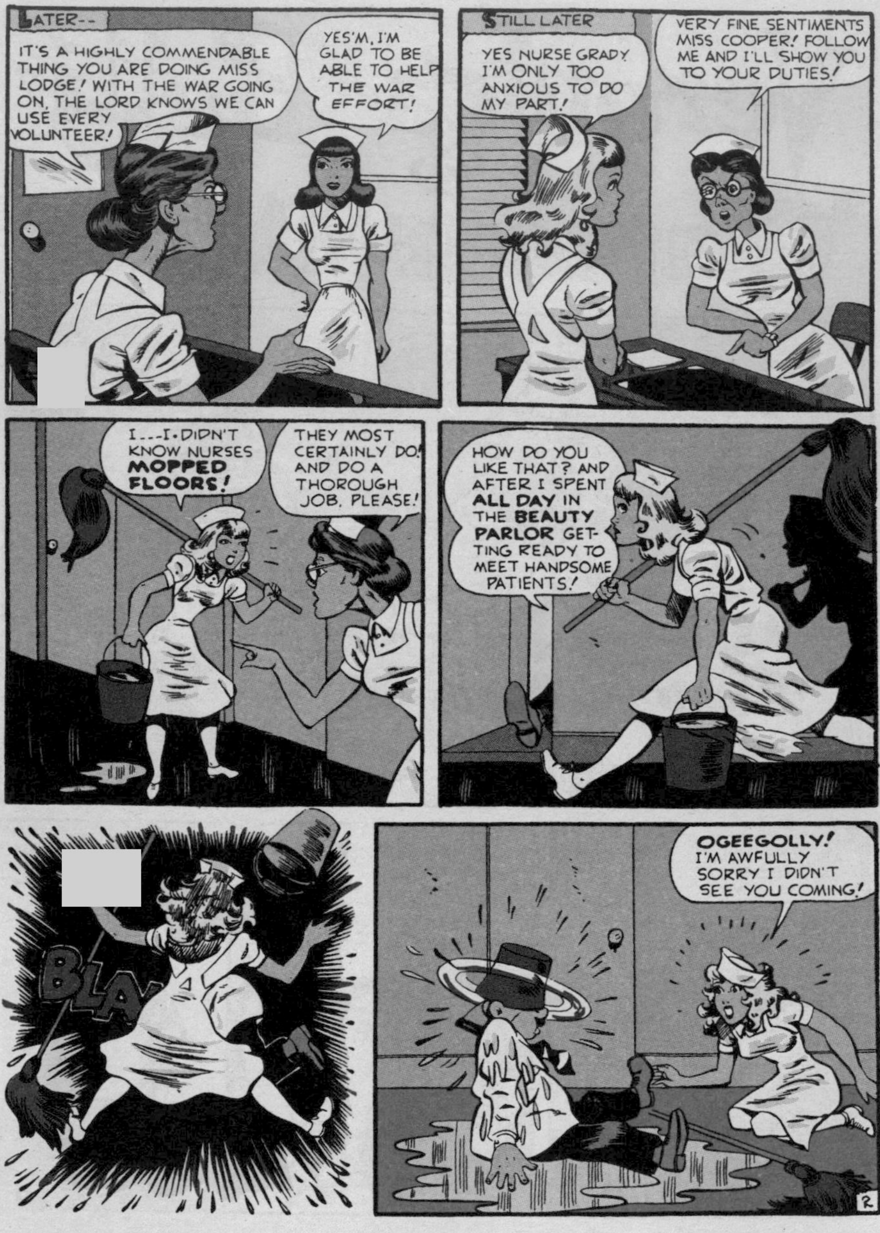
LATER--
IT'S A HIGHLY COMMENDABLE THING YOU ARE DOING MISS LODGE! WITH THE WAR GOING ON, THE LORD KNOWS WE CAN USE EVERY VOLUNTEER!
YES'M, I'M GLAD TO BE ABLE TO HELP THE WAR EFFORT!
STILL LATER
YES NURSE GRADY. I'M ONLY TOO ANXIOUS TO DO MY PART!
VERY FINE SENTIMENTS MISS COOPER! FOLLOW ME AND I'LL SHOW YOU TO YOUR DUTIES!
I---I-DIDN'T KNOW NURSES **MOPPED FLOORS!**
THEY MOST CERTAINLY DO! AND DO A THOROUGH JOB, PLEASE!
HOW DO YOU LIKE THAT? AND AFTER I SPENT **ALL DAY** IN THE **BEAUTY PARLOR** GETTING READY TO MEET HANDSOME PATIENTS!
OGEEGOLLY! I'M AWFULLY SORRY I DIDN'T SEE YOU COMING!

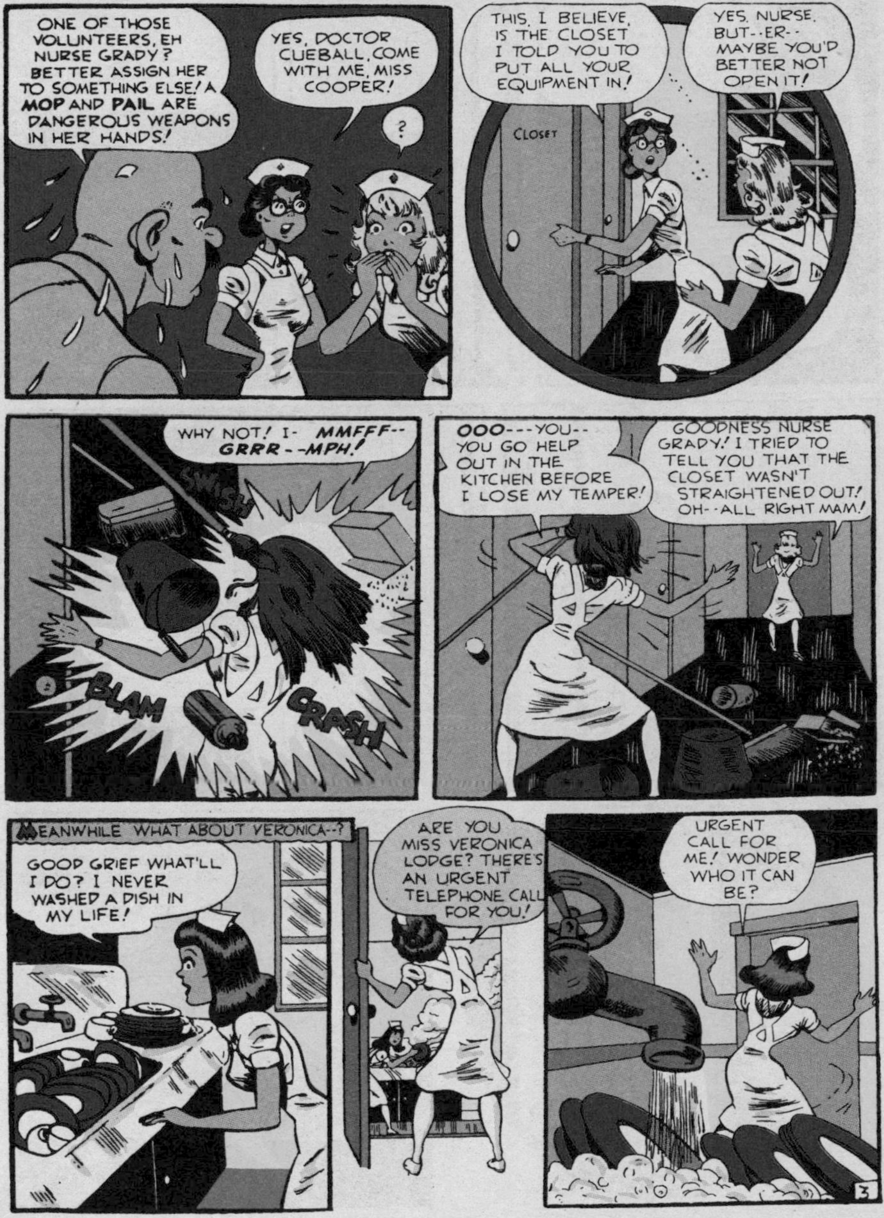
ONE OF THOSE VOLUNTEERS, EH NURSE GRADY? BETTER ASSIGN HER TO SOMETHING ELSE! A MOP AND PAIL ARE DANGEROUS WEAPONS IN HER HANDS!
YES, DOCTOR CUEBALL, COME WITH ME, MISS COOPER!
?
THIS, I BELIEVE, IS THE CLOSET I TOLD YOU TO PUT ALL YOUR EQUIPMENT IN!
YES, NURSE. BUT--ER--MAYBE YOU'D BETTER NOT OPEN IT!
CLOSET
WHY NOT! I- MMFFF--GRRR--MPH!
SWISH
BLAM
CRASH
OOO---YOU--YOU GO HELP OUT IN THE KITCHEN BEFORE I LOSE MY TEMPER!
GOODNESS NURSE GRADY! I TRIED TO TELL YOU THAT THE CLOSET WASN'T STRAIGHTENED OUT! OH--ALL RIGHT MAM!
MEANWHILE WHAT ABOUT VERONICA--?
GOOD GRIEF WHAT'LL I DO? I NEVER WASHED A DISH IN MY LIFE!
ARE YOU MISS VERONICA LODGE? THERE'S AN URGENT TELEPHONE CALL FOR YOU!
URGENT CALL FOR ME! WONDER WHO IT CAN BE?
3

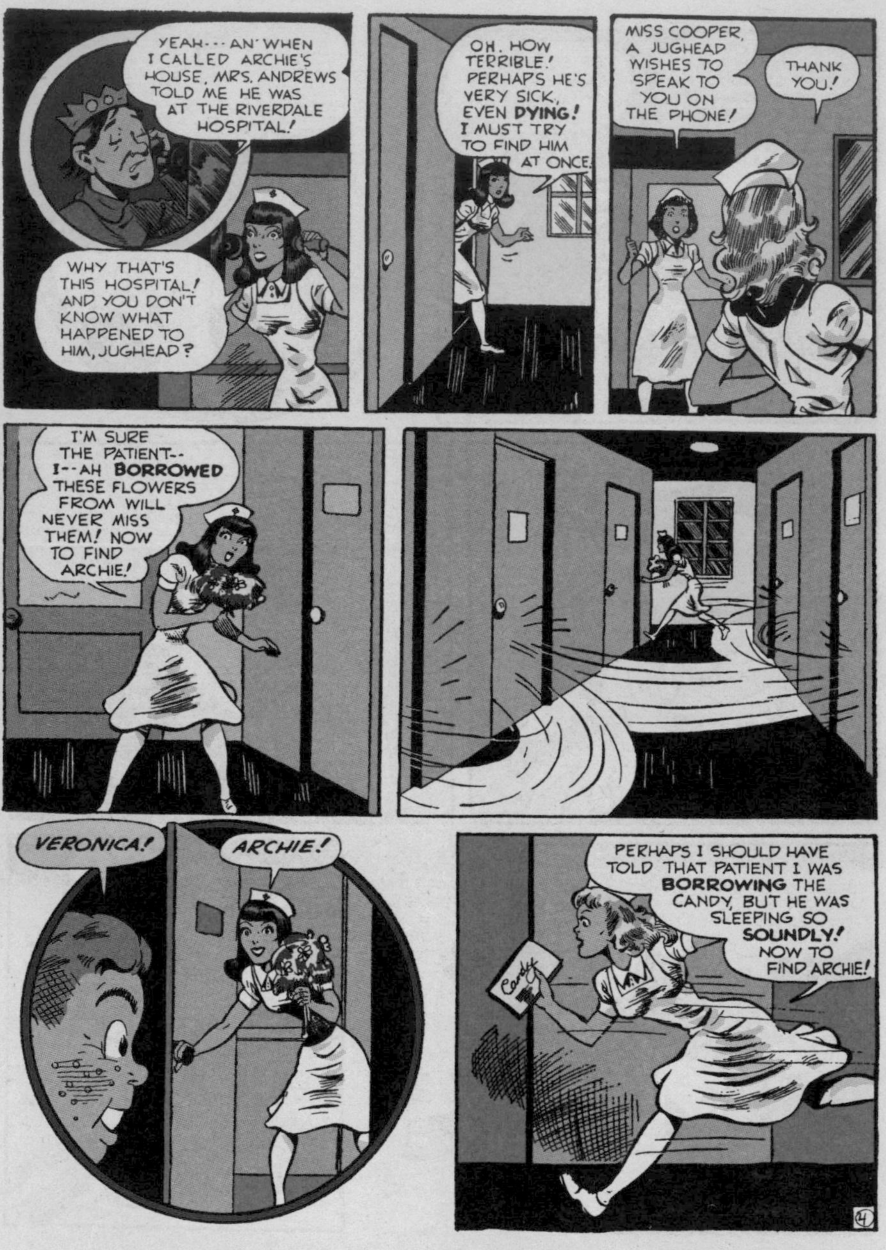
YEAH--- AN' WHEN I CALLED ARCHIE'S HOUSE, MRS. ANDREWS TOLD ME HE WAS AT THE RIVERDALE HOSPITAL!
WHY THAT'S THIS HOSPITAL! AND YOU DON'T KNOW WHAT HAPPENED TO HIM, JUGHEAD?
OH, HOW TERRIBLE! PERHAPS HE'S VERY SICK, EVEN DYING! I MUST TRY TO FIND HIM AT ONCE.
MISS COOPER, A JUGHEAD WISHES TO SPEAK TO YOU ON THE PHONE!
THANK YOU!
I'M SURE THE PATIENT-- I--AH BORROWED THESE FLOWERS FROM WILL NEVER MISS THEM! NOW TO FIND ARCHIE!
VERONICA!
ARCHIE!
PERHAPS I SHOULD HAVE TOLD THAT PATIENT I WAS BORROWING THE CANDY, BUT HE WAS SLEEPING SO SOUNDLY! NOW TO FIND ARCHIE!
Candy
4

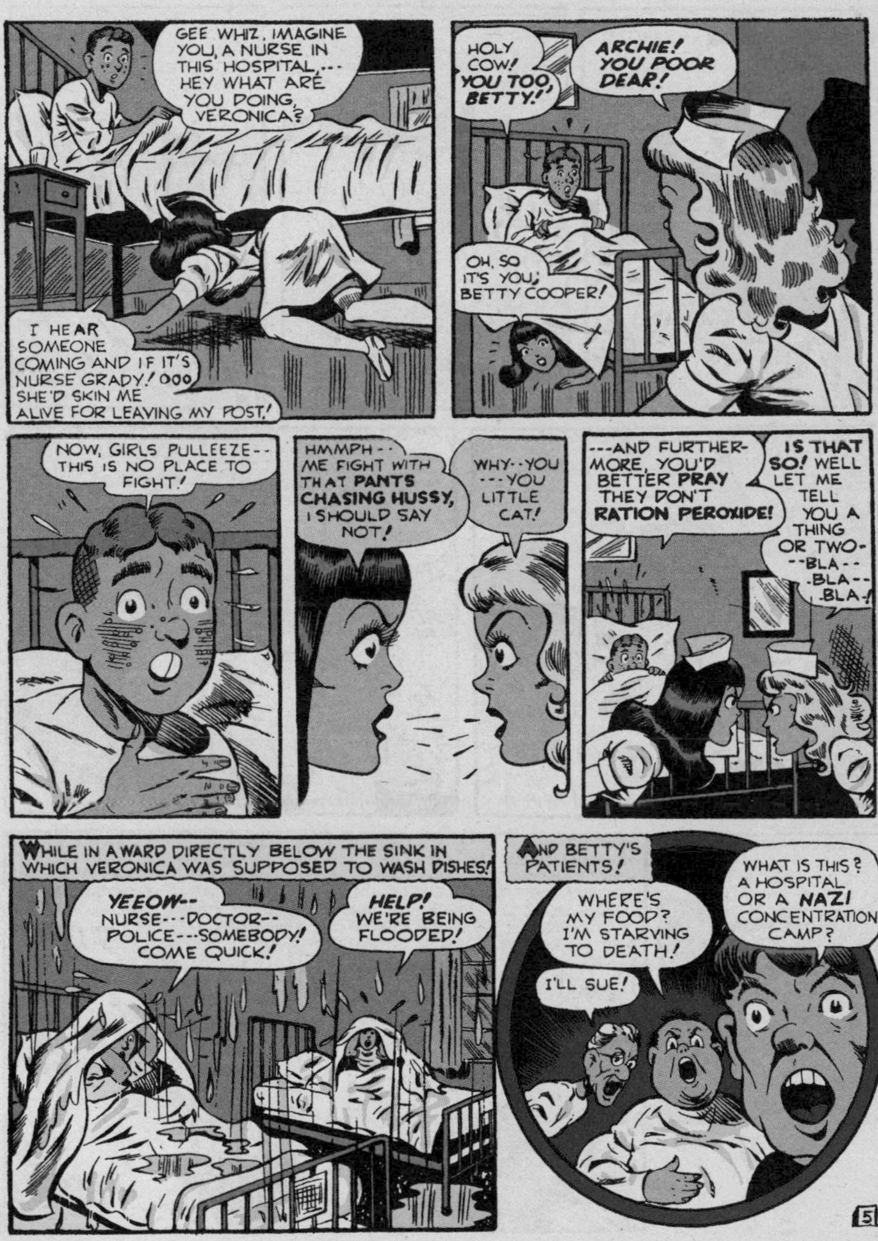
GEE WHIZ, IMAGINE YOU, A NURSE IN THIS HOSPITAL,--- HEY WHAT ARE YOU DOING, VERONICA?
I HEAR SOMEONE COMING AND IF IT'S NURSE GRADY! OOO SHE'D SKIN ME ALIVE FOR LEAVING MY POST!
HOLY COW! YOU TOO, BETTY!
ARCHIE! YOU POOR DEAR!
OH, SO IT'S YOU, BETTY COOPER!
NOW, GIRLS PULLEEZE-- THIS IS NO PLACE TO FIGHT!
HMMPH-- ME FIGHT WITH THAT PANTS CHASING HUSSY, I SHOULD SAY NOT!
WHY--YOU ---YOU LITTLE CAT!
---AND FURTHERMORE, YOU'D BETTER PRAY THEY DON'T RATION PEROXIDE!
IS THAT SO! WELL LET ME TELL YOU A THING OR TWO---BLA---BLA---BLA-!
WHILE IN A WARD DIRECTLY BELOW THE SINK IN WHICH VERONICA WAS SUPPOSED TO WASH DISHES!
YEEOW-- NURSE---DOCTOR-- POLICE---SOMEBODY! COME QUICK!
HELP! WE'RE BEING FLOODED!
AND BETTY'S PATIENTS!
WHERE'S MY FOOD? I'M STARVING TO DEATH!
WHAT IS THIS? A HOSPITAL OR A NAZI CONCENTRATION CAMP?
I'LL SUE!
5

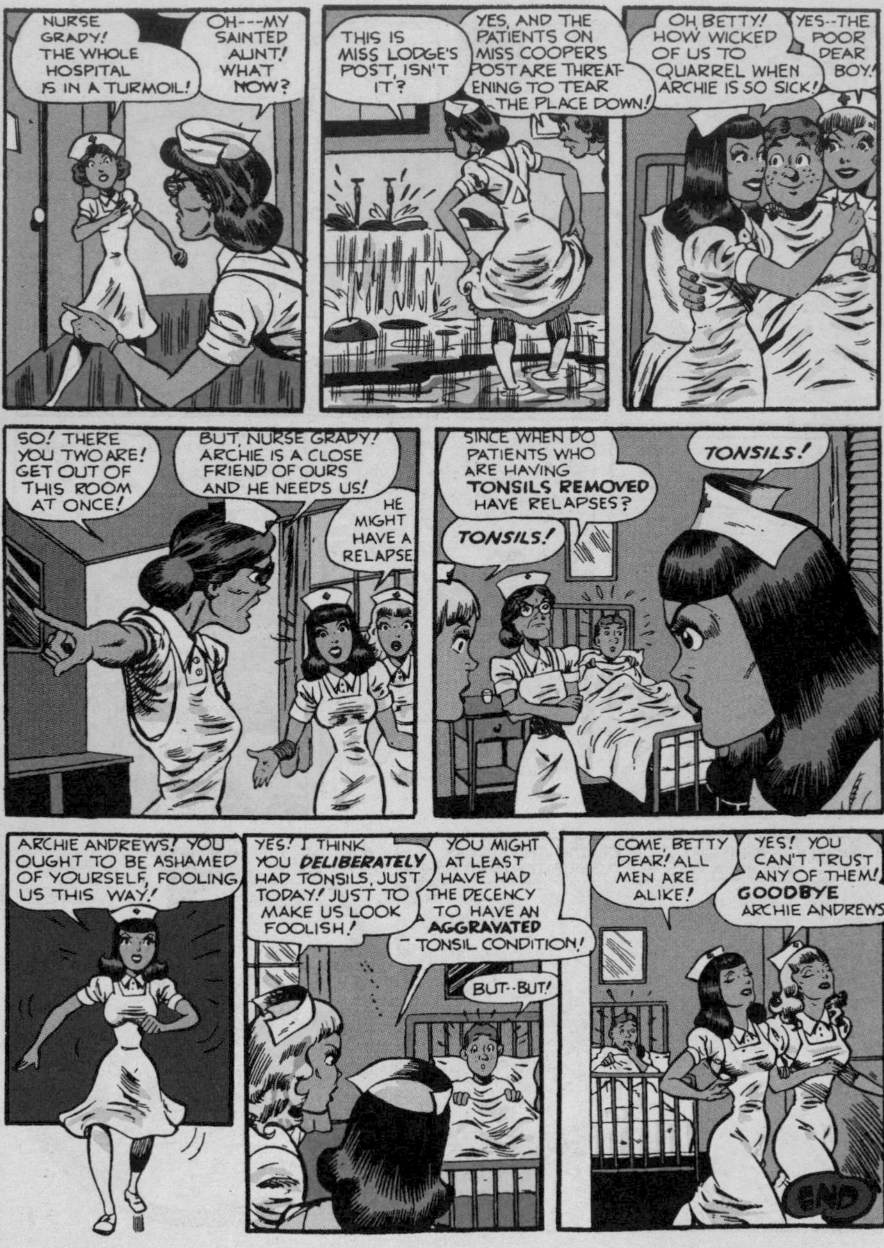
NURSE GRADY! THE WHOLE HOSPITAL IS IN A TURMOIL!
OH---MY SAINTED AUNT! WHAT NOW?
THIS IS MISS LODGE'S POST, ISN'T IT?
YES, AND THE PATIENTS ON MISS COOPER'S POST ARE THREATENING TO TEAR THE PLACE DOWN!
OH BETTY! HOW WICKED OF US TO QUARREL WHEN ARCHIE IS SO SICK!
YES--THE POOR DEAR BOY!
SO! THERE YOU TWO ARE! GET OUT OF THIS ROOM AT ONCE!
BUT, NURSE GRADY! ARCHIE IS A CLOSE FRIEND OF OURS AND HE NEEDS US!
HE MIGHT HAVE A RELAPSE
SINCE WHEN DO PATIENTS WHO ARE HAVING TONSILS REMOVED HAVE RELAPSES?
TONSILS!
TONSILS!
ARCHIE ANDREWS! YOU OUGHT TO BE ASHAMED OF YOURSELF, FOOLING US THIS WAY!
YES! I THINK YOU DELIBERATELY HAD TONSILS, JUST TODAY! JUST TO MAKE US LOOK FOOLISH!
YOU MIGHT AT LEAST HAVE HAD THE DECENCY TO HAVE AN AGGRAVATED TONSIL CONDITION!
BUT--BUT!
COME, BETTY DEAR! ALL MEN ARE ALIKE!
YES! YOU CAN'T TRUST ANY OF THEM! GOODBYE ARCHIE ANDREWS!
END

Archie starring Betty & Veronica
Archie #5, 1943
by Harry Sahle & Janice Valleau (Ginger)

Betty and Veronica (as well as Archie, Jughead, and the gang) were everywhere when I was growing up in Tennessee. My mom would often get the comics for me at the local TG&Y, but I never really paid attention to particular stories. I guess my earliest memory of really noticing Betty and Veronica was the live-action variety show that came out in 1978. I remember being really excited about a comic being on TV (*Legends of the Superheroes, Shazam* and *Wonder Woman* were already favorites) and eager to watch it. I think Veronica was the funniest one on the show, mostly because she got to play off Betty being so straight-laced, so I obviously took a shining to her. I was only five years old, so I wasn't as interested in the "girls" thing yet, so it was mostly all the humor and black hair of Veronica.

-- Mike Norton
Eisner Award-winning Artist, Battlepug, Revival

Betty & Veronica
Archie #15, 1945
by Bill Vigoda & Eleanor Woik
-and-
Of Men and Mermaids
Archie #17, 1945
by Bill Vigoda & Al McLean

Great classic stories. They have all the elements that you don't see often nowadays. Betty and Veronica really go at each other both verbally and physically with a lot of fun slapstick bits that makes this a great read. My favorite part is Archie pretending to drown, then getting knocked out by Betty in "Of Men and Mermaids." I mean, honestly, how often have you seen Betty socking people in the jaw recently? It really shows off her early feisty side.

-- Stephen Oswald
Production Manager, Archie Comics

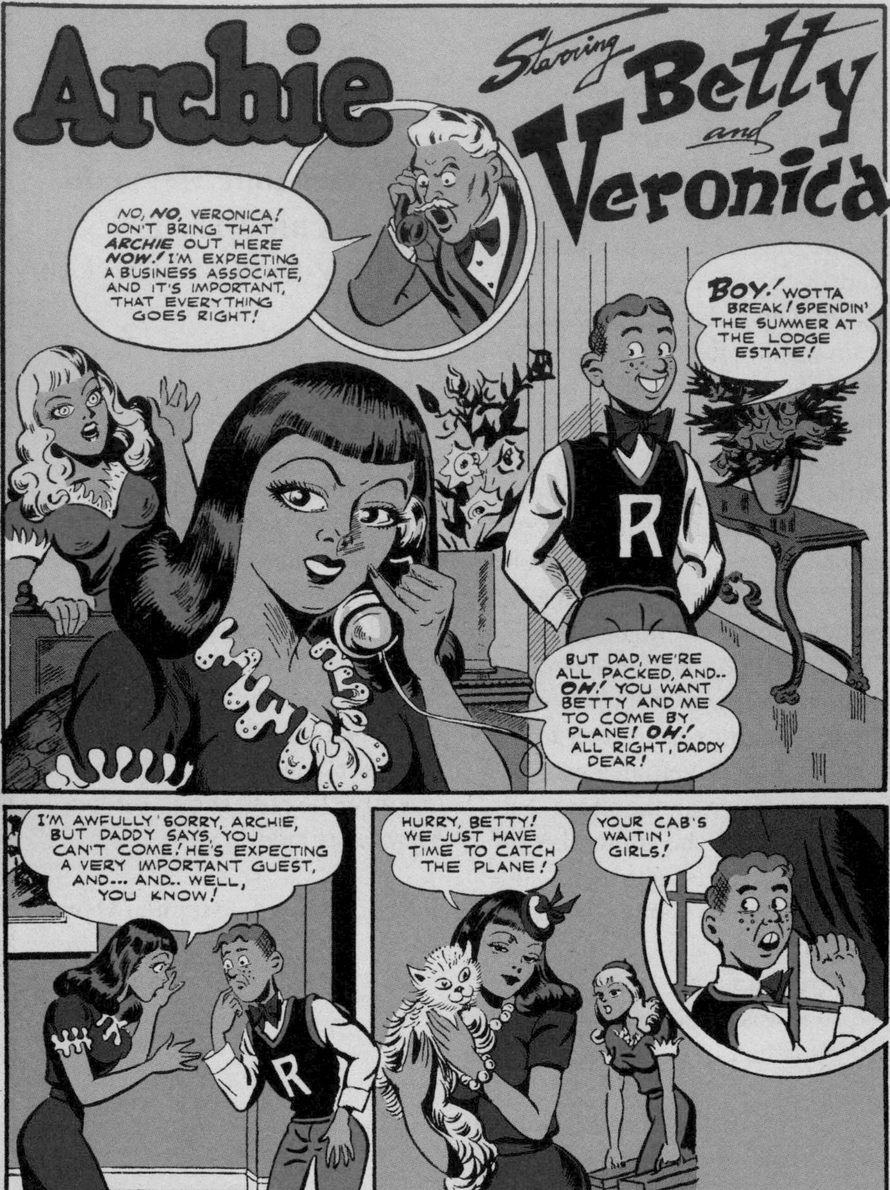
Archie
Starring Betty and Veronica
NO, NO, VERONICA! DON'T BRING THAT ARCHIE OUT HERE NOW! I'M EXPECTING A BUSINESS ASSOCIATE, AND IT'S IMPORTANT, THAT EVERYTHING GOES RIGHT!
BOY! WOTTA BREAK! SPENDIN' THE SUMMER AT THE LODGE ESTATE!
BUT DAD, WE'RE ALL PACKED, AND.. OH! YOU WANT BETTY AND ME TO COME BY PLANE! OH! ALL RIGHT, DADDY DEAR!
I'M AWFULLY SORRY, ARCHIE, BUT DADDY SAYS, YOU CAN'T COME! HE'S EXPECTING A VERY IMPORTANT GUEST, AND... AND.. WELL, YOU KNOW!
HURRY, BETTY! WE JUST HAVE TIME TO CATCH THE PLANE!
YOUR CAB'S WAITIN' GIRLS!

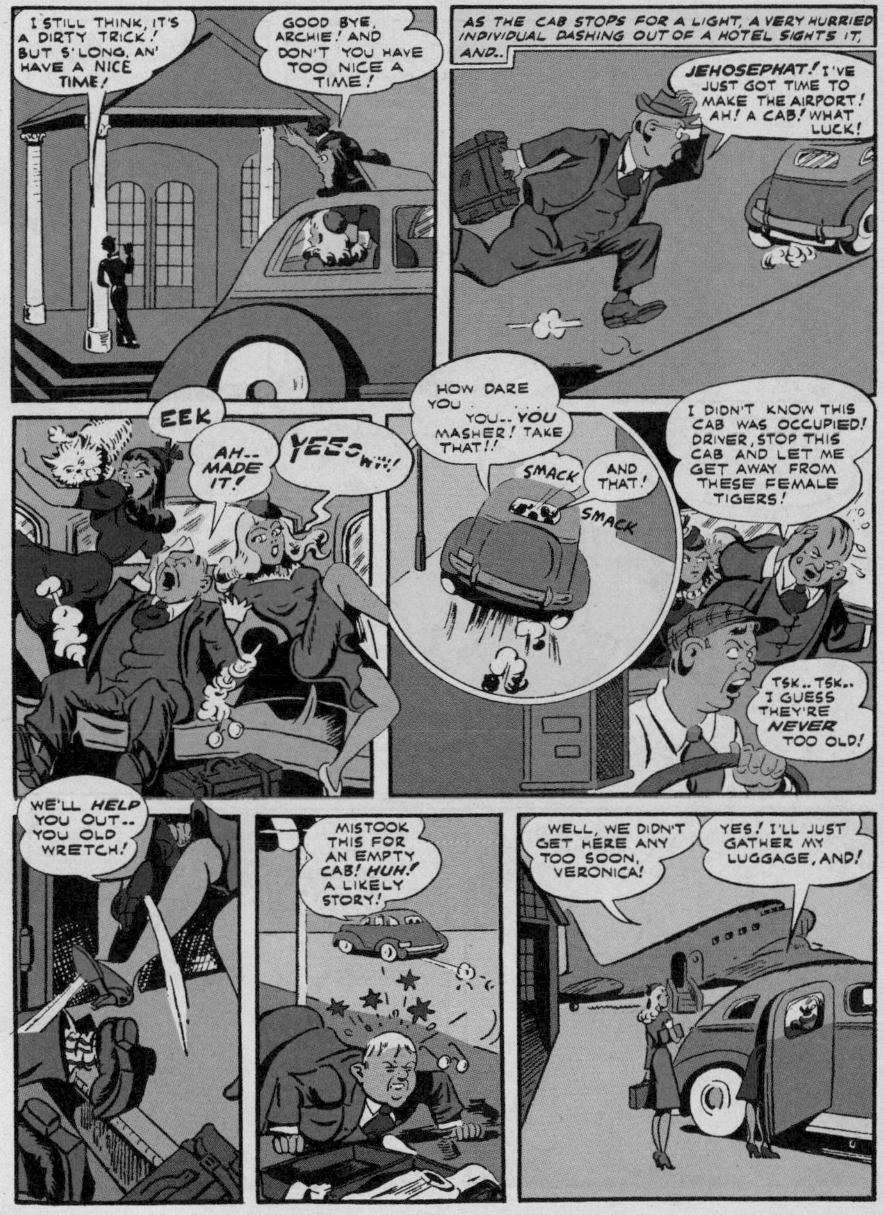
I STILL THINK, IT'S A DIRTY TRICK! BUT S'LONG, AN' HAVE A NICE TIME!
GOOD BYE, ARCHIE! AND DON'T YOU HAVE TOO NICE A TIME!
AS THE CAB STOPS FOR A LIGHT, A VERY HURRIED INDIVIDUAL DASHING OUT OF A HOTEL SIGHTS IT, AND..
JEHOSEPHAT! I'VE JUST GOT TIME TO MAKE THE AIRPORT! AH! A CAB! WHAT LUCK!
EEK
AH-- MADE IT!
YEEOWW!
HOW DARE YOU . . . . YOU-- YOU MASHER! TAKE THAT!!
SMACK
AND THAT!
SMACK
I DIDN'T KNOW THIS CAB WAS OCCUPIED! DRIVER, STOP THIS CAB AND LET ME GET AWAY FROM THESE FEMALE TIGERS!
TSK.. TSK.. I GUESS THEY'RE NEVER TOO OLD!
WE'LL HELP YOU OUT-- YOU OLD WRETCH!
MISTOOK THIS FOR AN EMPTY CAB! HUH! A LIKELY STORY!
WELL, WE DIDN'T GET HERE ANY TOO SOON, VERONICA!
YES! I'LL JUST GATHER MY LUGGAGE, AND!

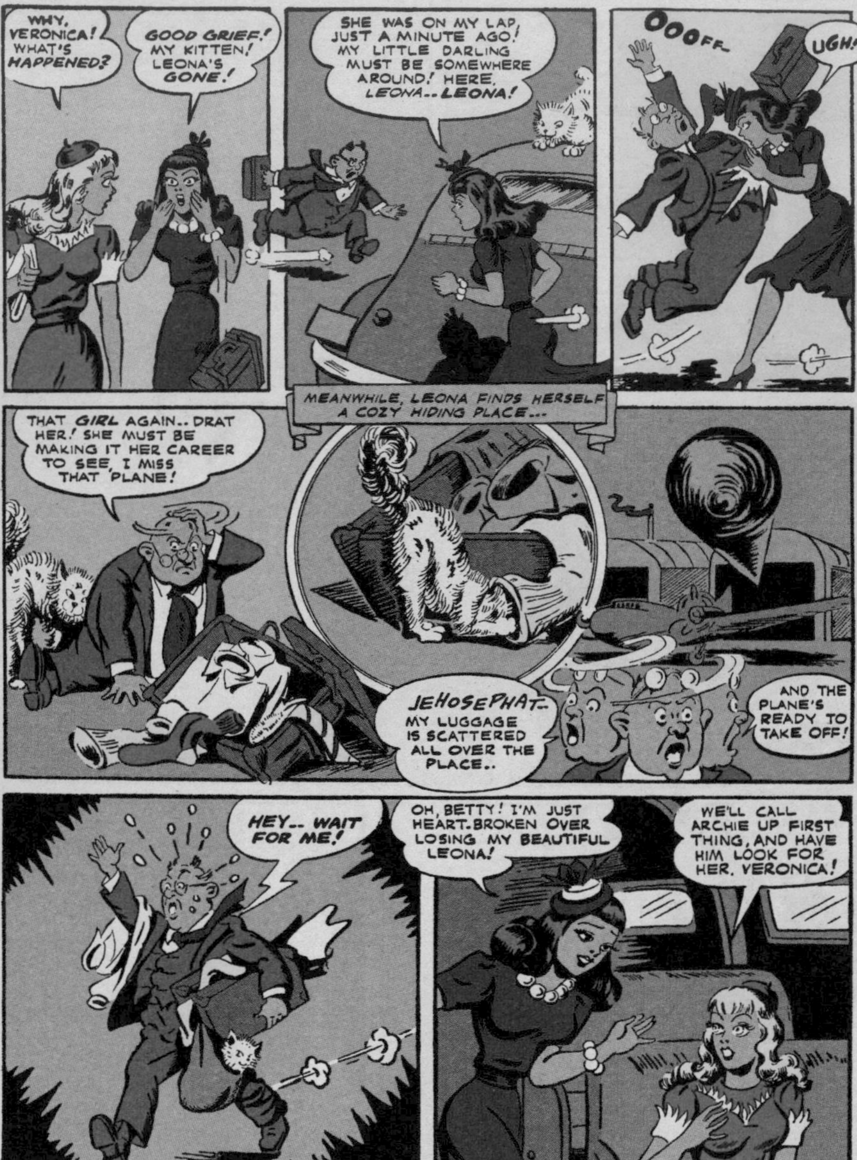
WHY, VERONICA! WHAT'S HAPPENED?
GOOD GRIEF! MY KITTEN! LEONA'S GONE!
SHE WAS ON MY LAP, JUST A MINUTE AGO! MY LITTLE DARLING MUST BE SOMEWHERE AROUND! HERE, LEONA.. LEONA!
OOOFF
UGH!
MEANWHILE, LEONA FINDS HERSELF A COZY HIDING PLACE...
THAT GIRL AGAIN.. DRAT HER! SHE MUST BE MAKING IT HER CAREER TO SEE, I MISS THAT 'PLANE!
JEHOSEPHAT-- MY LUGGAGE IS SCATTERED ALL OVER THE PLACE..
AND THE PLANE'S READY TO TAKE OFF!
HEY.. WAIT FOR ME!
OH, BETTY! I'M JUST HEART-BROKEN OVER LOSING MY BEAUTIFUL LEONA!
WE'LL CALL ARCHIE UP FIRST THING, AND HAVE HIM LOOK FOR HER, VERONICA!

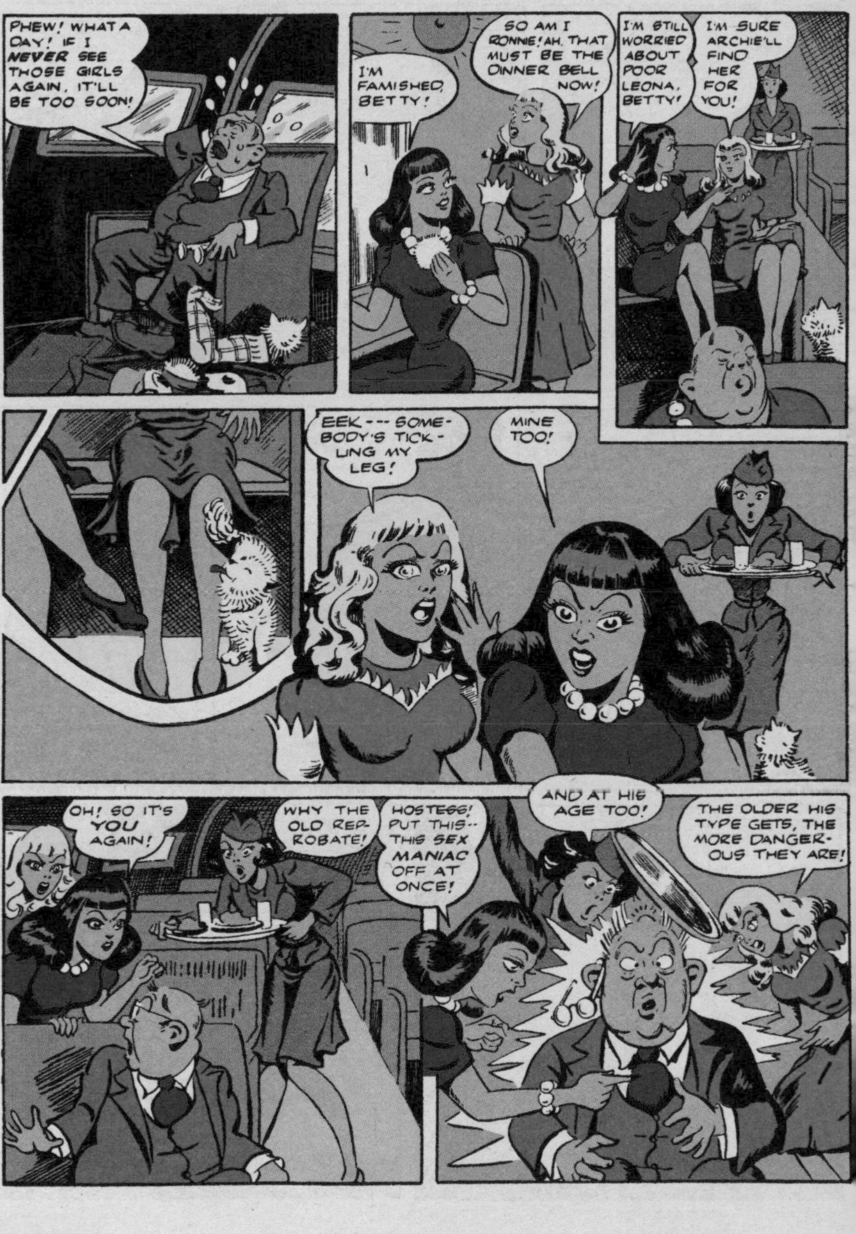
PHEW! WHAT A DAY! IF I NEVER SEE THOSE GIRLS AGAIN, IT'LL BE TOO SOON!
I'M FAMISHED, BETTY!
SO AM I RONNIE! AH. THAT MUST BE THE DINNER BELL NOW!
I'M STILL WORRIED ABOUT POOR LEONA, BETTY!
I'M SURE ARCHIE'LL FIND HER FOR YOU!
EEK --- SOMEBODY'S TICKLING MY LEG!
MINE TOO!
OH! SO IT'S YOU AGAIN!
WHY THE OLD REPROBATE!
HOSTESS! PUT THIS-- THIS SEX MANIAC OFF AT ONCE!
AND AT HIS AGE TOO!
THE OLDER HIS TYPE GETS, THE MORE DANGEROUS THEY ARE!

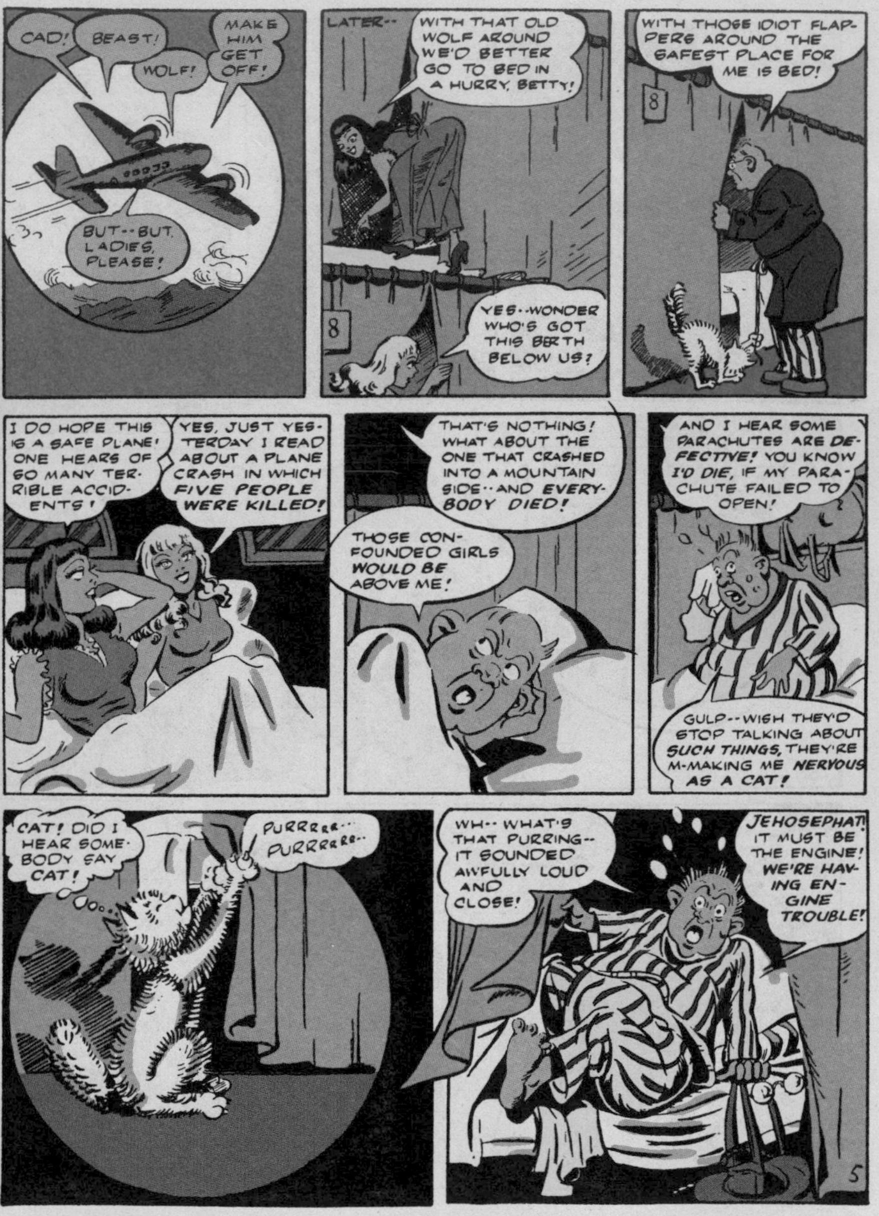
CAD!
BEAST!
WOLF!
MAKE HIM GET OFF!
BUT--BUT, LADIES, PLEASE!
LATER--
WITH THAT OLD WOLF AROUND WE'D BETTER GO TO BED IN A HURRY, BETTY!
YES--WONDER WHO'S GOT THIS BERTH BELOW US?
WITH THOSE IDIOT FLAPPERS AROUND THE SAFEST PLACE FOR ME IS BED!
I DO HOPE THIS IS A SAFE PLANE! ONE HEARS OF SO MANY TERRIBLE ACCIDENTS!
YES, JUST YESTERDAY I READ ABOUT A PLANE CRASH IN WHICH FIVE PEOPLE WERE KILLED!
THAT'S NOTHING! WHAT ABOUT THE ONE THAT CRASHED INTO A MOUNTAIN SIDE--AND EVERYBODY DIED!
THOSE CONFOUNDED GIRLS WOULD BE ABOVE ME!
AND I HEAR SOME PARACHUTES ARE DEFECTIVE! YOU KNOW I'D DIE, IF MY PARACHUTE FAILED TO OPEN!
GULP--WISH THEY'D STOP TALKING ABOUT SUCH THINGS, THEY'RE M-MAKING ME NERVOUS AS A CAT!
CAT! DID I HEAR SOMEBODY SAY CAT!
PURRRRRR--
PURRRRRRR--
WH--WHAT'S THAT PURRING--IT SOUNDED AWFULLY LOUD AND CLOSE!
JEHOSEPHAT! IT MUST BE THE ENGINE! WE'RE HAVING ENGINE TROUBLE!
5

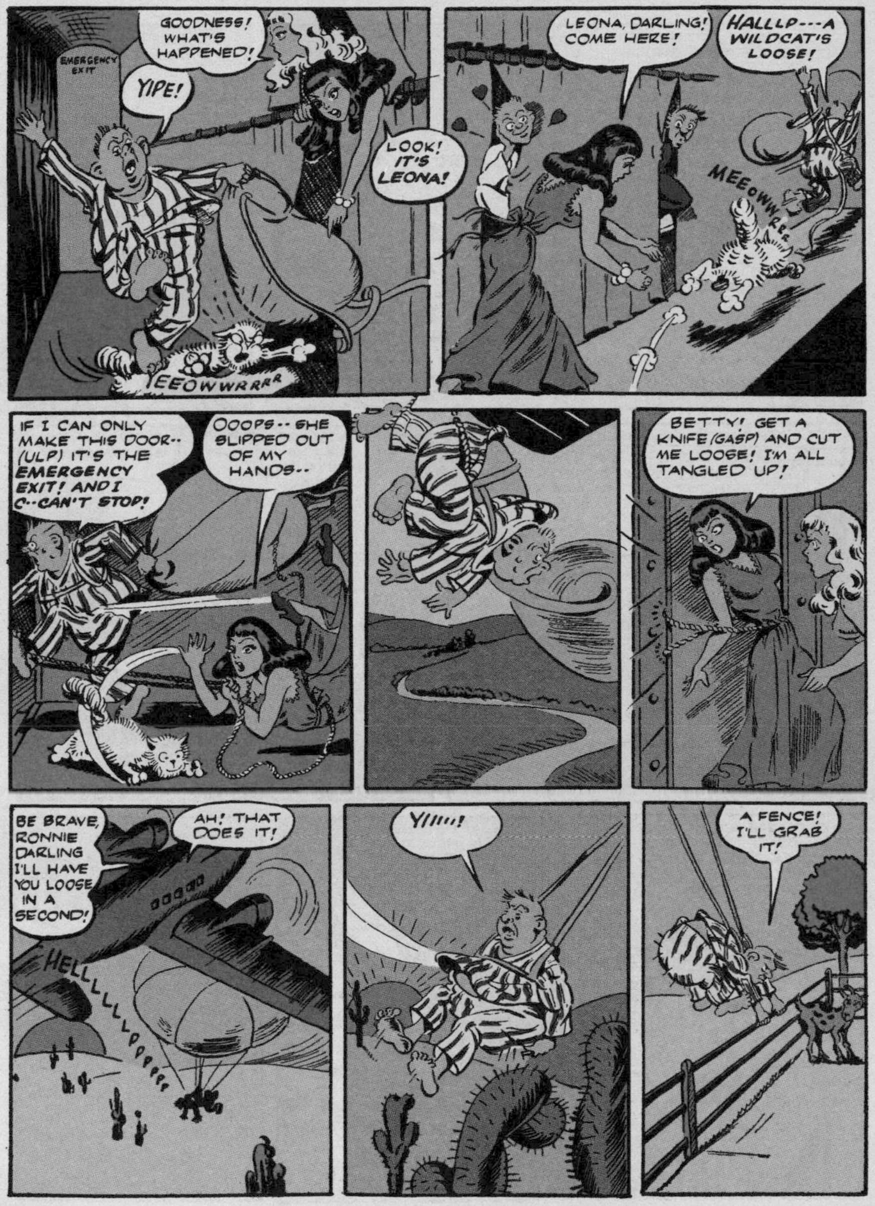
GOODNESS! WHAT'S HAPPENED!
EMERGENCY EXIT
YIPE!
LOOK! IT'S LEONA!
YEEOWWRRRR
LEONA, DARLING! COME HERE!
HALLLP---A WILDCAT'S LOOSE!
MEEOWWRRR
IF I CAN ONLY MAKE THIS DOOR-- (ULP) IT'S THE EMERGENCY EXIT! AND I C--CAN'T STOP!
OOOPS-- SHE SLIPPED OUT OF MY HANDS--
BETTY! GET A KNIFE (GASP) AND CUT ME LOOSE! I'M ALL TANGLED UP!
BE BRAVE, RONNIE DARLING I'LL HAVE YOU LOOSE IN A SECOND!
AH! THAT DOES IT!
HELLLLLLPPPPP
YIIIII!
A FENCE! I'LL GRAB IT!

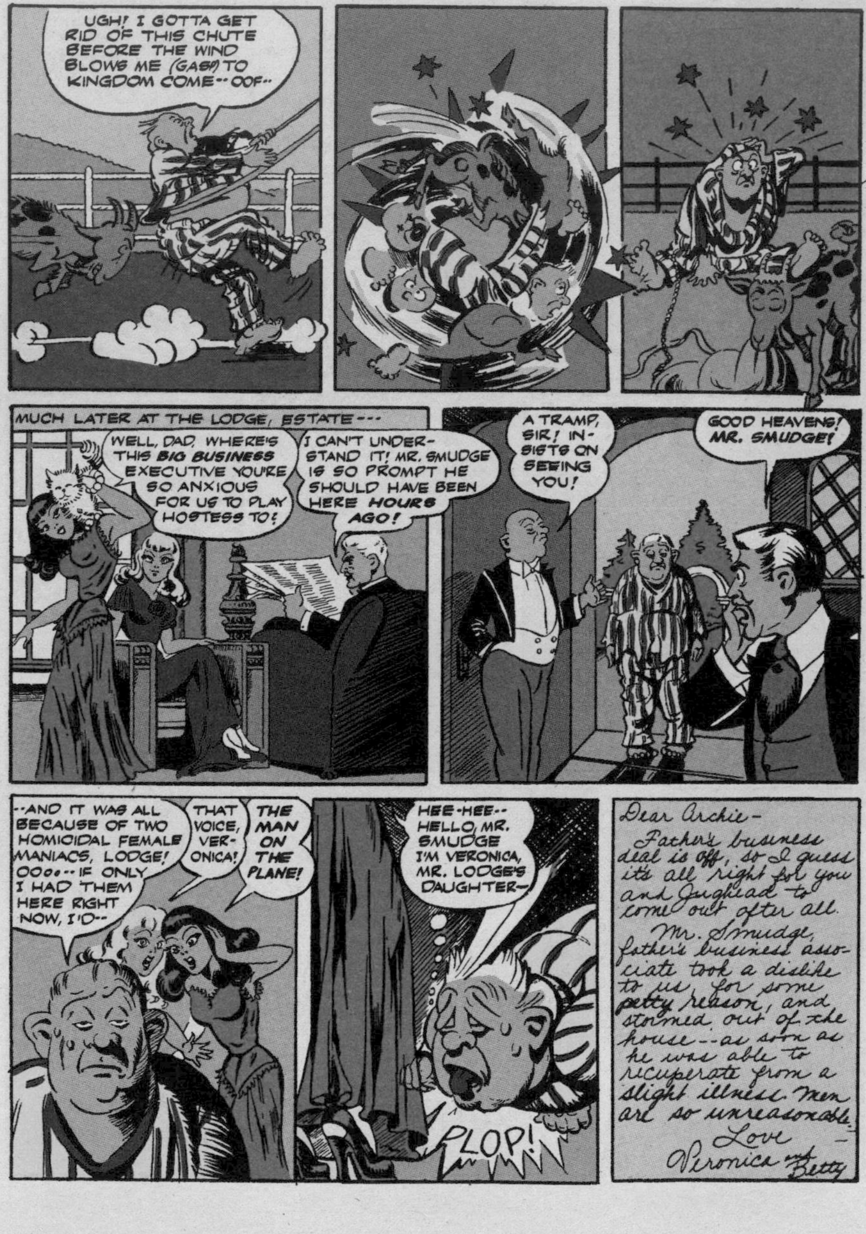
UGH! I GOTTA GET RID OF THIS CHUTE BEFORE THE WIND BLOWS ME (GASP) TO KINGDOM COME--OOF--
MUCH LATER AT THE LODGE ESTATE---
WELL, DAD, WHERE'S THIS BIG BUSINESS EXECUTIVE YOU'RE SO ANXIOUS FOR US TO PLAY HOSTESS TO?
I CAN'T UNDERSTAND IT! MR. SMUDGE IS SO PROMPT HE SHOULD HAVE BEEN HERE HOURS AGO!
A TRAMP, SIR! INSISTS ON SEEING YOU!
GOOD HEAVENS! MR. SMUDGE!
--AND IT WAS ALL BECAUSE OF TWO HOMICIDAL FEMALE MANIACS, LODGE! OOOo--IF ONLY I HAD THEM HERE RIGHT NOW, I'D--
THAT VOICE, VERONICA!
THE MAN ON THE PLANE!
HEE-HEE--HELLO, MR. SMUDGE I'M VERONICA, MR. LODGE'S DAUGHTER--
PLOP!
Dear Archie-
Father's business deal is off, so I guess it's all right for you and Jughead to come out after all.
Mr. Smudge, father's business associate took a dislike to us for some petty reason, and stormed out of the house--as soon as he was able to recuperate from a slight illness. Men are so unreasonable.
Love
Veronica and Betty

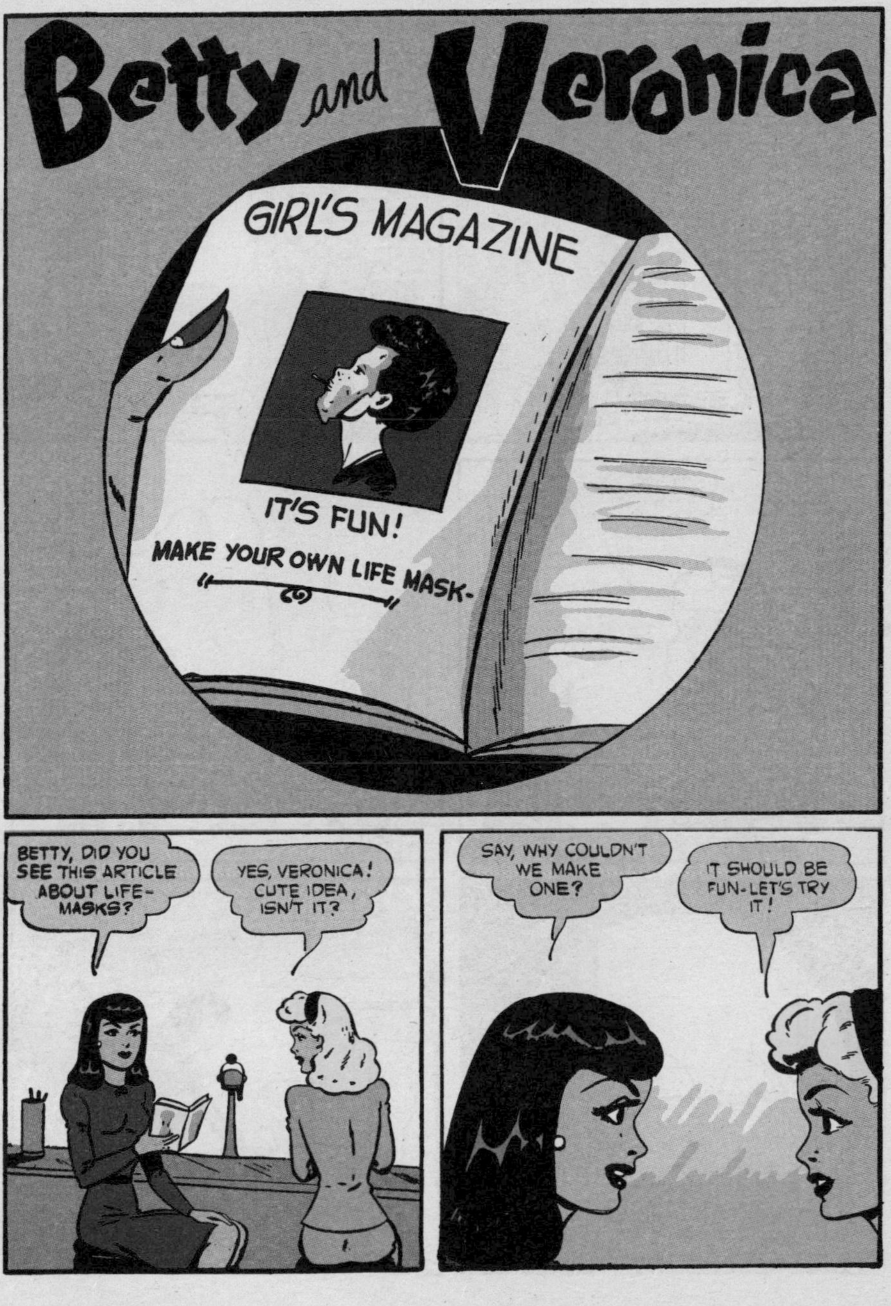
Betty and Veronica
GIRL'S MAGAZINE
IT'S FUN!
MAKE YOUR OWN LIFE MASK-
BETTY, DID YOU SEE THIS ARTICLE ABOUT LIFE-MASKS?
YES, VERONICA! CUTE IDEA, ISN'T IT?
SAY, WHY COULDN'T WE MAKE ONE?
IT SHOULD BE FUN-LET'S TRY IT!

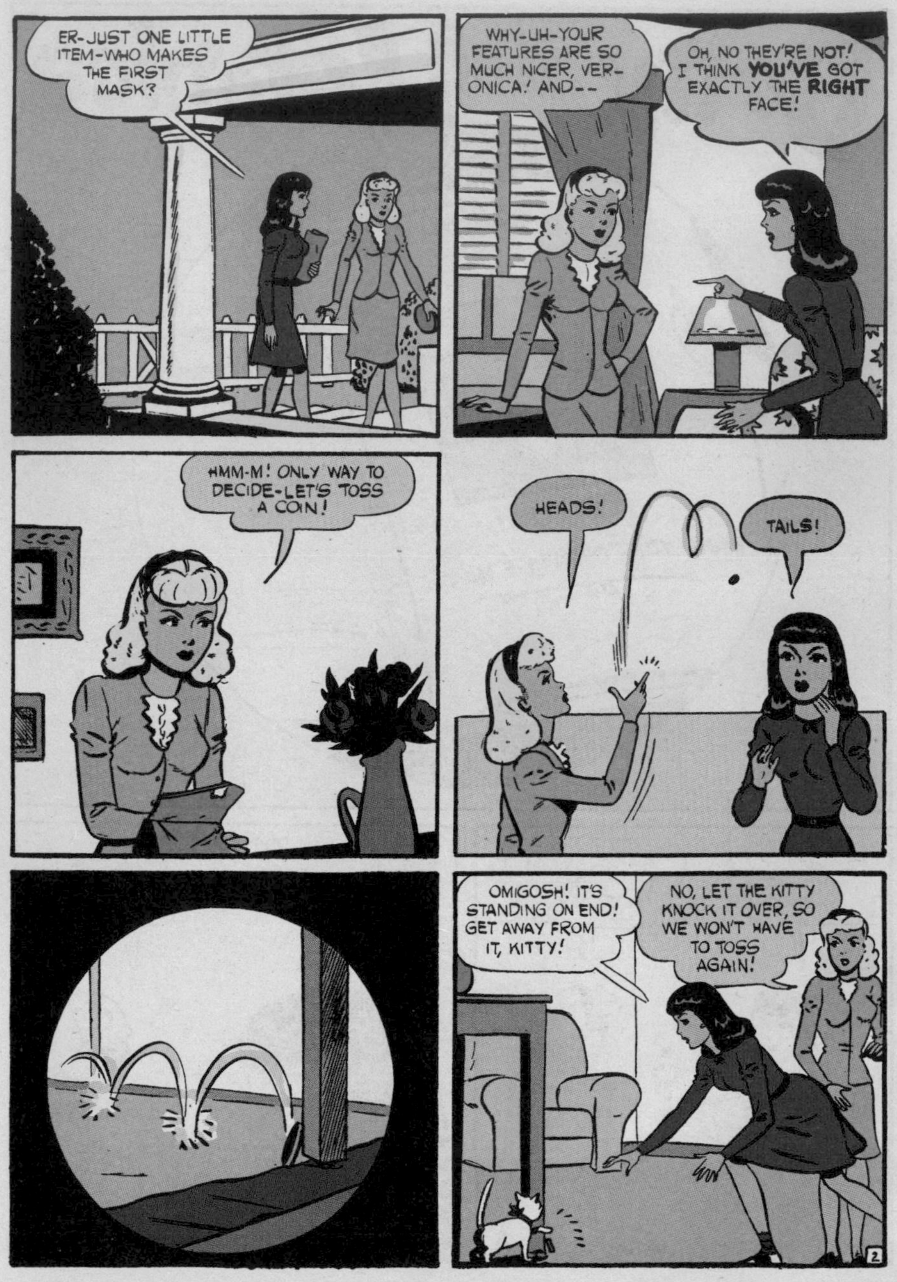
ER-JUST ONE LITTLE ITEM-WHO MAKES THE FIRST MASK?
WHY-UH-YOUR FEATURES ARE SO MUCH NICER, VERONICA! AND--
OH, NO THEY'RE NOT! I THINK YOU'VE GOT EXACTLY THE RIGHT FACE!
HMM-M! ONLY WAY TO DECIDE-LET'S TOSS A COIN!
HEADS!
TAILS!
OMIGOSH! IT'S STANDING ON END! GET AWAY FROM IT, KITTY!
NO, LET THE KITTY KNOCK IT OVER, SO WE WON'T HAVE TO TOSS AGAIN!
2

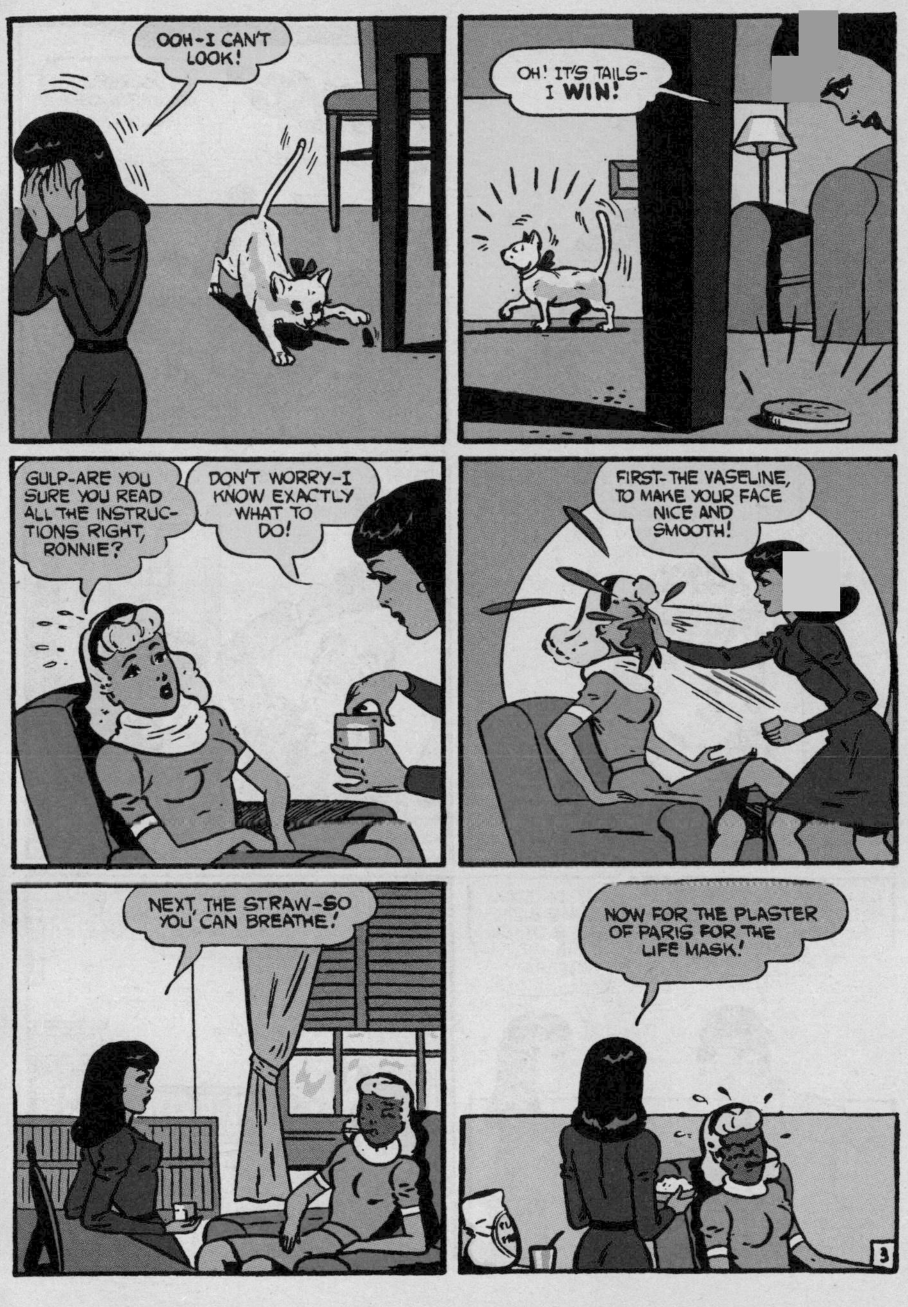
OOH-I CAN'T LOOK!
OH! IT'S TAILS- I WIN!
GULP-ARE YOU SURE YOU READ ALL THE INSTRUCTIONS RIGHT, RONNIE?
DON'T WORRY-I KNOW EXACTLY WHAT TO DO!
FIRST-THE VASELINE, TO MAKE YOUR FACE NICE AND SMOOTH!
NEXT, THE STRAW-SO YOU CAN BREATHE!
NOW FOR THE PLASTER OF PARIS FOR THE LIFE MASK!
3

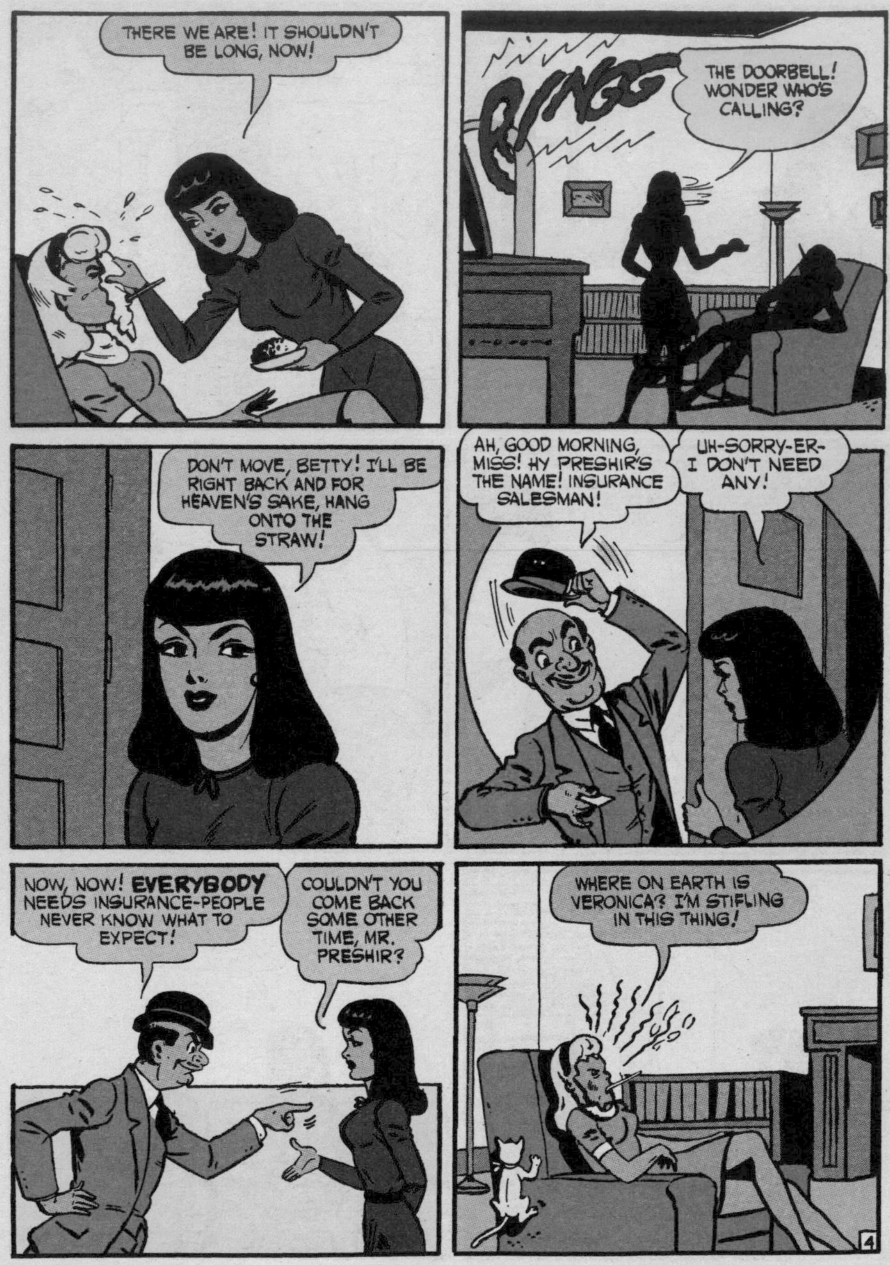
THERE WE ARE! IT SHOULDN'T BE LONG, NOW!
RINGG
THE DOORBELL! WONDER WHO'S CALLING?
DON'T MOVE, BETTY! I'LL BE RIGHT BACK AND FOR HEAVEN'S SAKE, HANG ONTO THE STRAW!
AH, GOOD MORNING, MISS! HY PRESHIR'S THE NAME! INSURANCE SALESMAN!
UH-SORRY-ER- I DON'T NEED ANY!
NOW, NOW! **EVERYBODY** NEEDS INSURANCE-PEOPLE NEVER KNOW WHAT TO EXPECT!
COULDN'T YOU COME BACK SOME OTHER TIME, MR. PRESHIR?
WHERE ON EARTH IS VERONICA? I'M STIFLING IN THIS THING!
4

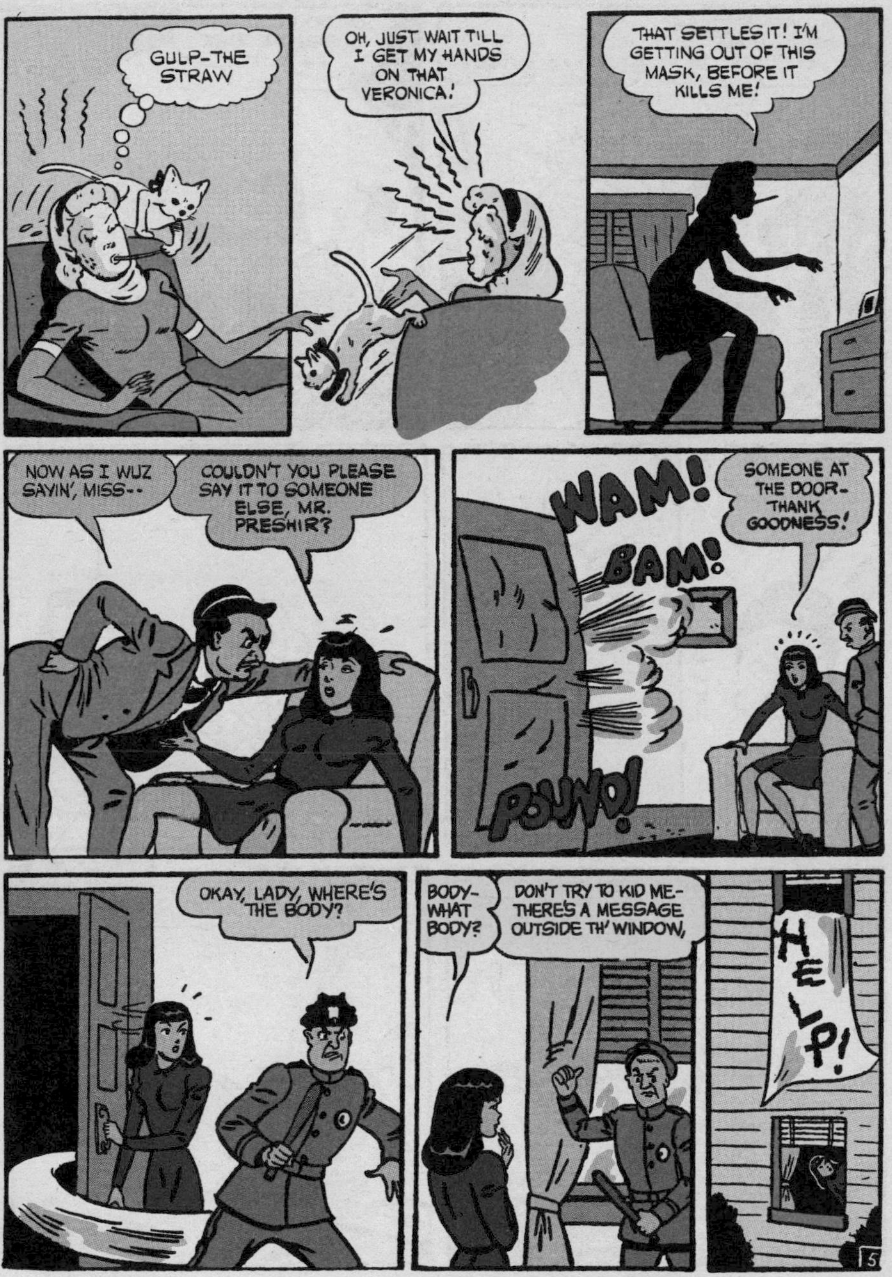
GULP-THE STRAW
OH, JUST WAIT TILL I GET MY HANDS ON THAT VERONICA!
THAT SETTLES IT! I'M GETTING OUT OF THIS MASK, BEFORE IT KILLS ME!
NOW AS I WUZ SAYIN', MISS--
COULDN'T YOU PLEASE SAY IT TO SOMEONE ELSE, MR. PRESHIR?
WAM!
BAM!
POUND!
SOMEONE AT THE DOOR-THANK GOODNESS!
OKAY, LADY, WHERE'S THE BODY?
BODY-WHAT BODY?
DON'T TRY TO KID ME-THERE'S A MESSAGE OUTSIDE TH' WINDOW,
HELP!
5

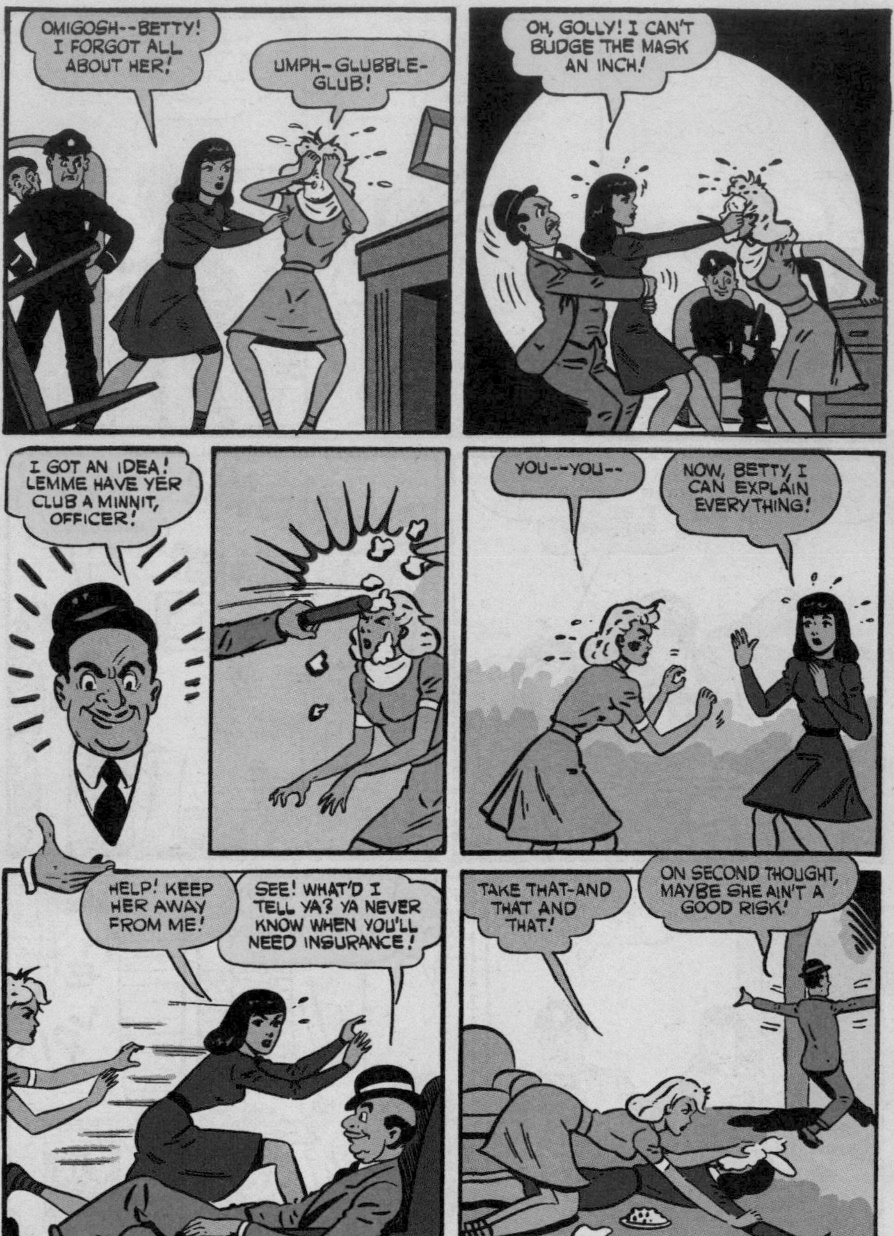
OMIGOSH--BETTY! I FORGOT ALL ABOUT HER!
UMPH-GLUBBLE-GLUB!
OH, GOLLY! I CAN'T BUDGE THE MASK AN INCH!
I GOT AN IDEA! LEMME HAVE YER CLUB A MINNIT, OFFICER!
YOU--YOU--
NOW, BETTY, I CAN EXPLAIN EVERYTHING!
HELP! KEEP HER AWAY FROM ME!
SEE! WHAT'D I TELL YA? YA NEVER KNOW WHEN YOU'LL NEED INSURANCE!
TAKE THAT-AND THAT AND THAT!
ON SECOND THOUGHT, MAYBE SHE AIN'T A GOOD RISK!
6

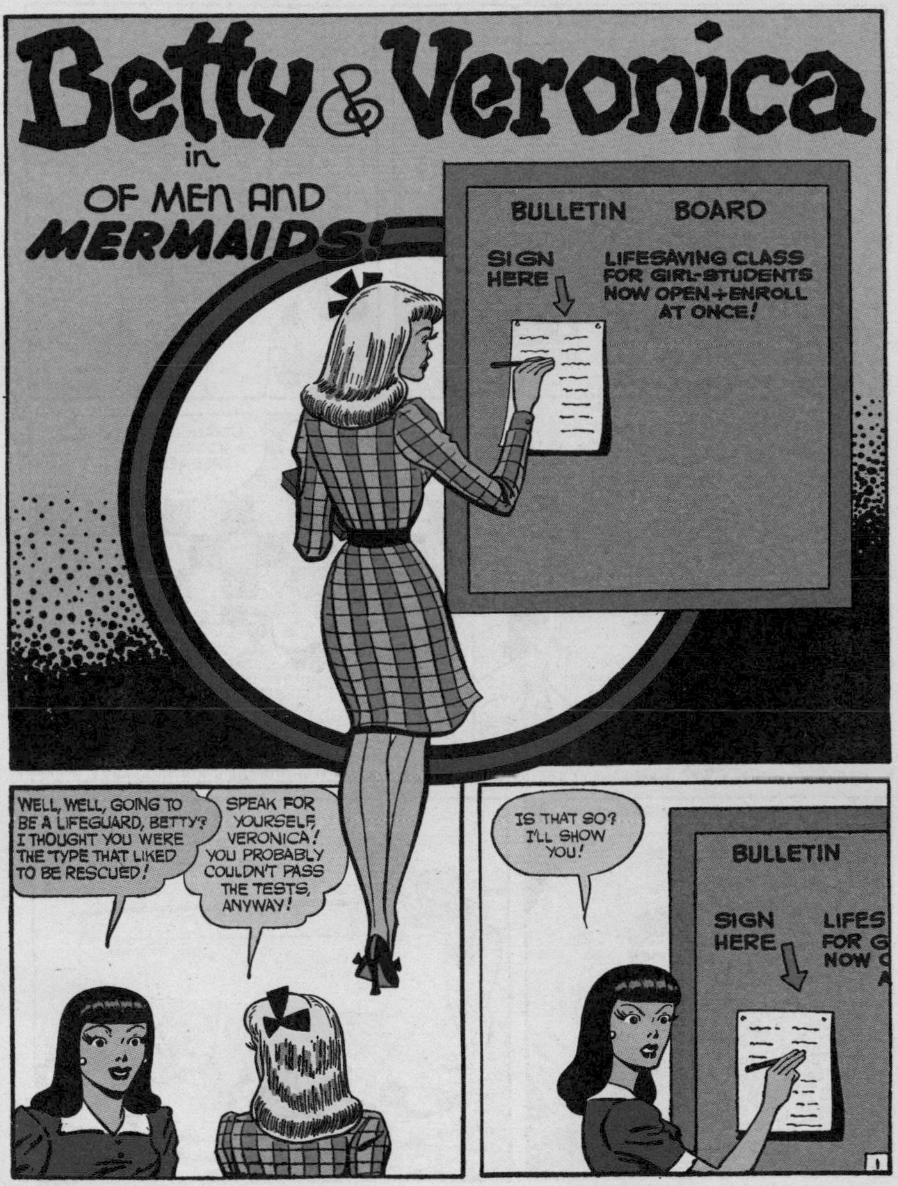
Betty & Veronica
in
OF MEN AND MERMAIDS!
BULLETIN BOARD
SIGN HERE
LIFESAVING CLASS FOR GIRL-STUDENTS NOW OPEN-ENROLL AT ONCE!
WELL, WELL, GOING TO BE A LIFEGUARD, BETTY? I THOUGHT YOU WERE THE TYPE THAT LIKED TO BE RESCUED!
SPEAK FOR YOURSELF, VERONICA! YOU PROBABLY COULDN'T PASS THE TESTS, ANYWAY!
IS THAT SO? I'LL SHOW YOU!
BULLETIN
SIGN HERE
1

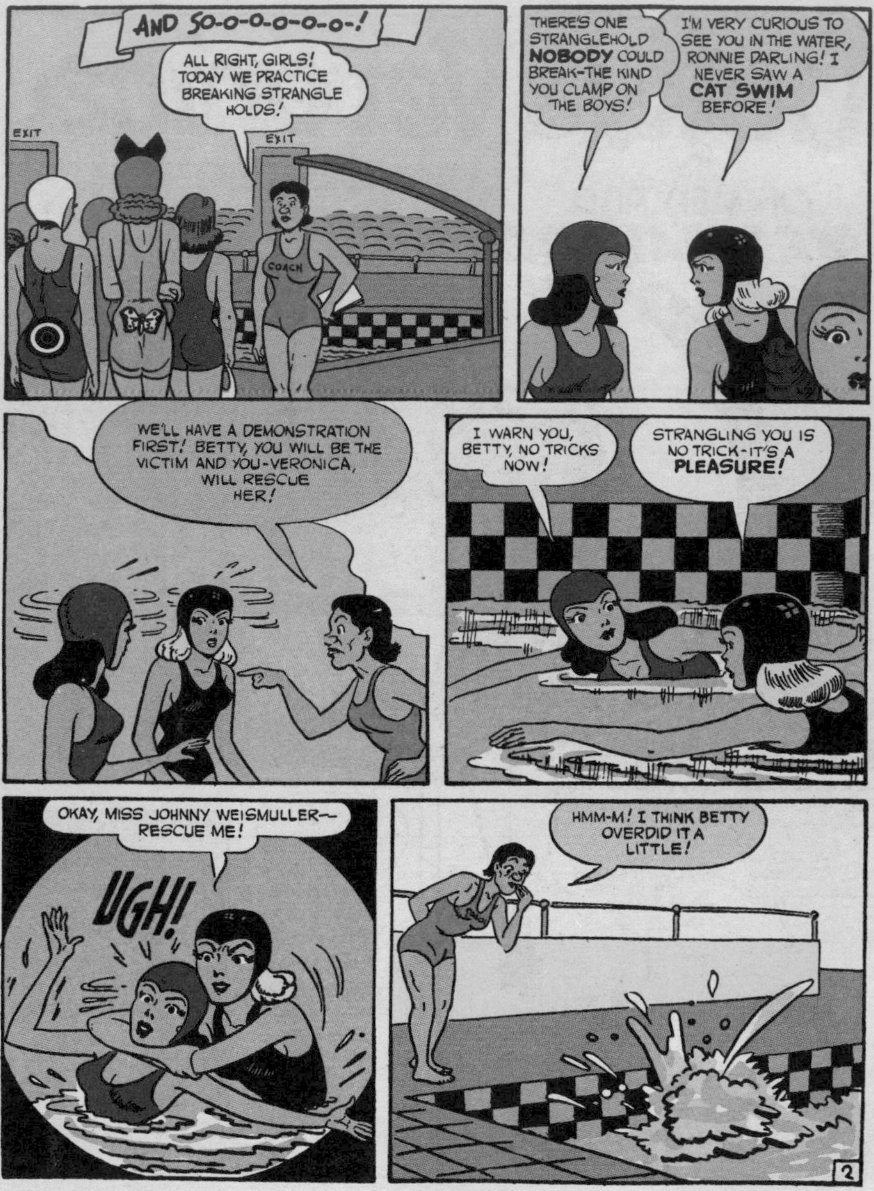
AND SO-O-O-O-O-O-!
ALL RIGHT, GIRLS! TODAY WE PRACTICE BREAKING STRANGLE HOLDS!
EXIT
EXIT
COACH
THERE'S ONE STRANGLEHOLD NOBODY COULD BREAK—THE KIND YOU CLAMP ON THE BOYS!
I'M VERY CURIOUS TO SEE YOU IN THE WATER, RONNIE DARLING! I NEVER SAW A CAT SWIM BEFORE!
WE'LL HAVE A DEMONSTRATION FIRST! BETTY, YOU WILL BE THE VICTIM AND YOU-VERONICA, WILL RESCUE HER!
I WARN YOU, BETTY, NO TRICKS NOW!
STRANGLING YOU IS NO TRICK-IT'S A PLEASURE!
OKAY, MISS JOHNNY WEISMULLER— RESCUE ME!
UGH!
HMM-M! I THINK BETTY OVERDID IT A LITTLE!
2

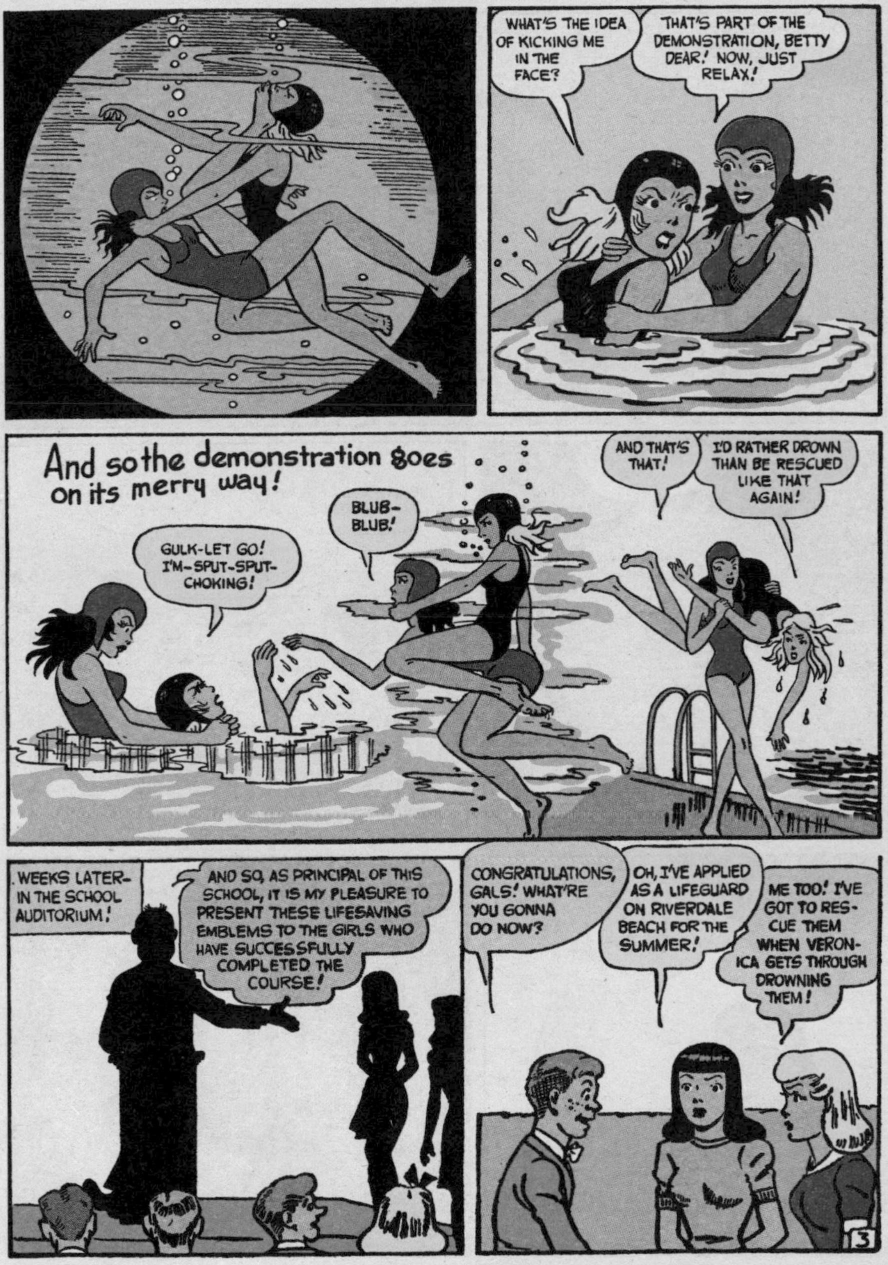
WHAT'S THE IDEA OF KICKING ME IN THE FACE?
THAT'S PART OF THE DEMONSTRATION, BETTY DEAR! NOW, JUST RELAX!
And so the demonstration goes on its merry way!
GULK-LET GO! I'M-SPUT-SPUT-CHOKING!
BLUB-BLUB!
AND THAT'S THAT!
I'D RATHER DROWN THAN BE RESCUED LIKE THAT AGAIN!
WEEKS LATER-IN THE SCHOOL AUDITORIUM!
AND SO, AS PRINCIPAL OF THIS SCHOOL, IT IS MY PLEASURE TO PRESENT THESE LIFESAVING EMBLEMS TO THE GIRLS WHO HAVE SUCCESSFULLY COMPLETED THE COURSE!
CONGRATULATIONS, GALS! WHAT'RE YOU GONNA DO NOW?
OH, I'VE APPLIED AS A LIFEGUARD ON RIVERDALE BEACH FOR THE SUMMER!
ME TOO! I'VE GOT TO RESCUE THEM WHEN VERONICA GETS THROUGH DROWNING THEM!
3

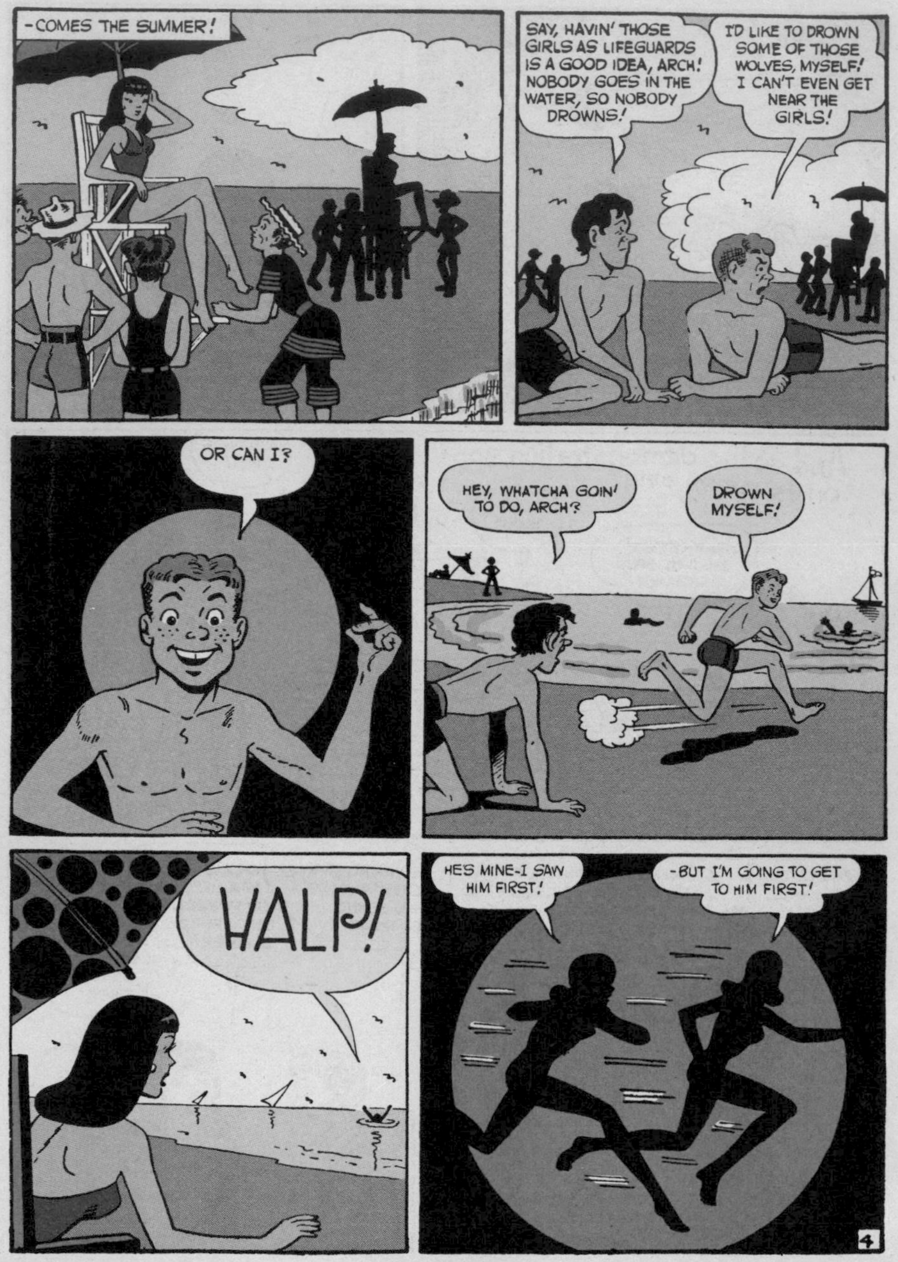
-COMES THE SUMMER!
SAY, HAVIN' THOSE GIRLS AS LIFEGUARDS IS A GOOD IDEA, ARCH! NOBODY GOES IN THE WATER, SO NOBODY DROWNS!
I'D LIKE TO DROWN SOME OF THOSE WOLVES, MYSELF! I CAN'T EVEN GET NEAR THE GIRLS!
OR CAN I?
HEY, WHATCHA GOIN' TO DO, ARCH?
DROWN MYSELF!
HALP!
HE'S MINE-I SAW HIM FIRST!
-BUT I'M GOING TO GET TO HIM FIRST!
4

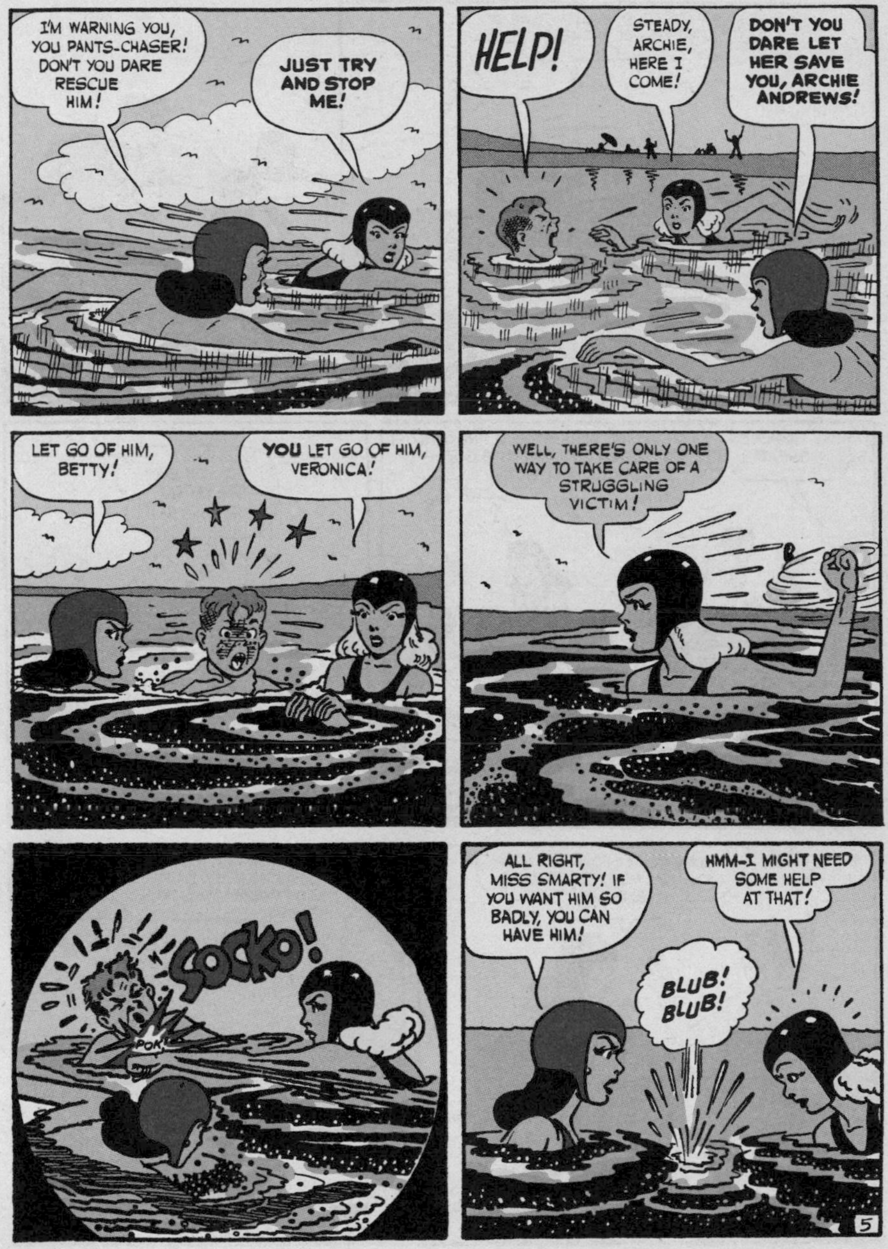
I'M WARNING YOU, YOU PANTS-CHASER! DON'T YOU DARE RESCUE HIM!
JUST TRY AND STOP ME!
HELP!
STEADY, ARCHIE, HERE I COME!
DON'T YOU DARE LET HER SAVE YOU, ARCHIE ANDREWS!
LET GO OF HIM, BETTY!
YOU LET GO OF HIM, VERONICA!
WELL, THERE'S ONLY ONE WAY TO TAKE CARE OF A STRUGGLING VICTIM!
SOCKO!
POK
ALL RIGHT, MISS SMARTY! IF YOU WANT HIM SO BADLY, YOU CAN HAVE HIM!
HMM-I MIGHT NEED SOME HELP AT THAT!
BLUB! BLUB!
5

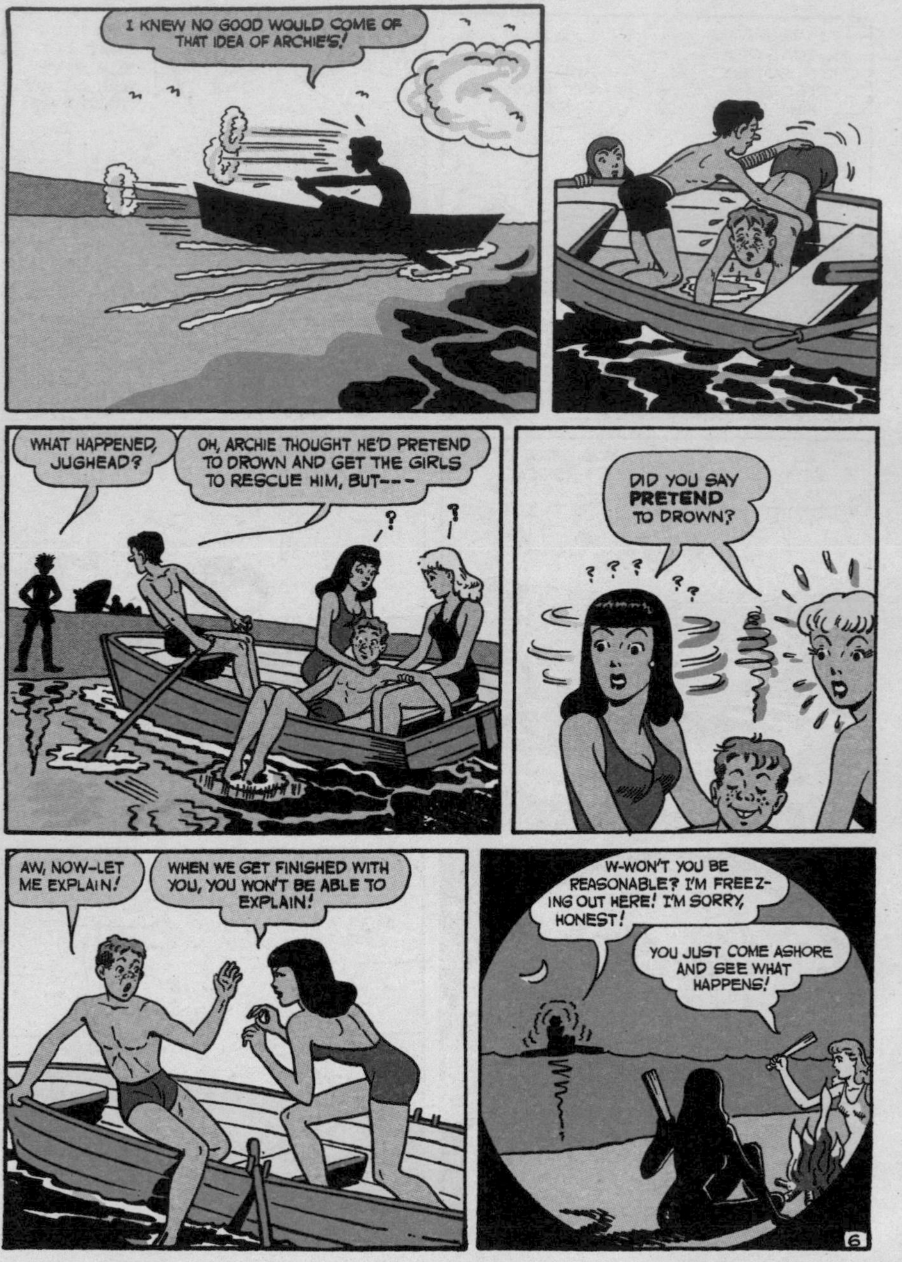
I KNEW NO GOOD WOULD COME OF THAT IDEA OF ARCHIE'S!
WHAT HAPPENED, JUGHEAD?
OH, ARCHIE THOUGHT HE'D PRETEND TO DROWN AND GET THE GIRLS TO RESCUE HIM, BUT---
DID YOU SAY **PRETEND** TO DROWN?
AW, NOW--LET ME EXPLAIN!
WHEN WE GET FINISHED WITH YOU, YOU WON'T BE ABLE TO EXPLAIN!
W-WON'T YOU BE REASONABLE? I'M FREEZ-ING OUT HERE! I'M SORRY, HONEST!
YOU JUST COME ASHORE AND SEE WHAT HAPPENS!
6

Women Flyers
Archie #19, 1946
by Bill Vigoda

The thing I love best about Betty and Veronica is that they're best friends despite being polar opposites. Their constant rivalry adds a good dose of tension and humor to every story, but I always loved knowing that, despite their competitiveness, they were still fast friends at the end of the day. Growing up, they also reminded me of my own best friend and myself. I was definitely more like Betty: a goody two shoes. My best friend was more like Veronica: bolder and more outspoken. I used to envy that quality and wanted to be more like her (and Veronica). But, since then, I've learned that both Betty and Veronica have traits that can go too far in either direction: Betty can be a bit too naïve, and Veronica can be a bit too overbearing. The ideal balance is a mix between the two girls' personalities, which explains why their friendship works — and why I'm still best friends with my own Veronica after all these years!

-- **Tania del Rio**
Writer/Artist,
Archie Comics

Go To The Dogs
Archie #23, 1946
by Bill Woggon
-and-
Betty & Veronica
Laugh #20, 1946
by Irv Novick

Exams can be *ruff* for anyone, especially when you can't seem to get your mind off of them. And who hasn't had a parent yell at them to get a job when it's time to pay the bills? Yet through and through Betty & Veronica seem to find a way to make the best of things, even if they end up seeing their teacher's heads on animal bodies and getting into all kinds of trouble looking for the right job.

In these classic B&V stories, Bill Woggon brings his famous pin-up art style from the world of super-model Katy Keene into the *dog eat dog* world of Betty & Veronica, while Irv Novick proves that knock-down, drag-out brawls aren't just for super heroes!

-- **Joe Morciglio**
Project Coordinator,
Archie Comics

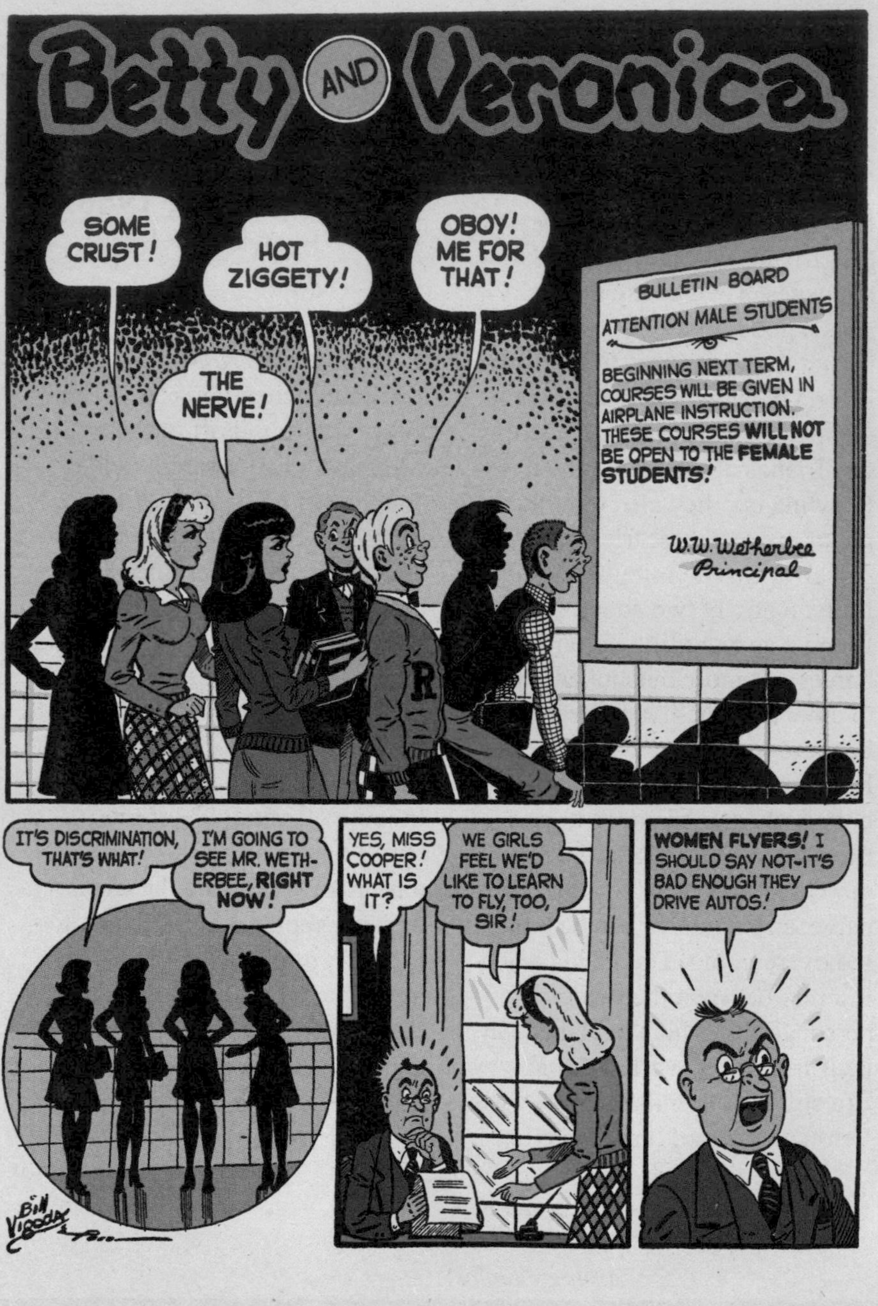
Betty AND Veronica
SOME CRUST!
HOT ZIGGETY!
OBOY! ME FOR THAT!
THE NERVE!
BULLETIN BOARD
ATTENTION MALE STUDENTS
BEGINNING NEXT TERM, COURSES WILL BE GIVEN IN AIRPLANE INSTRUCTION. THESE COURSES WILL NOT BE OPEN TO THE FEMALE STUDENTS!
W.W. Wetherbee Principal
IT'S DISCRIMINATION, THAT'S WHAT!
I'M GOING TO SEE MR. WETHERBEE, RIGHT NOW!
Bill Vigoda
YES, MISS COOPER! WHAT IS IT?
WE GIRLS FEEL WE'D LIKE TO LEARN TO FLY, TOO, SIR!
WOMEN FLYERS! I SHOULD SAY NOT-IT'S BAD ENOUGH THEY DRIVE AUTOS!

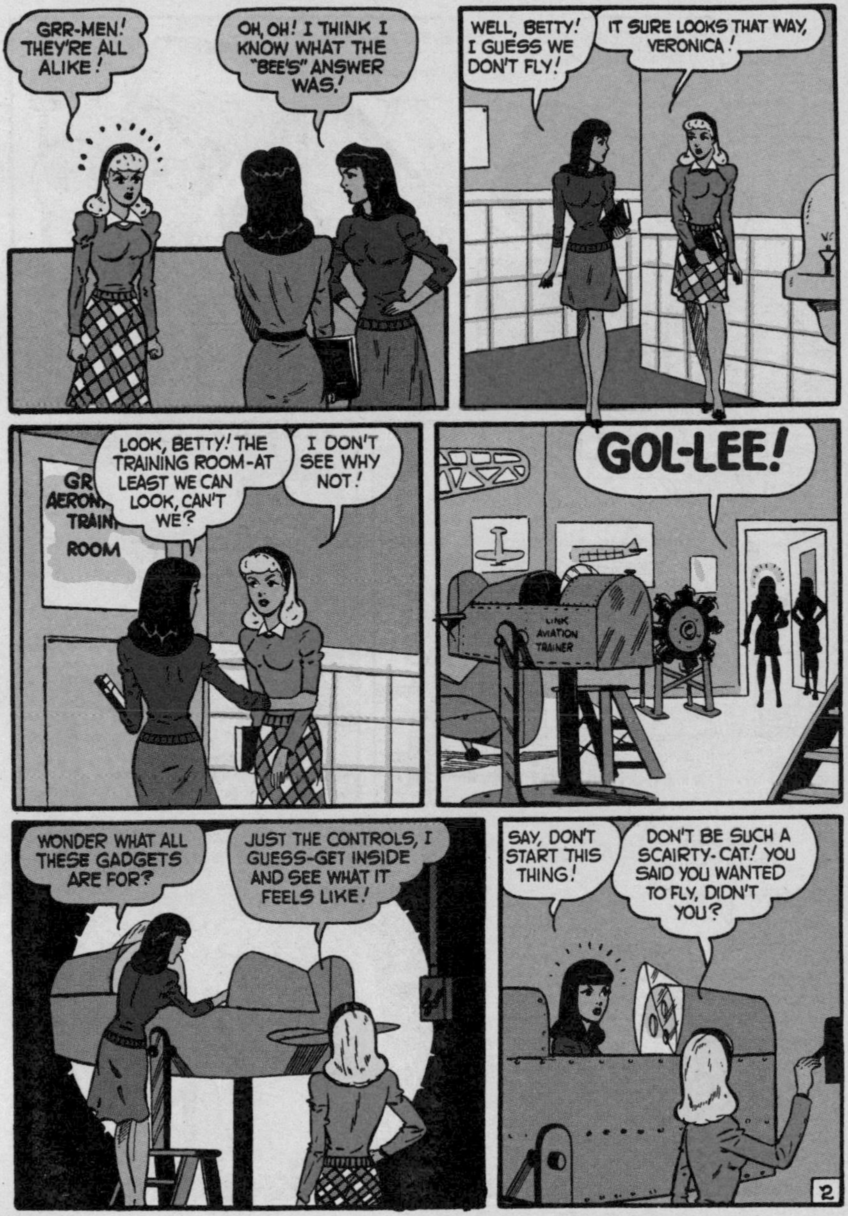
GRR-MEN! THEY'RE ALL ALIKE!
OH, OH! I THINK I KNOW WHAT THE "BEE'S" ANSWER WAS!
WELL, BETTY! I GUESS WE DON'T FLY!
IT SURE LOOKS THAT WAY, VERONICA!
LOOK, BETTY! THE TRAINING ROOM-AT LEAST WE CAN LOOK, CAN'T WE?
I DON'T SEE WHY NOT!
ROOM
GOL-LEE!
LINK AVIATION TRAINER
WONDER WHAT ALL THESE GADGETS ARE FOR?
JUST THE CONTROLS, I GUESS-GET INSIDE AND SEE WHAT IT FEELS LIKE!
SAY, DON'T START THIS THING!
DON'T BE SUCH A SCAIRTY-CAT! YOU SAID YOU WANTED TO FLY, DIDN'T YOU?
2

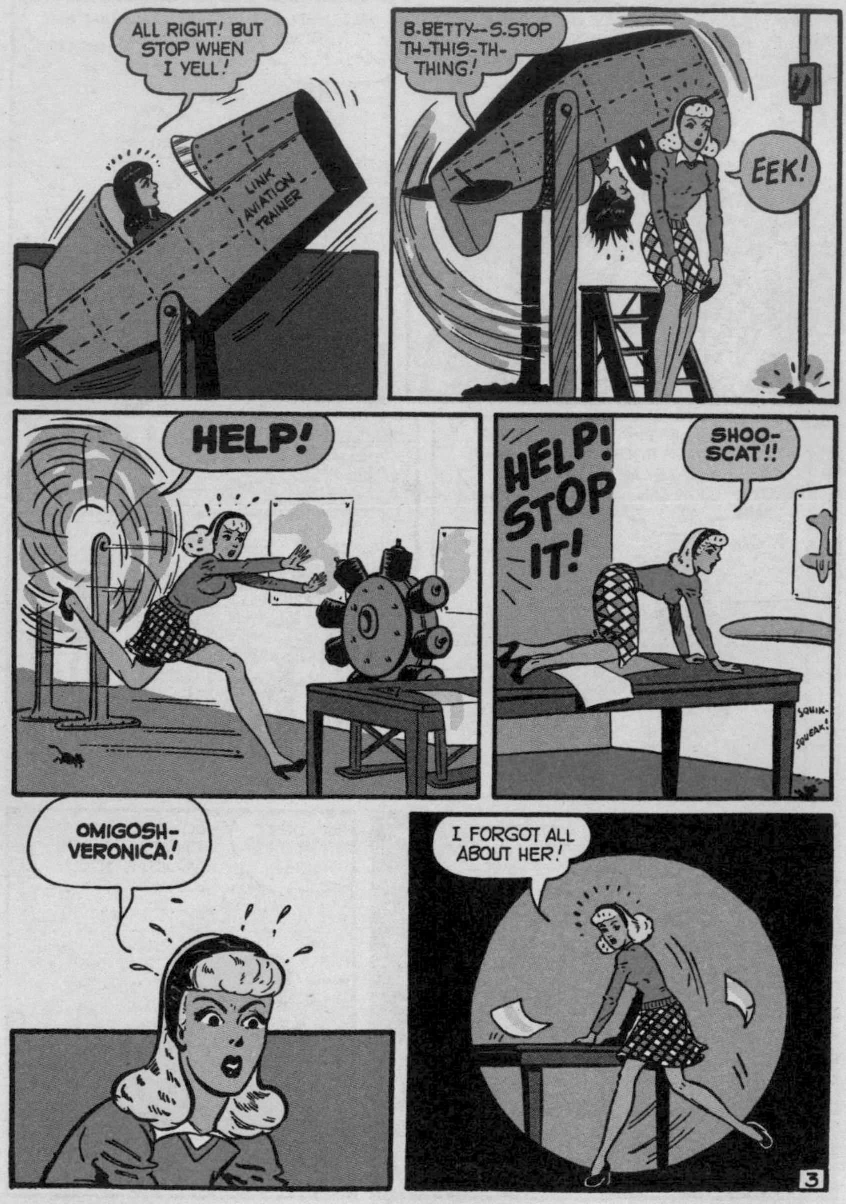
ALL RIGHT! BUT STOP WHEN I YELL!
LINK AVIATION TRAINER
B.BETTY--S.STOP TH-THIS-TH-THING!
EEK!
HELP!
HELP! STOP IT!
SHOO-SCAT!!
SQUIK-SQUEAK!
OMIGOSH-VERONICA!
I FORGOT ALL ABOUT HER!
3

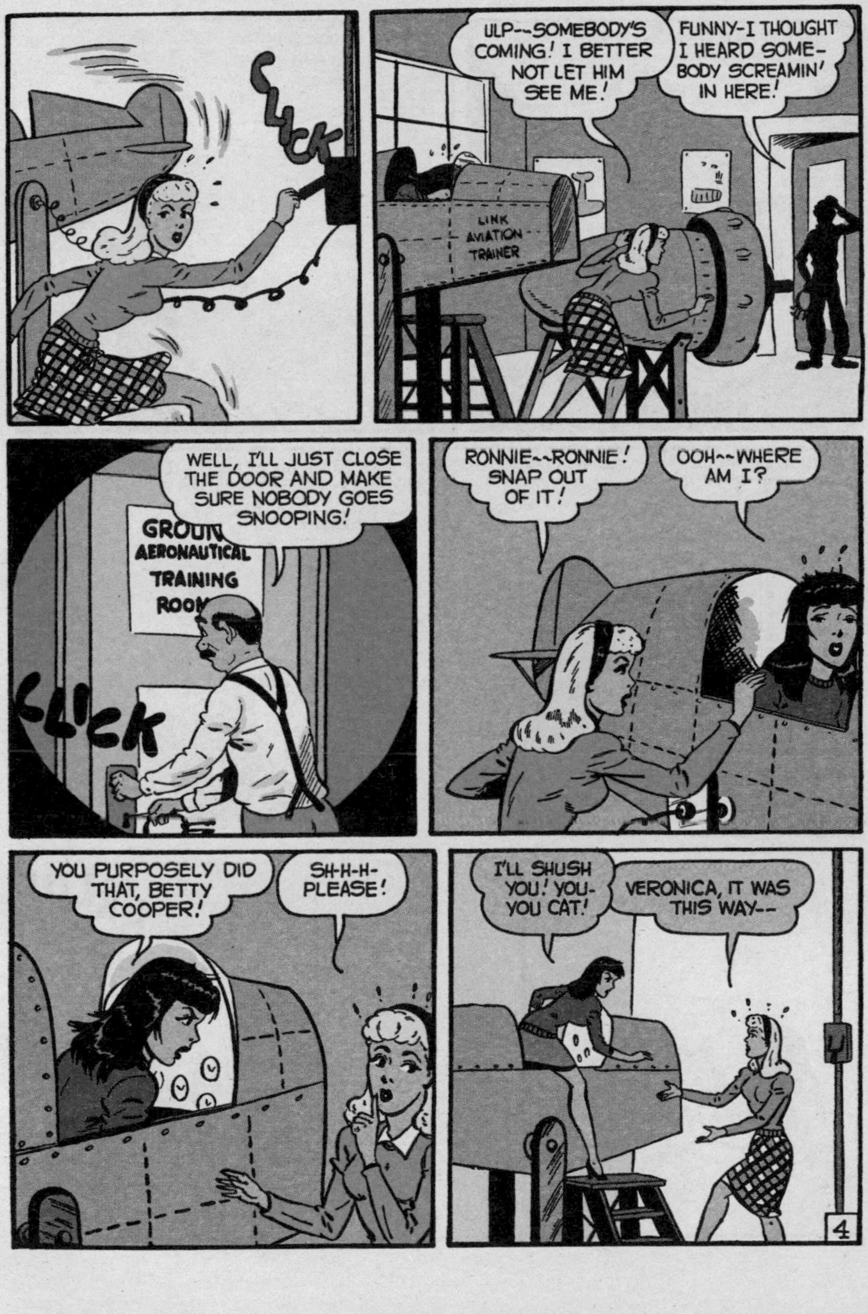
CLICK
ULP--SOMEBODY'S COMING! I BETTER NOT LET HIM SEE ME!
FUNNY-I THOUGHT I HEARD SOME-BODY SCREAMIN' IN HERE!
LINK AVIATION TRAINER
WELL, I'LL JUST CLOSE THE DOOR AND MAKE SURE NOBODY GOES SNOOPING!
AERONAUTICAL TRAINING
CLICK
RONNIE--RONNIE! SNAP OUT OF IT!
OOH--WHERE AM I?
YOU PURPOSELY DID THAT, BETTY COOPER!
SH-H-H- PLEASE!
I'LL SHUSH YOU! YOU-YOU CAT!
VERONICA, IT WAS THIS WAY--
4

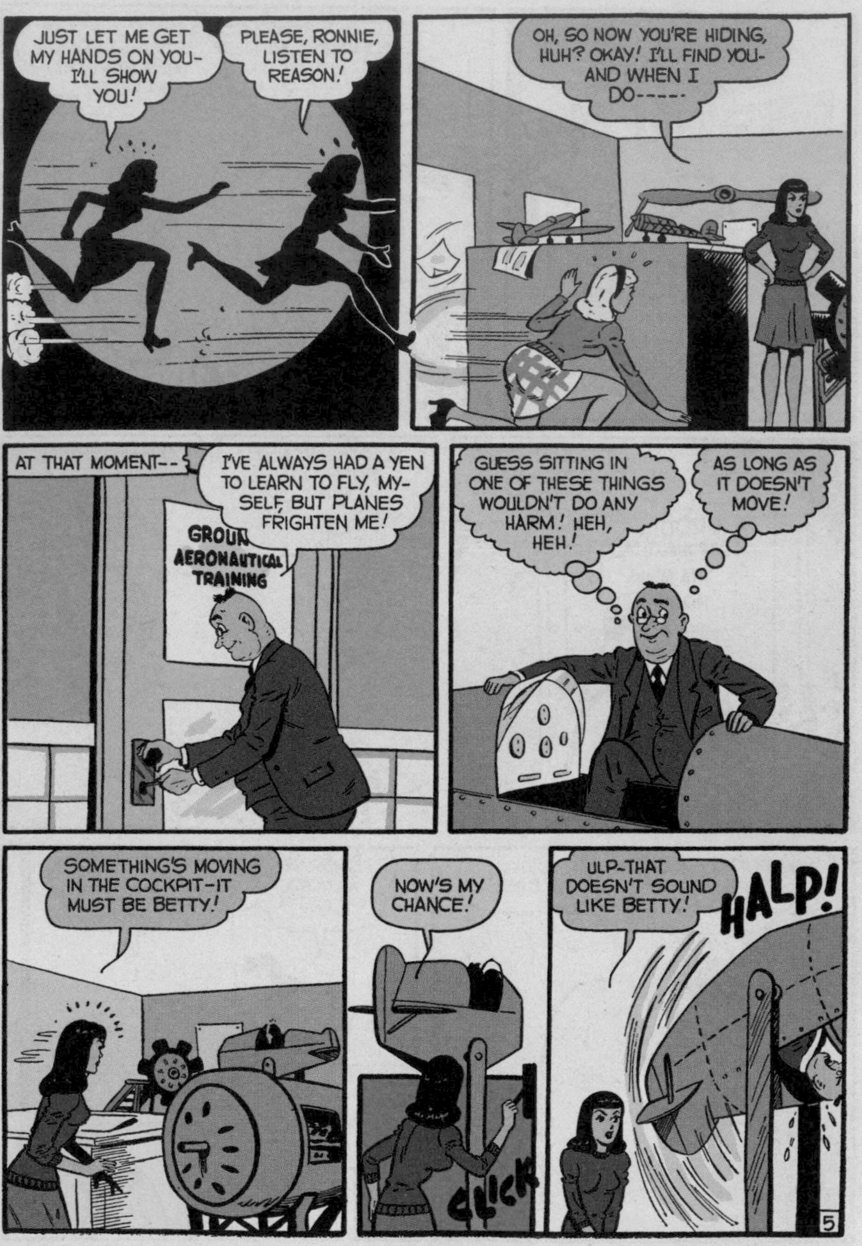
JUST LET ME GET MY HANDS ON YOU- I'LL SHOW YOU!
PLEASE, RONNIE, LISTEN TO REASON!
OH, SO NOW YOU'RE HIDING, HUH? OKAY! I'LL FIND YOU- AND WHEN I DO-----
AT THAT MOMENT--
I'VE ALWAYS HAD A YEN TO LEARN TO FLY, MY-SELF, BUT PLANES FRIGHTEN ME!
GROUN
AERONAUTICAL TRAINING
GUESS SITTING IN ONE OF THESE THINGS WOULDN'T DO ANY HARM! HEH, HEH!
AS LONG AS IT DOESN'T MOVE!
SOMETHING'S MOVING IN THE COCKPIT-IT MUST BE BETTY!
NOW'S MY CHANCE!
CLICK
ULP-THAT DOESN'T SOUND LIKE BETTY!
HALP!
5

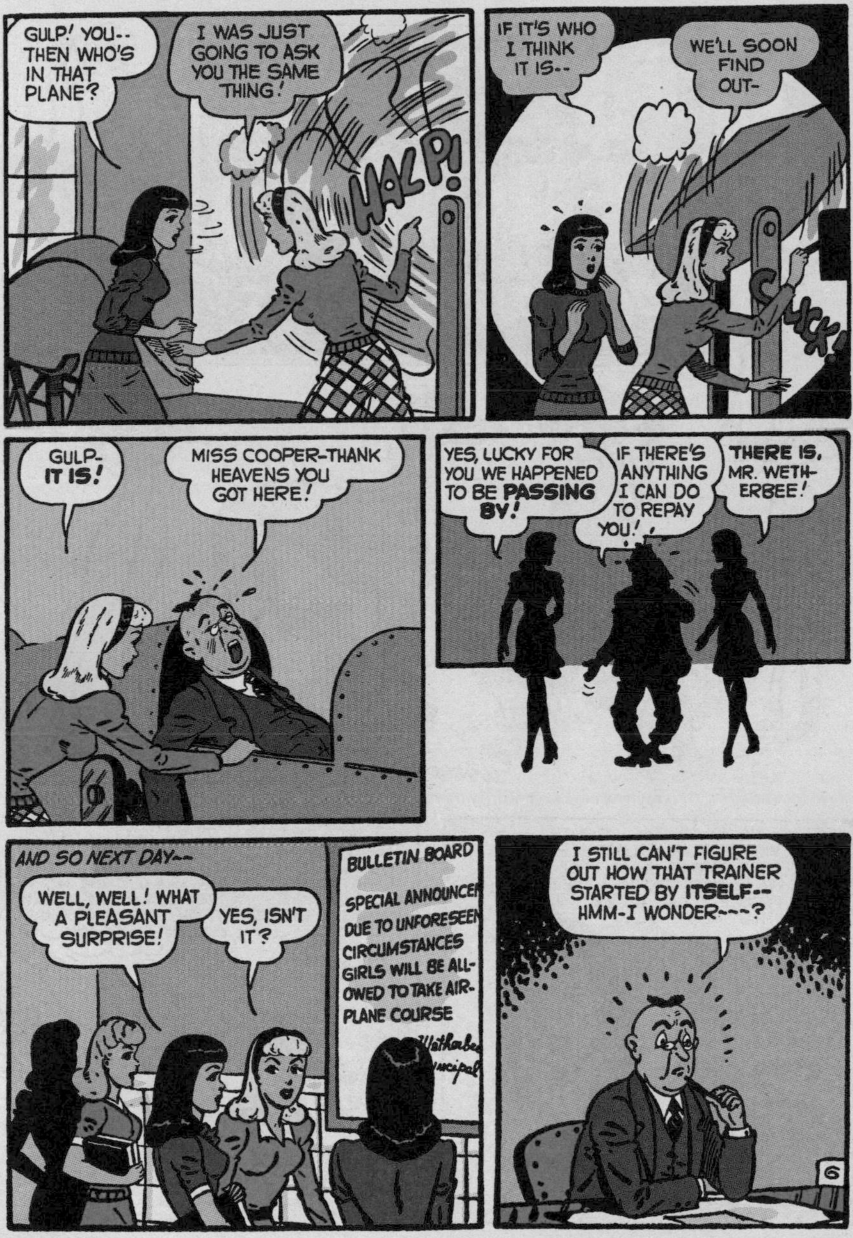
GULP! YOU-- THEN WHO'S IN THAT PLANE?
I WAS JUST GOING TO ASK YOU THE SAME THING!
HALP!
IF IT'S WHO I THINK IT IS--
WE'LL SOON FIND OUT-
CLICK!
GULP- IT IS!
MISS COOPER-THANK HEAVENS YOU GOT HERE!
YES, LUCKY FOR YOU WE HAPPENED TO BE PASSING BY!
IF THERE'S ANYTHING I CAN DO TO REPAY YOU!
THERE IS, MR. WETH-ERBEE!
AND SO NEXT DAY--
WELL, WELL! WHAT A PLEASANT SURPRISE!
YES, ISN'T IT?
BULLETIN BOARD
SPECIAL ANNOUNCE
DUE TO UNFORESEEN
CIRCUMSTANCES
GIRLS WILL BE ALL-
OWED TO TAKE AIR-
PLANE COURSE
I STILL CAN'T FIGURE OUT HOW THAT TRAINER STARTED BY ITSELF-- HMM-I WONDER---?

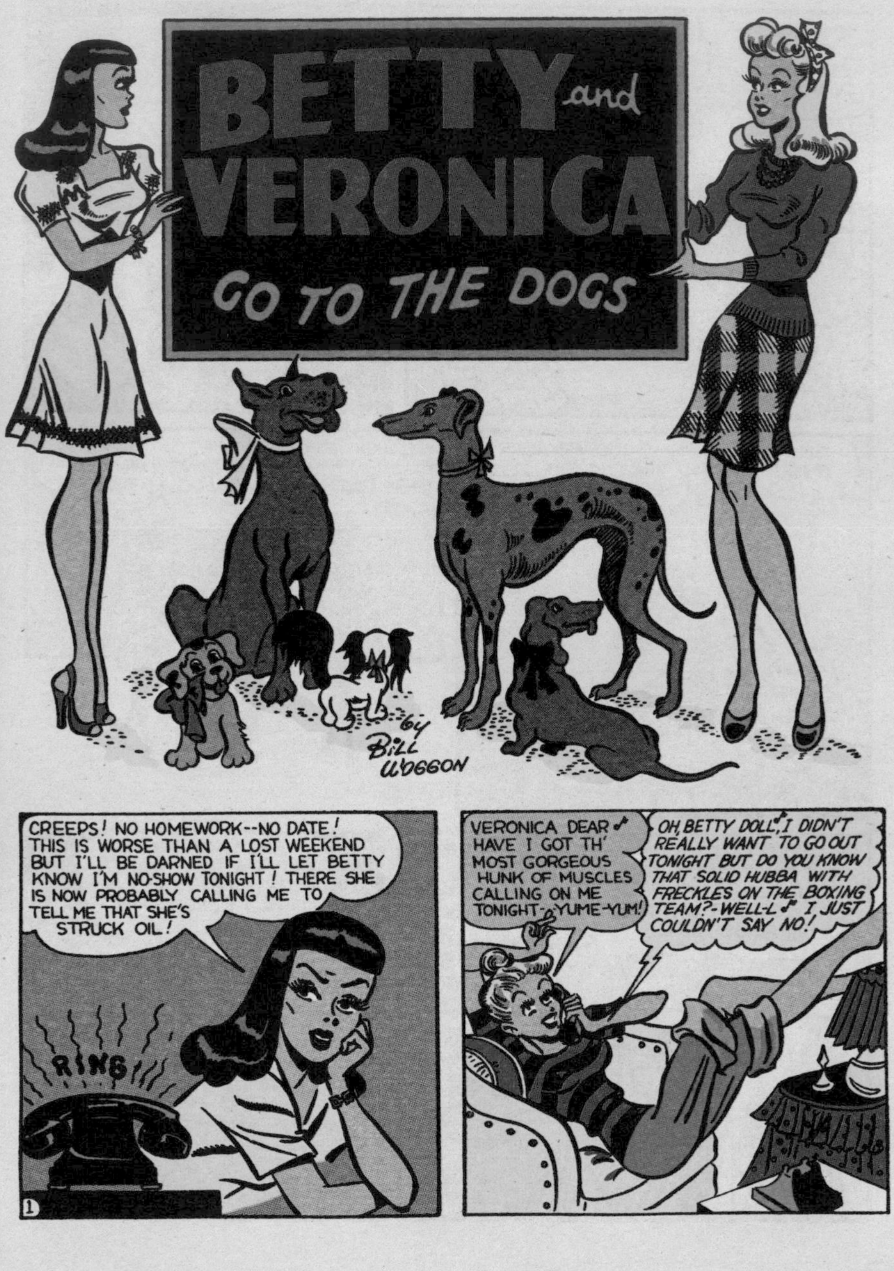
BETTY and VERONICA
GO TO THE DOGS
'64
BILL WOGGON
CREEPS! NO HOMEWORK--NO DATE! THIS IS WORSE THAN A LOST WEEKEND BUT I'LL BE DARNED IF I'LL LET BETTY KNOW I'M NO-SHOW TONIGHT! THERE SHE IS NOW PROBABLY CALLING ME TO TELL ME THAT SHE'S STRUCK OIL!
RING
VERONICA DEAR HAVE I GOT TH' MOST GORGEOUS HUNK OF MUSCLES CALLING ON ME TONIGHT-YUME-YUM!
OH, BETTY DOLL, I DIDN'T REALLY WANT TO GO OUT TONIGHT BUT DO YOU KNOW THAT SOLID HUBBA WITH FRECKLES ON THE BOXING TEAM?-WELL-L I JUST COULDN'T SAY NO!

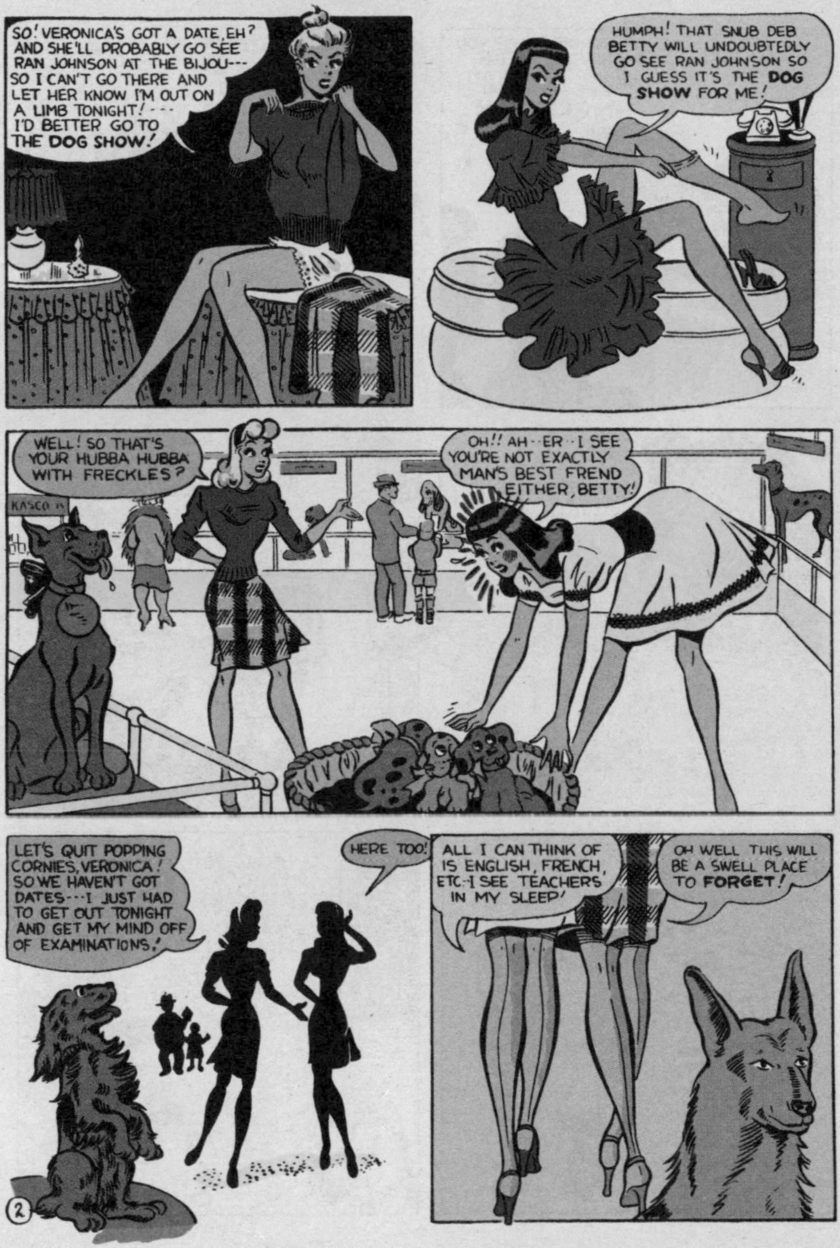
SO! VERONICA'S GOT A DATE, EH? AND SHE'LL PROBABLY GO SEE RAN JOHNSON AT THE BIJOU--- SO I CAN'T GO THERE AND LET HER KNOW I'M OUT ON A LIMB TONIGHT! --- I'D BETTER GO TO THE DOG SHOW!
HUMPH! THAT SNUB DEB BETTY WILL UNDOUBTEDLY GO SEE RAN JOHNSON SO I GUESS IT'S THE DOG SHOW FOR ME!
WELL! SO THAT'S YOUR HUBBA HUBBA WITH FRECKLES?
OH!! AH--ER--I SEE YOU'RE NOT EXACTLY MAN'S BEST FREND EITHER, BETTY!
KASCO
LET'S QUIT POPPING CORNIES, VERONICA! SO WE HAVEN'T GOT DATES---I JUST HAD TO GET OUT TONIGHT AND GET MY MIND OFF OF EXAMINATIONS!
HERE TOO!
2
ALL I CAN THINK OF IS ENGLISH, FRENCH, ETC.--I SEE TEACHERS IN MY SLEEP!
OH WELL THIS WILL BE A SWELL PLACE TO FORGET!

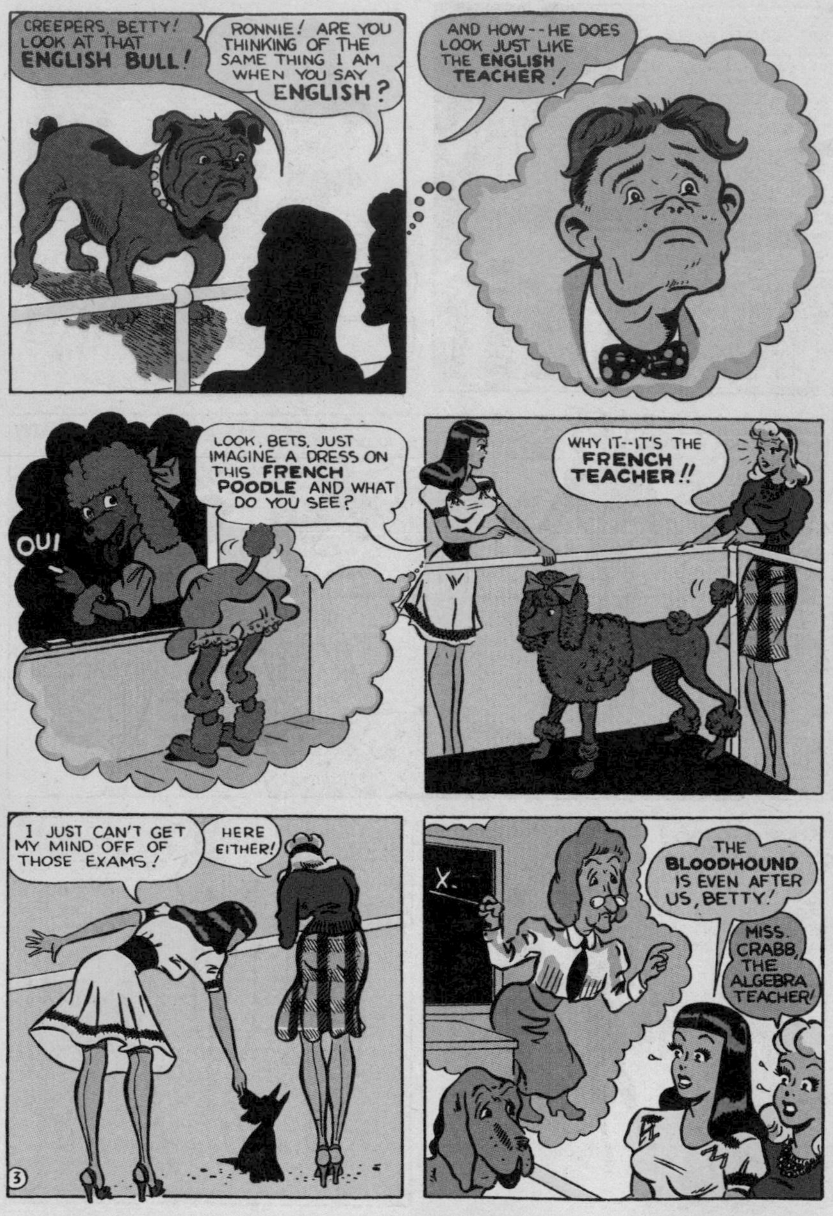
CREEPERS, BETTY! LOOK AT THAT ENGLISH BULL!
RONNIE! ARE YOU THINKING OF THE SAME THING I AM WHEN YOU SAY ENGLISH?
AND HOW--HE DOES LOOK JUST LIKE THE ENGLISH TEACHER!
LOOK, BETS, JUST IMAGINE A DRESS ON THIS FRENCH POODLE AND WHAT DO YOU SEE?
OUI
WHY IT--IT'S THE FRENCH TEACHER!!
I JUST CAN'T GET MY MIND OFF OF THOSE EXAMS!
HERE EITHER!
3
X
THE BLOODHOUND IS EVEN AFTER US, BETTY!
MISS. CRABB, THE ALGEBRA TEACHER!

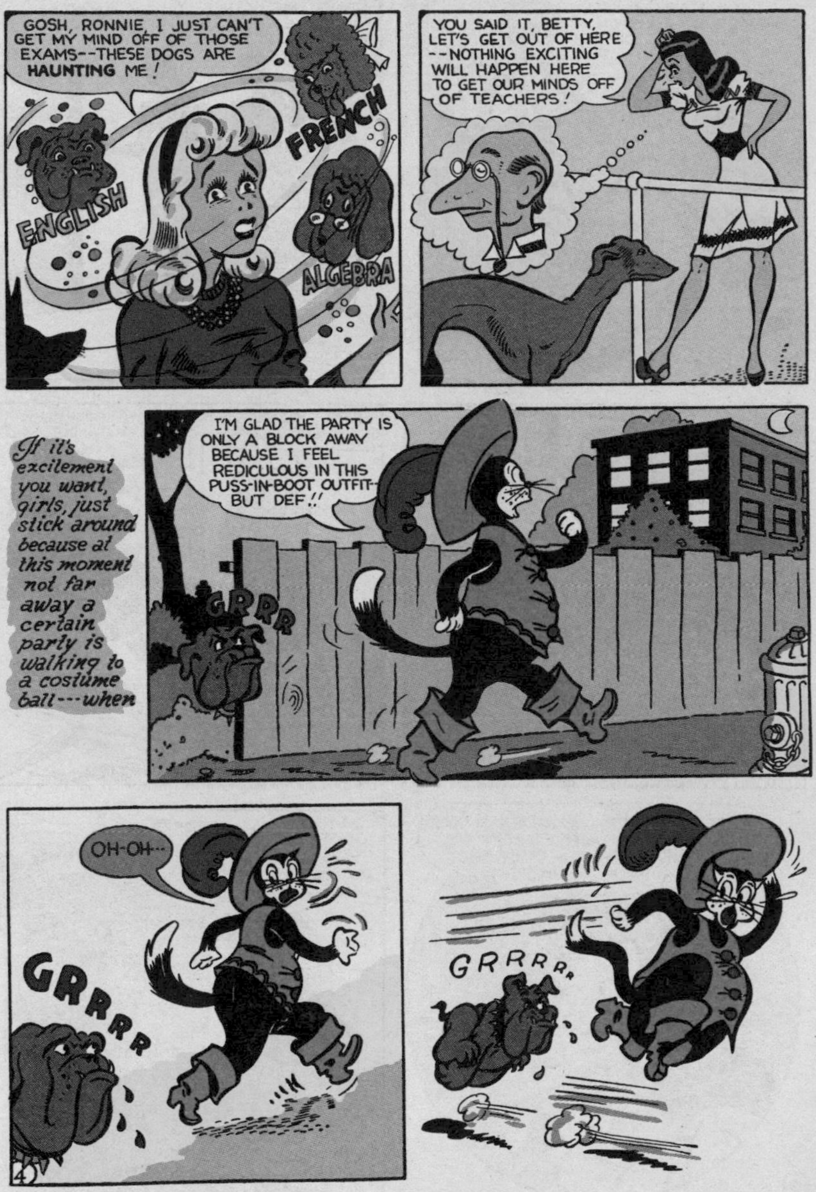
GOSH, RONNIE, I JUST CAN'T GET MY MIND OFF OF THOSE EXAMS--THESE DOGS ARE HAUNTING ME!
FRENCH
ENGLISH
ALGEBRA
YOU SAID IT, BETTY, LET'S GET OUT OF HERE --NOTHING EXCITING WILL HAPPEN HERE TO GET OUR MINDS OFF OF TEACHERS!
If it's excitement you want, girls, just stick around because at this moment not far away a certain party is walking to a costume ball---when
I'M GLAD THE PARTY IS ONLY A BLOCK AWAY BECAUSE I FEEL REDICULOUS IN THIS PUSS-IN-BOOT OUTFIT-BUT DEF!!
GRRR
OH-OH---
GRRRR
GRRRRR

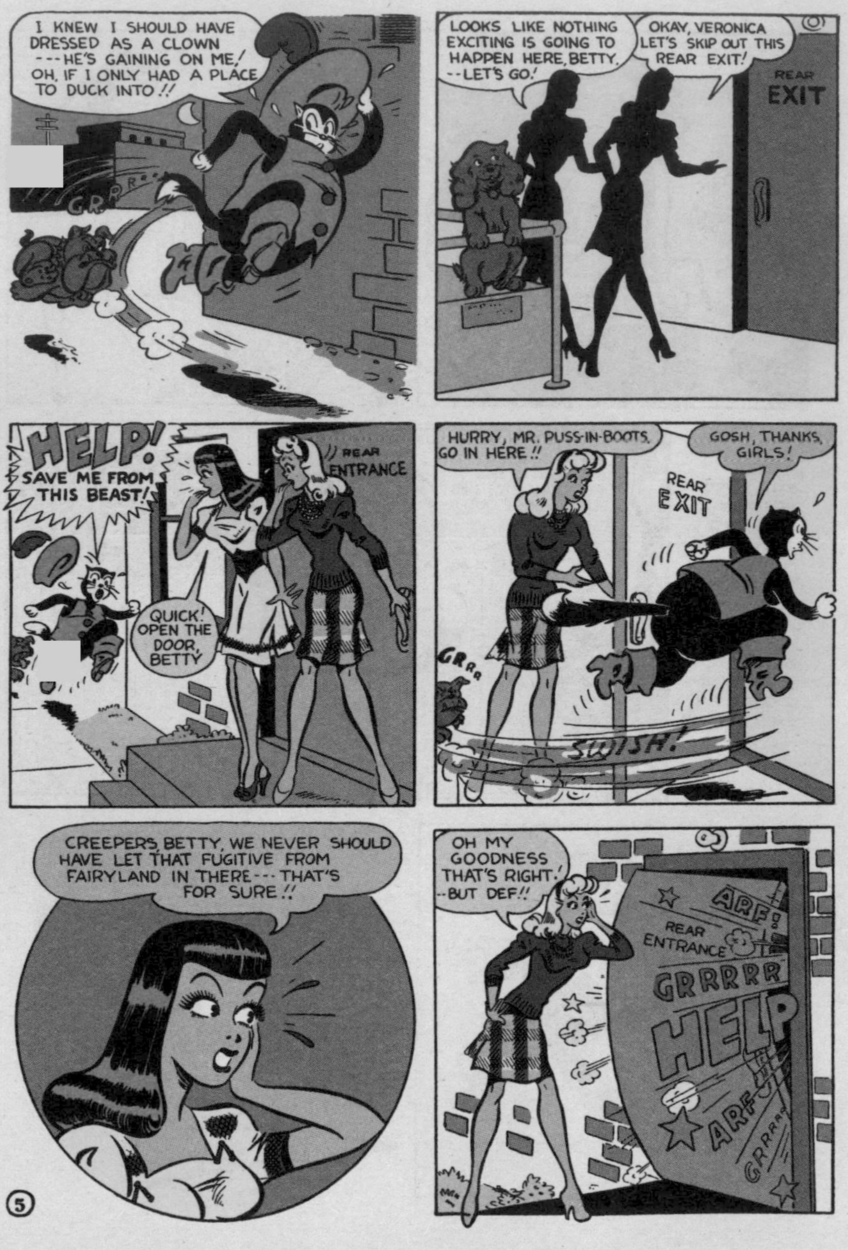
I KNEW I SHOULD HAVE DRESSED AS A CLOWN ---HE'S GAINING ON ME! OH, IF I ONLY HAD A PLACE TO DUCK INTO!!
GRRR...
LOOKS LIKE NOTHING EXCITING IS GOING TO HAPPEN HERE, BETTY. --LET'S GO!
OKAY, VERONICA LET'S SKIP OUT THIS REAR EXIT!
REAR EXIT
HELP! SAVE ME FROM THIS BEAST!
REAR ENTRANCE
QUICK! OPEN THE DOOR, BETTY
HURRY, MR. PUSS-IN-BOOTS, GO IN HERE!!
GOSH, THANKS, GIRLS!
REAR EXIT
GRRR
SWISH!
CREEPERS, BETTY, WE NEVER SHOULD HAVE LET THAT FUGITIVE FROM FAIRYLAND IN THERE---THAT'S FOR SURE!!
OH MY GOODNESS THAT'S RIGHT! --BUT DEF!!
ARF!
REAR ENTRANCE
GRRRRR
HELP
ARF
GRRRR
5

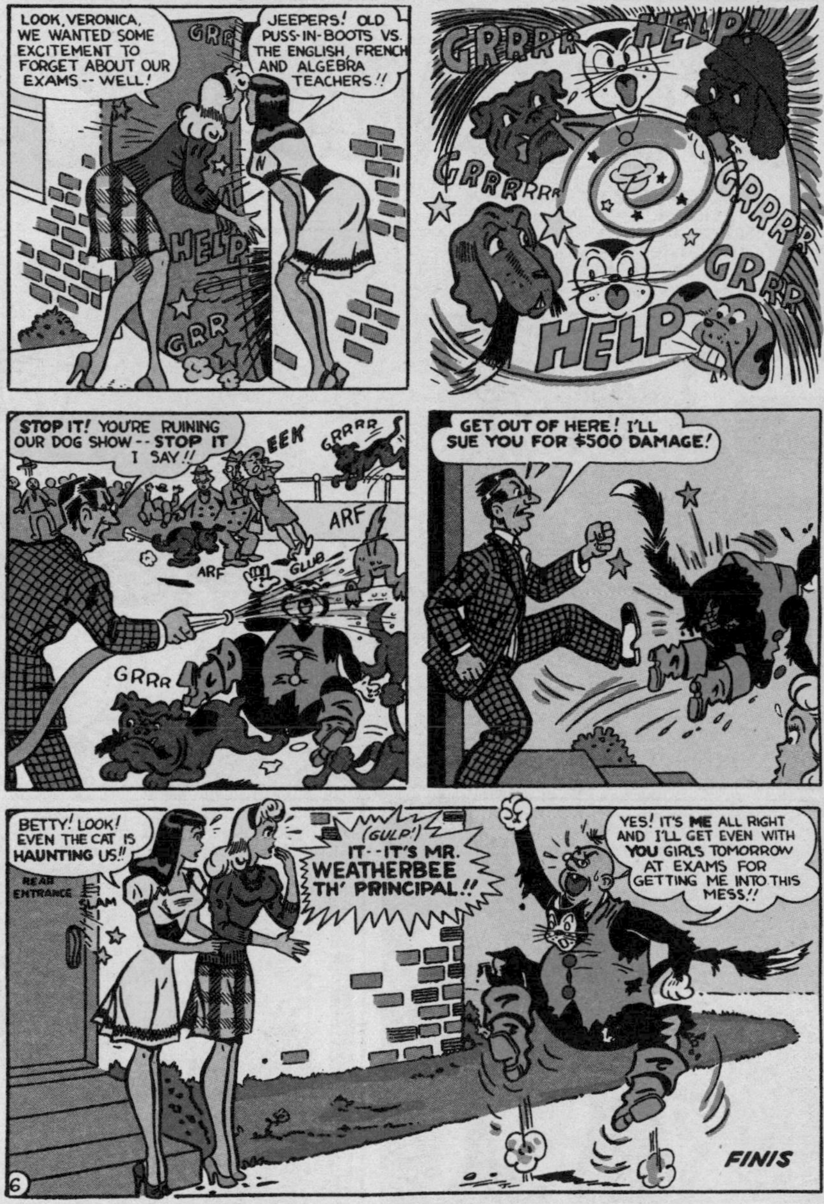
LOOK, VERONICA, WE WANTED SOME EXCITEMENT TO FORGET ABOUT OUR EXAMS -- WELL!
JEEPERS! OLD PUSS-IN-BOOTS VS. THE ENGLISH, FRENCH AND ALGEBRA TEACHERS!!
GRR
HELP
GRR
GRRRRR HELP!
GRRRRRRR
GRRRR
GRRR
HELP
STOP IT! YOU'RE RUINING OUR DOG SHOW -- STOP IT I SAY!!
EEK
GRRRR
ARF
ARF
GLUB
GRRR
GET OUT OF HERE! I'LL SUE YOU FOR $500 DAMAGE!
BETTY! LOOK! EVEN THE CAT IS HAUNTING US!!
REAR ENTRANCE
SLAM
(GULP!)
IT--IT'S MR. WEATHERBEE TH' PRINCIPAL!!
YES! IT'S ME ALL RIGHT AND I'LL GET EVEN WITH YOU GIRLS TOMORROW AT EXAMS FOR GETTING ME INTO THIS MESS!!
6
FINIS

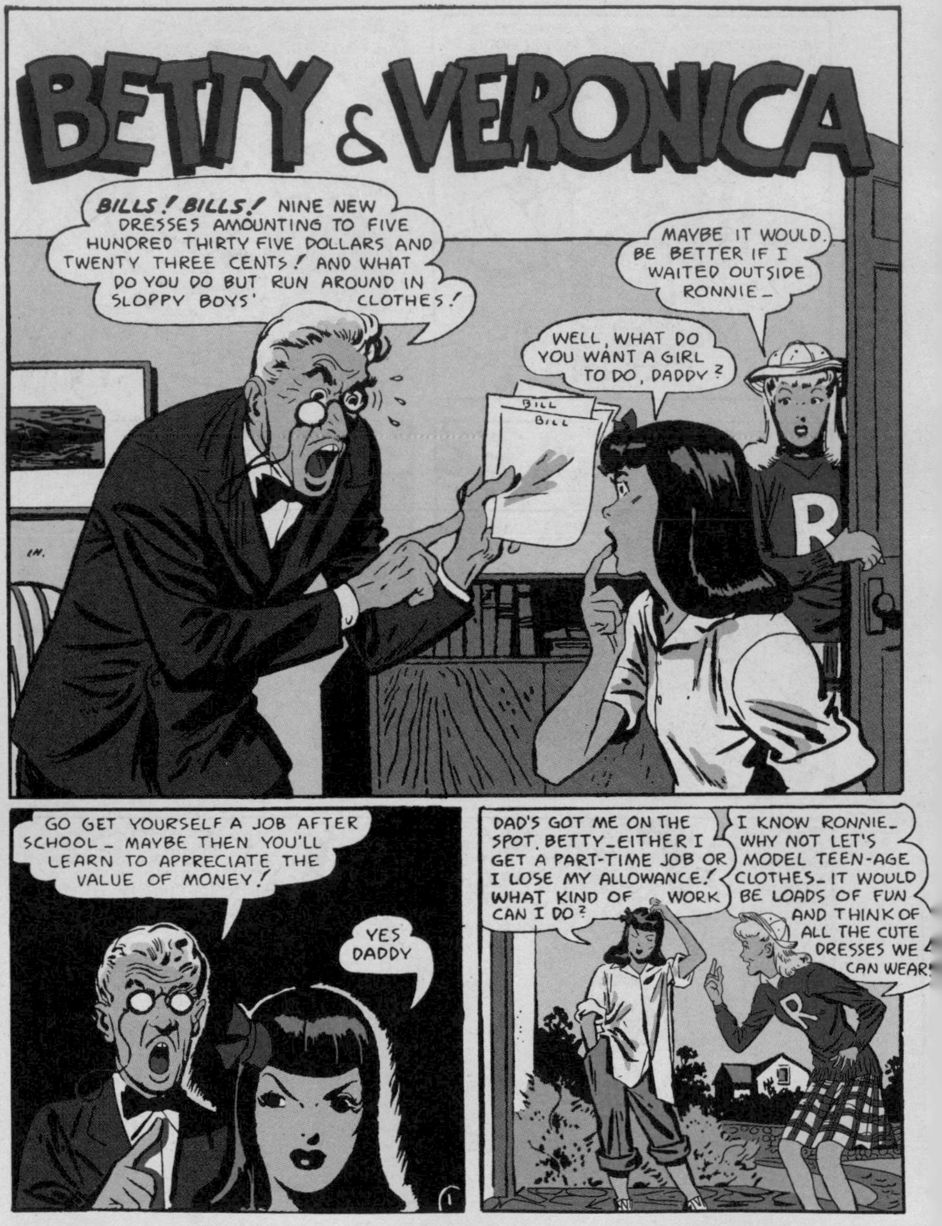
BETTY & VERONICA
BILLS! BILLS! NINE NEW DRESSES AMOUNTING TO FIVE HUNDRED THIRTY FIVE DOLLARS AND TWENTY THREE CENTS! AND WHAT DO YOU DO BUT RUN AROUND IN SLOPPY BOYS' CLOTHES!
MAYBE IT WOULD BE BETTER IF I WAITED OUTSIDE RONNIE_
WELL, WHAT DO YOU WANT A GIRL TO DO, DADDY?
BILL
BILL
R
GO GET YOURSELF A JOB AFTER SCHOOL_ MAYBE THEN YOU'LL LEARN TO APPRECIATE THE VALUE OF MONEY!
YES DADDY
DAD'S GOT ME ON THE SPOT, BETTY_EITHER I GET A PART-TIME JOB OR I LOSE MY ALLOWANCE! WHAT KIND OF WORK CAN I DO?
I KNOW RONNIE_ WHY NOT LET'S MODEL TEEN-AGE CLOTHES_ IT WOULD BE LOADS OF FUN AND THINK OF ALL THE CUTE DRESSES WE CAN WEAR!
R

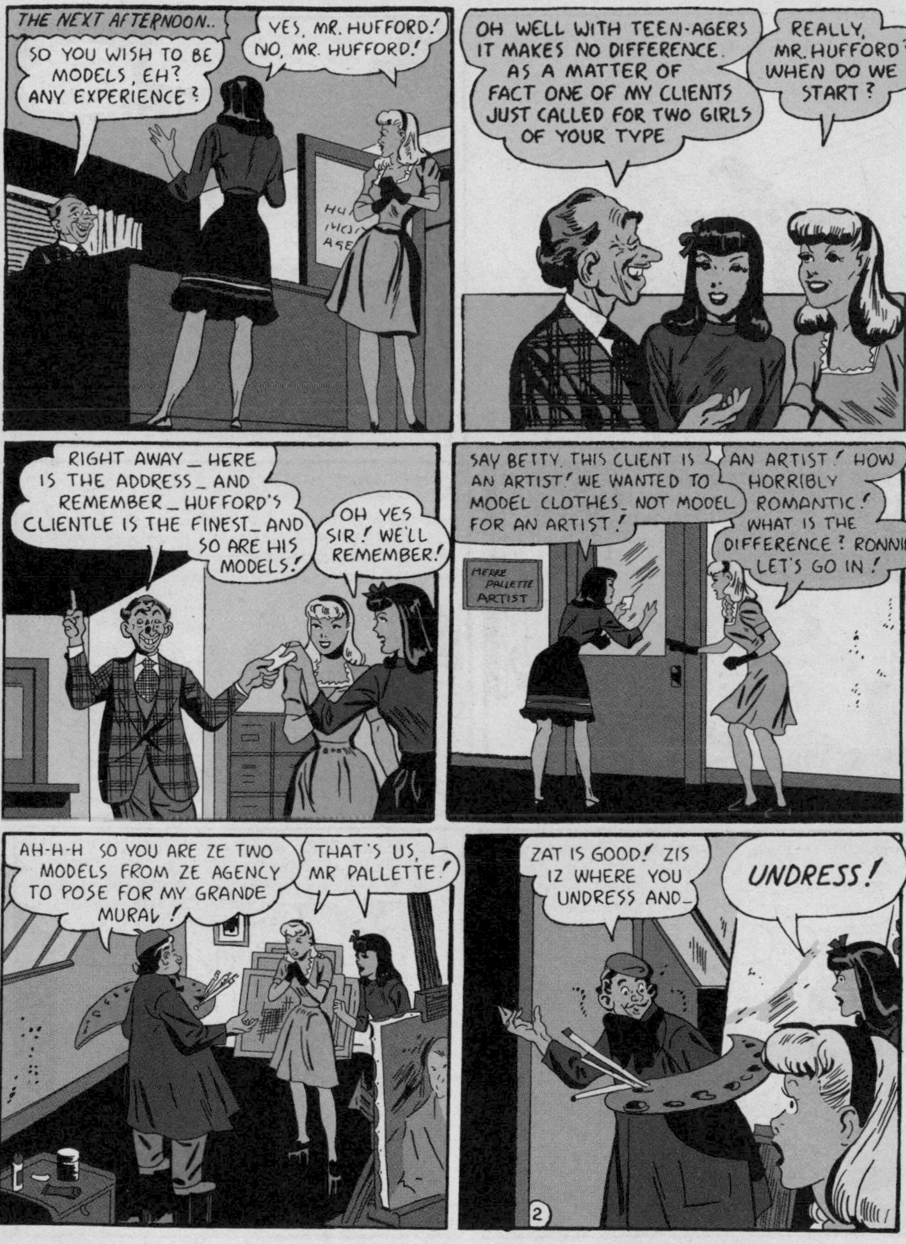
THE NEXT AFTERNOON..
SO YOU WISH TO BE MODELS, EH? ANY EXPERIENCE?
YES, MR. HUFFORD! NO, MR. HUFFORD!
OH WELL WITH TEEN-AGERS IT MAKES NO DIFFERENCE. AS A MATTER OF FACT ONE OF MY CLIENTS JUST CALLED FOR TWO GIRLS OF YOUR TYPE
REALLY, MR. HUFFORD? WHEN DO WE START?
RIGHT AWAY_ HERE IS THE ADDRESS_ AND REMEMBER_ HUFFORD'S CLIENTLE IS THE FINEST_ AND SO ARE HIS MODELS!
OH YES SIR! WE'LL REMEMBER!
SAY BETTY, THIS CLIENT IS AN ARTIST! WE WANTED TO MODEL CLOTHES_ NOT MODEL FOR AN ARTIST!
AN ARTIST! HOW HORRIBLY ROMANTIC! WHAT IS THE DIFFERENCE? RONNIE, LET'S GO IN!
ARTIST
AH-H-H SO YOU ARE ZE TWO MODELS FROM ZE AGENCY TO POSE FOR MY GRANDE MURAL!
THAT'S US, MR PALLETTE!
ZAT IS GOOD! ZIS IZ WHERE YOU UNDRESS AND_
UNDRESS!
2

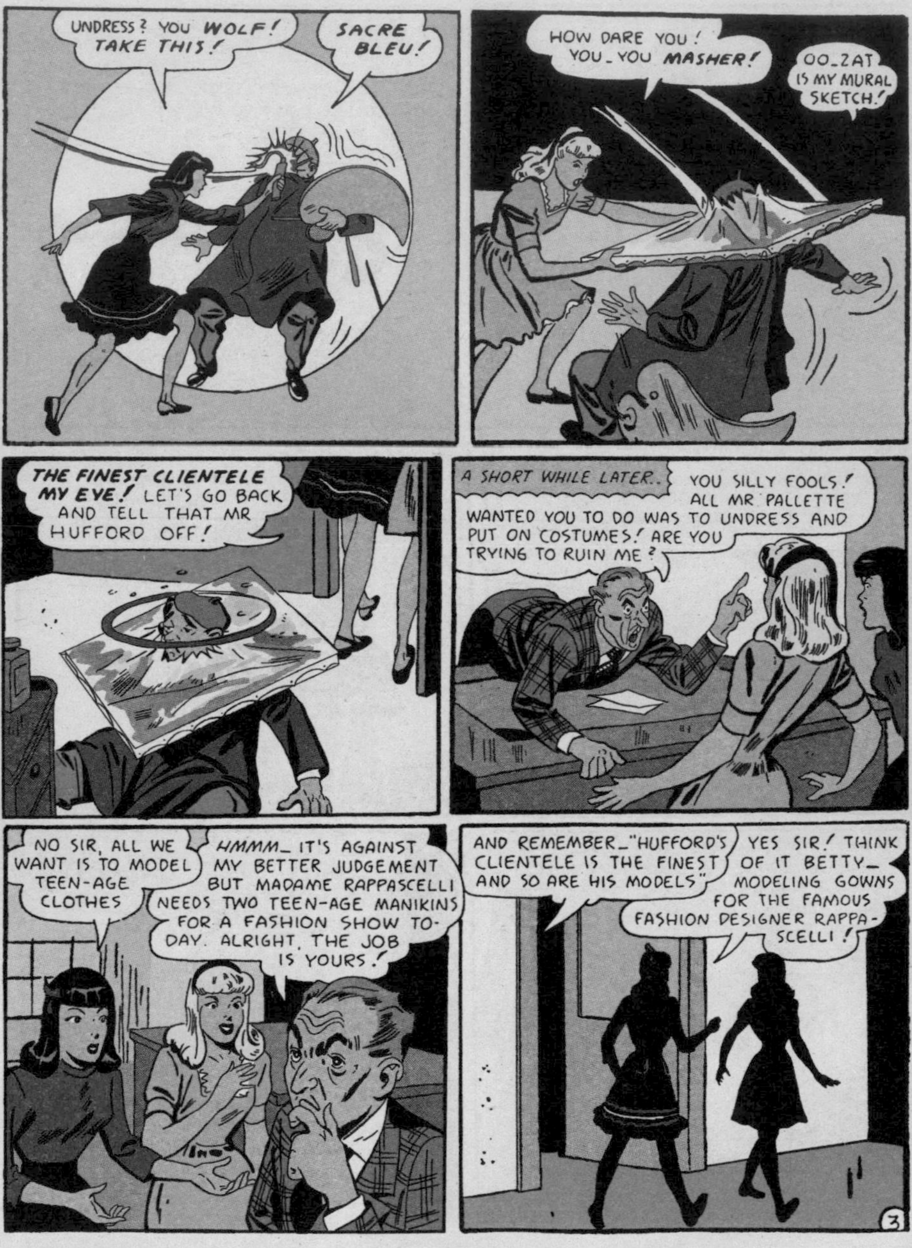
UNDRESS? YOU WOLF! TAKE THIS!
SACRE BLEU!
HOW DARE YOU! YOU_YOU MASHER!
OO_ZAT IS MY MURAL SKETCH!
THE FINEST CLIENTELE MY EYE! LET'S GO BACK AND TELL THAT MR HUFFORD OFF!
A SHORT WHILE LATER..
YOU SILLY FOOLS! ALL MR PALLETTE WANTED YOU TO DO WAS TO UNDRESS AND PUT ON COSTUMES! ARE YOU TRYING TO RUIN ME?
NO SIR, ALL WE WANT IS TO MODEL TEEN-AGE CLOTHES
HMMM_ IT'S AGAINST MY BETTER JUDGEMENT BUT MADAME RAPPASCELLI NEEDS TWO TEEN-AGE MANIKINS FOR A FASHION SHOW TO-DAY. ALRIGHT, THE JOB IS YOURS!
AND REMEMBER_"HUFFORD'S CLIENTELE IS THE FINEST AND SO ARE HIS MODELS"
YES SIR! THINK OF IT BETTY_ MODELING GOWNS FOR THE FAMOUS FASHION DESIGNER RAPPA-SCELLI!
3

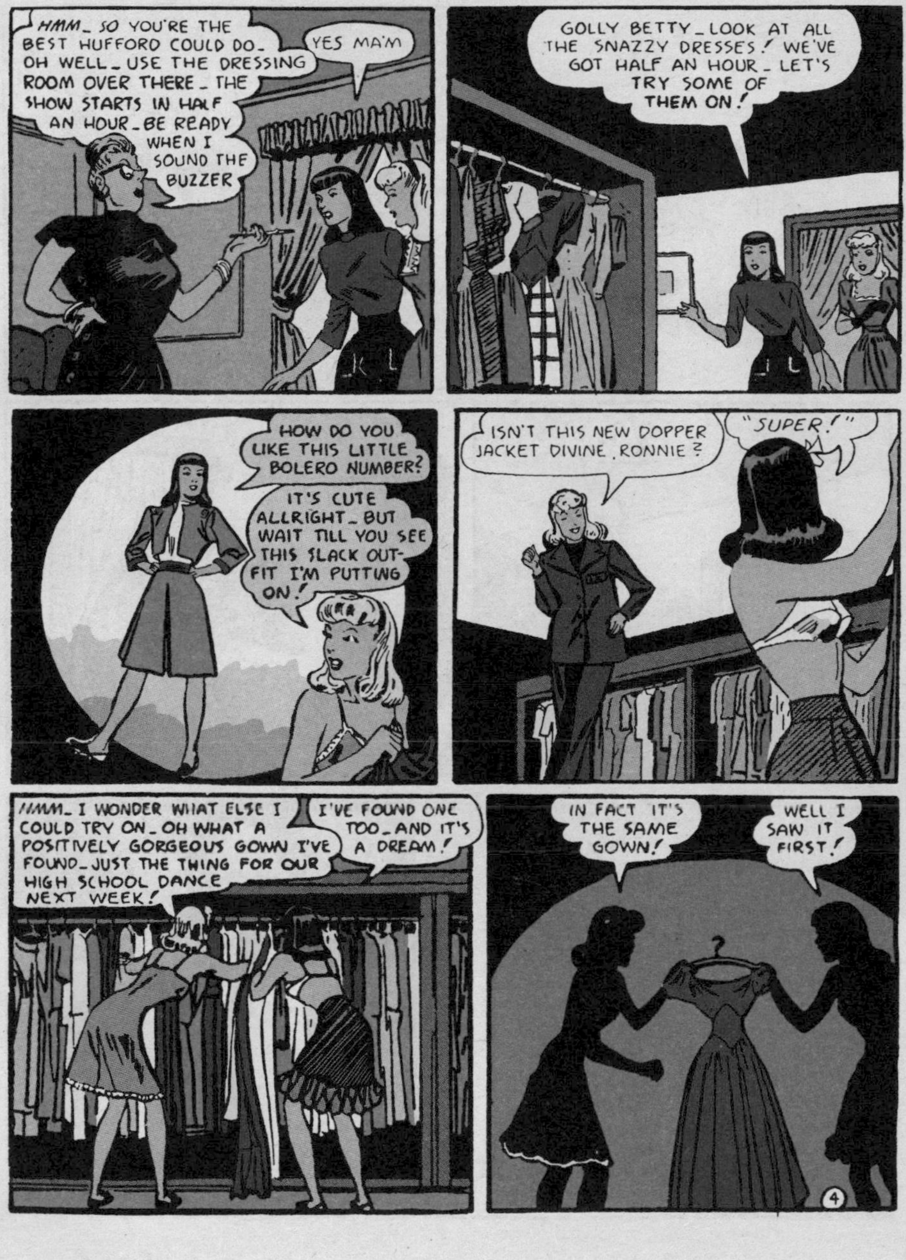
HMM_ SO YOU'RE THE BEST HUFFORD COULD DO_ OH WELL_ USE THE DRESSING ROOM OVER THERE_ THE SHOW STARTS IN HALF AN HOUR_ BE READY WHEN I SOUND THE BUZZER
YES MA'M
GOLLY BETTY_ LOOK AT ALL THE SNAZZY DRESSES! WE'VE GOT HALF AN HOUR_ LET'S TRY SOME OF THEM ON!
HOW DO YOU LIKE THIS LITTLE BOLERO NUMBER?
IT'S CUTE ALLRIGHT_ BUT WAIT TILL YOU SEE THIS SLACK OUT-FIT I'M PUTTING ON!
ISN'T THIS NEW DOPPER JACKET DIVINE, RONNIE?
"SUPER!"
HMM_ I WONDER WHAT ELSE I COULD TRY ON_ OH WHAT A POSITIVELY GORGEOUS GOWN I'VE FOUND_ JUST THE THING FOR OUR HIGH SCHOOL DANCE NEXT WEEK!
I'VE FOUND ONE TOO_ AND IT'S A DREAM!
IN FACT IT'S THE SAME GOWN!
WELL I SAW IT FIRST!
4

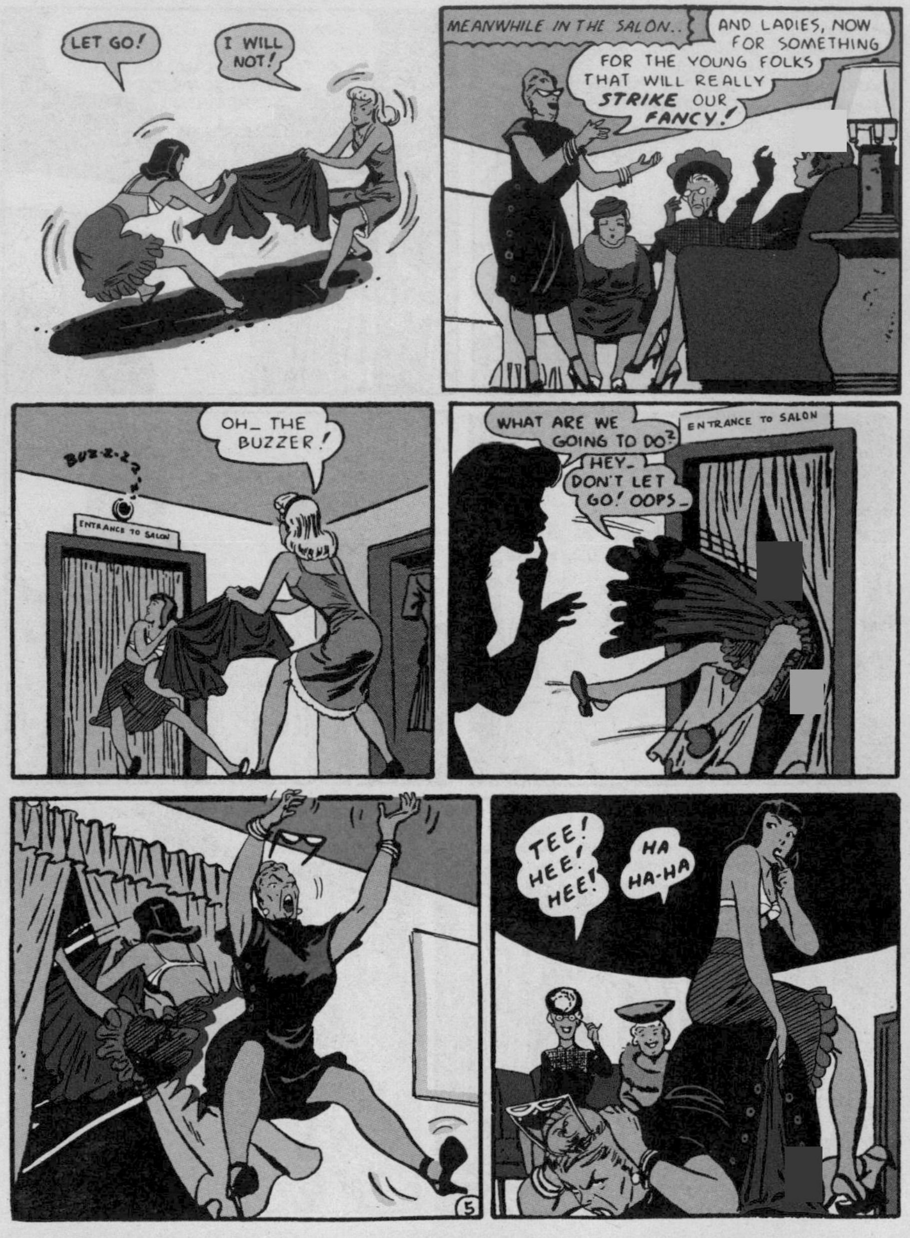
LET GO!
I WILL NOT!
MEANWHILE IN THE SALON..
AND LADIES, NOW FOR SOMETHING FOR THE YOUNG FOLKS THAT WILL REALLY STRIKE OUR FANCY!
BUZ-Z-Z
OH_ THE BUZZER!
ENTRANCE TO SALON
WHAT ARE WE GOING TO DO?
ENTRANCE TO SALON
HEY_ DON'T LET GO! OOPS_
5
TEE! HEE! HEE!
HA HA-HA

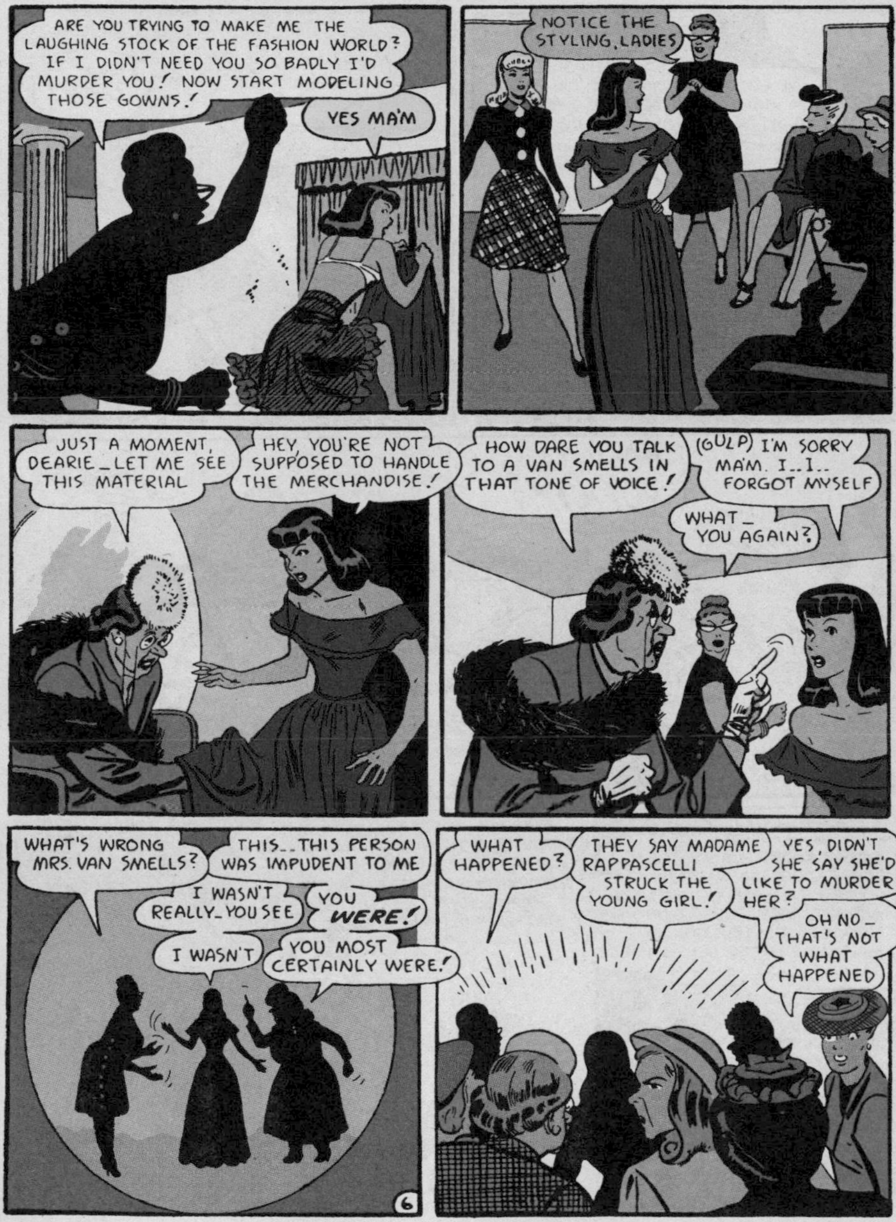
ARE YOU TRYING TO MAKE ME THE LAUGHING STOCK OF THE FASHION WORLD? IF I DIDN'T NEED YOU SO BADLY I'D MURDER YOU! NOW START MODELING THOSE GOWNS!
YES MA'M
NOTICE THE STYLING, LADIES
JUST A MOMENT, DEARIE_LET ME SEE THIS MATERIAL
HEY, YOU'RE NOT SUPPOSED TO HANDLE THE MERCHANDISE!
HOW DARE YOU TALK TO A VAN SMELLS IN THAT TONE OF VOICE!
(GULP) I'M SORRY MA'M. I..I.. FORGOT MYSELF
WHAT_ YOU AGAIN?
WHAT'S WRONG MRS. VAN SMELLS?
THIS..THIS PERSON WAS IMPUDENT TO ME
I WASN'T REALLY_YOU SEE
YOU WERE!
I WASN'T
YOU MOST CERTAINLY WERE!
6
WHAT HAPPENED?
THEY SAY MADAME RAPPASCELLI STRUCK THE YOUNG GIRL!
YES, DIDN'T SHE SAY SHE'D LIKE TO MURDER HER?
OH NO_ THAT'S NOT WHAT HAPPENED

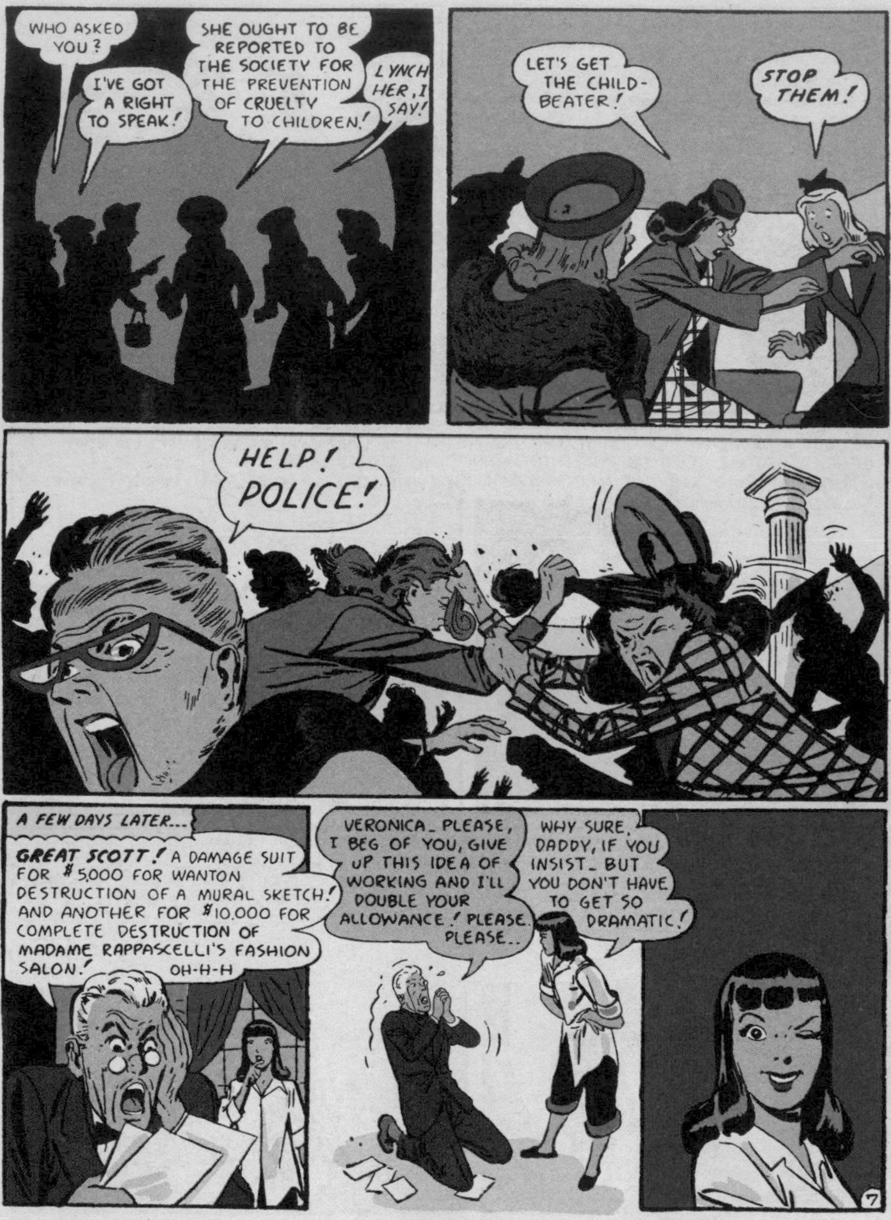
WHO ASKED YOU?
I'VE GOT A RIGHT TO SPEAK!
SHE OUGHT TO BE REPORTED TO THE SOCIETY FOR THE PREVENTION OF CRUELTY TO CHILDREN!
LYNCH HER, I SAY!
LET'S GET THE CHILD-BEATER!
STOP THEM!
HELP! POLICE!
A FEW DAYS LATER...
GREAT SCOTT! A DAMAGE SUIT FOR $5,000 FOR WANTON DESTRUCTION OF A MURAL SKETCH! AND ANOTHER FOR $10,000 FOR COMPLETE DESTRUCTION OF MADAME RAPPASCELLI'S FASHION SALON! OH-H-H
VERONICA_ PLEASE, I BEG OF YOU, GIVE UP THIS IDEA OF WORKING AND I'LL DOUBLE YOUR ALLOWANCE! PLEASE. PLEASE..
WHY SURE, DADDY, IF YOU INSIST_ BUT YOU DON'T HAVE TO GET SO DRAMATIC!
7

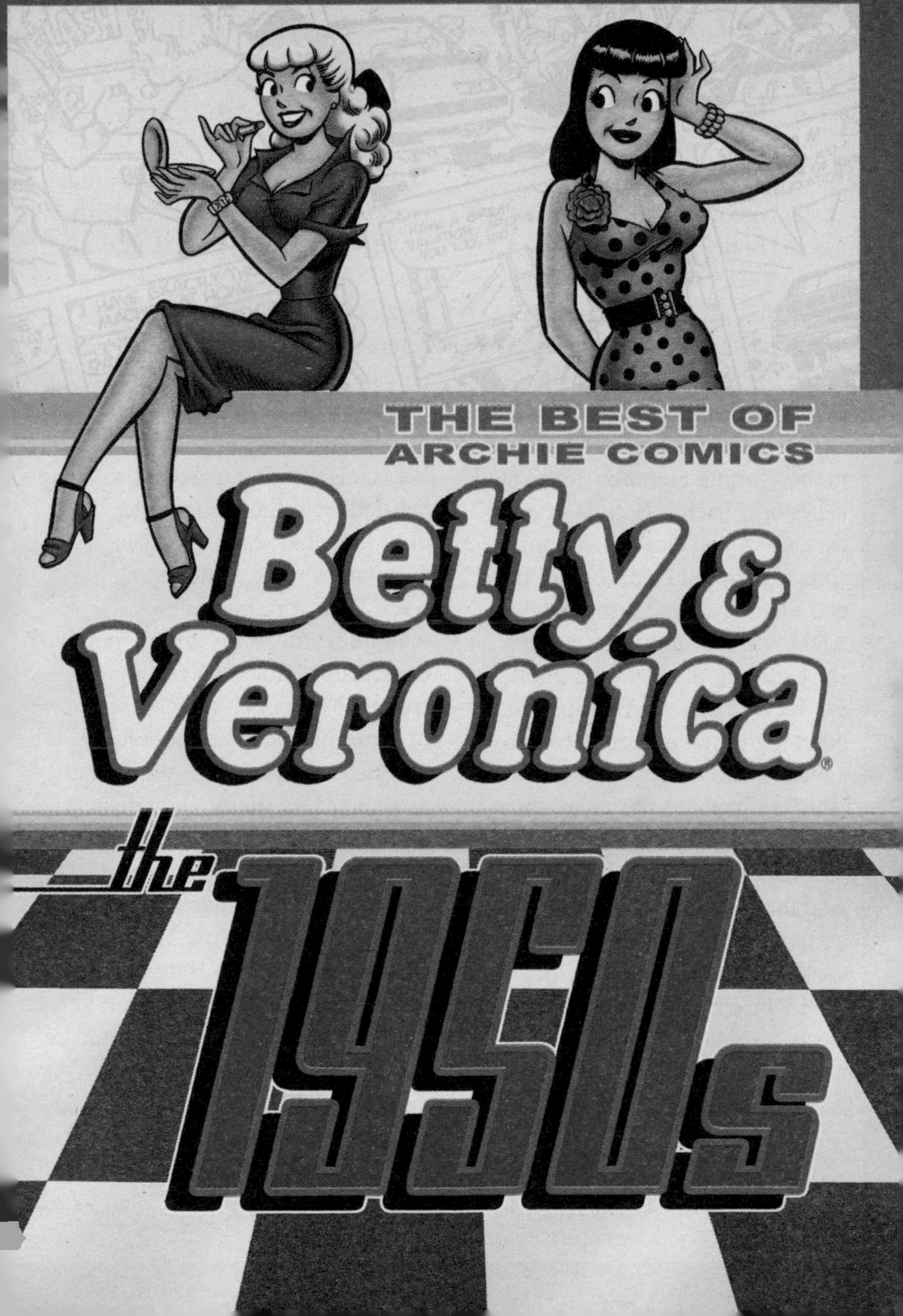

THE BEST OF ARCHIE COMICS

Betty & Veronica®

the 1950s

Poor Little Rich Girl
Betty & Veronica #1, 1950
by George Frese

This type of story has been tackled many times over in the many decades of Betty and Veronica's iconic friendship, but this one is notable because it's one of the first to truly acknowledge this aspect of their relationship. Veronica flaunts her lavish lifestyle to the "simple common-folk" that is her best friend, Betty — costly cars, the finest clothes, shopping sprees, people to wait on her hand and foot. She even turns down Archie just to show Betty that she can. Yet, it's a simple phone call by Betty to wish her parents good night that makes Veronica collapse into a tantrum of tears. Why? Because money can't buy you happiness. And that is where Veronica will always lose to Betty. And that's why both girls need each other. Veronica gives Betty confidence to break out of her shell while Betty brings Veronica crashing down to earth when she needs it the most. Two peas in a pod, so to speak.

-- **Jonathan Gray**
Production Artist,
Archie Comics

The Rain Maker
Betty & Veronica #1, 1950
by George Frese

The Betty Cooper we know today is super smart, nice to everybody and good at everything. But the Betty Cooper of yore used to be crazy obsessive, hilarious and prone to acting rather 'blonde.' One of the stories that helped to establish classic Betty's crazy personality was 'The Rainmaker.' We see Betty going around carrying her dad's shotgun, completely oblivious that she was scaring everyone she was interacting with! The story has snappy dialogue, amazingly funny facial expressions, and a suitably great ending. With time, the character of Betty has become more level-headed, well-rounded. While that made her less funny, it made her more relatable. The perception is that most young female readers identify with her character; Betty is the girl we all know, the girl we all have been. I like Betty as the girl-next-door, but I also want her to retain some of her kooky, quirky personality that made her one of the most beloved and iconic female characters in comic book history.

-- **Sina Tahmi**
Archie Comics Fan

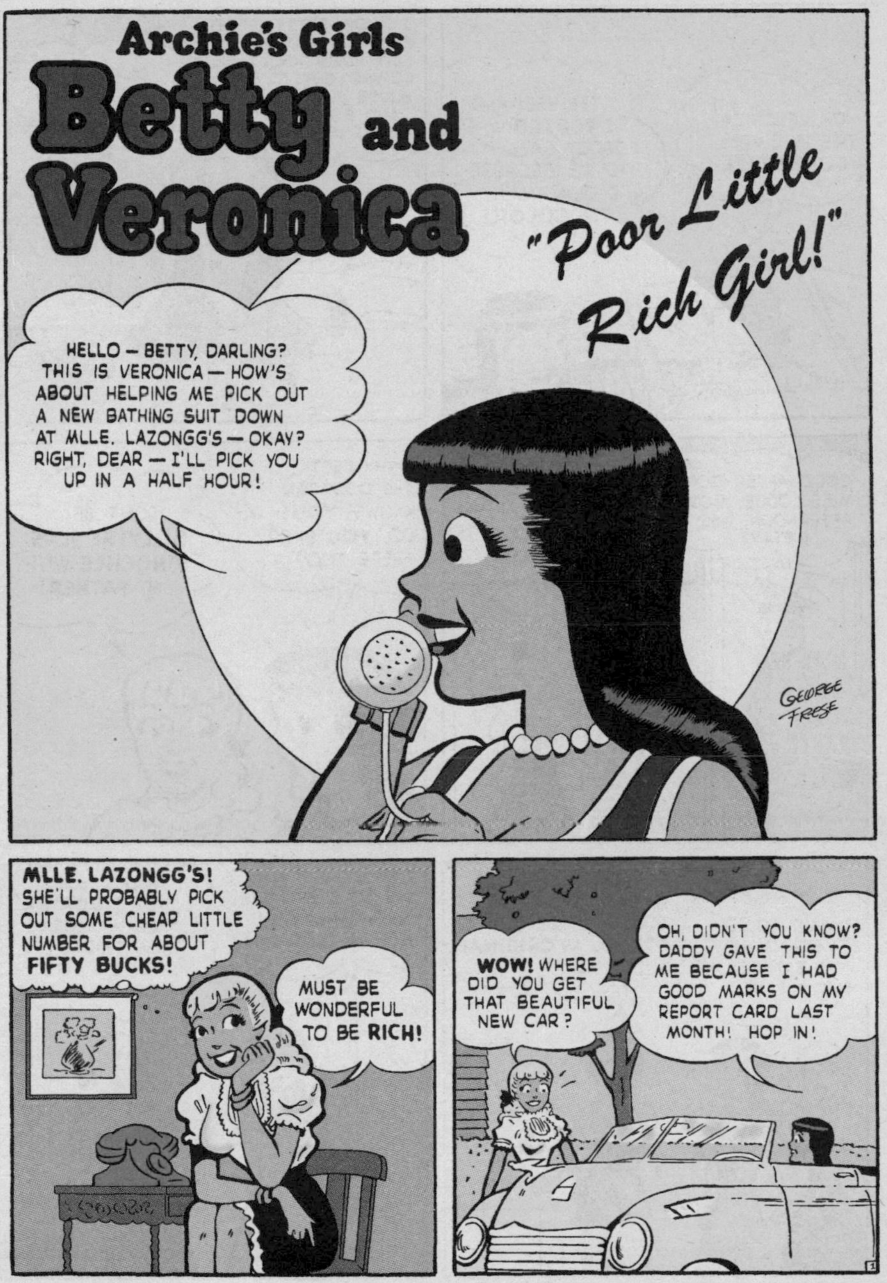
Archie's Girls
Betty and Veronica
"Poor Little Rich Girl!"
HELLO — BETTY, DARLING? THIS IS VERONICA — HOW'S ABOUT HELPING ME PICK OUT A NEW BATHING SUIT DOWN AT MLLE. LAZONGG'S — OKAY? RIGHT, DEAR — I'LL PICK YOU UP IN A HALF HOUR!
GEORGE FRESE
MLLE. LAZONGG'S! SHE'LL PROBABLY PICK OUT SOME CHEAP LITTLE NUMBER FOR ABOUT FIFTY BUCKS!
MUST BE WONDERFUL TO BE RICH!
WOW! WHERE DID YOU GET THAT BEAUTIFUL NEW CAR?
OH, DIDN'T YOU KNOW? DADDY GAVE THIS TO ME BECAUSE I HAD GOOD MARKS ON MY REPORT CARD LAST MONTH! HOP IN!

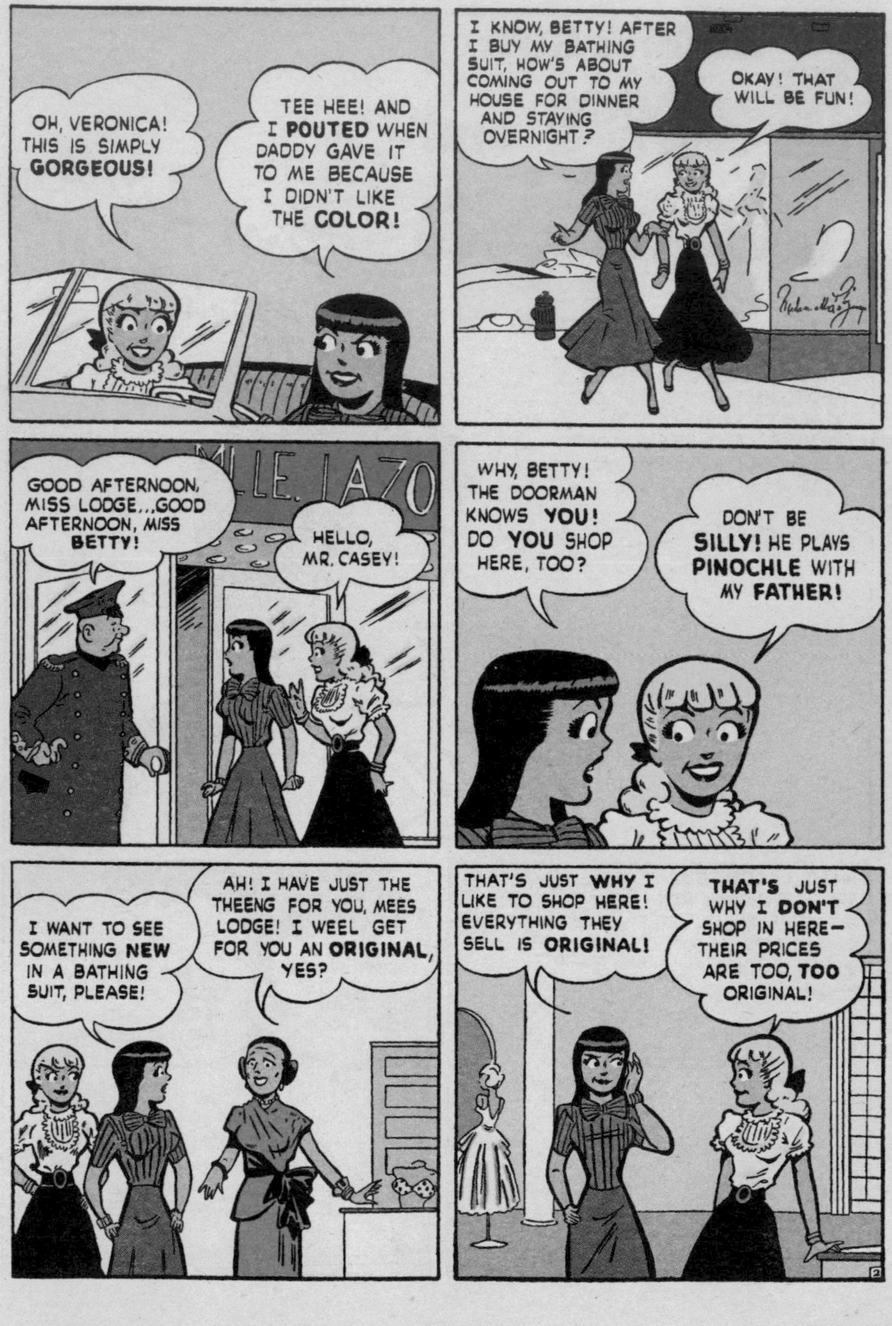
OH, VERONICA! THIS IS SIMPLY GORGEOUS!
TEE HEE! AND I POUTED WHEN DADDY GAVE IT TO ME BECAUSE I DIDN'T LIKE THE COLOR!
I KNOW, BETTY! AFTER I BUY MY BATHING SUIT, HOW'S ABOUT COMING OUT TO MY HOUSE FOR DINNER AND STAYING OVERNIGHT?
OKAY! THAT WILL BE FUN!
MLLE. LAZO
GOOD AFTERNOON, MISS LODGE...GOOD AFTERNOON, MISS BETTY!
HELLO, MR. CASEY!
WHY, BETTY! THE DOORMAN KNOWS YOU! DO YOU SHOP HERE, TOO?
DON'T BE SILLY! HE PLAYS PINOCHLE WITH MY FATHER!
I WANT TO SEE SOMETHING NEW IN A BATHING SUIT, PLEASE!
AH! I HAVE JUST THE THEENG FOR YOU, MEES LODGE! I WEEL GET FOR YOU AN ORIGINAL, YES?
THAT'S JUST WHY I LIKE TO SHOP HERE! EVERYTHING THEY SELL IS ORIGINAL!
THAT'S JUST WHY I DON'T SHOP IN HERE— THEIR PRICES ARE TOO, TOO ORIGINAL!

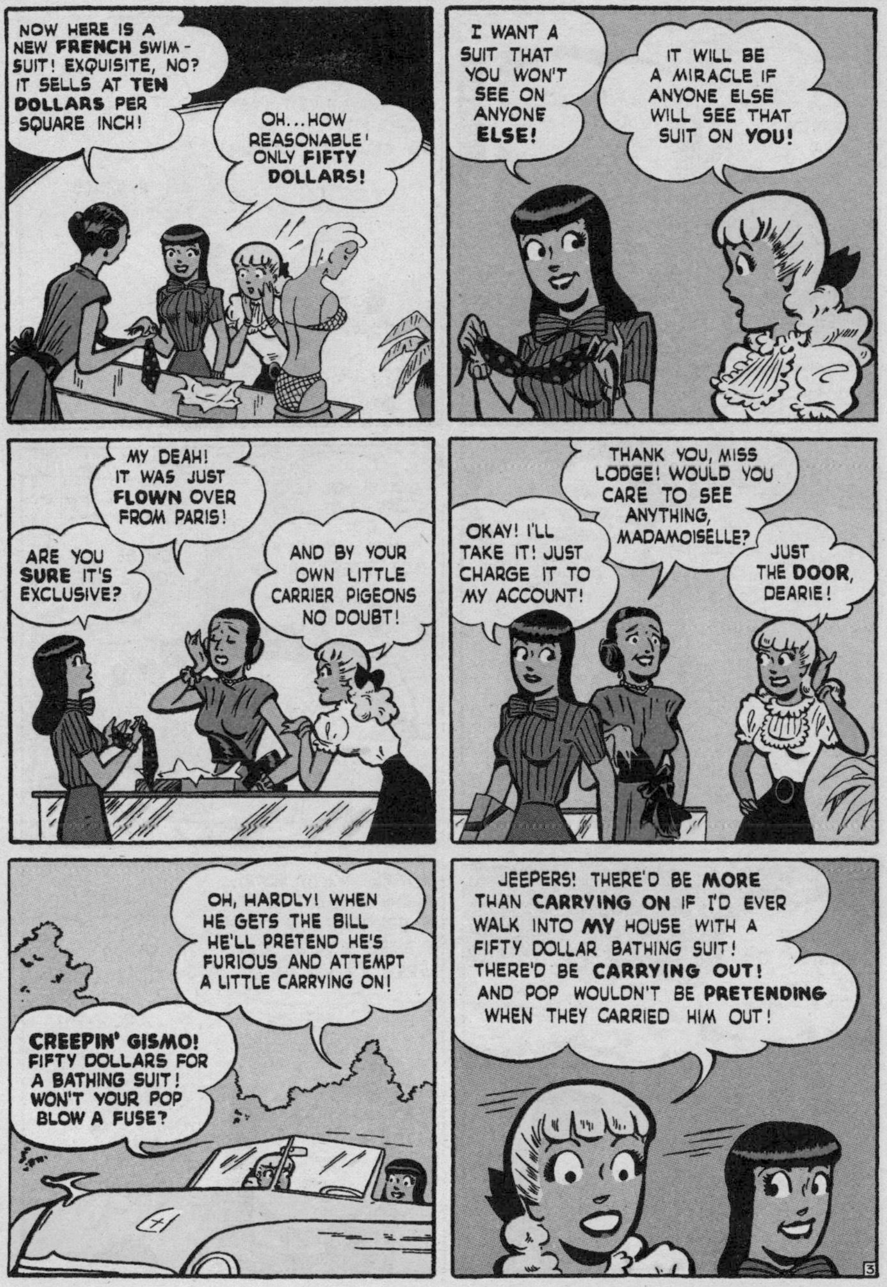
NOW HERE IS A NEW FRENCH SWIM-SUIT! EXQUISITE, NO? IT SELLS AT TEN DOLLARS PER SQUARE INCH!
OH...HOW REASONABLE! ONLY FIFTY DOLLARS!
I WANT A SUIT THAT YOU WON'T SEE ON ANYONE ELSE!
IT WILL BE A MIRACLE IF ANYONE ELSE WILL SEE THAT SUIT ON YOU!
MY DEAH! IT WAS JUST FLOWN OVER FROM PARIS!
ARE YOU SURE IT'S EXCLUSIVE?
AND BY YOUR OWN LITTLE CARRIER PIGEONS NO DOUBT!
THANK YOU, MISS LODGE! WOULD YOU CARE TO SEE ANYTHING, MADAMOISELLE?
OKAY! I'LL TAKE IT! JUST CHARGE IT TO MY ACCOUNT!
JUST THE DOOR, DEARIE!
OH, HARDLY! WHEN HE GETS THE BILL HE'LL PRETEND HE'S FURIOUS AND ATTEMPT A LITTLE CARRYING ON!
CREEPIN' GISMO! FIFTY DOLLARS FOR A BATHING SUIT! WON'T YOUR POP BLOW A FUSE?
JEEPERS! THERE'D BE MORE THAN CARRYING ON IF I'D EVER WALK INTO MY HOUSE WITH A FIFTY DOLLAR BATHING SUIT! THERE'D BE CARRYING OUT! AND POP WOULDN'T BE PRETENDING WHEN THEY CARRIED HIM OUT!
3

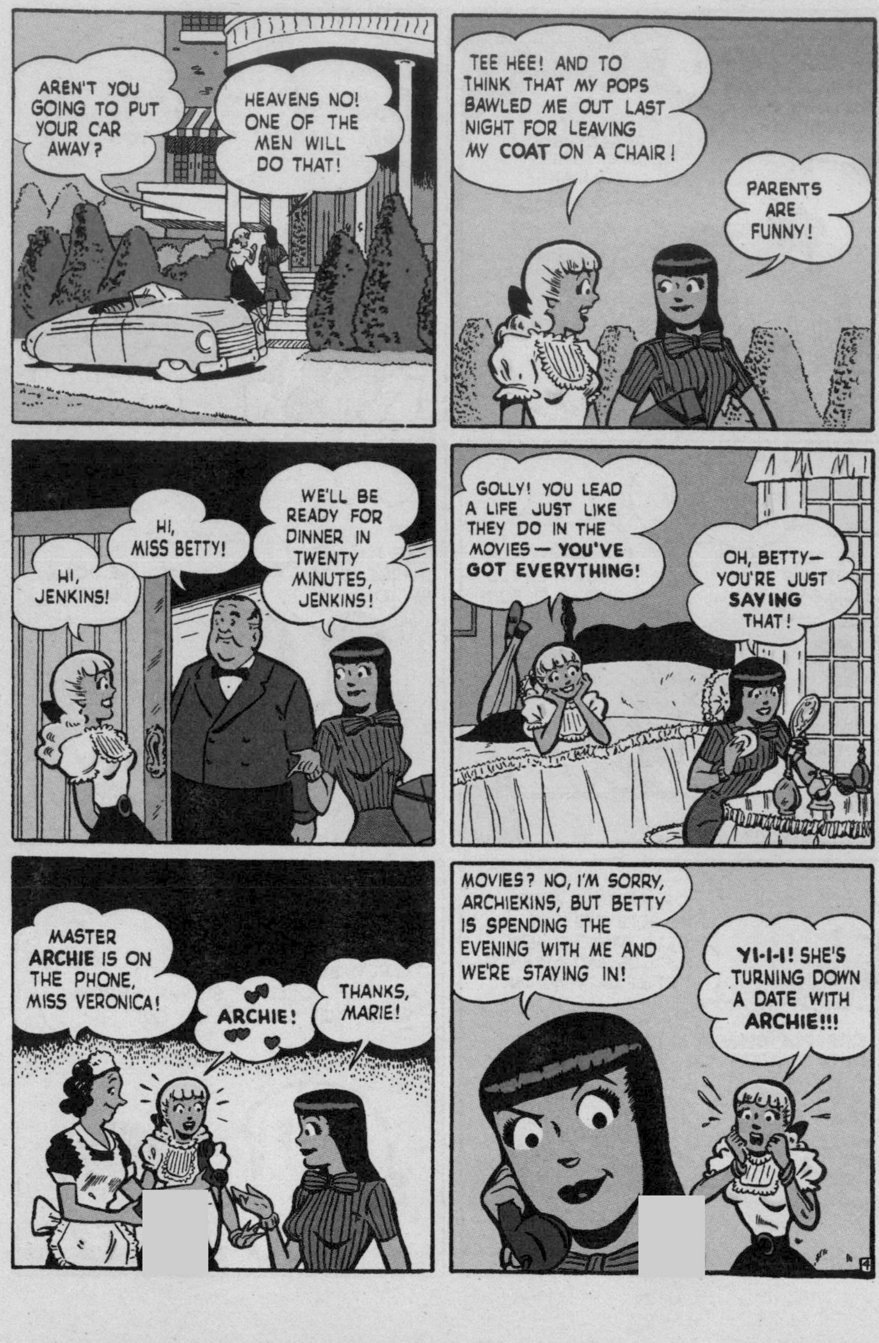
AREN'T YOU GOING TO PUT YOUR CAR AWAY?
HEAVENS NO! ONE OF THE MEN WILL DO THAT!
TEE HEE! AND TO THINK THAT MY POPS BAWLED ME OUT LAST NIGHT FOR LEAVING MY COAT ON A CHAIR!
PARENTS ARE FUNNY!
HI, JENKINS!
HI, MISS BETTY!
WE'LL BE READY FOR DINNER IN TWENTY MINUTES, JENKINS!
GOLLY! YOU LEAD A LIFE JUST LIKE THEY DO IN THE MOVIES — YOU'VE GOT EVERYTHING!
OH, BETTY— YOU'RE JUST SAYING THAT!
MASTER ARCHIE IS ON THE PHONE, MISS VERONICA!
ARCHIE!
THANKS, MARIE!
MOVIES? NO, I'M SORRY, ARCHIEKINS, BUT BETTY IS SPENDING THE EVENING WITH ME AND WE'RE STAYING IN!
YI-I-I! SHE'S TURNING DOWN A DATE WITH ARCHIE!!!
4

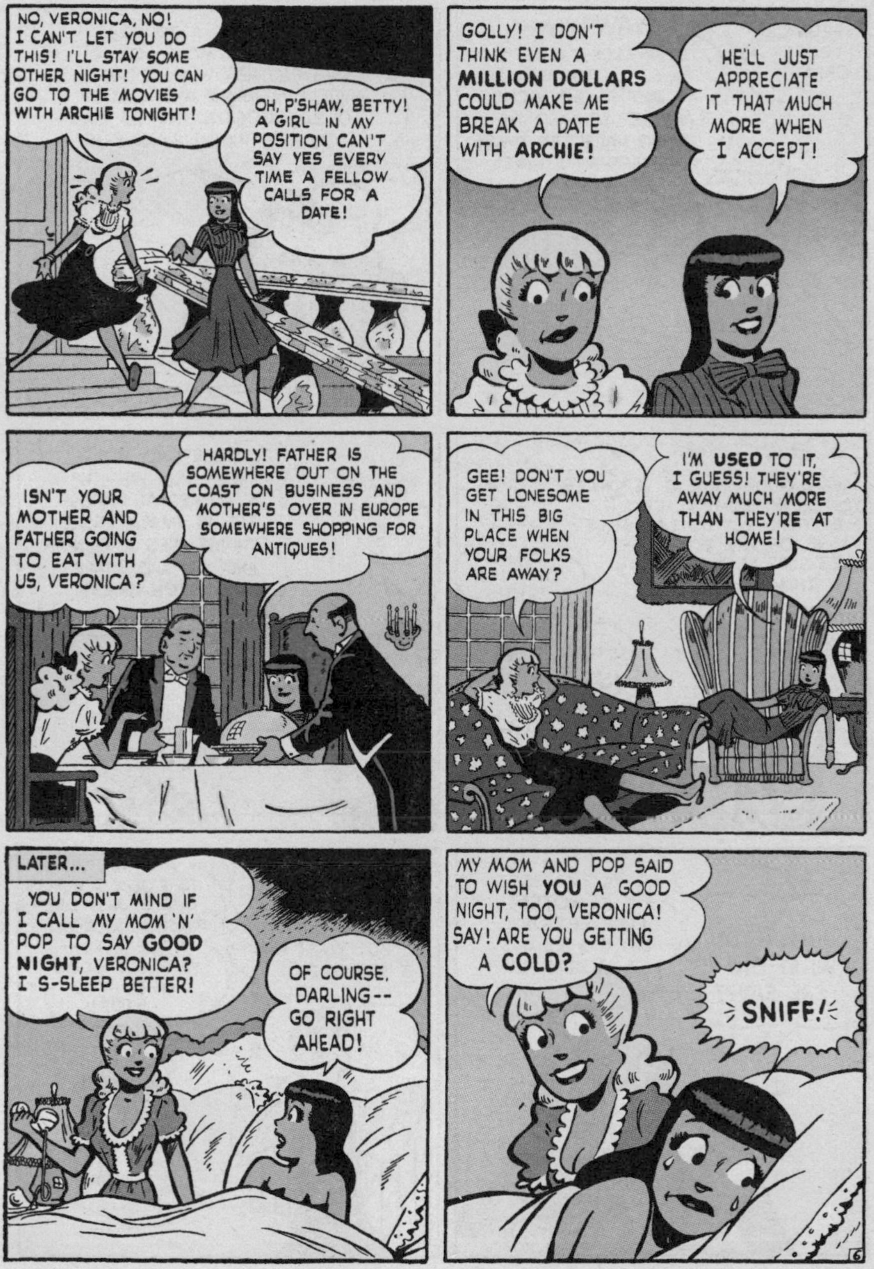
NO, VERONICA, NO! I CAN'T LET YOU DO THIS! I'LL STAY SOME OTHER NIGHT! YOU CAN GO TO THE MOVIES WITH ARCHIE TONIGHT!
OH, P'SHAW, BETTY! A GIRL IN MY POSITION CAN'T SAY YES EVERY TIME A FELLOW CALLS FOR A DATE!
GOLLY! I DON'T THINK EVEN A MILLION DOLLARS COULD MAKE ME BREAK A DATE WITH ARCHIE!
HE'LL JUST APPRECIATE IT THAT MUCH MORE WHEN I ACCEPT!
ISN'T YOUR MOTHER AND FATHER GOING TO EAT WITH US, VERONICA?
HARDLY! FATHER IS SOMEWHERE OUT ON THE COAST ON BUSINESS AND MOTHER'S OVER IN EUROPE SOMEWHERE SHOPPING FOR ANTIQUES!
GEE! DON'T YOU GET LONESOME IN THIS BIG PLACE WHEN YOUR FOLKS ARE AWAY?
I'M USED TO IT, I GUESS! THEY'RE AWAY MUCH MORE THAN THEY'RE AT HOME!
LATER...
YOU DON'T MIND IF I CALL MY MOM 'N' POP TO SAY GOOD NIGHT, VERONICA? I S-SLEEP BETTER!
OF COURSE, DARLING-- GO RIGHT AHEAD!
MY MOM AND POP SAID TO WISH YOU A GOOD NIGHT, TOO, VERONICA! SAY! ARE YOU GETTING A COLD?
SNIFF!
6

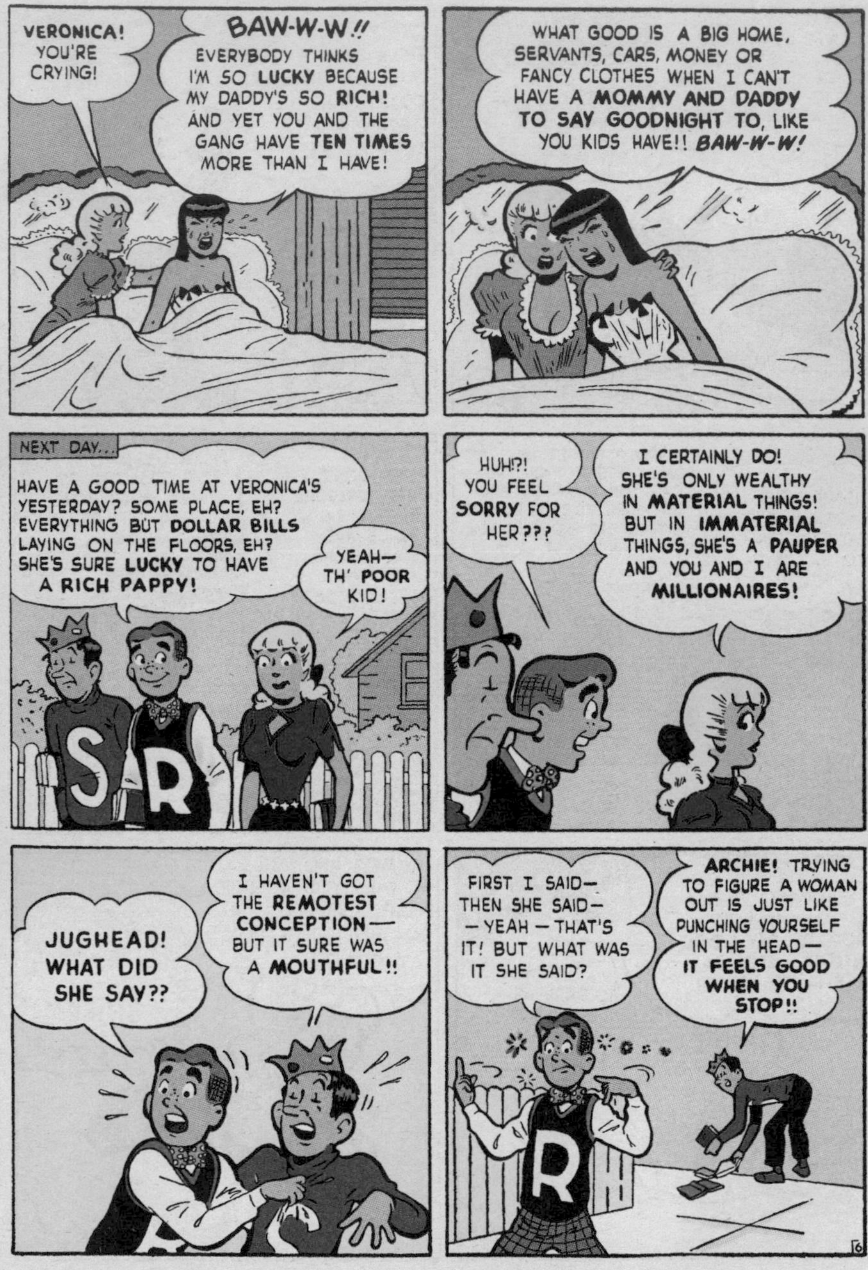
VERONICA! YOU'RE CRYING!
BAW-W-W!! EVERYBODY THINKS I'M SO LUCKY BECAUSE MY DADDY'S SO RICH! AND YET YOU AND THE GANG HAVE TEN TIMES MORE THAN I HAVE!
WHAT GOOD IS A BIG HOME, SERVANTS, CARS, MONEY OR FANCY CLOTHES WHEN I CAN'T HAVE A MOMMY AND DADDY TO SAY GOODNIGHT TO, LIKE YOU KIDS HAVE!! BAW-W-W!
NEXT DAY...
HAVE A GOOD TIME AT VERONICA'S YESTERDAY? SOME PLACE, EH? EVERYTHING BUT DOLLAR BILLS LAYING ON THE FLOORS, EH? SHE'S SURE LUCKY TO HAVE A RICH PAPPY!
YEAH— TH' POOR KID!
S
R
HUH!?! YOU FEEL SORRY FOR HER???
I CERTAINLY DO! SHE'S ONLY WEALTHY IN MATERIAL THINGS! BUT IN IMMATERIAL THINGS, SHE'S A PAUPER AND YOU AND I ARE MILLIONAIRES!
JUGHEAD! WHAT DID SHE SAY??
I HAVEN'T GOT THE REMOTEST CONCEPTION— BUT IT SURE WAS A MOUTHFUL!!
FIRST I SAID— THEN SHE SAID— —YEAH —THAT'S IT! BUT WHAT WAS IT SHE SAID?
ARCHIE! TRYING TO FIGURE A WOMAN OUT IS JUST LIKE PUNCHING YOURSELF IN THE HEAD— IT FEELS GOOD WHEN YOU STOP!!
R
6

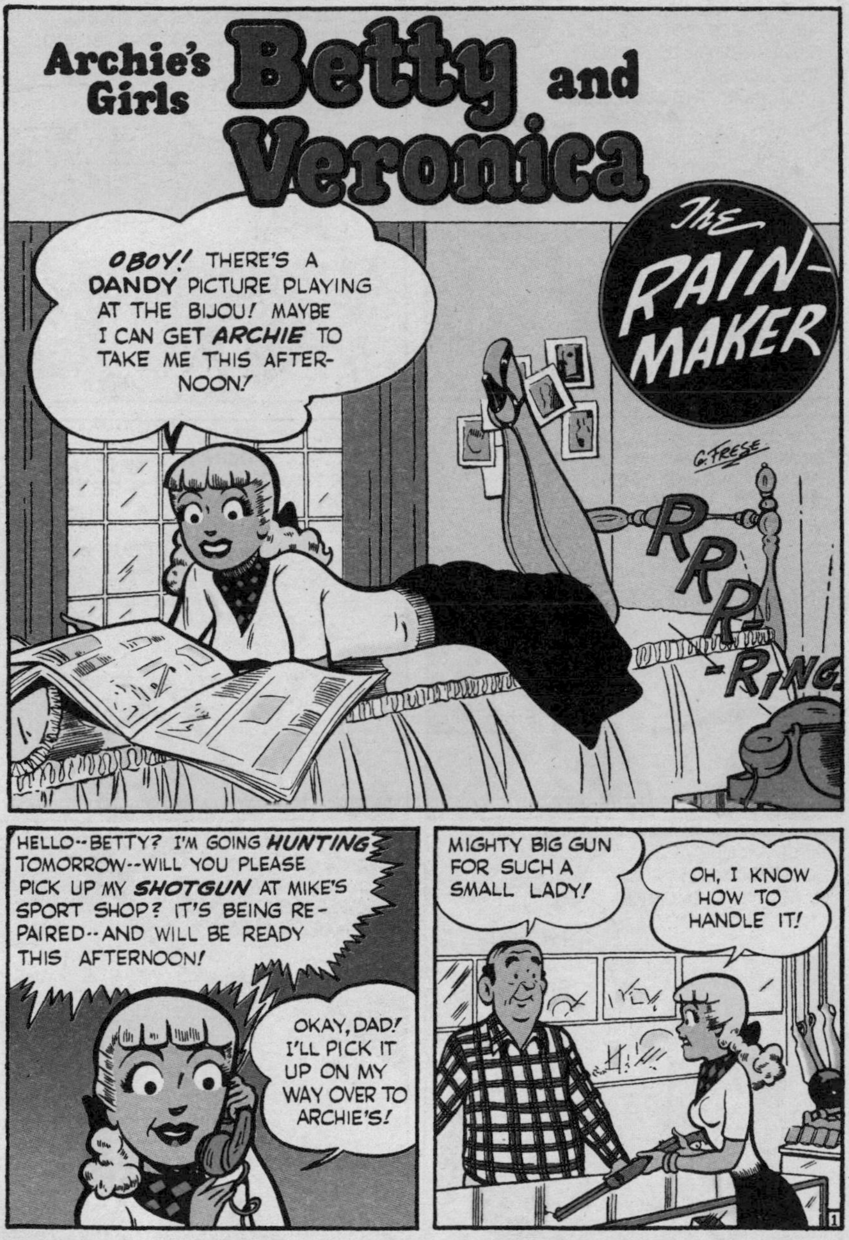
Archie's Girls Betty and Veronica
THE RAIN-MAKER
OBOY! THERE'S A DANDY PICTURE PLAYING AT THE BIJOU! MAYBE I CAN GET ARCHIE TO TAKE ME THIS AFTER-NOON!
G. FRESE
RRR-RING
HELLO--BETTY? I'M GOING HUNTING TOMORROW--WILL YOU PLEASE PICK UP MY SHOTGUN AT MIKE'S SPORT SHOP? IT'S BEING RE-PAIRED--AND WILL BE READY THIS AFTERNOON!
OKAY, DAD! I'LL PICK IT UP ON MY WAY OVER TO ARCHIE'S!
MIGHTY BIG GUN FOR SUCH A SMALL LADY!
OH, I KNOW HOW TO HANDLE IT!
1

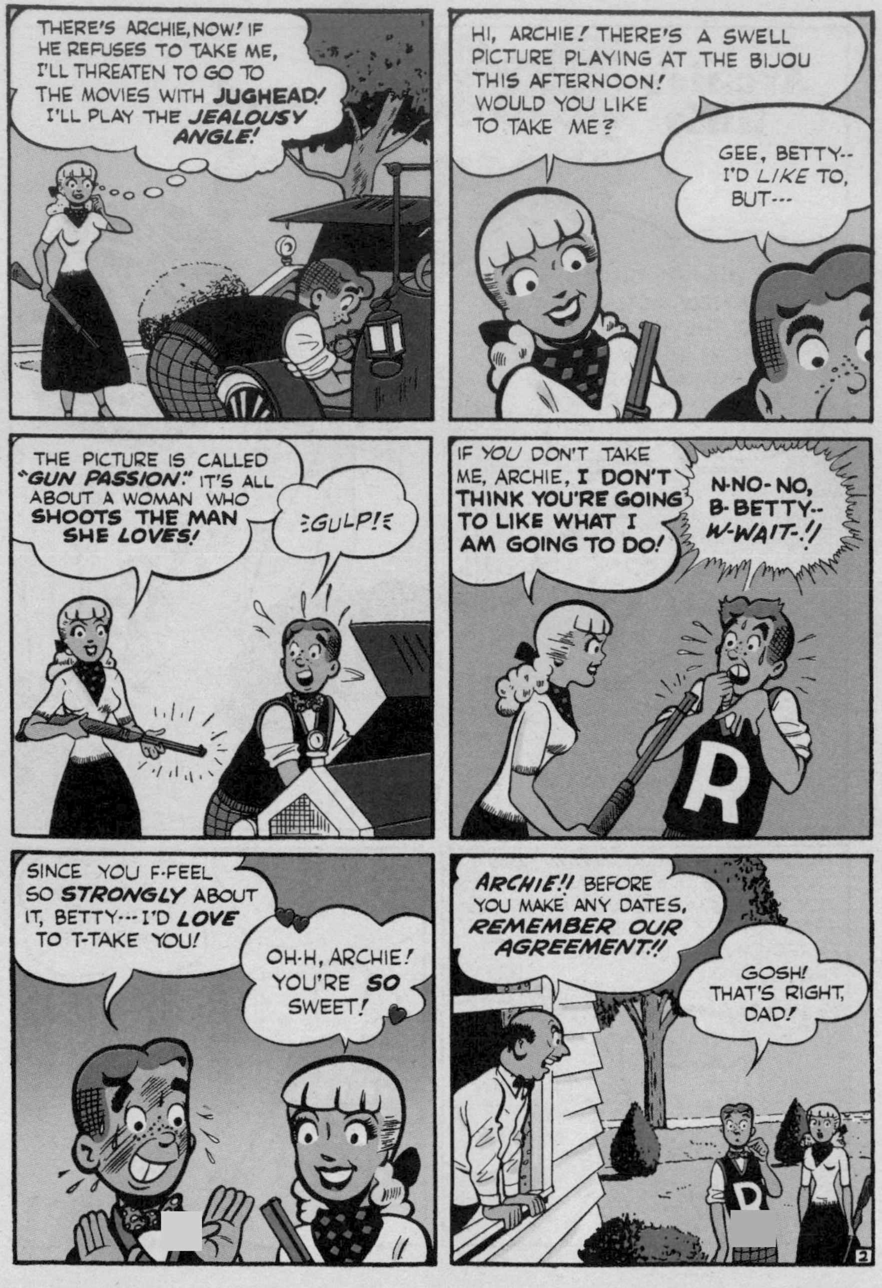
THERE'S ARCHIE, NOW! IF HE REFUSES TO TAKE ME, I'LL THREATEN TO GO TO THE MOVIES WITH JUGHEAD! I'LL PLAY THE JEALOUSY ANGLE!
HI, ARCHIE! THERE'S A SWELL PICTURE PLAYING AT THE BIJOU THIS AFTERNOON! WOULD YOU LIKE TO TAKE ME?
GEE, BETTY-- I'D LIKE TO, BUT---
THE PICTURE IS CALLED "GUN PASSION." IT'S ALL ABOUT A WOMAN WHO SHOOTS THE MAN SHE LOVES!
GULP!
IF YOU DON'T TAKE ME, ARCHIE, I DON'T THINK YOU'RE GOING TO LIKE WHAT I AM GOING TO DO!
N-NO- NO, B- BETTY-- W-WAIT-!!
SINCE YOU F-FEEL SO STRONGLY ABOUT IT, BETTY--- I'D LOVE TO T-TAKE YOU!
OH-H, ARCHIE! YOU'RE SO SWEET!
ARCHIE!! BEFORE YOU MAKE ANY DATES, REMEMBER OUR AGREEMENT!!
GOSH! THAT'S RIGHT, DAD!
2

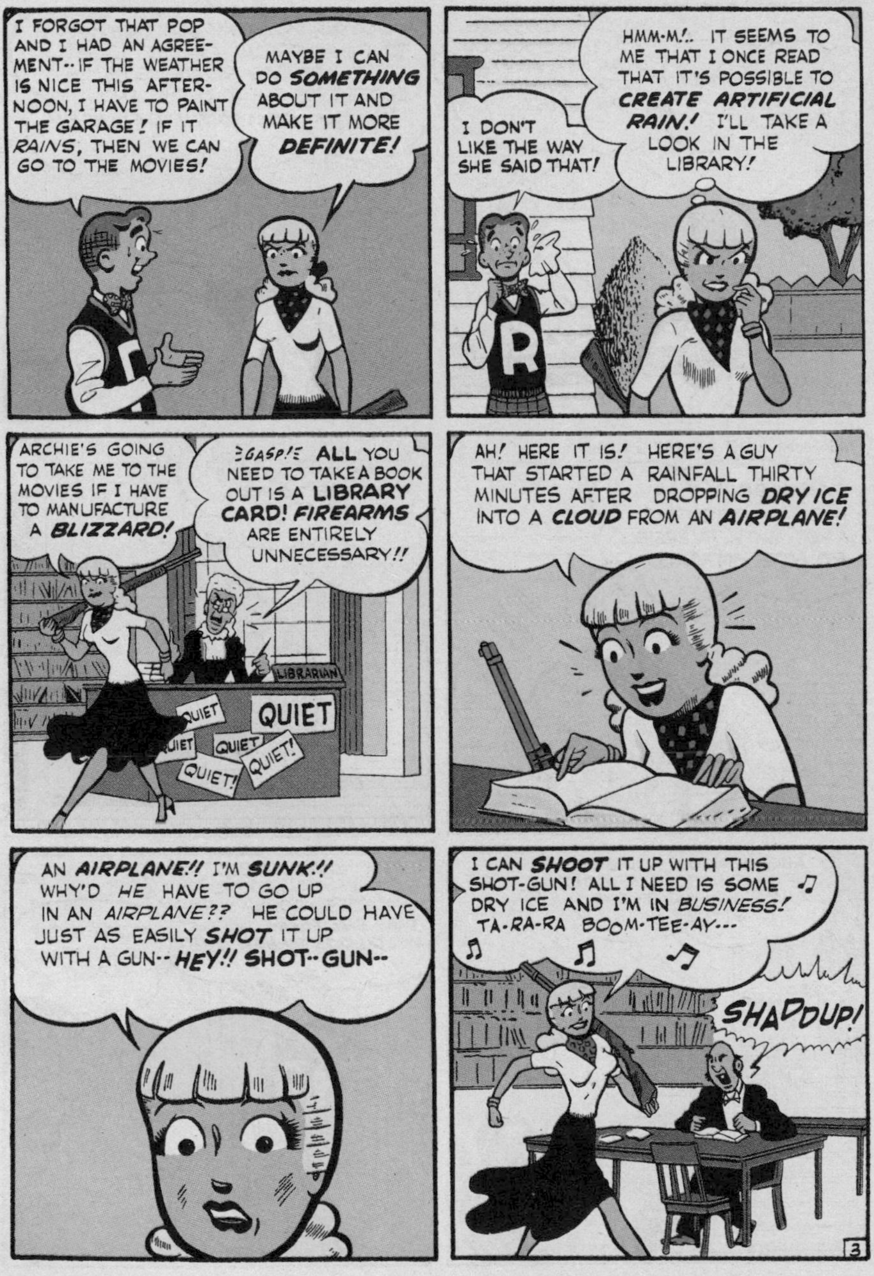
I FORGOT THAT POP AND I HAD AN AGREEMENT-- IF THE WEATHER IS NICE THIS AFTERNOON, I HAVE TO PAINT THE GARAGE! IF IT RAINS, THEN WE CAN GO TO THE MOVIES!
MAYBE I CAN DO SOMETHING ABOUT IT AND MAKE IT MORE DEFINITE!
HMM-M!.. IT SEEMS TO ME THAT I ONCE READ THAT IT'S POSSIBLE TO CREATE ARTIFICIAL RAIN! I'LL TAKE A LOOK IN THE LIBRARY!
I DON'T LIKE THE WAY SHE SAID THAT!
ARCHIE'S GOING TO TAKE ME TO THE MOVIES IF I HAVE TO MANUFACTURE A BLIZZARD!
GASP! ALL YOU NEED TO TAKE A BOOK OUT IS A LIBRARY CARD! FIREARMS ARE ENTIRELY UNNECESSARY!!
LIBRARIAN
QUIET
QUIET
QUIET
QUIET
QUIET!
QUIET!
AH! HERE IT IS! HERE'S A GUY THAT STARTED A RAINFALL THIRTY MINUTES AFTER DROPPING DRY ICE INTO A CLOUD FROM AN AIRPLANE!
AN AIRPLANE!! I'M SUNK!! WHY'D HE HAVE TO GO UP IN AN AIRPLANE?? HE COULD HAVE JUST AS EASILY SHOT IT UP WITH A GUN-- HEY!! SHOT--GUN--
I CAN SHOOT IT UP WITH THIS SHOT-GUN! ALL I NEED IS SOME DRY ICE AND I'M IN BUSINESS! TA-RA-RA BOOM-TEE-AY---
SHADDUP!
3

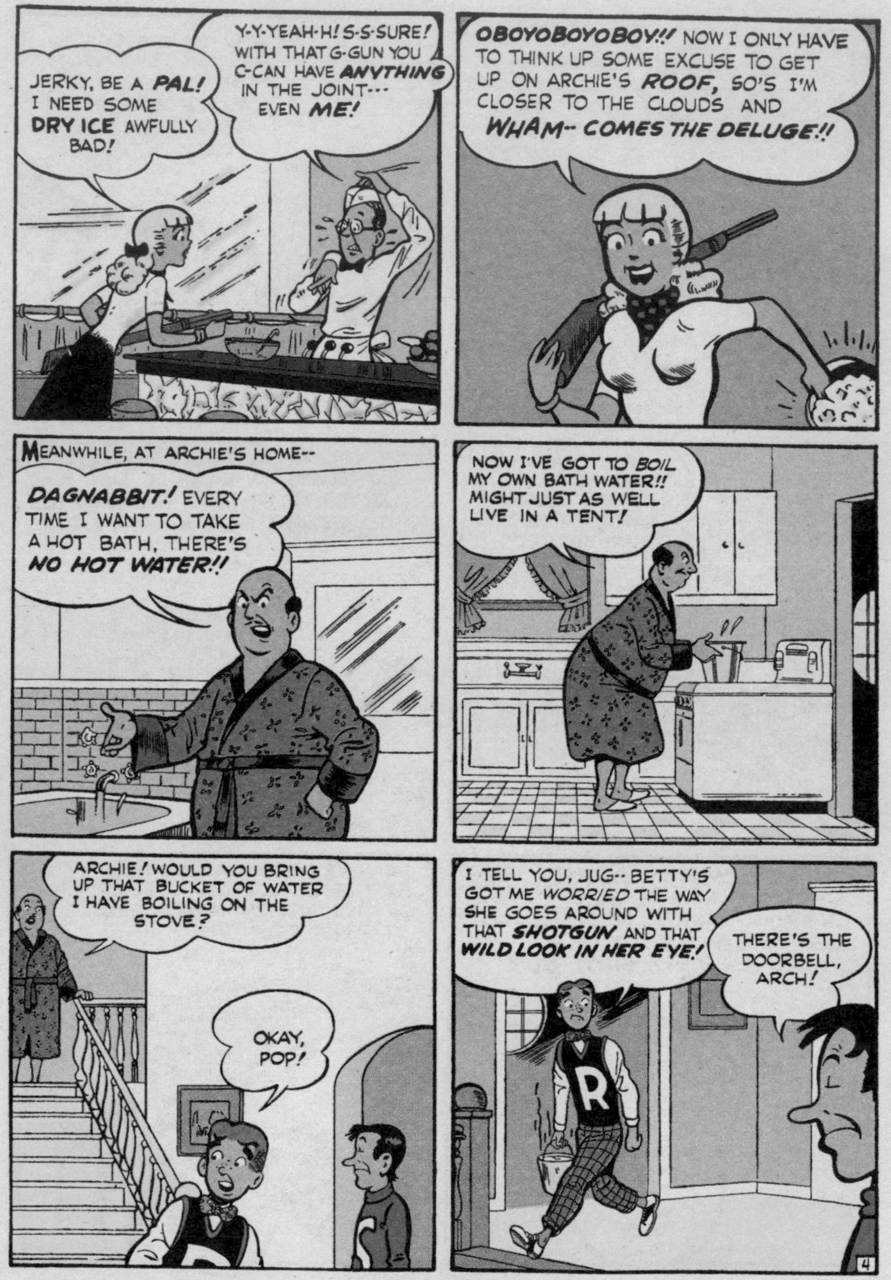
JERKY, BE A PAL! I NEED SOME DRY ICE AWFULLY BAD!
Y-Y-YEAH-H! S-S-SURE! WITH THAT G-GUN YOU C-CAN HAVE ANYTHING IN THE JOINT--- EVEN ME!
OBOYOBOYOBOY!! NOW I ONLY HAVE TO THINK UP SOME EXCUSE TO GET UP ON ARCHIE'S ROOF, SO'S I'M CLOSER TO THE CLOUDS AND WHAM-- COMES THE DELUGE!!
MEANWHILE, AT ARCHIE'S HOME--
DAGNABBIT! EVERY TIME I WANT TO TAKE A HOT BATH, THERE'S NO HOT WATER!!
NOW I'VE GOT TO BOIL MY OWN BATH WATER!! MIGHT JUST AS WELL LIVE IN A TENT!
ARCHIE! WOULD YOU BRING UP THAT BUCKET OF WATER I HAVE BOILING ON THE STOVE?
OKAY, POP!
I TELL YOU, JUG-- BETTY'S GOT ME WORRIED THE WAY SHE GOES AROUND WITH THAT SHOTGUN AND THAT WILD LOOK IN HER EYE!
THERE'S THE DOORBELL, ARCH!
4

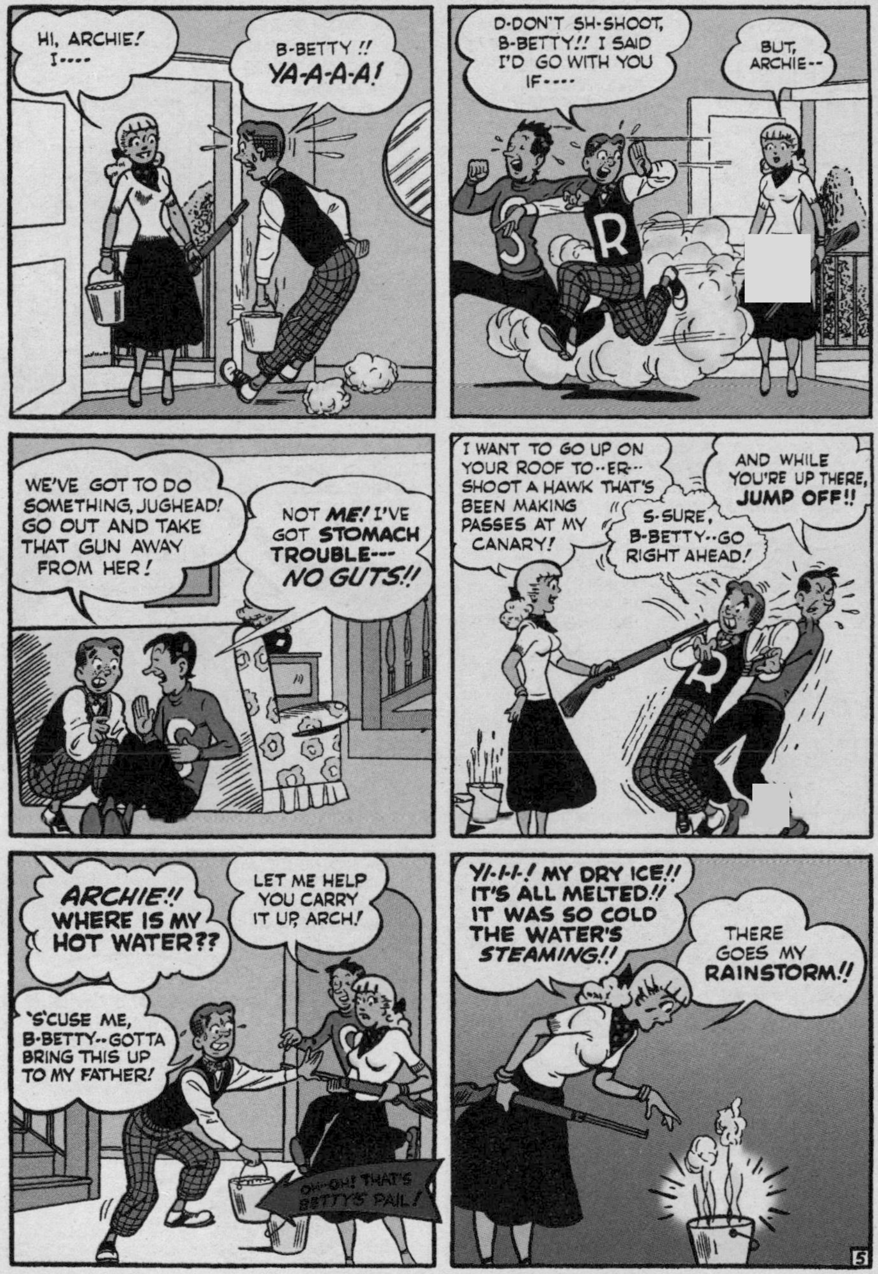
HI, ARCHIE! I----
B-BETTY !! YA-A-A-A!
D-DON'T SH-SHOOT, B-BETTY!! I SAID I'D GO WITH YOU IF----
BUT, ARCHIE--
WE'VE GOT TO DO SOMETHING, JUGHEAD! GO OUT AND TAKE THAT GUN AWAY FROM HER!
NOT ME! I'VE GOT STOMACH TROUBLE--- NO GUTS!!
I WANT TO GO UP ON YOUR ROOF TO--ER-- SHOOT A HAWK THAT'S BEEN MAKING PASSES AT MY CANARY!
AND WHILE YOU'RE UP THERE, JUMP OFF!!
S-SURE, B-BETTY--GO RIGHT AHEAD!
ARCHIE!! WHERE IS MY HOT WATER??
LET ME HELP YOU CARRY IT UP, ARCH!
'S'CUSE ME, B-BETTY--GOTTA BRING THIS UP TO MY FATHER!
OH-OH! THAT'S BETTY'S PAIL!
YI-I-I-! MY DRY ICE!! IT'S ALL MELTED!! IT WAS SO COLD THE WATER'S STEAMING!!
THERE GOES MY RAINSTORM!!
5

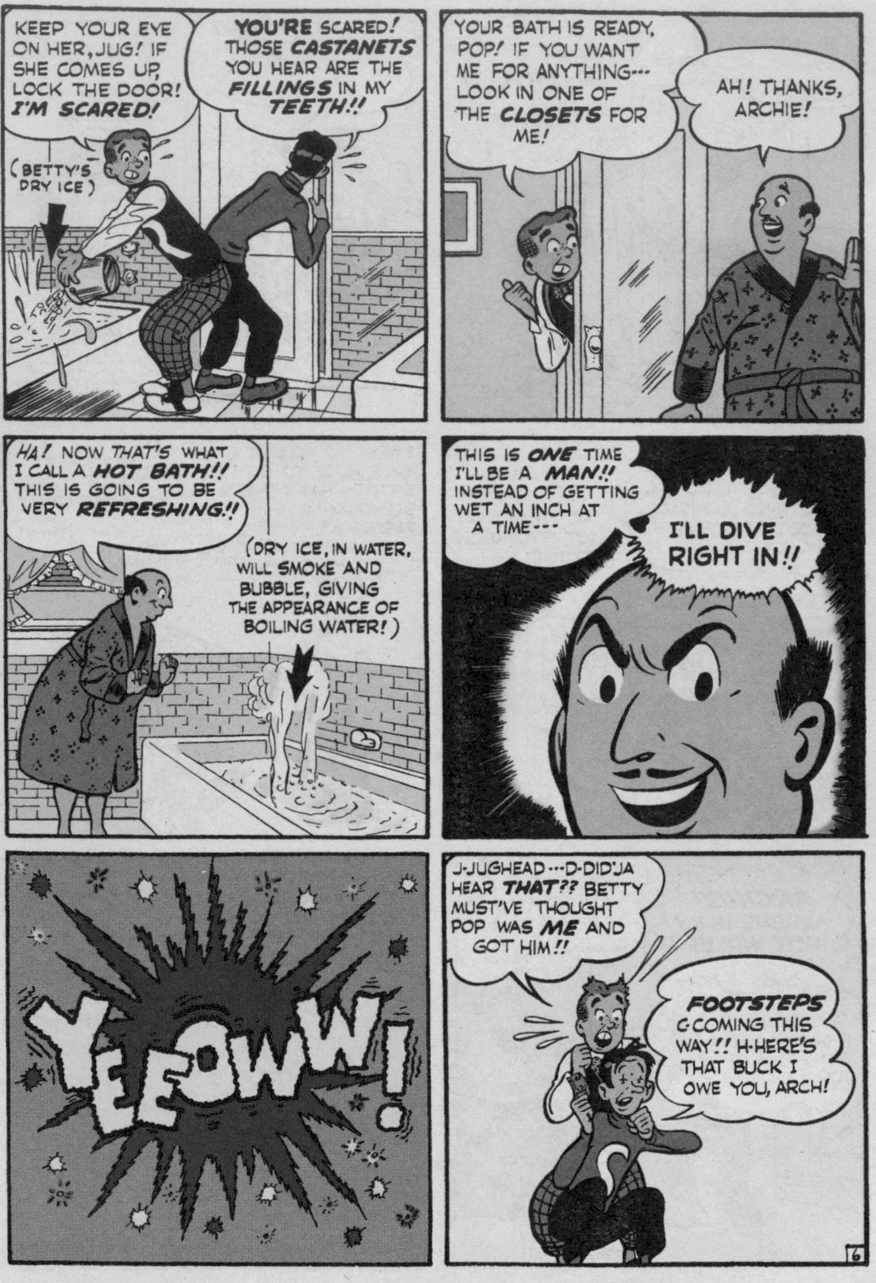
KEEP YOUR EYE ON HER, JUG! IF SHE COMES UP, LOCK THE DOOR! I'M SCARED!
YOU'RE SCARED! THOSE CASTANETS YOU HEAR ARE THE FILLINGS IN MY TEETH!!
(BETTY'S DRY ICE)
YOUR BATH IS READY, POP! IF YOU WANT ME FOR ANYTHING--- LOOK IN ONE OF THE CLOSETS FOR ME!
AH! THANKS, ARCHIE!
HA! NOW THAT'S WHAT I CALL A HOT BATH!! THIS IS GOING TO BE VERY REFRESHING!!
(DRY ICE, IN WATER, WILL SMOKE AND BUBBLE, GIVING THE APPEARANCE OF BOILING WATER!)
THIS IS ONE TIME I'LL BE A MAN!! INSTEAD OF GETTING WET AN INCH AT A TIME---
I'LL DIVE RIGHT IN!!
YEEOWW!
J-JUGHEAD---D-DID'JA HEAR THAT?? BETTY MUST'VE THOUGHT POP WAS ME AND GOT HIM!!
FOOTSTEPS C-COMING THIS WAY!! H-HERE'S THAT BUCK I OWE YOU, ARCH!
6

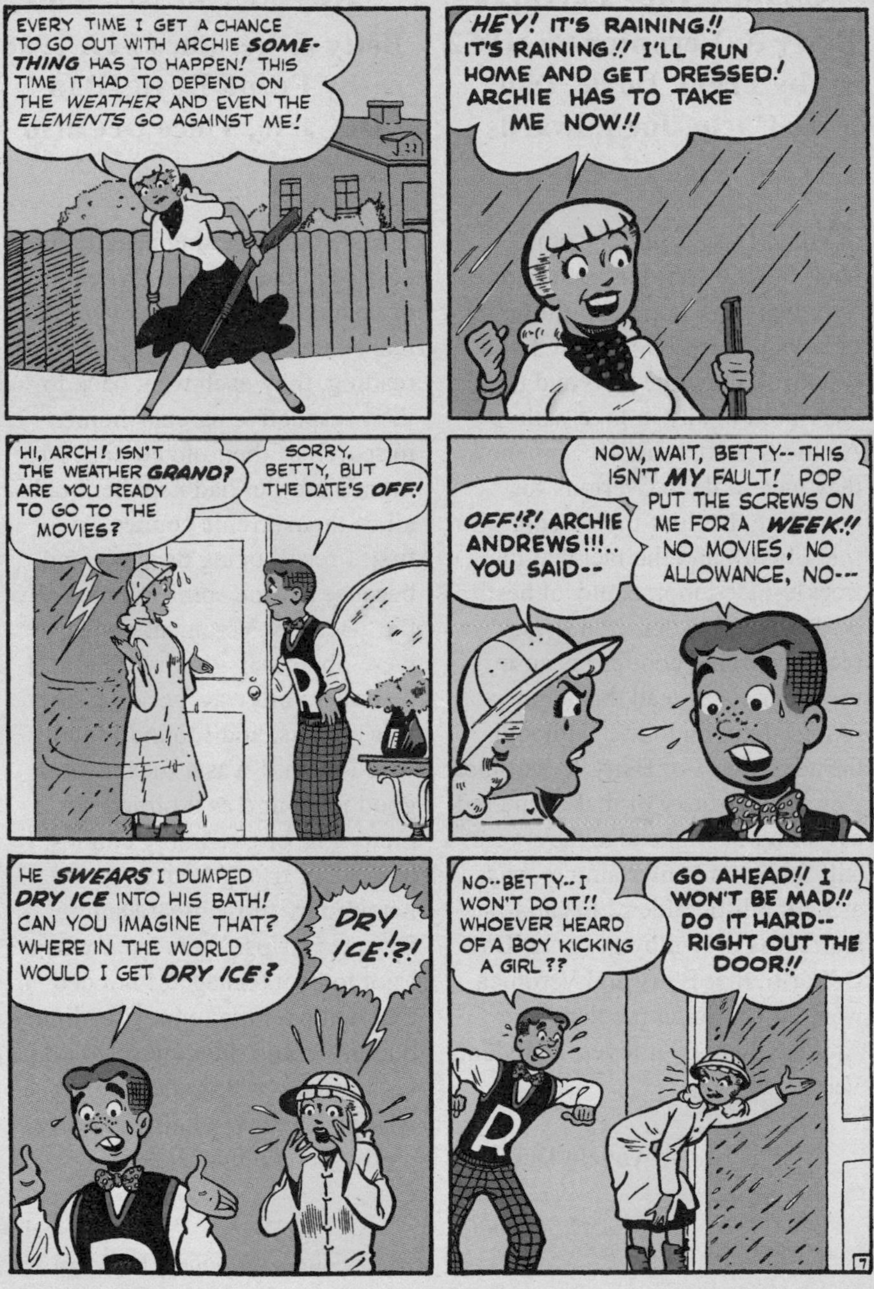
EVERY TIME I GET A CHANCE TO GO OUT WITH ARCHIE **SOMETHING** HAS TO HAPPEN! THIS TIME IT HAD TO DEPEND ON THE *WEATHER* AND EVEN THE *ELEMENTS* GO AGAINST ME!
HEY! IT'S RAINING!! IT'S RAINING!! I'LL RUN HOME AND GET DRESSED! ARCHIE HAS TO TAKE ME NOW!!
HI, ARCH! ISN'T THE WEATHER **GRAND?** ARE YOU READY TO GO TO THE MOVIES?
SORRY, BETTY, BUT THE DATE'S **OFF!**
OFF!?! ARCHIE ANDREWS!!!.. YOU SAID--
NOW, WAIT, BETTY-- THIS ISN'T **MY** FAULT! POP PUT THE SCREWS ON ME FOR A **WEEK!!** NO MOVIES, NO ALLOWANCE, NO---
HE **SWEARS** I DUMPED **DRY ICE** INTO HIS BATH! CAN YOU IMAGINE THAT? WHERE IN THE WORLD WOULD I GET **DRY ICE?**
DRY ICE!?!
NO--BETTY--I WON'T DO IT!! WHOEVER HEARD OF A BOY KICKING A GIRL??
GO AHEAD!! I WON'T BE MAD!! DO IT HARD-- RIGHT OUT THE DOOR!!
7

Change Your Partners
Betty & Veronica #6, 1952
by Frank Doyle, Dan DeCarlo, Joe Edwards

When I was a young comic book fanatic…er, fan, Betty and Veronica gave hope to millions of boys like me. Here were two beautiful, dynamic girls and they were both madly in love with Archie….ARCHIE!!!!! Somehow, they were able to overlook his bumbling, his less-than-stellar schoolwork and the fact that his freckle-faced look could, at best, be described as "cute." I began reading Archie comics because my older sister read them and passed them on to me. Although the adventures of Betty & Veronica weren't as wacky or male-centered as Archie or Jughead's, they were still funny and entertaining. And, as I got a little older, I began to realize, as drawn by the great Dan DeCarlo, that Betty and Veronica were HOT! So let me thank Archie's two great loves, Betty and Veronica.

-- **Angelo Decesare**
Writer,
Archie Comics

Rhyme Nor Reason
Betty & Veronica #27, 1956
by Frank Doyle, Dan DeCarlo, Vince DeCarlo

I first started getting heavily into comics at the age of 5. When my parents happily discovered I had a new hobby, and it involved reading, they each went back to their respective parents' homes in search of their old comics. My mom's mother had kept her books, all of them Archie comics. At first, I recall being disappointed, because Archie comics, especially the "Betty & Veronica" series, were obviously girls' stuff. But, I read them anyway, because, hey, free comics, and I found I totally loved them. I was a sucker for a good joke, and as it turned out, a pretty girl or two in my comics. I remember trying to draw women inspired by those great Dan DeCarlo strips. Years later, when I got to be a teenager, I noticed that while a lot of comic reading buddies could draw muscled dudes with grimaces, I was the only one who could draw a halfway decent pretty girl. So thanks B&V!

-- **Tim Seeley**
Award-winning Writer/Artist,
Hack/Slash

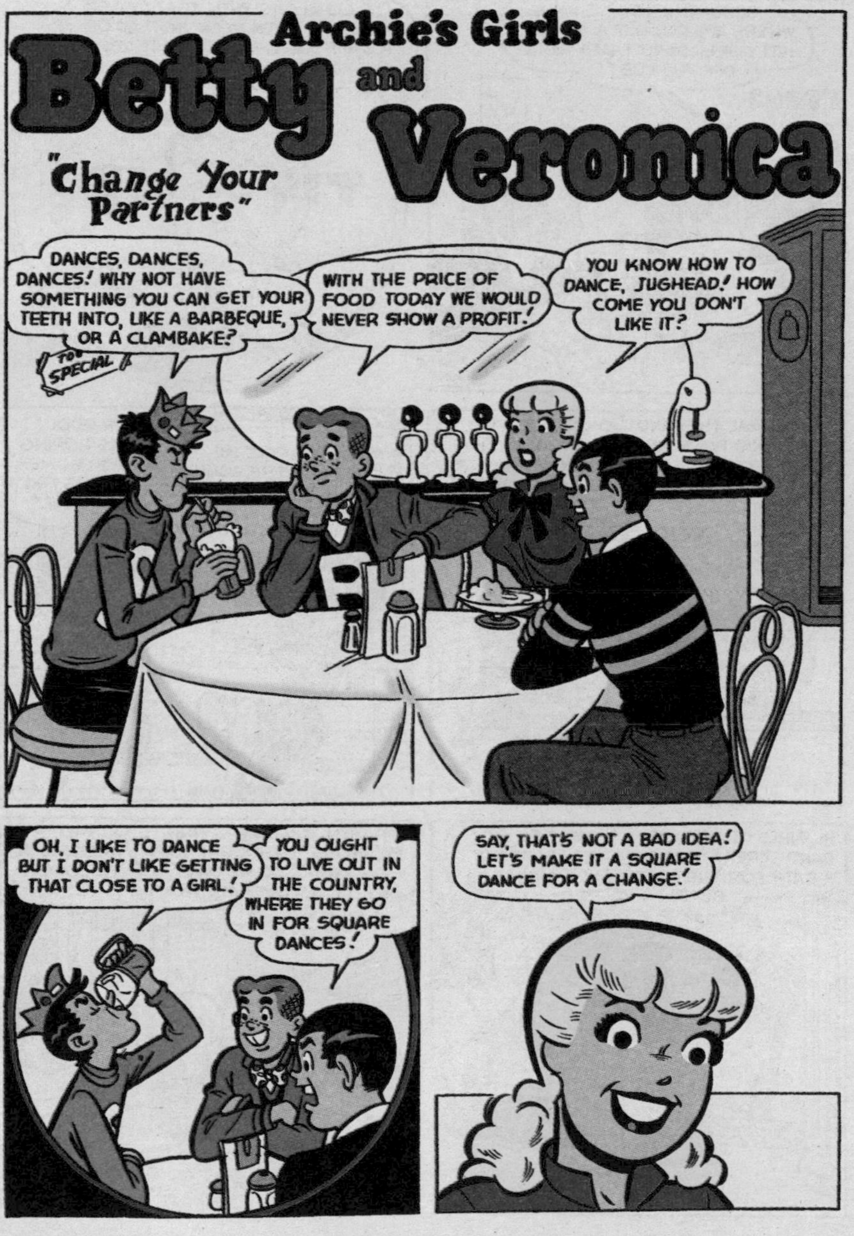
Archie's Girls
Betty and Veronica
"Change Your Partners"
DANCES, DANCES, DANCES! WHY NOT HAVE SOMETHING YOU CAN GET YOUR TEETH INTO, LIKE A BARBEQUE, OR A CLAMBAKE?
WITH THE PRICE OF FOOD TODAY WE WOULD NEVER SHOW A PROFIT!
YOU KNOW HOW TO DANCE, JUGHEAD! HOW COME YOU DON'T LIKE IT?
SPECIAL
OH, I LIKE TO DANCE BUT I DON'T LIKE GETTING THAT CLOSE TO A GIRL!
YOU OUGHT TO LIVE OUT IN THE COUNTRY, WHERE THEY GO IN FOR SQUARE DANCES!
SAY, THAT'S NOT A BAD IDEA! LET'S MAKE IT A SQUARE DANCE FOR A CHANGE!

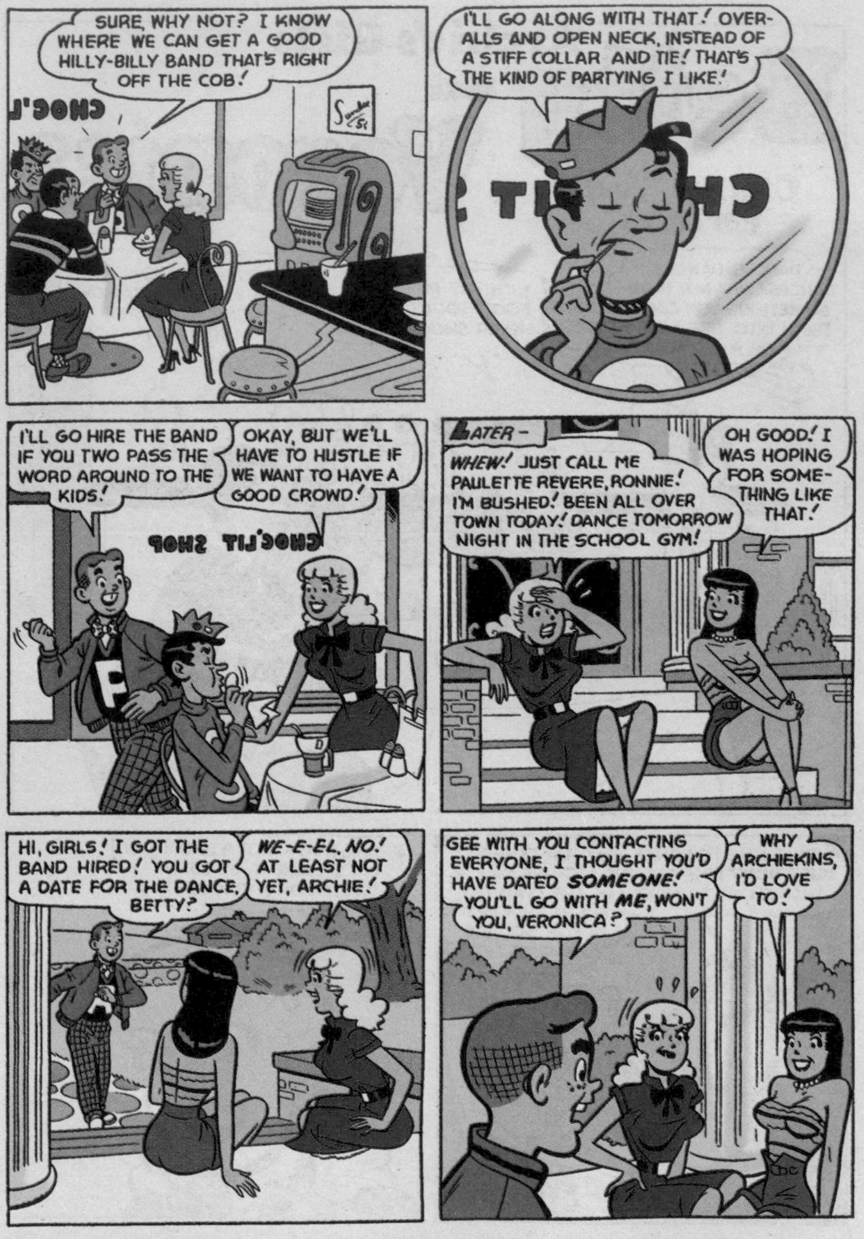
SURE, WHY NOT? I KNOW WHERE WE CAN GET A GOOD HILLY-BILLY BAND THAT'S RIGHT OFF THE COB!
I'LL GO ALONG WITH THAT! OVER-ALLS AND OPEN NECK, INSTEAD OF A STIFF COLLAR AND TIE! THAT'S THE KIND OF PARTYING I LIKE!
I'LL GO HIRE THE BAND IF YOU TWO PASS THE WORD AROUND TO THE KIDS!
OKAY, BUT WE'LL HAVE TO HUSTLE IF WE WANT TO HAVE A GOOD CROWD!
LATER -
WHEW! JUST CALL ME PAULETTE REVERE, RONNIE! I'M BUSHED! BEEN ALL OVER TOWN TODAY! DANCE TOMORROW NIGHT IN THE SCHOOL GYM!
OH GOOD! I WAS HOPING FOR SOME-THING LIKE THAT!
HI, GIRLS! I GOT THE BAND HIRED! YOU GOT A DATE FOR THE DANCE, BETTY?
WE-E-EL, NO! AT LEAST NOT YET, ARCHIE!
GEE WITH YOU CONTACTING EVERYONE, I THOUGHT YOU'D HAVE DATED SOMEONE! YOU'LL GO WITH ME, WON'T YOU, VERONICA?
WHY ARCHIEKINS, I'D LOVE TO!

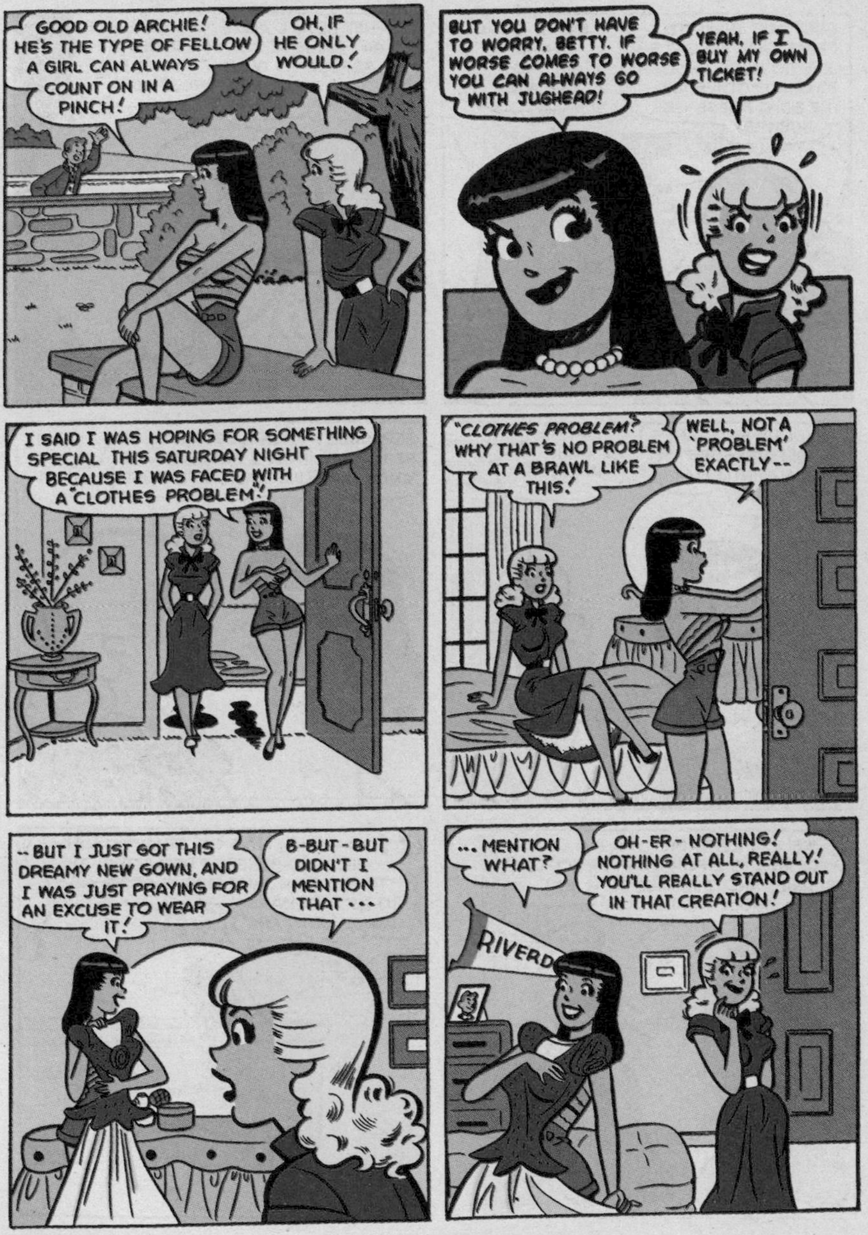
GOOD OLD ARCHIE! HE'S THE TYPE OF FELLOW A GIRL CAN ALWAYS COUNT ON IN A PINCH!
OH, IF HE ONLY WOULD!
BUT YOU DON'T HAVE TO WORRY, BETTY. IF WORSE COMES TO WORSE YOU CAN ALWAYS GO WITH JUGHEAD!
YEAH, IF I BUY MY OWN TICKET!
I SAID I WAS HOPING FOR SOMETHING SPECIAL THIS SATURDAY NIGHT BECAUSE I WAS FACED WITH A "CLOTHES PROBLEM"!
"CLOTHES PROBLEM"? WHY THAT'S NO PROBLEM AT A BRAWL LIKE THIS!
WELL, NOT A 'PROBLEM' EXACTLY --
-- BUT I JUST GOT THIS DREAMY NEW GOWN, AND I WAS JUST PRAYING FOR AN EXCUSE TO WEAR IT!
B-BUT-BUT DIDN'T I MENTION THAT ...
... MENTION WHAT?
OH-ER- NOTHING! NOTHING AT ALL, REALLY! YOU'LL REALLY STAND OUT IN THAT CREATION!
RIVERD

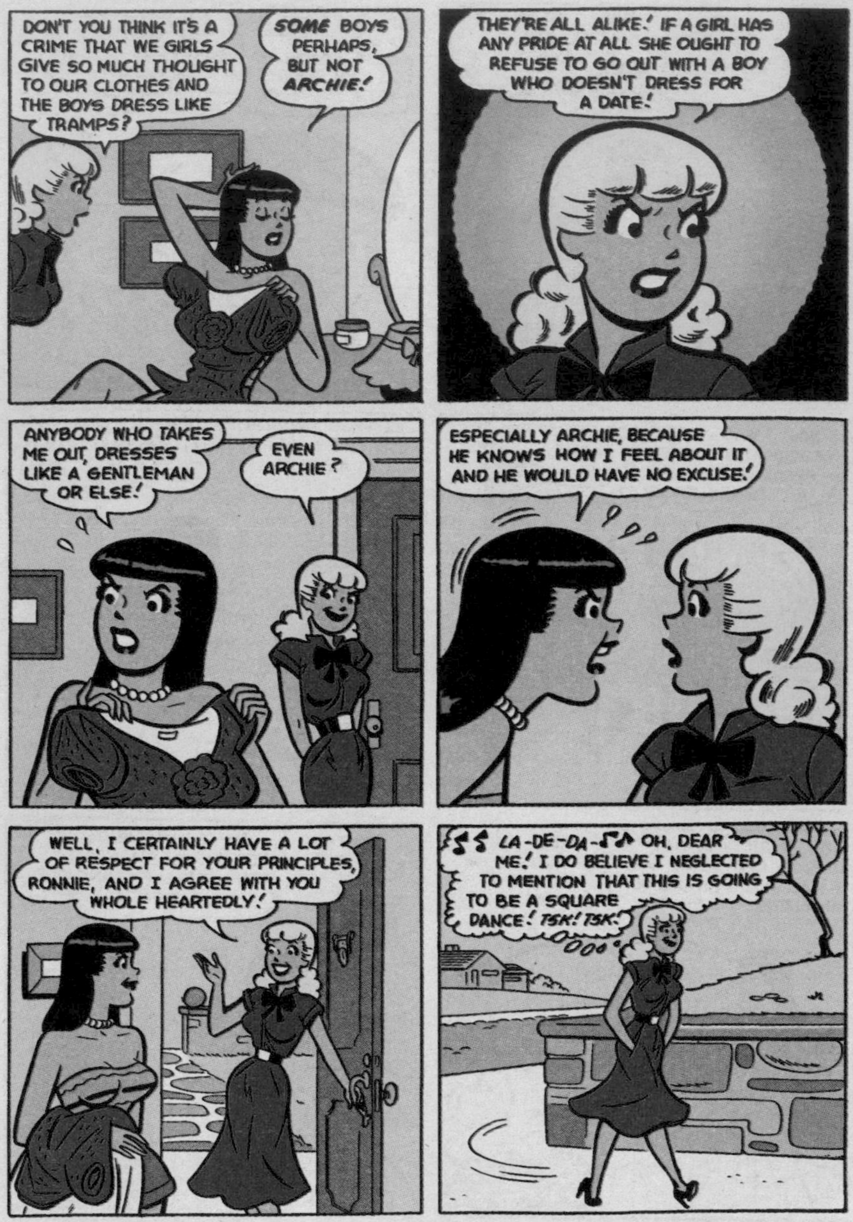
DON'T YOU THINK IT'S A CRIME THAT WE GIRLS GIVE SO MUCH THOUGHT TO OUR CLOTHES AND THE BOYS DRESS LIKE TRAMPS?
SOME BOYS PERHAPS, BUT NOT ARCHIE!
THEY'RE ALL ALIKE! IF A GIRL HAS ANY PRIDE AT ALL SHE OUGHT TO REFUSE TO GO OUT WITH A BOY WHO DOESN'T DRESS FOR A DATE!
ANYBODY WHO TAKES ME OUT, DRESSES LIKE A GENTLEMAN OR ELSE!
EVEN ARCHIE?
ESPECIALLY ARCHIE, BECAUSE HE KNOWS HOW I FEEL ABOUT IT AND HE WOULD HAVE NO EXCUSE!
WELL, I CERTAINLY HAVE A LOT OF RESPECT FOR YOUR PRINCIPLES, RONNIE, AND I AGREE WITH YOU WHOLE HEARTEDLY!
LA-DE-DA- OH, DEAR ME! I DO BELIEVE I NEGLECTED TO MENTION THAT THIS IS GOING TO BE A SQUARE DANCE! TSK! TSK!

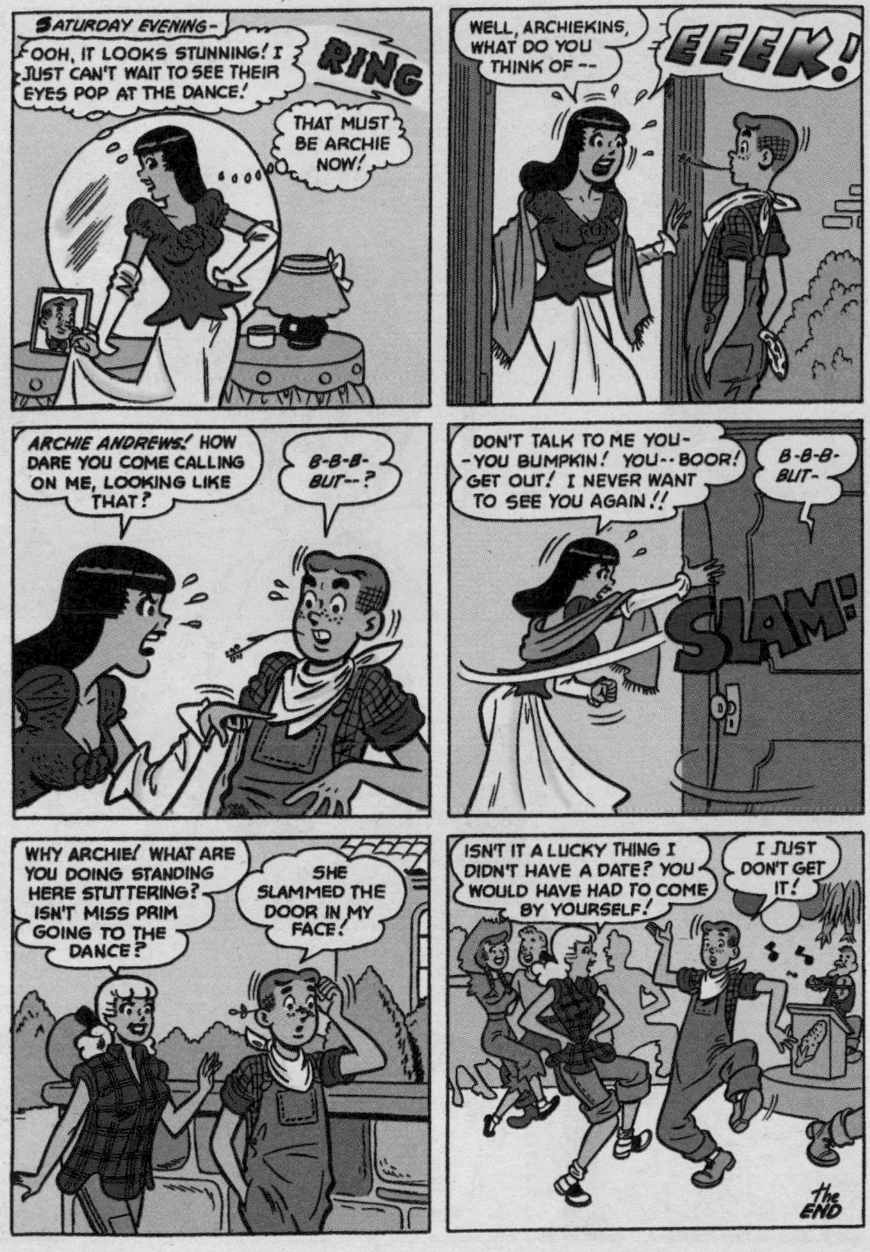
SATURDAY EVENING-
OOH, IT LOOKS STUNNING! I JUST CAN'T WAIT TO SEE THEIR EYES POP AT THE DANCE!
RING
THAT MUST BE ARCHIE NOW!
WELL, ARCHIEKINS, WHAT DO YOU THINK OF --
EEEK!
ARCHIE ANDREWS! HOW DARE YOU COME CALLING ON ME, LOOKING LIKE THAT?
B-B-B-BUT--?
DON'T TALK TO ME YOU--YOU BUMPKIN! YOU--BOOR! GET OUT! I NEVER WANT TO SEE YOU AGAIN!!
B-B-B-BUT-
SLAM!
WHY ARCHIE! WHAT ARE YOU DOING STANDING HERE STUTTERING? ISN'T MISS PRIM GOING TO THE DANCE?
SHE SLAMMED THE DOOR IN MY FACE!
ISN'T IT A LUCKY THING I DIDN'T HAVE A DATE? YOU WOULD HAVE HAD TO COME BY YOURSELF!
I JUST DON'T GET IT!
the END

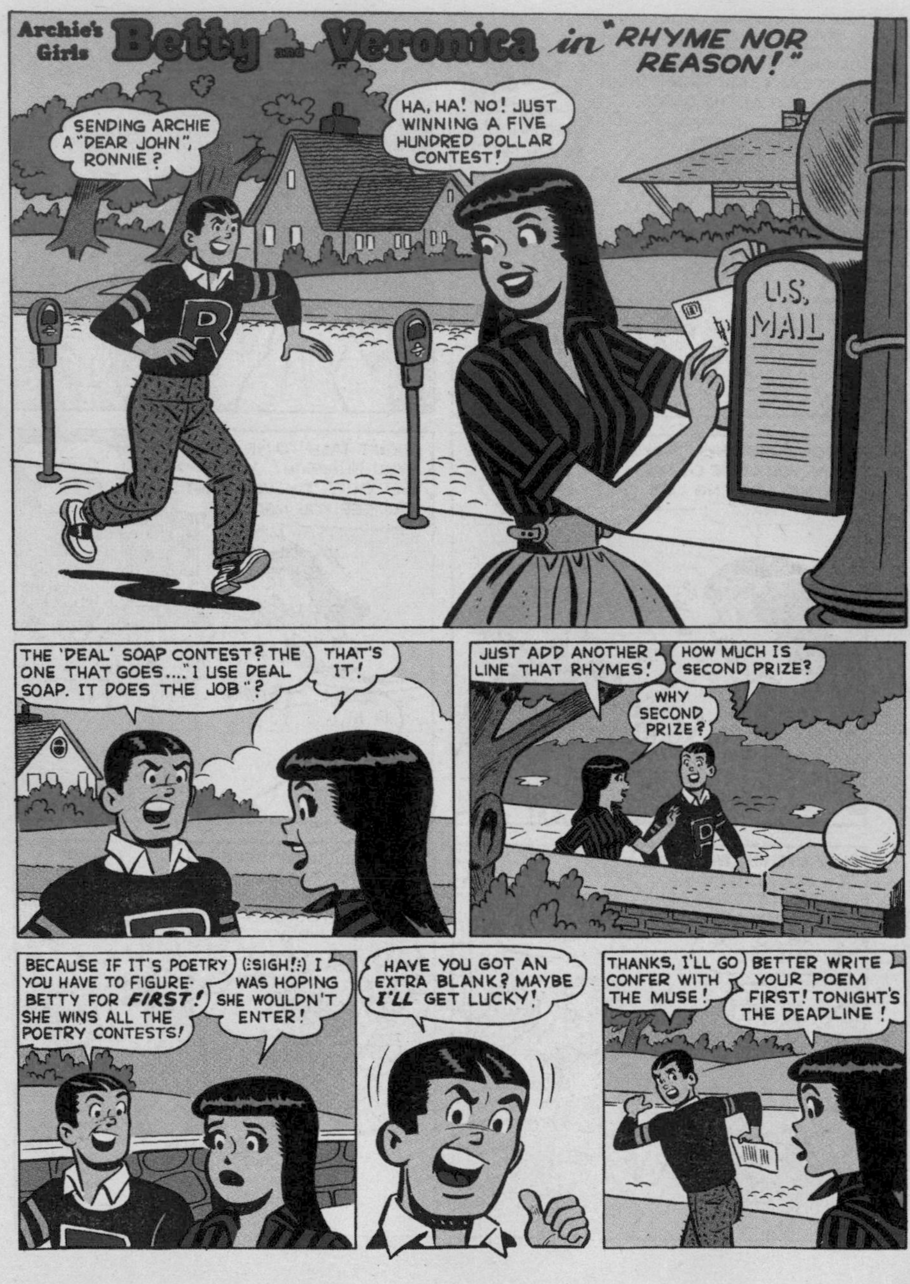
Archie's Girls Betty and Veronica in "RHYME NOR REASON!"
SENDING ARCHIE A "DEAR JOHN", RONNIE ?
HA, HA! NO! JUST WINNING A FIVE HUNDRED DOLLAR CONTEST!
U.S. MAIL
THE 'DEAL' SOAP CONTEST? THE ONE THAT GOES...."I USE DEAL SOAP. IT DOES THE JOB"?
THAT'S IT!
JUST ADD ANOTHER LINE THAT RHYMES!
HOW MUCH IS SECOND PRIZE?
WHY SECOND PRIZE?
BECAUSE IF IT'S POETRY YOU HAVE TO FIGURE BETTY FOR FIRST! SHE WINS ALL THE POETRY CONTESTS!
(:SIGH!:) I WAS HOPING SHE WOULDN'T ENTER!
HAVE YOU GOT AN EXTRA BLANK? MAYBE I'LL GET LUCKY!
THANKS, I'LL GO CONFER WITH THE MUSE!
BETTER WRITE YOUR POEM FIRST! TONIGHT'S THE DEADLINE!

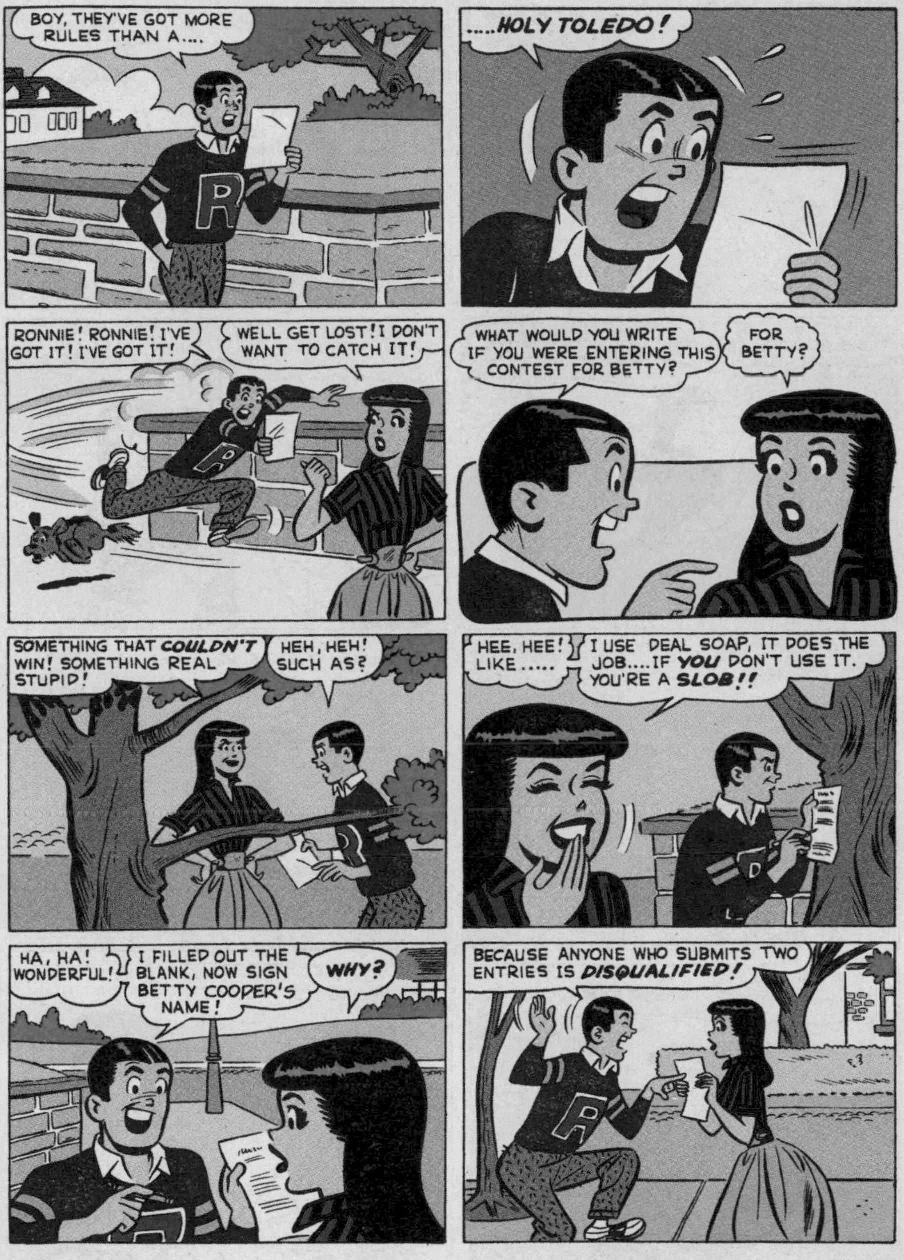
BOY, THEY'VE GOT MORE RULES THAN A....
.....HOLY TOLEDO!
RONNIE! RONNIE! I'VE GOT IT! I'VE GOT IT!
WELL GET LOST! I DON'T WANT TO CATCH IT!
WHAT WOULD YOU WRITE IF YOU WERE ENTERING THIS CONTEST FOR BETTY?
FOR BETTY?
SOMETHING THAT COULDN'T WIN! SOMETHING REAL STUPID!
HEH, HEH! SUCH AS?
HEE, HEE! LIKE .....
I USE DEAL SOAP, IT DOES THE JOB....IF YOU DON'T USE IT. YOU'RE A SLOB!!
HA, HA! WONDERFUL!
I FILLED OUT THE BLANK, NOW SIGN BETTY COOPER'S NAME!
WHY?
BECAUSE ANYONE WHO SUBMITS TWO ENTRIES IS DISQUALIFIED!

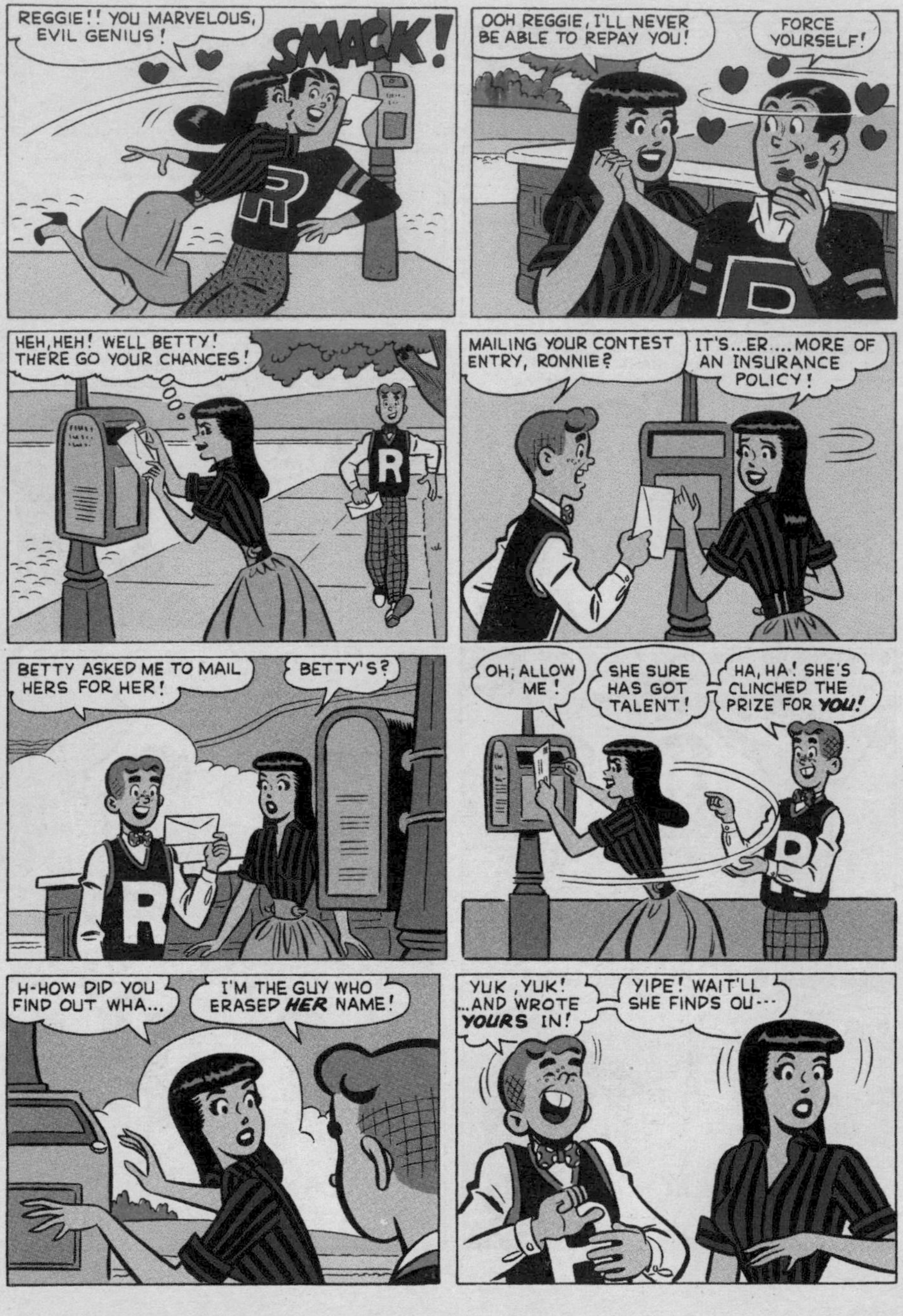
REGGIE!! YOU MARVELOUS, EVIL GENIUS!
SMACK!
OOH REGGIE, I'LL NEVER BE ABLE TO REPAY YOU!
FORCE YOURSELF!
HEH, HEH! WELL BETTY! THERE GO YOUR CHANCES!
MAILING YOUR CONTEST ENTRY, RONNIE?
IT'S...ER....MORE OF AN INSURANCE POLICY!
BETTY ASKED ME TO MAIL HERS FOR HER!
BETTY'S?
OH, ALLOW ME!
SHE SURE HAS GOT TALENT!
HA, HA! SHE'S CLINCHED THE PRIZE FOR YOU!
H-HOW DID YOU FIND OUT WHA...
I'M THE GUY WHO ERASED HER NAME!
YUK, YUK! ...AND WROTE YOURS IN!
YIPE! WAIT'LL SHE FINDS OU---

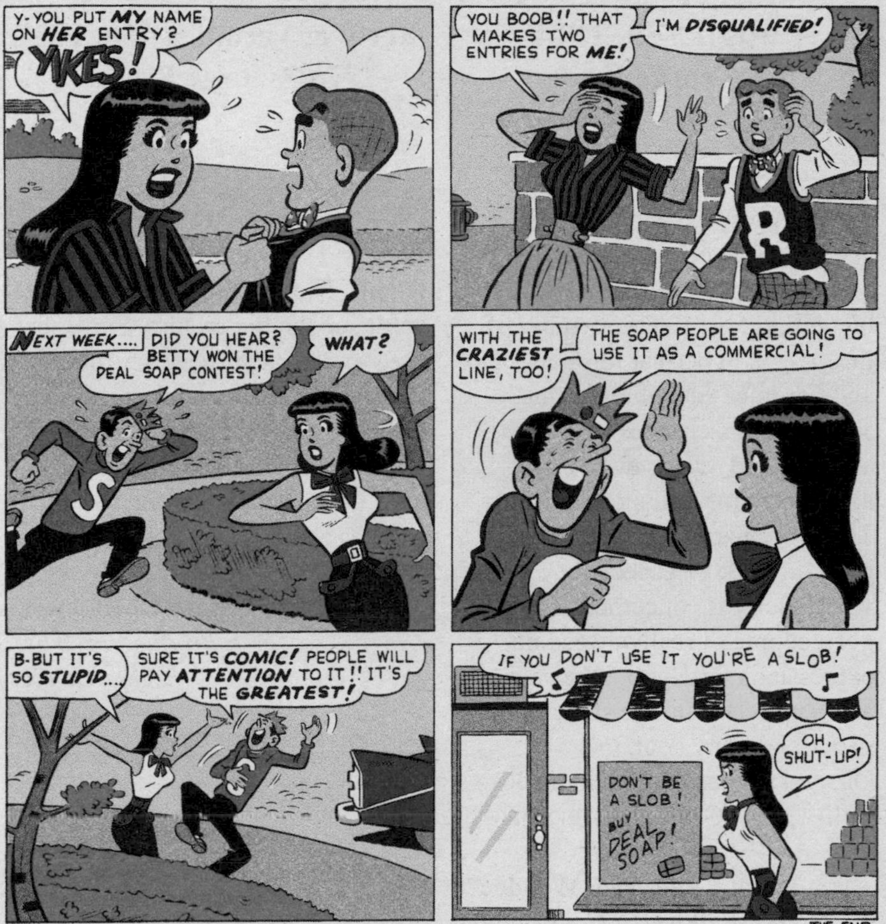
Y-YOU PUT MY NAME ON HER ENTRY?
YIKES!
YOU BOOB!! THAT MAKES TWO ENTRIES FOR ME!
I'M DISQUALIFIED!
NEXT WEEK....
DID YOU HEAR? BETTY WON THE DEAL SOAP CONTEST!
WHAT?
WITH THE CRAZIEST LINE, TOO!
THE SOAP PEOPLE ARE GOING TO USE IT AS A COMMERCIAL!
B-BUT IT'S SO STUPID...
SURE IT'S COMIC! PEOPLE WILL PAY ATTENTION TO IT!! IT'S THE GREATEST!
IF YOU DON'T USE IT YOU'RE A SLOB!
OH, SHUT-UP!
DON'T BE A SLOB! BUY DEAL SOAP!

THE END

REGGIE

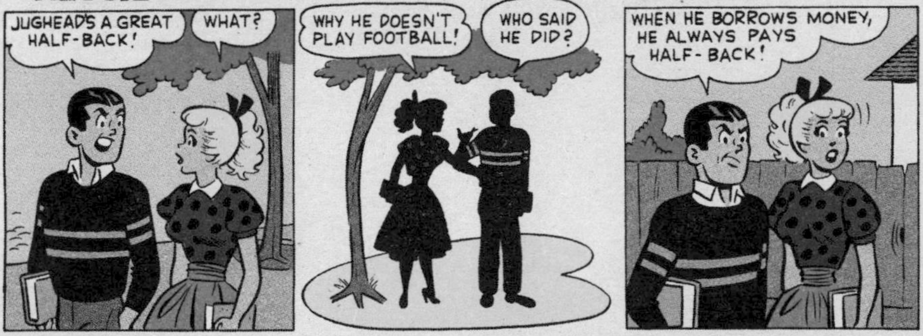
JUGHEAD'S A GREAT HALF-BACK!
WHAT?
WHY HE DOESN'T PLAY FOOTBALL!
WHO SAID HE DID?
WHEN HE BORROWS MONEY, HE ALWAYS PAYS HALF-BACK!

Skip, Hop & Thump
Laugh #75, 1956
by George Frese

Rage Before Beauty
Betty & Veronica #30, 1957
by George Frese

In this story, the gang is head over heels for the sock hop, a weird school dance craze that was pretty big in the '50s! Every member of the gang is in perfect form, as Betty and Veronica squabble, Archie screws up his chances with both, and Jughead avoids everything altogether (for as long as he can). This story packs some seriously great artwork — especially where Betty is concerned! She's got a couple of really awesome expressions throughout the story, and her dress with the static plaid pattern is pretty cool, too. Oh, and Jughead? A pack of socks is, like, $15. Get it together, man!

-- Patrick Woodruff
Digital Publishing Coordinator,
Archie Comics

A lot of people would read this story and see Veronica as the villain. Then again, a lot of people don't see the big picture. Sure, she tried to sabotage Betty's birthday and play on the boys' naivety of fashion... but no one ever stopped to consider what Veronica would like! Poor Veronica. Poor Veronica and her comically backfiring ways.

-- Steve Golebiewski
Production Artist,
Archie Comics

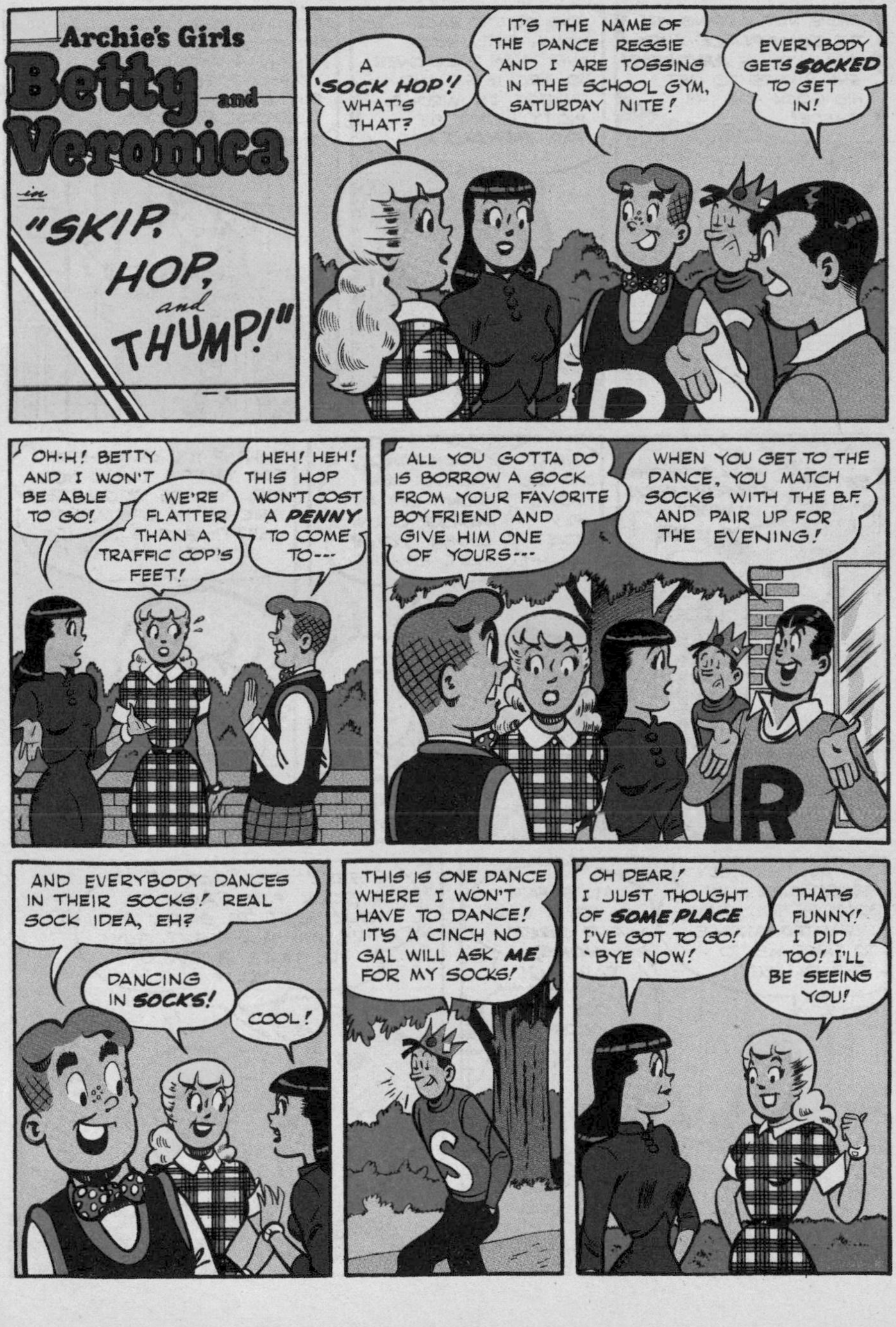
Archie's Girls
Betty and Veronica
in
"SKIP, HOP, and THUMP!"
A 'SOCK HOP'! WHAT'S THAT?
IT'S THE NAME OF THE DANCE REGGIE AND I ARE TOSSING IN THE SCHOOL GYM, SATURDAY NITE!
EVERYBODY GETS SOCKED TO GET IN!
OH-H! BETTY AND I WON'T BE ABLE TO GO!
WE'RE FLATTER THAN A TRAFFIC COP'S FEET!
HEH! HEH! THIS HOP WON'T COST A PENNY TO COME TO---
ALL YOU GOTTA DO IS BORROW A SOCK FROM YOUR FAVORITE BOY FRIEND AND GIVE HIM ONE OF YOURS---
WHEN YOU GET TO THE DANCE, YOU MATCH SOCKS WITH THE B.F. AND PAIR UP FOR THE EVENING!
AND EVERYBODY DANCES IN THEIR SOCKS! REAL SOCK IDEA, EH?
DANCING IN SOCKS!
COOL!
THIS IS ONE DANCE WHERE I WON'T HAVE TO DANCE! IT'S A CINCH NO GAL WILL ASK ME FOR MY SOCKS!
OH DEAR! I JUST THOUGHT OF SOME PLACE I'VE GOT TO GO! 'BYE NOW!
THAT'S FUNNY! I DID TOO! I'LL BE SEEING YOU!

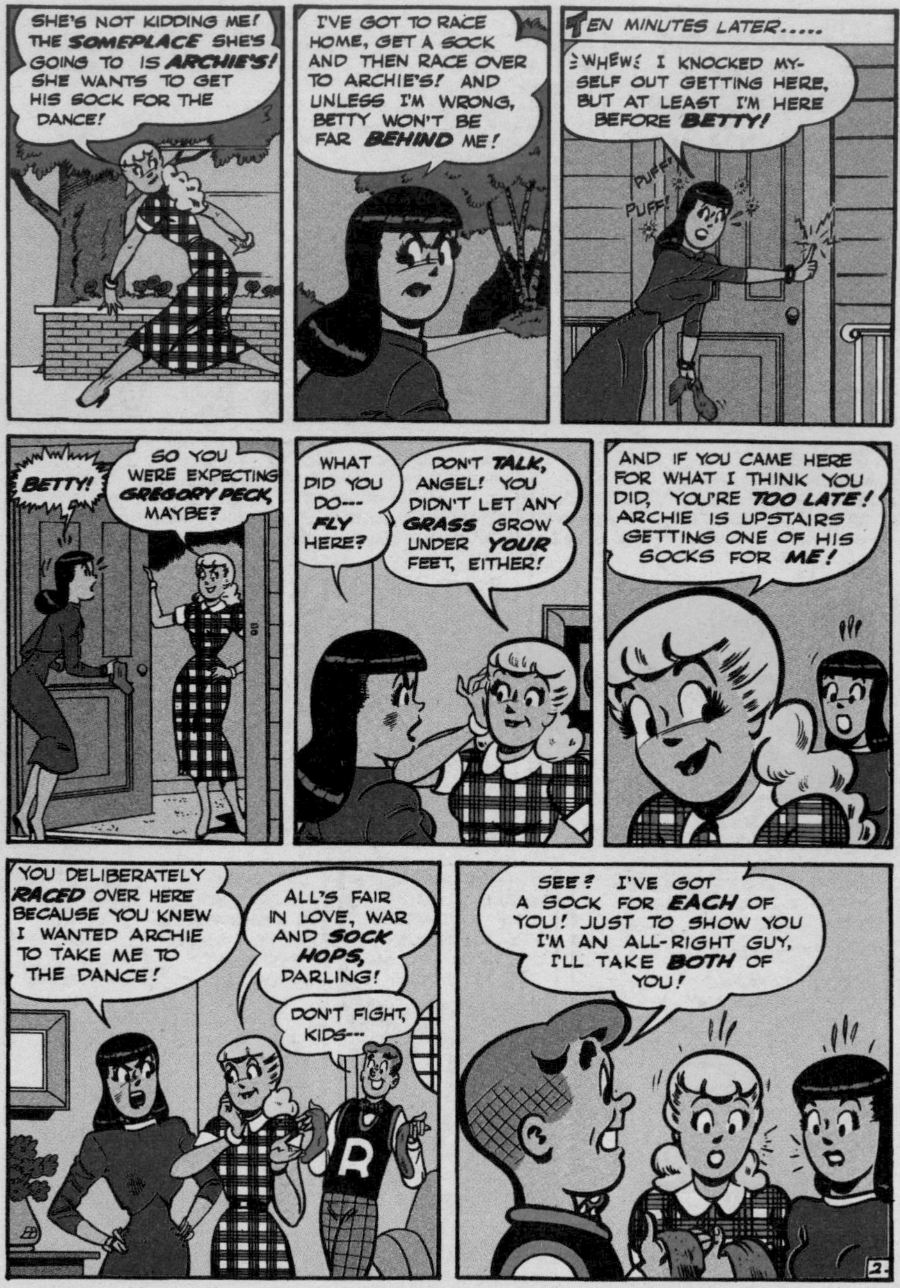
SHE'S NOT KIDDING ME! THE SOMEPLACE SHE'S GOING TO IS ARCHIE'S! SHE WANTS TO GET HIS SOCK FOR THE DANCE!
I'VE GOT TO RACE HOME, GET A SOCK AND THEN RACE OVER TO ARCHIE'S! AND UNLESS I'M WRONG, BETTY WON'T BE FAR BEHIND ME!
TEN MINUTES LATER.....
WHEW! I KNOCKED MYSELF OUT GETTING HERE, BUT AT LEAST I'M HERE BEFORE BETTY!
PUFF! PUFF!
BETTY!
SO YOU WERE EXPECTING GREGORY PECK, MAYBE?
WHAT DID YOU DO--- FLY HERE?
DON'T TALK, ANGEL! YOU DIDN'T LET ANY GRASS GROW UNDER YOUR FEET, EITHER!
AND IF YOU CAME HERE FOR WHAT I THINK YOU DID, YOU'RE TOO LATE! ARCHIE IS UPSTAIRS GETTING ONE OF HIS SOCKS FOR ME!
YOU DELIBERATELY RACED OVER HERE BECAUSE YOU KNEW I WANTED ARCHIE TO TAKE ME TO THE DANCE!
ALL'S FAIR IN LOVE, WAR AND SOCK HOPS, DARLING!
DON'T FIGHT, KIDS---
SEE? I'VE GOT A SOCK FOR EACH OF YOU! JUST TO SHOW YOU I'M AN ALL-RIGHT GUY, I'LL TAKE BOTH OF YOU!
2

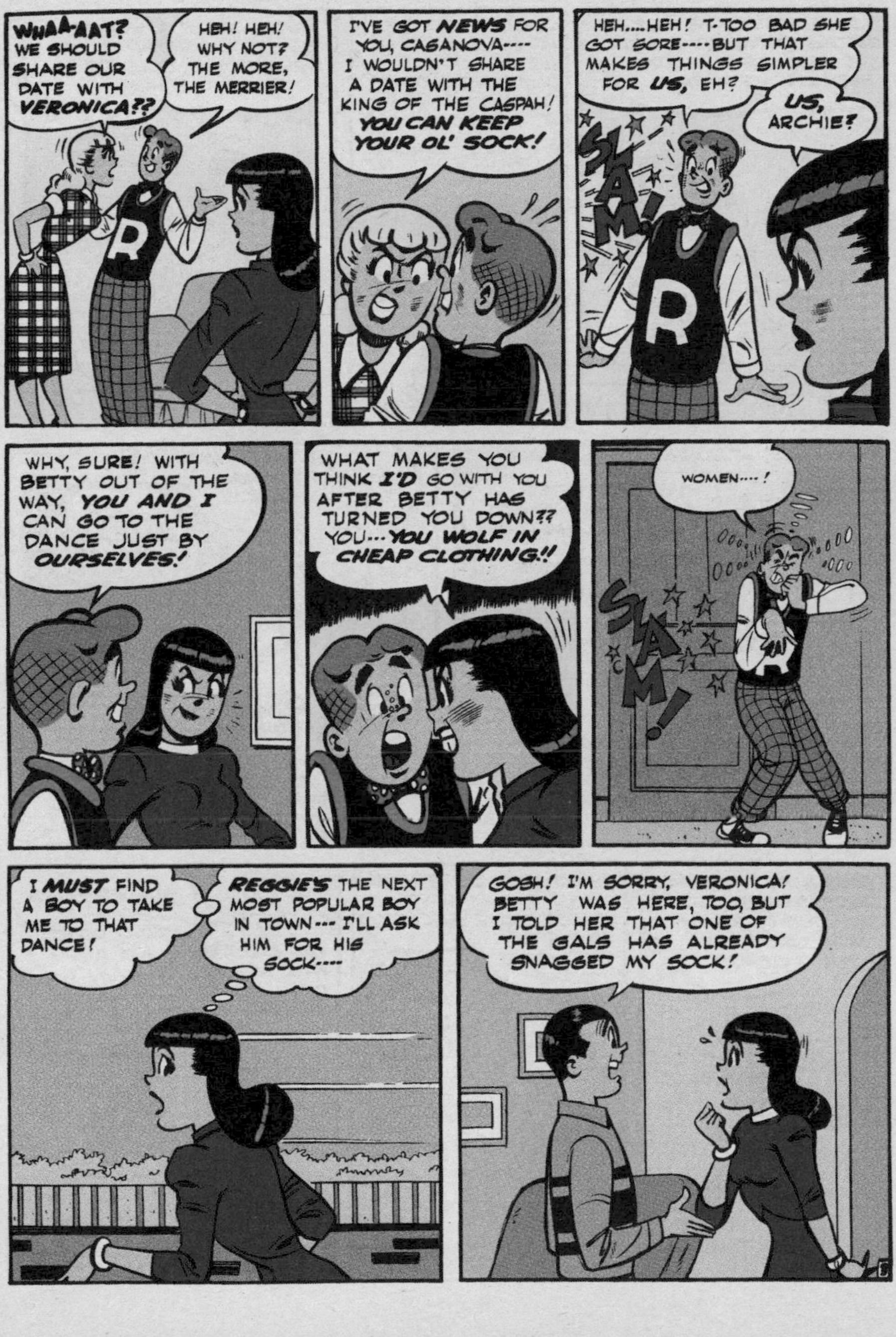
WHAA-AAT? WE SHOULD SHARE OUR DATE WITH VERONICA??
HEH! HEH! WHY NOT? THE MORE, THE MERRIER!
I'VE GOT NEWS FOR YOU, CASANOVA---- I WOULDN'T SHARE A DATE WITH THE KING OF THE CASPAH! YOU CAN KEEP YOUR OL' SOCK!
HEH....HEH! T-TOO BAD SHE GOT SORE----BUT THAT MAKES THINGS SIMPLER FOR US, EH?
SLAM!
US, ARCHIE?
WHY, SURE! WITH BETTY OUT OF THE WAY, YOU AND I CAN GO TO THE DANCE JUST BY OURSELVES!
WHAT MAKES YOU THINK I'D GO WITH YOU AFTER BETTY HAS TURNED YOU DOWN?? YOU---YOU WOLF IN CHEAP CLOTHING!!
WOMEN----!
SLAM!
I MUST FIND A BOY TO TAKE ME TO THAT DANCE!
REGGIE'S THE NEXT MOST POPULAR BOY IN TOWN--- I'LL ASK HIM FOR HIS SOCK----
GOSH! I'M SORRY, VERONICA! BETTY WAS HERE, TOO, BUT I TOLD HER THAT ONE OF THE GALS HAS ALREADY SNAGGED MY SOCK!

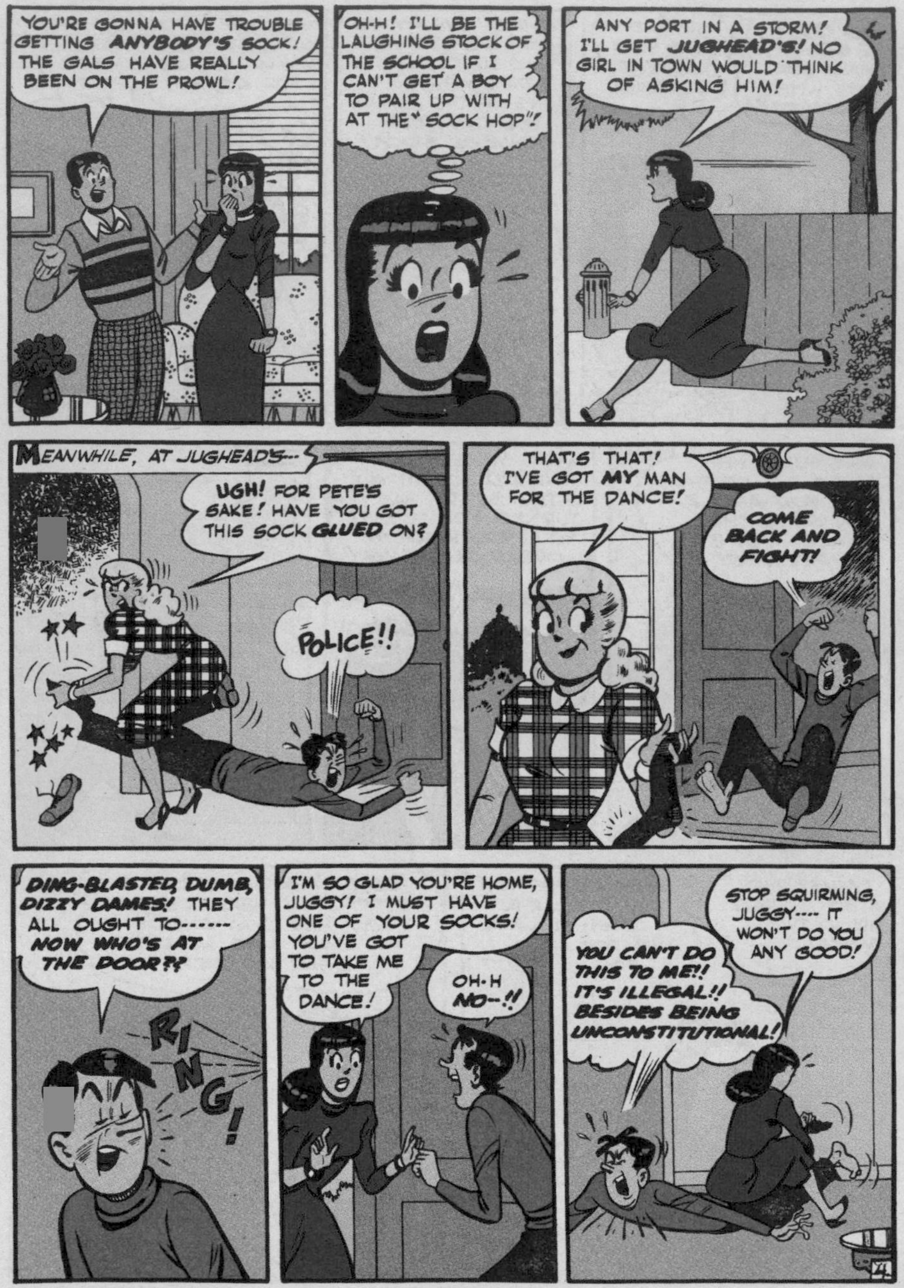

YOU'RE GONNA HAVE TROUBLE GETTING ANYBODY'S SOCK! THE GALS HAVE REALLY BEEN ON THE PROWL!
OH-H! I'LL BE THE LAUGHING STOCK OF THE SCHOOL IF I CAN'T GET A BOY TO PAIR UP WITH AT THE "SOCK HOP"!
ANY PORT IN A STORM! I'LL GET JUGHEAD'S! NO GIRL IN TOWN WOULD THINK OF ASKING HIM!
MEANWHILE, AT JUGHEAD'S---
UGH! FOR PETE'S SAKE! HAVE YOU GOT THIS SOCK GLUED ON?
POLICE!!
THAT'S THAT! I'VE GOT MY MAN FOR THE DANCE!
COME BACK AND FIGHT!
DING-BLASTED, DUMB, DIZZY DAMES! THEY ALL OUGHT TO------ NOW WHO'S AT THE DOOR??
RING!
I'M SO GLAD YOU'RE HOME, JUGGY! I MUST HAVE ONE OF YOUR SOCKS! YOU'VE GOT TO TAKE ME TO THE DANCE!
OH-H NO--!!
STOP SQUIRMING, JUGGY---- IT WON'T DO YOU ANY GOOD!
YOU CAN'T DO THIS TO ME!! IT'S ILLEGAL!! BESIDES BEING UNCONSTITUTIONAL!
4

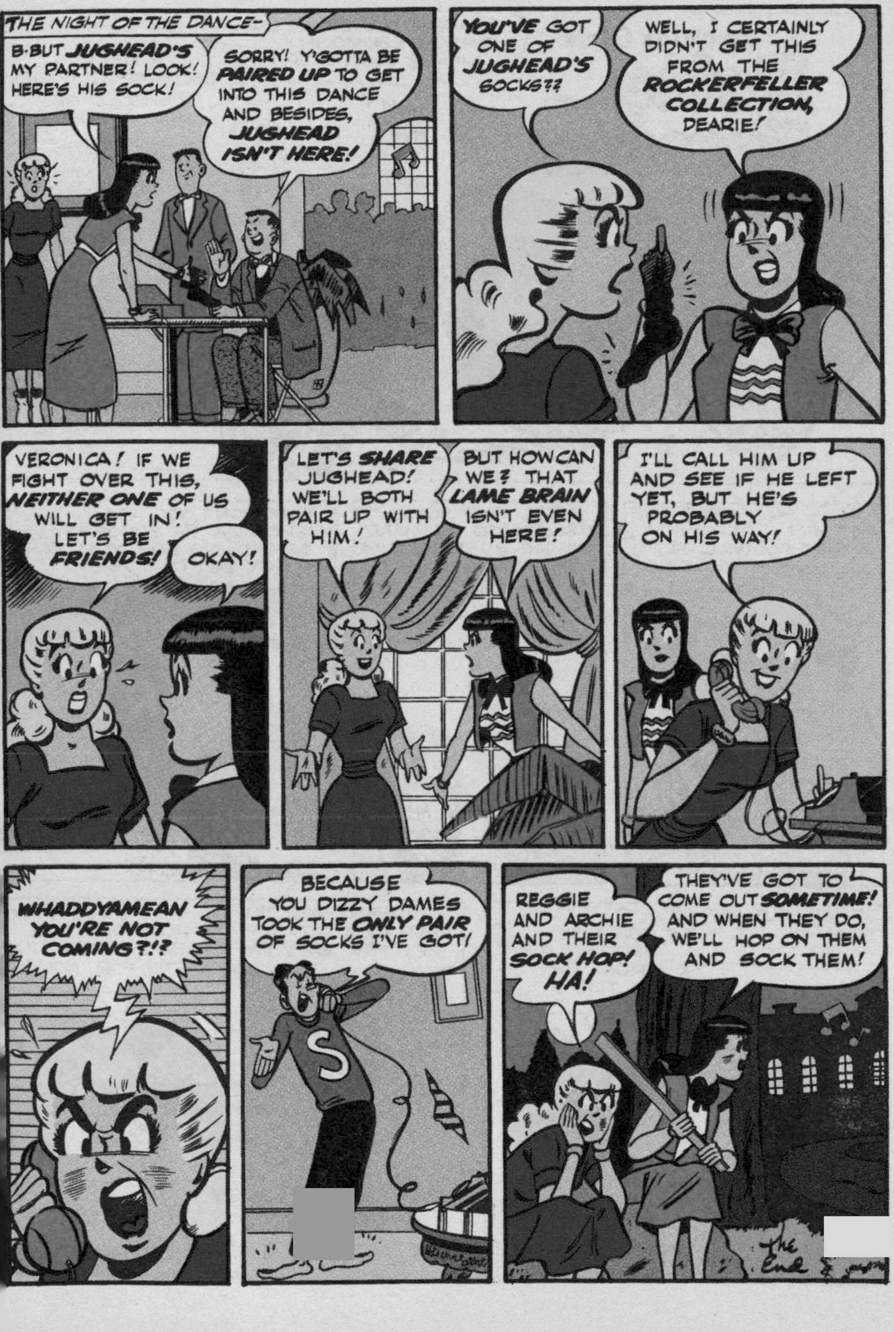
THE NIGHT OF THE DANCE-
B-BUT JUGHEAD'S MY PARTNER! LOOK! HERE'S HIS SOCK!
SORRY! Y'GOTTA BE PAIRED UP TO GET INTO THIS DANCE AND BESIDES, JUGHEAD ISN'T HERE!
YOU'VE GOT ONE OF JUGHEAD'S SOCKS??
WELL, I CERTAINLY DIDN'T GET THIS FROM THE ROCKERFELLER COLLECTION, DEARIE!
VERONICA! IF WE FIGHT OVER THIS, NEITHER ONE OF US WILL GET IN! LET'S BE FRIENDS!
OKAY!
LET'S SHARE JUGHEAD! WE'LL BOTH PAIR UP WITH HIM!
BUT HOW CAN WE? THAT LAME BRAIN ISN'T EVEN HERE!
I'LL CALL HIM UP AND SEE IF HE LEFT YET, BUT HE'S PROBABLY ON HIS WAY!
WHADDYAMEAN YOU'RE NOT COMING?!?
BECAUSE YOU DIZZY DAMES TOOK THE ONLY PAIR OF SOCKS I'VE GOT!
REGGIE AND ARCHIE AND THEIR SOCK HOP! HA!
THEY'VE GOT TO COME OUT SOMETIME! AND WHEN THEY DO, WE'LL HOP ON THEM AND SOCK THEM!
The End

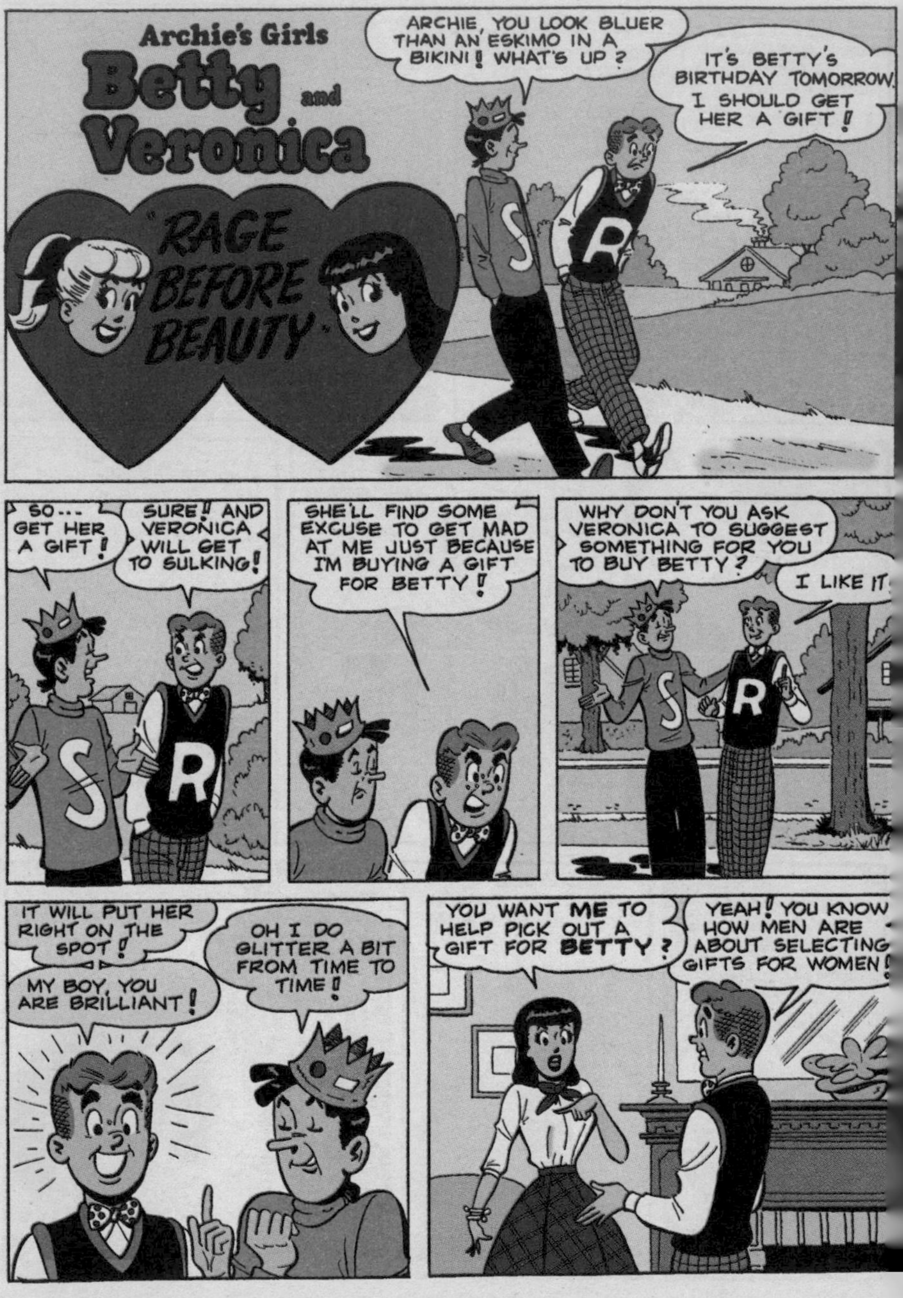
Archie's Girls
Betty and Veronica
"RAGE BEFORE BEAUTY"
ARCHIE, YOU LOOK BLUER THAN AN ESKIMO IN A BIKINI! WHAT'S UP ?
IT'S BETTY'S BIRTHDAY TOMORROW I SHOULD GET HER A GIFT!
SO... GET HER A GIFT!
SURE! AND VERONICA WILL GET TO SULKING!
SHE'LL FIND SOME EXCUSE TO GET MAD AT ME JUST BECAUSE I'M BUYING A GIFT FOR BETTY!
WHY DON'T YOU ASK VERONICA TO SUGGEST SOMETHING FOR YOU TO BUY BETTY ?
I LIKE IT
IT WILL PUT HER RIGHT ON THE SPOT!
MY BOY, YOU ARE BRILLIANT!
OH I DO GLITTER A BIT FROM TIME TO TIME!
YOU WANT ME TO HELP PICK OUT A GIFT FOR BETTY ?
YEAH! YOU KNOW HOW MEN ARE ABOUT SELECTING GIFTS FOR WOMEN!

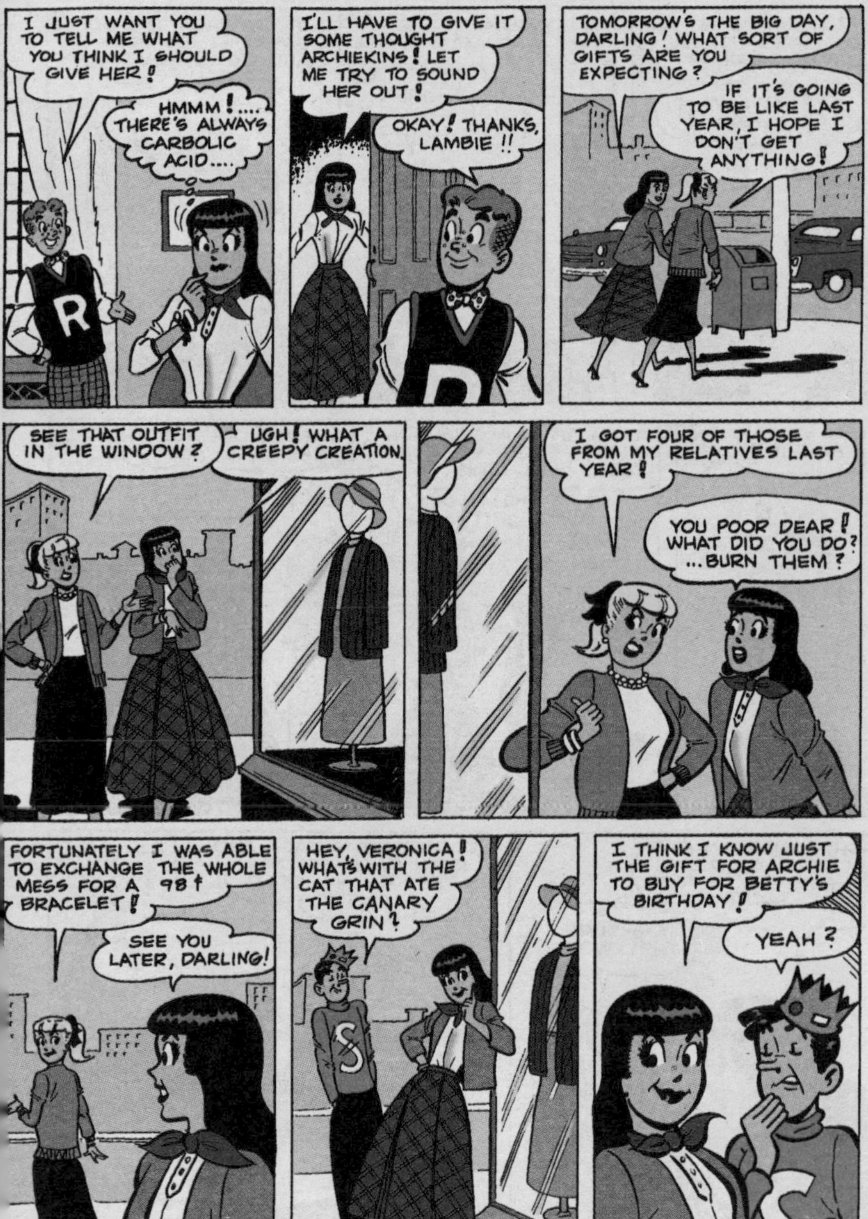

I JUST WANT YOU TO TELL ME WHAT YOU THINK I SHOULD GIVE HER!
HMMM!.... THERE'S ALWAYS CARBOLIC ACID....
I'LL HAVE TO GIVE IT SOME THOUGHT ARCHIEKINS! LET ME TRY TO SOUND HER OUT!
OKAY! THANKS, LAMBIE !!
TOMORROW'S THE BIG DAY, DARLING! WHAT SORT OF GIFTS ARE YOU EXPECTING?
IF IT'S GOING TO BE LIKE LAST YEAR, I HOPE I DON'T GET ANYTHING!
SEE THAT OUTFIT IN THE WINDOW?
UGH! WHAT A CREEPY CREATION!
I GOT FOUR OF THOSE FROM MY RELATIVES LAST YEAR!
YOU POOR DEAR! WHAT DID YOU DO? ...BURN THEM?
FORTUNATELY I WAS ABLE TO EXCHANGE THE WHOLE MESS FOR A 98¢ BRACELET!
SEE YOU LATER, DARLING!
HEY, VERONICA! WHAT'S WITH THE CAT THAT ATE THE CANARY GRIN?
I THINK I KNOW JUST THE GIFT FOR ARCHIE TO BUY FOR BETTY'S BIRTHDAY!
YEAH?

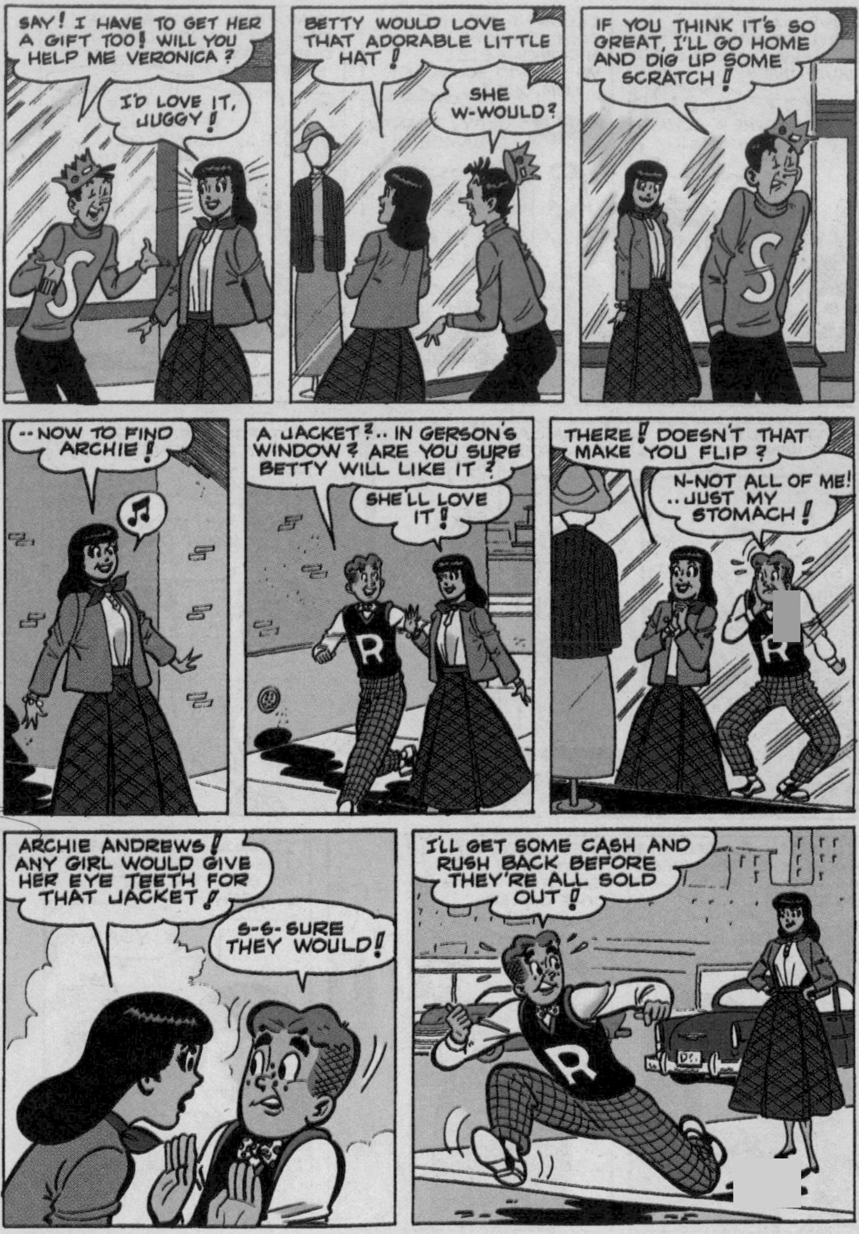
SAY! I HAVE TO GET HER A GIFT TOO! WILL YOU HELP ME VERONICA?
I'D LOVE IT, JUGGY!
BETTY WOULD LOVE THAT ADORABLE LITTLE HAT!
SHE W-WOULD?
IF YOU THINK IT'S SO GREAT, I'LL GO HOME AND DIG UP SOME SCRATCH!
-- NOW TO FIND ARCHIE!
A JACKET?.. IN GERSON'S WINDOW? ARE YOU SURE BETTY WILL LIKE IT?
SHE'LL LOVE IT!
THERE! DOESN'T THAT MAKE YOU FLIP?
N-NOT ALL OF ME! ..JUST MY STOMACH!
ARCHIE ANDREWS! ANY GIRL WOULD GIVE HER EYE TEETH FOR THAT JACKET!
S-S-SURE THEY WOULD!
I'LL GET SOME CASH AND RUSH BACK BEFORE THEY'RE ALL SOLD OUT!

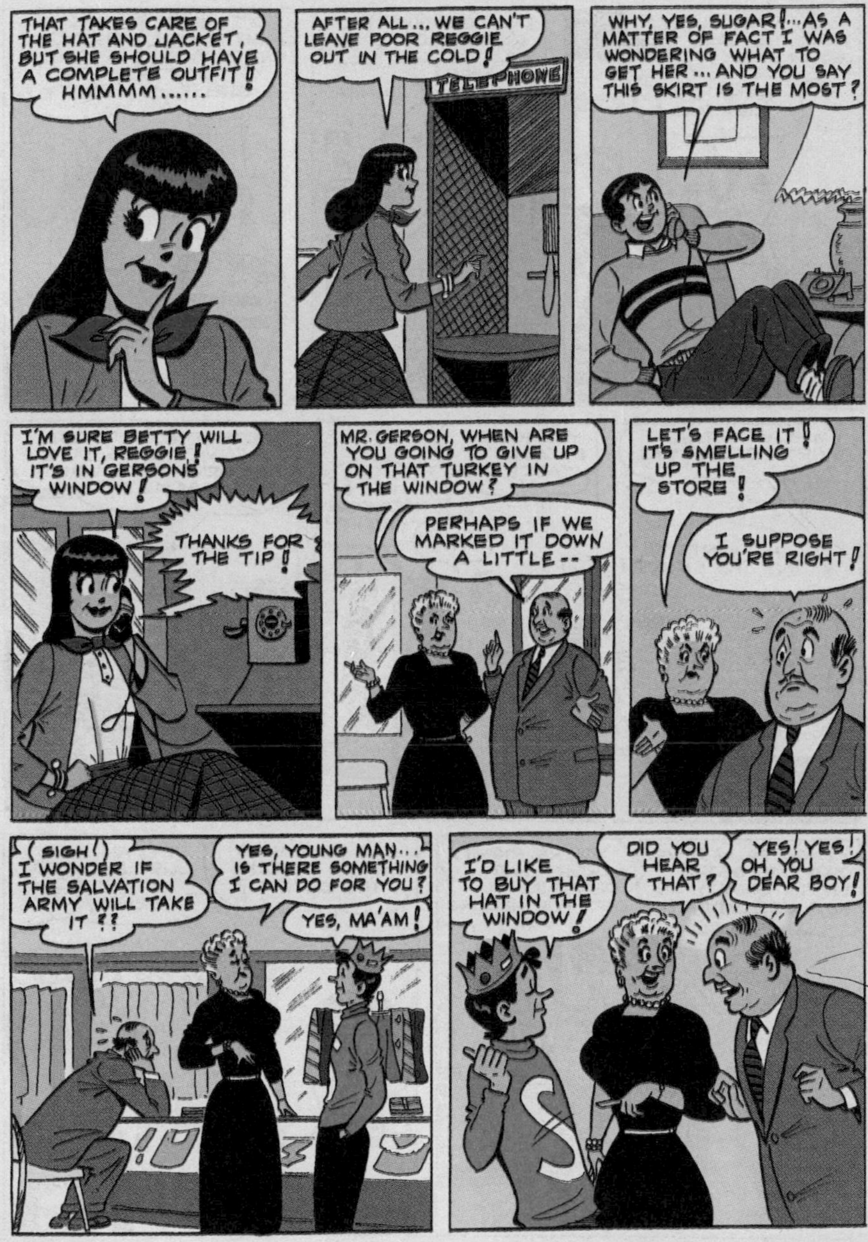
THAT TAKES CARE OF THE HAT AND JACKET, BUT SHE SHOULD HAVE A COMPLETE OUTFIT! HMMMM......
AFTER ALL... WE CAN'T LEAVE POOR REGGIE OUT IN THE COLD!
TELEPHONE
WHY, YES, SUGAR!...AS A MATTER OF FACT I WAS WONDERING WHAT TO GET HER... AND YOU SAY THIS SKIRT IS THE MOST?
I'M SURE BETTY WILL LOVE IT, REGGIE! IT'S IN GERSON'S WINDOW!
THANKS FOR THE TIP!
MR. GERSON, WHEN ARE YOU GOING TO GIVE UP ON THAT TURKEY IN THE WINDOW?
PERHAPS IF WE MARKED IT DOWN A LITTLE--
LET'S FACE IT! IT'S SMELLING UP THE STORE!
I SUPPOSE YOU'RE RIGHT!
(SIGH!) I WONDER IF THE SALVATION ARMY WILL TAKE IT ??
YES, YOUNG MAN... IS THERE SOMETHING I CAN DO FOR YOU?
YES, MA'AM!
I'D LIKE TO BUY THAT HAT IN THE WINDOW!
DID YOU HEAR THAT?
YES! YES! OH, YOU DEAR BOY!

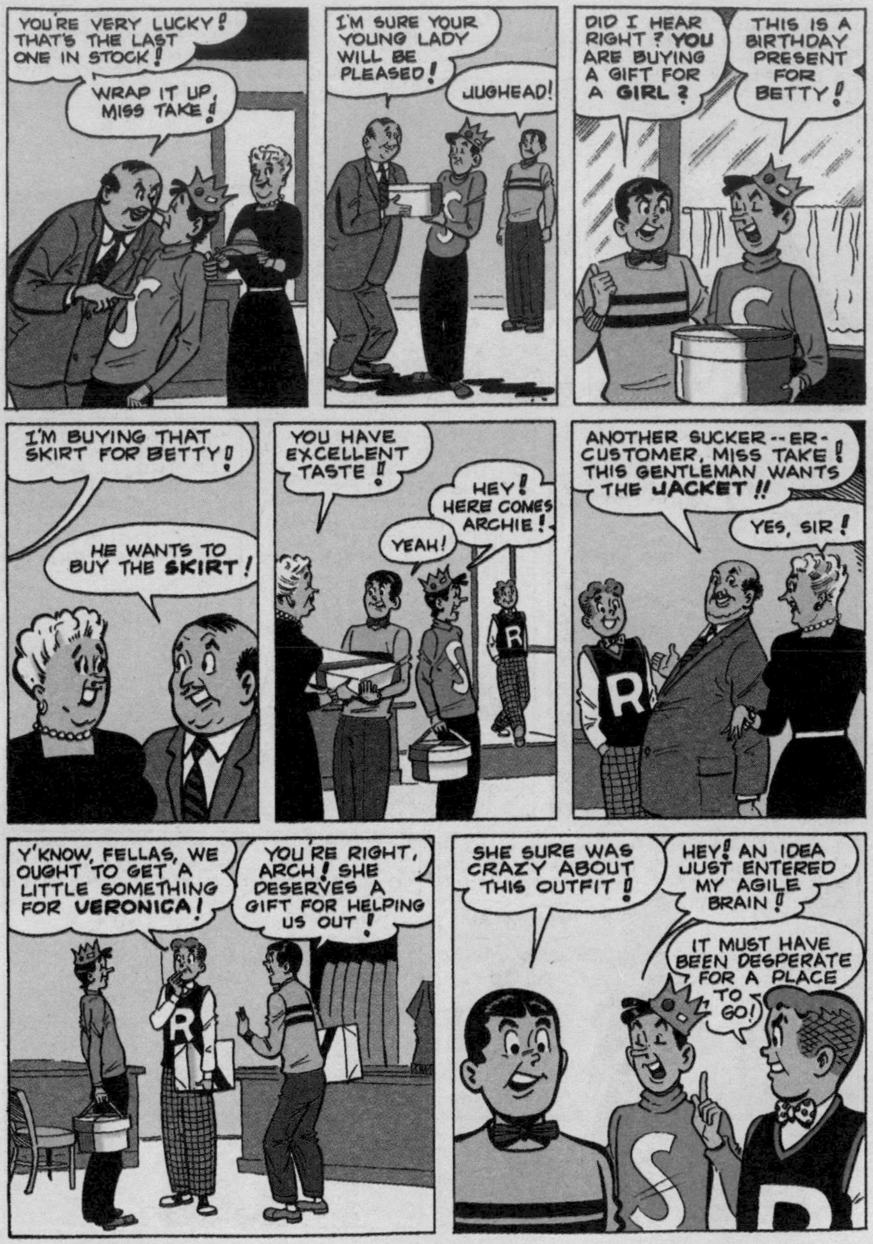
YOU'RE VERY LUCKY! THAT'S THE LAST ONE IN STOCK!
WRAP IT UP, MISS TAKE!
I'M SURE YOUR YOUNG LADY WILL BE PLEASED!
JUGHEAD!
DID I HEAR RIGHT? YOU ARE BUYING A GIFT FOR A GIRL?
THIS IS A BIRTHDAY PRESENT FOR BETTY!
I'M BUYING THAT SKIRT FOR BETTY!
HE WANTS TO BUY THE SKIRT!
YOU HAVE EXCELLENT TASTE!!
HEY! HERE COMES ARCHIE!
YEAH!
ANOTHER SUCKER -- ER - CUSTOMER, MISS TAKE! THIS GENTLEMAN WANTS THE JACKET!!
YES, SIR!
Y'KNOW, FELLAS, WE OUGHT TO GET A LITTLE SOMETHING FOR VERONICA!
YOU'RE RIGHT, ARCH! SHE DESERVES A GIFT FOR HELPING US OUT!
SHE SURE WAS CRAZY ABOUT THIS OUTFIT!
HEY! AN IDEA JUST ENTERED MY AGILE BRAIN!
IT MUST HAVE BEEN DESPERATE FOR A PLACE TO GO!

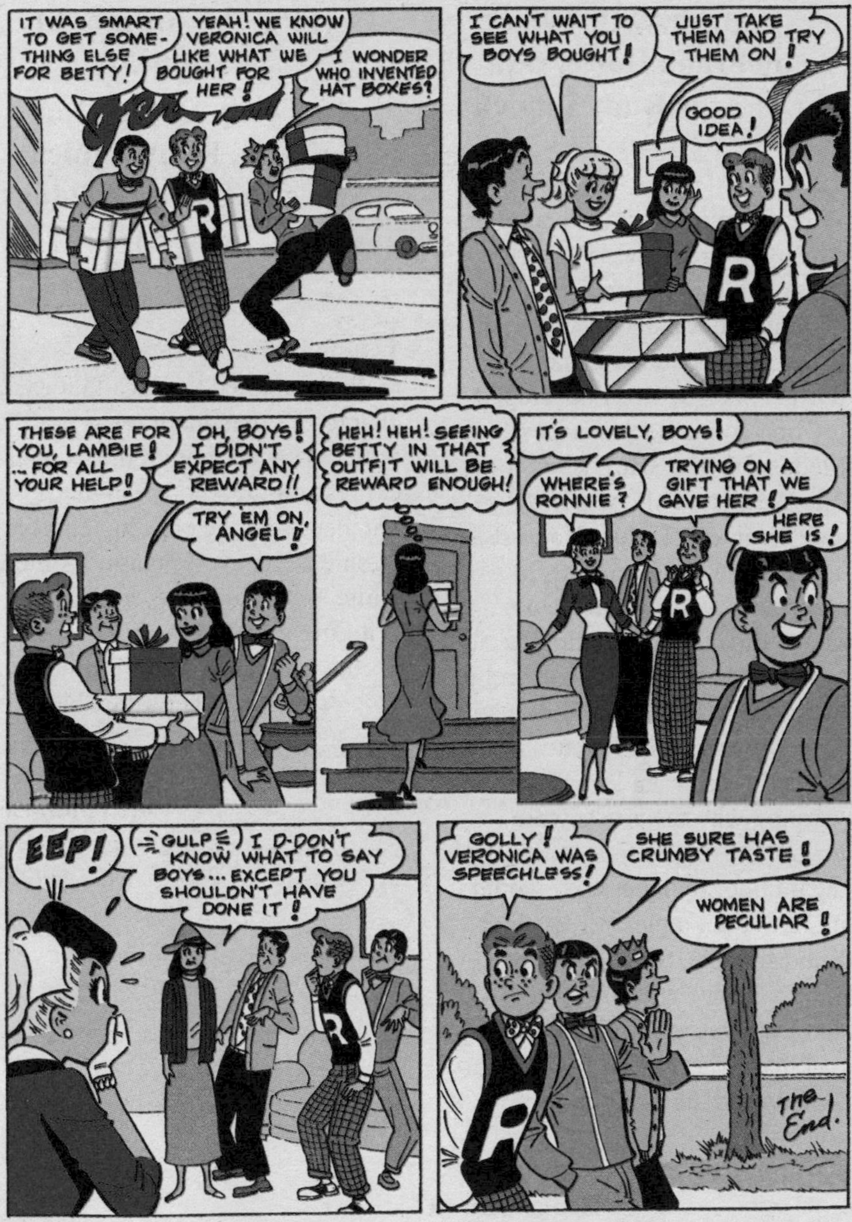
IT WAS SMART TO GET SOMETHING ELSE FOR BETTY!
YEAH! WE KNOW VERONICA WILL LIKE WHAT WE BOUGHT FOR HER!
I WONDER WHO INVENTED HAT BOXES?
I CAN'T WAIT TO SEE WHAT YOU BOYS BOUGHT!
JUST TAKE THEM AND TRY THEM ON!
GOOD IDEA!
THESE ARE FOR YOU, LAMBIE! ...FOR ALL YOUR HELP!
OH, BOYS! I DIDN'T EXPECT ANY REWARD!!
TRY 'EM ON, ANGEL!
HEH! HEH! SEEING BETTY IN THAT OUTFIT WILL BE REWARD ENOUGH!
IT'S LOVELY, BOYS!
WHERE'S RONNIE?
TRYING ON A GIFT THAT WE GAVE HER!
HERE SHE IS!
EEP!
GULP I D-DON'T KNOW WHAT TO SAY BOYS... EXCEPT YOU SHOULDN'T HAVE DONE IT!
GOLLY! VERONICA WAS SPEECHLESS!
SHE SURE HAS CRUMBY TASTE!
WOMEN ARE PECULIAR!
The End.

Going, Going, Gown
Laugh #80, 1957
by Frank Doyle, Dan DeCarlo, Rudy Lapick

The first time I remember being allowed to freely tear through comic books was the large stacks of comics our piano teacher had in her waiting room. What a thrill! This is where I developed my first comic book crushes: Medusa, Gwen Stacy, Sue Storm, The Wasp, and of course, Betty and Veronica! I adored, and still adore those two beauties! My allegiance would switch from one to the other depending on my mood, or how they treated Archie in any particular story. But, man! They always looked great! I was all grown up when I finally started learning who the artists were behind those gorgeous ladies, and the unique subtleties they would bring to their styles. Greats like Bob Montana, Stan Goldberg, Samm Schwartz, Harry Lucey, and Dan DeCarlo. Thank you for making me look forward to piano lessons and all the good times since!

-- Michael Allred
Writer/Artist,
Creator of Madman

The Peacemaker
Betty & Veronica #47, 1959
by Frank Doyle, Dan DeCarlo, Rudy Lapick, Vince DeCarlo, Sheldon Brodsky

For me, "The Peacemaker" really illustrated the idea that each character's personality was not only portrayed though their facial expressions and body language, but also from the clothing choices. Archie is the everyman in a simple white T-shirt and trousers, Reggie is a little more dressed up, Betty is cute and casual and Veronica is fancier still with her kitten heeled shoes.

--Jill Thompson
Award-winning Artist,
Scary Godmother

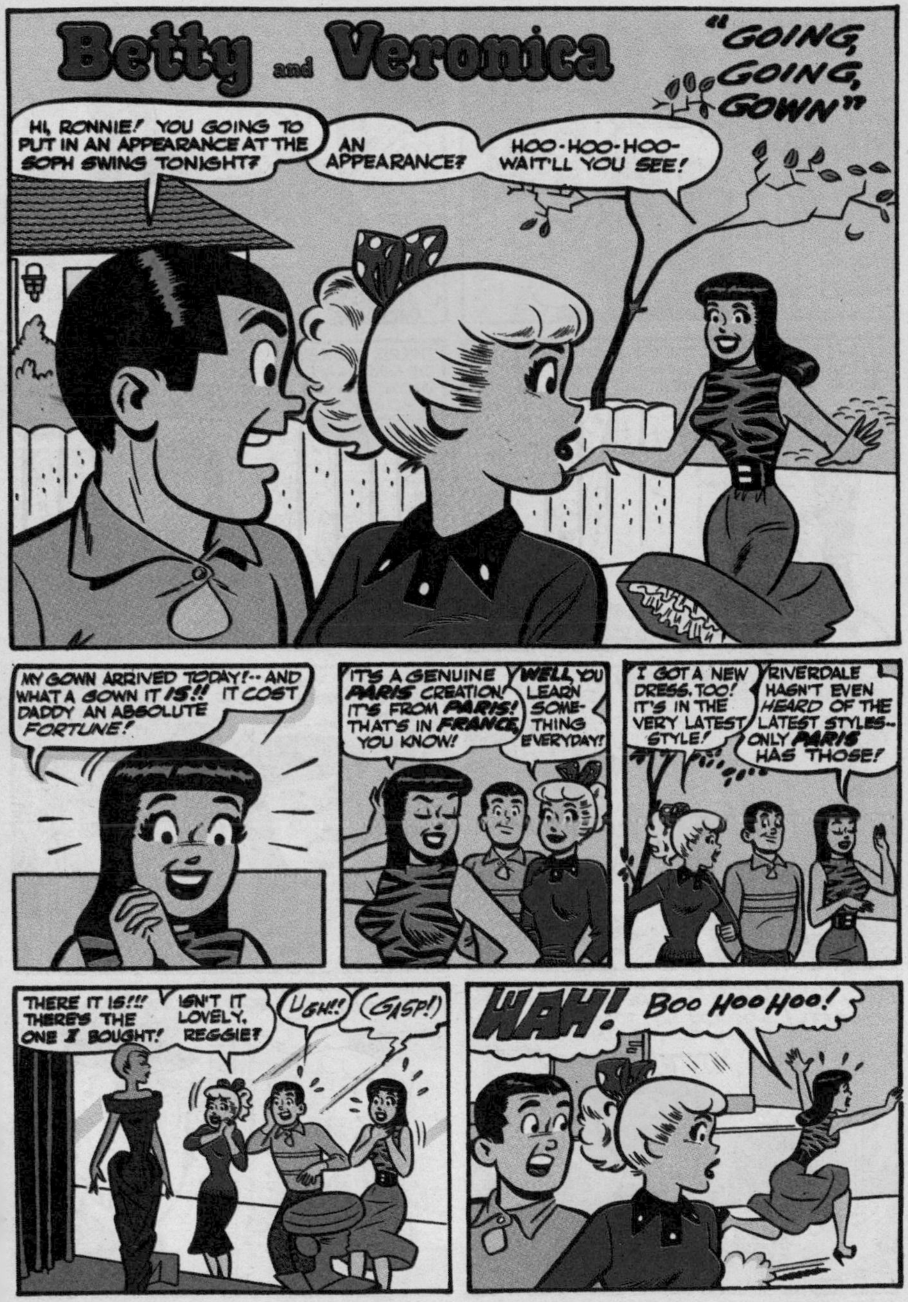
Betty and Veronica
"GOING, GOING, GOWN"
HI, RONNIE! YOU GOING TO PUT IN AN APPEARANCE AT THE SOPH SWING TONIGHT?
AN APPEARANCE?
HOO-HOO-HOO- WAIT'LL YOU SEE!
MY GOWN ARRIVED TODAY!-- AND WHAT A GOWN IT IS!! IT COST DADDY AN ABSOLUTE FORTUNE!
IT'S A GENUINE PARIS CREATION! IT'S FROM PARIS! THAT'S IN FRANCE, YOU KNOW!
WELL, YOU LEARN SOME-THING EVERYDAY!
I GOT A NEW DRESS, TOO! IT'S IN THE VERY LATEST STYLE!
RIVERDALE HASN'T EVEN HEARD OF THE LATEST STYLES-- ONLY PARIS HAS THOSE!
THERE IT IS!!! THERE'S THE ONE I BOUGHT!
ISN'T IT LOVELY, REGGIE?
UGH!!
(GASP!)
WAH!
BOO HOO HOO!

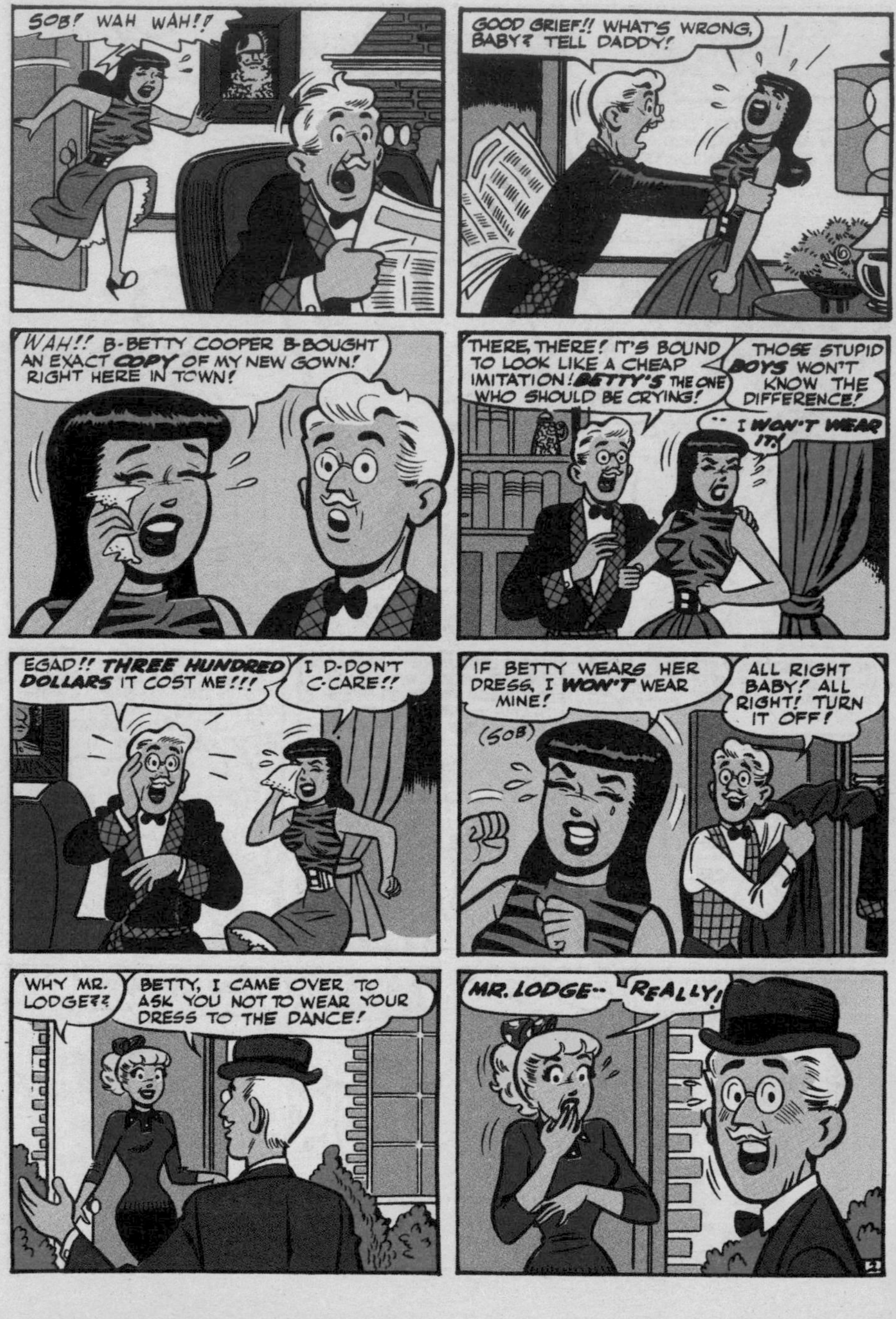
SOB! WAH WAH!!
GOOD GRIEF!! WHAT'S WRONG, BABY? TELL DADDY!
WAH!! B-BETTY COOPER B-BOUGHT AN EXACT COPY OF MY NEW GOWN! RIGHT HERE IN TOWN!
THERE, THERE! IT'S BOUND TO LOOK LIKE A CHEAP IMITATION! BETTY'S THE ONE WHO SHOULD BE CRYING!
THOSE STUPID BOYS WON'T KNOW THE DIFFERENCE!
.. I WON'T WEAR IT!
EGAD!! THREE HUNDRED DOLLARS IT COST ME!!!
I D-DON'T C-CARE!!
IF BETTY WEARS HER DRESS, I WON'T WEAR MINE!
(SOB)
ALL RIGHT BABY! ALL RIGHT! TURN IT OFF!
WHY MR. LODGE??
BETTY, I CAME OVER TO ASK YOU NOT TO WEAR YOUR DRESS TO THE DANCE!
MR. LODGE-- REALLY!

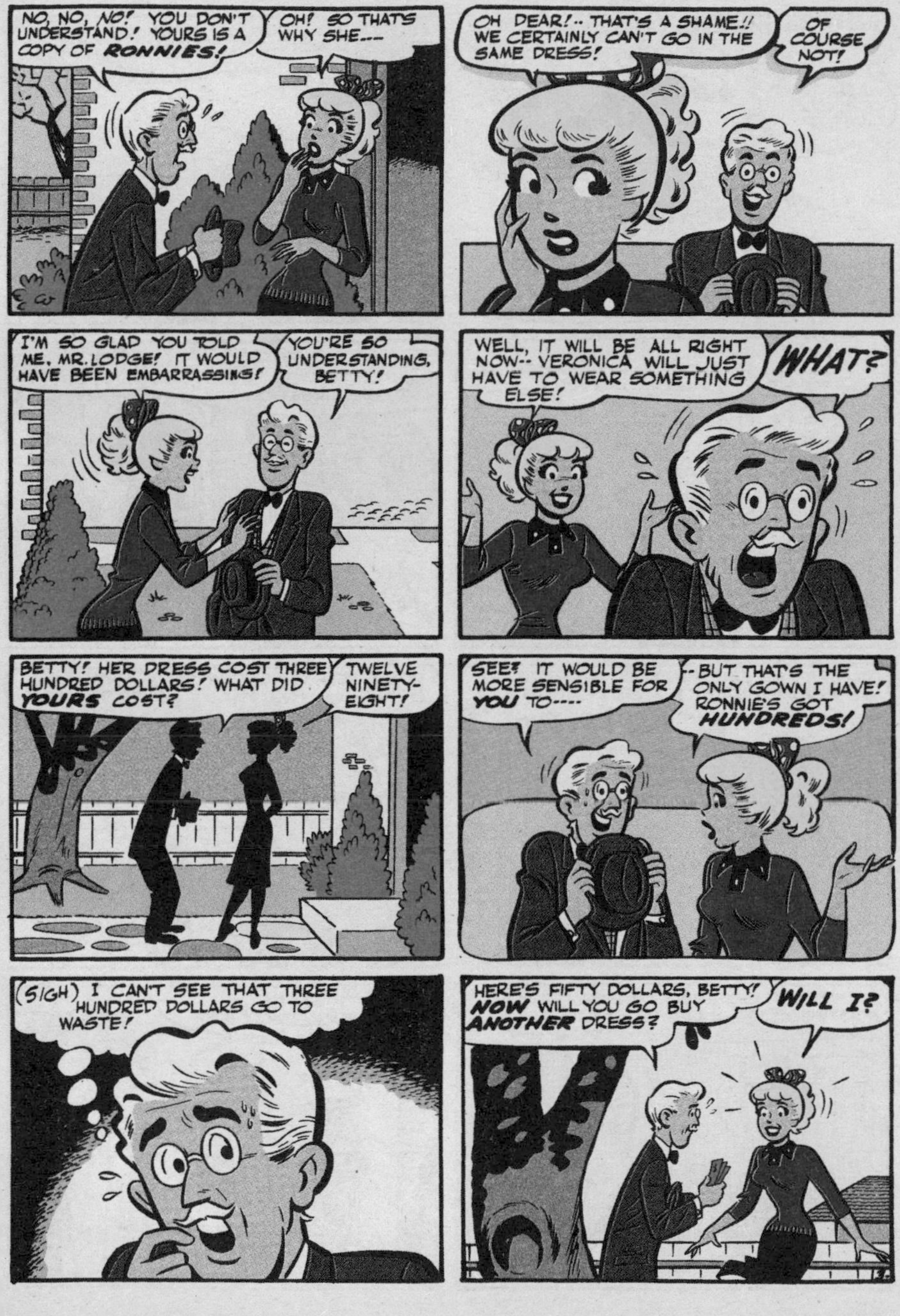
NO, NO, NO! YOU DON'T UNDERSTAND! YOURS IS A COPY OF RONNIES!
OH! SO THAT'S WHY SHE---
OH DEAR!.. THAT'S A SHAME!! WE CERTAINLY CAN'T GO IN THE SAME DRESS!
OF COURSE NOT!
I'M SO GLAD YOU TOLD ME, MR. LODGE! IT WOULD HAVE BEEN EMBARRASSING!
YOU'RE SO UNDERSTANDING, BETTY!
WELL, IT WILL BE ALL RIGHT NOW-- VERONICA WILL JUST HAVE TO WEAR SOMETHING ELSE!
WHAT?
BETTY! HER DRESS COST THREE HUNDRED DOLLARS! WHAT DID YOURS COST?
TWELVE NINETY-EIGHT!
SEE? IT WOULD BE MORE SENSIBLE FOR YOU TO----
--BUT THAT'S THE ONLY GOWN I HAVE! RONNIE'S GOT HUNDREDS!
(SIGH) I CAN'T SEE THAT THREE HUNDRED DOLLARS GO TO WASTE!
HERE'S FIFTY DOLLARS, BETTY! NOW WILL YOU GO BUY ANOTHER DRESS?
WILL I?

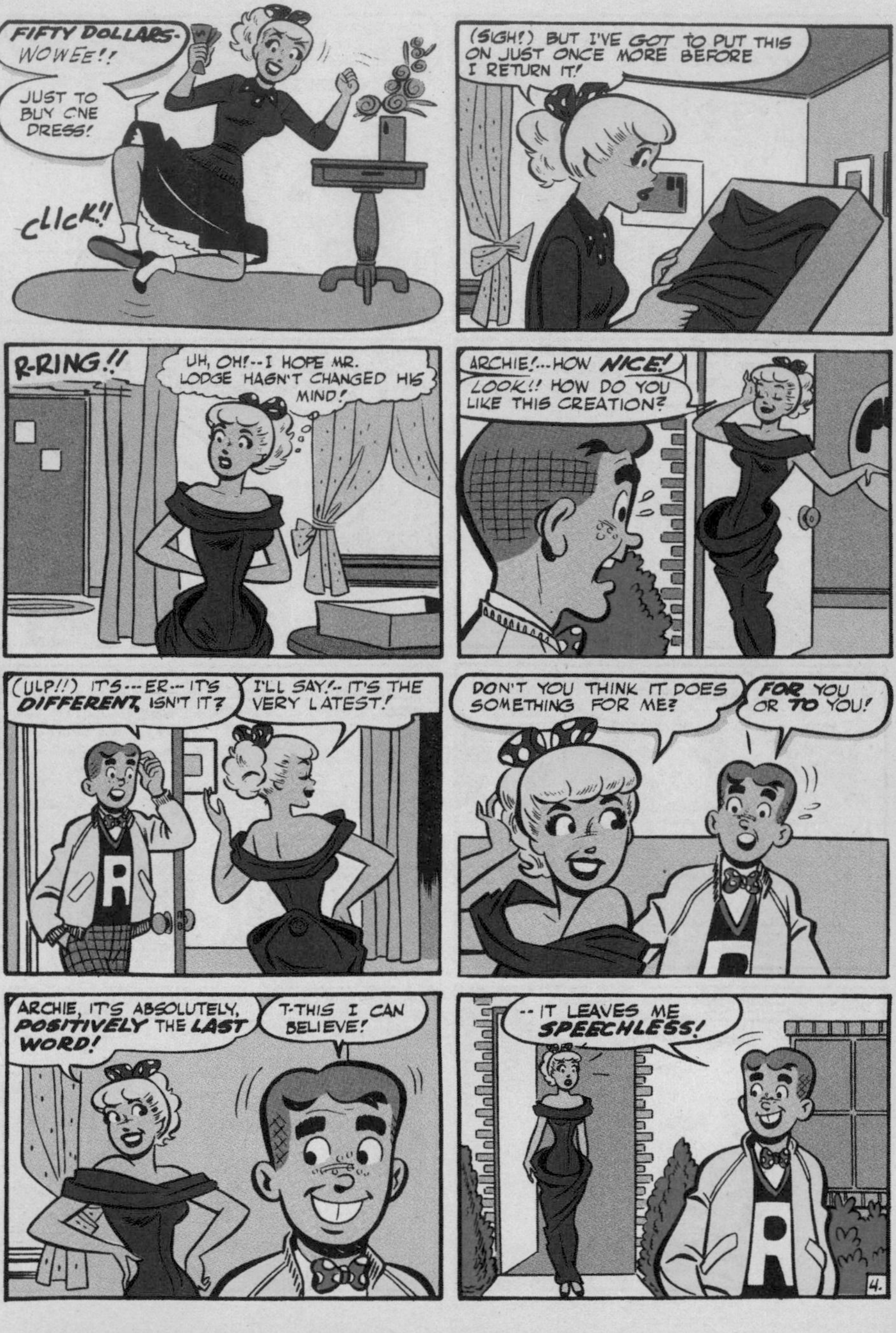
FIFTY DOLLARS-
WOWEE!!
JUST TO BUY ONE DRESS!
CLICK!!
(SIGH!) BUT I'VE GOT TO PUT THIS ON JUST ONCE MORE BEFORE I RETURN IT!
R-RING!!
UH, OH!--I HOPE MR. LODGE HASN'T CHANGED HIS MIND!
ARCHIE!...HOW NICE!
LOOK!! HOW DO YOU LIKE THIS CREATION?
(ULP!!) IT'S---ER--IT'S DIFFERENT, ISN'T IT?
I'LL SAY!--IT'S THE VERY LATEST!
DON'T YOU THINK IT DOES SOMETHING FOR ME?
FOR YOU OR TO YOU!
ARCHIE, IT'S ABSOLUTELY, POSITIVELY THE LAST WORD!
T-THIS I CAN BELIEVE!
--IT LEAVES ME SPEECHLESS!
4.

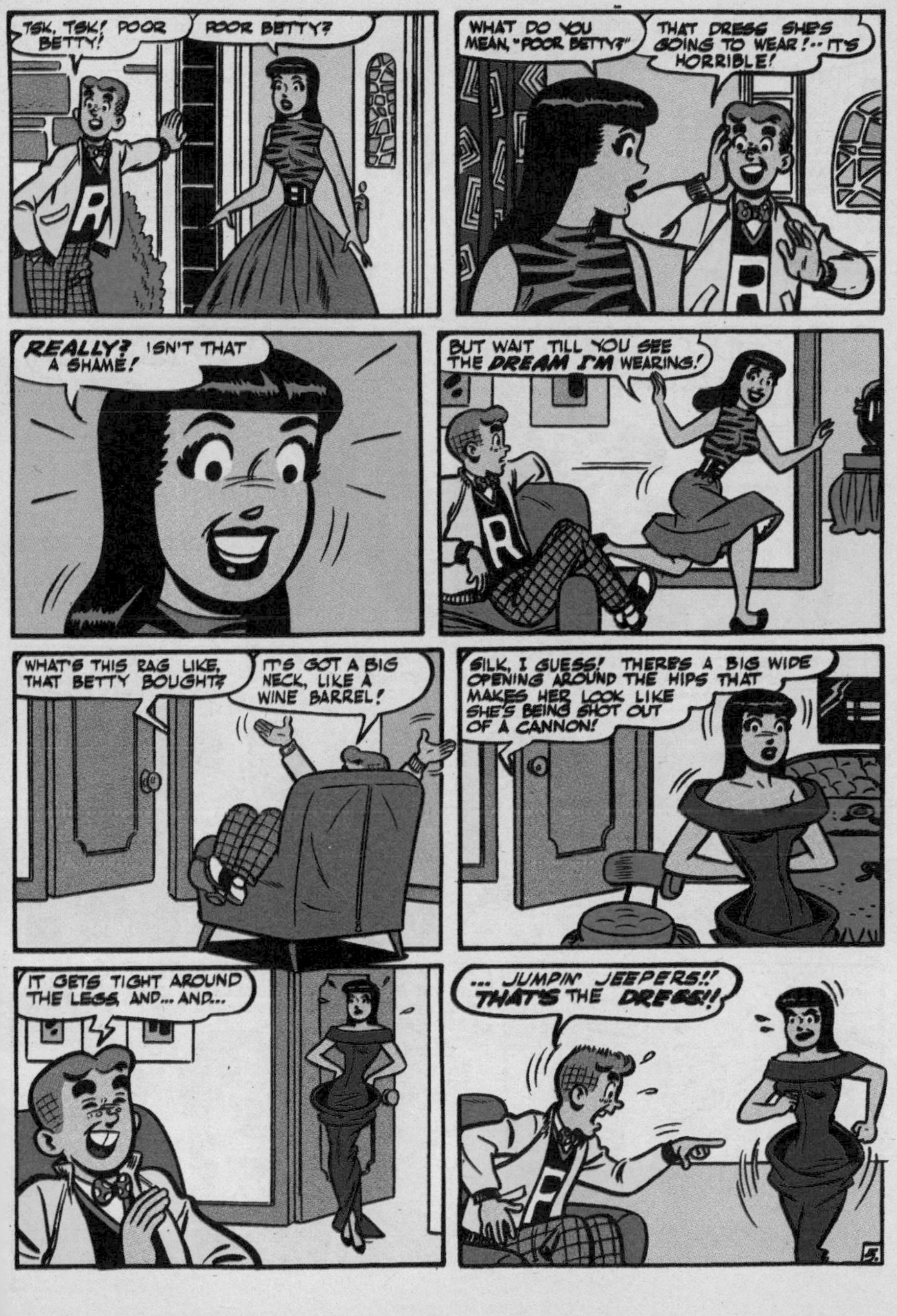
TSK, TSK! POOR BETTY!
POOR BETTY?
WHAT DO YOU MEAN, "POOR BETTY?"
THAT DRESS SHE'S GOING TO WEAR!-- IT'S HORRIBLE!
REALLY? ISN'T THAT A SHAME!
BUT WAIT TILL YOU SEE THE DREAM I'M WEARING!
WHAT'S THIS RAG LIKE, THAT BETTY BOUGHT?
IT'S GOT A BIG NECK, LIKE A WINE BARREL!
SILK, I GUESS! THERE'S A BIG WIDE OPENING AROUND THE HIPS THAT MAKES HER LOOK LIKE SHE'S BEING SHOT OUT OF A CANNON!
IT GETS TIGHT AROUND THE LEGS, AND... AND...
... JUMPIN' JEEPERS!! THAT'S THE DRESS!!
5.

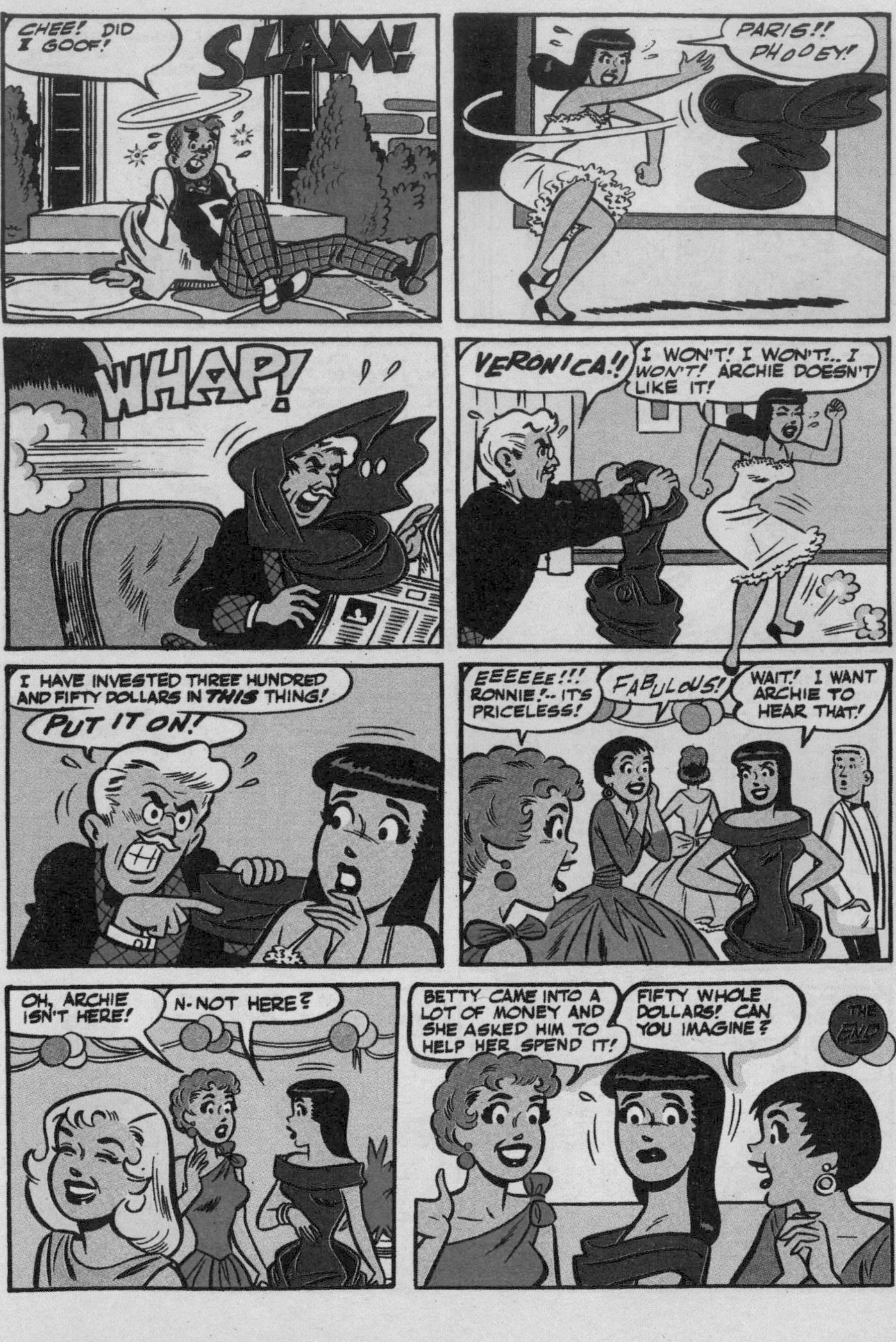
CHEE! DID I GOOF!
SLAM!
PARIS!! PHOOEY!
WHAP!
VERONICA!!
I WON'T! I WON'T!.. I WON'T! ARCHIE DOESN'T LIKE IT!
I HAVE INVESTED THREE HUNDRED AND FIFTY DOLLARS IN THIS THING!
PUT IT ON!
EEEEEE!!! RONNIE!-- IT'S PRICELESS!
FABULOUS!
WAIT! I WANT ARCHIE TO HEAR THAT!
OH, ARCHIE ISN'T HERE!
N-NOT HERE?
BETTY CAME INTO A LOT OF MONEY AND SHE ASKED HIM TO HELP HER SPEND IT!
FIFTY WHOLE DOLLARS! CAN YOU IMAGINE?
THE END

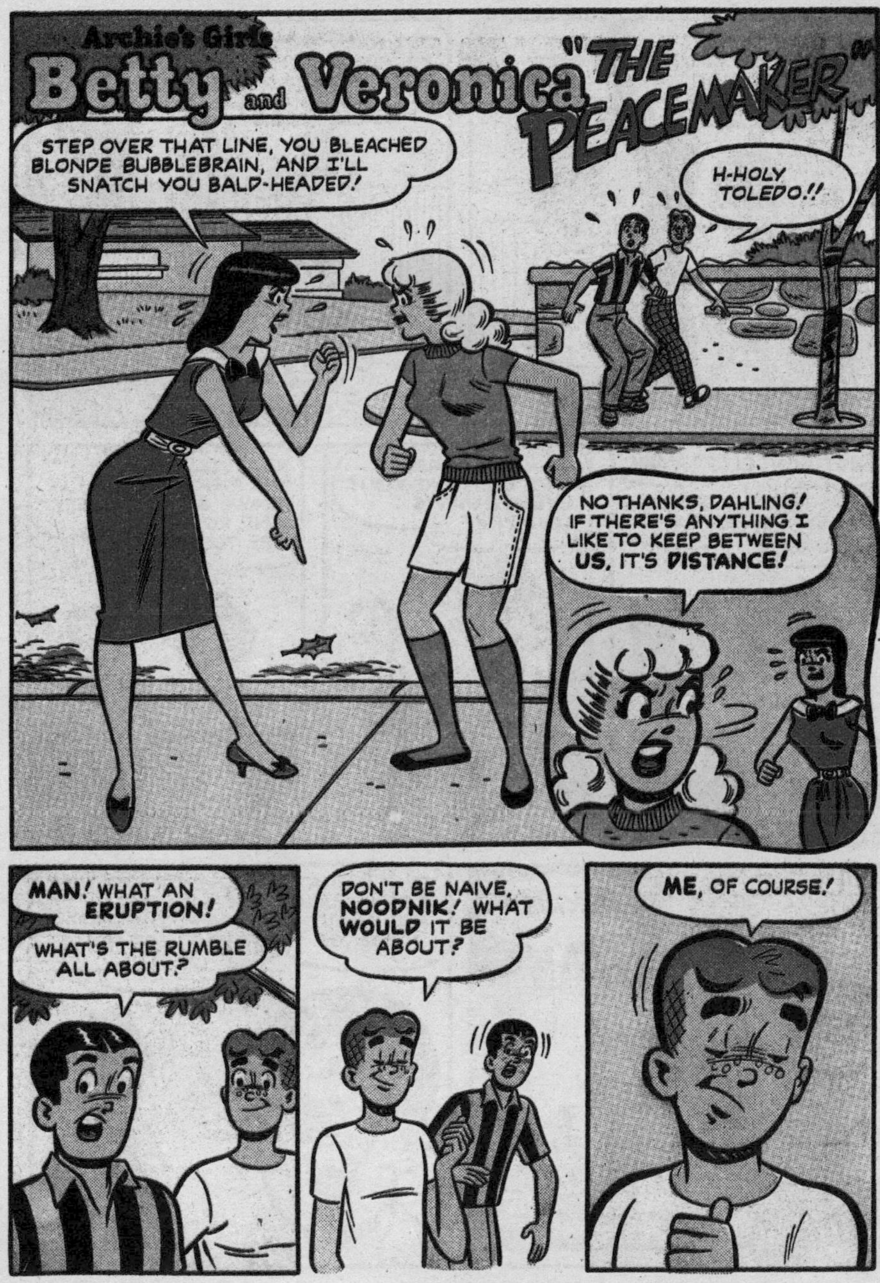
Archie's Girls
Betty and Veronica
"THE PEACEMAKER"
STEP OVER THAT LINE, YOU BLEACHED BLONDE BUBBLEBRAIN, AND I'LL SNATCH YOU BALD-HEADED!
H-HOLY TOLEDO.!!
NO THANKS, DAHLING! IF THERE'S ANYTHING I LIKE TO KEEP BETWEEN US, IT'S DISTANCE!
MAN! WHAT AN ERUPTION!
WHAT'S THE RUMBLE ALL ABOUT?
DON'T BE NAIVE, NOODNIK! WHAT WOULD IT BE ABOUT?
ME, OF COURSE!

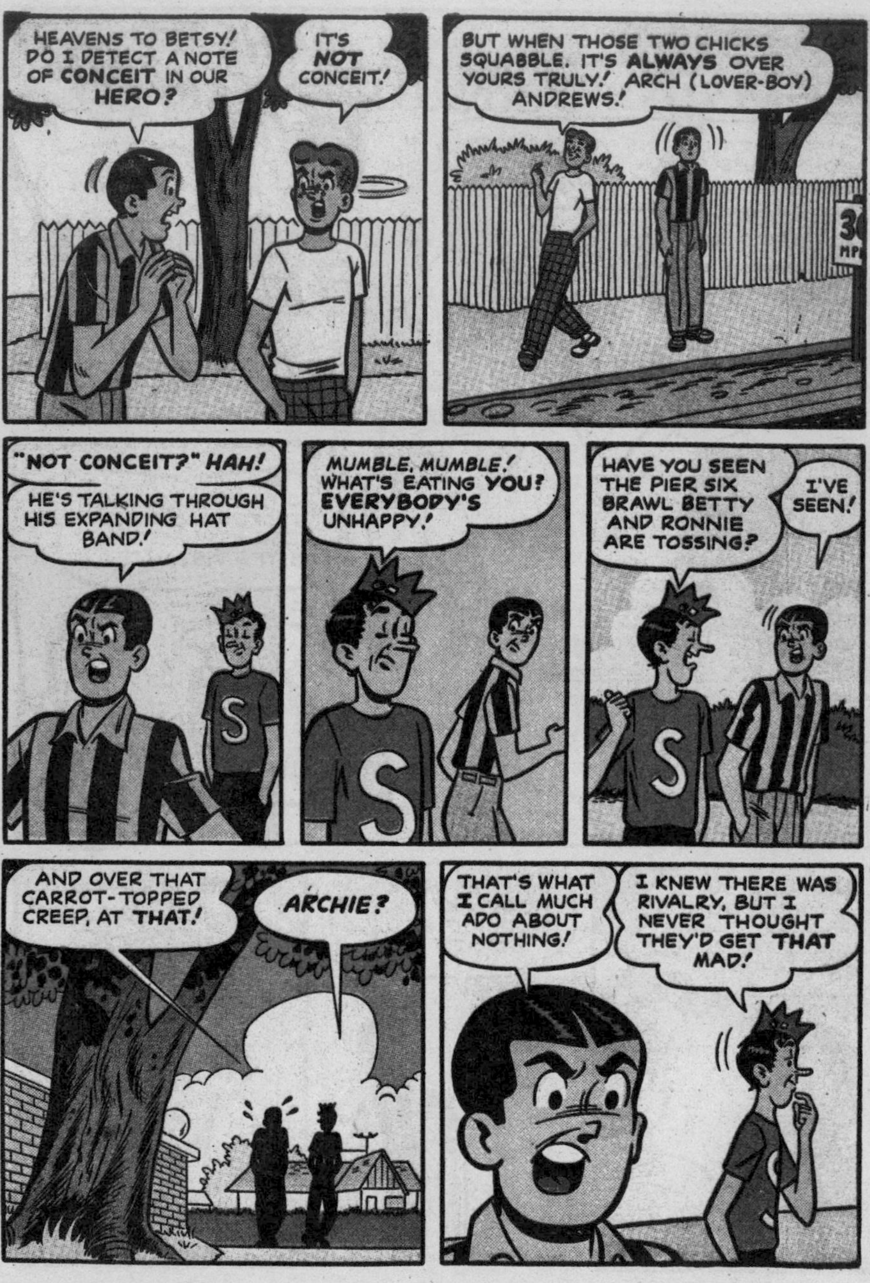
HEAVENS TO BETSY! DO I DETECT A NOTE OF CONCEIT IN OUR HERO?
IT'S NOT CONCEIT!
BUT WHEN THOSE TWO CHICKS SQUABBLE, IT'S ALWAYS OVER YOURS TRULY! ARCH (LOVER-BOY) ANDREWS!
"NOT CONCEIT?" HAH!
HE'S TALKING THROUGH HIS EXPANDING HAT BAND!
MUMBLE, MUMBLE! WHAT'S EATING YOU? EVERYBODY'S UNHAPPY!
HAVE YOU SEEN THE PIER SIX BRAWL BETTY AND RONNIE ARE TOSSING?
I'VE SEEN!
AND OVER THAT CARROT-TOPPED CREEP, AT THAT!
ARCHIE?
THAT'S WHAT I CALL MUCH ADO ABOUT NOTHING!
I KNEW THERE WAS RIVALRY, BUT I NEVER THOUGHT THEY'D GET THAT MAD!

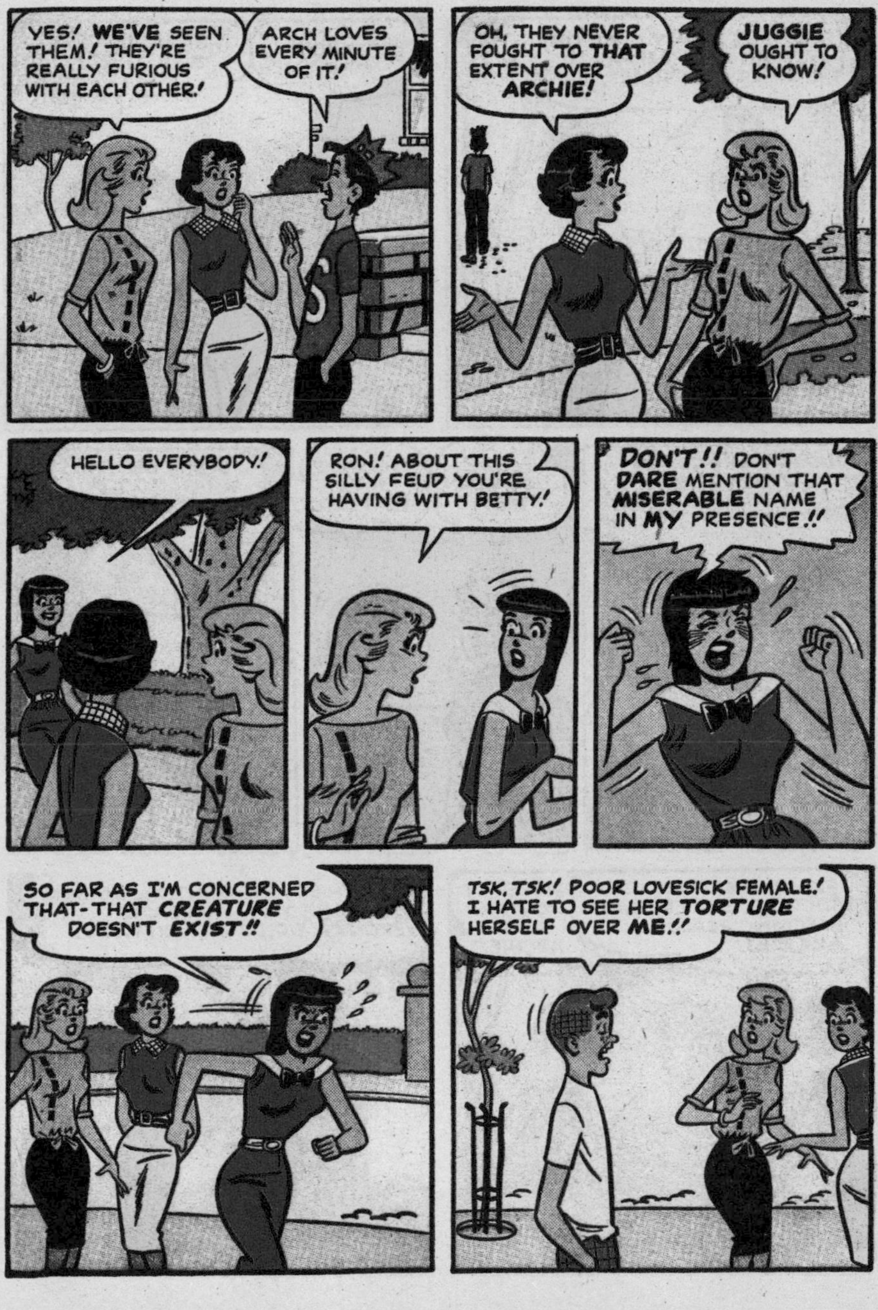
YES! WE'VE SEEN THEM! THEY'RE REALLY FURIOUS WITH EACH OTHER!
ARCH LOVES EVERY MINUTE OF IT!
OH, THEY NEVER FOUGHT TO THAT EXTENT OVER ARCHIE!
JUGGIE OUGHT TO KNOW!
HELLO EVERYBODY!
RON! ABOUT THIS SILLY FEUD YOU'RE HAVING WITH BETTY!
DON'T!! DON'T DARE MENTION THAT MISERABLE NAME IN MY PRESENCE!!
SO FAR AS I'M CONCERNED THAT-THAT CREATURE DOESN'T EXIST!!
TSK, TSK! POOR LOVESICK FEMALE! I HATE TO SEE HER TORTURE HERSELF OVER ME!!

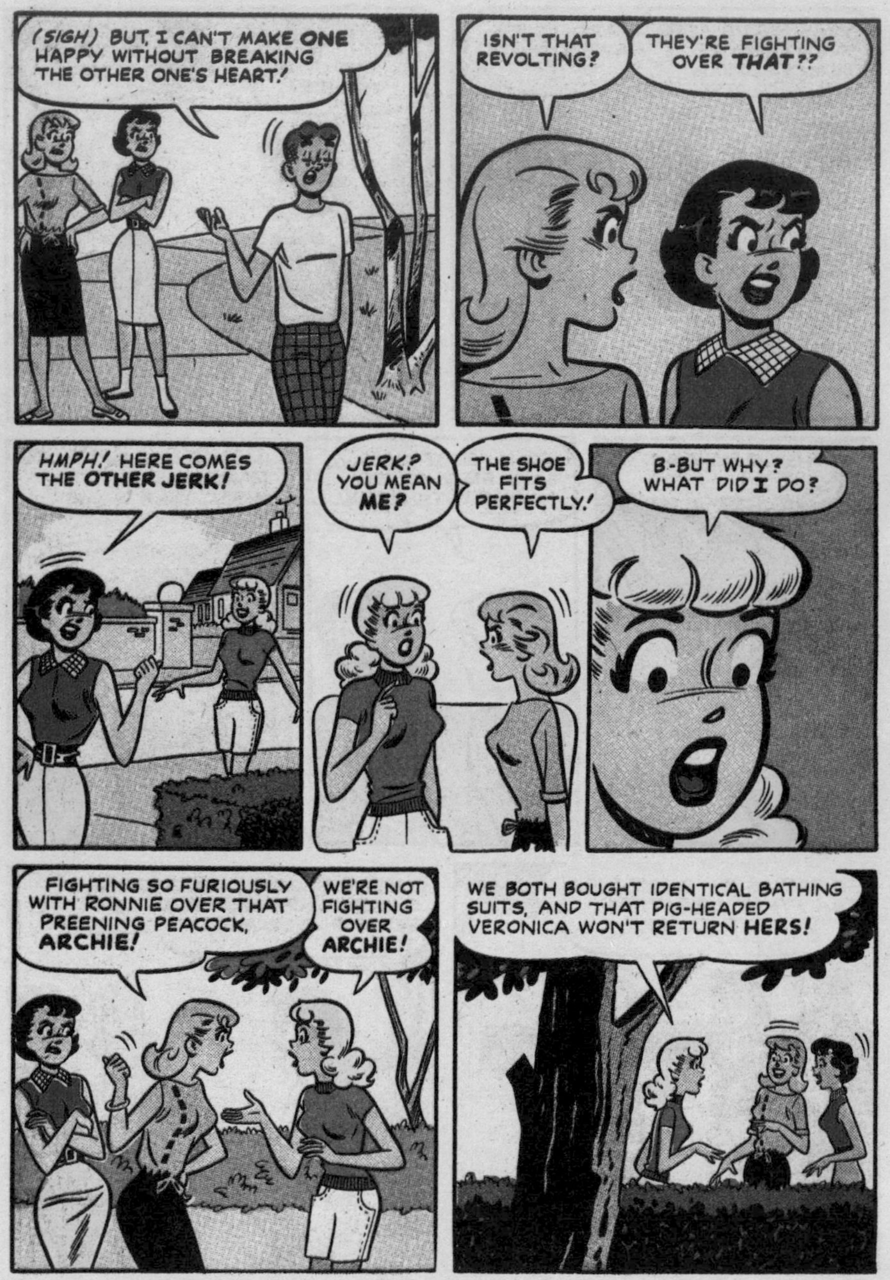
(SIGH) BUT, I CAN'T MAKE ONE HAPPY WITHOUT BREAKING THE OTHER ONE'S HEART!
ISN'T THAT REVOLTING?
THEY'RE FIGHTING OVER THAT??
HMPH! HERE COMES THE OTHER JERK!
JERK? YOU MEAN ME?
THE SHOE FITS PERFECTLY!
B-BUT WHY? WHAT DID I DO?
FIGHTING SO FURIOUSLY WITH RONNIE OVER THAT PREENING PEACOCK, ARCHIE!
WE'RE NOT FIGHTING OVER ARCHIE!
WE BOTH BOUGHT IDENTICAL BATHING SUITS, AND THAT PIG-HEADED VERONICA WON'T RETURN HERS!

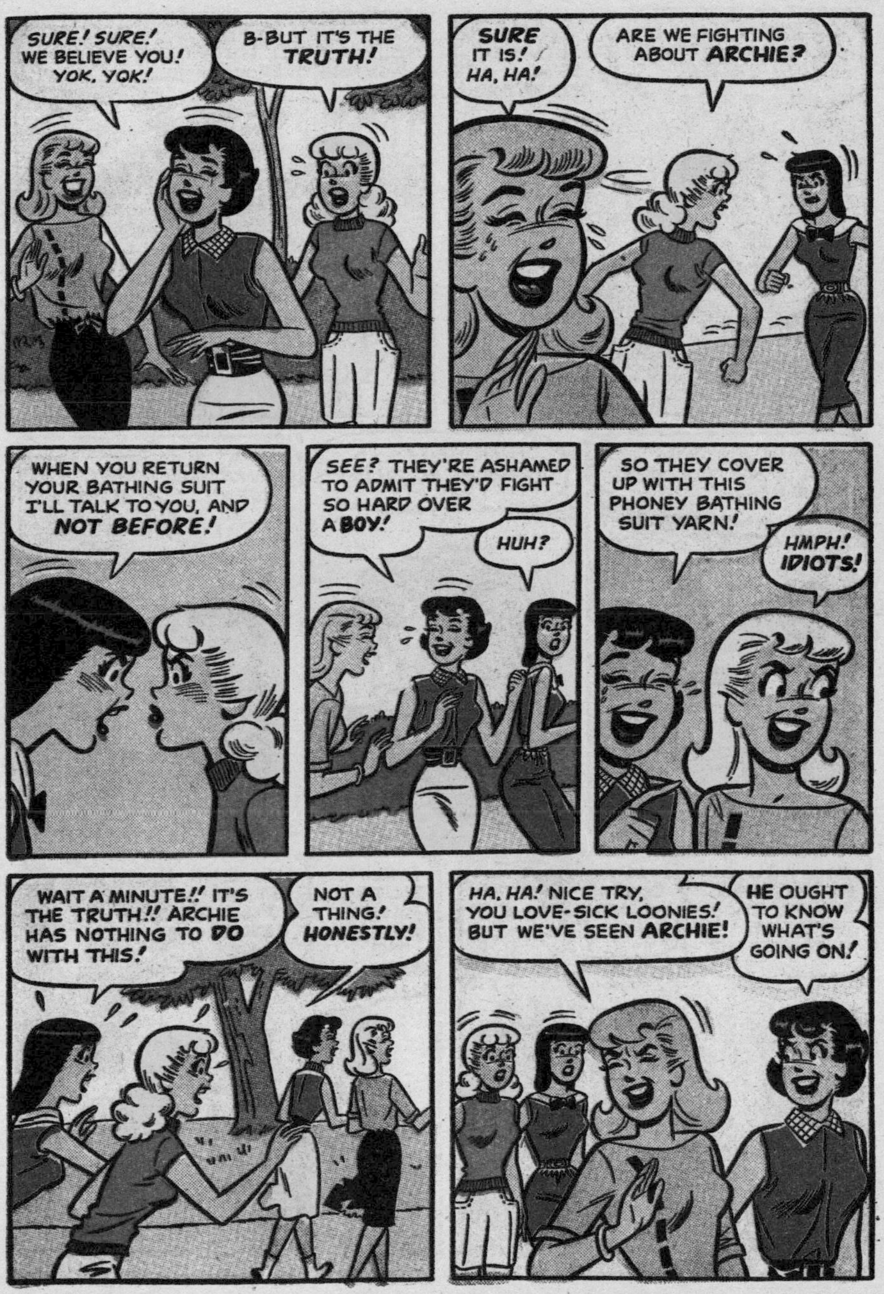
SURE! SURE! WE BELIEVE YOU! YOK, YOK!
B-BUT IT'S THE TRUTH!
SURE IT IS! HA, HA!
ARE WE FIGHTING ABOUT ARCHIE?
WHEN YOU RETURN YOUR BATHING SUIT I'LL TALK TO YOU, AND NOT BEFORE!
SEE? THEY'RE ASHAMED TO ADMIT THEY'D FIGHT SO HARD OVER A BOY!
HUH?
SO THEY COVER UP WITH THIS PHONEY BATHING SUIT YARN!
HMPH! IDIOTS!
WAIT A MINUTE!! IT'S THE TRUTH!! ARCHIE HAS NOTHING TO DO WITH THIS!
NOT A THING! HONESTLY!
HA, HA! NICE TRY, YOU LOVE-SICK LOONIES! BUT WE'VE SEEN ARCHIE!
HE OUGHT TO KNOW WHAT'S GOING ON!

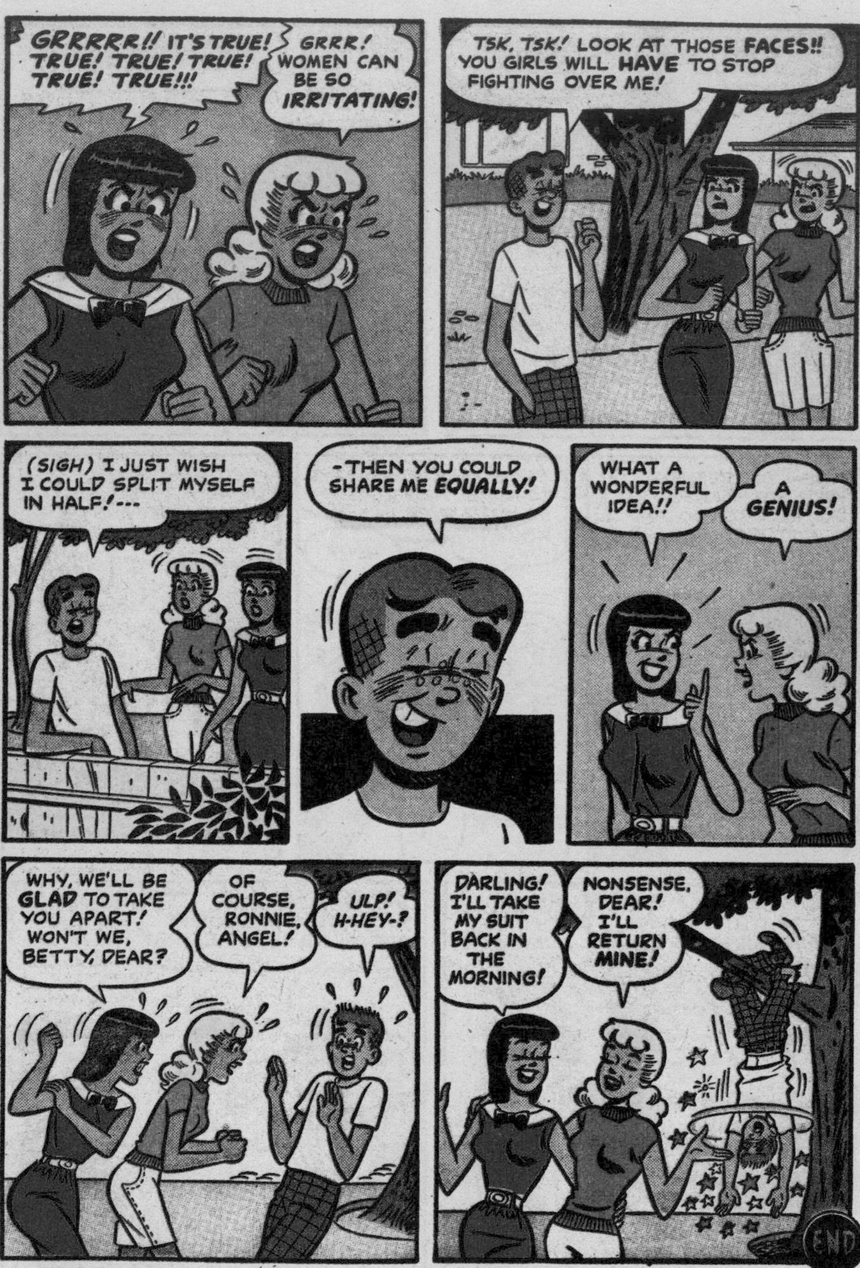
GRRRRR!! IT'S TRUE! TRUE! TRUE! TRUE! TRUE! TRUE!!!
GRRR! WOMEN CAN BE SO IRRITATING!
TSK, TSK! LOOK AT THOSE FACES!! YOU GIRLS WILL HAVE TO STOP FIGHTING OVER ME!
(SIGH) I JUST WISH I COULD SPLIT MYSELF IN HALF!---
-THEN YOU COULD SHARE ME EQUALLY!
WHAT A WONDERFUL IDEA!!
A GENIUS!
WHY, WE'LL BE GLAD TO TAKE YOU APART! WON'T WE, BETTY, DEAR?
OF COURSE, RONNIE, ANGEL!
ULP! H-HEY-?
DARLING! I'LL TAKE MY SUIT BACK IN THE MORNING!
NONSENSE, DEAR! I'LL RETURN MINE!
END

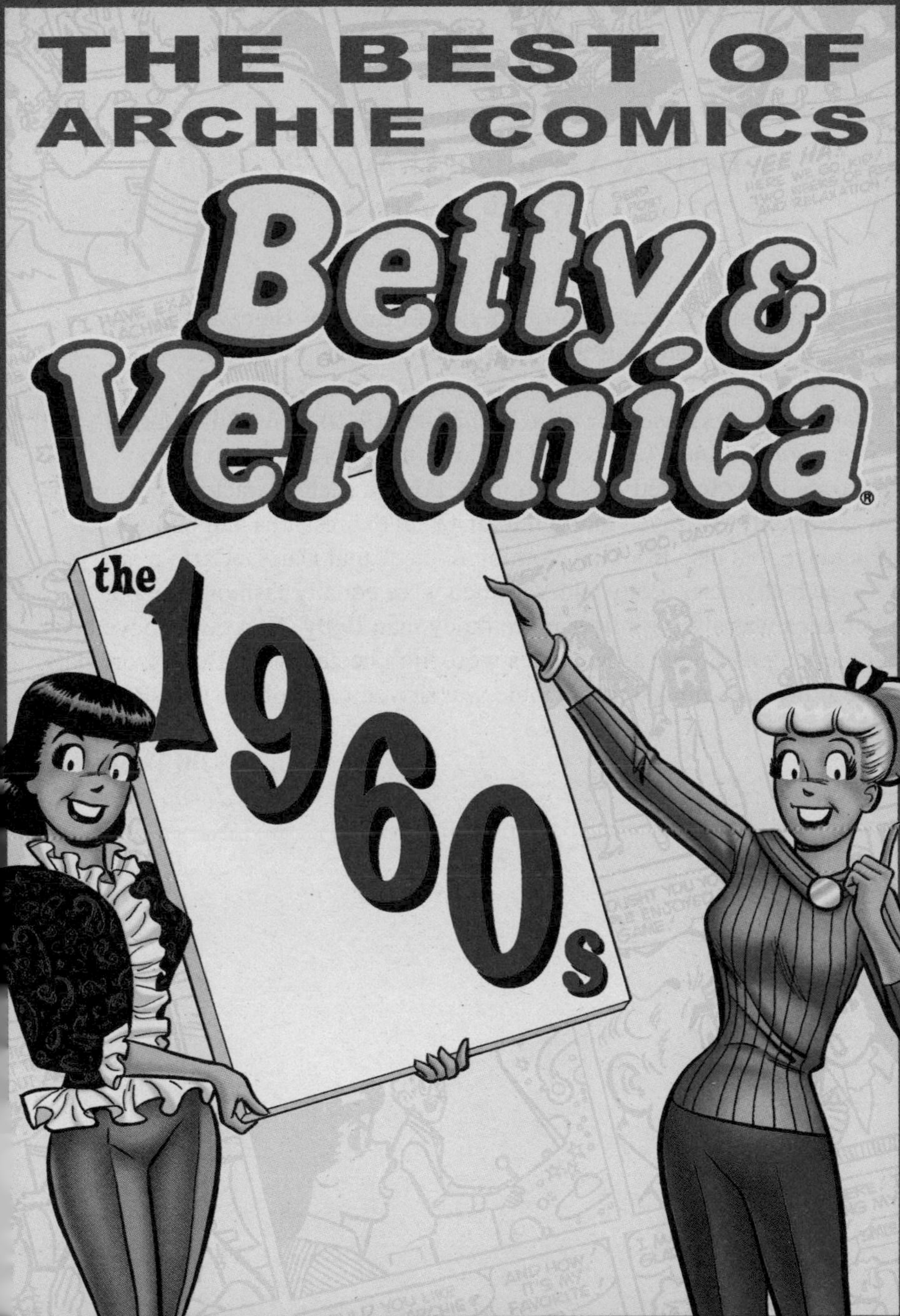
THE BEST OF
ARCHIE COMICS
Betty & Veronica®
the 1960s

Sweet Sorrow
-and-
The Kiss Off
Betty & Veronica Annual #8, 1960
by Bob Montana

The early sixties is my favorite period of time for Betty and Veronica stories, with the late sixties and early seventies coming in second.

I can say in *Betty and Veronica Annual #8* (1960) I loved the stories *Sweet Sorrow* and *The Kiss Off* because they represent some of my favorite looks for Betty and Veronica. For me each character's personality was not only portrayed through their facial expressions and body language, but also from the clothing choices that Dan DeCarlo made for each character. Betty and Veronica were equally fashionable, but Veronica was always a little more fancy than Betty. That might have been something as simple as her shoes were high heeled when Betty wore flats, but to me that showed that Ronnie was driven more places than Betty.

--Jill Thompson
Award-winning Artist,
Scary Godmother

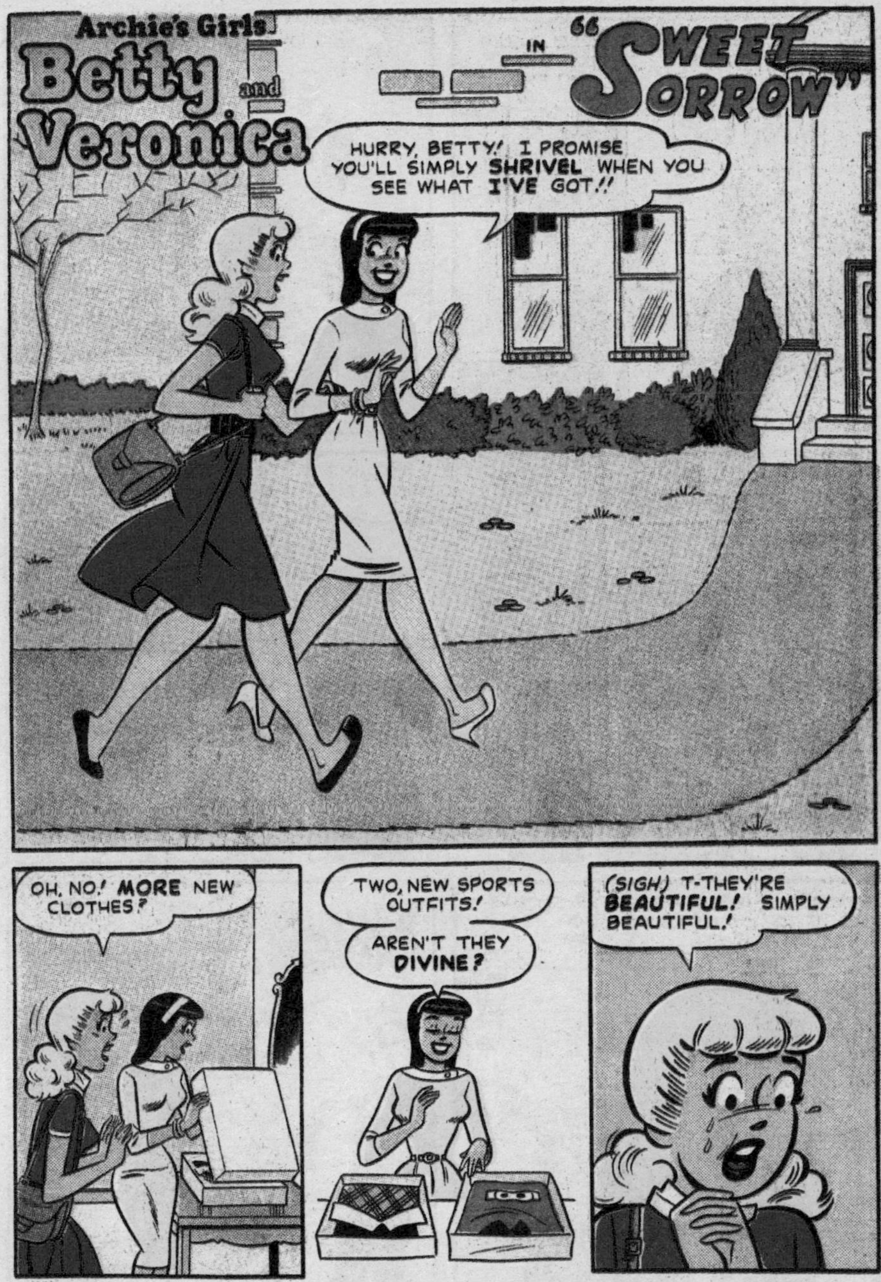
Archie's Girls Betty and Veronica
IN "SWEET SORROW"
HURRY, BETTY! I PROMISE YOU'LL SIMPLY SHRIVEL WHEN YOU SEE WHAT I'VE GOT!!
OH, NO! MORE NEW CLOTHES?
TWO, NEW SPORTS OUTFITS!
AREN'T THEY DIVINE?
(SIGH) T-THEY'RE BEAUTIFUL! SIMPLY BEAUTIFUL!

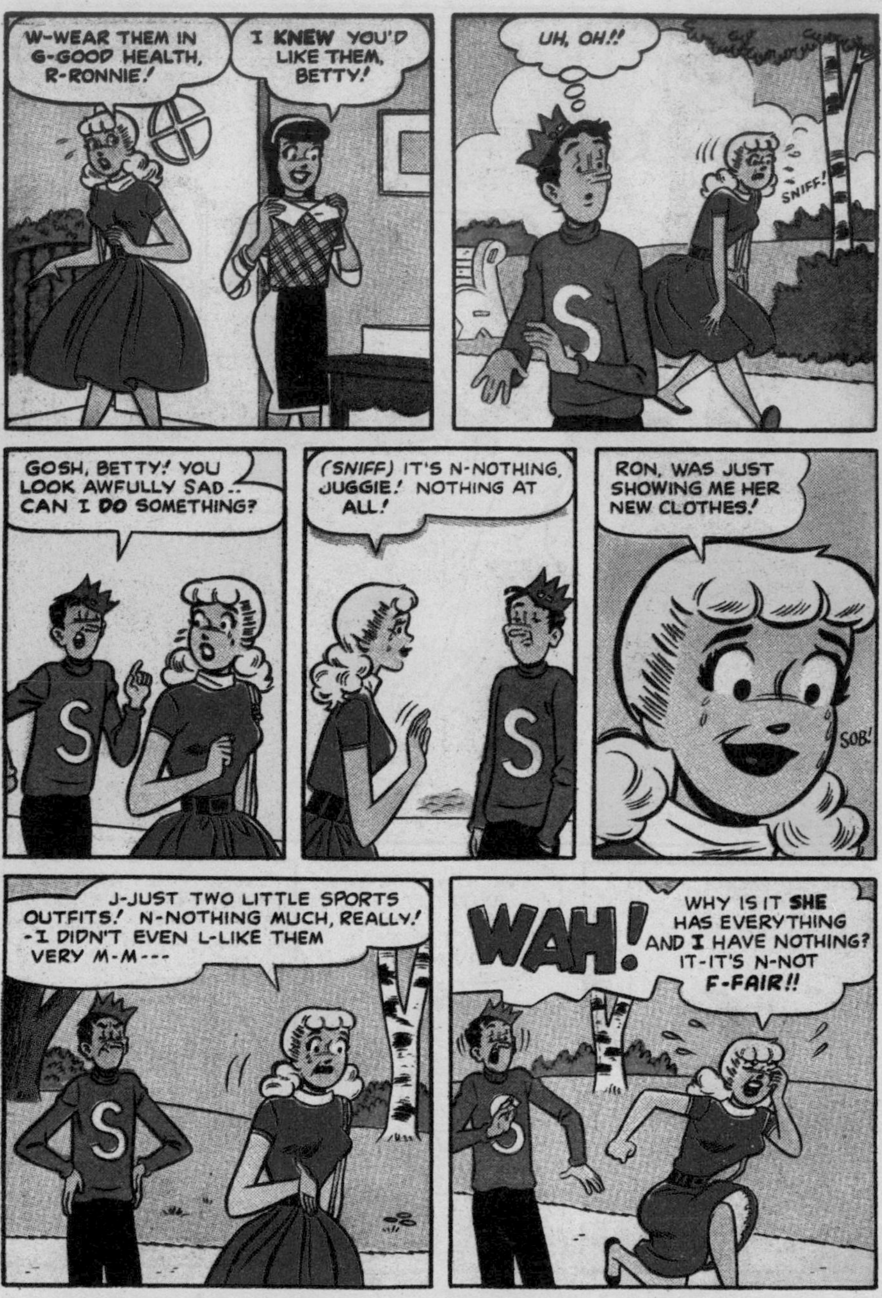
W-WEAR THEM IN G-GOOD HEALTH, R-RONNIE!
I KNEW YOU'D LIKE THEM, BETTY!
UH, OH!!
SNIFF!
GOSH, BETTY! YOU LOOK AWFULLY SAD.. CAN I DO SOMETHING?
(SNIFF) IT'S N-NOTHING, JUGGIE! NOTHING AT ALL!
RON, WAS JUST SHOWING ME HER NEW CLOTHES!
SOB!
J-JUST TWO LITTLE SPORTS OUTFITS! N-NOTHING MUCH, REALLY! -I DIDN'T EVEN L-LIKE THEM VERY M-M---
WAH!
WHY IS IT SHE HAS EVERYTHING AND I HAVE NOTHING? IT-IT'S N-NOT F-FAIR!!

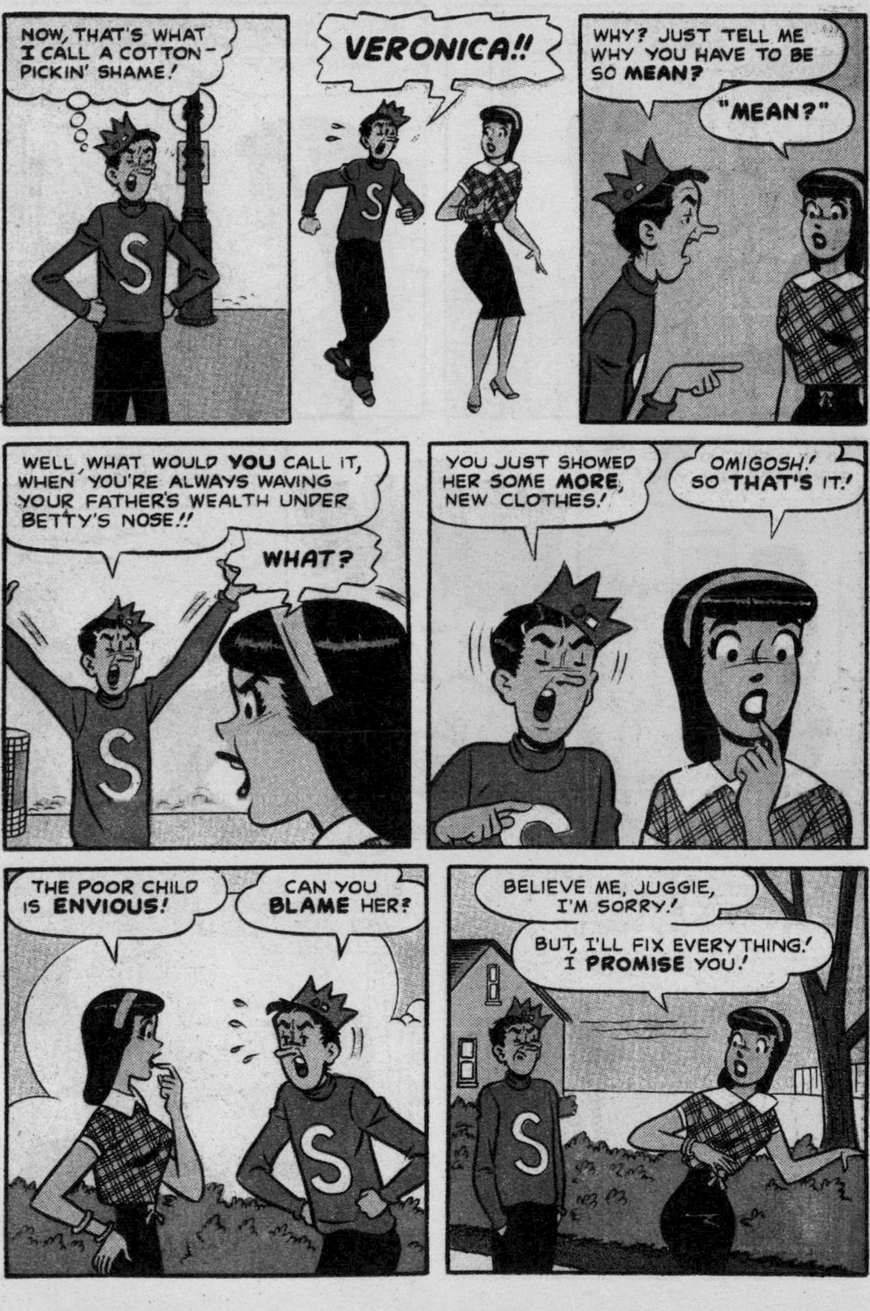
NOW, THAT'S WHAT I CALL A COTTON-PICKIN' SHAME!
VERONICA!!
WHY? JUST TELL ME WHY YOU HAVE TO BE SO MEAN?
"MEAN?"
WELL, WHAT WOULD YOU CALL IT, WHEN YOU'RE ALWAYS WAVING YOUR FATHER'S WEALTH UNDER BETTY'S NOSE!!
WHAT?
YOU JUST SHOWED HER SOME MORE, NEW CLOTHES!
OMIGOSH! SO THAT'S IT!
THE POOR CHILD IS ENVIOUS!
CAN YOU BLAME HER?
BELIEVE ME, JUGGIE, I'M SORRY!
BUT, I'LL FIX EVERYTHING! I PROMISE YOU!

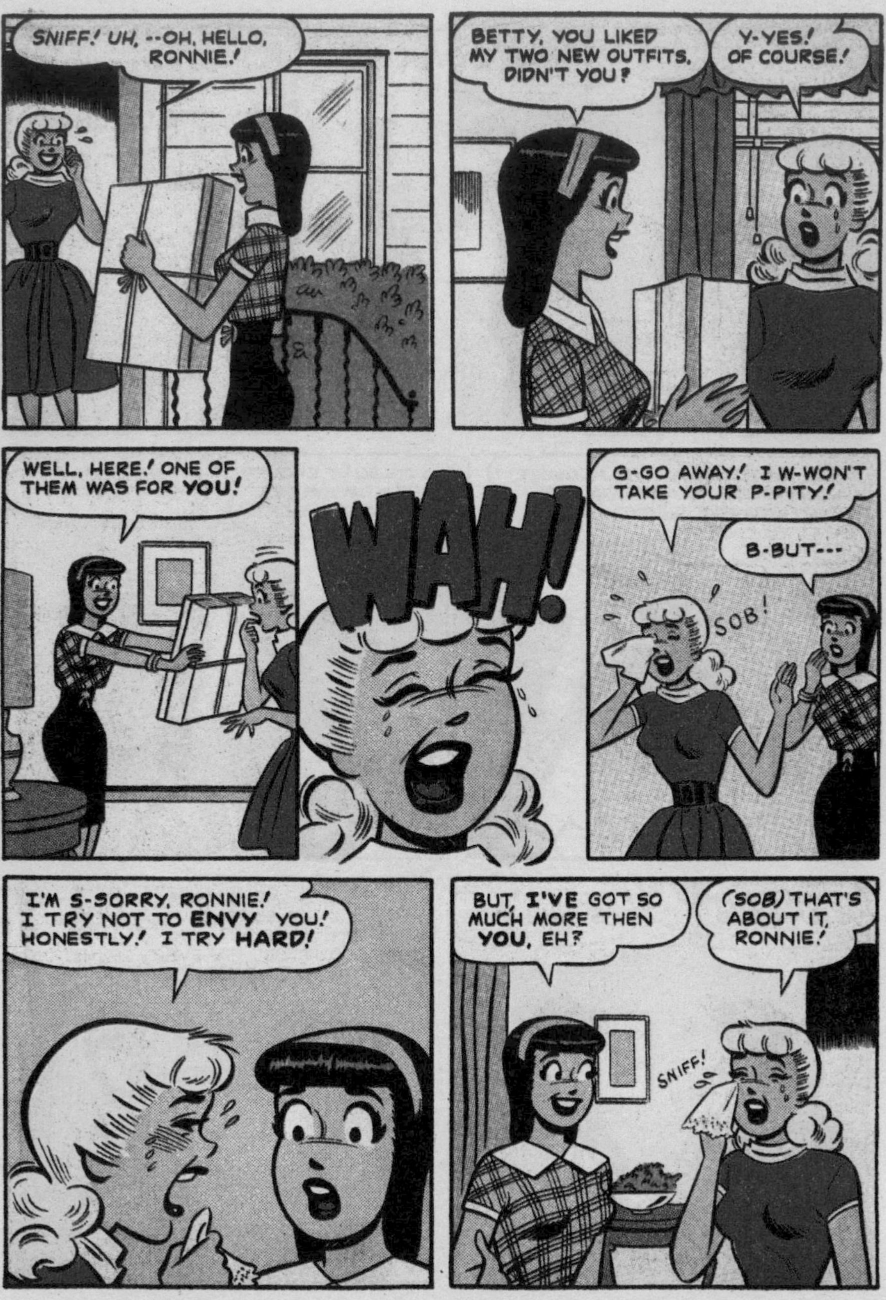
SNIFF! UH, --OH, HELLO, RONNIE!
BETTY, YOU LIKED MY TWO NEW OUTFITS, DIDN'T YOU?
Y-YES! OF COURSE!
WELL, HERE! ONE OF THEM WAS FOR YOU!
WAH!
G-GO AWAY! I W-WON'T TAKE YOUR P-PITY!
B-BUT---
SOB!
I'M S-SORRY, RONNIE! I TRY NOT TO ENVY YOU! HONESTLY! I TRY HARD!
BUT, I'VE GOT SO MUCH MORE THEN YOU, EH?
(SOB) THAT'S ABOUT IT, RONNIE!
SNIFF!

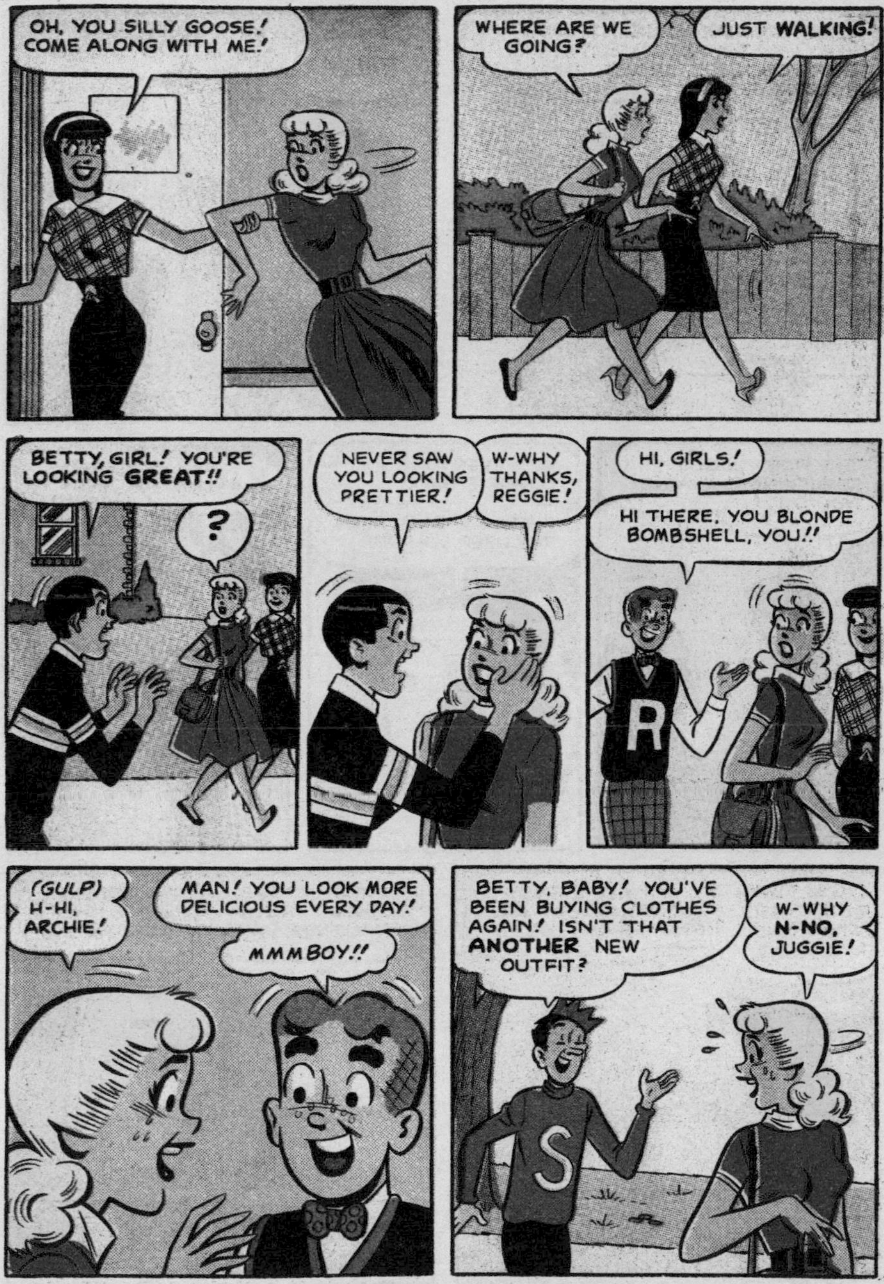
OH, YOU SILLY GOOSE! COME ALONG WITH ME!
WHERE ARE WE GOING?
JUST WALKING!
BETTY, GIRL! YOU'RE LOOKING GREAT!!
?
NEVER SAW YOU LOOKING PRETTIER!
W-WHY THANKS, REGGIE!
HI, GIRLS!
HI THERE, YOU BLONDE BOMBSHELL, YOU!!
(GULP) H-HI, ARCHIE!
MAN! YOU LOOK MORE DELICIOUS EVERY DAY!
MMMBOY!!
BETTY, BABY! YOU'VE BEEN BUYING CLOTHES AGAIN! ISN'T THAT ANOTHER NEW OUTFIT?
W-WHY N-NO, JUGGIE!

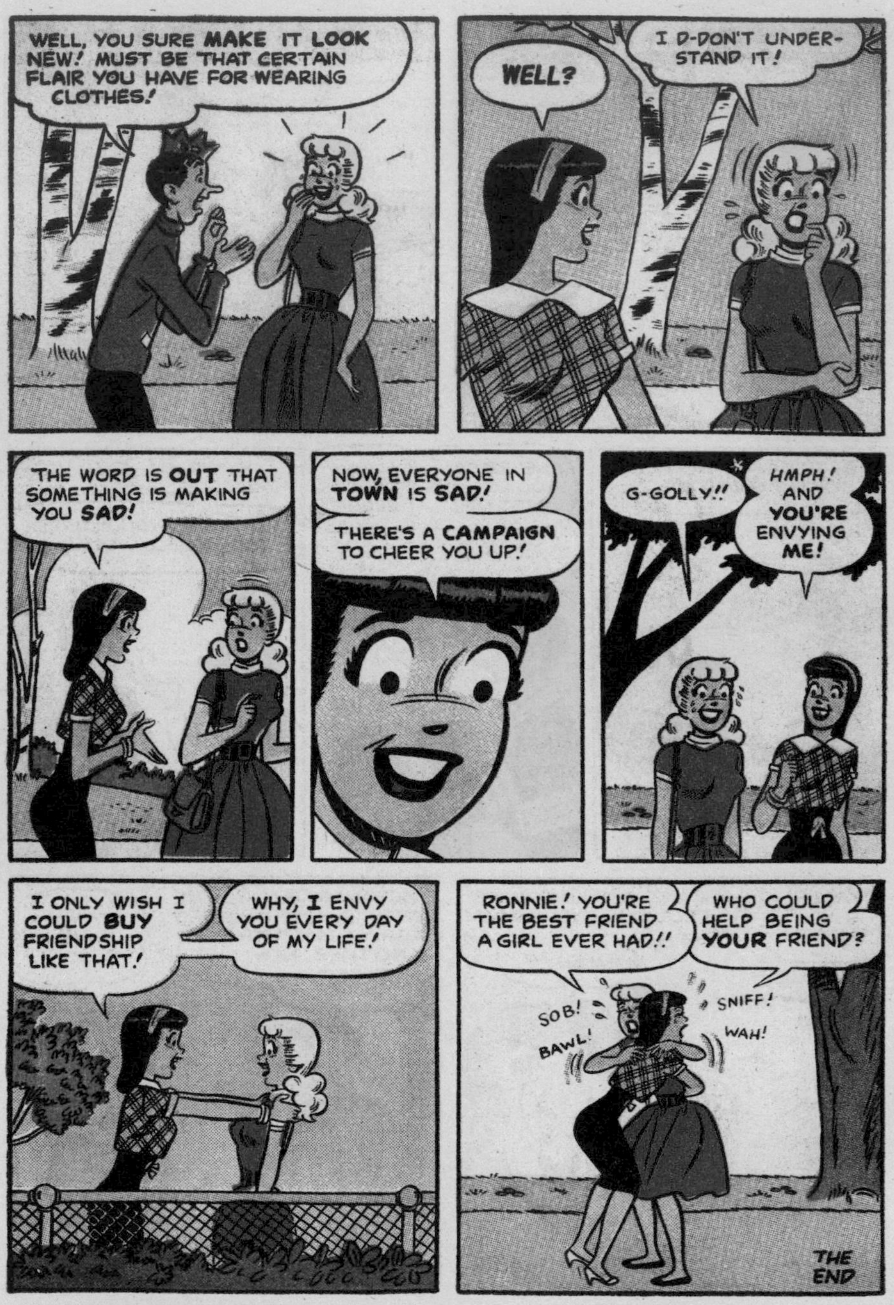
WELL, YOU SURE MAKE IT LOOK NEW! MUST BE THAT CERTAIN FLAIR YOU HAVE FOR WEARING CLOTHES!
WELL?
I D-DON'T UNDER-STAND IT!
THE WORD IS OUT THAT SOMETHING IS MAKING YOU SAD!
NOW, EVERYONE IN TOWN IS SAD!
THERE'S A CAMPAIGN TO CHEER YOU UP!
G-GOLLY!!
HMPH! AND YOU'RE ENVYING ME!
I ONLY WISH I COULD BUY FRIENDSHIP LIKE THAT!
WHY, I ENVY YOU EVERY DAY OF MY LIFE!
RONNIE! YOU'RE THE BEST FRIEND A GIRL EVER HAD!!
WHO COULD HELP BEING YOUR FRIEND?
SOB!
BAWL!
SNIFF!
WAH!
THE END

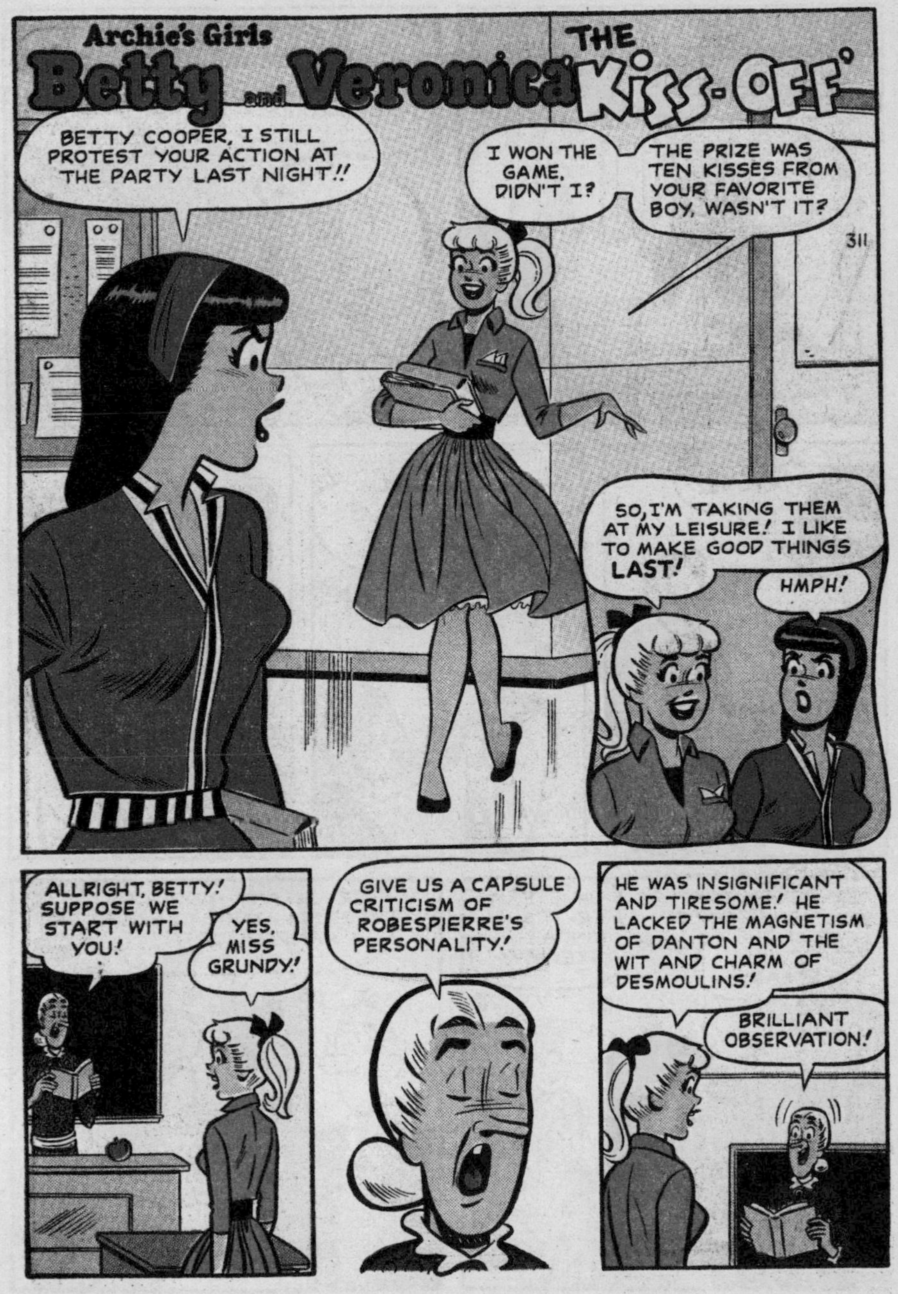
Archie's Girls Betty and Veronica
THE KISS-OFF
BETTY COOPER, I STILL PROTEST YOUR ACTION AT THE PARTY LAST NIGHT!!
I WON THE GAME, DIDN'T I?
THE PRIZE WAS TEN KISSES FROM YOUR FAVORITE BOY, WASN'T IT?
SO, I'M TAKING THEM AT MY LEISURE! I LIKE TO MAKE GOOD THINGS LAST!
HMPH!
ALLRIGHT, BETTY! SUPPOSE WE START WITH YOU!
YES, MISS GRUNDY!
GIVE US A CAPSULE CRITICISM OF ROBESPIERRE'S PERSONALITY!
HE WAS INSIGNIFICANT AND TIRESOME! HE LACKED THE MAGNETISM OF DANTON AND THE WIT AND CHARM OF DESMOULINS!
BRILLIANT OBSERVATION!

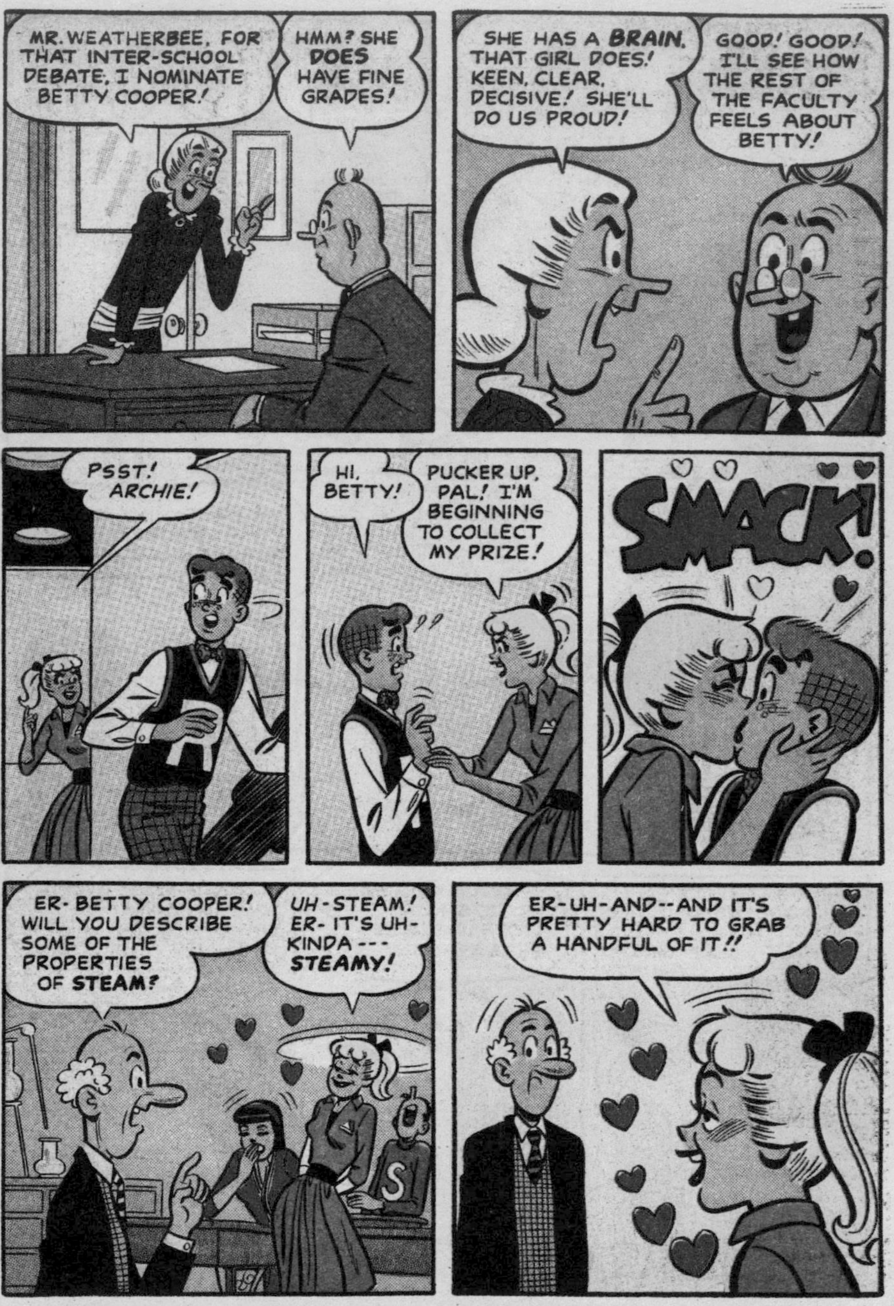
MR. WEATHERBEE, FOR THAT INTER-SCHOOL DEBATE, I NOMINATE BETTY COOPER!
HMM? SHE DOES HAVE FINE GRADES!
SHE HAS A BRAIN. THAT GIRL DOES! KEEN, CLEAR, DECISIVE! SHE'LL DO US PROUD!
GOOD! GOOD! I'LL SEE HOW THE REST OF THE FACULTY FEELS ABOUT BETTY!
PSST! ARCHIE!
HI, BETTY!
PUCKER UP, PAL! I'M BEGINNING TO COLLECT MY PRIZE!
SMACK!
ER- BETTY COOPER! WILL YOU DESCRIBE SOME OF THE PROPERTIES OF STEAM?
UH-STEAM! ER- IT'S UH- KINDA --- STEAMY!
ER-UH-AND--AND IT'S PRETTY HARD TO GRAB A HANDFUL OF IT!!

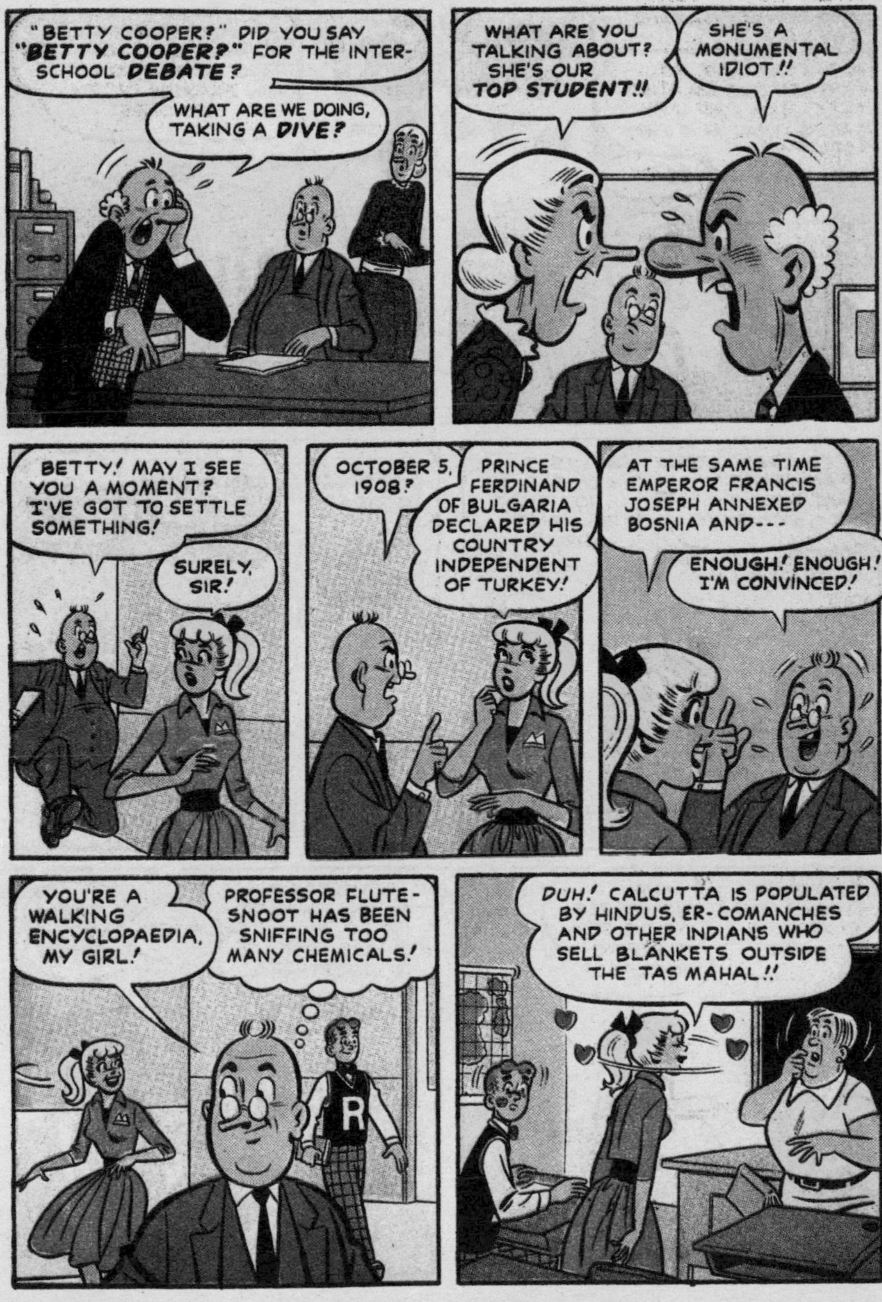
"BETTY COOPER?" DID YOU SAY "BETTY COOPER?" FOR THE INTER-SCHOOL DEBATE?
WHAT ARE WE DOING, TAKING A DIVE?
WHAT ARE YOU TALKING ABOUT? SHE'S OUR TOP STUDENT!!
SHE'S A MONUMENTAL IDIOT!!
BETTY! MAY I SEE YOU A MOMENT? I'VE GOT TO SETTLE SOMETHING!
SURELY, SIR!
OCTOBER 5, 1908?
PRINCE FERDINAND OF BULGARIA DECLARED HIS COUNTRY INDEPENDENT OF TURKEY!
AT THE SAME TIME EMPEROR FRANCIS JOSEPH ANNEXED BOSNIA AND---
ENOUGH! ENOUGH! I'M CONVINCED!
YOU'RE A WALKING ENCYCLOPAEDIA, MY GIRL!
PROFESSOR FLUTE-SNOOT HAS BEEN SNIFFING TOO MANY CHEMICALS!
R
DUH! CALCUTTA IS POPULATED BY HINDUS, ER-COMANCHES AND OTHER INDIANS WHO SELL BLANKETS OUTSIDE THE TAS MAHAL!!

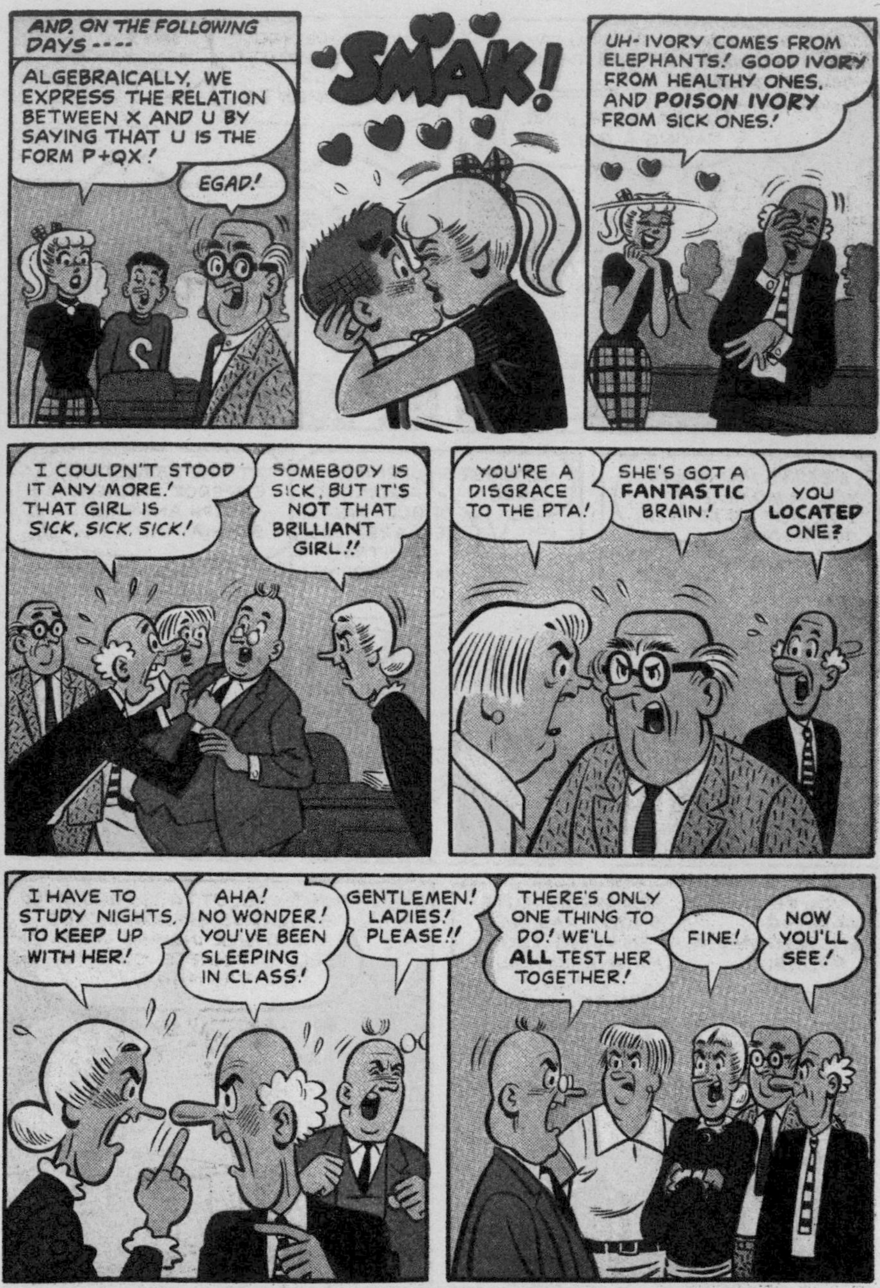
AND, ON THE FOLLOWING DAYS ----
ALGEBRAICALLY, WE EXPRESS THE RELATION BETWEEN X AND U BY SAYING THAT U IS THE FORM P+QX!
EGAD!
SMAK!
UH- IVORY COMES FROM ELEPHANTS! GOOD IVORY FROM HEALTHY ONES, AND POISON IVORY FROM SICK ONES!
I COULDN'T STOOD IT ANY MORE! THAT GIRL IS SICK, SICK, SICK!
SOMEBODY IS SICK, BUT IT'S NOT THAT BRILLIANT GIRL!!
YOU'RE A DISGRACE TO THE PTA!
SHE'S GOT A FANTASTIC BRAIN!
YOU LOCATED ONE?
I HAVE TO STUDY NIGHTS, TO KEEP UP WITH HER!
AHA! NO WONDER! YOU'VE BEEN SLEEPING IN CLASS!
GENTLEMEN! LADIES! PLEASE!!
THERE'S ONLY ONE THING TO DO! WE'LL ALL TEST HER TOGETHER!
FINE!
NOW YOU'LL SEE!

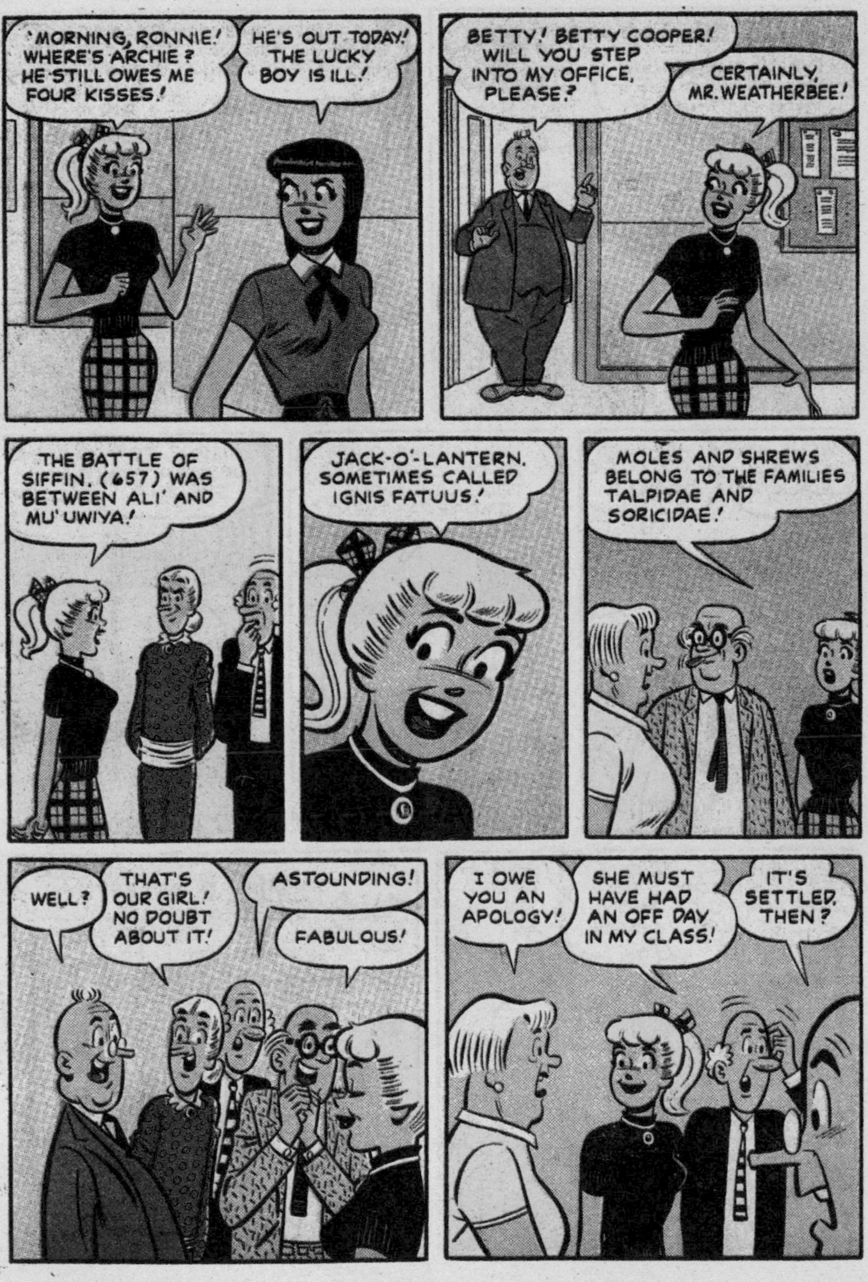
'MORNING, RONNIE! WHERE'S ARCHIE? HE STILL OWES ME FOUR KISSES!
HE'S OUT TODAY! THE LUCKY BOY IS ILL!
BETTY! BETTY COOPER! WILL YOU STEP INTO MY OFFICE, PLEASE?
CERTAINLY, MR. WEATHERBEE!
THE BATTLE OF SIFFIN. (657) WAS BETWEEN ALI' AND MU'UWIYA!
JACK-O'-LANTERN. SOMETIMES CALLED IGNIS FATUUS!
MOLES AND SHREWS BELONG TO THE FAMILIES TALPIDAE AND SORICIDAE!
WELL?
THAT'S OUR GIRL! NO DOUBT ABOUT IT!
ASTOUNDING!
FABULOUS!
I OWE YOU AN APOLOGY!
SHE MUST HAVE HAD AN OFF DAY IN MY CLASS!
IT'S SETTLED, THEN?

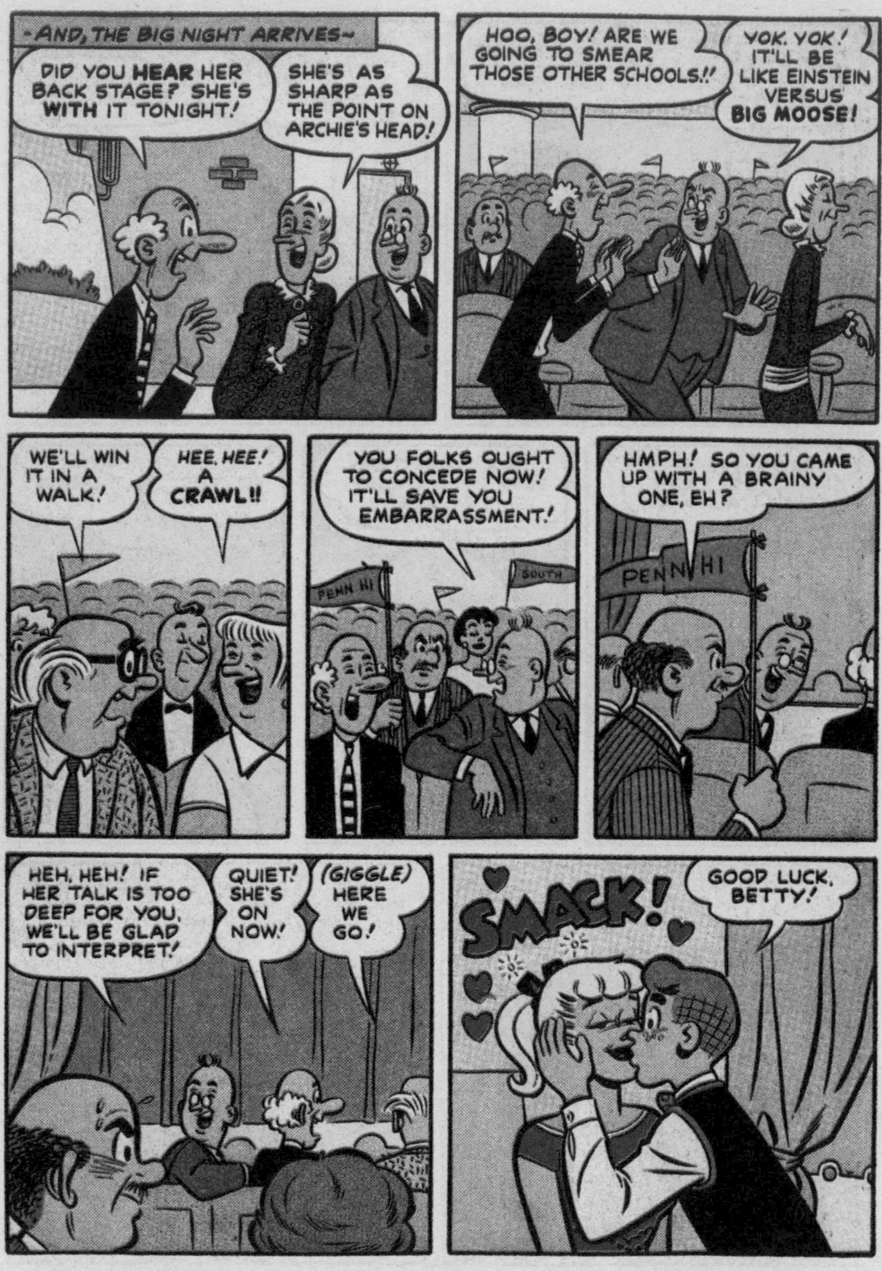
-AND, THE BIG NIGHT ARRIVES-
DID YOU HEAR HER BACK STAGE? SHE'S WITH IT TONIGHT!
SHE'S AS SHARP AS THE POINT ON ARCHIE'S HEAD!
HOO, BOY! ARE WE GOING TO SMEAR THOSE OTHER SCHOOLS!!
YOK. YOK! IT'LL BE LIKE EINSTEIN VERSUS BIG MOOSE!
WE'LL WIN IT IN A WALK!
HEE. HEE! A CRAWL!!
YOU FOLKS OUGHT TO CONCEDE NOW! IT'LL SAVE YOU EMBARRASSMENT!
PENN HI
SOUTH
HMPH! SO YOU CAME UP WITH A BRAINY ONE, EH?
PENN HI
HEH, HEH! IF HER TALK IS TOO DEEP FOR YOU, WE'LL BE GLAD TO INTERPRET!
QUIET! SHE'S ON NOW!
(GIGGLE) HERE WE GO!
SMACK!
GOOD LUCK, BETTY!

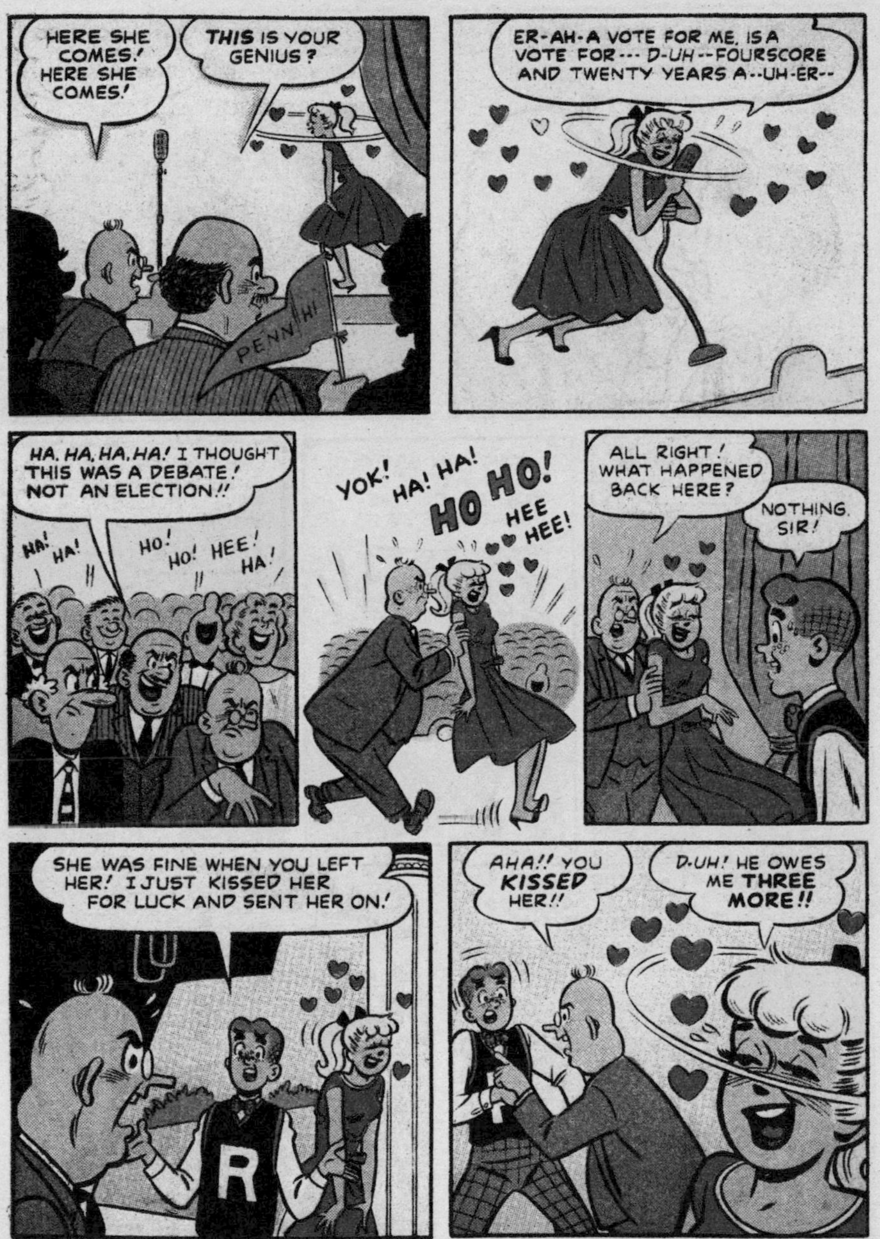
HERE SHE COMES! HERE SHE COMES!
THIS IS YOUR GENIUS?
PENN HI
ER-AH-A VOTE FOR ME, IS A VOTE FOR--- D-UH--FOURSCORE AND TWENTY YEARS A--UH-ER--
HA. HA. HA. HA! I THOUGHT THIS WAS A DEBATE! NOT AN ELECTION!!
HA! HA!
HO! HO! HEE! HA!
YOK! HA! HA! HO HO! HEE HEE!
ALL RIGHT! WHAT HAPPENED BACK HERE?
NOTHING, SIR!
SHE WAS FINE WHEN YOU LEFT HER! I JUST KISSED HER FOR LUCK AND SENT HER ON!
AHA!! YOU KISSED HER!!
D-UH! HE OWES ME THREE MORE!!

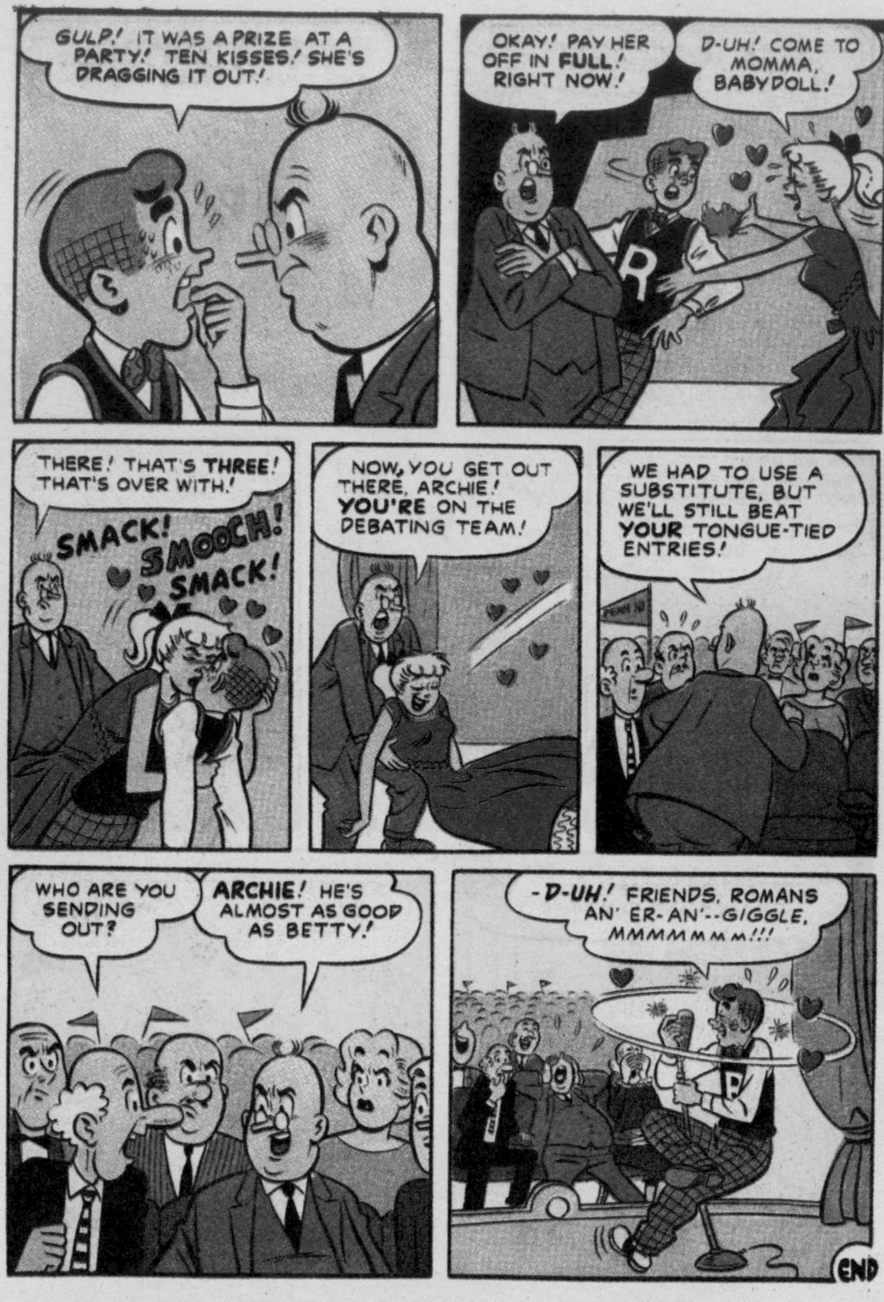
GULP! IT WAS A PRIZE AT A PARTY! TEN KISSES! SHE'S DRAGGING IT OUT!
OKAY! PAY HER OFF IN FULL! RIGHT NOW!
D-UH! COME TO MOMMA, BABYDOLL!
THERE! THAT'S THREE! THAT'S OVER WITH!
SMACK!
SMOOCH!
SMACK!
NOW, YOU GET OUT THERE, ARCHIE! YOU'RE ON THE DEBATING TEAM!
WE HAD TO USE A SUBSTITUTE, BUT WE'LL STILL BEAT YOUR TONGUE-TIED ENTRIES!
WHO ARE YOU SENDING OUT?
ARCHIE! HE'S ALMOST AS GOOD AS BETTY!
-D-UH! FRIENDS, ROMANS AN' ER-AN'--GIGGLE, MMMMMMM!!!
END

Sight for Sore Eyes
Betty & Veronica #67, 1961 by Frank Doyle, Dan DeCarlo, Rudy Lapick, Vince DeCarlo

Comics are known for their entertainment value, but I've always found their abilities to be time capsules really fascinating. For example, this little tale has some of the wacky lingo and hairdos (or should I say, a particular hair-don't) found in the far-out '60s. The girls act as trendsetters, also acting as a microcosm for teenagers of that time. Now that this has become rather academic, let me just end with a traditional '60s sentence. Ahem. "Unless you're thicker than a $5 malt, you should start reading this outta sight story!"

-- Jonathan Betancourt
Publishing Coordinator,
Archie Comics

Too Close For Comfort
Betty & Veronica #67, 1961 by Frank Doyle, Dan DeCarlo, Rudy Lapick, Vince DeCarlo

A classic Betty & Veronica story. The art is early Dan DeCarlo. The story was written by Frank Doyle. I like this story for a few things. First, the two main characters show their individual personalities on the first page. A new reader sees Veronica as being critical and Betty vulnerable and trusting. If you're already a Betty, Veronica and Archie fan you know what these characters are all about. The theme of this story is about fashion. Specifically, tight fitting pants called "Slim Jims." Fashion has always been an important part of what has made Archie Comics so popular. Then Archie and Jughead come along with a practical joke and a few wise guy remarks. But Betty & Veronica are not pushovers when it comes to the boys. Or maybe in some way they are. You decide after you read the story. In the end, "Too Close For Comfort" made me laugh. Laughing makes me feel good.

-- Victor Gorelick
Co-President/Editor-in-Chief,
Archie Comics

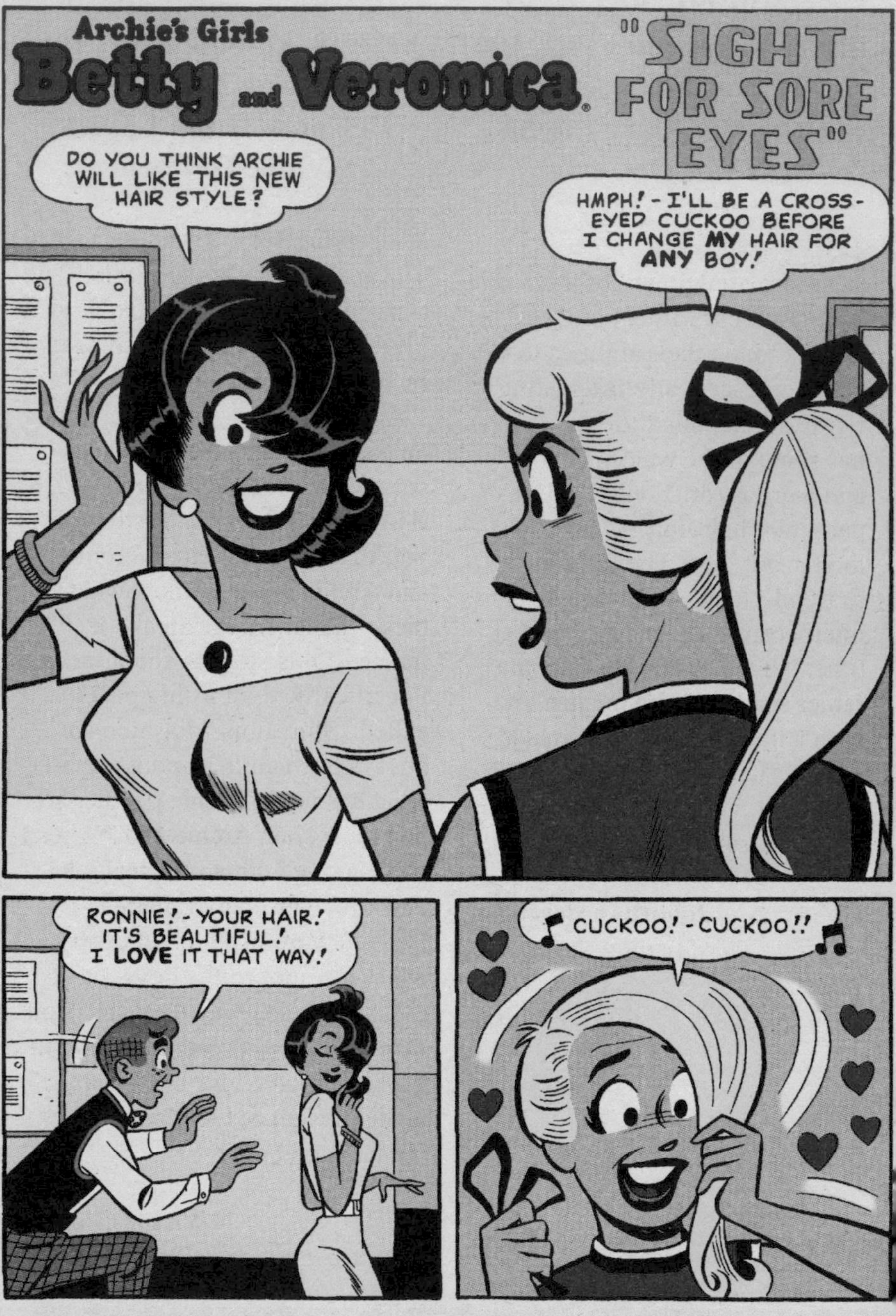
Archie's Girls Betty and Veronica
"SIGHT FOR SORE EYES"
DO YOU THINK ARCHIE WILL LIKE THIS NEW HAIR STYLE?
HMPH! - I'LL BE A CROSS-EYED CUCKOO BEFORE I CHANGE MY HAIR FOR ANY BOY!
RONNIE! - YOUR HAIR! IT'S BEAUTIFUL! I LOVE IT THAT WAY!
CUCKOO! - CUCKOO!!

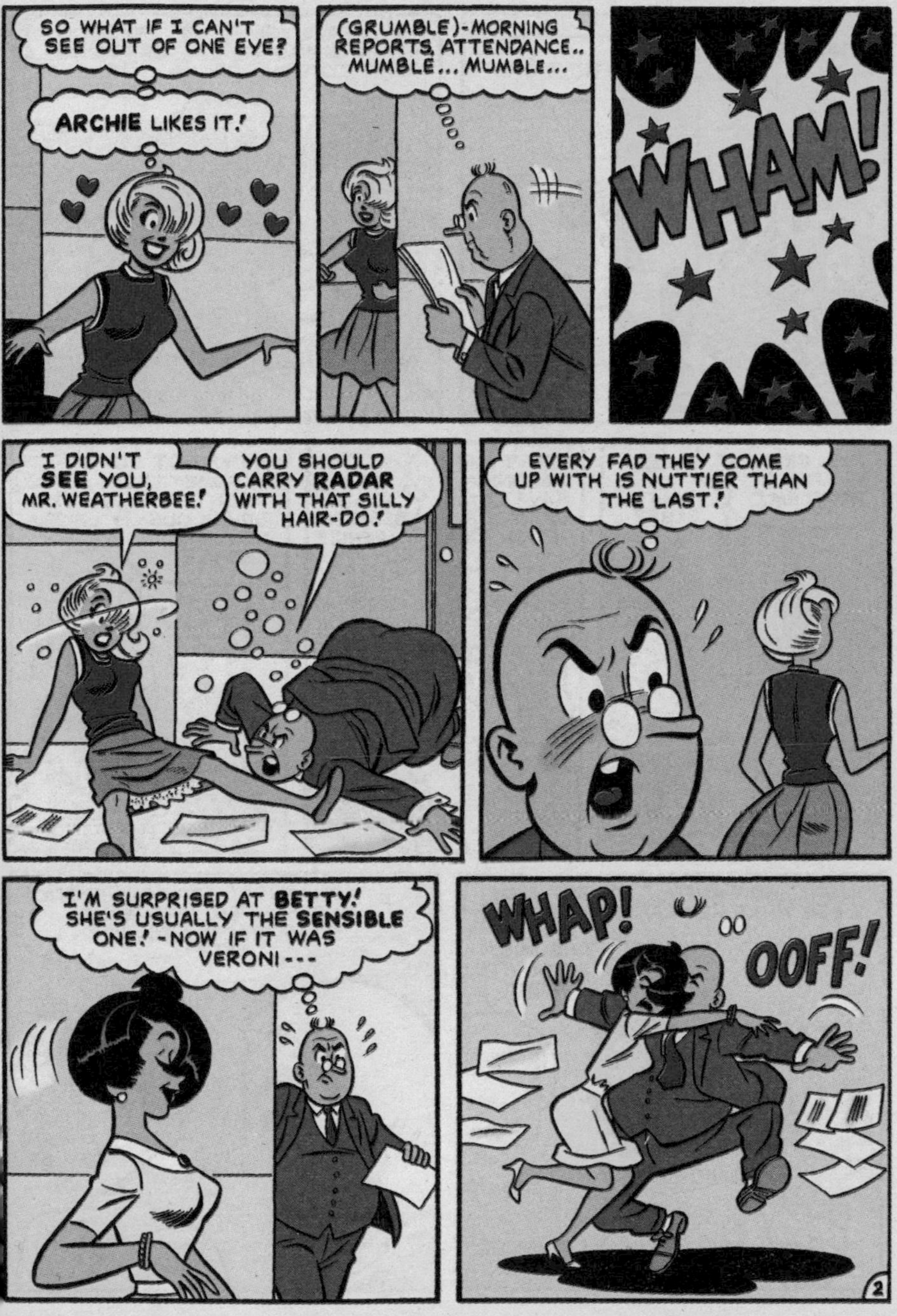
SO WHAT IF I CAN'T SEE OUT OF ONE EYE?
ARCHIE LIKES IT!
(GRUMBLE)-MORNING REPORTS, ATTENDANCE.. MUMBLE... MUMBLE...
WHAM!
I DIDN'T SEE YOU, MR. WEATHERBEE!
YOU SHOULD CARRY RADAR WITH THAT SILLY HAIR-DO!
EVERY FAD THEY COME UP WITH IS NUTTIER THAN THE LAST!
I'M SURPRISED AT BETTY! SHE'S USUALLY THE SENSIBLE ONE! -NOW IF IT WAS VERONI---
WHAP!
OOFF!
2

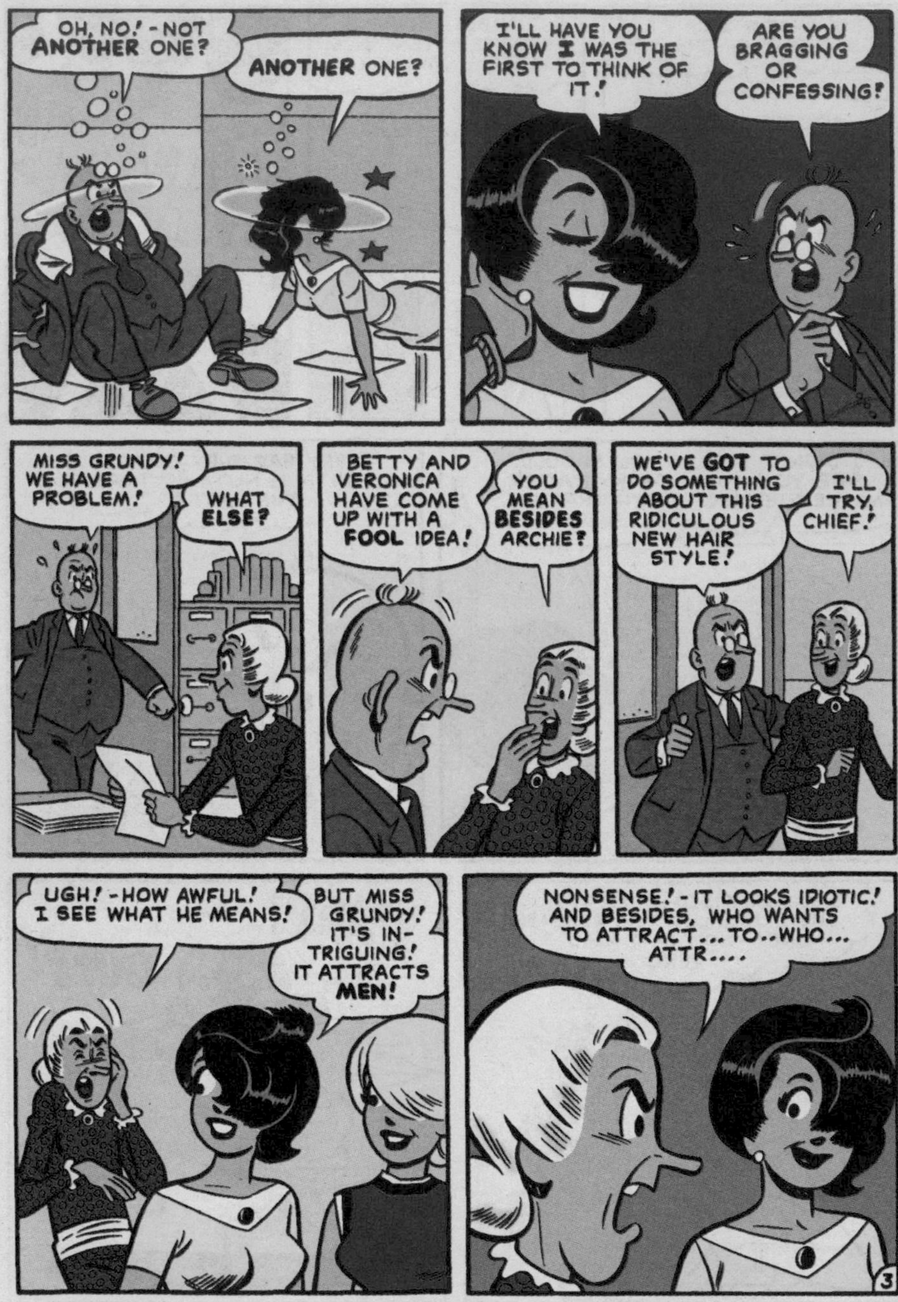
OH, NO! -NOT ANOTHER ONE?
ANOTHER ONE?
I'LL HAVE YOU KNOW I WAS THE FIRST TO THINK OF IT!
ARE YOU BRAGGING OR CONFESSING?
MISS GRUNDY! WE HAVE A PROBLEM!
WHAT ELSE?
BETTY AND VERONICA HAVE COME UP WITH A FOOL IDEA!
YOU MEAN BESIDES ARCHIE?
WE'VE GOT TO DO SOMETHING ABOUT THIS RIDICULOUS NEW HAIR STYLE!
I'LL TRY, CHIEF!
UGH! -HOW AWFUL! I SEE WHAT HE MEANS!
BUT MISS GRUNDY! IT'S IN-TRIGUING! IT ATTRACTS MEN!
NONSENSE! - IT LOOKS IDIOTIC! AND BESIDES, WHO WANTS TO ATTRACT... TO..WHO... ATTR....
3

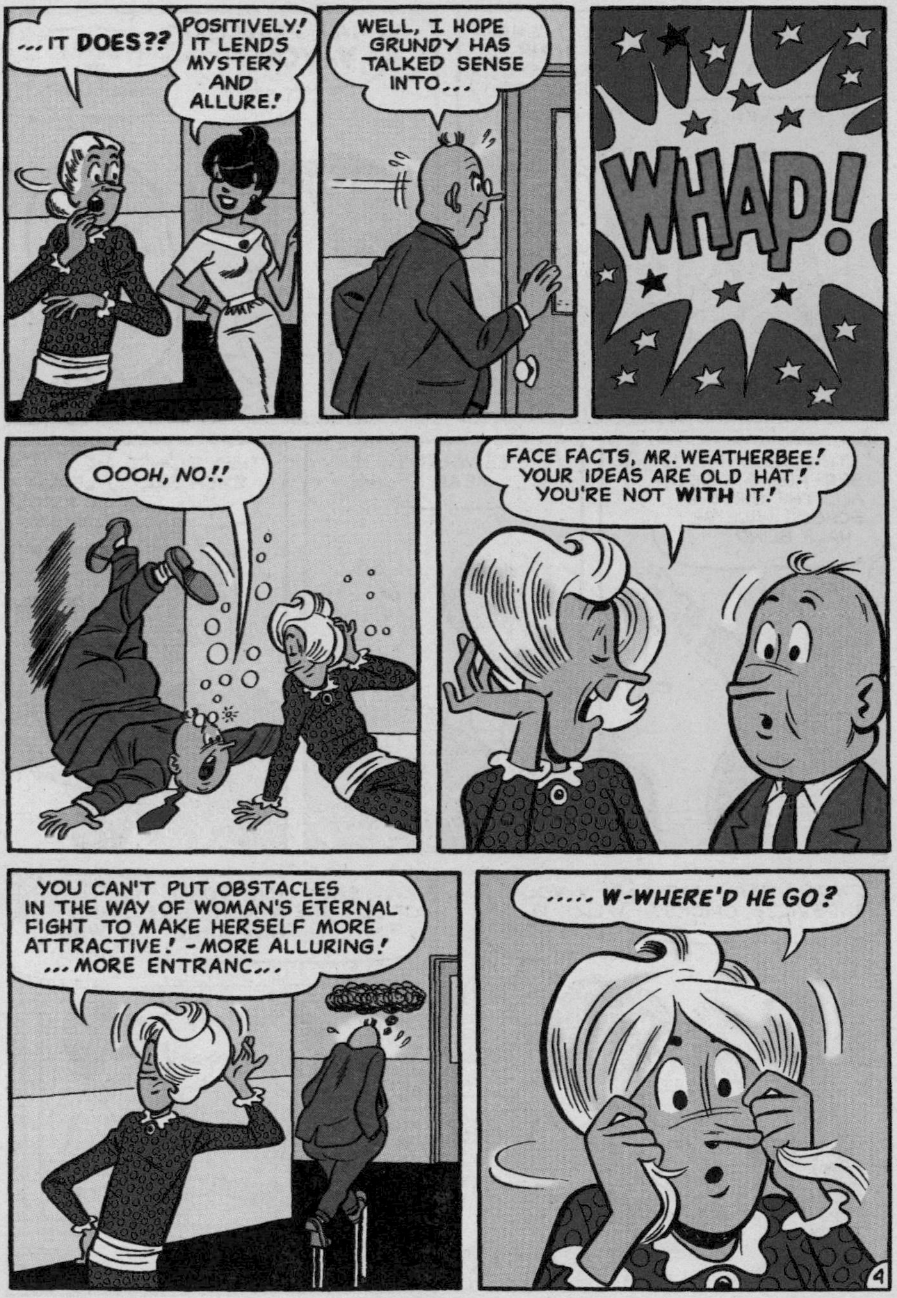
... IT DOES??
POSITIVELY! IT LENDS MYSTERY AND ALLURE!
WELL, I HOPE GRUNDY HAS TALKED SENSE INTO...
WHAP!
OOOH, NO!!
FACE FACTS, MR. WEATHERBEE! YOUR IDEAS ARE OLD HAT! YOU'RE NOT WITH IT!
YOU CAN'T PUT OBSTACLES IN THE WAY OF WOMAN'S ETERNAL FIGHT TO MAKE HERSELF MORE ATTRACTIVE! -MORE ALLURING! ...MORE ENTRANC...
..... W-WHERE'D HE GO?
4

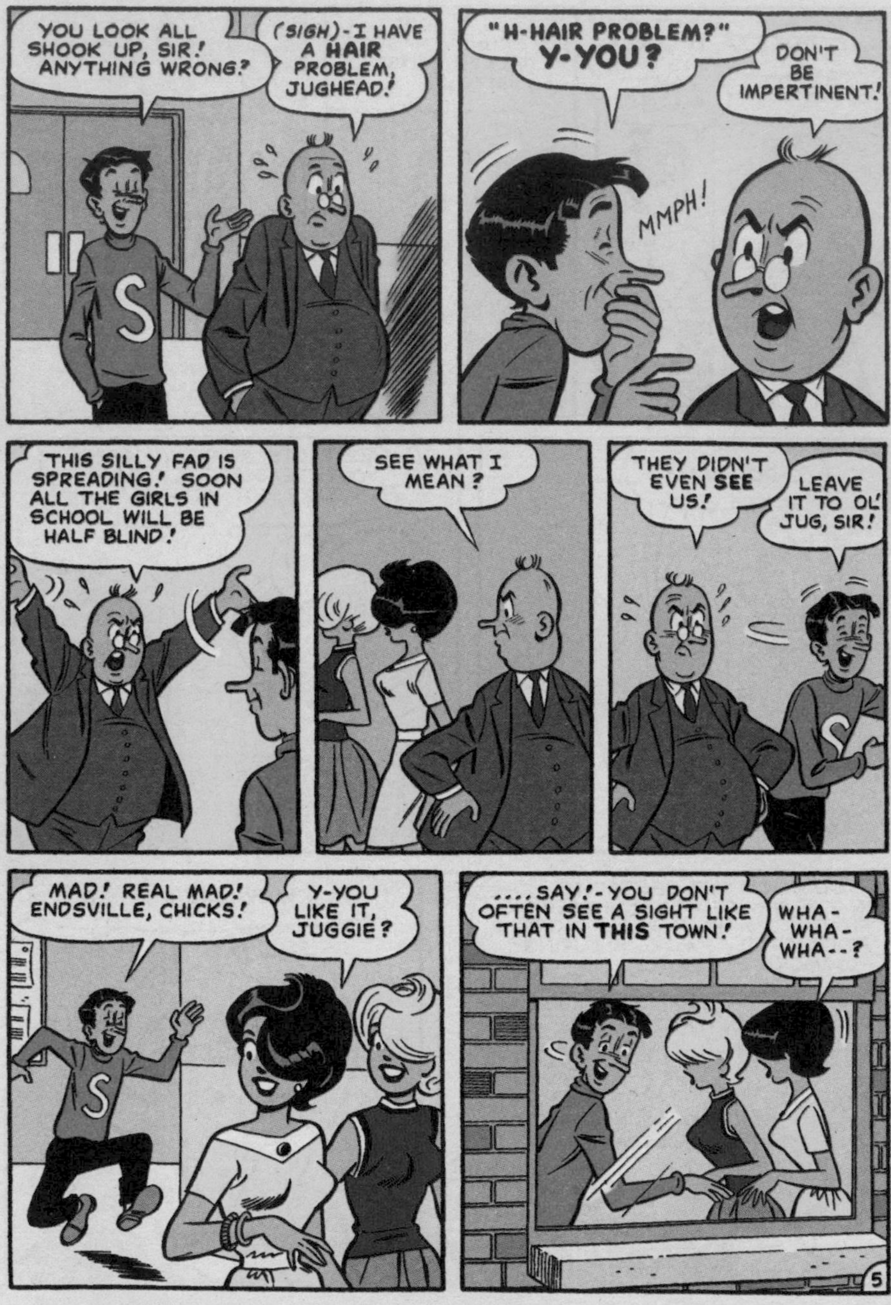
YOU LOOK ALL SHOOK UP, SIR! ANYTHING WRONG?
(SIGH) - I HAVE A HAIR PROBLEM, JUGHEAD!
"H-HAIR PROBLEM?" Y-YOU?
MMPH!
DON'T BE IMPERTINENT!
THIS SILLY FAD IS SPREADING! SOON ALL THE GIRLS IN SCHOOL WILL BE HALF BLIND!
SEE WHAT I MEAN?
THEY DIDN'T EVEN SEE US!
LEAVE IT TO OL' JUG, SIR!
MAD! REAL MAD! ENDSVILLE, CHICKS!
Y-YOU LIKE IT, JUGGIE?
....SAY! - YOU DON'T OFTEN SEE A SIGHT LIKE THAT IN THIS TOWN!
WHA-WHA-WHA--?
5

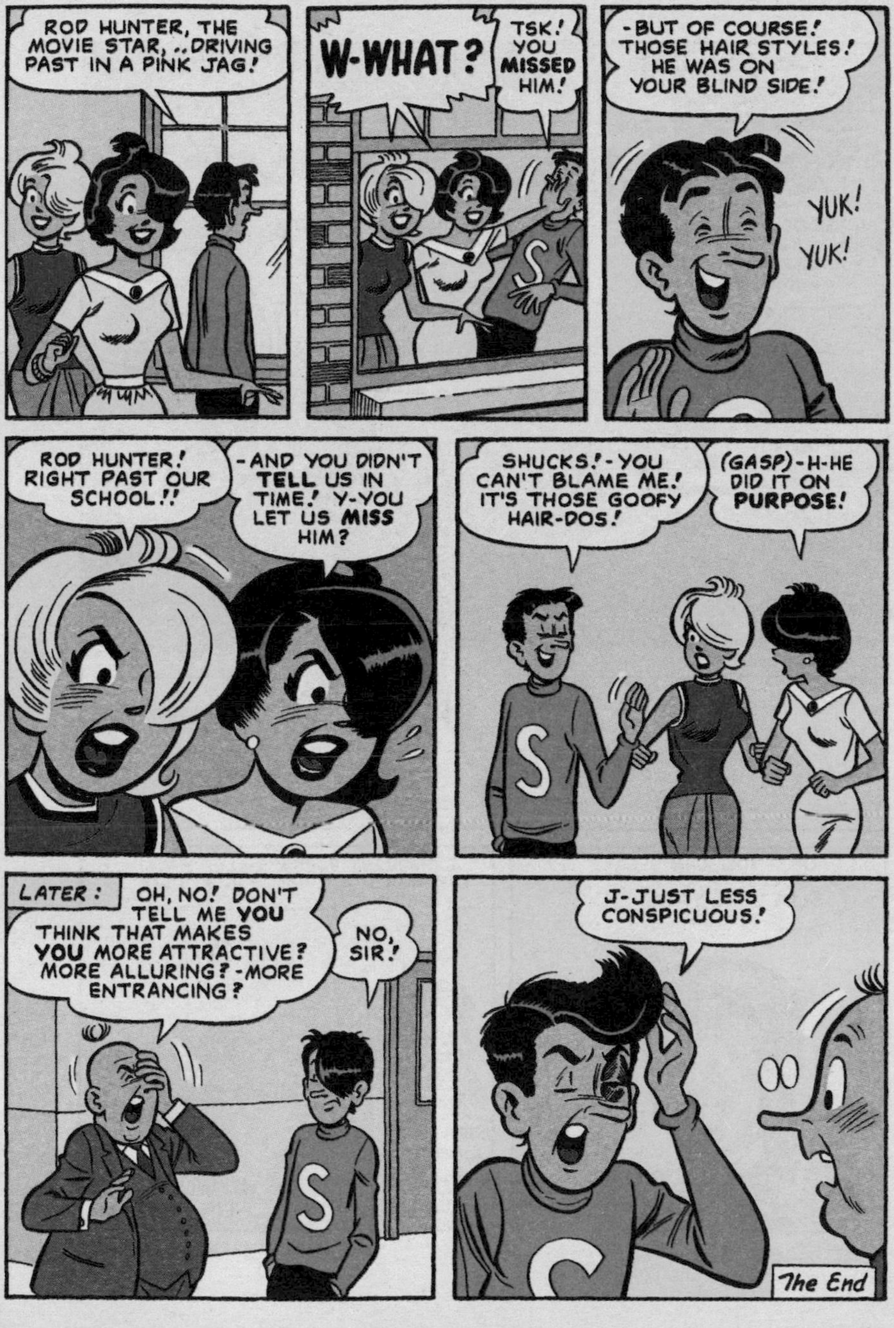
ROD HUNTER, THE MOVIE STAR, ..DRIVING PAST IN A PINK JAG!
W-WHAT?
TSK! YOU MISSED HIM!
-BUT OF COURSE! THOSE HAIR STYLES! HE WAS ON YOUR BLIND SIDE!
YUK!
YUK!
ROD HUNTER! RIGHT PAST OUR SCHOOL!!
-AND YOU DIDN'T TELL US IN TIME! Y-YOU LET US MISS HIM?
SHUCKS!-YOU CAN'T BLAME ME! IT'S THOSE GOOFY HAIR-DOS!
(GASP)-H-HE DID IT ON PURPOSE!
LATER:
OH, NO! DON'T TELL ME YOU THINK THAT MAKES YOU MORE ATTRACTIVE? MORE ALLURING?-MORE ENTRANCING?
NO, SIR!
J-JUST LESS CONSPICUOUS!
The End

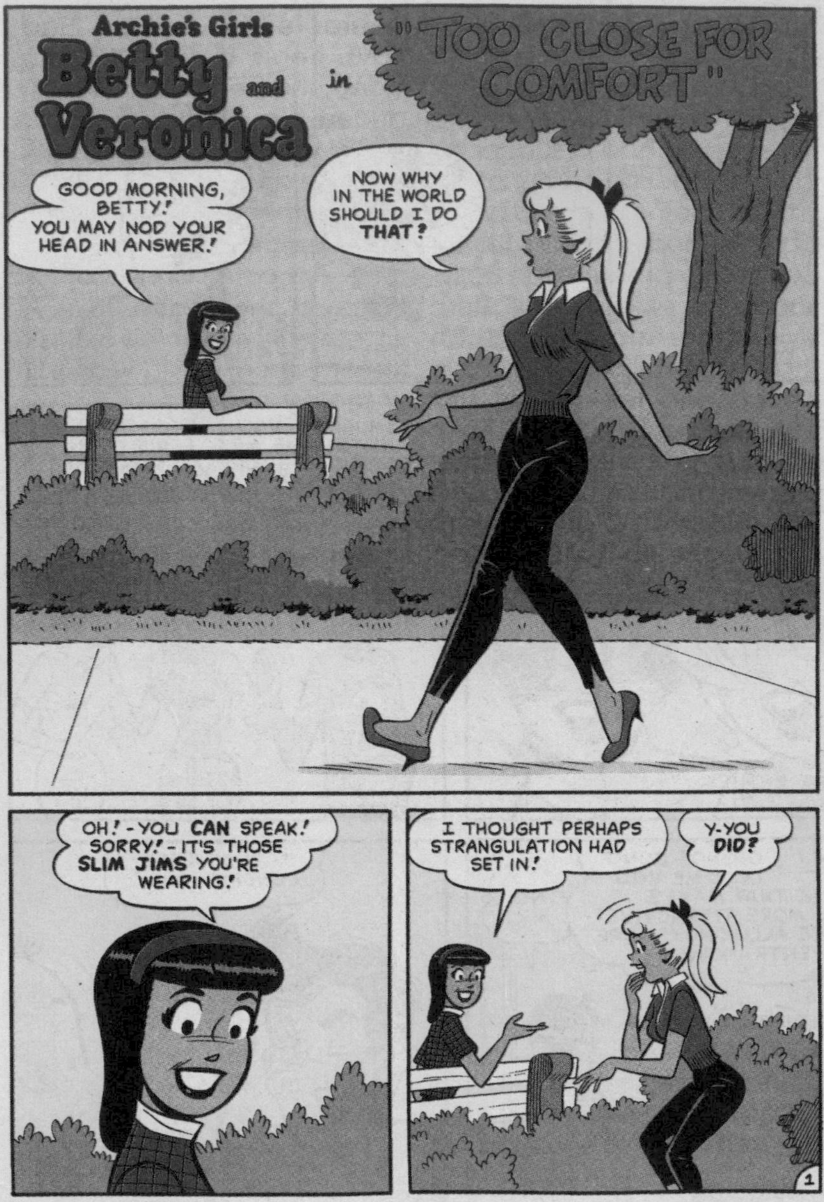
Archie's Girls
Betty and Veronica
in
"TOO CLOSE FOR COMFORT"
GOOD MORNING, BETTY! YOU MAY NOD YOUR HEAD IN ANSWER!
NOW WHY IN THE WORLD SHOULD I DO THAT?
OH! - YOU CAN SPEAK! SORRY! - IT'S THOSE SLIM JIMS YOU'RE WEARING!
I THOUGHT PERHAPS STRANGULATION HAD SET IN!
Y-YOU DID?
1

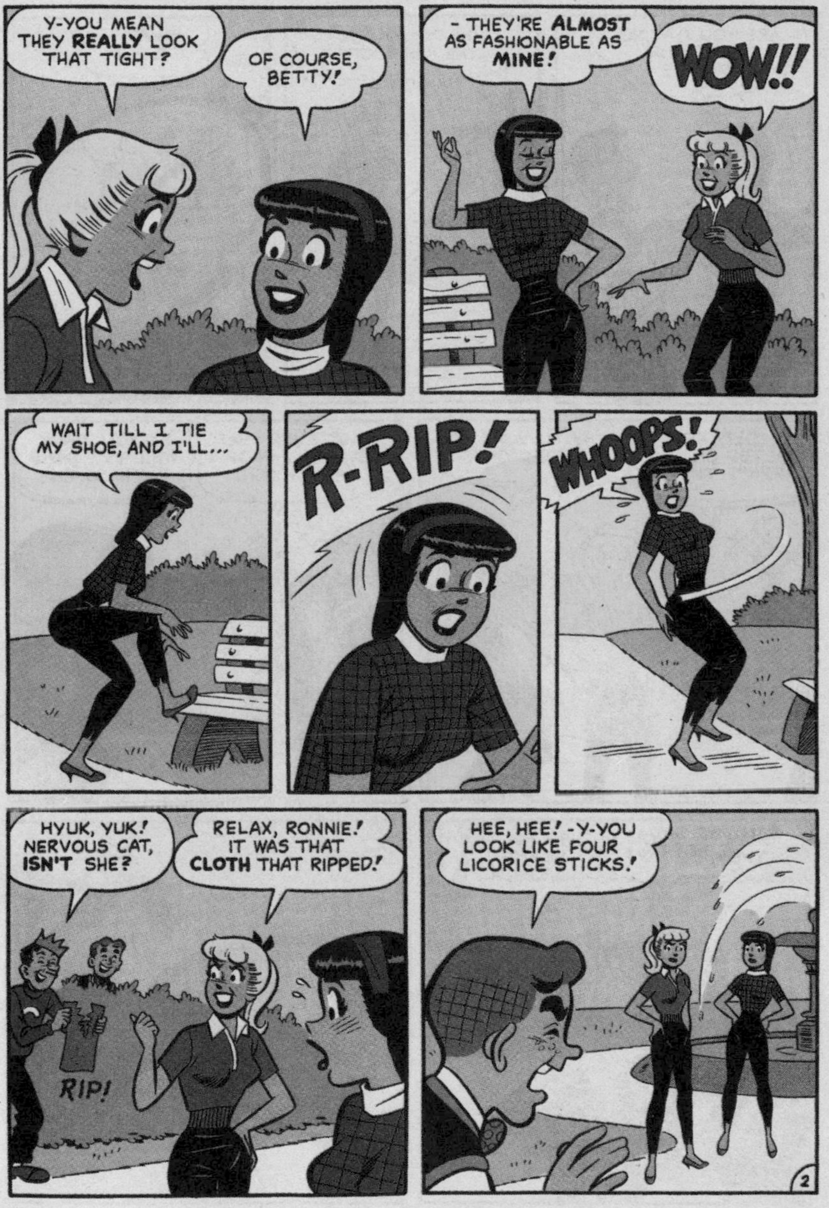
Y-YOU MEAN THEY REALLY LOOK THAT TIGHT?
OF COURSE, BETTY!
- THEY'RE ALMOST AS FASHIONABLE AS MINE!
WOW!!
WAIT TILL I TIE MY SHOE, AND I'LL...
R-RIP!
WHOOPS!
HYUK, YUK! NERVOUS CAT, ISN'T SHE?
RELAX, RONNIE! IT WAS THAT CLOTH THAT RIPPED!
RIP!
HEE, HEE! -Y-YOU LOOK LIKE FOUR LICORICE STICKS!
2

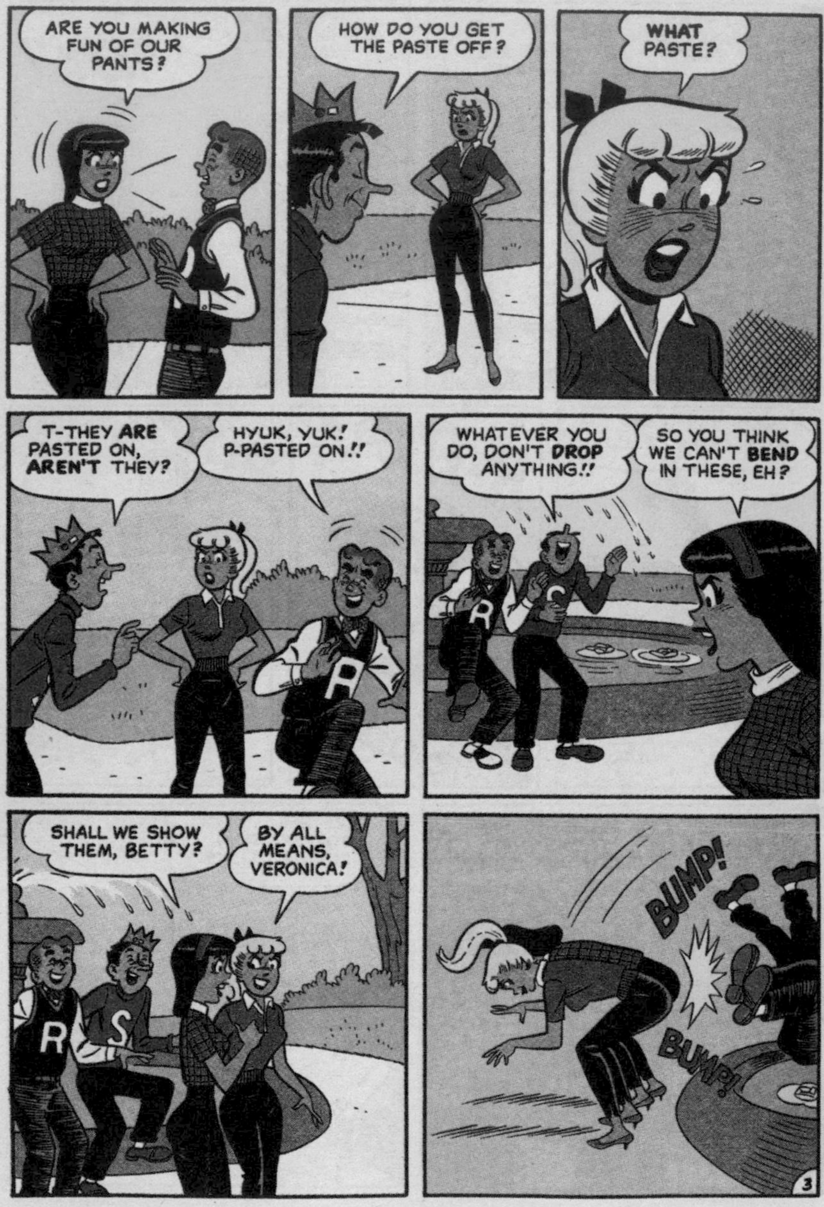
ARE YOU MAKING FUN OF OUR PANTS?
HOW DO YOU GET THE PASTE OFF?
WHAT PASTE?
T-THEY ARE PASTED ON, AREN'T THEY?
HYUK, YUK! P-PASTED ON.!!
WHATEVER YOU DO, DON'T DROP ANYTHING.!!
SO YOU THINK WE CAN'T BEND IN THESE, EH?
SHALL WE SHOW THEM, BETTY?
BY ALL MEANS, VERONICA!
BUMP!
BUMP!
3

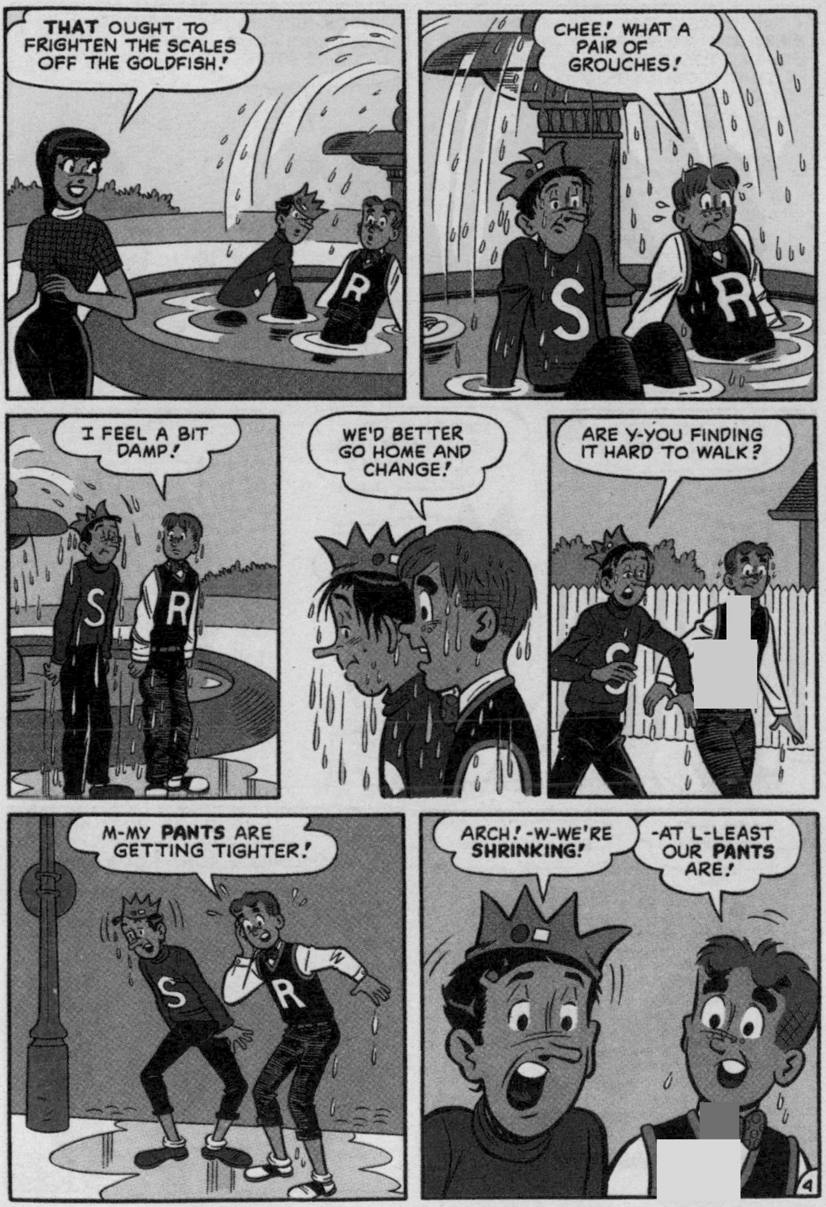
THAT OUGHT TO FRIGHTEN THE SCALES OFF THE GOLDFISH!
CHEE! WHAT A PAIR OF GROUCHES!
I FEEL A BIT DAMP!
WE'D BETTER GO HOME AND CHANGE!
ARE Y-YOU FINDING IT HARD TO WALK?
M-MY PANTS ARE GETTING TIGHTER!
ARCH! -W-WE'RE SHRINKING!
-AT L-LEAST OUR PANTS ARE!
4

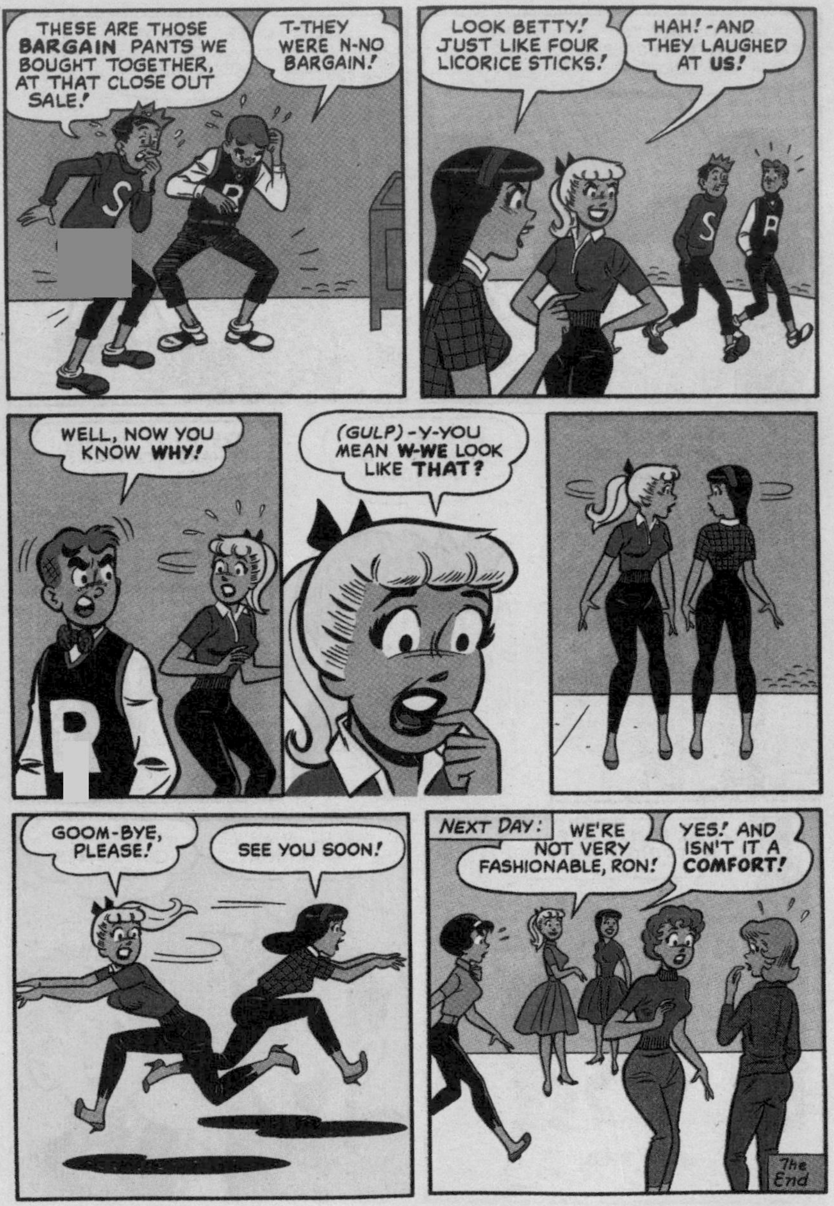
THESE ARE THOSE BARGAIN PANTS WE BOUGHT TOGETHER, AT THAT CLOSE OUT SALE!
T-THEY WERE N-NO BARGAIN!
LOOK BETTY! JUST LIKE FOUR LICORICE STICKS!
HAH! -AND THEY LAUGHED AT US!
WELL, NOW YOU KNOW WHY!
(GULP) -Y-YOU MEAN W-WE LOOK LIKE THAT?
GOOM-BYE, PLEASE!
SEE YOU SOON!
NEXT DAY:
WE'RE NOT VERY FASHIONABLE, RON!
YES! AND ISN'T IT A COMFORT!
The End

Clothes Make the Man
Jughead #82, 1962
by Samm Schwartz

Schwartz might be best known for his work on Jughead and the boys, but I love the way he drew Betty and Veronica. While he presented the guys as lanky, angular, wildly gesticulating figures with arms and legs everywhere, I think he tended to treat the girls with more restraint. They were poised, sometimes even prim, and their deadpan deliveries of punchlines were killer. Sometimes their facial expressions as they reacted to the guys' antics were funnier than the jokes themselves.

Betty & Veronica digests are a treasure trove of great cartoonists, and to this day they're teaching me to be a better artist!

--Fiona Staples
Award-winning Artist,
Saga

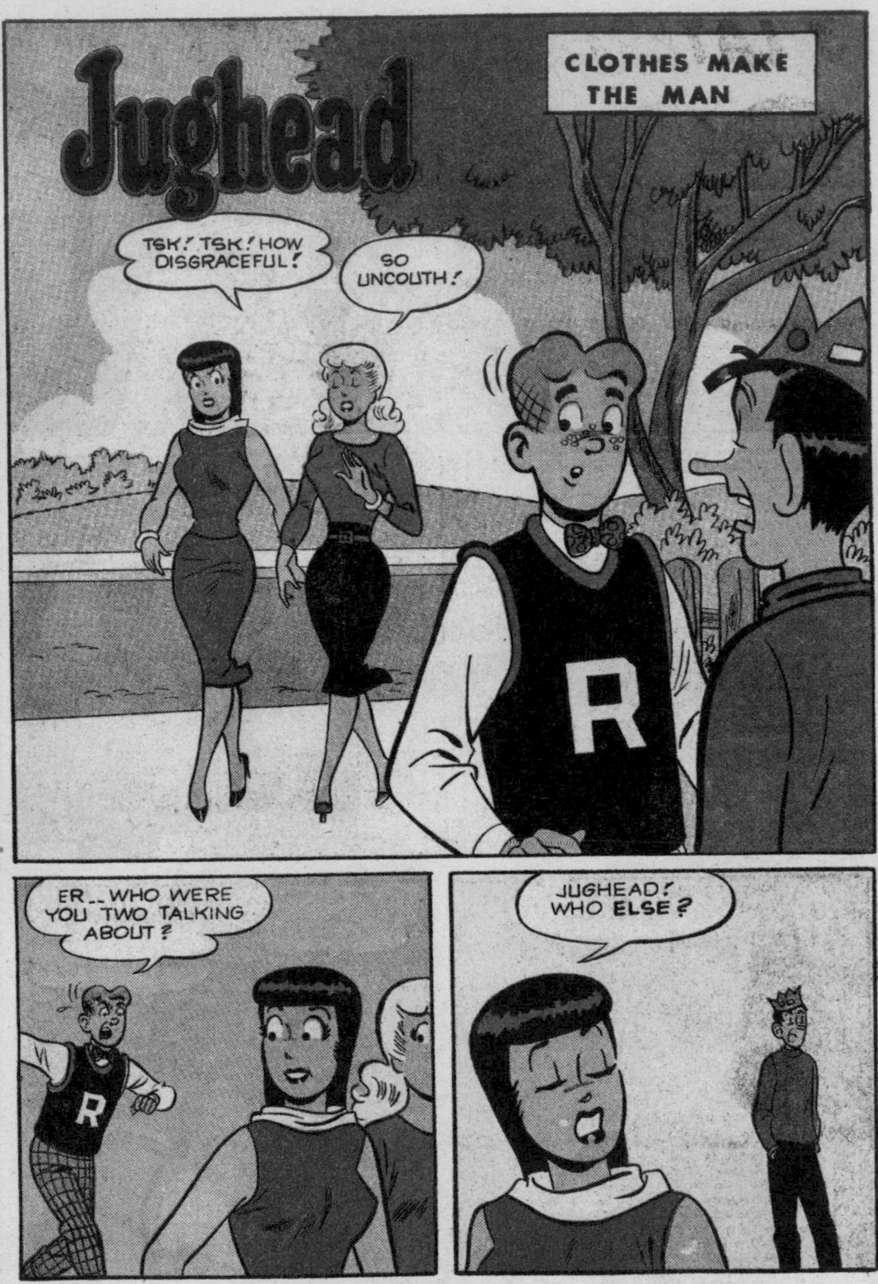
Jughead
CLOTHES MAKE THE MAN
TSK! TSK! HOW DISGRACEFUL!
SO UNCOUTH!
ER -- WHO WERE YOU TWO TALKING ABOUT?
JUGHEAD! WHO ELSE?

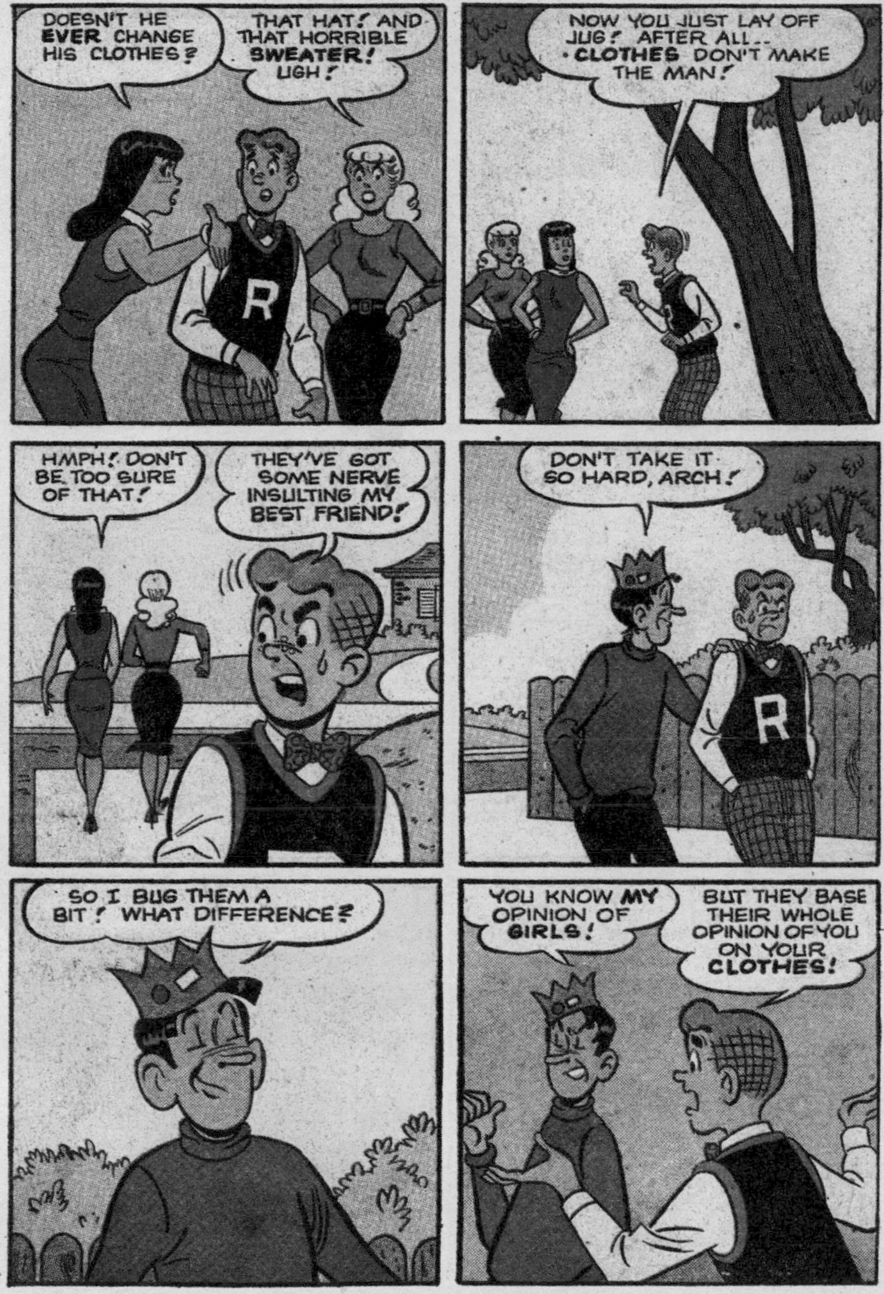
DOESN'T HE EVER CHANGE HIS CLOTHES?
THAT HAT! AND THAT HORRIBLE SWEATER! UGH!
NOW YOU JUST LAY OFF JUG! AFTER ALL... CLOTHES DON'T MAKE THE MAN!
HMPH! DON'T BE TOO SURE OF THAT!
THEY'VE GOT SOME NERVE INSULTING MY BEST FRIEND!
DON'T TAKE IT SO HARD, ARCH!
SO I BUG THEM A BIT! WHAT DIFFERENCE?
YOU KNOW MY OPINION OF GIRLS!
BUT THEY BASE THEIR WHOLE OPINION OF YOU ON YOUR CLOTHES!

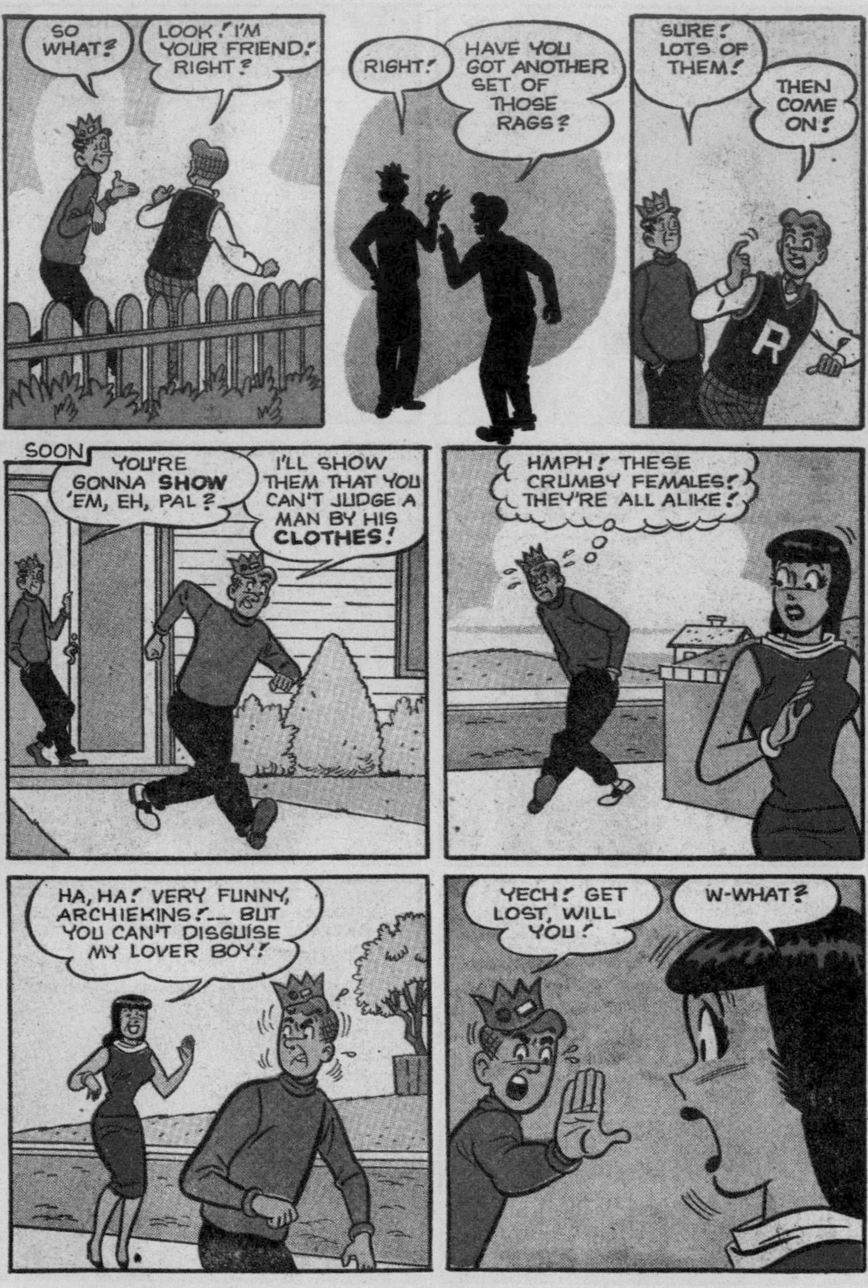
SO WHAT?
LOOK! I'M YOUR FRIEND! RIGHT?
RIGHT!
HAVE YOU GOT ANOTHER SET OF THOSE RAGS?
SURE! LOTS OF THEM!
THEN COME ON!
SOON
YOU'RE GONNA SHOW 'EM, EH, PAL?
I'LL SHOW THEM THAT YOU CAN'T JUDGE A MAN BY HIS CLOTHES!
HMPH! THESE CRUMBY FEMALES! THEY'RE ALL ALIKE!
HA, HA! VERY FUNNY, ARCHIEKINS!... BUT YOU CAN'T DISGUISE MY LOVER BOY!
YECH! GET LOST, WILL YOU!
W-WHAT?

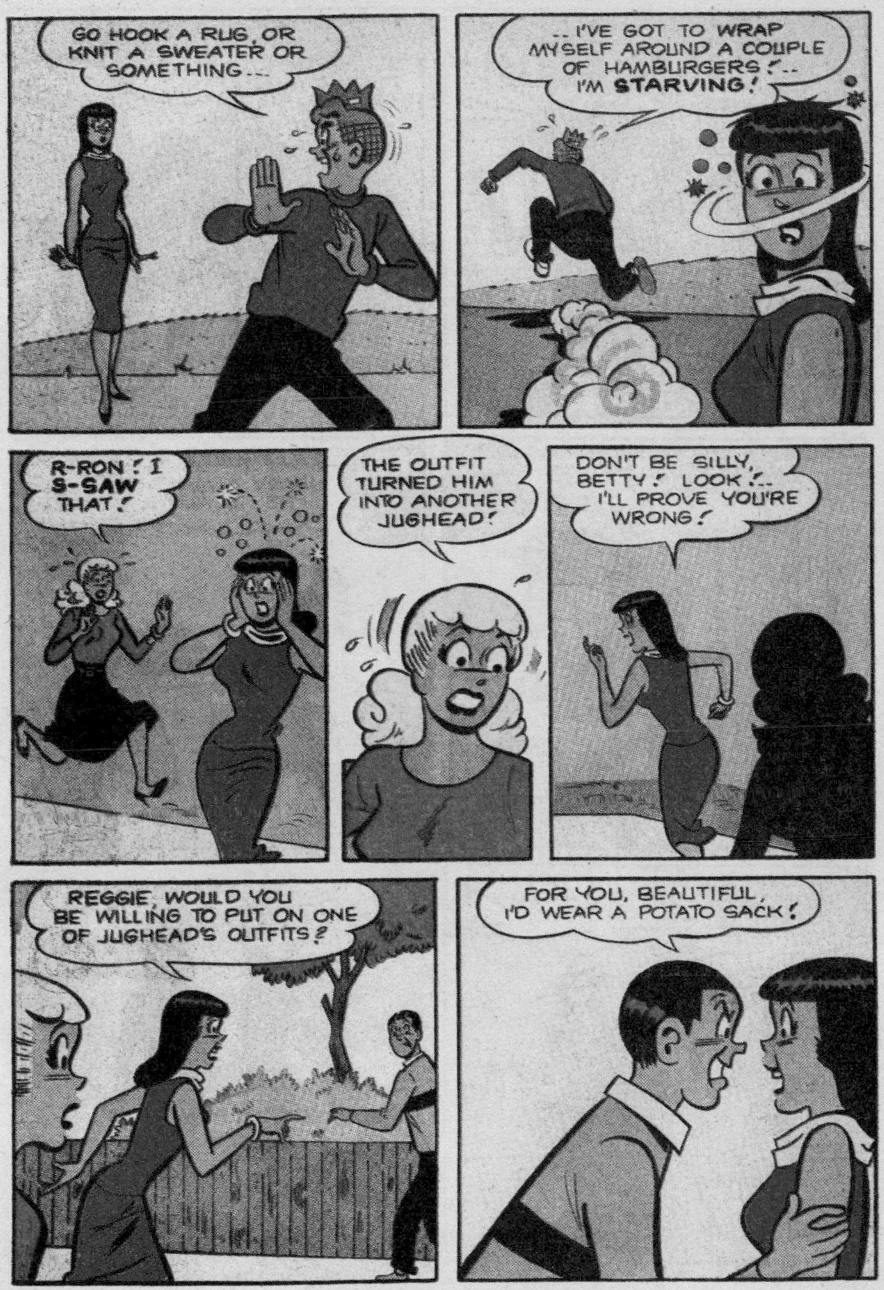
GO HOOK A RUG, OR KNIT A SWEATER OR SOMETHING...
..I'VE GOT TO WRAP MYSELF AROUND A COUPLE OF HAMBURGERS!.. I'M STARVING!
R-RON! I S-SAW THAT!
THE OUTFIT TURNED HIM INTO ANOTHER JUGHEAD!
DON'T BE SILLY, BETTY! LOOK!.. I'LL PROVE YOU'RE WRONG!
REGGIE, WOULD YOU BE WILLING TO PUT ON ONE OF JUGHEAD'S OUTFITS?
FOR YOU, BEAUTIFUL, I'D WEAR A POTATO SACK!

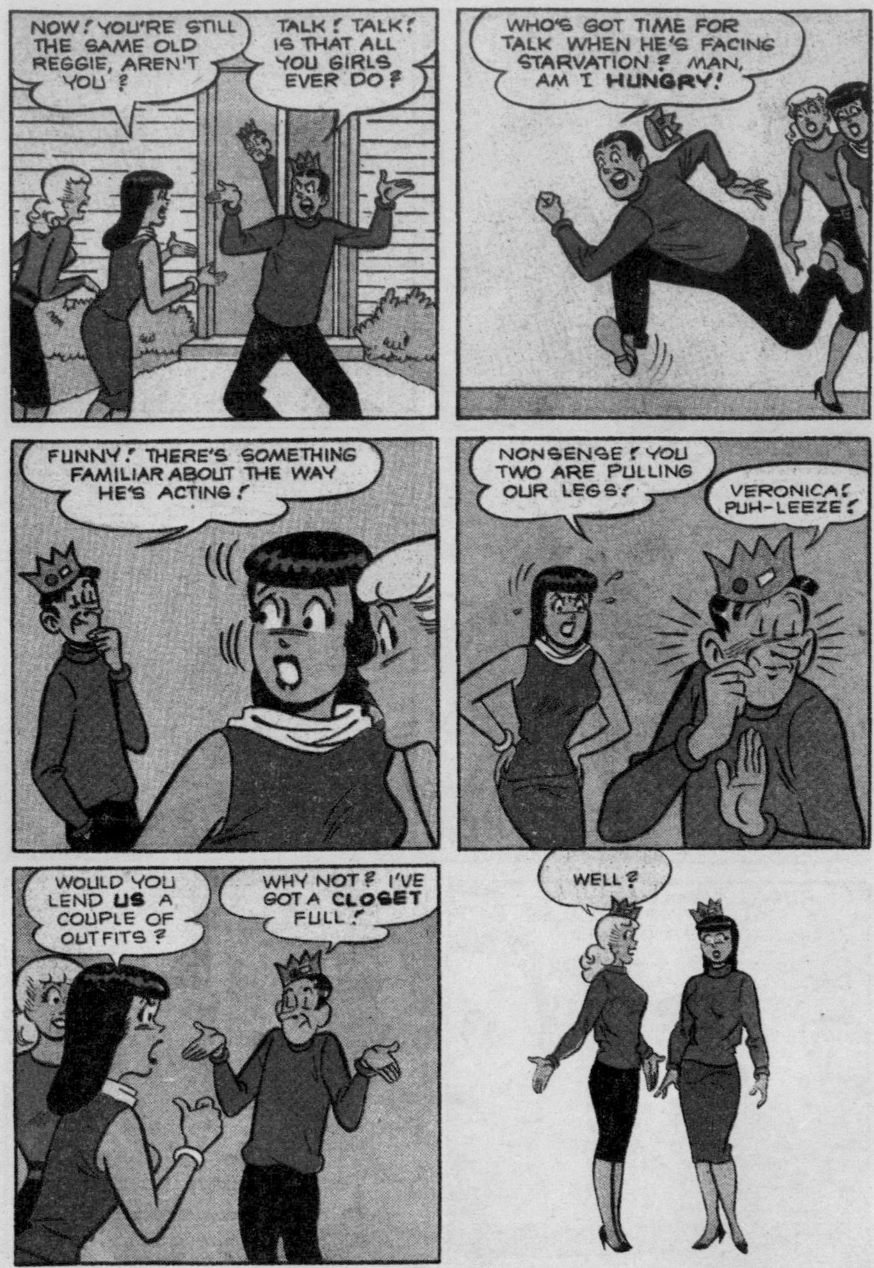
NOW! YOU'RE STILL THE SAME OLD REGGIE, AREN'T YOU?
TALK! TALK! IS THAT ALL YOU GIRLS EVER DO?
WHO'S GOT TIME FOR TALK WHEN HE'S FACING STARVATION? MAN, AM I HUNGRY!
FUNNY! THERE'S SOMETHING FAMILIAR ABOUT THE WAY HE'S ACTING!
NONSENSE! YOU TWO ARE PULLING OUR LEGS!
VERONICA! PUH-LEEZE!
WOULD YOU LEND US A COUPLE OF OUTFITS?
WHY NOT? I'VE GOT A CLOSET FULL!
WELL?

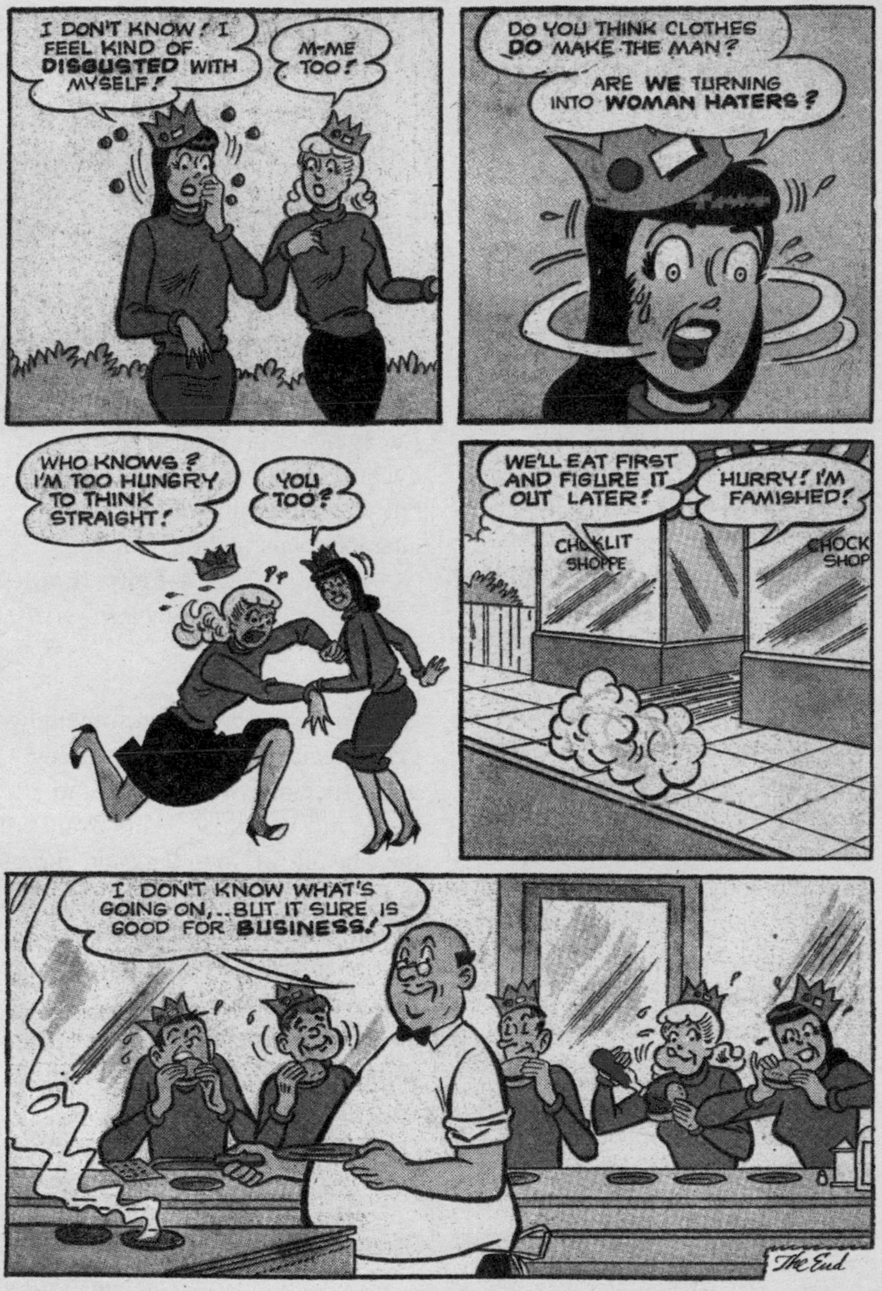
I DON'T KNOW! I FEEL KIND OF DISGUSTED WITH MYSELF!
M-ME TOO!
DO YOU THINK CLOTHES DO MAKE THE MAN?
ARE WE TURNING INTO WOMAN HATERS?
WHO KNOWS? I'M TOO HUNGRY TO THINK STRAIGHT!
YOU TOO?
WE'LL EAT FIRST AND FIGURE IT OUT LATER!
HURRY! I'M FAMISHED!
CHOCKLIT SHOPPE
I DON'T KNOW WHAT'S GOING ON,..BUT IT SURE IS GOOD FOR BUSINESS!
The End

Guess Again
Laugh #142, 1963
by Frank Doyle, Harry Lucey, Terry Szenics

"Guess again" features Archie and Reggie trying to get an impartial person to choose which of them will take Veronica to their dance, and to me it spotlights some of my favorite drawings of Betty and Veronica. I think it's the combo of fashion and hairstyles and drawing and storytelling as well as the simple and fun stories that still hold up today.

-- **Jill Thompson**
Award-winning Artist,
Scary Godmother

The 1960s was a great time for the Archie company and its fans. The artists and writers who helped build these titles had matured into the styles that would define them. DeCarlo could draw girls. Schwartz could do zany Jughead material, and Bolling handled all those great Little Archie stories. But it was Harry Lucey who could handle everything from great looking girls to physical comedy to pantomime silliness better than the rest. Did we mention he drew great looking girls? Enjoy!

-- **Pat & Tim Kennedy**
Artists, Archie Comics

The Kisser Strikes /
Strike One Kisser
Archie #143, 1964
by Frank Doyle, Harry Lucey, Terry Szenics

Lucey's Betty and Veronica could be graceful and delicate when they were flirting and formidable when they were angry. Not to mention all those subtler emotions in between! They were perfectly conveyed. Lucey never drew a hand or an eyebrow or an ankle that didn't tell you something about what a character was feeling.

--**Fiona Staples**
Award-winning Artist,
Saga

There has always been something very special about a Harry Lucey girl, especially when it came to Betty and Veronica. Aside from their beautiful, long legs and curves designed for caressing, his girls had a unique quality all their own. His Veronica seemed more determined, strong-willed and sarcastic, while his Betty seemed more naïve, compassionate and sweet. He drew both girls with these "knowing" expressions that made it very clear that they were always in charge.

-- **Tom DeFalco**
Legendary comic book
writer and editor

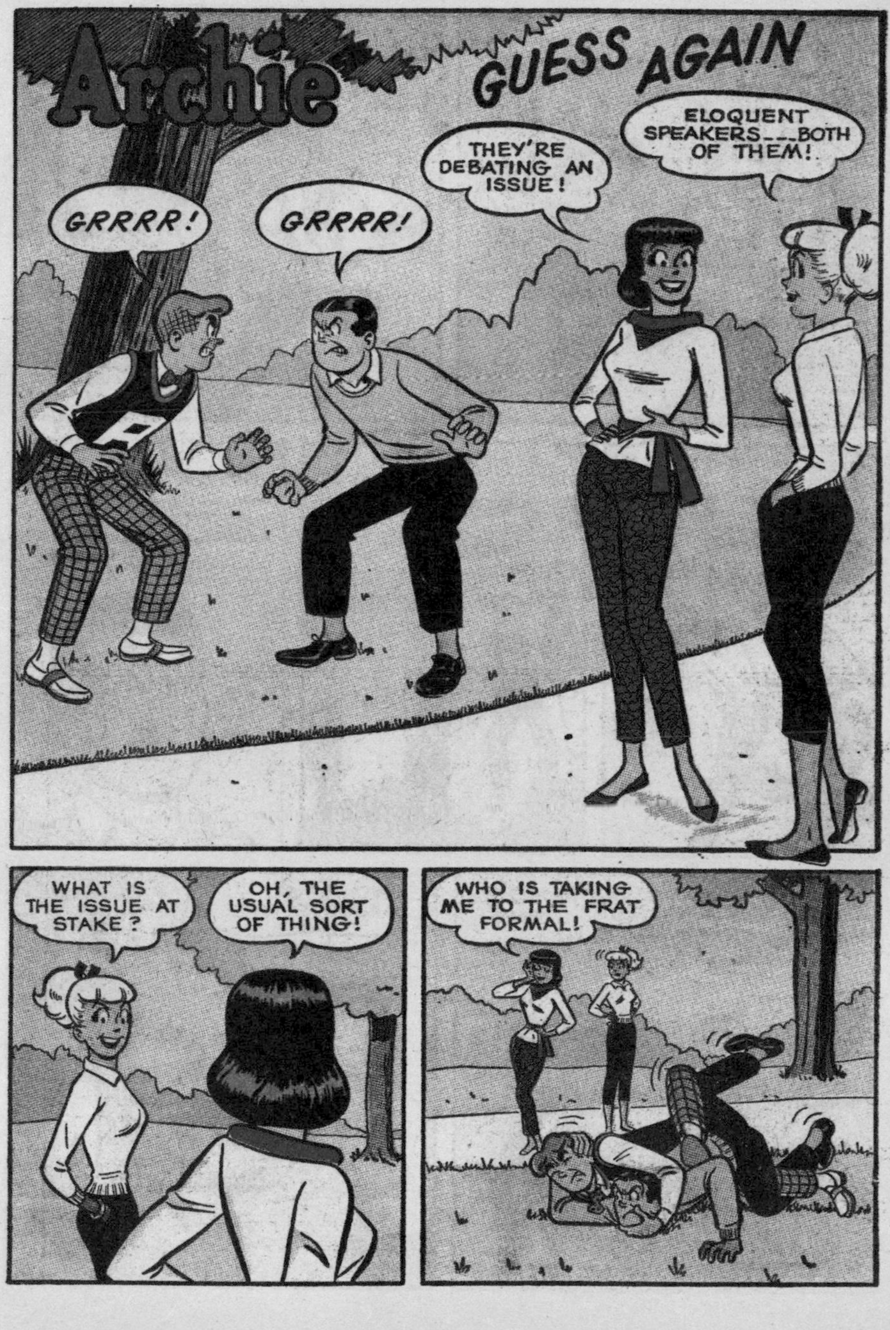
Archie
GUESS AGAIN
GRRRR!
GRRRR!
THEY'RE DEBATING AN ISSUE!
ELOQUENT SPEAKERS---BOTH OF THEM!
WHAT IS THE ISSUE AT STAKE?
OH, THE USUAL SORT OF THING!
WHO IS TAKING ME TO THE FRAT FORMAL!

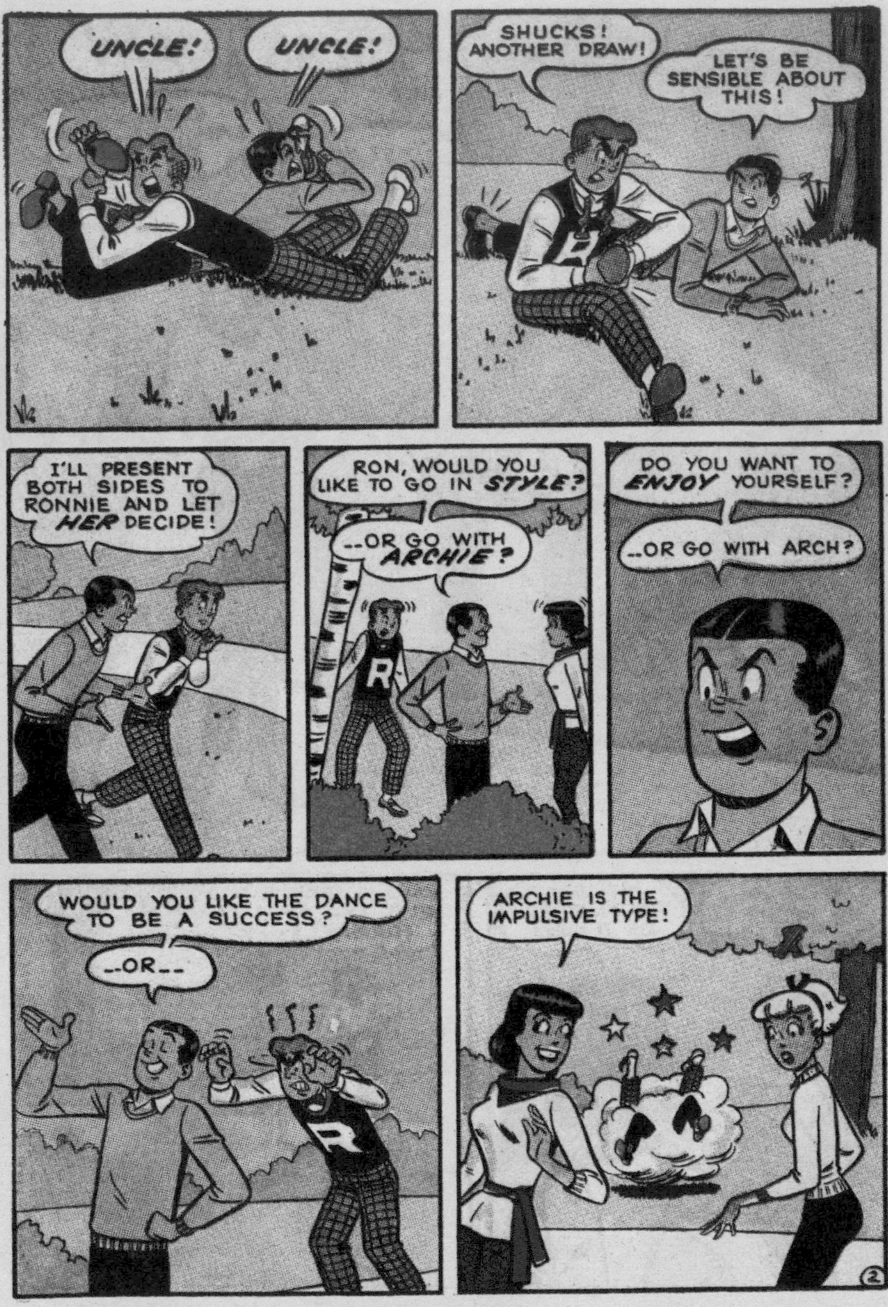
UNCLE!
UNCLE!
SHUCKS! ANOTHER DRAW!
LET'S BE SENSIBLE ABOUT THIS!
I'LL PRESENT BOTH SIDES TO RONNIE AND LET HER DECIDE!
RON, WOULD YOU LIKE TO GO IN STYLE?
--OR GO WITH ARCHIE?
DO YOU WANT TO ENJOY YOURSELF?
--OR GO WITH ARCH?
WOULD YOU LIKE THE DANCE TO BE A SUCCESS?
--OR--
ARCHIE IS THE IMPULSIVE TYPE!
2

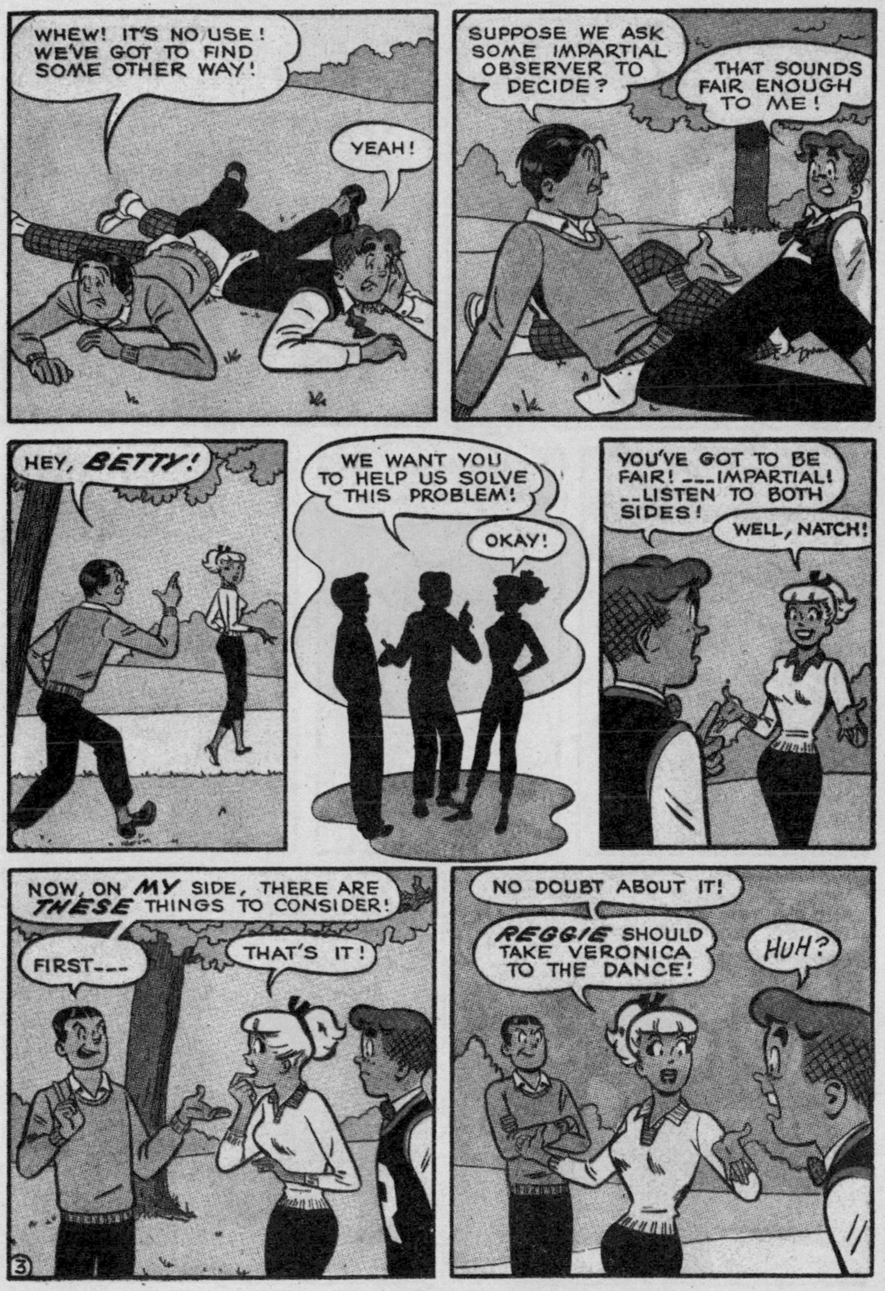
WHEW! IT'S NO USE! WE'VE GOT TO FIND SOME OTHER WAY!
YEAH!
SUPPOSE WE ASK SOME IMPARTIAL OBSERVER TO DECIDE?
THAT SOUNDS FAIR ENOUGH TO ME!
HEY, BETTY!
WE WANT YOU TO HELP US SOLVE THIS PROBLEM!
OKAY!
YOU'VE GOT TO BE FAIR! ---IMPARTIAL! --LISTEN TO BOTH SIDES!
WELL, NATCH!
NOW, ON MY SIDE, THERE ARE THESE THINGS TO CONSIDER!
FIRST---
THAT'S IT!
NO DOUBT ABOUT IT!
REGGIE SHOULD TAKE VERONICA TO THE DANCE!
HUH?
3

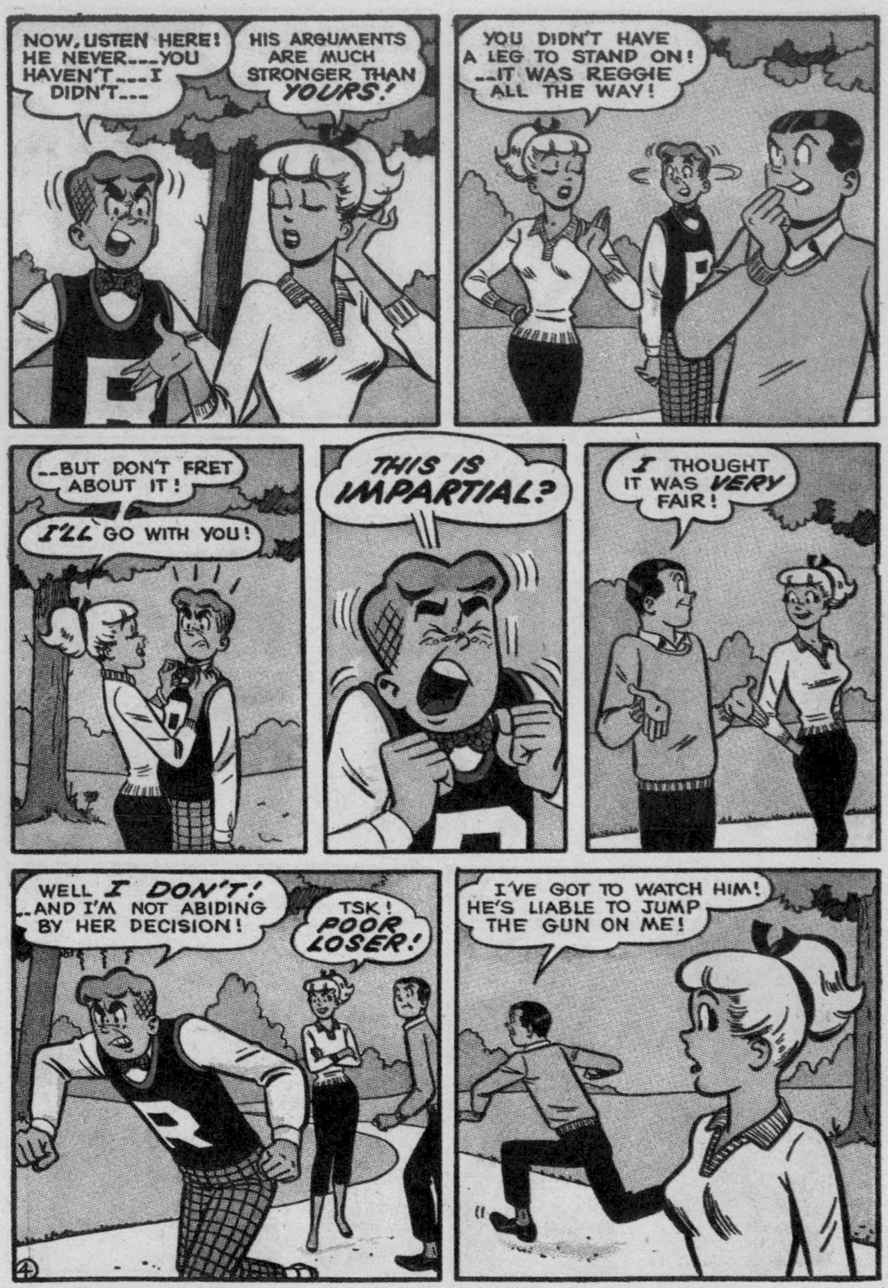
NOW, LISTEN HERE! HE NEVER---YOU HAVEN'T---I DIDN'T---
HIS ARGUMENTS ARE MUCH STRONGER THAN YOURS!
YOU DIDN'T HAVE A LEG TO STAND ON! --IT WAS REGGIE ALL THE WAY!
--BUT DON'T FRET ABOUT IT!
I'LL GO WITH YOU!
THIS IS IMPARTIAL?
I THOUGHT IT WAS VERY FAIR!
WELL I DON'T! ..AND I'M NOT ABIDING BY HER DECISION!
TSK! POOR LOSER!
I'VE GOT TO WATCH HIM! HE'S LIABLE TO JUMP THE GUN ON ME!
4

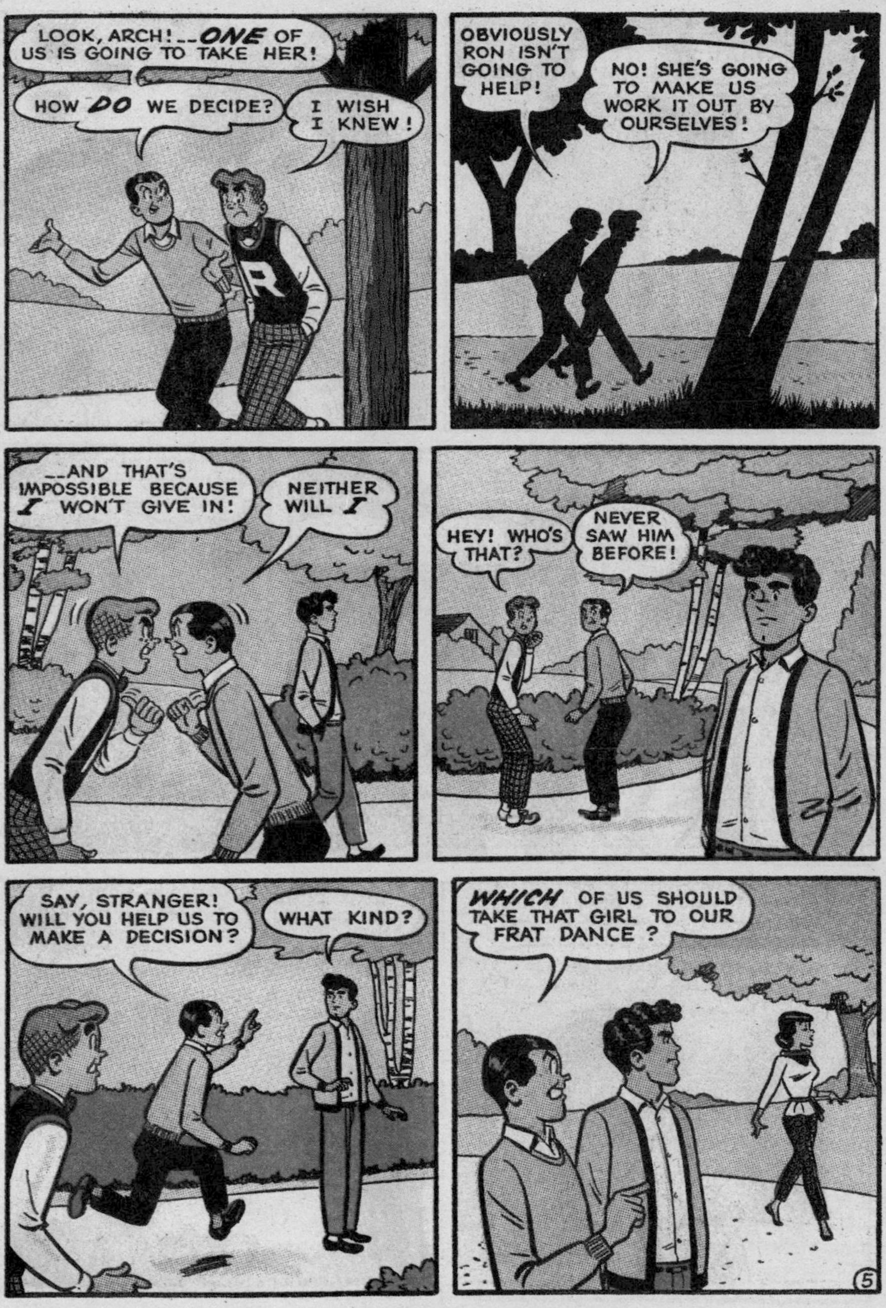
LOOK, ARCH! --ONE OF US IS GOING TO TAKE HER!
HOW DO WE DECIDE?
I WISH I KNEW!
OBVIOUSLY RON ISN'T GOING TO HELP!
NO! SHE'S GOING TO MAKE US WORK IT OUT BY OURSELVES!
--AND THAT'S IMPOSSIBLE BECAUSE I WON'T GIVE IN!
NEITHER WILL I
HEY! WHO'S THAT?
NEVER SAW HIM BEFORE!
SAY, STRANGER! WILL YOU HELP US TO MAKE A DECISION?
WHAT KIND?
WHICH OF US SHOULD TAKE THAT GIRL TO OUR FRAT DANCE?
5

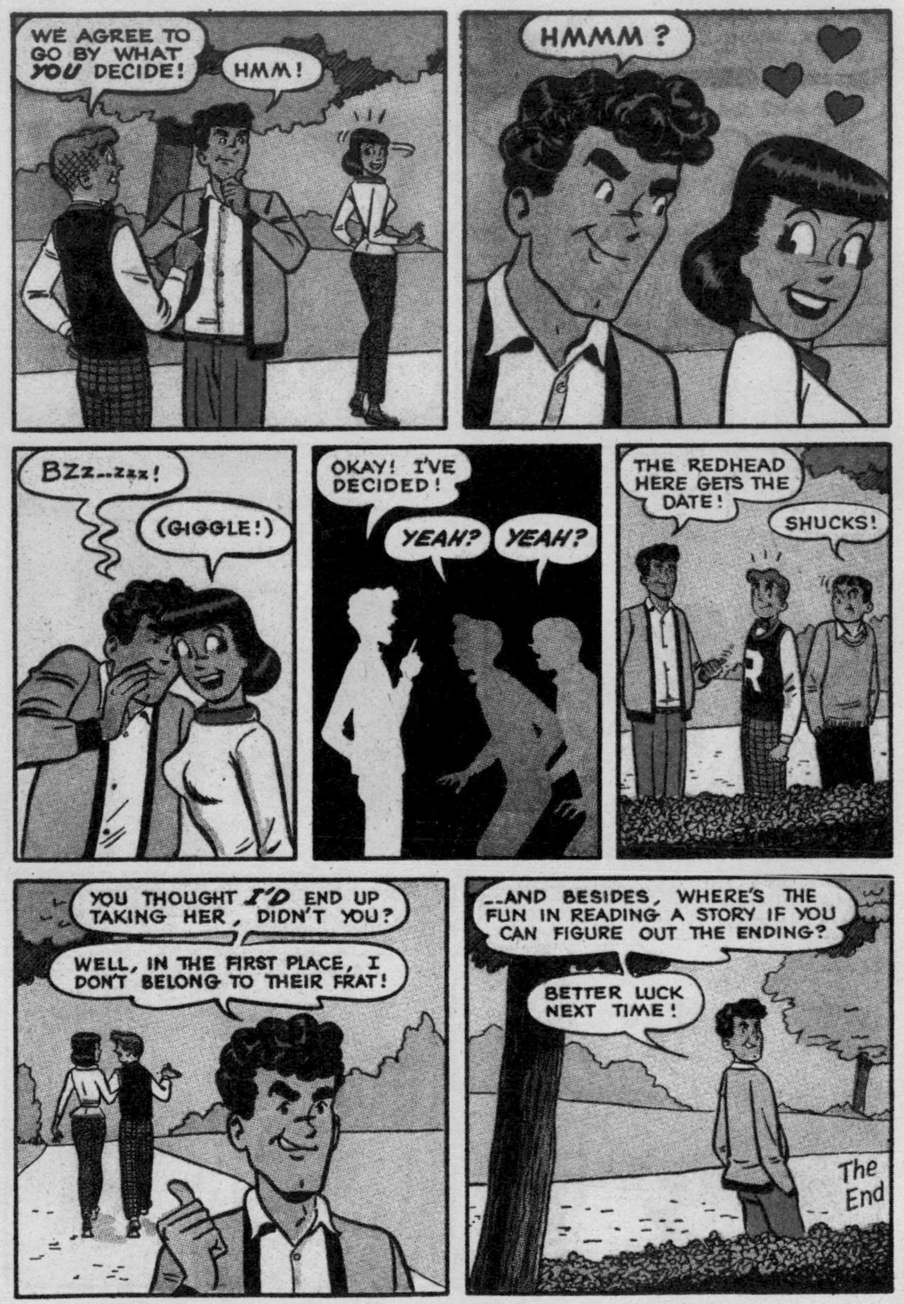
WE AGREE TO GO BY WHAT YOU DECIDE!
HMM!
HMMM ?
BZz--zzz!
(GIGGLE!)
OKAY! I'VE DECIDED!
YEAH?
YEAH?
THE REDHEAD HERE GETS THE DATE!
SHUCKS!
YOU THOUGHT I'D END UP TAKING HER, DIDN'T YOU?
WELL, IN THE FIRST PLACE, I DON'T BELONG TO THEIR FRAT!
--AND BESIDES, WHERE'S THE FUN IN READING A STORY IF YOU CAN FIGURE OUT THE ENDING?
BETTER LUCK NEXT TIME!
The End

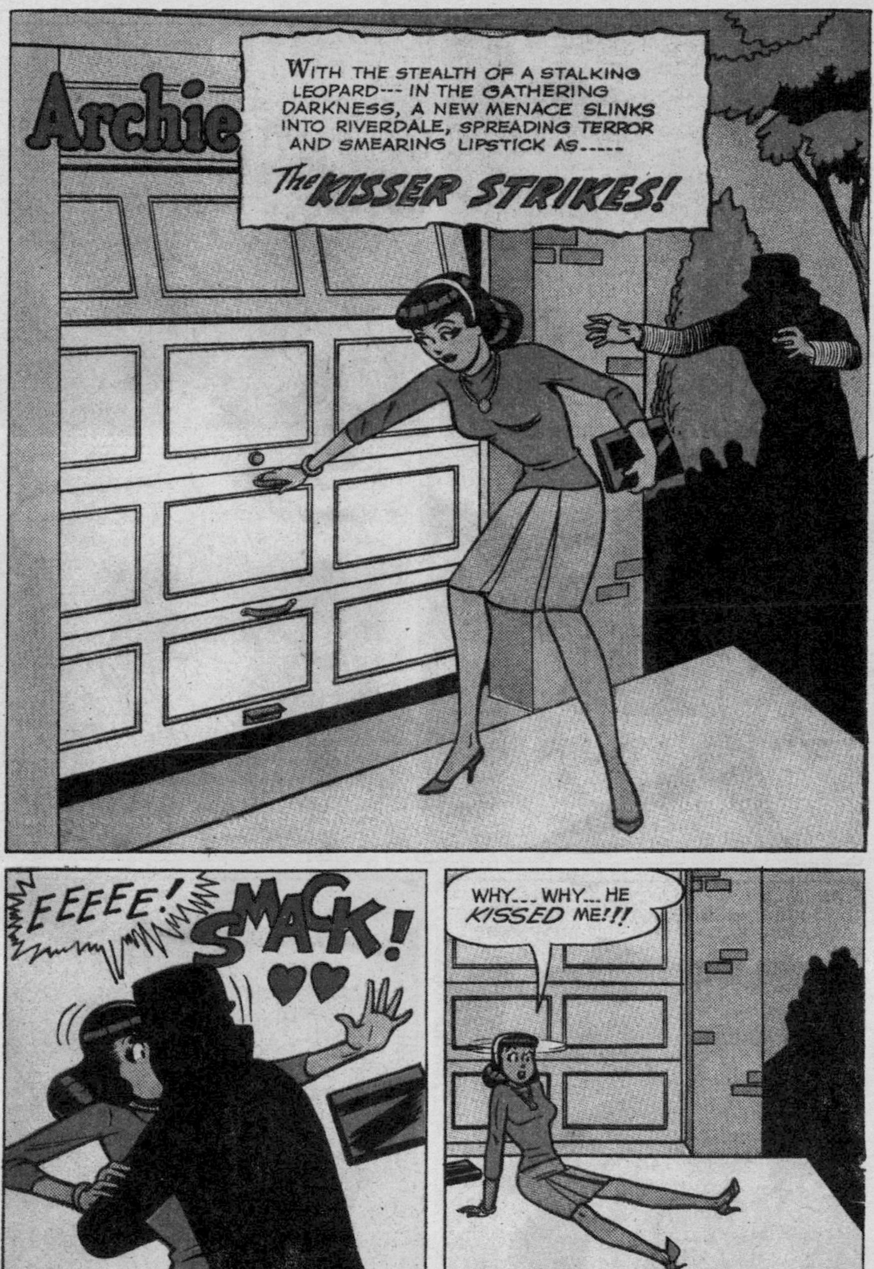
Archie
WITH THE STEALTH OF A STALKING LEOPARD--- IN THE GATHERING DARKNESS, A NEW MENACE SLINKS INTO RIVERDALE, SPREADING TERROR AND SMEARING LIPSTICK AS-----
The KISSER STRIKES!
EEEEE!
SMACK!
WHY--- WHY--- HE KISSED ME!!!

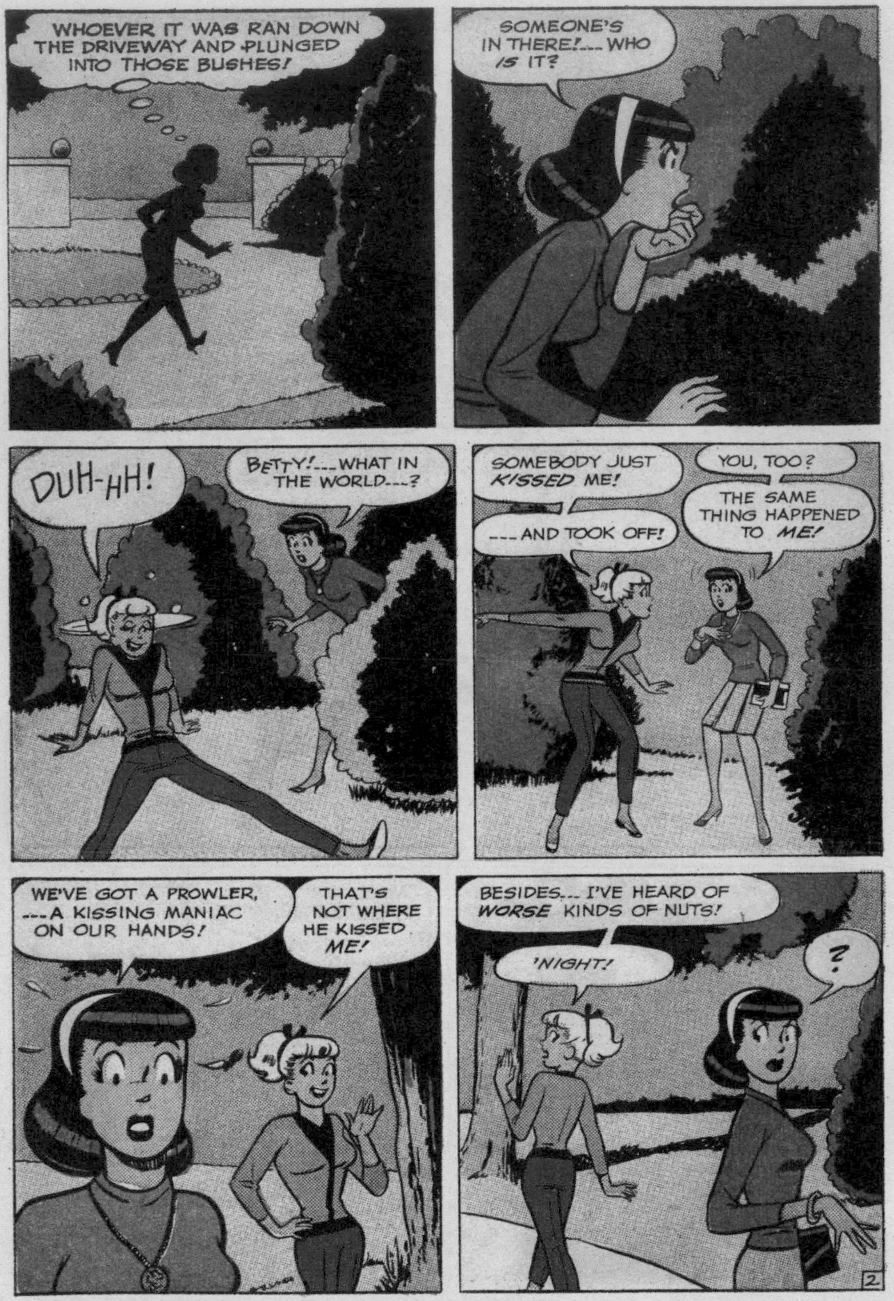
WHOEVER IT WAS RAN DOWN THE DRIVEWAY AND PLUNGED INTO THOSE BUSHES!
SOMEONE'S IN THERE!--- WHO IS IT?
DUH-HH!
BETTY!---WHAT IN THE WORLD---?
SOMEBODY JUST KISSED ME!
---AND TOOK OFF!
YOU, TOO?
THE SAME THING HAPPENED TO ME!
WE'VE GOT A PROWLER, ---A KISSING MANIAC ON OUR HANDS!
THAT'S NOT WHERE HE KISSED ME!
BESIDES... I'VE HEARD OF WORSE KINDS OF NUTS!
'NIGHT!
?
2

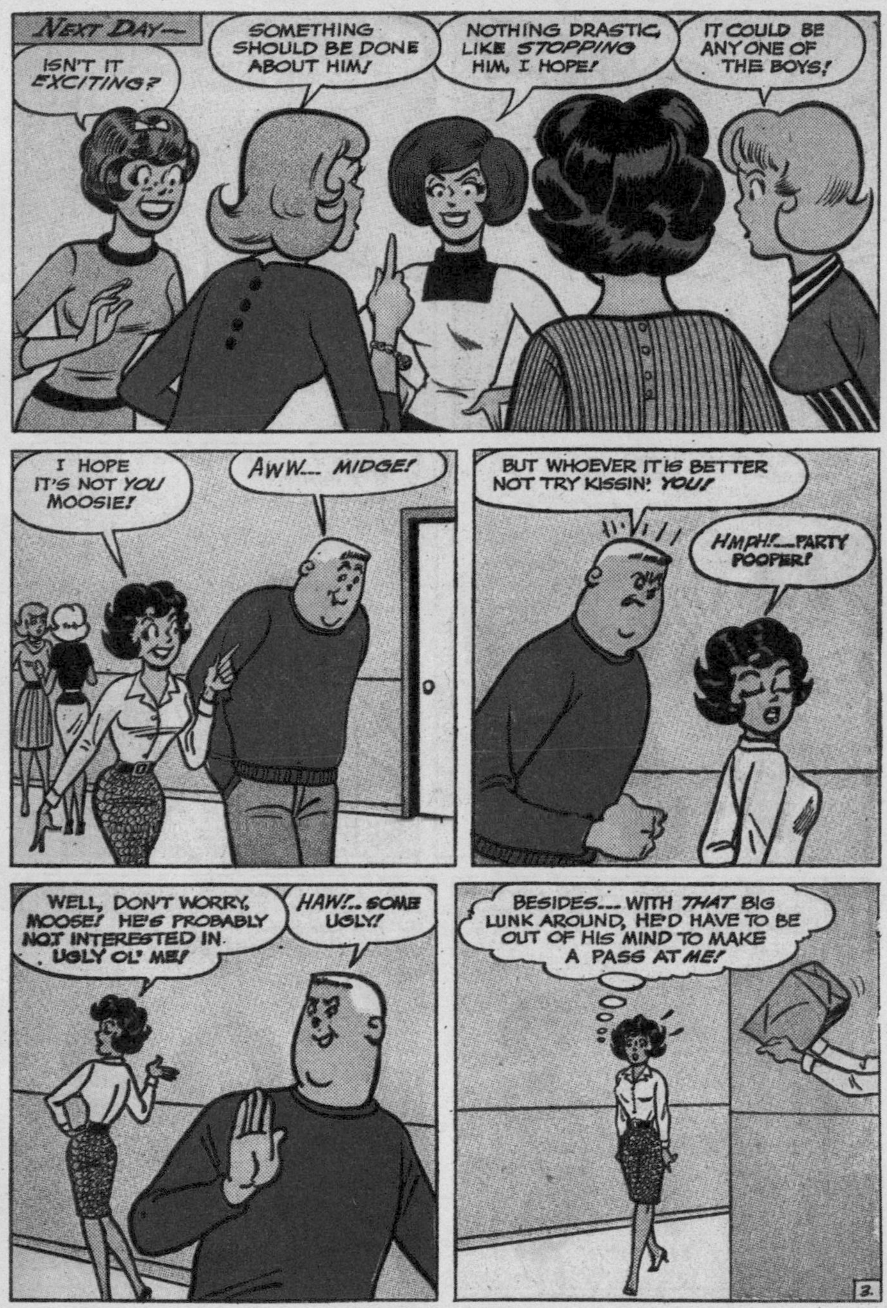
NEXT DAY—
ISN'T IT EXCITING?
SOMETHING SHOULD BE DONE ABOUT HIM!
NOTHING DRASTIC, LIKE STOPPING HIM, I HOPE!
IT COULD BE ANY ONE OF THE BOYS!
I HOPE IT'S NOT YOU MOOSIE!
AWW.... MIDGE!
BUT WHOEVER IT IS BETTER NOT TRY KISSIN' YOU!
HMPH!....PARTY POOPER!
WELL, DON'T WORRY, MOOSE! HE'S PROBABLY NOT INTERESTED IN UGLY OL' ME!
HAW!.. SOME UGLY!
BESIDES.... WITH THAT BIG LUNK AROUND, HE'D HAVE TO BE OUT OF HIS MIND TO MAKE A PASS AT ME!
3.

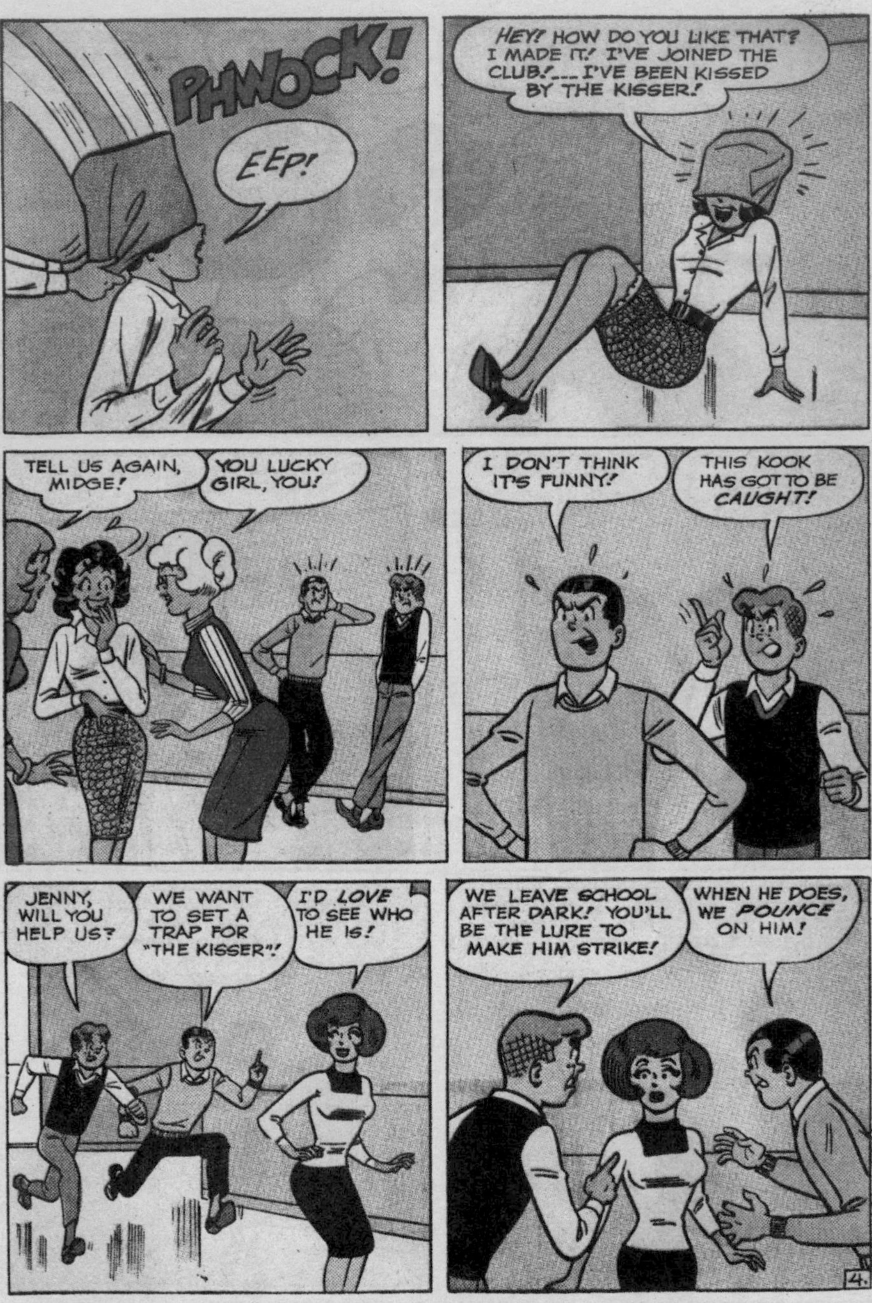
PHWOCK!
EEP!
HEY! HOW DO YOU LIKE THAT? I MADE IT! I'VE JOINED THE CLUB!... I'VE BEEN KISSED BY THE KISSER!
TELL US AGAIN, MIDGE!
YOU LUCKY GIRL, YOU!
I DON'T THINK IT'S FUNNY!
THIS KOOK HAS GOT TO BE CAUGHT!
JENNY, WILL YOU HELP US?
WE WANT TO SET A TRAP FOR "THE KISSER"!
I'D LOVE TO SEE WHO HE IS!
WE LEAVE SCHOOL AFTER DARK! YOU'LL BE THE LURE TO MAKE HIM STRIKE!
WHEN HE DOES, WE POUNCE ON HIM!
4.

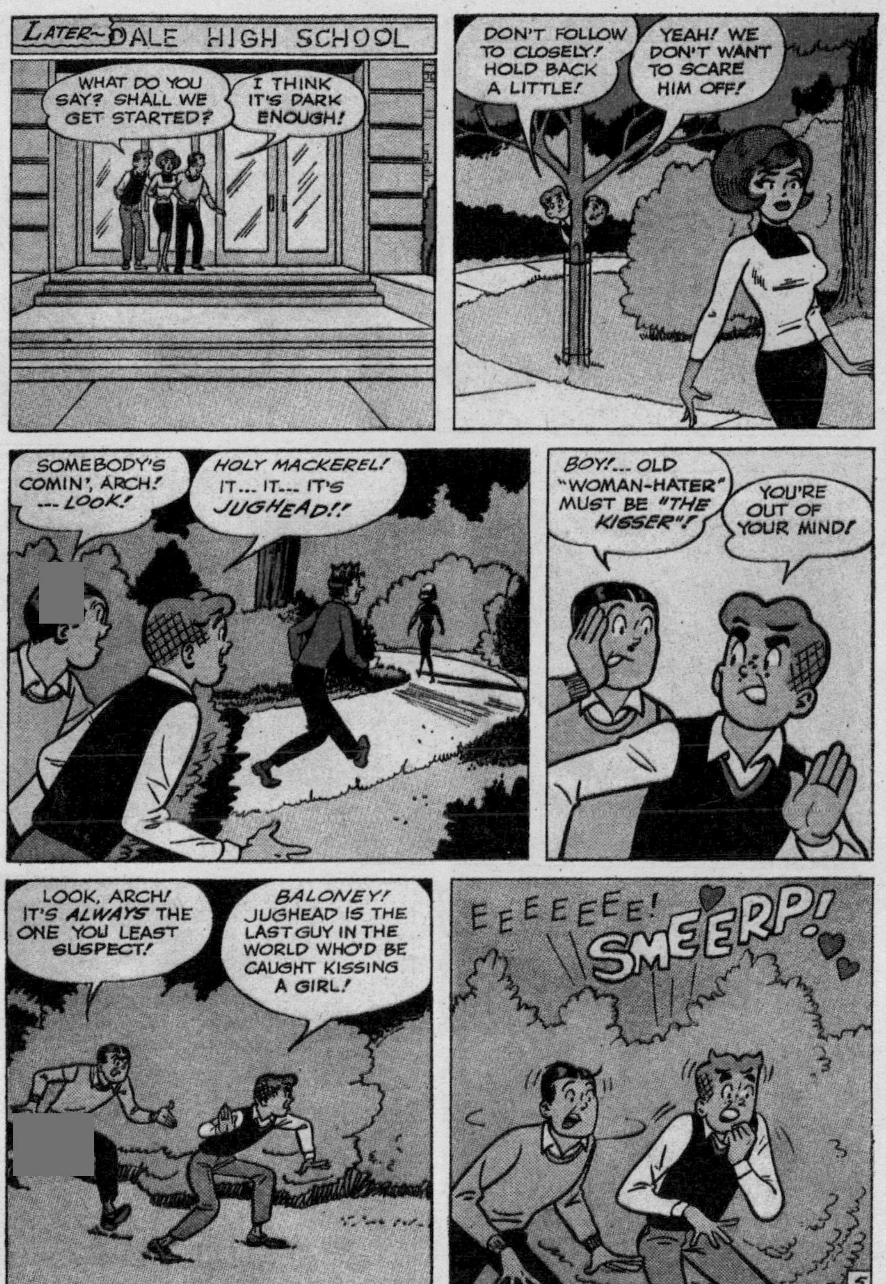
LATER~ DALE HIGH SCHOOL
WHAT DO YOU SAY? SHALL WE GET STARTED?
I THINK IT'S DARK ENOUGH!
DON'T FOLLOW TO CLOSELY! HOLD BACK A LITTLE!
YEAH! WE DON'T WANT TO SCARE HIM OFF!
SOMEBODY'S COMIN', ARCH! --- LOOK!
HOLY MACKEREL! IT... IT... IT'S JUGHEAD!!
BOY!... OLD "WOMAN-HATER" MUST BE "THE KISSER"!
YOU'RE OUT OF YOUR MIND!
LOOK, ARCH! IT'S ALWAYS THE ONE YOU LEAST SUSPECT!
BALONEY! JUGHEAD IS THE LAST GUY IN THE WORLD WHO'D BE CAUGHT KISSING A GIRL!
EEEEEEEE!
SMEERP!
5

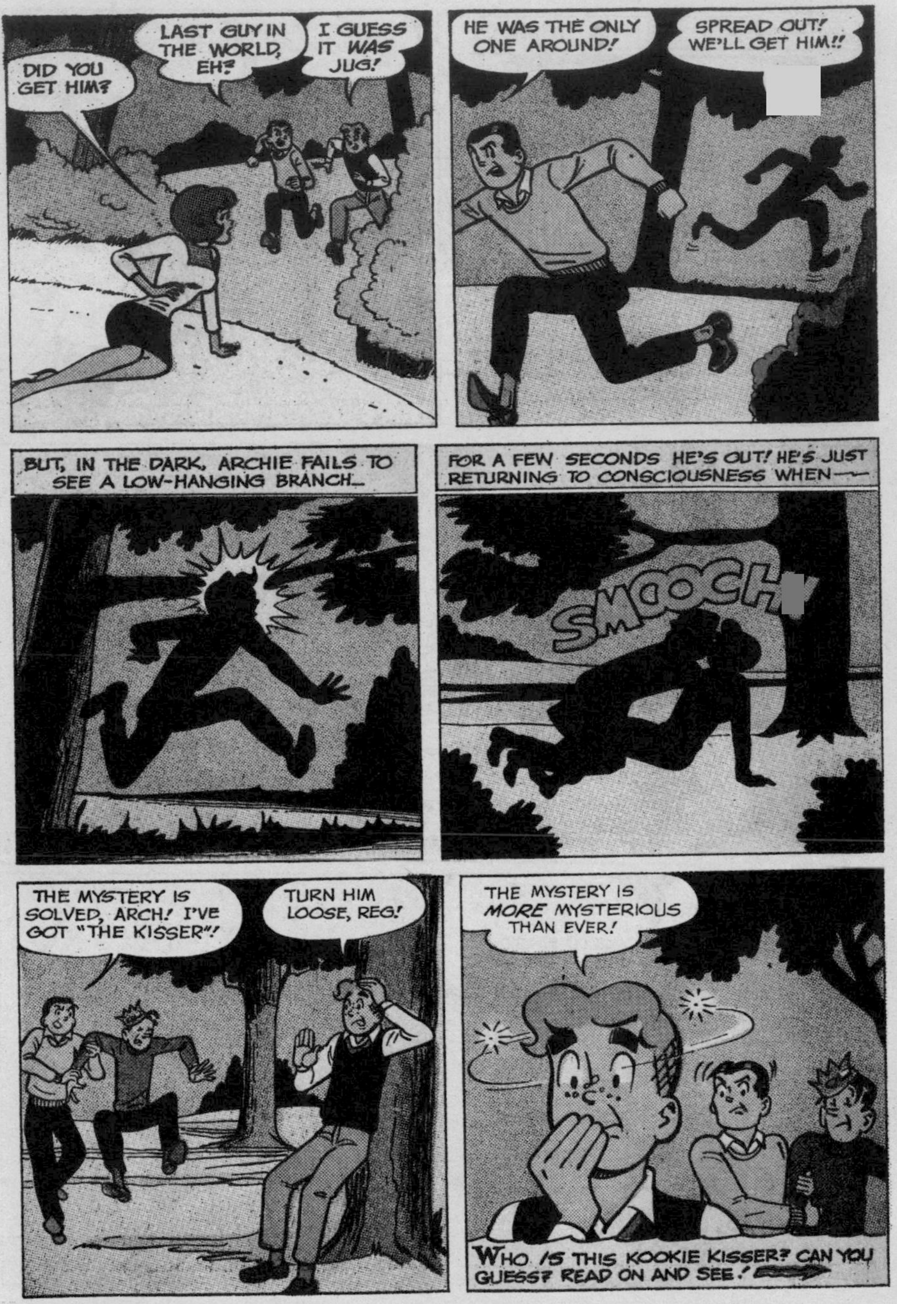
DID YOU GET HIM?
LAST GUY IN THE WORLD, EH?
I GUESS IT *WAS* JUG!
HE WAS THE ONLY ONE AROUND!
SPREAD OUT! WE'LL GET HIM!!
BUT, IN THE DARK, ARCHIE FAILS TO SEE A LOW-HANGING BRANCH...
FOR A FEW SECONDS HE'S OUT! HE'S JUST RETURNING TO CONSCIOUSNESS WHEN—
SMOOCH
THE MYSTERY IS SOLVED, ARCH! I'VE GOT "THE KISSER"!
TURN HIM LOOSE, REG!
THE MYSTERY IS *MORE* MYSTERIOUS THAN EVER!
WHO *IS* THIS KOOKIE KISSER? CAN YOU GUESS? READ ON AND SEE!

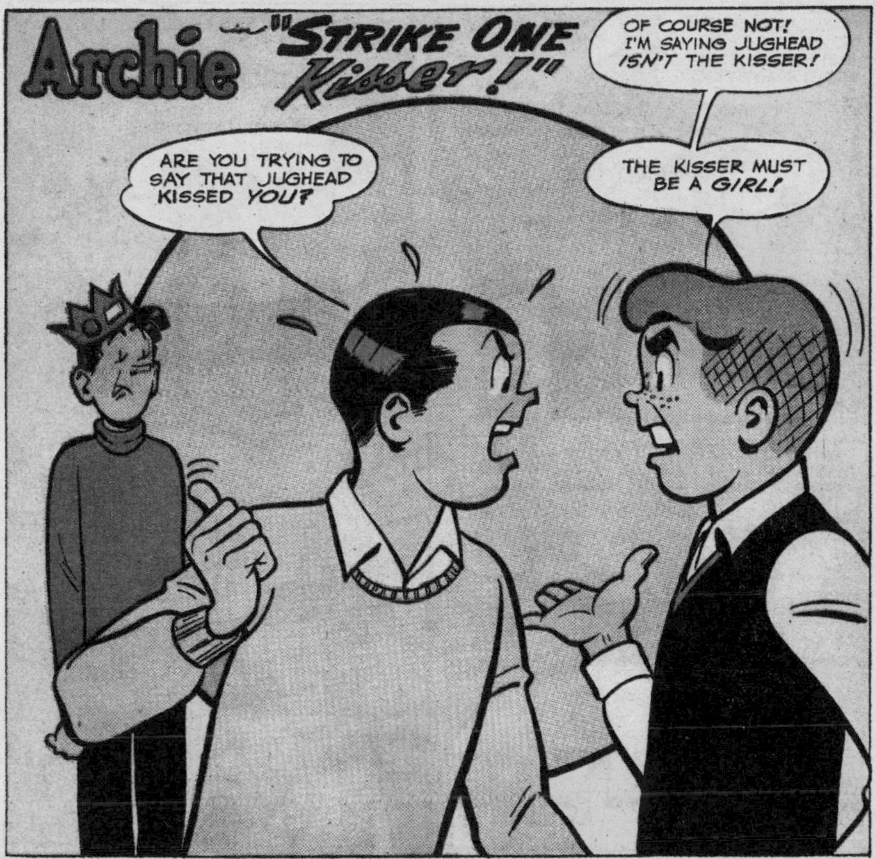
Archie in "STRIKE ONE Kisser!"
ARE YOU TRYING TO SAY THAT JUGHEAD KISSED YOU?
OF COURSE NOT! I'M SAYING JUGHEAD ISN'T THE KISSER!
THE KISSER MUST BE A GIRL!

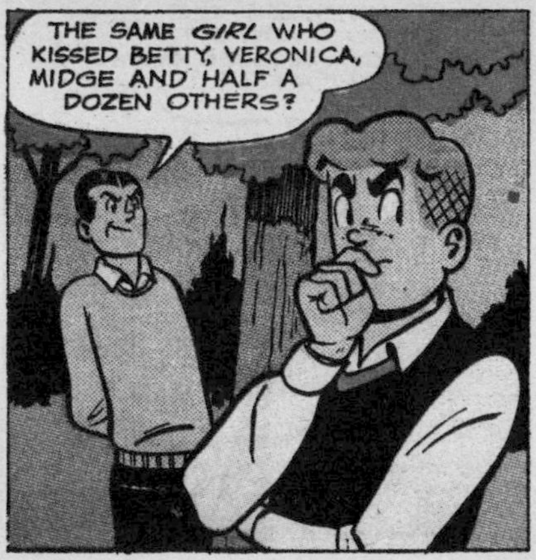
THE SAME GIRL WHO KISSED BETTY, VERONICA, MIDGE AND HALF A DOZEN OTHERS?

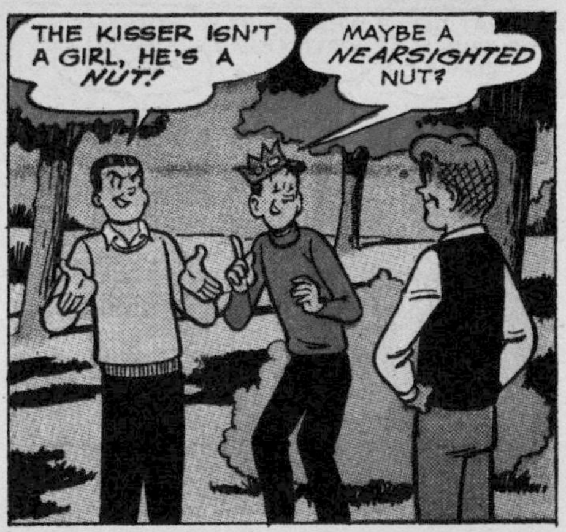
THE KISSER ISN'T A GIRL, HE'S A NUT!
MAYBE A NEARSIGHTED NUT?

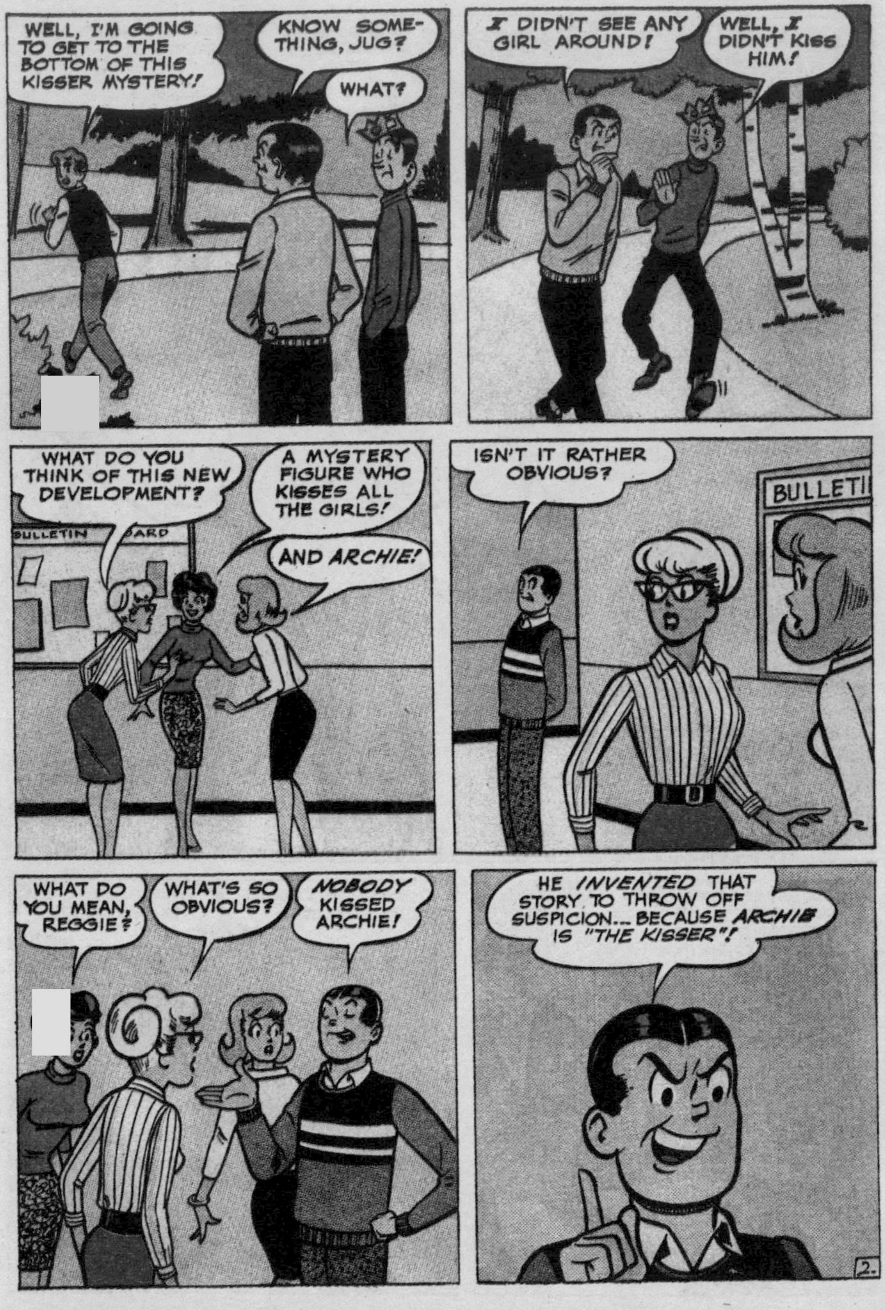
WELL, I'M GOING TO GET TO THE BOTTOM OF THIS KISSER MYSTERY!
KNOW SOMETHING, JUG?
WHAT?
I DIDN'T SEE ANY GIRL AROUND!
WELL, I DIDN'T KISS HIM!
WHAT DO YOU THINK OF THIS NEW DEVELOPMENT?
A MYSTERY FIGURE WHO KISSES ALL THE GIRLS!
AND ARCHIE!
BULLETIN BOARD
ISN'T IT RATHER OBVIOUS?
BULLETI
WHAT DO YOU MEAN, REGGIE?
WHAT'S SO OBVIOUS?
NOBODY KISSED ARCHIE!
HE INVENTED THAT STORY TO THROW OFF SUSPICION... BECAUSE ARCHIE IS "THE KISSER"!
2.

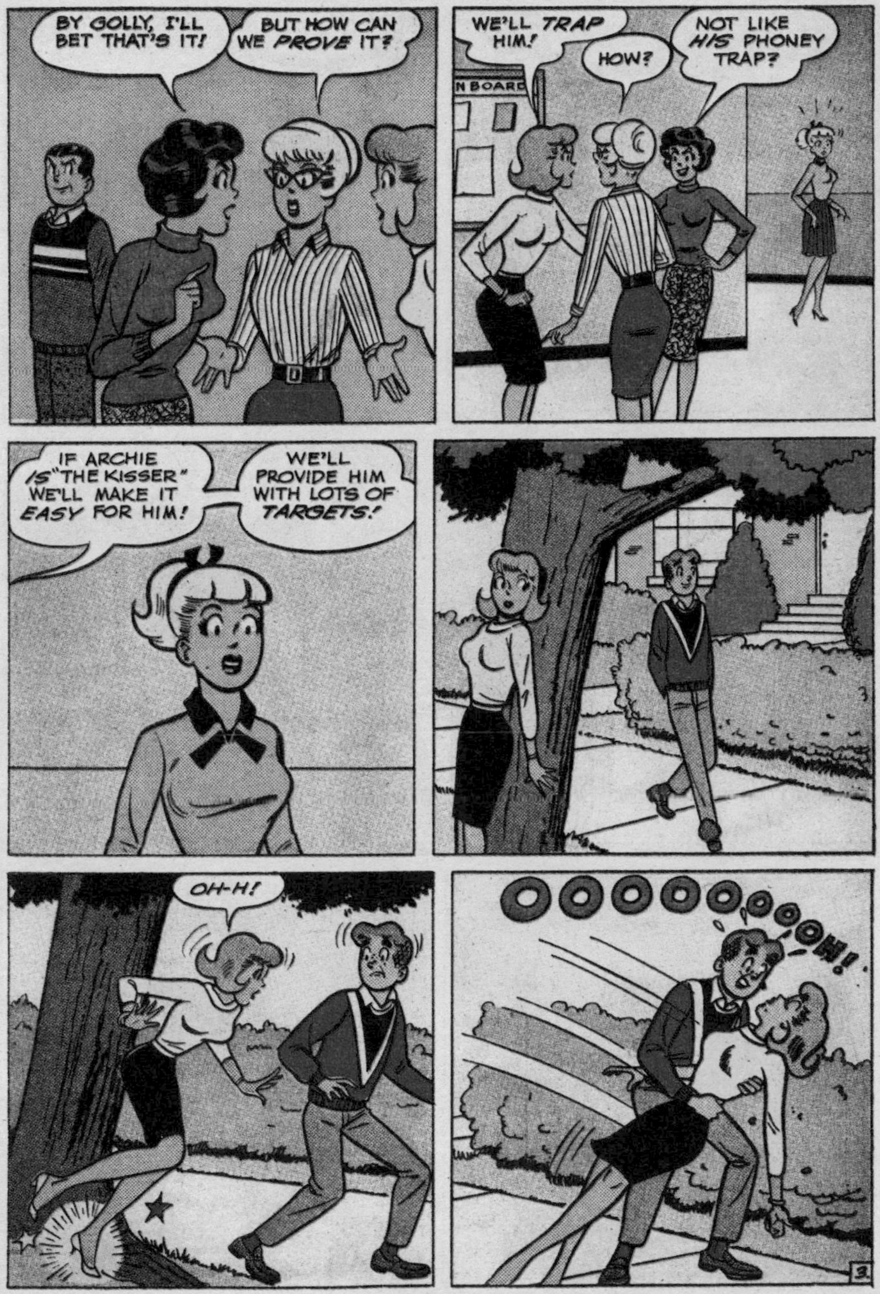
BY GOLLY, I'LL BET THAT'S IT!
BUT HOW CAN WE PROVE IT?
WE'LL TRAP HIM!
HOW?
NOT LIKE HIS PHONEY TRAP?
N BOARD
IF ARCHIE IS "THE KISSER" WE'LL MAKE IT EASY FOR HIM!
WE'LL PROVIDE HIM WITH LOTS OF TARGETS!
OH-H!
OOOOOOOOOH!
3

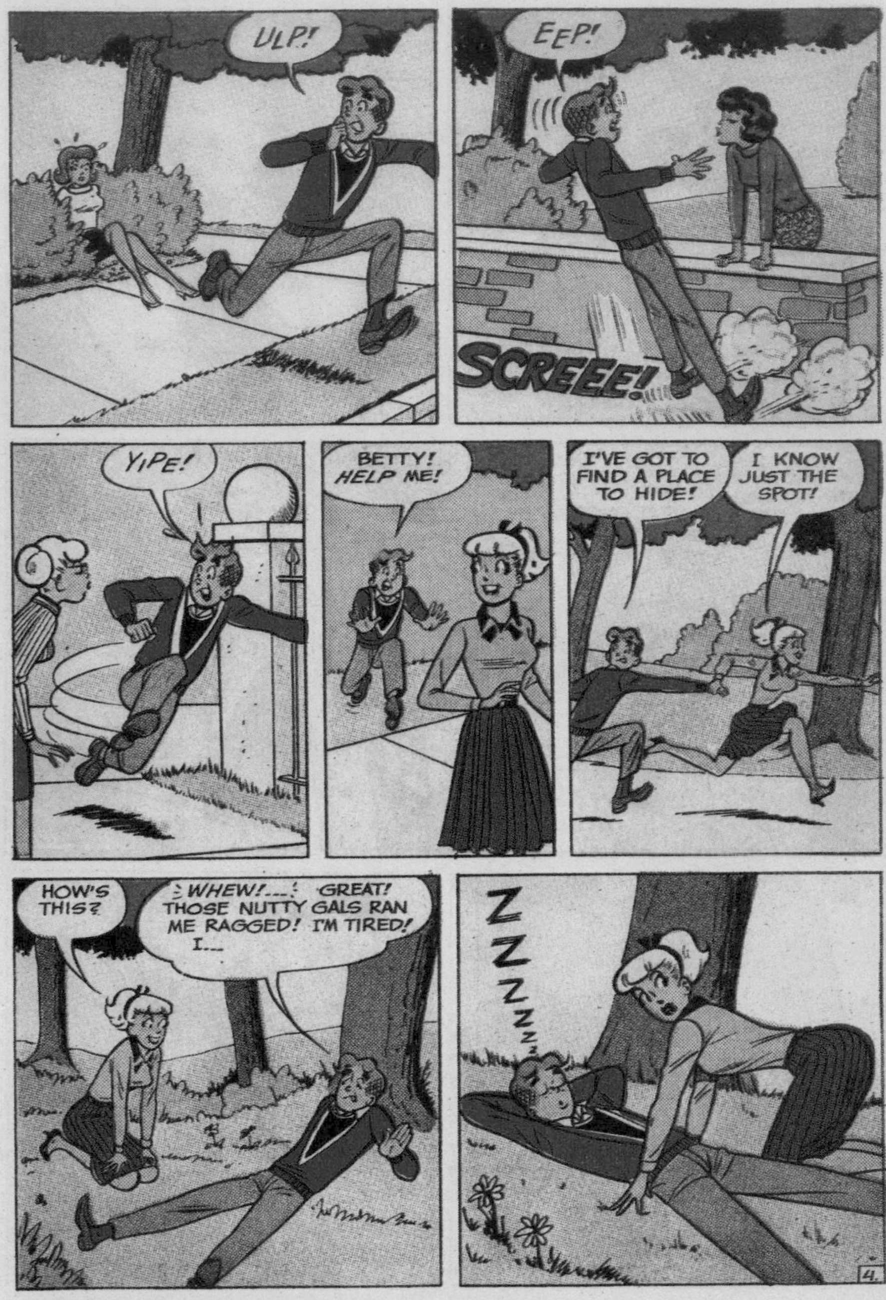
ULP!
EEP!
SCREEE!
YIPE!
BETTY! HELP ME!
I'VE GOT TO FIND A PLACE TO HIDE!
I KNOW JUST THE SPOT!
HOW'S THIS?
WHEW!... GREAT! THOSE NUTTY GALS RAN ME RAGGED! I'M TIRED! I...
Z Z Z Z Z
4

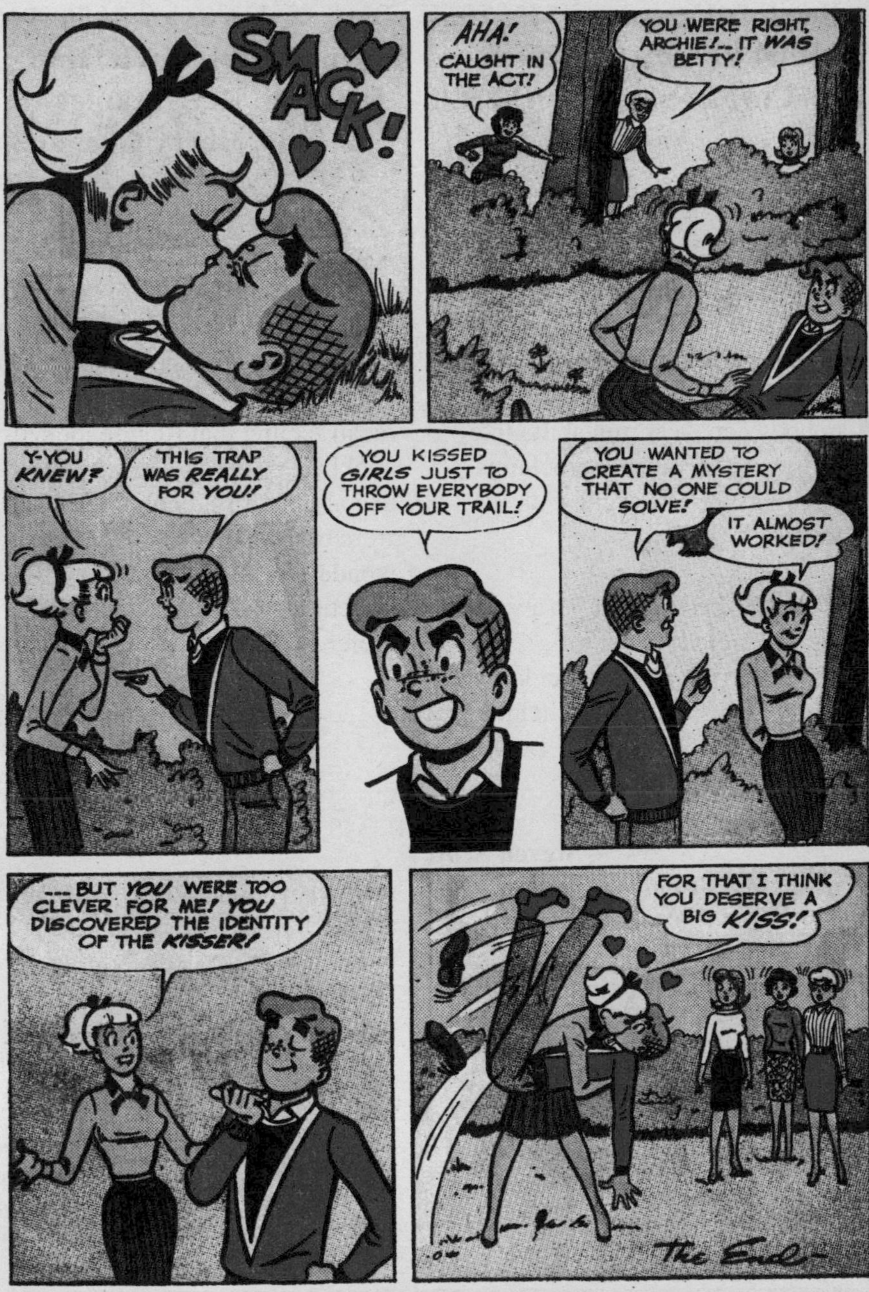
SMACK!
AHA! CAUGHT IN THE ACT!
YOU WERE RIGHT, ARCHIE!... IT WAS BETTY!
Y-YOU KNEW?
THIS TRAP WAS REALLY FOR YOU!
YOU KISSED GIRLS JUST TO THROW EVERYBODY OFF YOUR TRAIL!
YOU WANTED TO CREATE A MYSTERY THAT NO ONE COULD SOLVE!
IT ALMOST WORKED!
...BUT YOU WERE TOO CLEVER FOR ME! YOU DISCOVERED THE IDENTITY OF THE KISSER!
FOR THAT I THINK YOU DESERVE A BIG KISS!
The End

Miniskirt Madness
Betty & Veronica #142, 1967 by Frank Doyle, Dan DeCarlo, Rudy Lapick, Bill Yoshida

Everyone discovers Betty and Veronica at some point in time. It's just a part of life. And anyone who grew up a little girl-crazy can relate to Archie and Reggie. "Nobody but nobody can wear miniskirts like Betty and Veronica!" proclaims Archie. Who can argue with that logic?

Well, maybe Jughead. To answer his oft-quoted "What girls?" line in this story (which I've decided just might be his unofficial catchphrase) there's only one reply — Betty and Veronica, that's who!

-- Steven Scott
Director of Publicity & Marketing, Archie Comics

Time of Your Life
Betty & Veronica #156, 1968 by Frank Doyle, Dan DeCarlo, Rudy Lapick, Bill Yoshida, Barry Grossman

I remember reading Archie comics when I was a very little kid (around six years old or so), and to me at that young age the characters seemed close to adults to me. I recall feeling that Reggie looked cool but Archie was clearly nicer, and although Betty and Veronica were both very pretty, I've often wondered if Betty's greater sweetness gave me a lifelong preference for blondes!

-- Norm Breyfogle
Award-winning Artist, Batman / Life with Archie

Archie Comics stories were often accused of being formulaic, but writer Frank Doyle, supported by artist Dan DeCarlo, knew how to finesse the formula for inventive impact.

-- Craig Boldman
Writer, Archie Comics

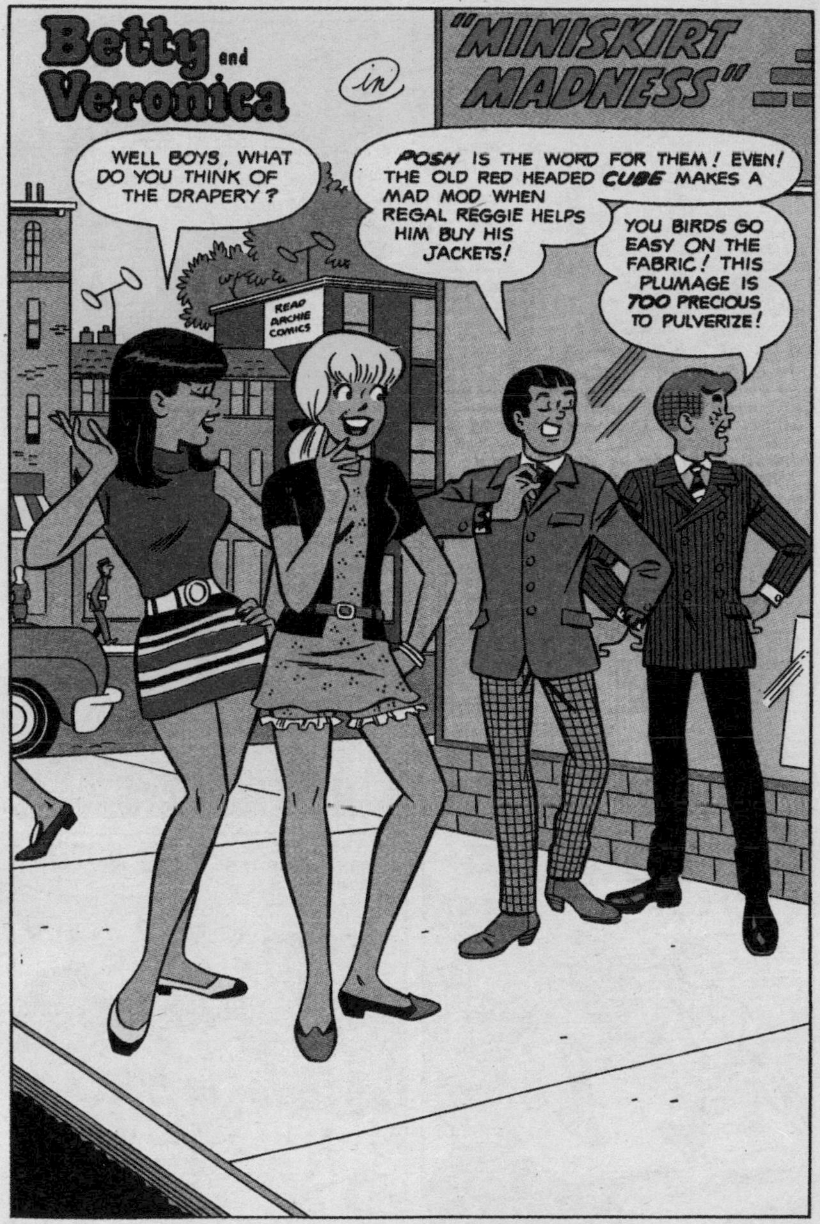
Betty and Veronica
in
"MINISKIRT MADNESS"
WELL BOYS, WHAT DO YOU THINK OF THE DRAPERY?
POSH IS THE WORD FOR THEM! EVEN! THE OLD RED HEADED CUBE MAKES A MAD MOD WHEN REGAL REGGIE HELPS HIM BUY HIS JACKETS!
YOU BIRDS GO EASY ON THE FABRIC! THIS PLUMAGE IS TOO PRECIOUS TO PULVERIZE!
READ ARCHIE COMICS

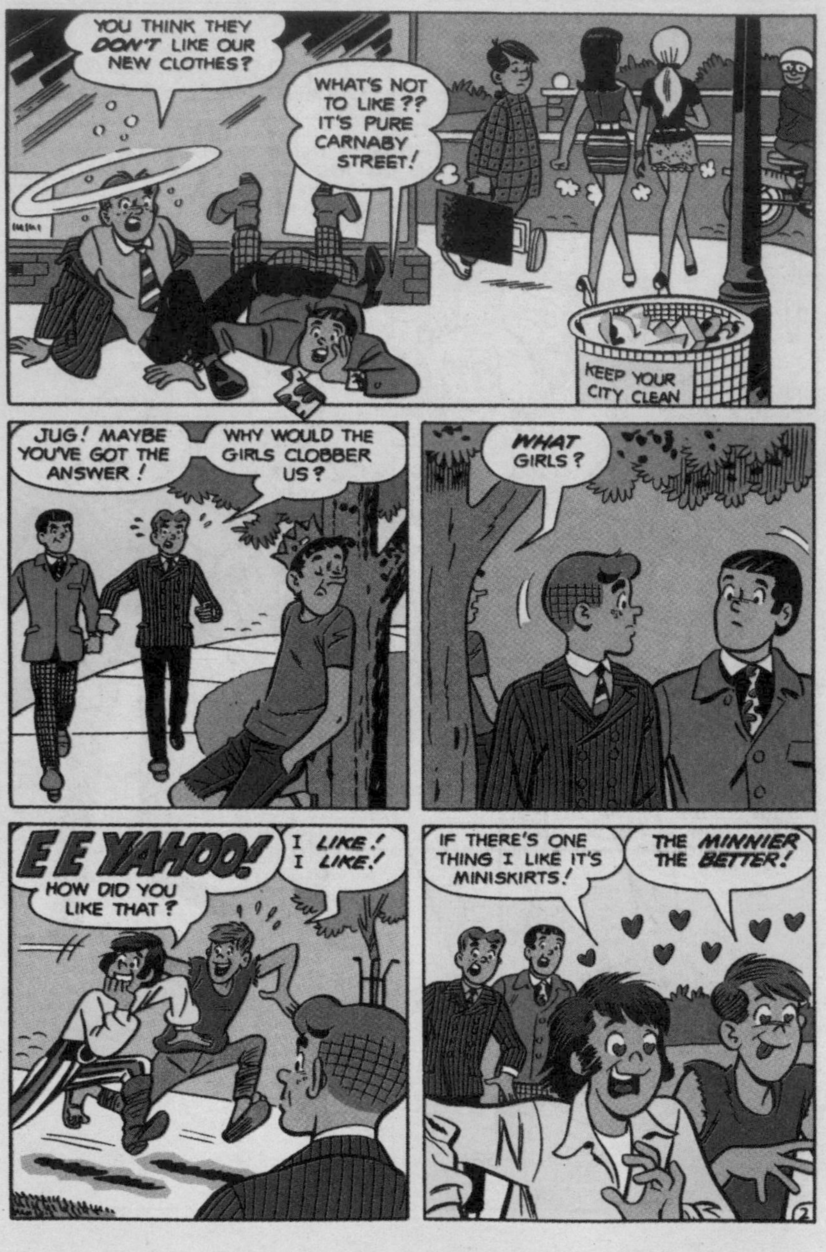
YOU THINK THEY DON'T LIKE OUR NEW CLOTHES?
WHAT'S NOT TO LIKE?? IT'S PURE CARNABY STREET!
KEEP YOUR CITY CLEAN
JUG! MAYBE YOU'VE GOT THE ANSWER!
WHY WOULD THE GIRLS CLOBBER US?
WHAT GIRLS?
E E YAHOO! HOW DID YOU LIKE THAT?
I LIKE! I LIKE!
IF THERE'S ONE THING I LIKE IT'S MINISKIRTS!
THE MINNIER THE BETTER!
2

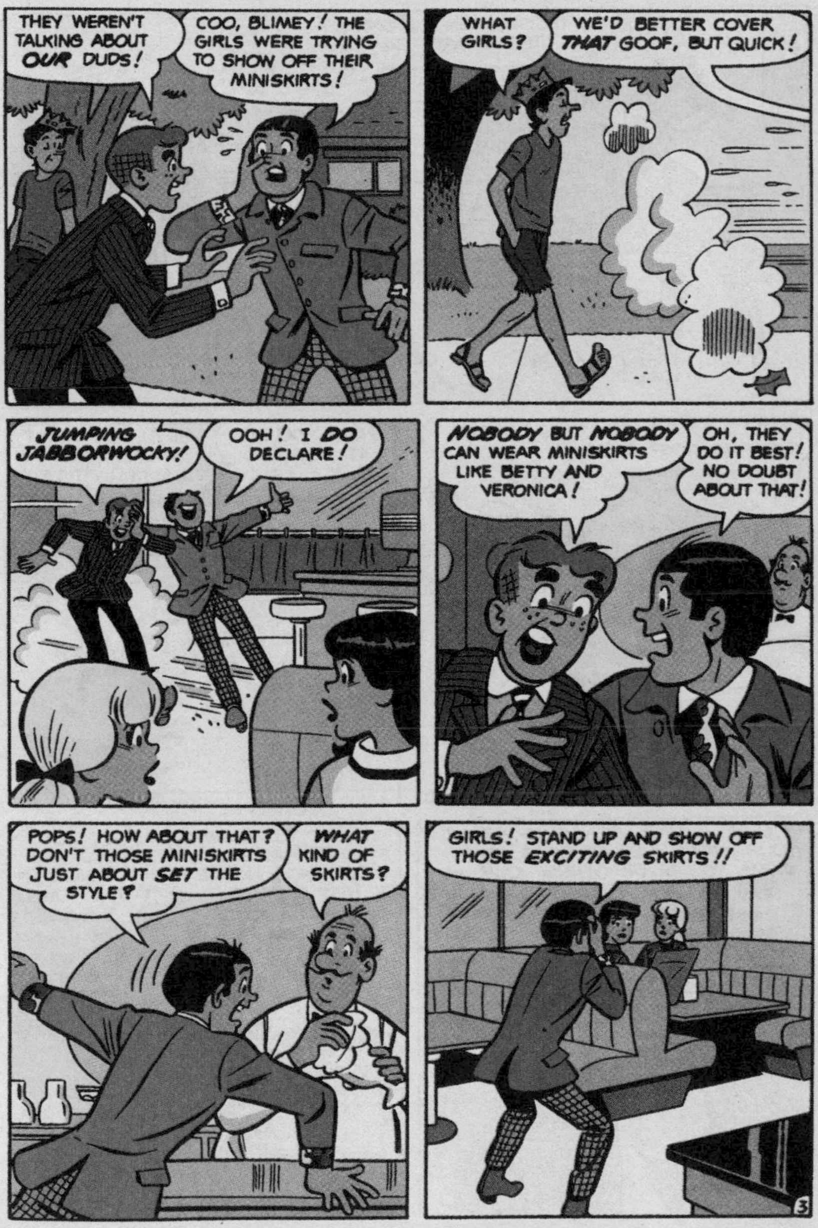
THEY WEREN'T TALKING ABOUT OUR DUDS!
COO, BLIMEY! THE GIRLS WERE TRYING TO SHOW OFF THEIR MINISKIRTS!
WHAT GIRLS?
WE'D BETTER COVER THAT GOOF, BUT QUICK!
JUMPING JABBORWOCKY!
OOH! I DO DECLARE!
NOBODY BUT NOBODY CAN WEAR MINISKIRTS LIKE BETTY AND VERONICA!
OH, THEY DO IT BEST! NO DOUBT ABOUT THAT!
POPS! HOW ABOUT THAT? DON'T THOSE MINISKIRTS JUST ABOUT SET THE STYLE?
WHAT KIND OF SKIRTS?
GIRLS! STAND UP AND SHOW OFF THOSE EXCITING SKIRTS!!
3

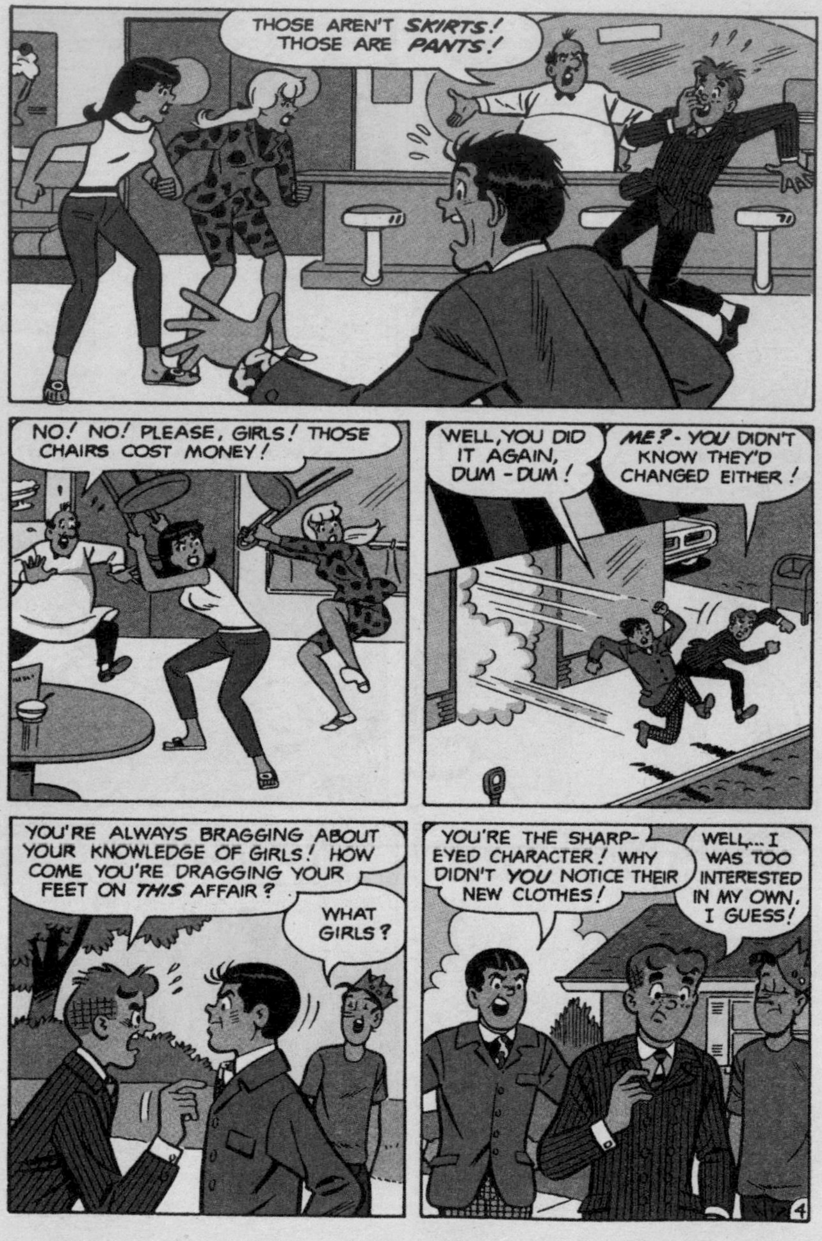
THOSE AREN'T *SKIRTS*! THOSE ARE *PANTS*!
NO! NO! PLEASE, GIRLS! THOSE CHAIRS COST MONEY!
WELL, YOU DID IT AGAIN, DUM-DUM!
ME? - *YOU* DIDN'T KNOW THEY'D CHANGED EITHER!
YOU'RE ALWAYS BRAGGING ABOUT YOUR KNOWLEDGE OF GIRLS! HOW COME YOU'RE DRAGGING YOUR FEET ON *THIS* AFFAIR?
WHAT GIRLS?
YOU'RE THE SHARP-EYED CHARACTER! WHY DIDN'T *YOU* NOTICE THEIR NEW CLOTHES!
WELL... I WAS TOO INTERESTED IN MY OWN, I GUESS!
4

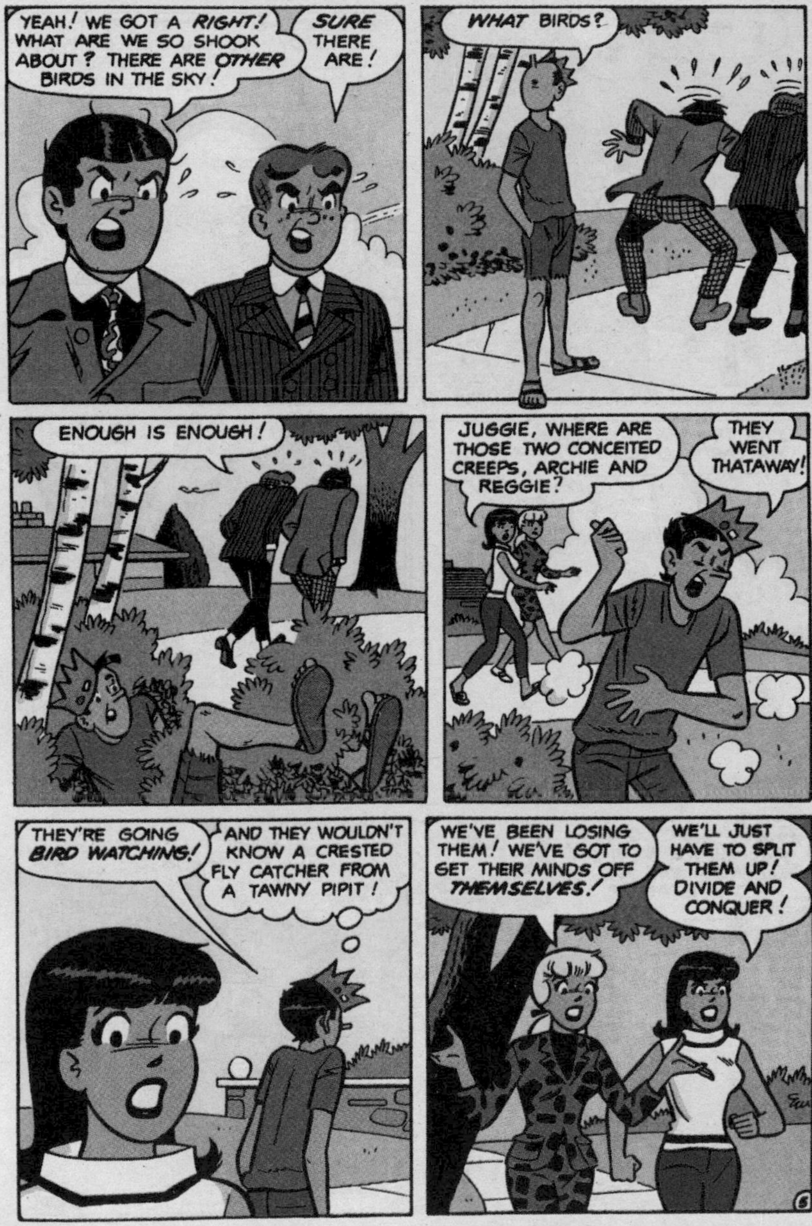
YEAH! WE GOT A RIGHT! WHAT ARE WE SO SHOOK ABOUT? THERE ARE OTHER BIRDS IN THE SKY!
SURE THERE ARE!
WHAT BIRDS?
ENOUGH IS ENOUGH!
JUGGIE, WHERE ARE THOSE TWO CONCEITED CREEPS, ARCHIE AND REGGIE?
THEY WENT THATAWAY!
THEY'RE GOING BIRD WATCHING!
AND THEY WOULDN'T KNOW A CRESTED FLY CATCHER FROM A TAWNY PIPIT!
WE'VE BEEN LOSING THEM! WE'VE GOT TO GET THEIR MINDS OFF THEMSELVES!
WE'LL JUST HAVE TO SPLIT THEM UP! DIVIDE AND CONQUER!
5

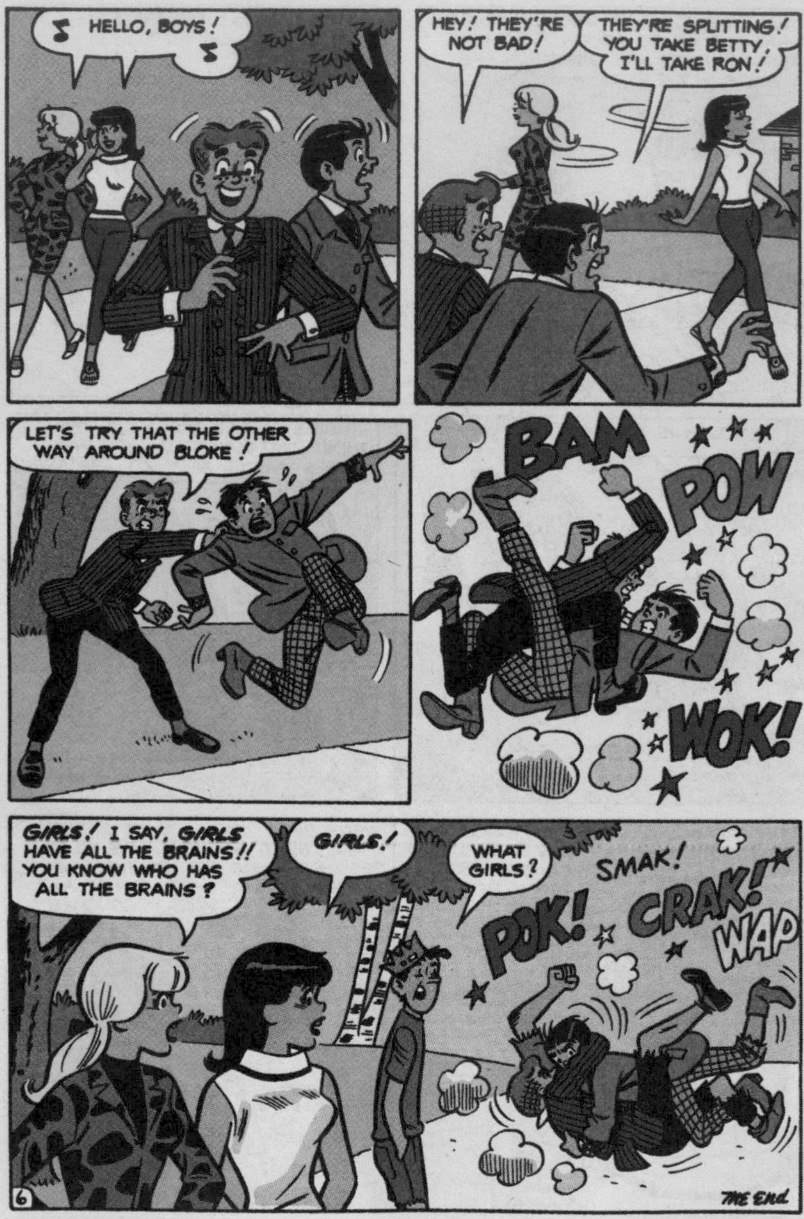
HELLO, BOYS!
HEY! THEY'RE NOT BAD!
THEY'RE SPLITTING! YOU TAKE BETTY, I'LL TAKE RON!
LET'S TRY THAT THE OTHER WAY AROUND BLOKE!
BAM
POW
WOK!
GIRLS! I SAY, GIRLS HAVE ALL THE BRAINS!! YOU KNOW WHO HAS ALL THE BRAINS?
GIRLS!
WHAT GIRLS?
SMAK!
POK!
CRAK!
WAP
6
THE End

Betty -in- THE TIME OF YOUR LIFE

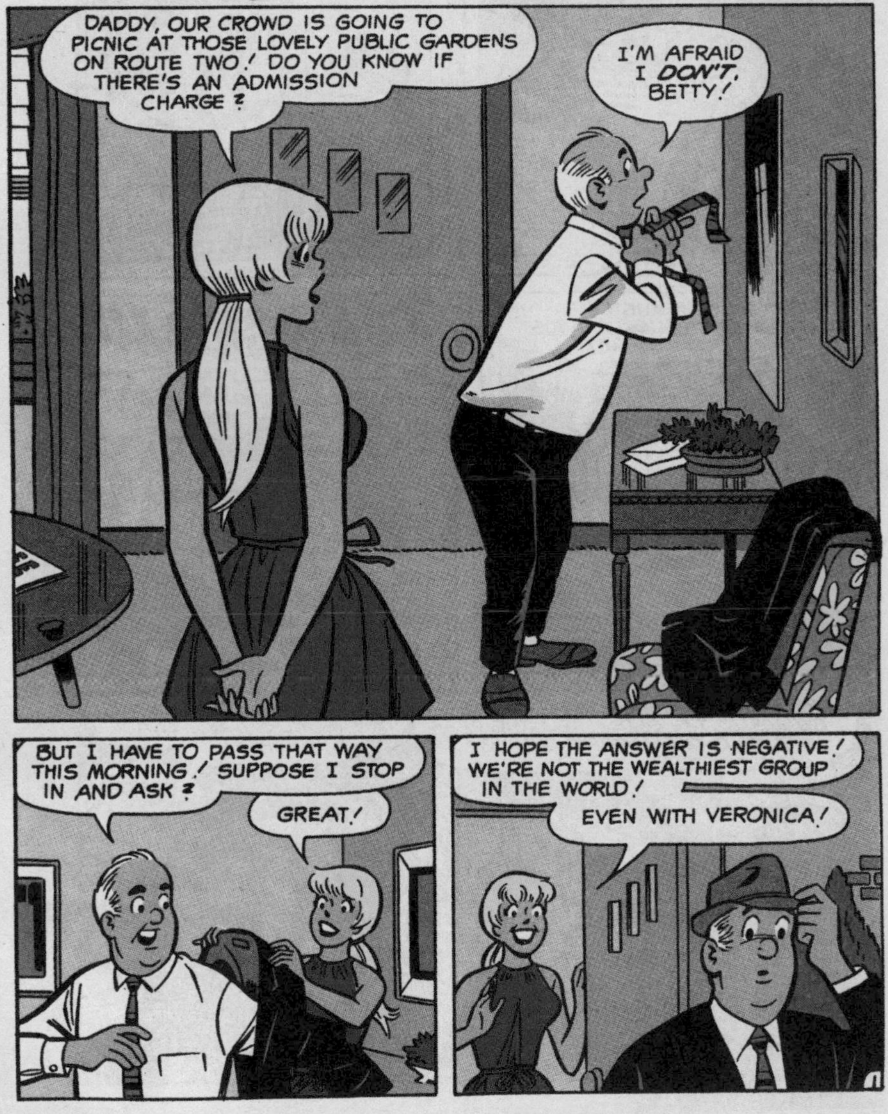
DADDY, OUR CROWD IS GOING TO PICNIC AT THOSE LOVELY PUBLIC GARDENS ON ROUTE TWO! DO YOU KNOW IF THERE'S AN ADMISSION CHARGE?
I'M AFRAID I DON'T, BETTY!
BUT I HAVE TO PASS THAT WAY THIS MORNING! SUPPOSE I STOP IN AND ASK?
GREAT!
I HOPE THE ANSWER IS NEGATIVE! WE'RE NOT THE WEALTHIEST GROUP IN THE WORLD!
EVEN WITH VERONICA!

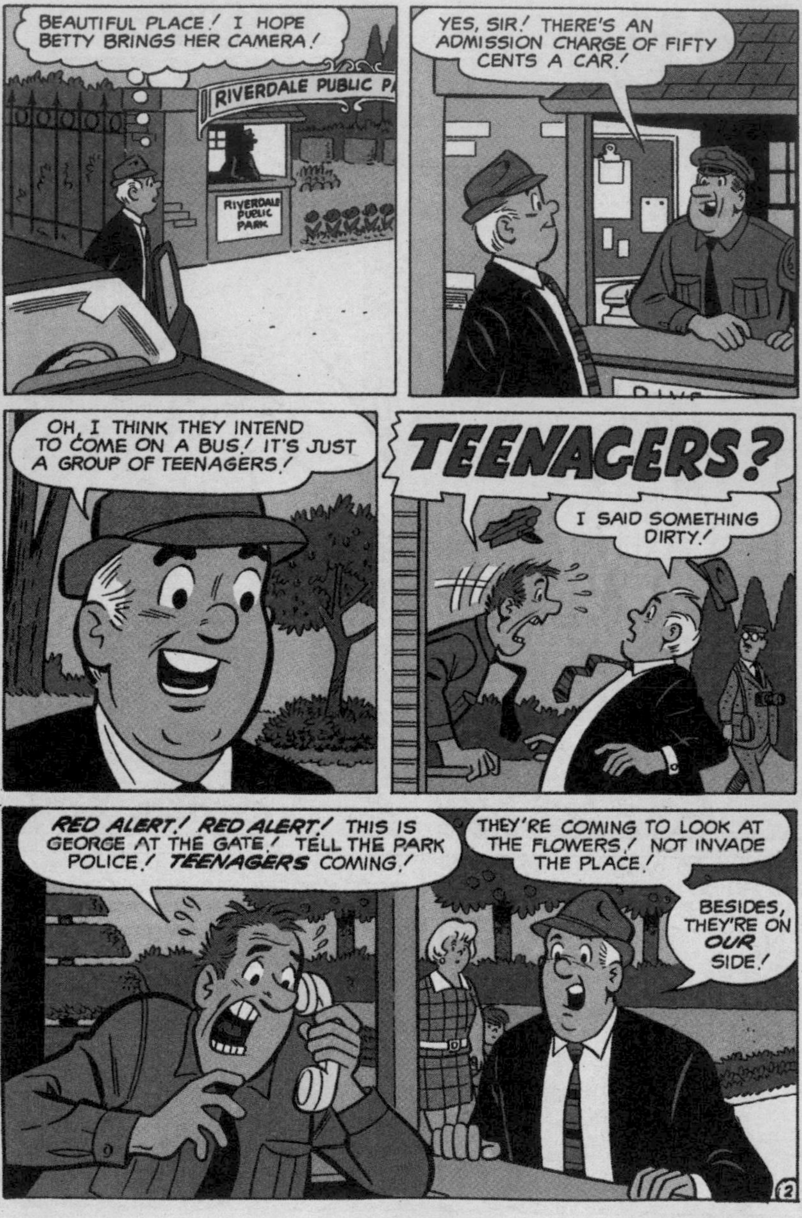
BEAUTIFUL PLACE! I HOPE BETTY BRINGS HER CAMERA!
RIVERDALE PUBLIC P
RIVERDALE PUBLIC PARK
YES, SIR! THERE'S AN ADMISSION CHARGE OF FIFTY CENTS A CAR!
OH, I THINK THEY INTEND TO COME ON A BUS! IT'S JUST A GROUP OF TEENAGERS!
TEENAGERS?
I SAID SOMETHING DIRTY!
RED ALERT! RED ALERT! THIS IS GEORGE AT THE GATE! TELL THE PARK POLICE! TEENAGERS COMING!
THEY'RE COMING TO LOOK AT THE FLOWERS! NOT INVADE THE PLACE!
BESIDES, THEY'RE ON OUR SIDE!
2

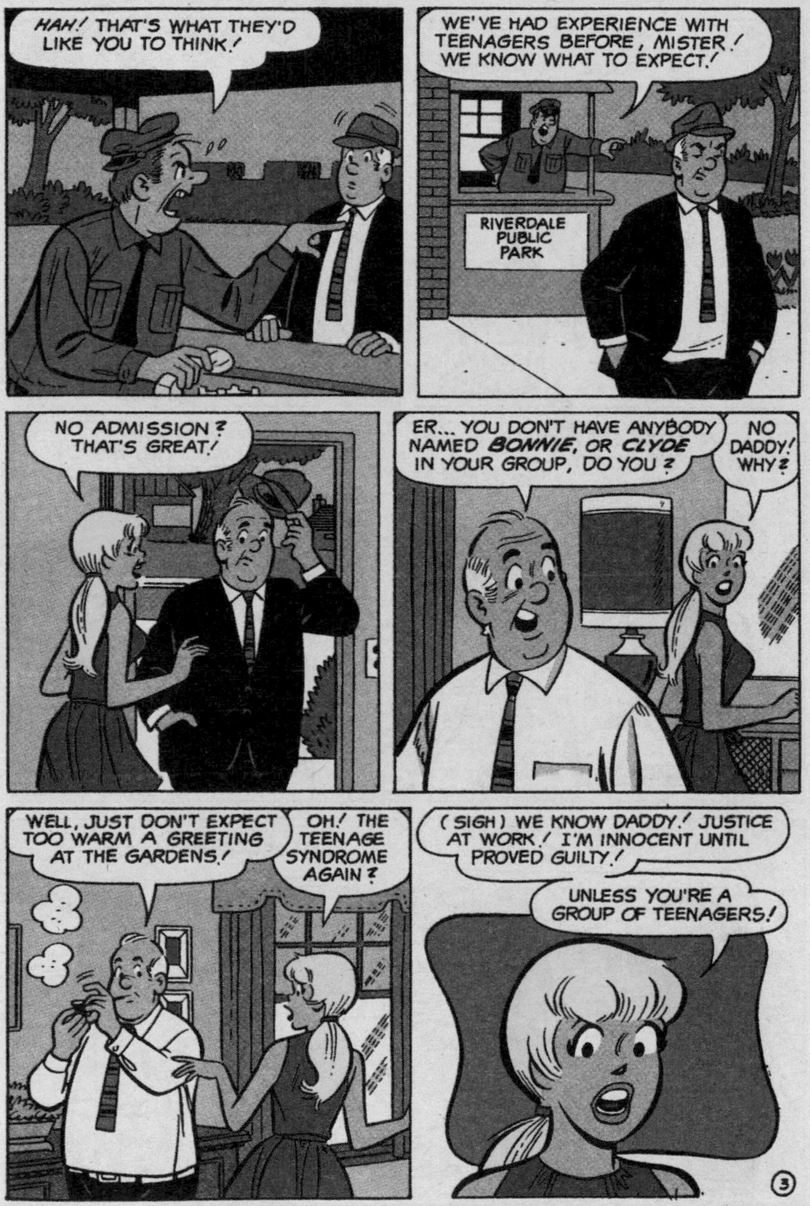
HAH! THAT'S WHAT THEY'D LIKE YOU TO THINK!
WE'VE HAD EXPERIENCE WITH TEENAGERS BEFORE, MISTER! WE KNOW WHAT TO EXPECT!
RIVERDALE PUBLIC PARK
NO ADMISSION? THAT'S GREAT!
ER... YOU DON'T HAVE ANYBODY NAMED BONNIE, OR CLYDE IN YOUR GROUP, DO YOU?
NO DADDY! WHY?
WELL, JUST DON'T EXPECT TOO WARM A GREETING AT THE GARDENS!
OH! THE TEENAGE SYNDROME AGAIN?
(SIGH) WE KNOW DADDY! JUSTICE AT WORK! I'M INNOCENT UNTIL PROVED GUILTY!
UNLESS YOU'RE A GROUP OF TEENAGERS!
3

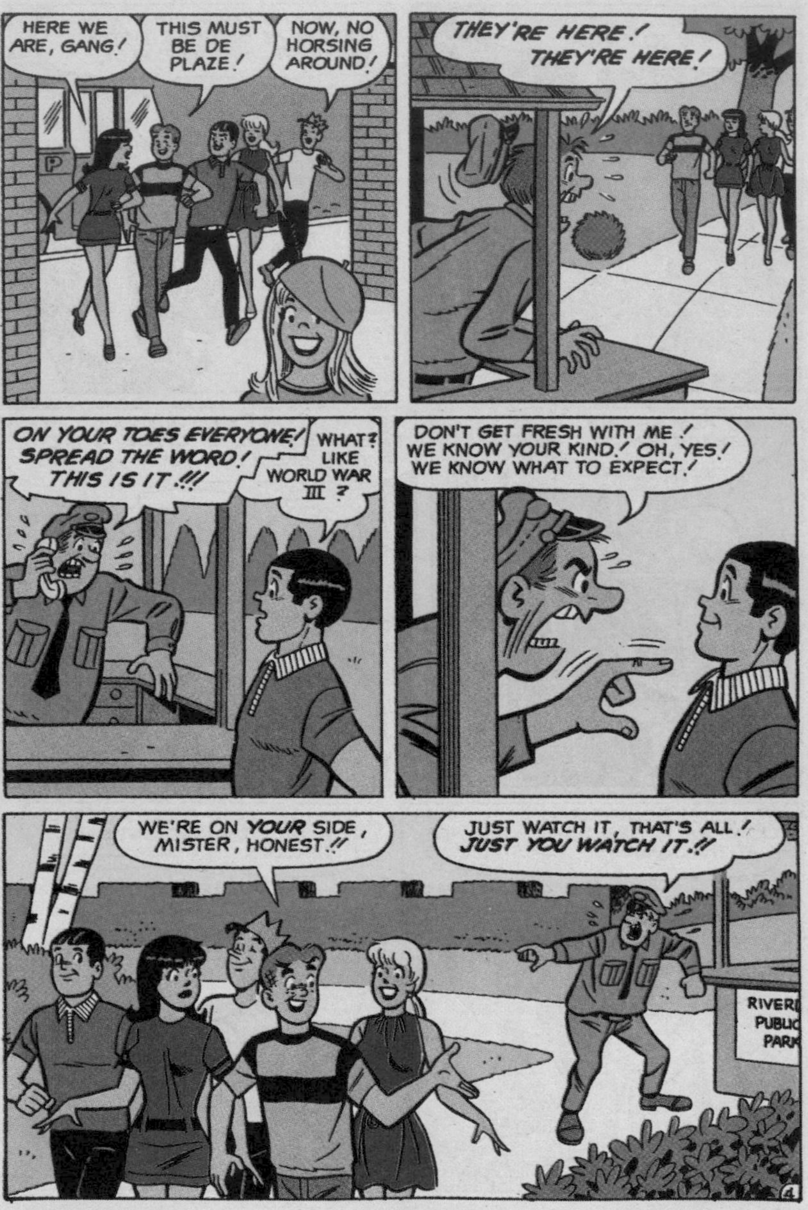
HERE WE ARE, GANG!
THIS MUST BE DE PLAZE!
NOW, NO HORSING AROUND!
THEY'RE HERE! THEY'RE HERE!
ON YOUR TOES EVERYONE! SPREAD THE WORD! THIS IS IT!!!
WHAT? LIKE WORLD WAR III?
DON'T GET FRESH WITH ME! WE KNOW YOUR KIND! OH, YES! WE KNOW WHAT TO EXPECT!
WE'RE ON YOUR SIDE, MISTER, HONEST!!
JUST WATCH IT, THAT'S ALL! JUST YOU WATCH IT!!
RIVERD PUBLIC PARK
4

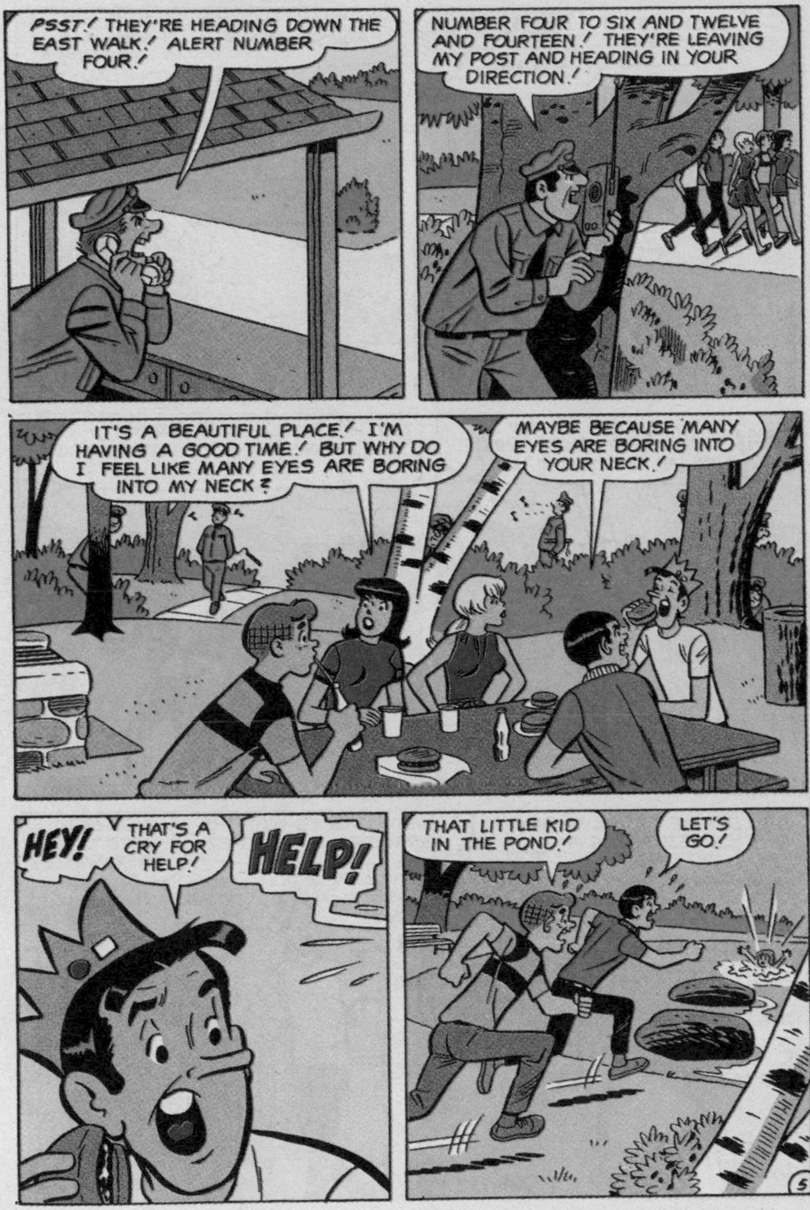
PSST! THEY'RE HEADING DOWN THE EAST WALK! ALERT NUMBER FOUR!
NUMBER FOUR TO SIX AND TWELVE AND FOURTEEN! THEY'RE LEAVING MY POST AND HEADING IN YOUR DIRECTION!
IT'S A BEAUTIFUL PLACE! I'M HAVING A GOOD TIME! BUT WHY DO I FEEL LIKE MANY EYES ARE BORING INTO MY NECK?
MAYBE BECAUSE MANY EYES ARE BORING INTO YOUR NECK!
HEY!
THAT'S A CRY FOR HELP!
HELP!
THAT LITTLE KID IN THE POND!
LET'S GO!
5

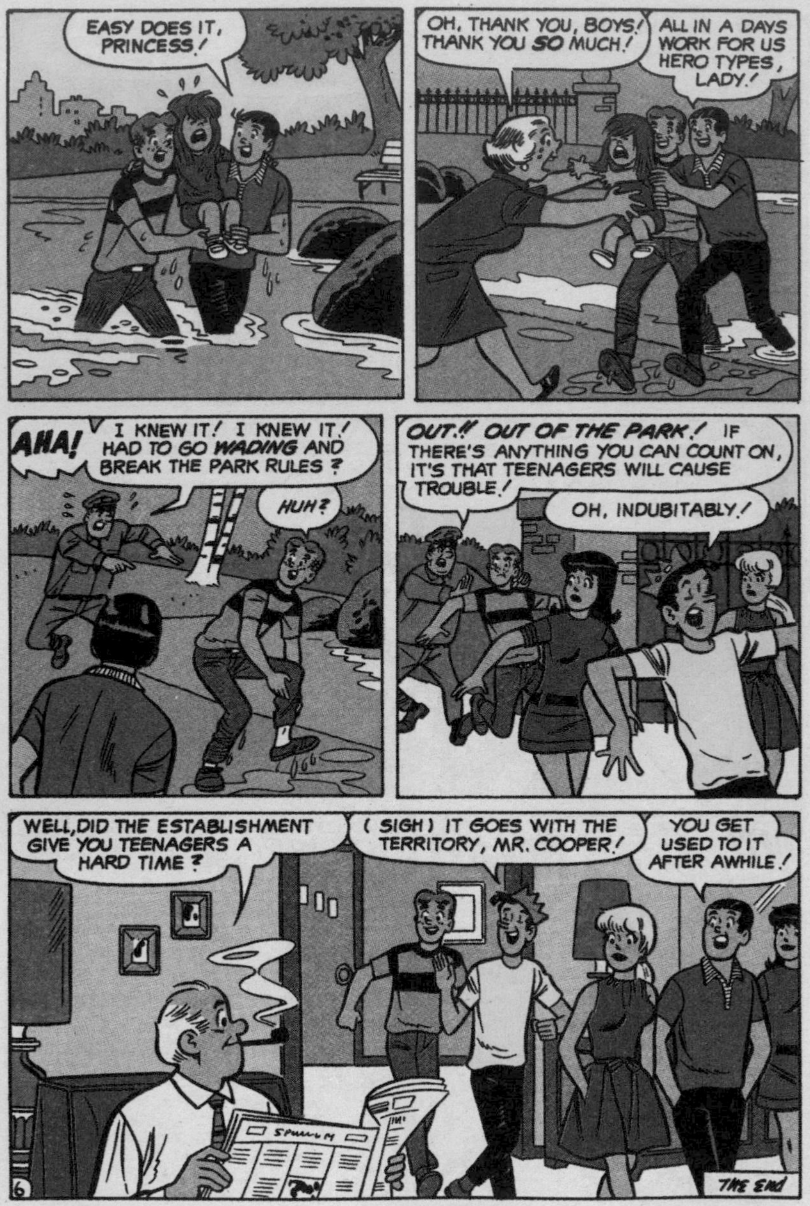
EASY DOES IT, PRINCESS!
OH, THANK YOU, BOYS! THANK YOU SO MUCH!
ALL IN A DAYS WORK FOR US HERO TYPES, LADY!
AHA!
I KNEW IT! I KNEW IT! HAD TO GO WADING AND BREAK THE PARK RULES?
HUH?
OUT!! OUT OF THE PARK! IF THERE'S ANYTHING YOU CAN COUNT ON, IT'S THAT TEENAGERS WILL CAUSE TROUBLE!
OH, INDUBITABLY!
WELL, DID THE ESTABLISHMENT GIVE YOU TEENAGERS A HARD TIME?
(SIGH) IT GOES WITH THE TERRITORY, MR. COOPER!
YOU GET USED TO IT AFTER AWHILE!
6
THE END

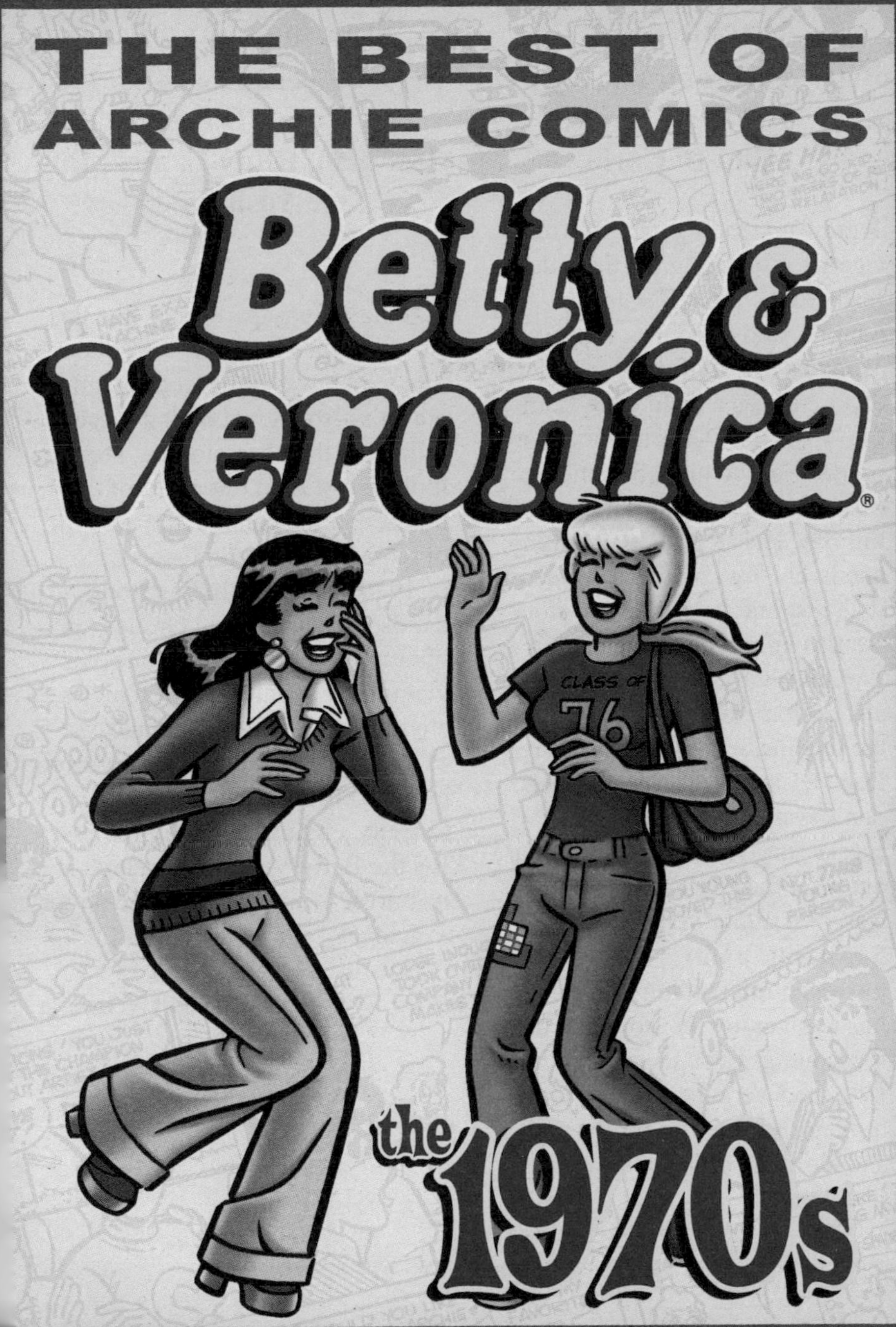
THE BEST OF ARCHIE COMICS
Betty & Veronica®
CLASS OF 76
the 1970s

Archie's Gift
Betty & Veronica #174, 1970 by Frank Doyle, Dan DeCarlo

I grew up reading a lot of Archie Comics, especially the titles that featured the girls, like Josie, Sabrina, and of course, Betty & Veronica. Most of the stories I was exposed to as a child were from the '70s. Dan DeCarlo, the artist on B&V at the time, became one of my favorite artists, and still is to this day. His art was so charming and lively. I was stuck to come up with just one favorite B&V story — it's really hard! I decided on "Archie's Gift," as it's a story I've always remembered, and it shows the liveliness, I so appreciate in Dan DeCarlo's art. Some panels don't even have words, the art speaks for itself! I never did figure out what the "Gift" in the title was — it might've been a typo for "Archie's Girl" — but I had too much fun reading it to care. I hope you enjoy the story and that it encourages you to seek out more Betty and Veronica stories. They truly are a lot of fun for the young and old. I know I'm still reading them.

--Gisele Lagace
Artist,
Archie Comics

Steering Committee
Betty & Veronica #186, 1971 by Frank Doyle, Dan DeCarlo, Rudy Lapick, Bill Yoshida

Being a Betty partisan, I like this story because Betty comes out on top, which was unusual during this era. It's also a great period piece, reflecting the obsession with teen idols that was so big a part of the times, and the panel at the bottom of page 3 is like a mini-survey of 1970s fashions. In this story, handsome singer Tom Grones (an obvious takeoff on Tom Jones) is visiting Riverdale, and Veronica's attempt to steer Betty and the rest of the Riverdale females away from him backfires massively, due purely to Betty's naïveté and helpfulness. It's the Betty/Veronica dynamic at its purest — and without Archie for a change!

--Brigid Alverson
Writer,
CBR's Robot 6 &
SLJ's Good Comics for Kids

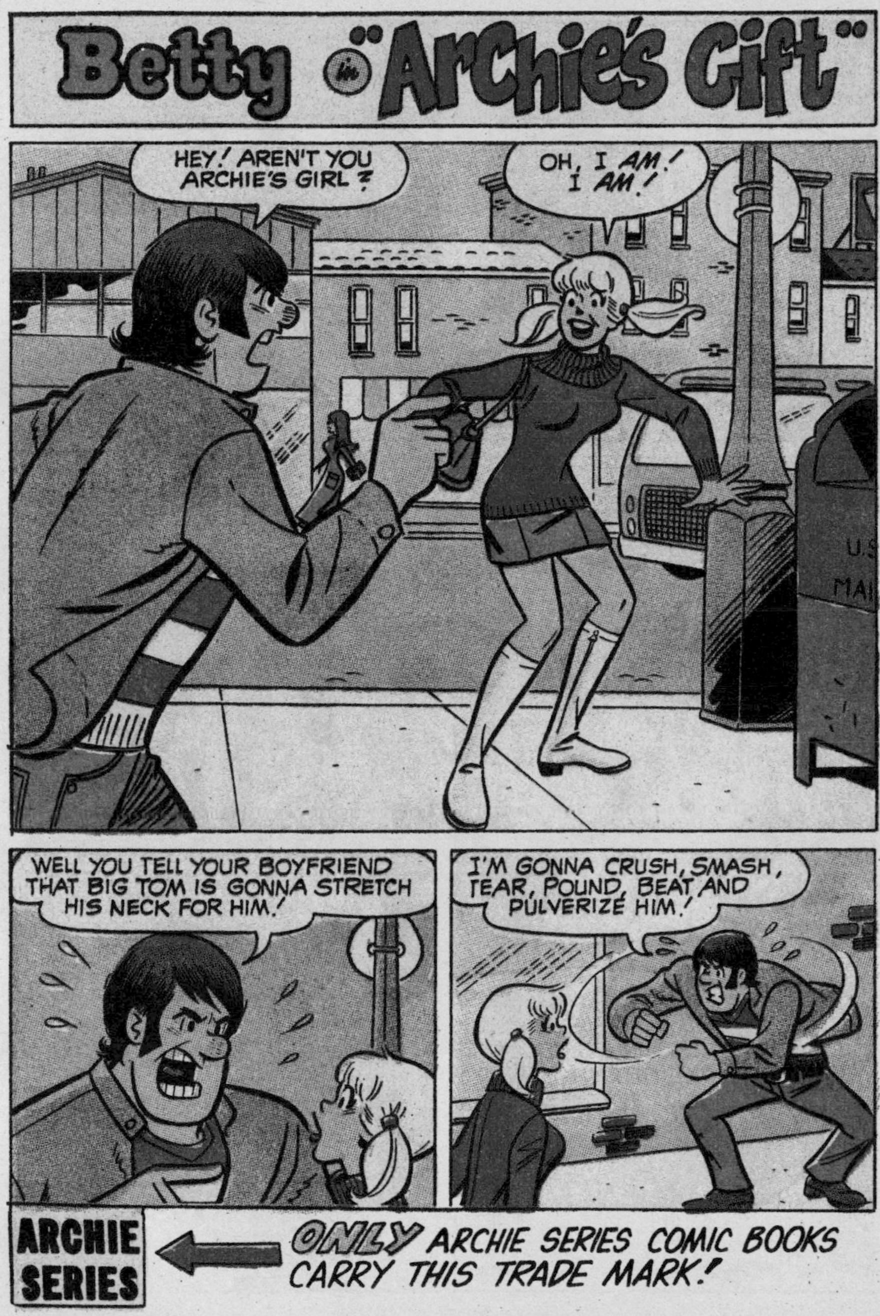
Betty in "Archie's Gift"
HEY! AREN'T YOU ARCHIE'S GIRL?
OH, I AM! I AM!
U.S. MAI
WELL YOU TELL YOUR BOYFRIEND THAT BIG TOM IS GONNA STRETCH HIS NECK FOR HIM!
I'M GONNA CRUSH, SMASH, TEAR, POUND, BEAT AND PULVERIZE HIM!

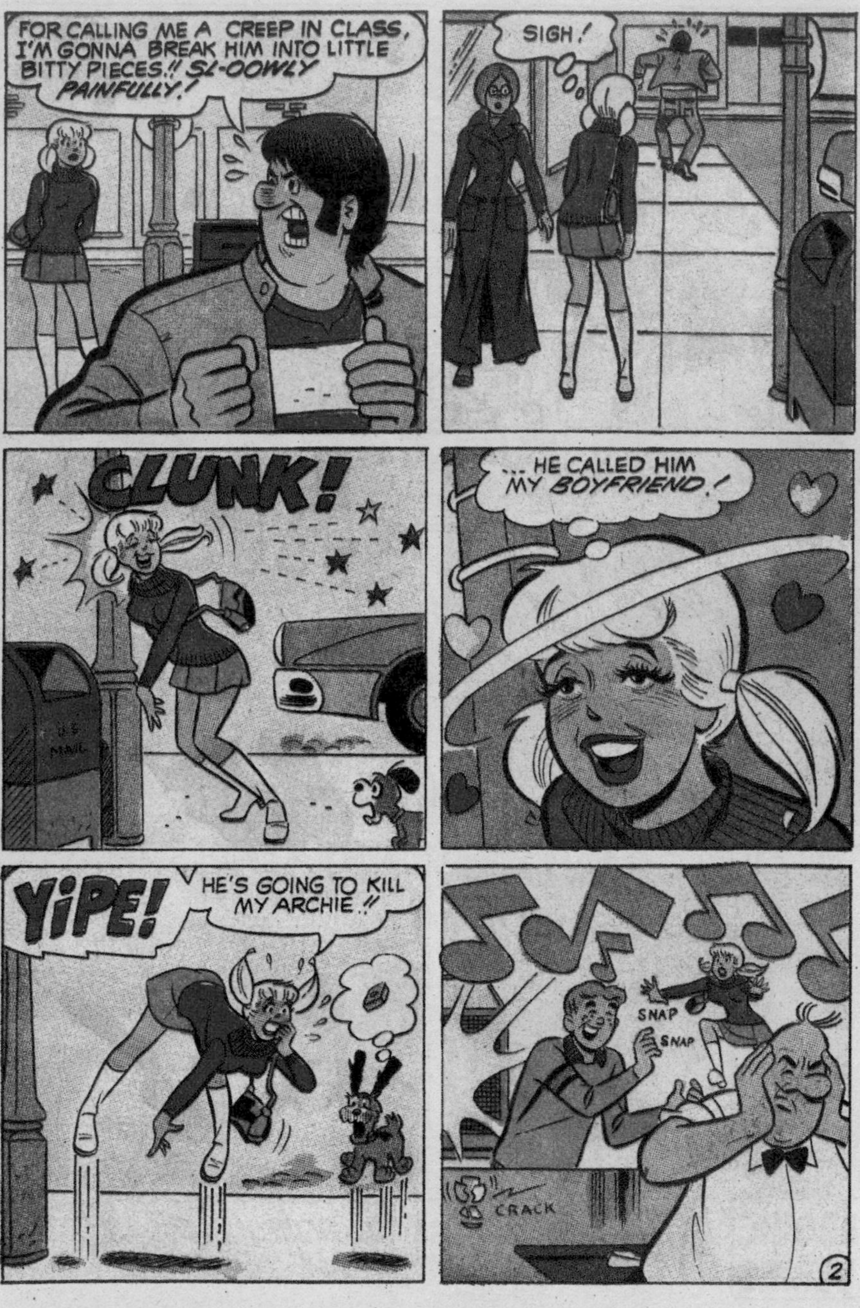
FOR CALLING ME A CREEP IN CLASS, I'M GONNA BREAK HIM INTO LITTLE BITTY PIECES.!! SL-OOWLY PAINFULLY.!
SIGH!
CLUNK!
... HE CALLED HIM MY BOYFRIEND.!
YiPE!
HE'S GOING TO KILL MY ARCHIE.!!
SNAP
SNAP
CRACK
2

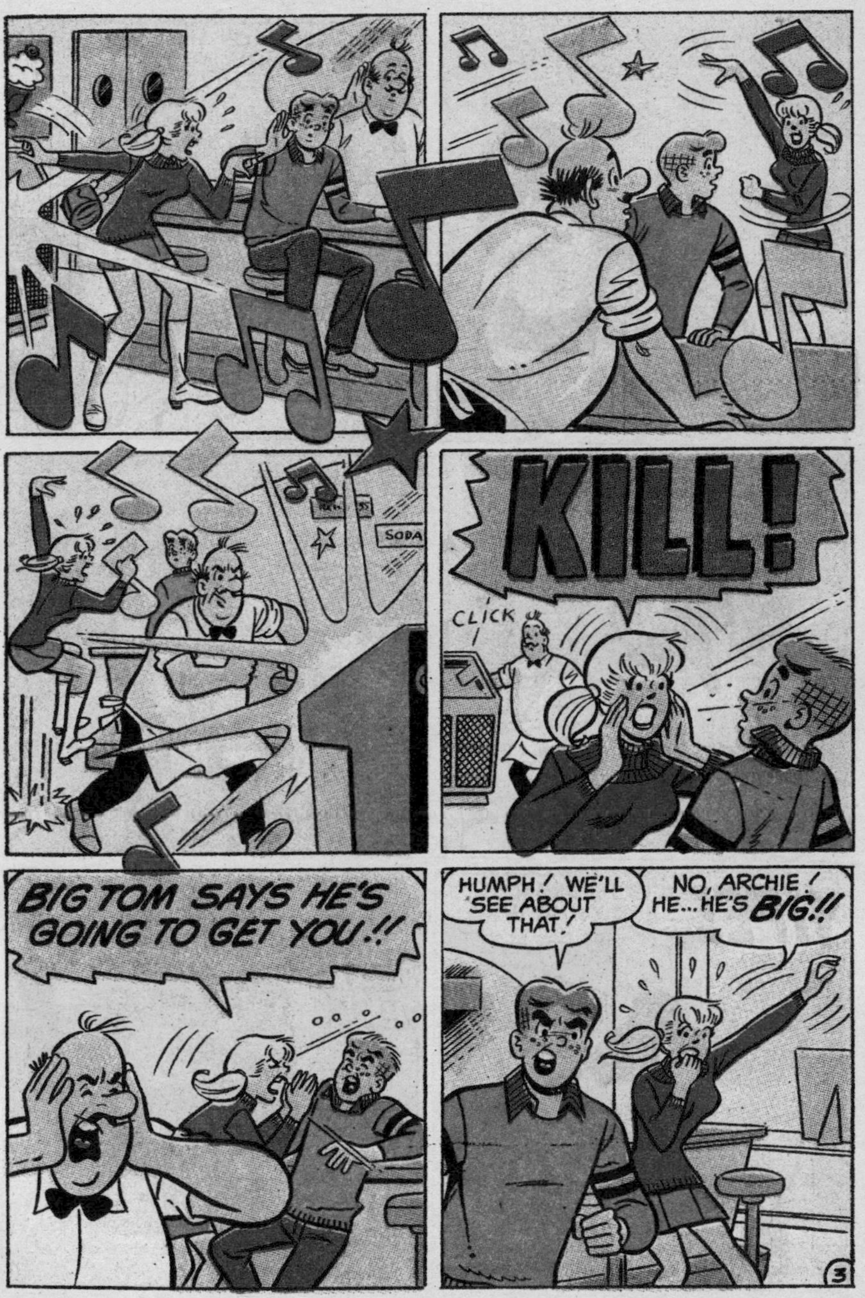
SODA
KILL!
CLICK
BIG TOM SAYS HE'S GOING TO GET YOU !!
HUMPH ! WE'LL SEE ABOUT THAT !
NO, ARCHIE ! HE... HE'S BIG !!
3

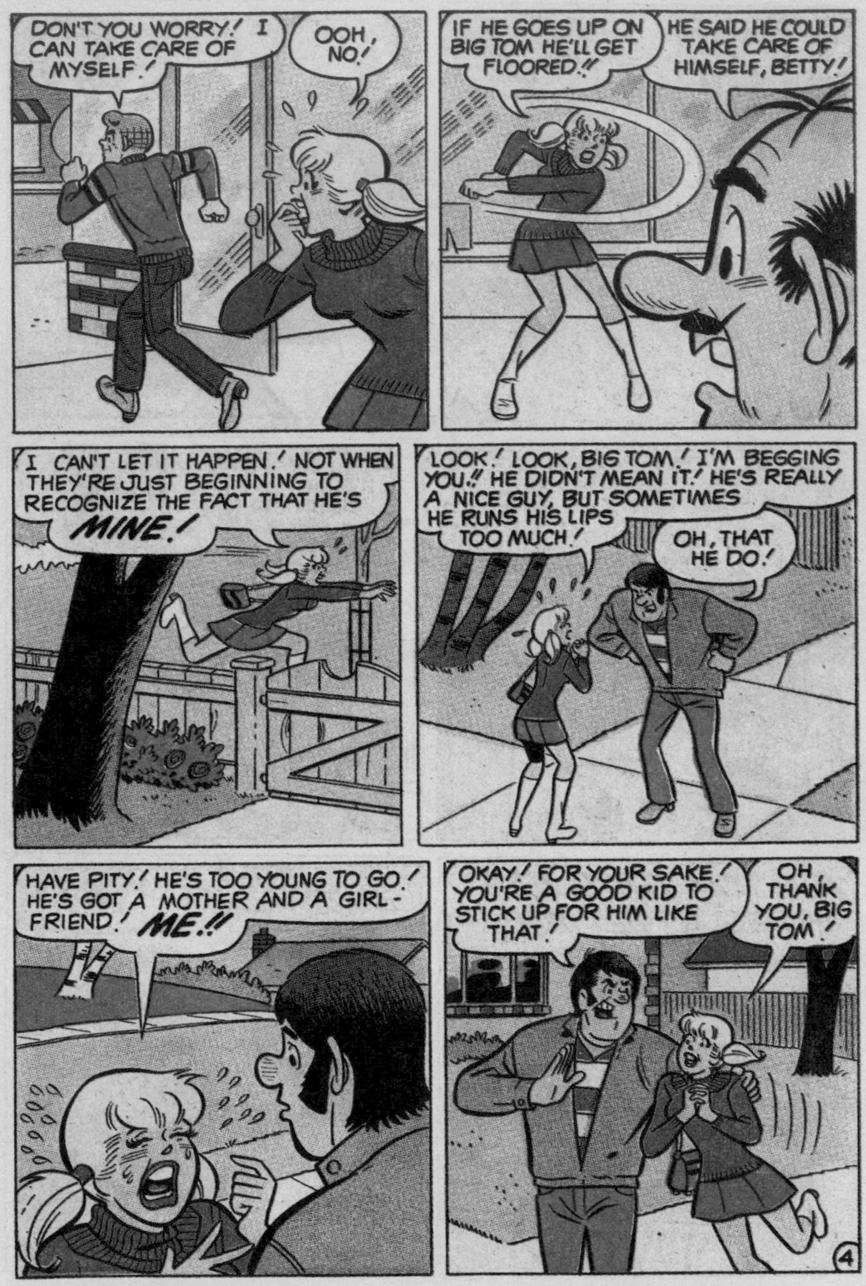
DON'T YOU WORRY! I CAN TAKE CARE OF MYSELF!
OOH, NO!
IF HE GOES UP ON BIG TOM HE'LL GET FLOORED!!
HE SAID HE COULD TAKE CARE OF HIMSELF, BETTY!
I CAN'T LET IT HAPPEN! NOT WHEN THEY'RE JUST BEGINNING TO RECOGNIZE THE FACT THAT HE'S MINE!
LOOK! LOOK, BIG TOM! I'M BEGGING YOU!! HE DIDN'T MEAN IT! HE'S REALLY A NICE GUY, BUT SOMETIMES HE RUNS HIS LIPS TOO MUCH!
OH, THAT HE DO!
HAVE PITY! HE'S TOO YOUNG TO GO! HE'S GOT A MOTHER AND A GIRL-FRIEND! ME!!
OKAY! FOR YOUR SAKE! YOU'RE A GOOD KID TO STICK UP FOR HIM LIKE THAT!
OH, THANK YOU, BIG TOM!
4

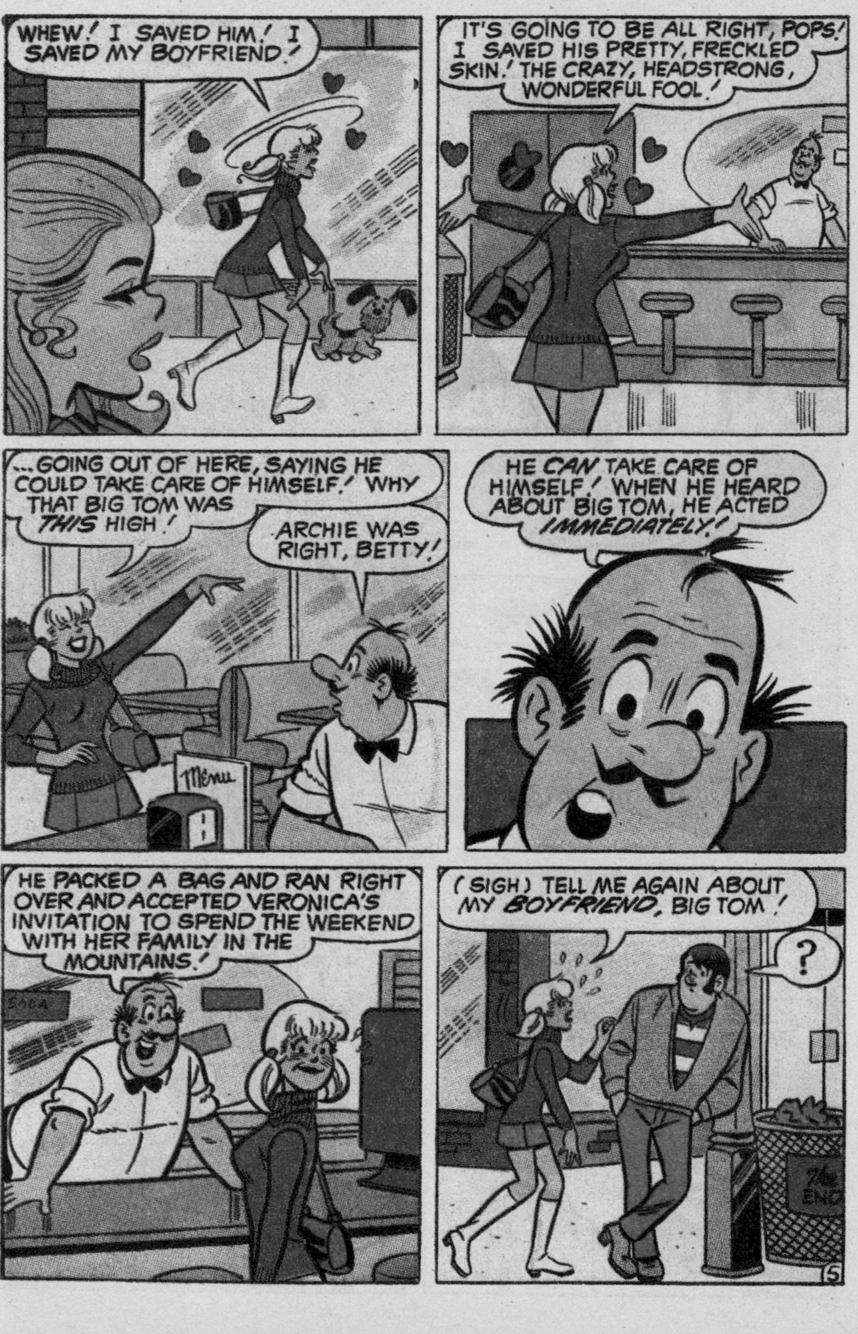
WHEW! I SAVED HIM! I SAVED MY BOYFRIEND!
IT'S GOING TO BE ALL RIGHT, POPS! I SAVED HIS PRETTY, FRECKLED SKIN! THE CRAZY, HEADSTRONG, WONDERFUL FOOL!
...GOING OUT OF HERE, SAYING HE COULD TAKE CARE OF HIMSELF! WHY THAT BIG TOM WAS THIS HIGH!
ARCHIE WAS RIGHT, BETTY!
Menu
HE CAN TAKE CARE OF HIMSELF! WHEN HE HEARD ABOUT BIG TOM, HE ACTED IMMEDIATELY!
HE PACKED A BAG AND RAN RIGHT OVER AND ACCEPTED VERONICA'S INVITATION TO SPEND THE WEEKEND WITH HER FAMILY IN THE MOUNTAINS!
SODA
(SIGH) TELL ME AGAIN ABOUT MY BOYFRIEND, BIG TOM!
?
The END
5

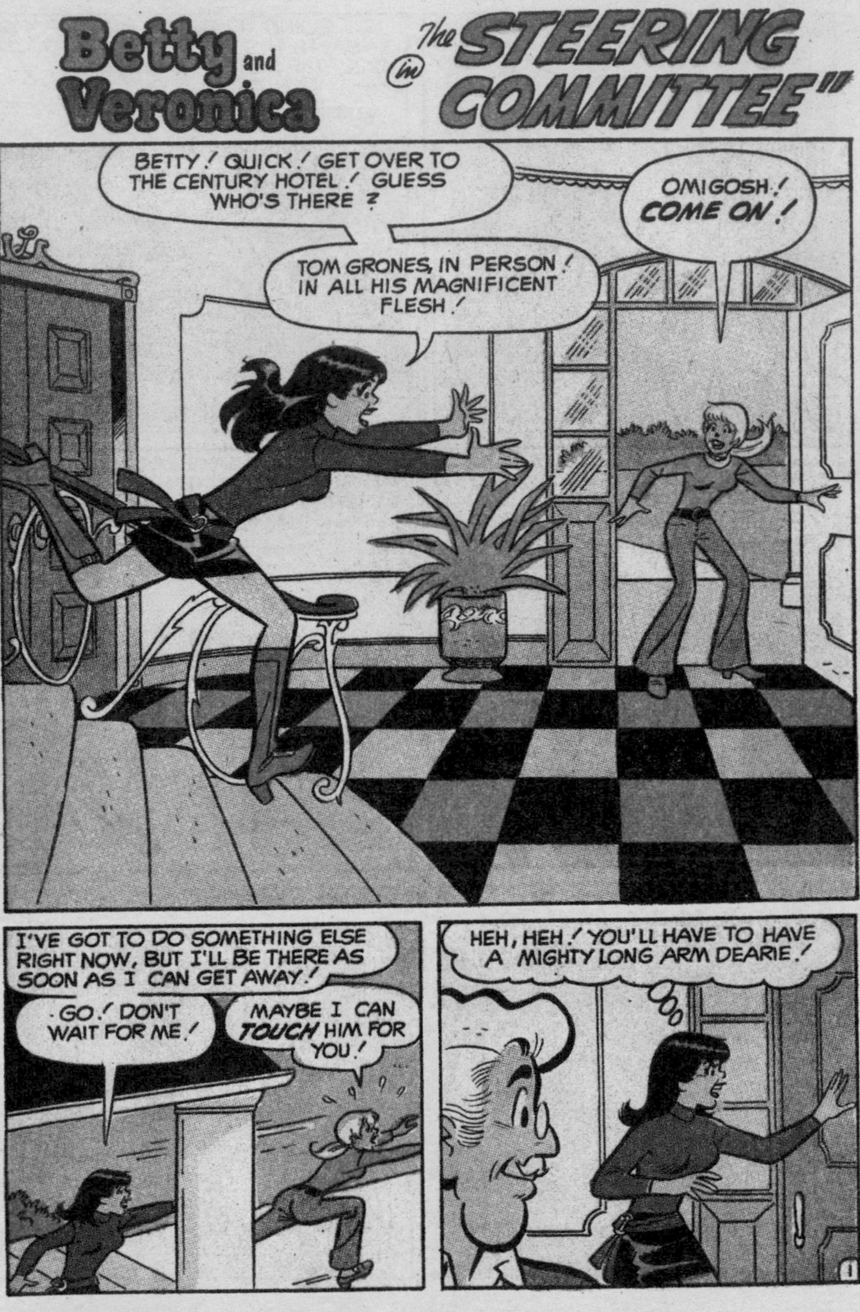
Betty and Veronica
in "The STEERING COMMITTEE"
BETTY! QUICK! GET OVER TO THE CENTURY HOTEL! GUESS WHO'S THERE?
TOM GRONES, IN PERSON! IN ALL HIS MAGNIFICENT FLESH!
OMIGOSH! COME ON!
I'VE GOT TO DO SOMETHING ELSE RIGHT NOW, BUT I'LL BE THERE AS SOON AS I CAN GET AWAY!
GO! DON'T WAIT FOR ME!
MAYBE I CAN TOUCH HIM FOR YOU!
HEH, HEH! YOU'LL HAVE TO HAVE A MIGHTY LONG ARM DEARIE!
1

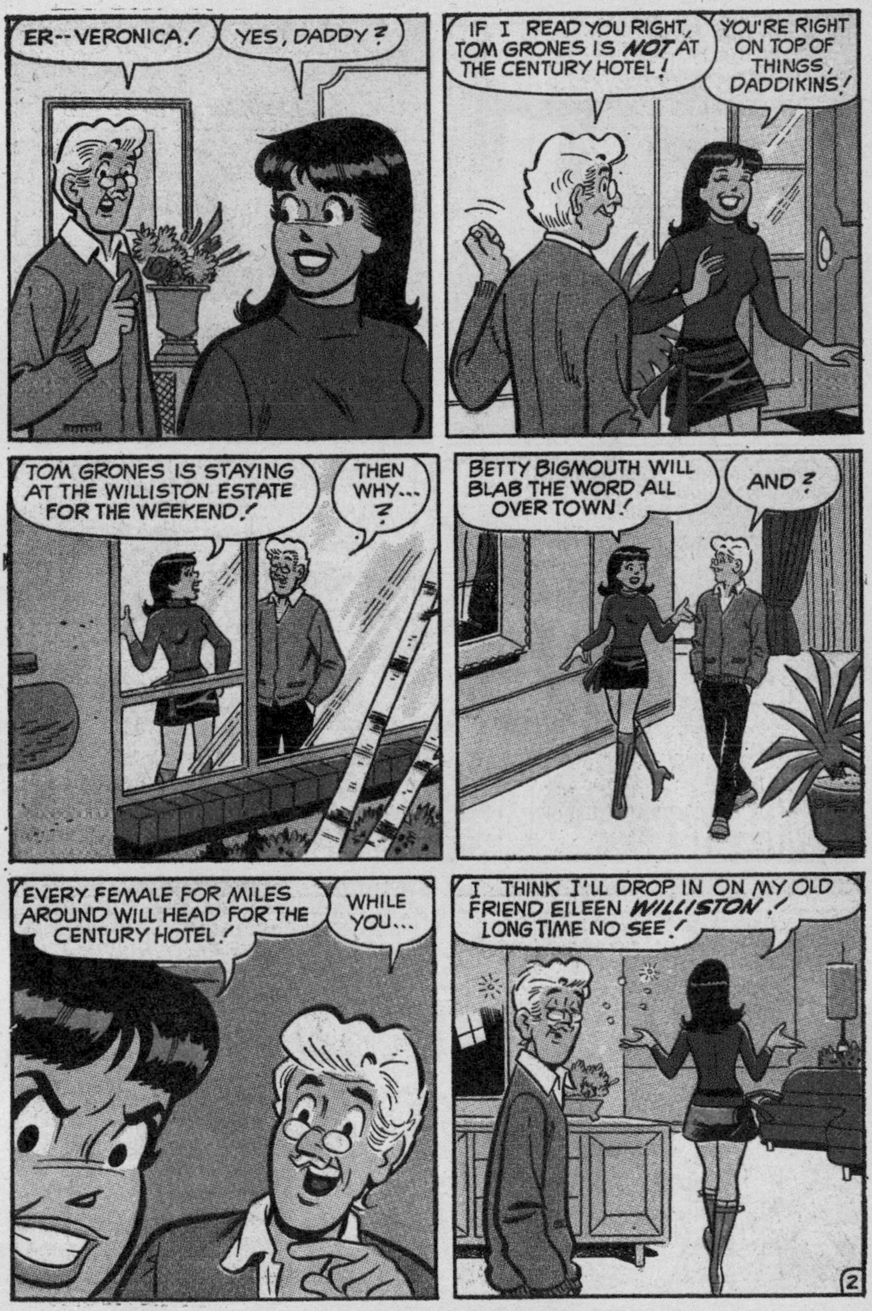
ER--VERONICA!
YES, DADDY?
IF I READ YOU RIGHT, TOM GRONES IS NOT AT THE CENTURY HOTEL!
YOU'RE RIGHT ON TOP OF THINGS, DADDIKINS!
TOM GRONES IS STAYING AT THE WILLISTON ESTATE FOR THE WEEKEND!
THEN WHY...?
BETTY BIGMOUTH WILL BLAB THE WORD ALL OVER TOWN!
AND?
EVERY FEMALE FOR MILES AROUND WILL HEAD FOR THE CENTURY HOTEL!
WHILE YOU...
I THINK I'LL DROP IN ON MY OLD FRIEND EILEEN WILLISTON! LONG TIME NO SEE!
2

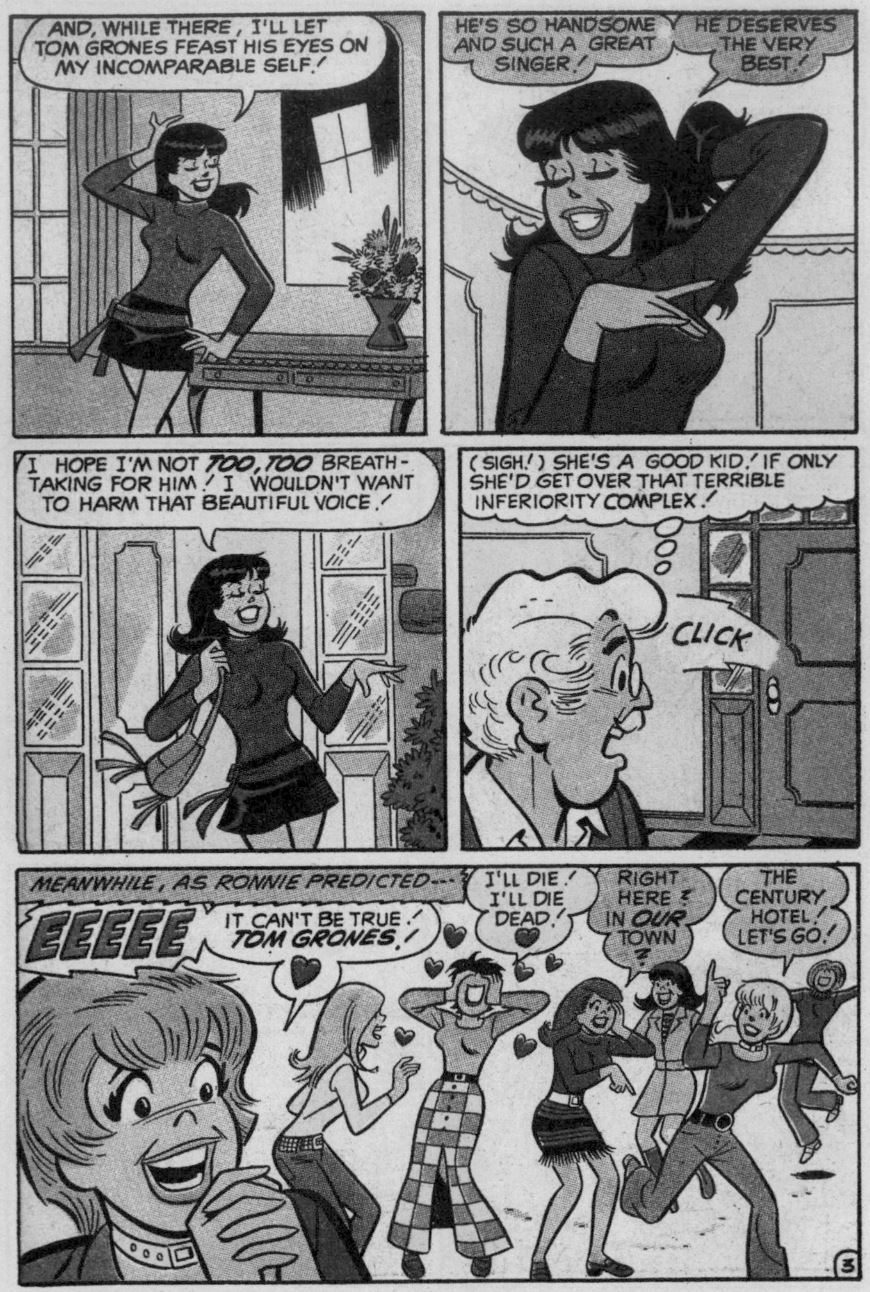
AND, WHILE THERE, I'LL LET TOM GRONES FEAST HIS EYES ON MY INCOMPARABLE SELF.!
HE'S SO HANDSOME AND SUCH A GREAT SINGER!
HE DESERVES THE VERY BEST!
I HOPE I'M NOT TOO, TOO BREATH-TAKING FOR HIM! I WOULDN'T WANT TO HARM THAT BEAUTIFUL VOICE!
(SIGH!) SHE'S A GOOD KID! IF ONLY SHE'D GET OVER THAT TERRIBLE INFERIORITY COMPLEX!
CLICK
MEANWHILE, AS RONNIE PREDICTED---
EEEEE
IT CAN'T BE TRUE! TOM GRONES!
I'LL DIE! I'LL DIE DEAD!
RIGHT HERE? IN OUR TOWN?
THE CENTURY HOTEL! LET'S GO!
3

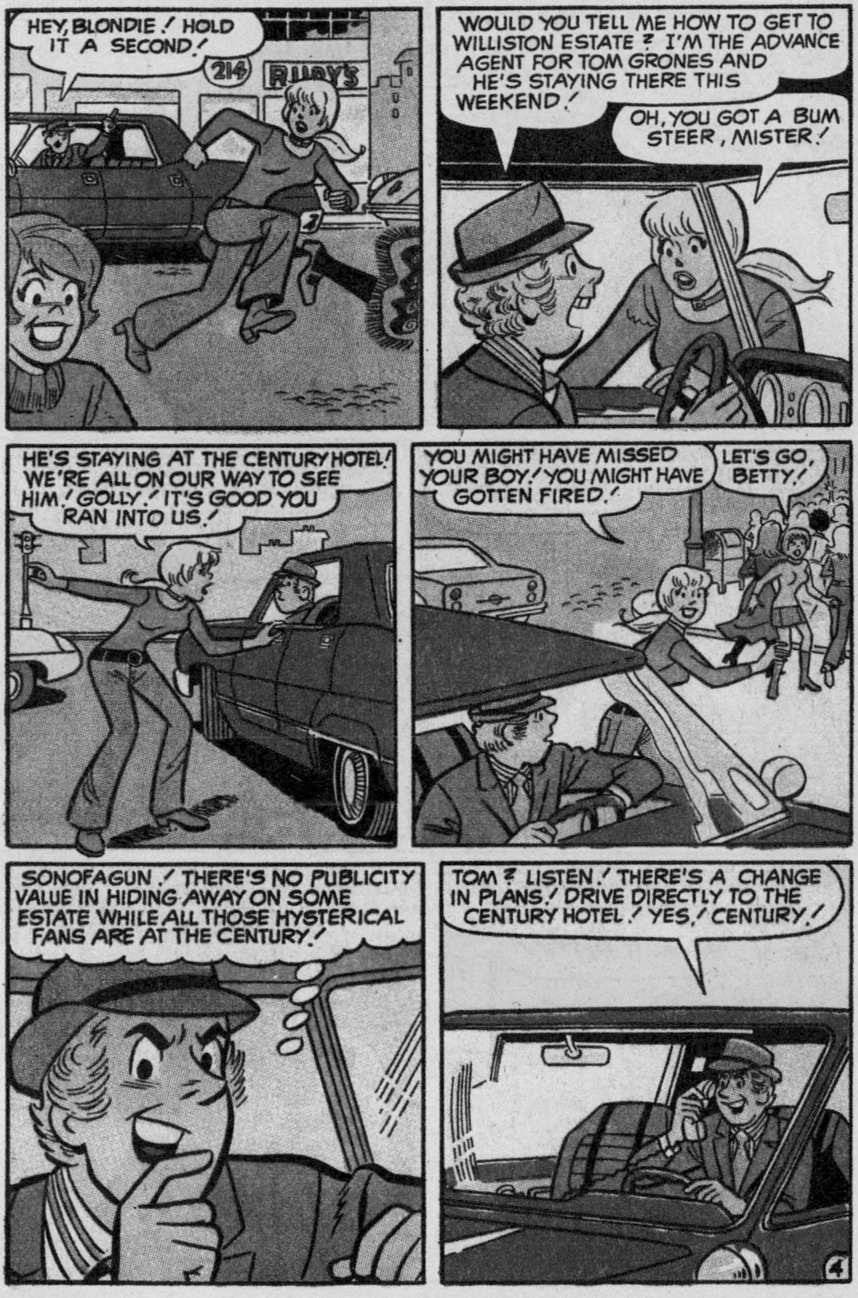
HEY, BLONDIE! HOLD IT A SECOND!
214
RUDY'S
WOULD YOU TELL ME HOW TO GET TO WILLISTON ESTATE? I'M THE ADVANCE AGENT FOR TOM GRONES AND HE'S STAYING THERE THIS WEEKEND!
OH, YOU GOT A BUM STEER, MISTER!
HE'S STAYING AT THE CENTURY HOTEL! WE'RE ALL ON OUR WAY TO SEE HIM! GOLLY! IT'S GOOD YOU RAN INTO US!
YOU MIGHT HAVE MISSED YOUR BOY! YOU MIGHT HAVE GOTTEN FIRED!
LET'S GO, BETTY!
SONOFAGUN! THERE'S NO PUBLICITY VALUE IN HIDING AWAY ON SOME ESTATE WHILE ALL THOSE HYSTERICAL FANS ARE AT THE CENTURY!
TOM? LISTEN! THERE'S A CHANGE IN PLANS! DRIVE DIRECTLY TO THE CENTURY HOTEL! YES, CENTURY!
4

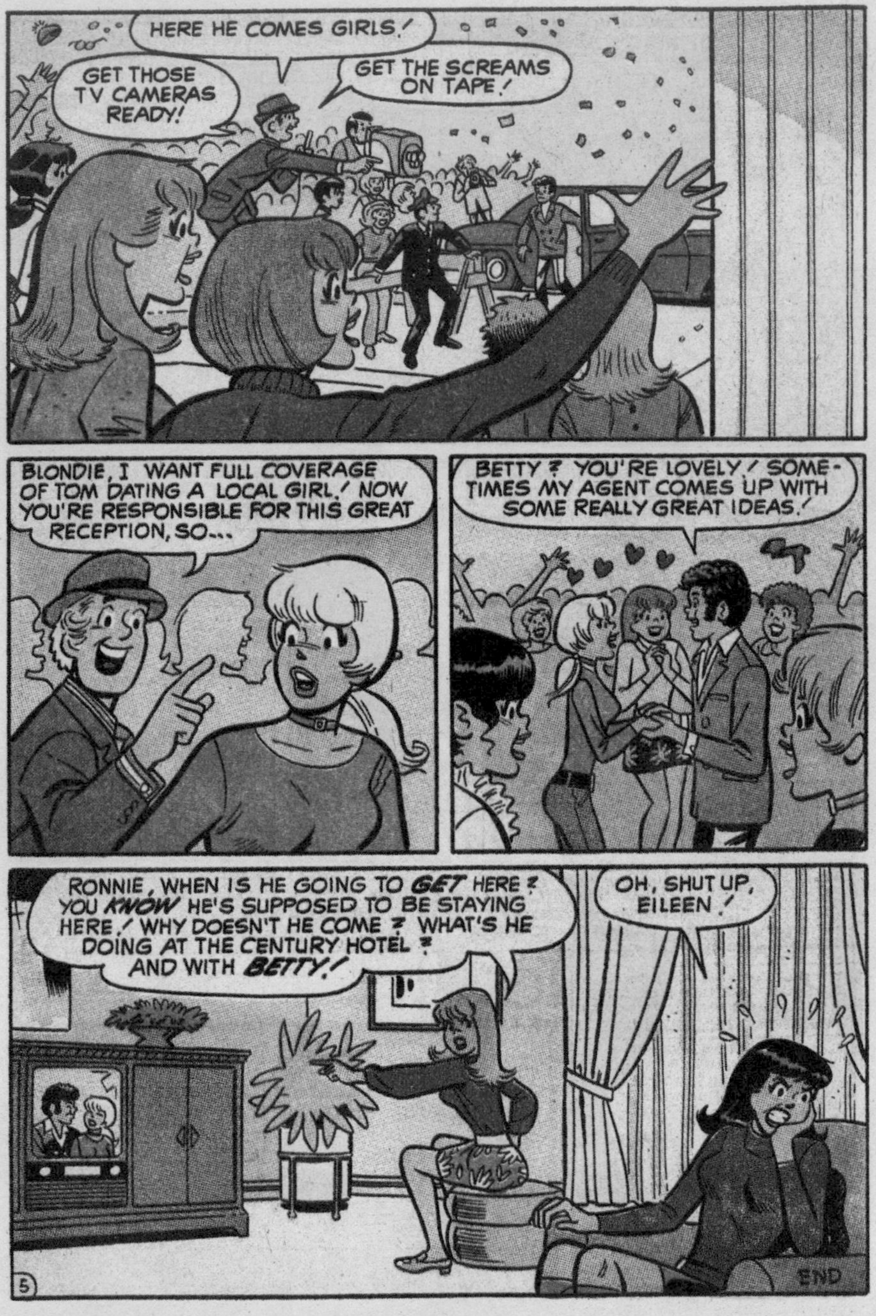
HERE HE COMES GIRLS!
GET THOSE TV CAMERAS READY!
GET THE SCREAMS ON TAPE!
BLONDIE, I WANT FULL COVERAGE OF TOM DATING A LOCAL GIRL! NOW YOU'RE RESPONSIBLE FOR THIS GREAT RECEPTION, SO...
BETTY? YOU'RE LOVELY! SOMETIMES MY AGENT COMES UP WITH SOME REALLY GREAT IDEAS!
RONNIE, WHEN IS HE GOING TO GET HERE? YOU KNOW HE'S SUPPOSED TO BE STAYING HERE! WHY DOESN'T HE COME? WHAT'S HE DOING AT THE CENTURY HOTEL? AND WITH BETTY!
OH, SHUT UP, EILEEN!
5
END

Star Struck
Laugh #267, 1973
by Stan Goldberg, Jon D'Agostino

This story is very much of its time in a lot of ways: the fashions, the pop idols du jour, and the less-than-PC teasing banter between sexes (which probably wouldn't make it into print these days. The girls do get the last word, though!). One thing is timeless, however—teen boys and girls will likely always scoff at each other's celebrity crushes.

-- Duncan McLachlan
Graphic Novel Development,
Archie Comics

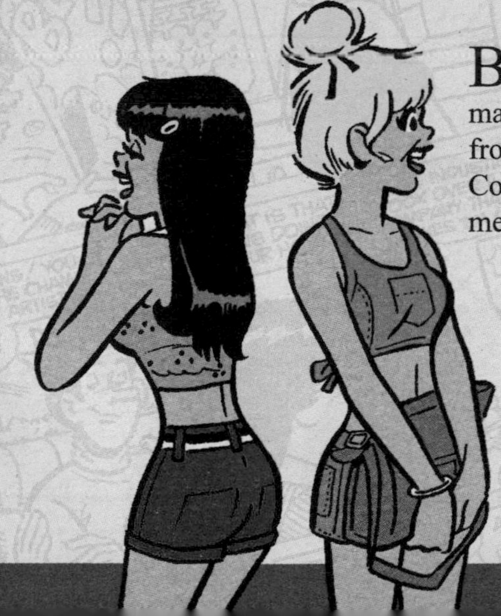

Riverdale Rock
Betty & Veronica #224, 1974
by Dan DeCarlo

Another great outcome in which Veronica gets her just desserts. It's so great when she's so sure of herself and sweet, unassuming Betty gets the prize instead.

-- Ellen Leonforte
Senior Art Director,
Archie Comics

Video Vexation
Betty & Veronica #263, 1977
by George Gladir, Dan DeCarlo, Barry Grossman

Betty & Veronica learn how to master video games with help from Dilton. Ask anyone at Archie Comics—this story was made for me.

-- Jonathan Betancourt
Publishing Coordinator,
Archie Comics

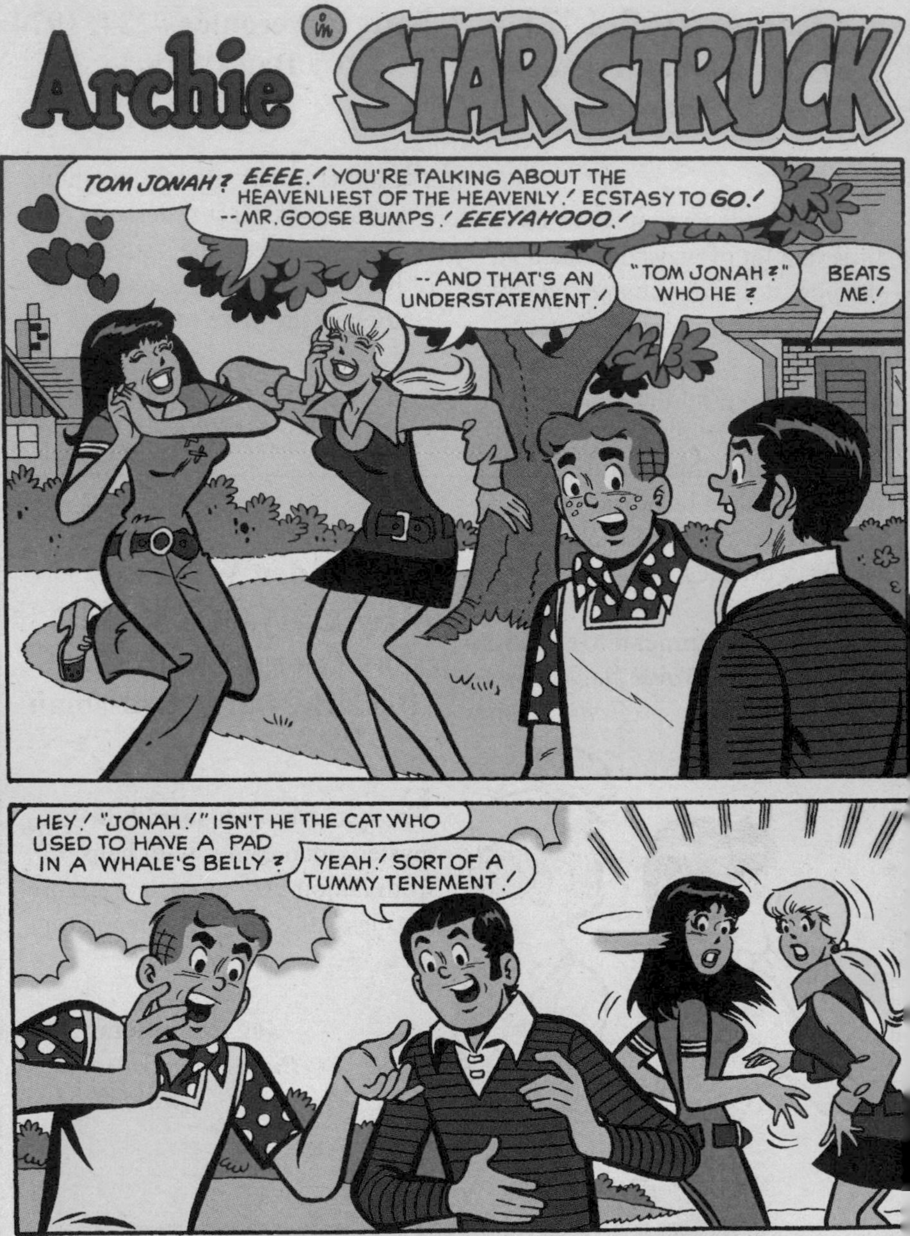
Archie in STAR STRUCK
TOM JONAH? EEEE.! YOU'RE TALKING ABOUT THE HEAVENLIEST OF THE HEAVENLY.! ECSTASY TO GO.! --MR. GOOSE BUMPS.! EEEYAHOOO.!
-- AND THAT'S AN UNDERSTATEMENT.!
"TOM JONAH?" WHO HE?
BEATS ME.!
HEY.! "JONAH.!" ISN'T HE THE CAT WHO USED TO HAVE A PAD IN A WHALE'S BELLY?
YEAH.! SORT OF A TUMMY TENEMENT.!

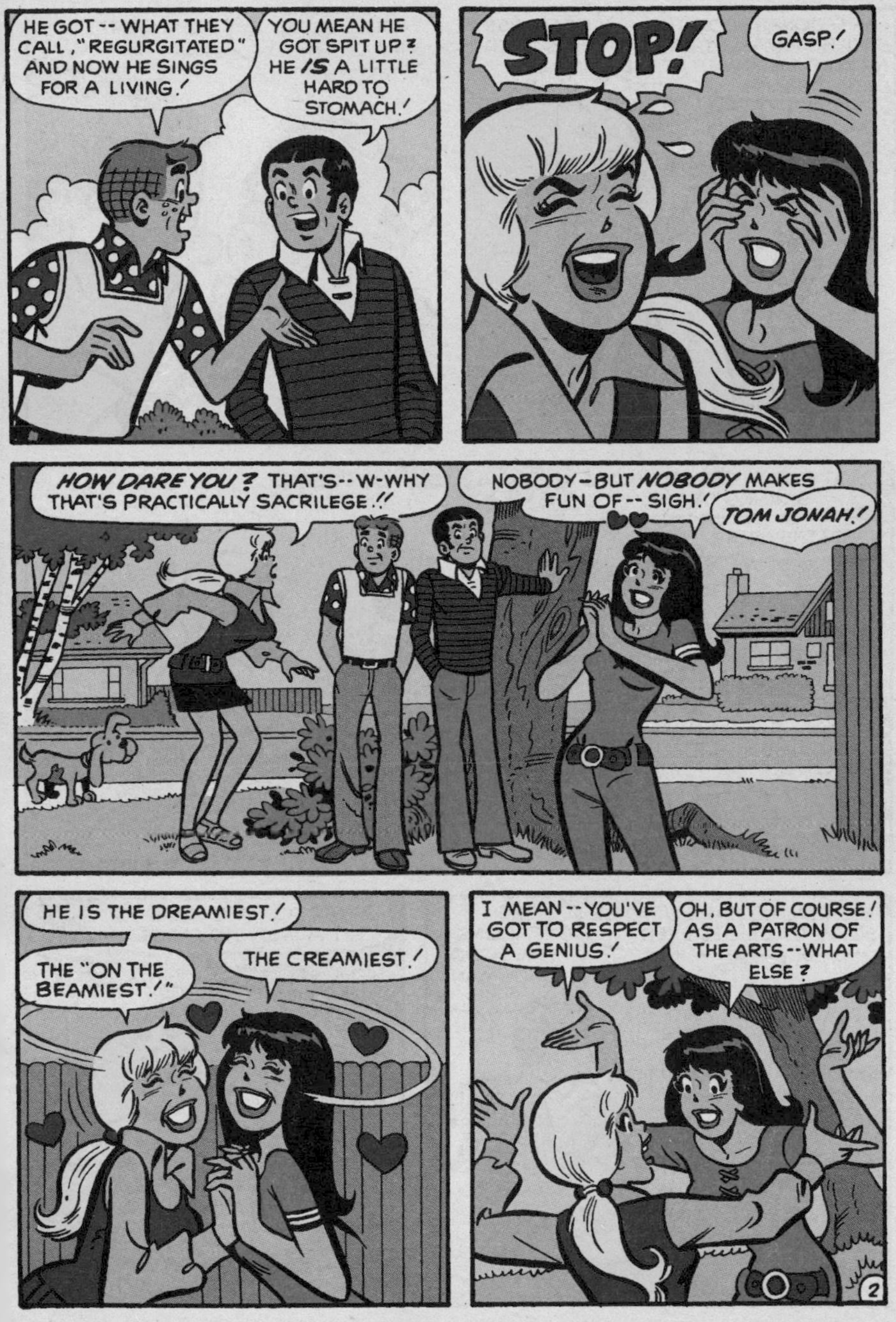
HE GOT -- WHAT THEY CALL, "REGURGITATED" AND NOW HE SINGS FOR A LIVING!
YOU MEAN HE GOT SPIT UP? HE IS A LITTLE HARD TO STOMACH!
STOP!
GASP!
HOW DARE YOU? THAT'S-- W-WHY THAT'S PRACTICALLY SACRILEGE!!
NOBODY-- BUT NOBODY MAKES FUN OF -- SIGH!
TOM JONAH!
HE IS THE DREAMIEST!
THE "ON THE BEAMIEST!"
THE CREAMIEST!
I MEAN -- YOU'VE GOT TO RESPECT A GENIUS!
OH, BUT OF COURSE! AS A PATRON OF THE ARTS -- WHAT ELSE?
2

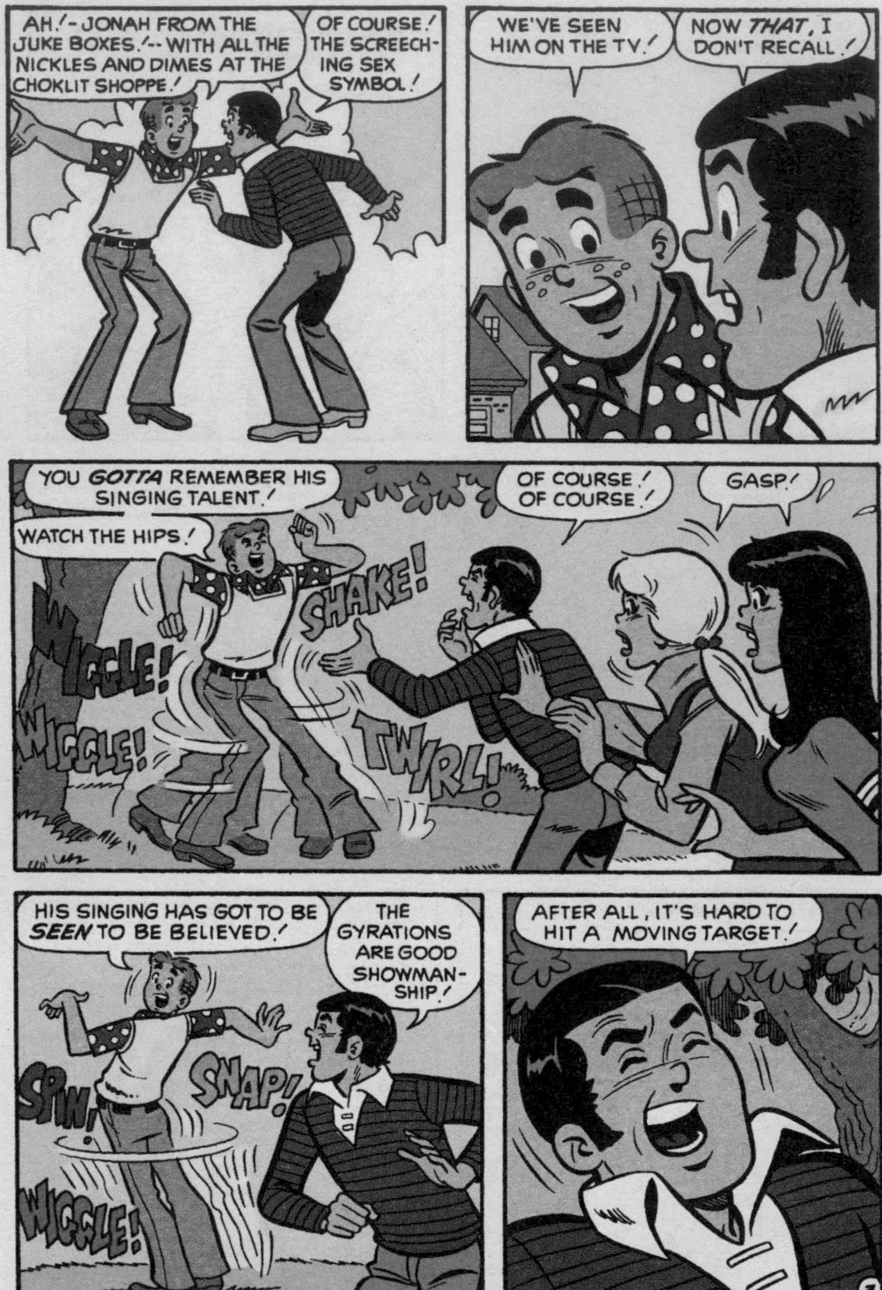
AH!-JONAH FROM THE JUKE BOXES!--WITH ALL THE NICKLES AND DIMES AT THE CHOKLIT SHOPPE!
OF COURSE! THE SCREECHING SEX SYMBOL!
WE'VE SEEN HIM ON THE TV!
NOW THAT, I DON'T RECALL!
YOU GOTTA REMEMBER HIS SINGING TALENT!
WATCH THE HIPS!
OF COURSE! OF COURSE!
GASP!
SHAKE!
WIGGLE!
WIGGLE!
TWIRL!
HIS SINGING HAS GOT TO BE SEEN TO BE BELIEVED!
THE GYRATIONS ARE GOOD SHOWMANSHIP!
SPIN!
SNAP!
WIGGLE!
AFTER ALL, IT'S HARD TO HIT A MOVING TARGET!
3

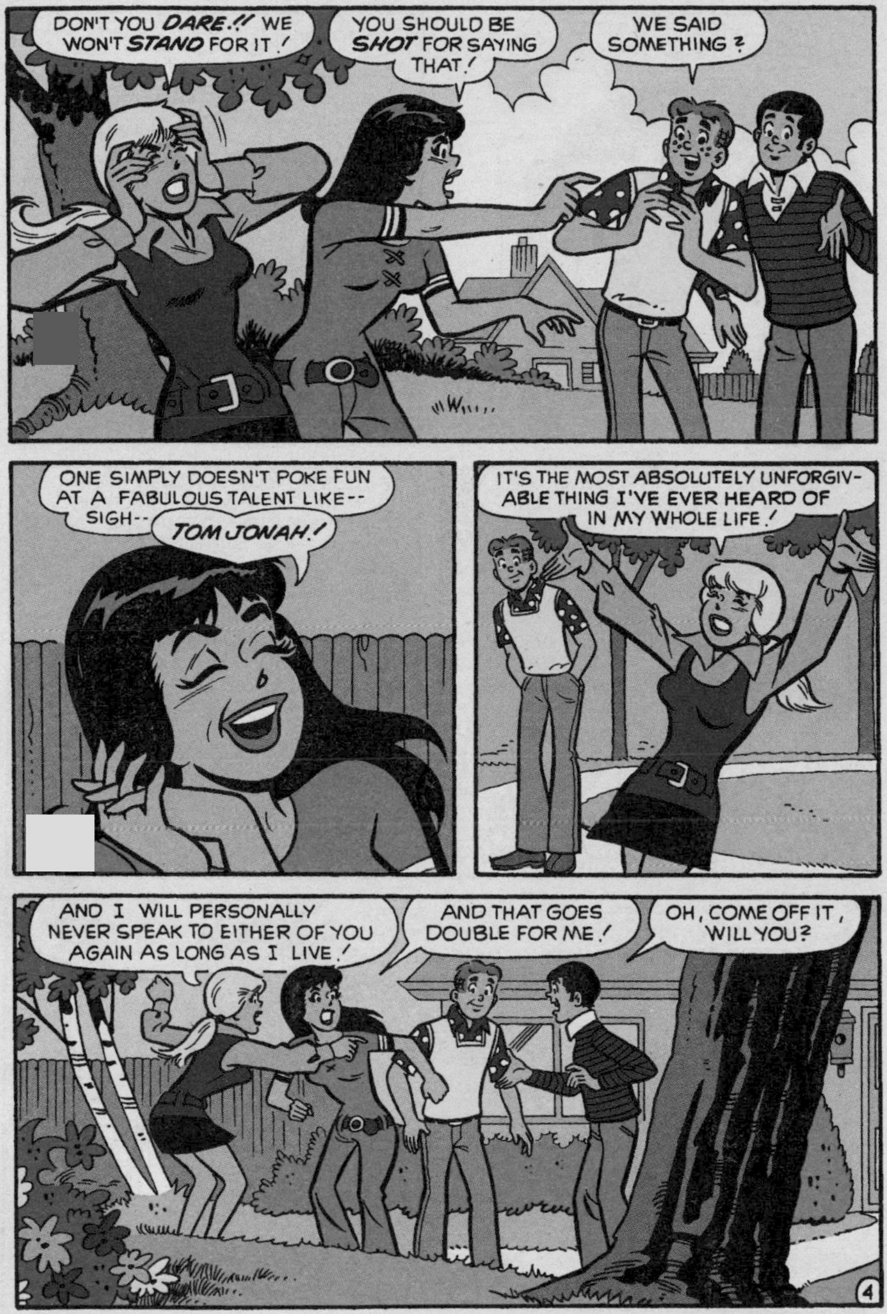
DON'T YOU DARE.!! WE WON'T STAND FOR IT.!
YOU SHOULD BE SHOT FOR SAYING THAT.!
WE SAID SOMETHING ?
ONE SIMPLY DOESN'T POKE FUN AT A FABULOUS TALENT LIKE-- SIGH--
TOM JONAH.!
IT'S THE MOST ABSOLUTELY UNFORGIV-ABLE THING I'VE EVER HEARD OF IN MY WHOLE LIFE.!
AND I WILL PERSONALLY NEVER SPEAK TO EITHER OF YOU AGAIN AS LONG AS I LIVE.!
AND THAT GOES DOUBLE FOR ME.!
OH, COME OFF IT, WILL YOU?
4

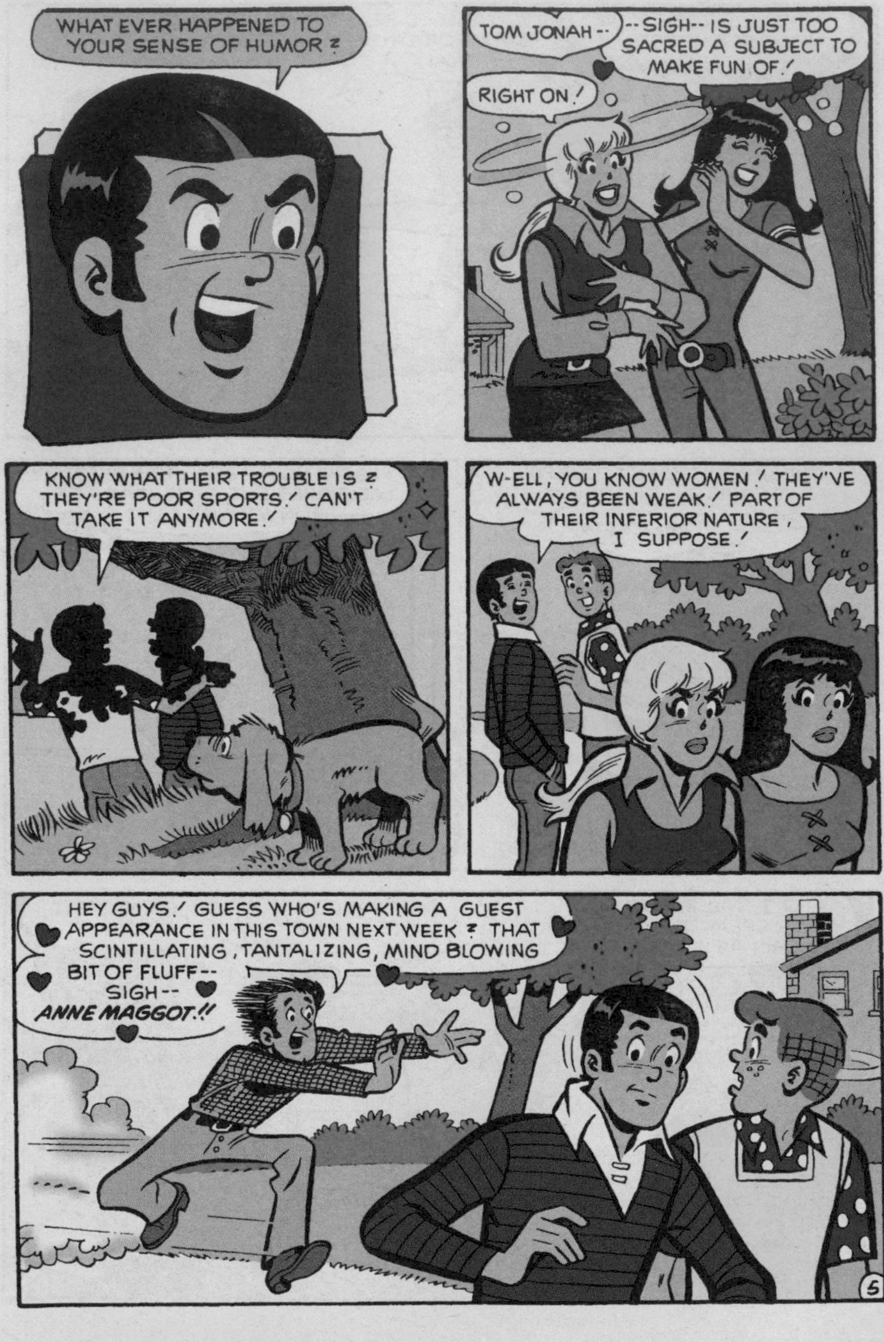
WHAT EVER HAPPENED TO YOUR SENSE OF HUMOR ?
TOM JONAH --
-- SIGH -- IS JUST TOO SACRED A SUBJECT TO MAKE FUN OF!
RIGHT ON!
KNOW WHAT THEIR TROUBLE IS ? THEY'RE POOR SPORTS! CAN'T TAKE IT ANYMORE!
W-ELL, YOU KNOW WOMEN! THEY'VE ALWAYS BEEN WEAK! PART OF THEIR INFERIOR NATURE, I SUPPOSE!
HEY GUYS! GUESS WHO'S MAKING A GUEST APPEARANCE IN THIS TOWN NEXT WEEK ? THAT SCINTILLATING, TANTALIZING, MIND BLOWING BIT OF FLUFF -- SIGH -- ANNE MAGGOT!!
5

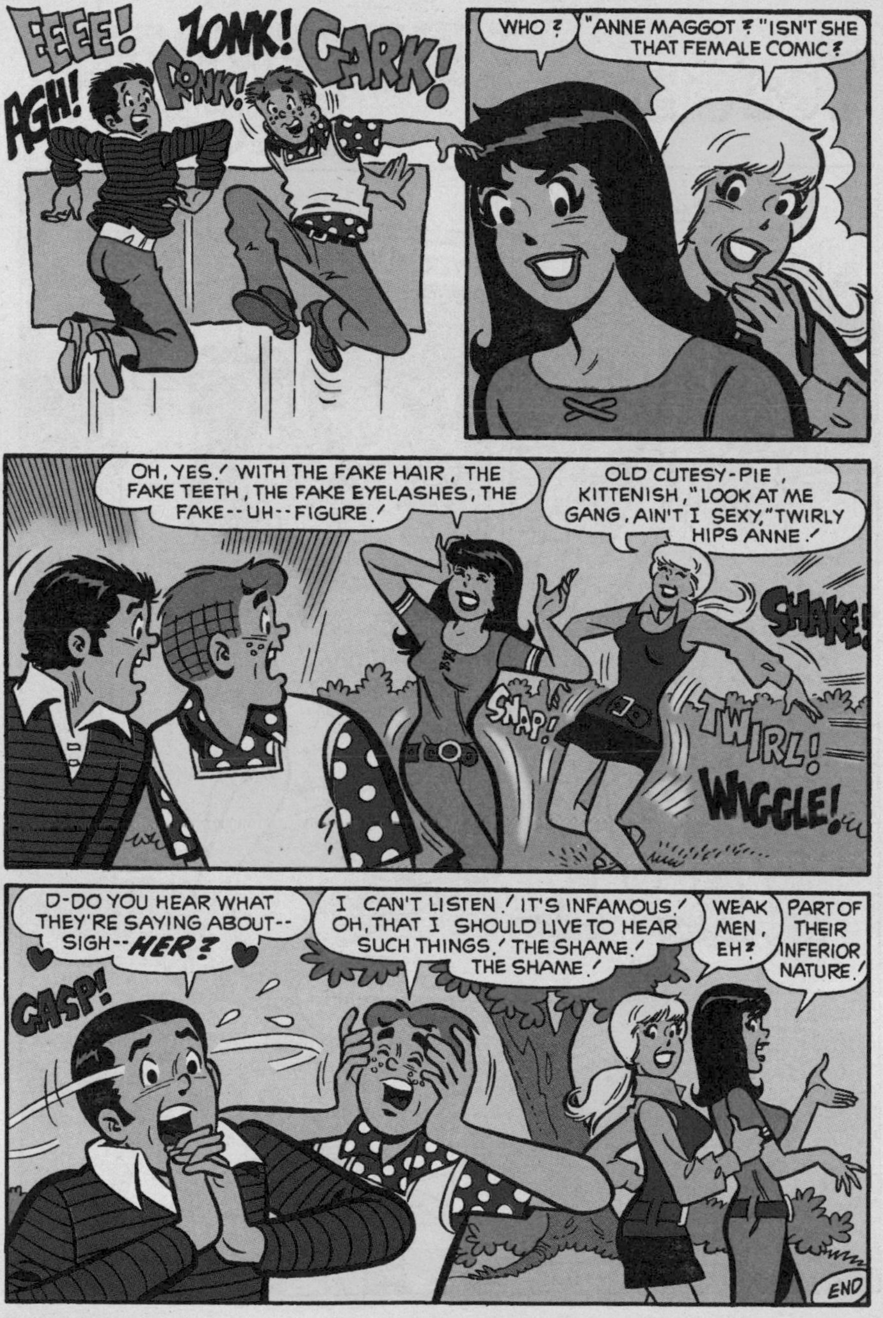
EEEE!
AGH!
ZONK!
CONK!
GARK!
WHO?
"ANNE MAGGOT?" ISN'T SHE THAT FEMALE COMIC?
OH, YES! WITH THE FAKE HAIR, THE FAKE TEETH, THE FAKE EYELASHES, THE FAKE--UH--FIGURE!
OLD CUTESY-PIE, KITTENISH, "LOOK AT ME GANG, AIN'T I SEXY," TWIRLY HIPS ANNE!
SHAKE!
SNAP!
TWIRL!
WIGGLE!
D-DO YOU HEAR WHAT THEY'RE SAYING ABOUT--SIGH--HER?
GASP!
I CAN'T LISTEN! IT'S INFAMOUS! OH, THAT I SHOULD LIVE TO HEAR SUCH THINGS! THE SHAME! THE SHAME!
WEAK MEN, EH?
PART OF THEIR INFERIOR NATURE!
END

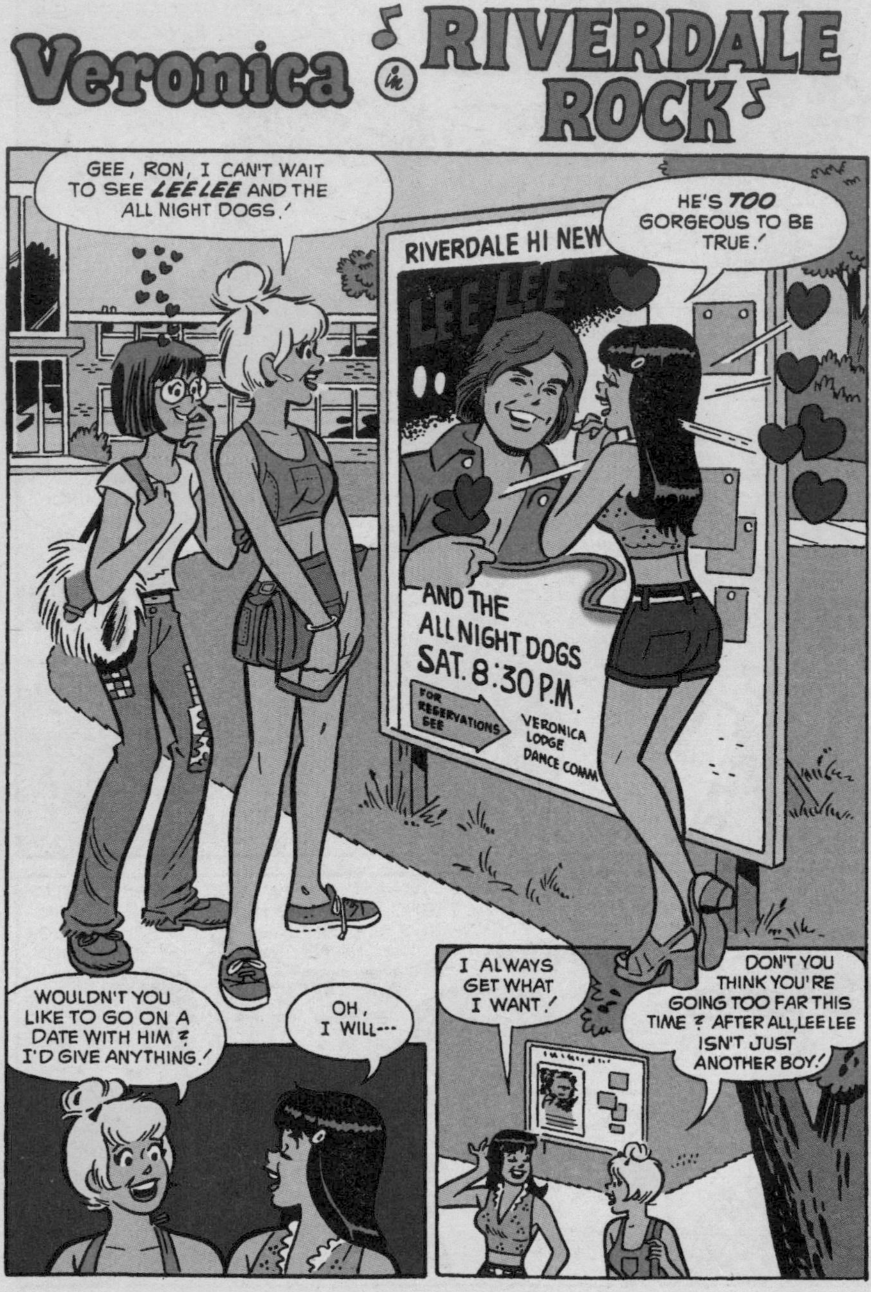
Veronica in RIVERDALE ROCK
GEE, RON, I CAN'T WAIT TO SEE LEE LEE AND THE ALL NIGHT DOGS!
HE'S TOO GORGEOUS TO BE TRUE!
RIVERDALE HI NEW
LEE LEE
AND THE ALL NIGHT DOGS
SAT. 8:30 P.M.
FOR RESERVATIONS SEE
VERONICA LODGE
DANCE COMM
WOULDN'T YOU LIKE TO GO ON A DATE WITH HIM? I'D GIVE ANYTHING!
OH, I WILL---
I ALWAYS GET WHAT I WANT!
DON'T YOU THINK YOU'RE GOING TOO FAR THIS TIME? AFTER ALL, LEE LEE ISN'T JUST ANOTHER BOY!

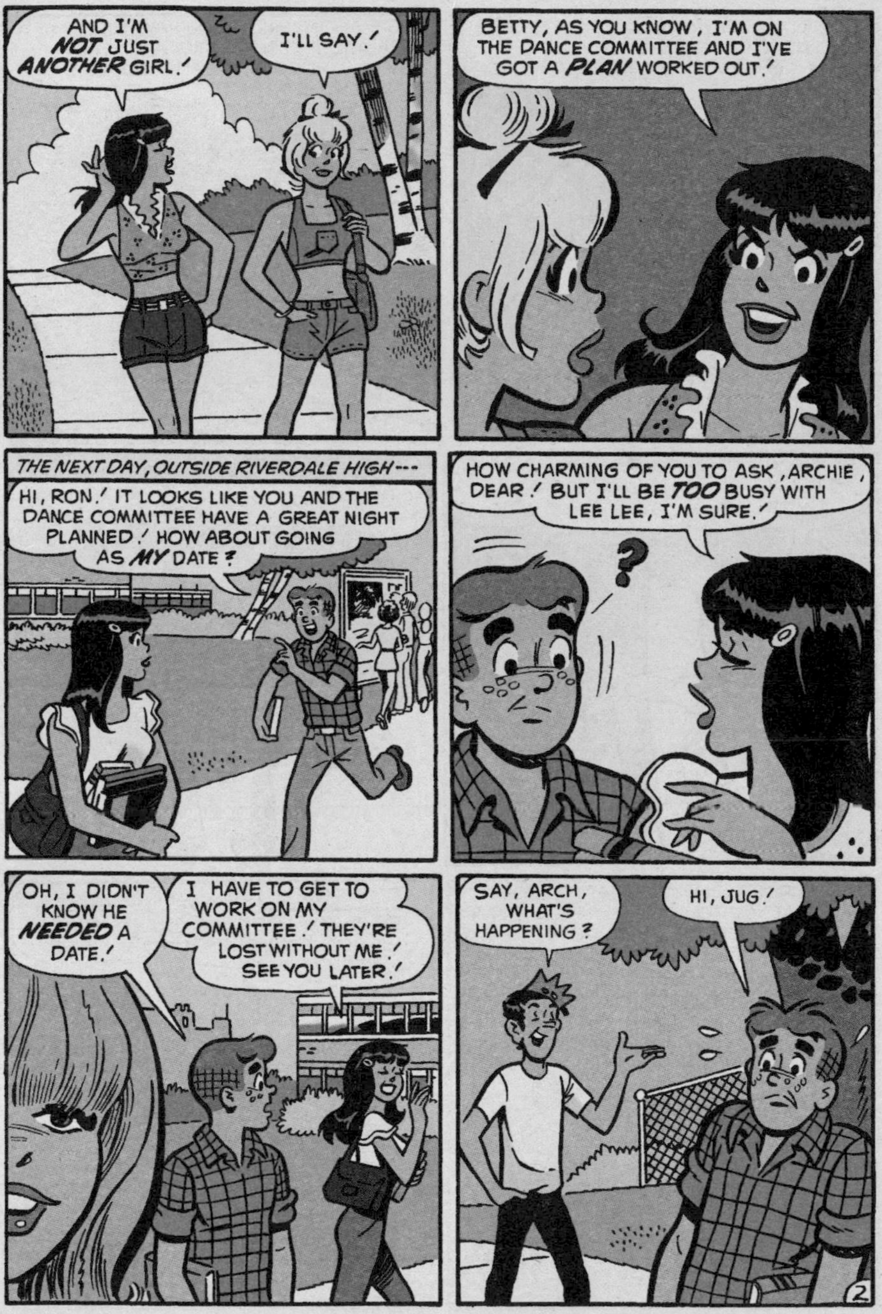
AND I'M NOT JUST ANOTHER GIRL!
I'LL SAY!
BETTY, AS YOU KNOW, I'M ON THE DANCE COMMITTEE AND I'VE GOT A PLAN WORKED OUT!
THE NEXT DAY, OUTSIDE RIVERDALE HIGH---
HI, RON! IT LOOKS LIKE YOU AND THE DANCE COMMITTEE HAVE A GREAT NIGHT PLANNED! HOW ABOUT GOING AS MY DATE?
HOW CHARMING OF YOU TO ASK, ARCHIE, DEAR! BUT I'LL BE TOO BUSY WITH LEE LEE, I'M SURE!
?
OH, I DIDN'T KNOW HE NEEDED A DATE!
I HAVE TO GET TO WORK ON MY COMMITTEE! THEY'RE LOST WITHOUT ME! SEE YOU LATER!
SAY, ARCH, WHAT'S HAPPENING?
HI, JUG!
2

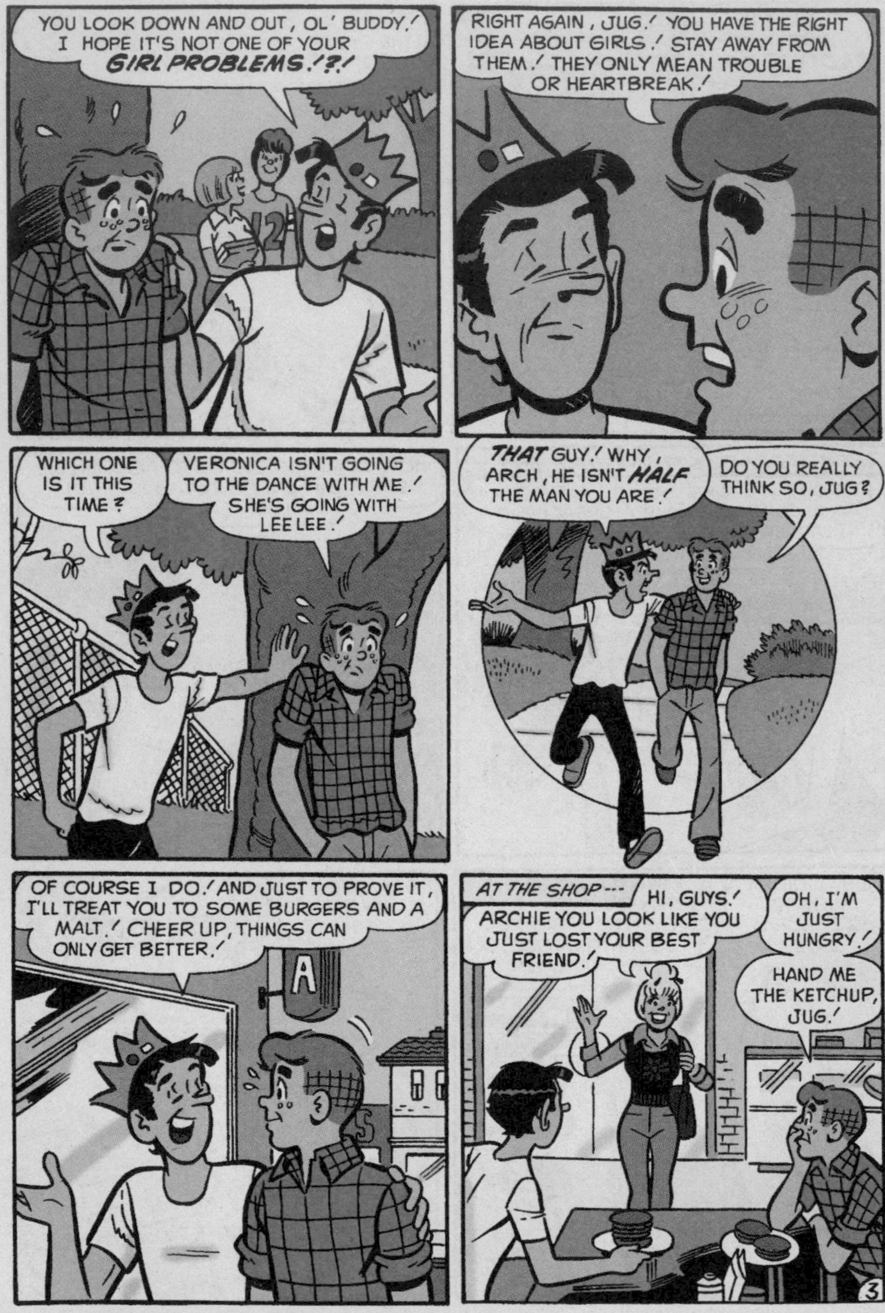
YOU LOOK DOWN AND OUT, OL' BUDDY! I HOPE IT'S NOT ONE OF YOUR GIRL PROBLEMS!?!
12
RIGHT AGAIN, JUG! YOU HAVE THE RIGHT IDEA ABOUT GIRLS! STAY AWAY FROM THEM! THEY ONLY MEAN TROUBLE OR HEARTBREAK!
WHICH ONE IS IT THIS TIME?
VERONICA ISN'T GOING TO THE DANCE WITH ME! SHE'S GOING WITH LEE LEE!
THAT GUY! WHY, ARCH, HE ISN'T HALF THE MAN YOU ARE!
DO YOU REALLY THINK SO, JUG?
OF COURSE I DO! AND JUST TO PROVE IT, I'LL TREAT YOU TO SOME BURGERS AND A MALT! CHEER UP, THINGS CAN ONLY GET BETTER!
A
AT THE SHOP---
HI, GUYS! ARCHIE YOU LOOK LIKE YOU JUST LOST YOUR BEST FRIEND!
OH, I'M JUST HUNGRY!
HAND ME THE KETCHUP, JUG!
3

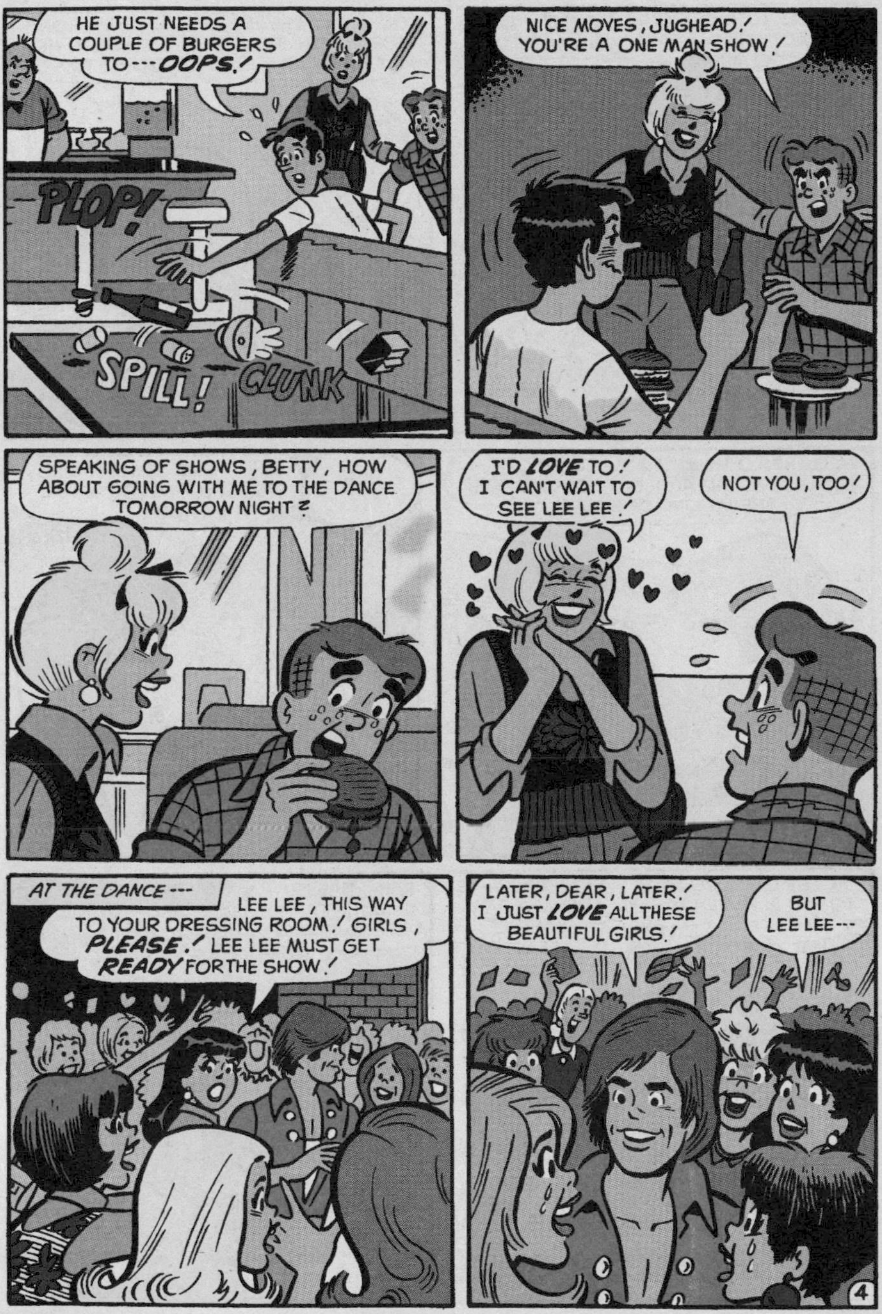
HE JUST NEEDS A COUPLE OF BURGERS TO---OOPS.!
PLOP!
SPILL!
CLUNK
NICE MOVES, JUGHEAD.! YOU'RE A ONE MAN SHOW.!
SPEAKING OF SHOWS, BETTY, HOW ABOUT GOING WITH ME TO THE DANCE TOMORROW NIGHT?
I'D LOVE TO.! I CAN'T WAIT TO SEE LEE LEE.!
NOT YOU, TOO.!
AT THE DANCE---
LEE LEE, THIS WAY TO YOUR DRESSING ROOM.! GIRLS, PLEASE.! LEE LEE MUST GET READY FOR THE SHOW.!
LATER, DEAR, LATER.! I JUST LOVE ALL THESE BEAUTIFUL GIRLS.!
BUT LEE LEE---
4

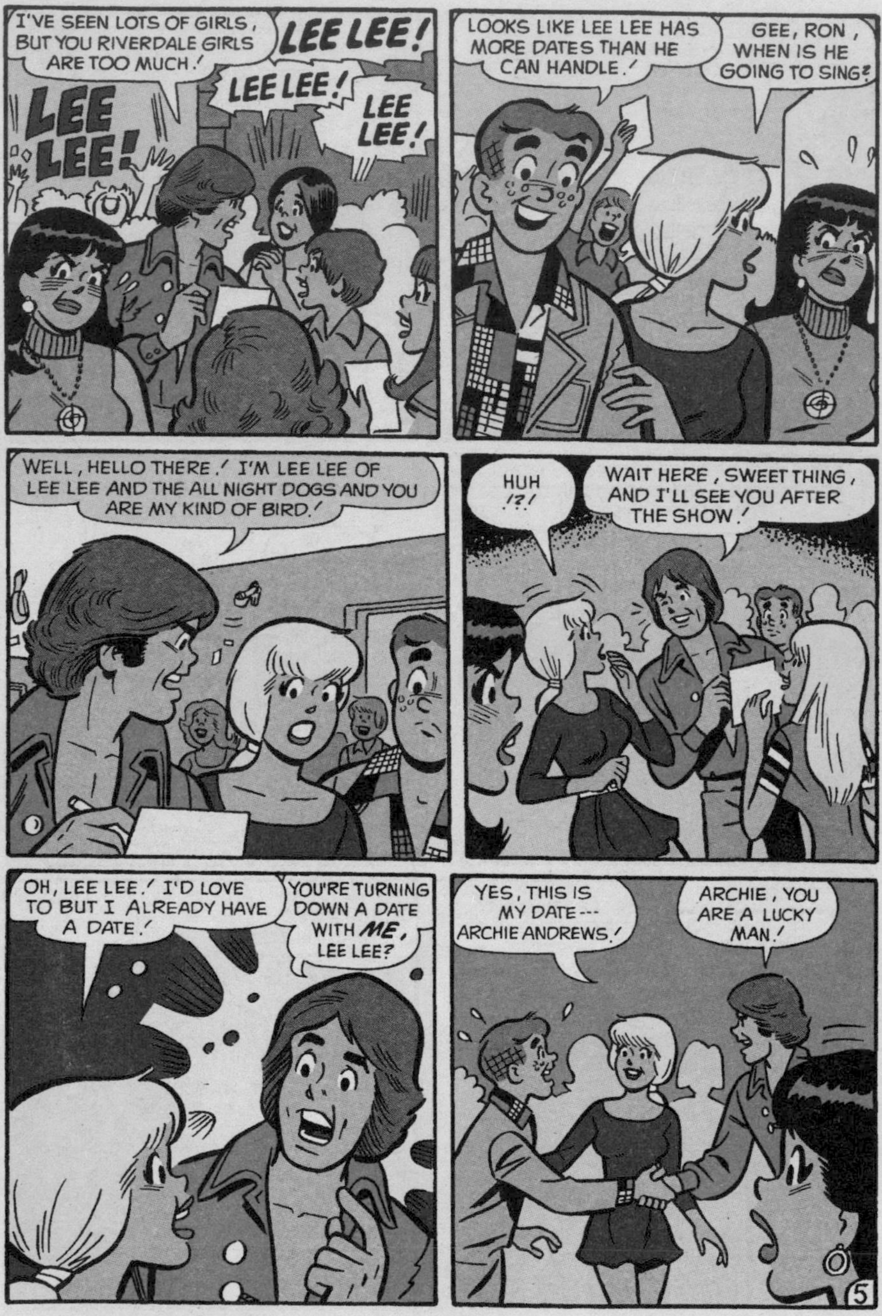
I'VE SEEN LOTS OF GIRLS, BUT YOU RIVERDALE GIRLS ARE TOO MUCH!
LEE LEE!
LEE LEE!
LEE LEE!
LEE LEE!
LOOKS LIKE LEE LEE HAS MORE DATES THAN HE CAN HANDLE!
GEE, RON, WHEN IS HE GOING TO SING?
WELL, HELLO THERE! I'M LEE LEE OF LEE LEE AND THE ALL NIGHT DOGS AND YOU ARE MY KIND OF BIRD!
HUH !?!
WAIT HERE, SWEET THING, AND I'LL SEE YOU AFTER THE SHOW!
OH, LEE LEE! I'D LOVE TO BUT I ALREADY HAVE A DATE!
YOU'RE TURNING DOWN A DATE WITH ME, LEE LEE?
YES, THIS IS MY DATE--- ARCHIE ANDREWS!
ARCHIE, YOU ARE A LUCKY MAN!
5

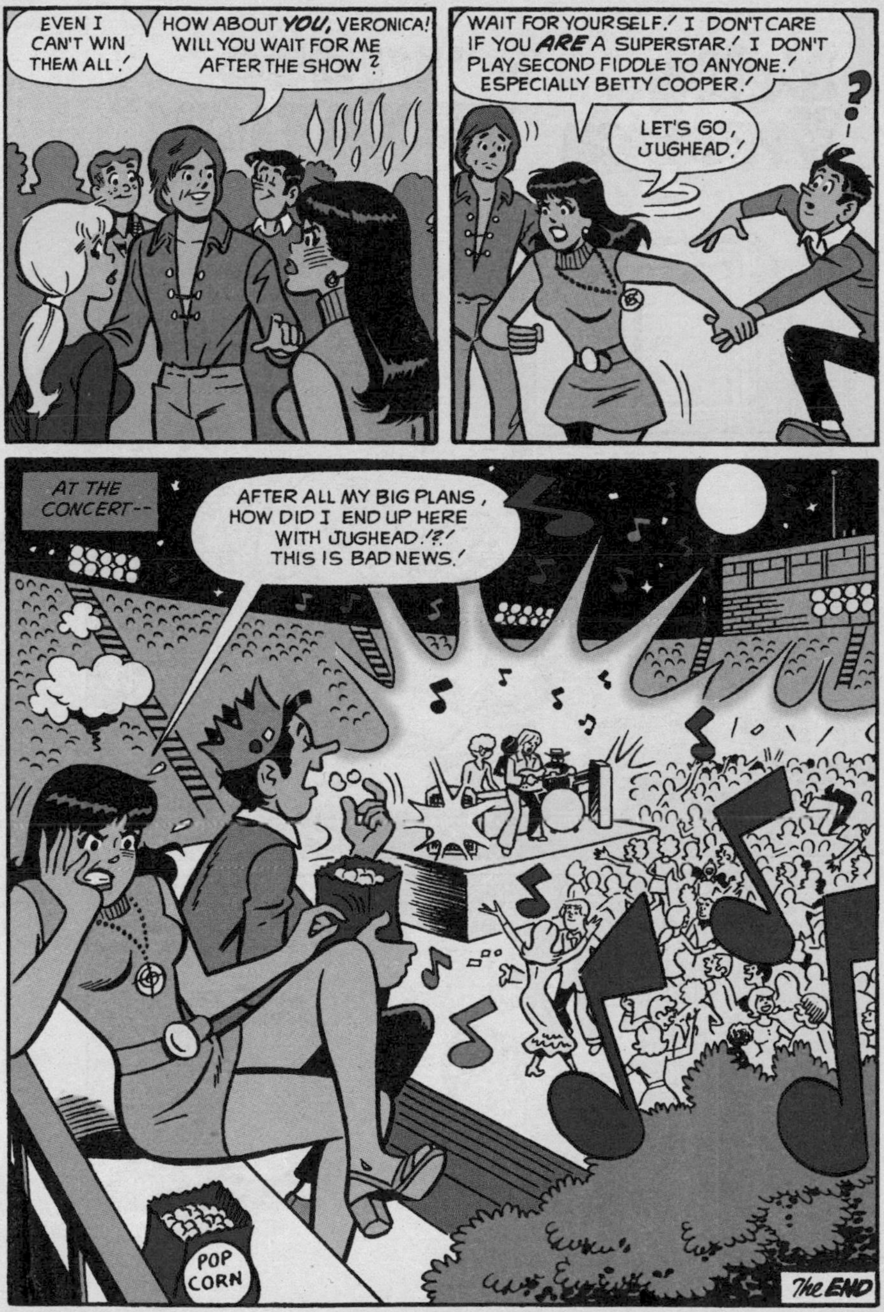
EVEN I CAN'T WIN THEM ALL!
HOW ABOUT YOU, VERONICA! WILL YOU WAIT FOR ME AFTER THE SHOW?
WAIT FOR YOURSELF! I DON'T CARE IF YOU ARE A SUPERSTAR! I DON'T PLAY SECOND FIDDLE TO ANYONE! ESPECIALLY BETTY COOPER!
LET'S GO, JUGHEAD!
?
AT THE CONCERT--
AFTER ALL MY BIG PLANS, HOW DID I END UP HERE WITH JUGHEAD!?! THIS IS BAD NEWS!
POP CORN
The END

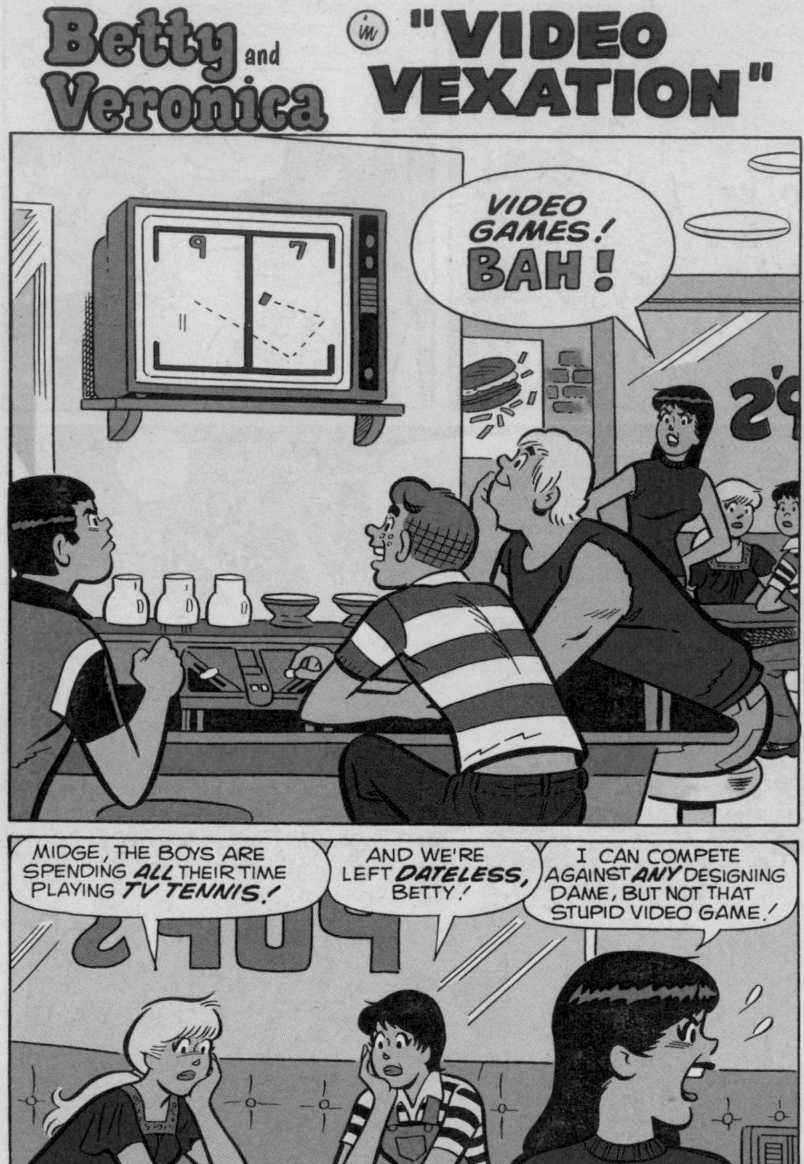
Betty and Veronica in "VIDEO VEXATION"
VIDEO GAMES! BAH!
MIDGE, THE BOYS ARE SPENDING ALL THEIR TIME PLAYING TV TENNIS!
AND WE'RE LEFT DATELESS, BETTY!
I CAN COMPETE AGAINST ANY DESIGNING DAME, BUT NOT THAT STUPID VIDEO GAME!

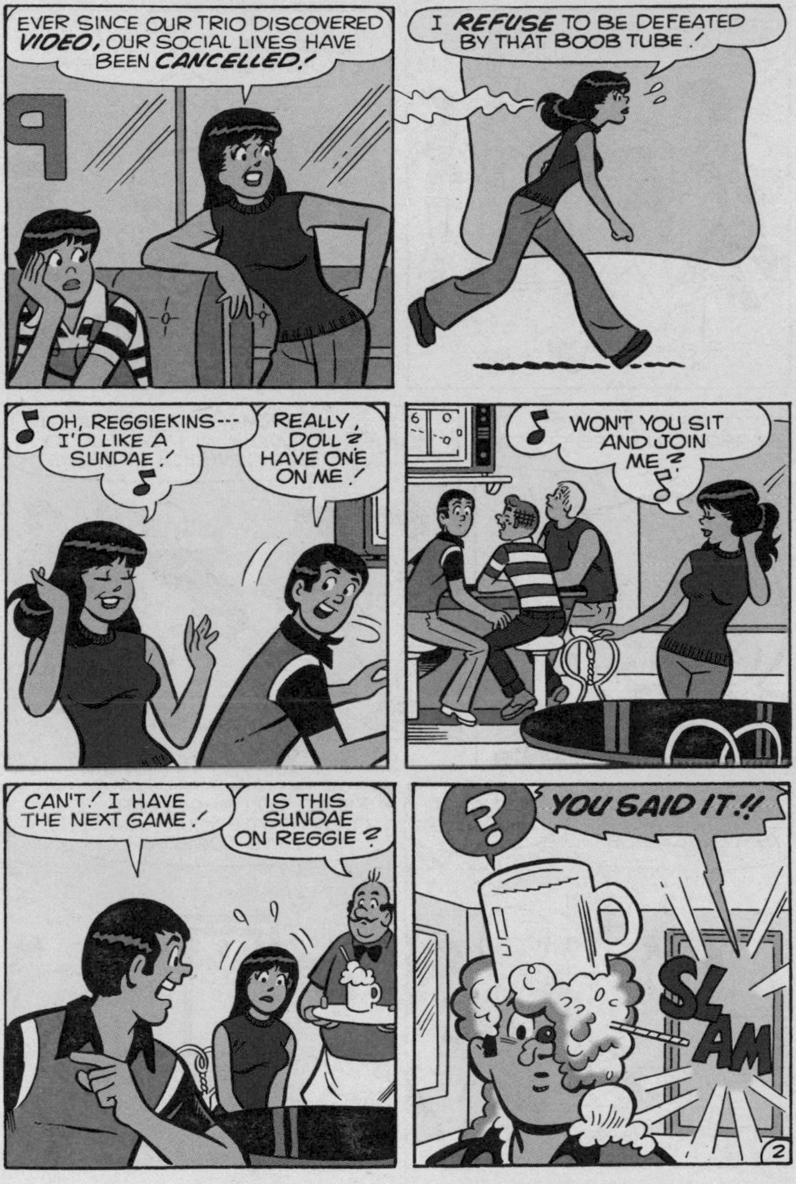
EVER SINCE OUR TRIO DISCOVERED VIDEO, OUR SOCIAL LIVES HAVE BEEN CANCELLED!
I REFUSE TO BE DEFEATED BY THAT BOOB TUBE!
OH, REGGIEKINS--- I'D LIKE A SUNDAE!
REALLY, DOLL? HAVE ONE ON ME!
WON'T YOU SIT AND JOIN ME?
CAN'T! I HAVE THE NEXT GAME!
IS THIS SUNDAE ON REGGIE?
?
YOU SAID IT!!
SLAM
2

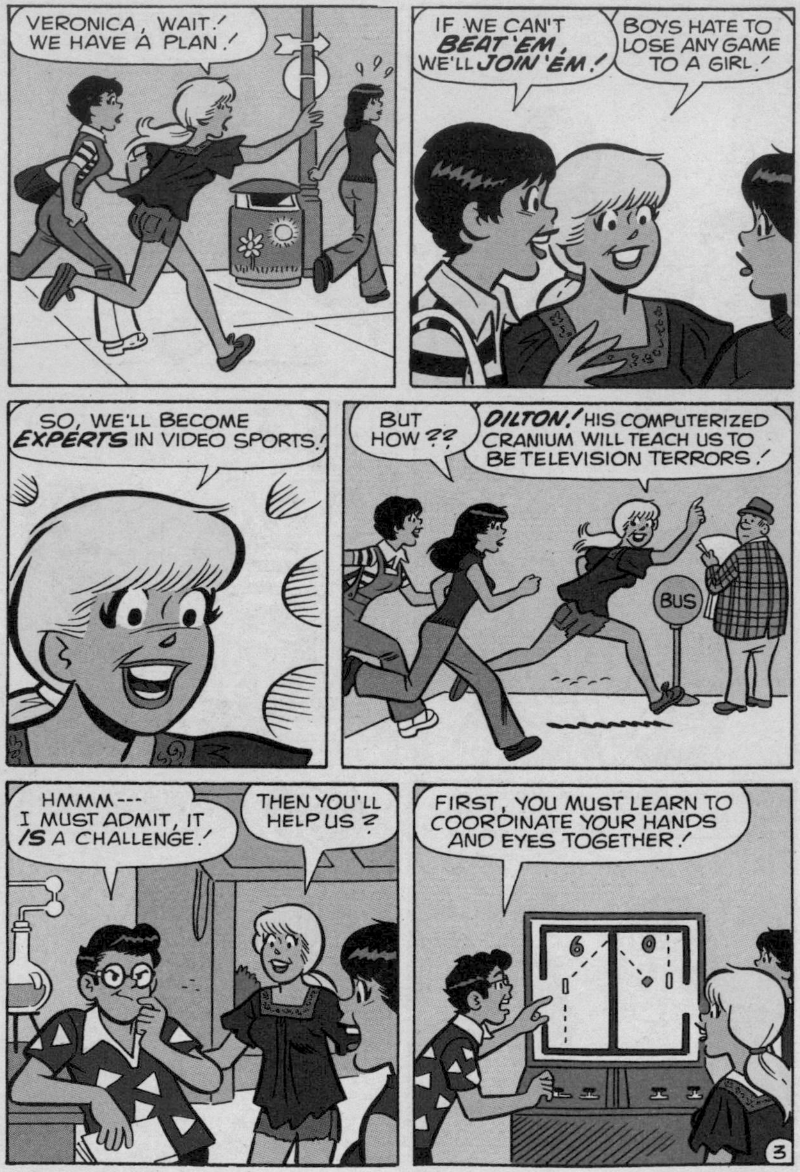
VERONICA, WAIT! WE HAVE A PLAN!
IF WE CAN'T BEAT 'EM, WE'LL JOIN 'EM!
BOYS HATE TO LOSE ANY GAME TO A GIRL!
SO, WE'LL BECOME EXPERTS IN VIDEO SPORTS!
BUT HOW??
DILTON! HIS COMPUTERIZED CRANIUM WILL TEACH US TO BE TELEVISION TERRORS!
BUS
HMMM--- I MUST ADMIT, IT IS A CHALLENGE!
THEN YOU'LL HELP US?
FIRST, YOU MUST LEARN TO COORDINATE YOUR HANDS AND EYES TOGETHER!
6
0
3

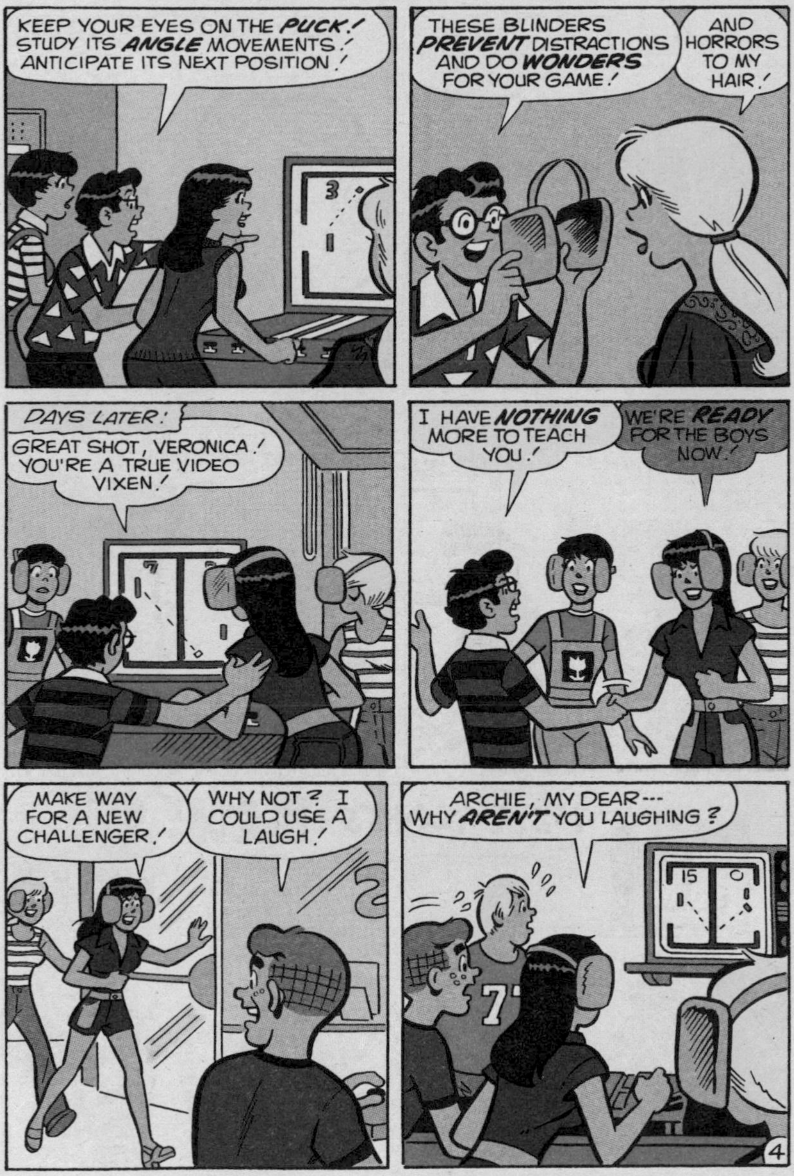
KEEP YOUR EYES ON THE PUCK! STUDY ITS ANGLE MOVEMENTS! ANTICIPATE ITS NEXT POSITION!
3
THESE BLINDERS PREVENT DISTRACTIONS AND DO WONDERS FOR YOUR GAME!
AND HORRORS TO MY HAIR!
DAYS LATER:
GREAT SHOT, VERONICA! YOU'RE A TRUE VIDEO VIXEN!
I HAVE NOTHING MORE TO TEACH YOU!
WE'RE READY FOR THE BOYS NOW!
MAKE WAY FOR A NEW CHALLENGER!
WHY NOT? I COULD USE A LAUGH!
ARCHIE, MY DEAR--- WHY AREN'T YOU LAUGHING?
15
0
4

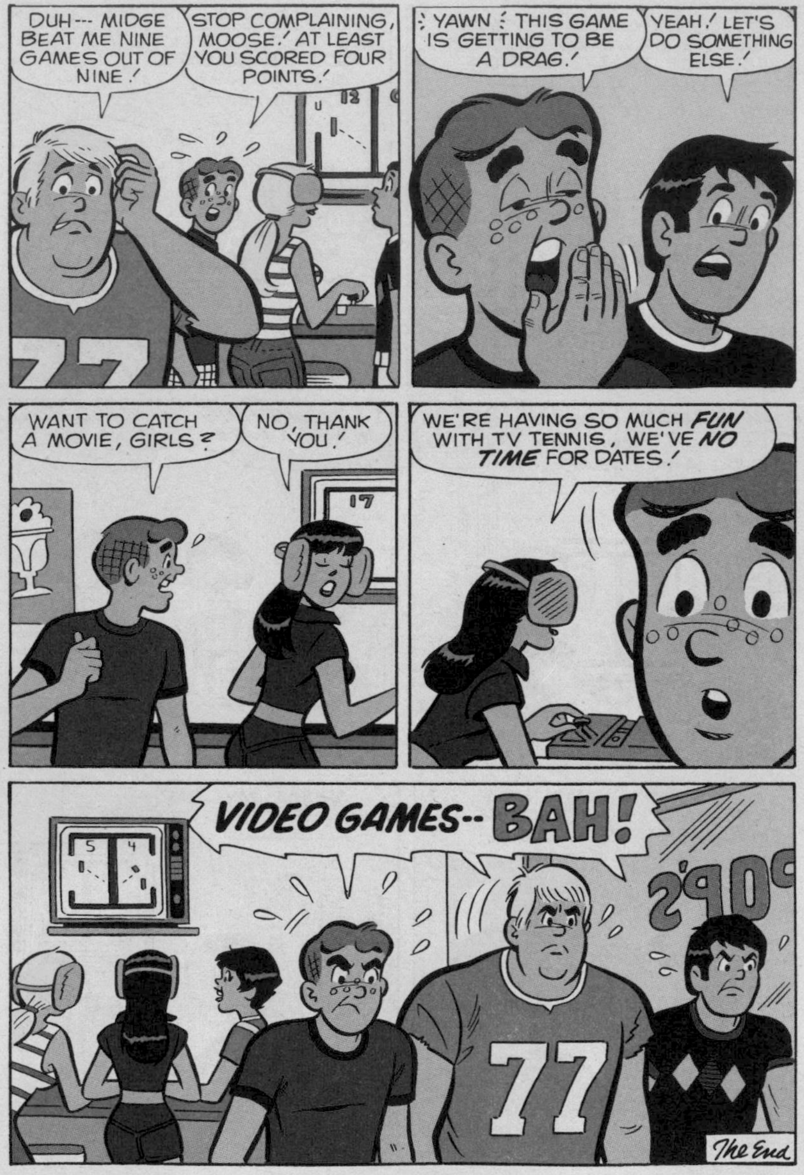
DUH--- MIDGE BEAT ME NINE GAMES OUT OF NINE!
STOP COMPLAINING, MOOSE! AT LEAST YOU SCORED FOUR POINTS!
YAWN! THIS GAME IS GETTING TO BE A DRAG!
YEAH! LET'S DO SOMETHING ELSE!
WANT TO CATCH A MOVIE, GIRLS?
NO, THANK YOU!
WE'RE HAVING SO MUCH FUN WITH TV TENNIS, WE'VE NO TIME FOR DATES!
VIDEO GAMES-- BAH!
POP'S
The End

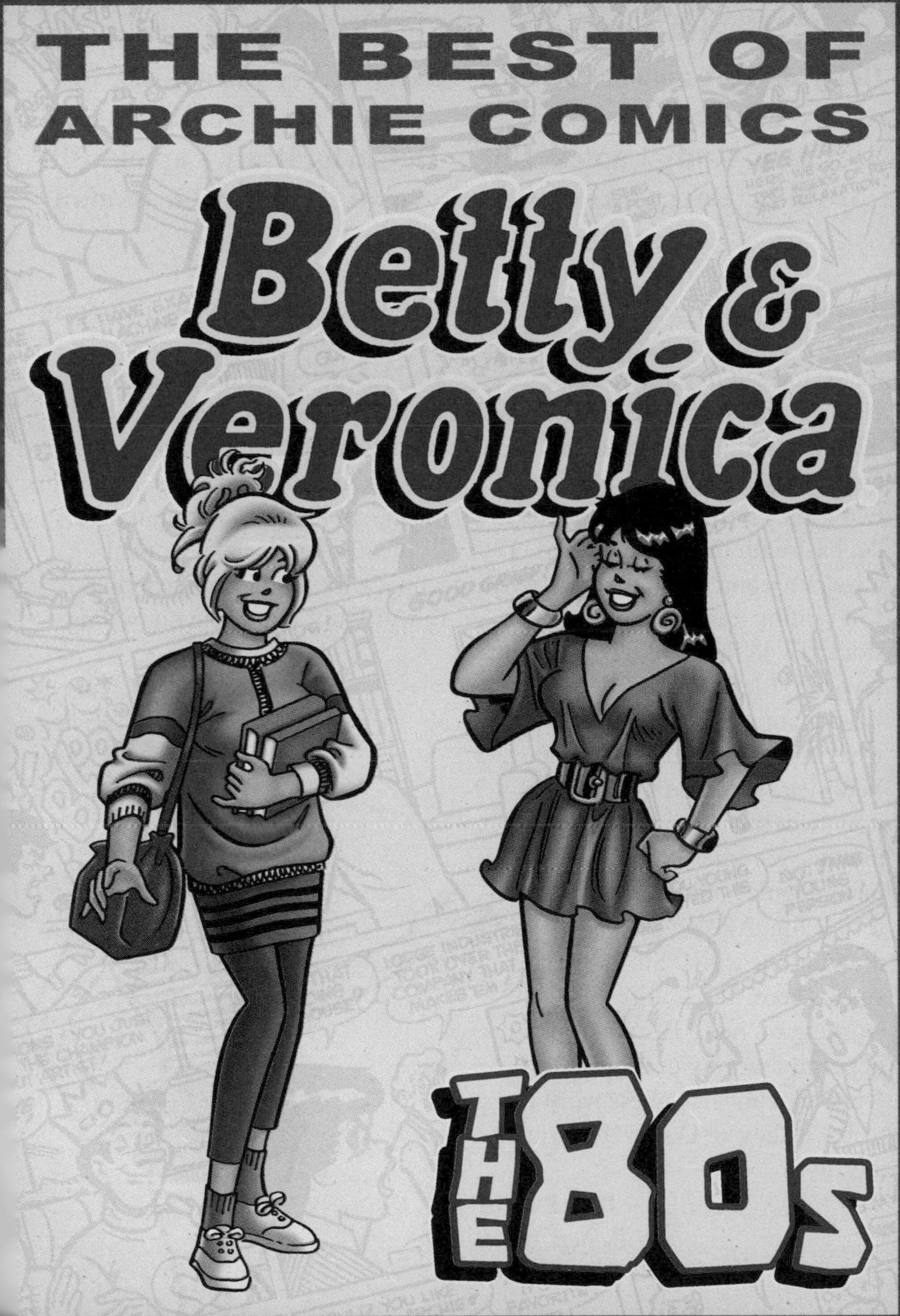
THE BEST OF
ARCHIE COMICS
Betty & Veronica
THE 80s

Health Nuts

Betty & Veronica #302, 1981
by Frank Doyle, Dan DeCarlo, Rudy Lapick, Bill Yoshida, Barry Grossman

Reading Betty and Veronica through the years, the best stories that stand out to me were the classics drawn by Dan DeCarlo and the ones written by Frank Doyle. Frank Doyle always displayed the two girls' contrasting personalities the best with the best dialogue. I always try and remember that when I'm writing a Betty and Veronica story. Even though I have a slight favorite (I lean towards Veronica) the dynamic between the two is what makes a good Betty and Veronica story, and I like to mix it up, whether it's a takeoff on spy movies, parodies of fairy tales or just a regular old Riverdale story, it's all fun. And nothing beats drawing the girls! So, enjoy the stories here! As I write this, I'm working on more B&V stories hopefully worthy of more "Best Of" collections! I guess we'll have to see if they're Doyle/DeCarlo worthy!

-- Dan Parent
Writer/Artist,
Archie Comics

Fleeting Meeting

Betty & Veronica #310, 1981
by Frank Doyle, Dan DeCarlo, Rudy Lapick, Bill Yoshida, Barry Grossman

Betty was probably my first crush (if you count comic characters!). She's sweet, considerate, and smart. I never liked Veronica much. Sure, she's cute, rich, and resourceful, but she's also mean, spoiled, and manipulative. Ironically, I married a woman who's a lot more Veronica than Betty! Wait, that came out wrong.

-- J. Torres
Writer,
Jinx

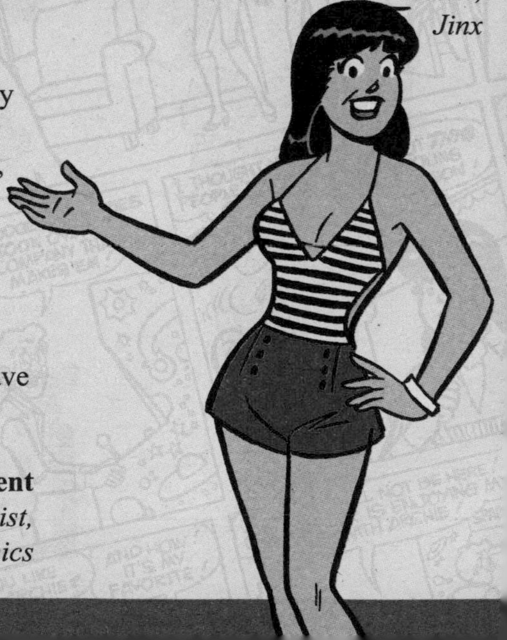

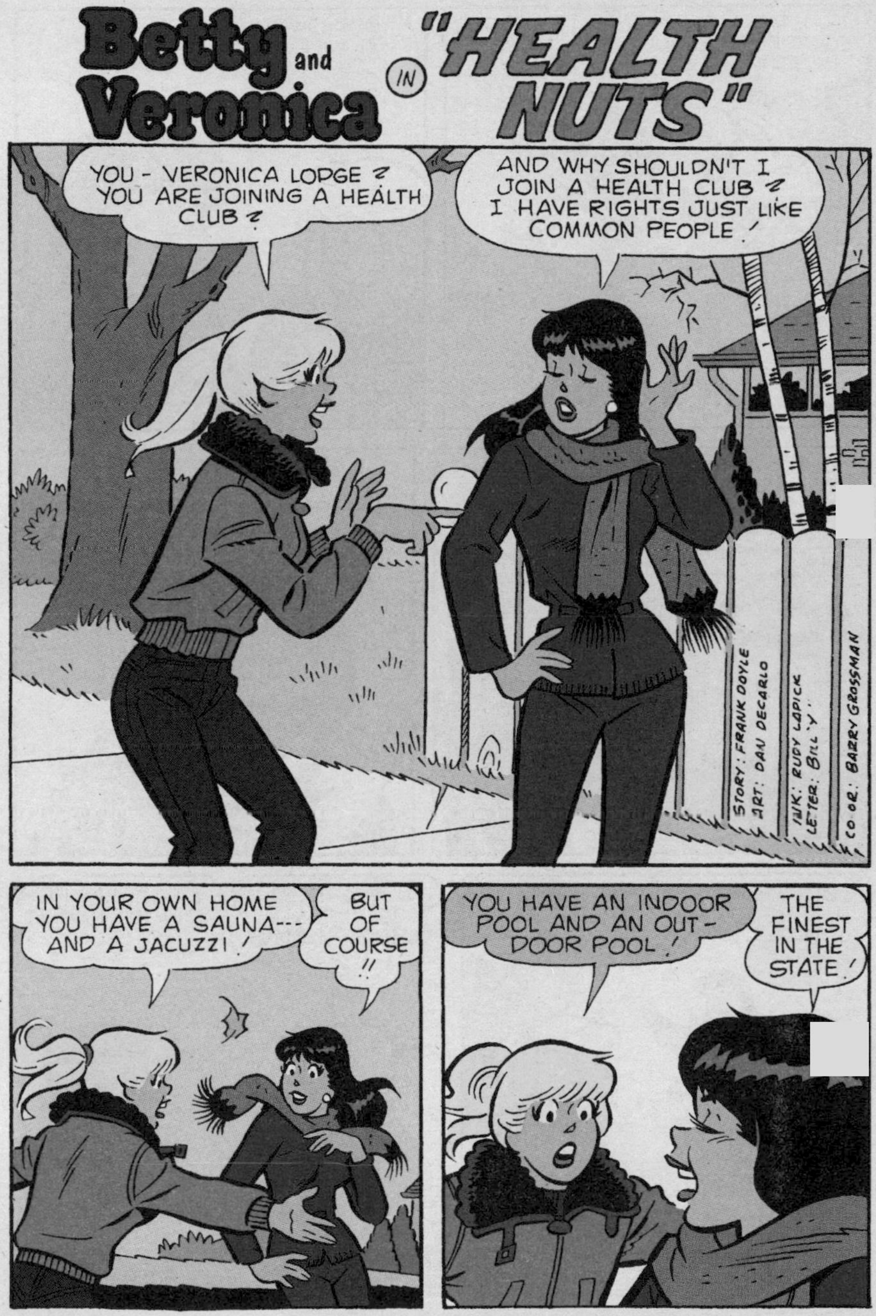
Betty and Veronica
IN
"HEALTH NUTS"
YOU - VERONICA LODGE ? YOU ARE JOINING A HEALTH CLUB ?
AND WHY SHOULDN'T I JOIN A HEALTH CLUB ? I HAVE RIGHTS JUST LIKE COMMON PEOPLE !
STORY: FRANK DOYLE
ART: DAN DECARLO
INK: RUDY LAPICK
LETTER: BILL 'Y'
CO-OR: BARRY GROSSMAN
IN YOUR OWN HOME YOU HAVE A SAUNA--- AND A JACUZZI !
BUT OF COURSE !!
YOU HAVE AN INDOOR POOL AND AN OUT-DOOR POOL !
THE FINEST IN THE STATE !

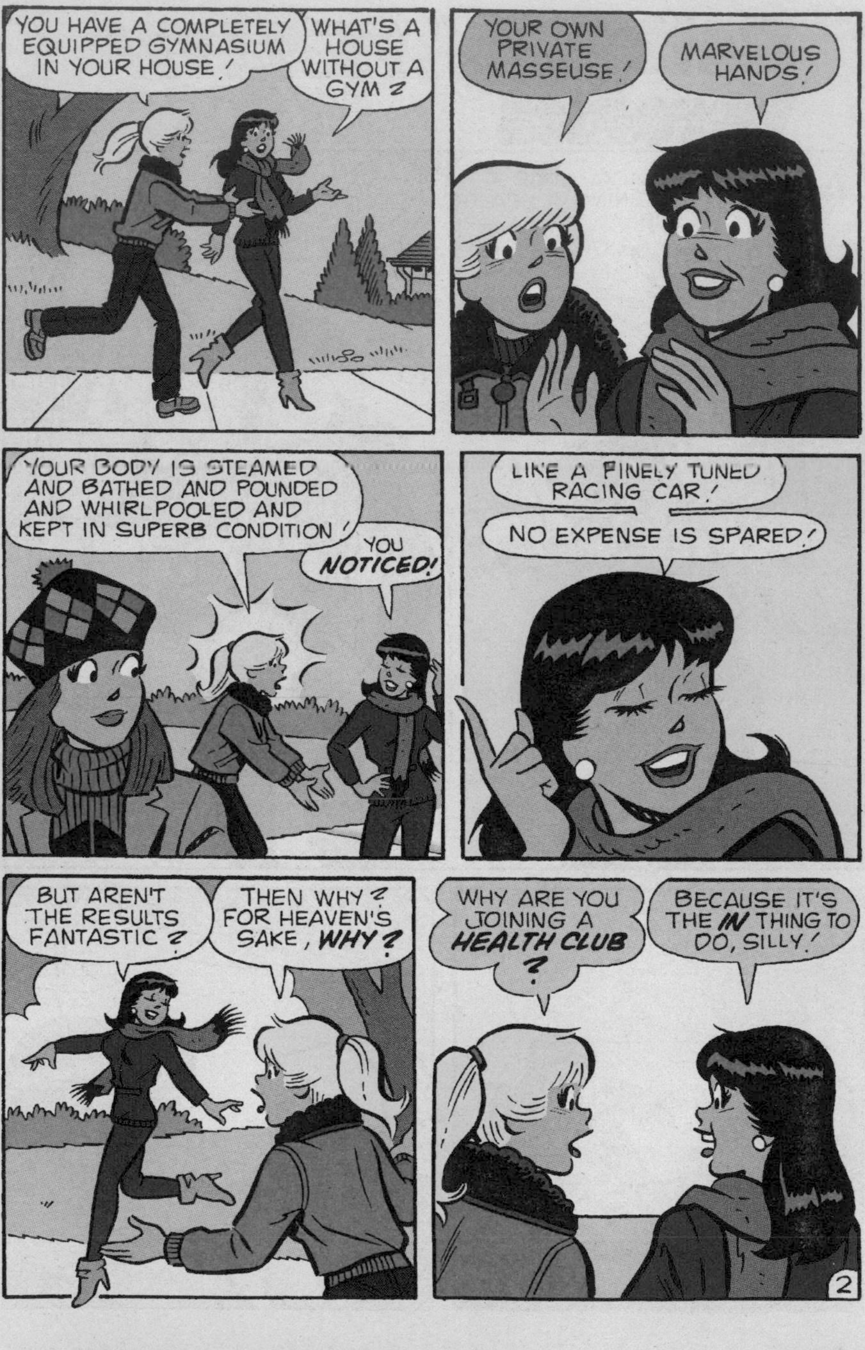
YOU HAVE A COMPLETELY EQUIPPED GYMNASIUM IN YOUR HOUSE!
WHAT'S A HOUSE WITHOUT A GYM?
YOUR OWN PRIVATE MASSEUSE!
MARVELOUS HANDS!
YOUR BODY IS STEAMED AND BATHED AND POUNDED AND WHIRLPOOLED AND KEPT IN SUPERB CONDITION!
YOU NOTICED!
LIKE A FINELY TUNED RACING CAR!
NO EXPENSE IS SPARED!
BUT AREN'T THE RESULTS FANTASTIC?
THEN WHY? FOR HEAVEN'S SAKE, WHY?
WHY ARE YOU JOINING A HEALTH CLUB?
BECAUSE IT'S THE IN THING TO DO, SILLY!
2

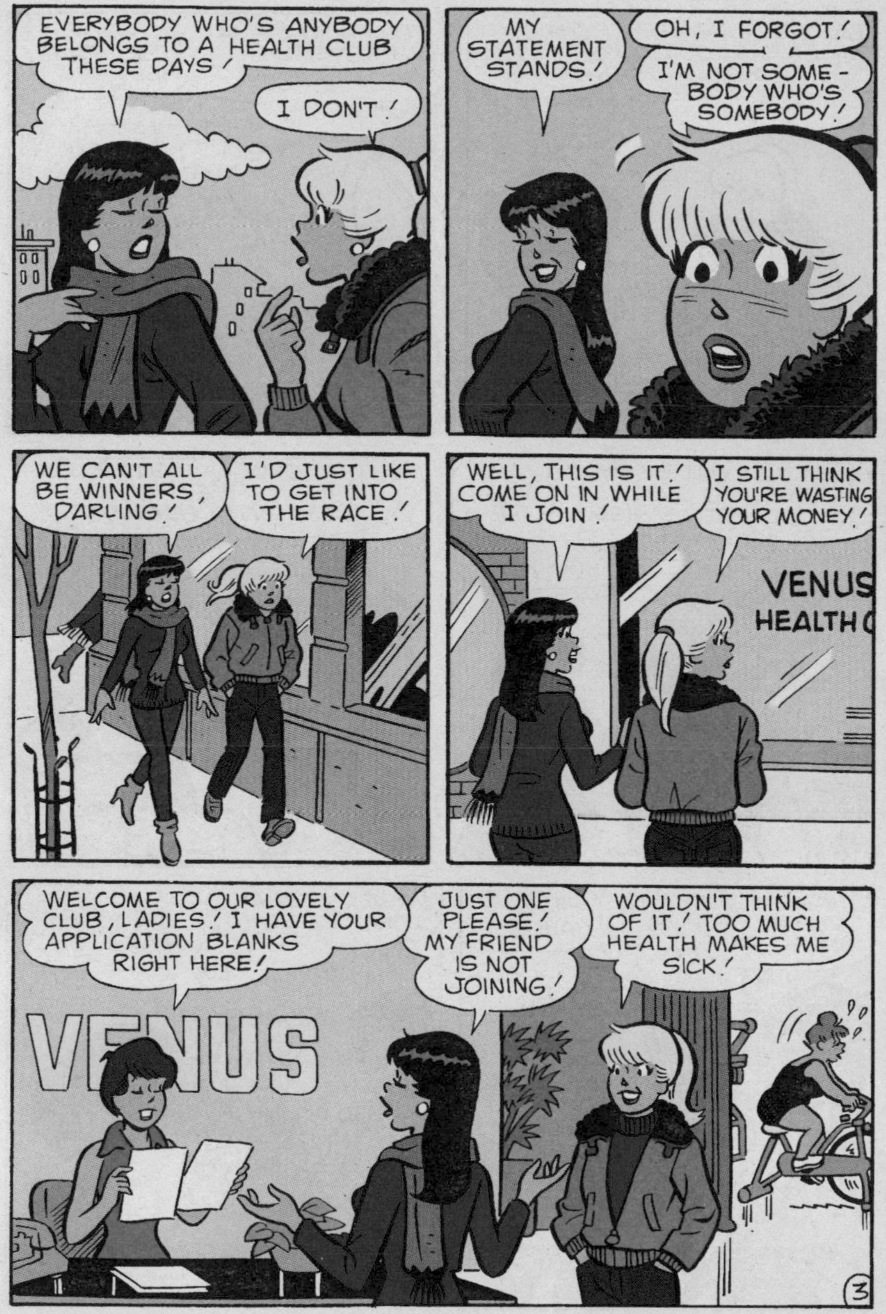
EVERYBODY WHO'S ANYBODY BELONGS TO A HEALTH CLUB THESE DAYS!
I DON'T!
MY STATEMENT STANDS!
OH, I FORGOT!
I'M NOT SOME-BODY WHO'S SOMEBODY!
WE CAN'T ALL BE WINNERS, DARLING!
I'D JUST LIKE TO GET INTO THE RACE!
WELL, THIS IS IT! COME ON IN WHILE I JOIN!
I STILL THINK YOU'RE WASTING YOUR MONEY!
VENUS
HEALTH C
WELCOME TO OUR LOVELY CLUB, LADIES! I HAVE YOUR APPLICATION BLANKS RIGHT HERE!
JUST ONE PLEASE! MY FRIEND IS NOT JOINING!
WOULDN'T THINK OF IT! TOO MUCH HEALTH MAKES ME SICK!
VENUS
3

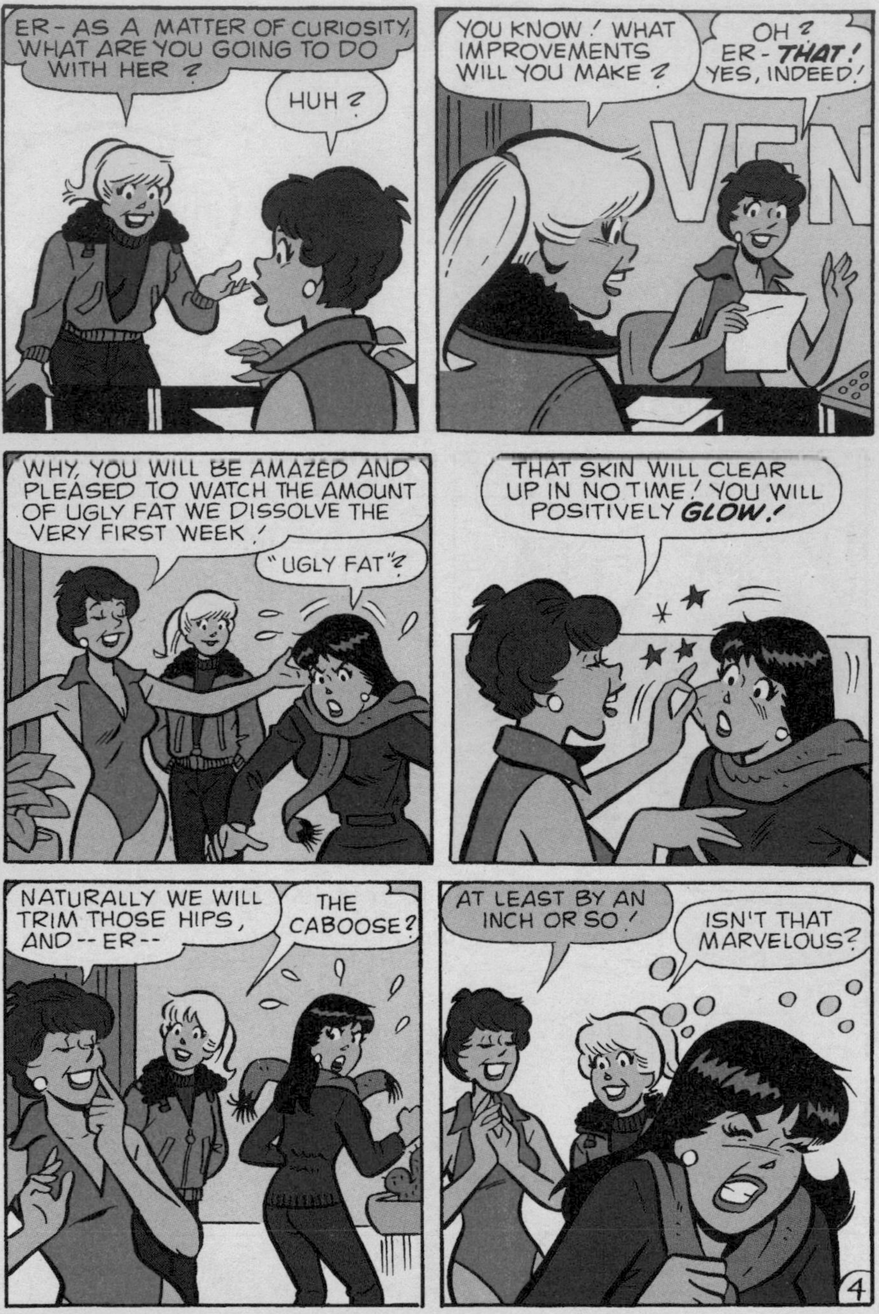
ER- AS A MATTER OF CURIOSITY, WHAT ARE YOU GOING TO DO WITH HER ?
HUH ?
YOU KNOW! WHAT IMPROVEMENTS WILL YOU MAKE ?
OH ? ER- THAT! YES, INDEED!
VEN
WHY, YOU WILL BE AMAZED AND PLEASED TO WATCH THE AMOUNT OF UGLY FAT WE DISSOLVE THE VERY FIRST WEEK!
"UGLY FAT"?
THAT SKIN WILL CLEAR UP IN NO TIME! YOU WILL POSITIVELY GLOW!
NATURALLY WE WILL TRIM THOSE HIPS, AND -- ER --
THE CABOOSE?
AT LEAST BY AN INCH OR SO!
ISN'T THAT MARVELOUS?
4

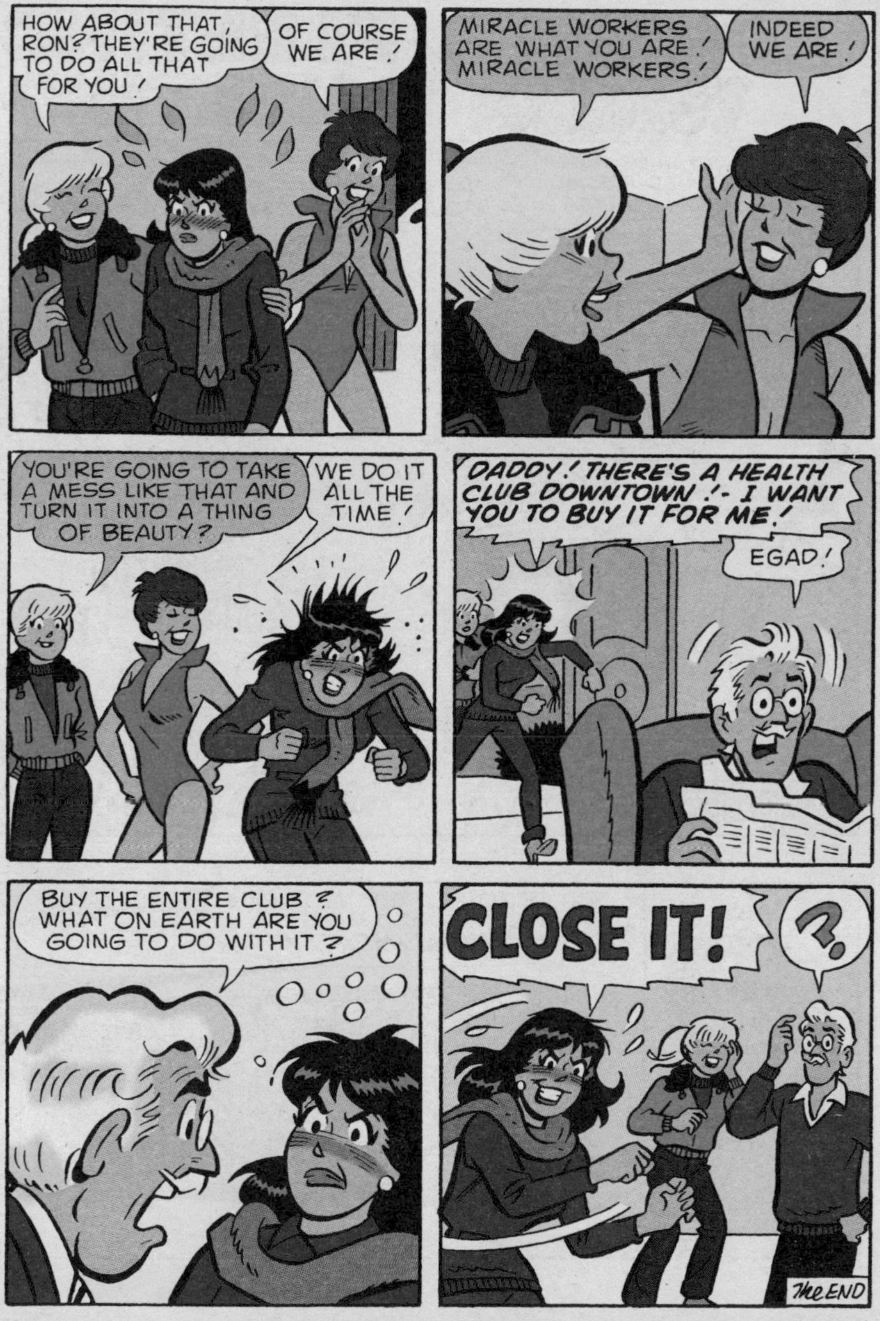
HOW ABOUT THAT, RON? THEY'RE GOING TO DO ALL THAT FOR YOU!
OF COURSE WE ARE!
MIRACLE WORKERS ARE WHAT YOU ARE! MIRACLE WORKERS!
INDEED WE ARE!
YOU'RE GOING TO TAKE A MESS LIKE THAT AND TURN IT INTO A THING OF BEAUTY?
WE DO IT ALL THE TIME!
DADDY! THERE'S A HEALTH CLUB DOWNTOWN!- I WANT YOU TO BUY IT FOR ME!
EGAD!
BUY THE ENTIRE CLUB? WHAT ON EARTH ARE YOU GOING TO DO WITH IT?
CLOSE IT!
?
The END

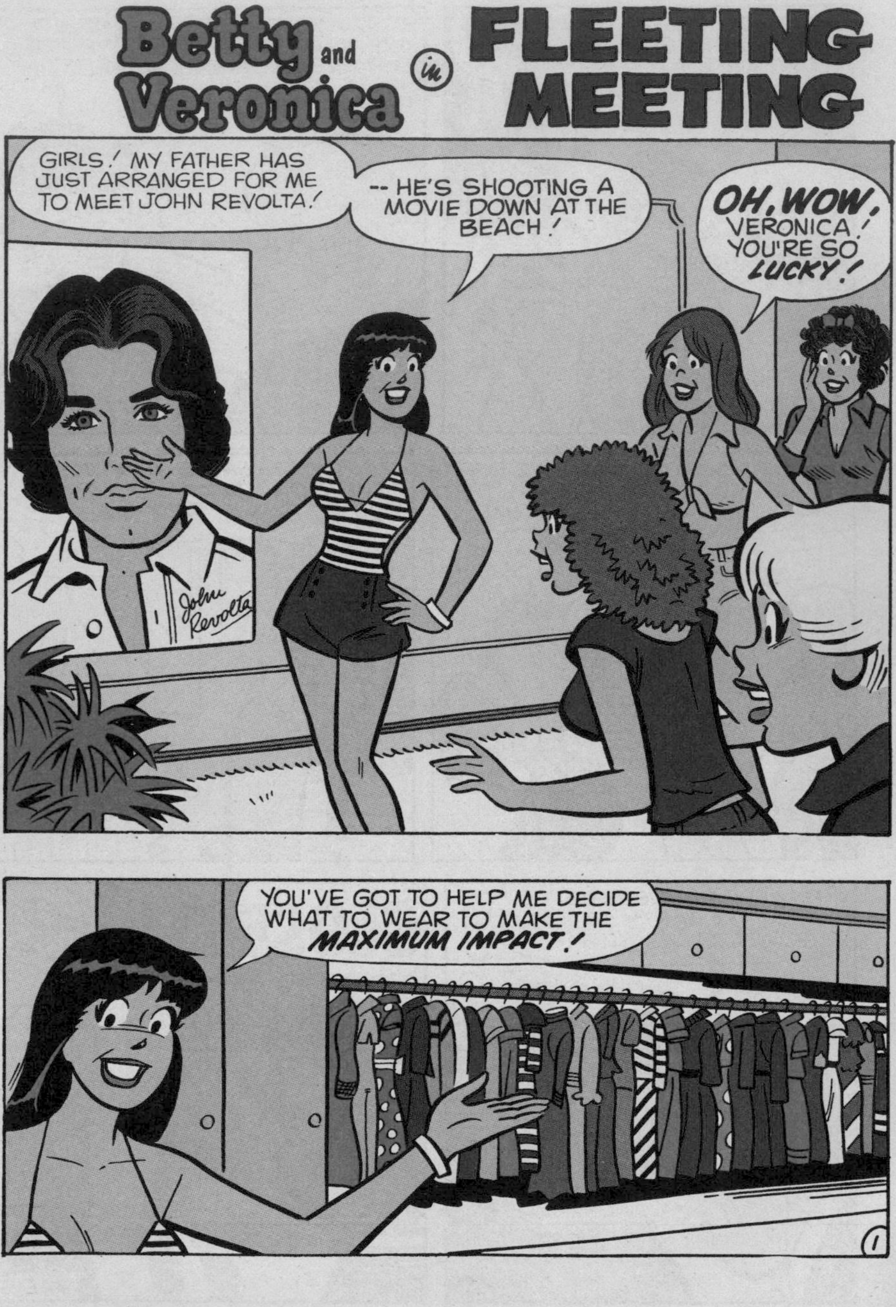
Betty and Veronica in
FLEETING MEETING
GIRLS! MY FATHER HAS JUST ARRANGED FOR ME TO MEET JOHN REVOLTA!
-- HE'S SHOOTING A MOVIE DOWN AT THE BEACH!
OH, WOW, VERONICA! YOU'RE SO LUCKY!
John Revolta
YOU'VE GOT TO HELP ME DECIDE WHAT TO WEAR TO MAKE THE MAXIMUM IMPACT!
1

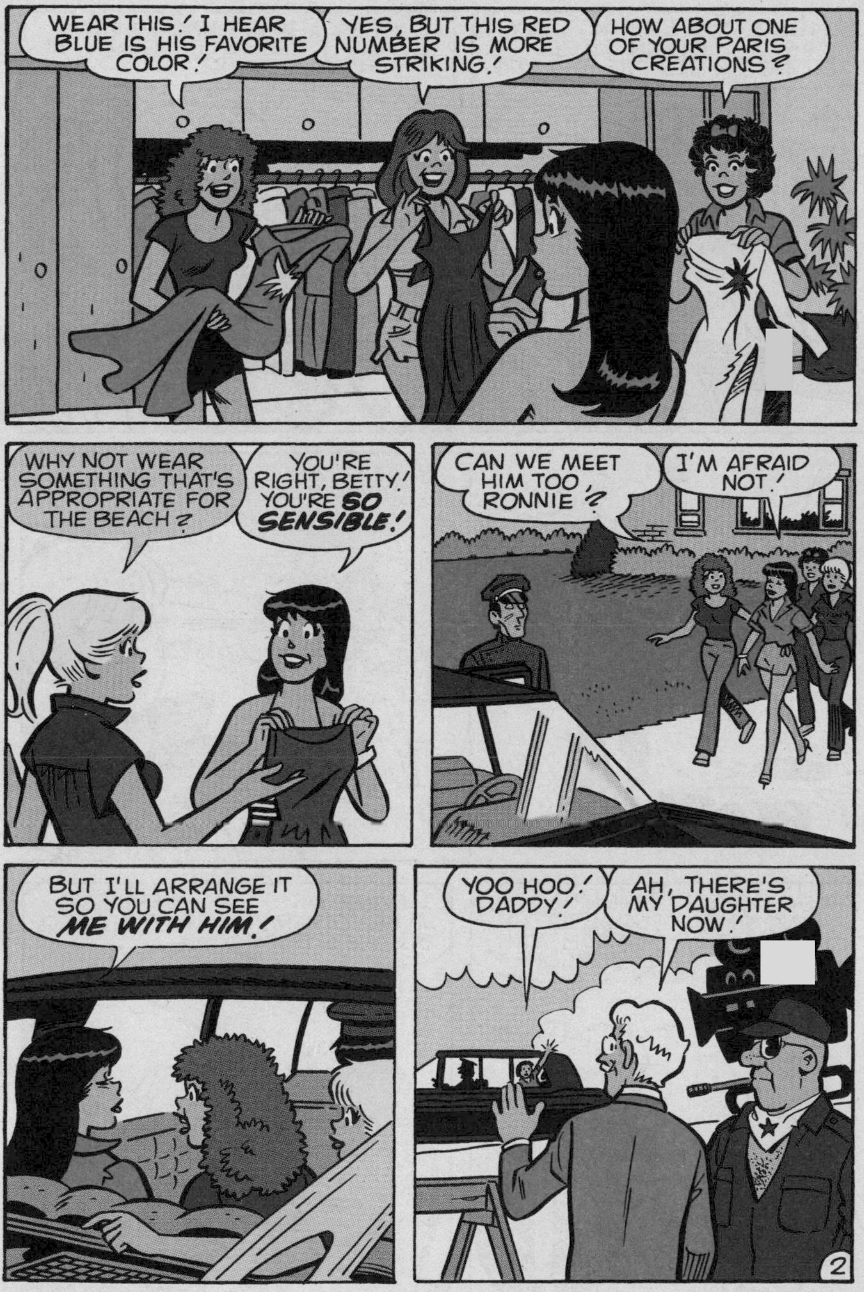
WEAR THIS! I HEAR BLUE IS HIS FAVORITE COLOR!
YES, BUT THIS RED NUMBER IS MORE STRIKING!
HOW ABOUT ONE OF YOUR PARIS CREATIONS?
WHY NOT WEAR SOMETHING THAT'S APPROPRIATE FOR THE BEACH?
YOU'RE RIGHT, BETTY! YOU'RE SO SENSIBLE!
CAN WE MEET HIM TOO, RONNIE?
I'M AFRAID NOT!
BUT I'LL ARRANGE IT SO YOU CAN SEE ME WITH HIM!
YOO HOO! DADDY!
AH, THERE'S MY DAUGHTER NOW!
2

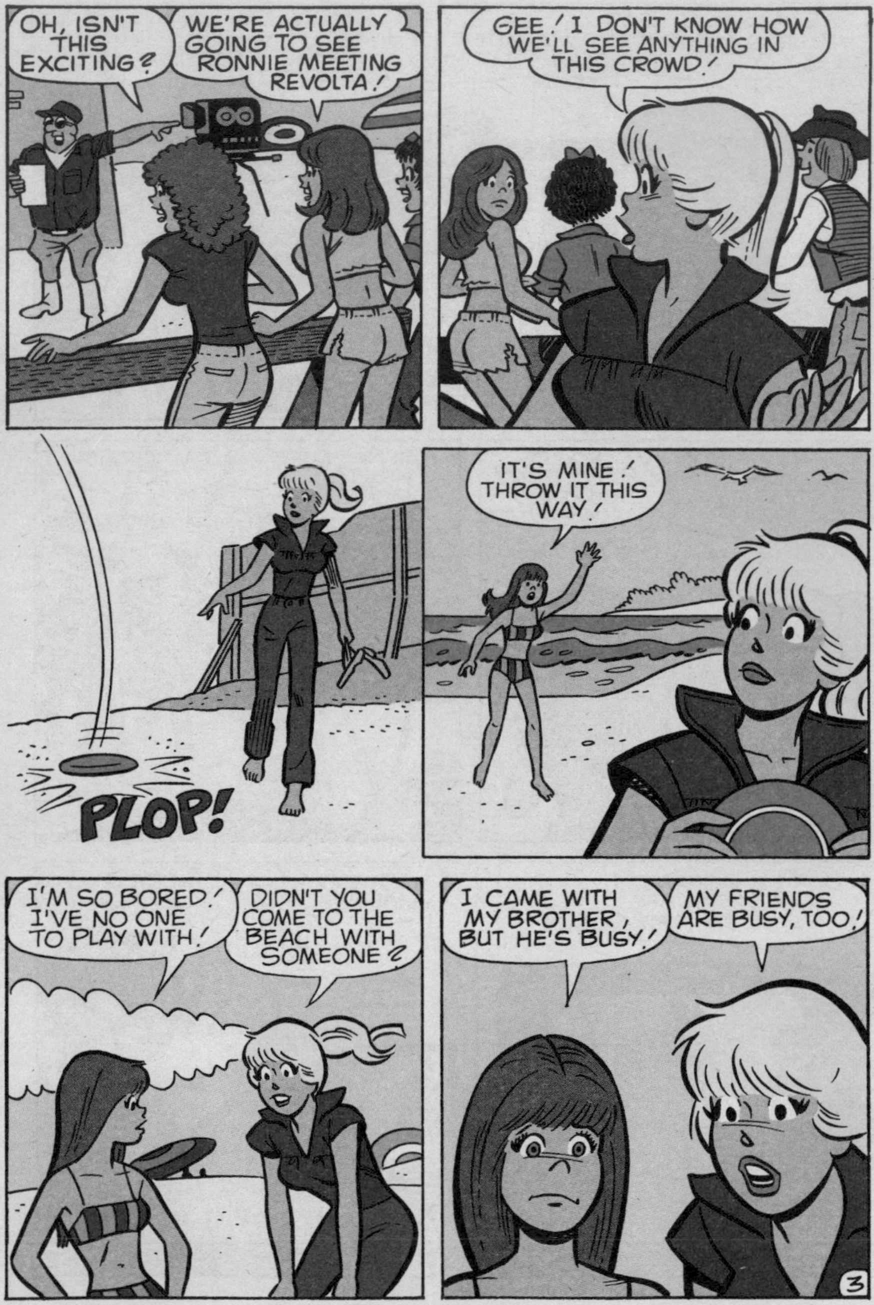
OH, ISN'T THIS EXCITING?
WE'RE ACTUALLY GOING TO SEE RONNIE MEETING REVOLTA!
GEE! I DON'T KNOW HOW WE'LL SEE ANYTHING IN THIS CROWD!
PLOP!
IT'S MINE! THROW IT THIS WAY!
I'M SO BORED! I'VE NO ONE TO PLAY WITH!
DIDN'T YOU COME TO THE BEACH WITH SOMEONE?
I CAME WITH MY BROTHER, BUT HE'S BUSY!
MY FRIENDS ARE BUSY, TOO!
3

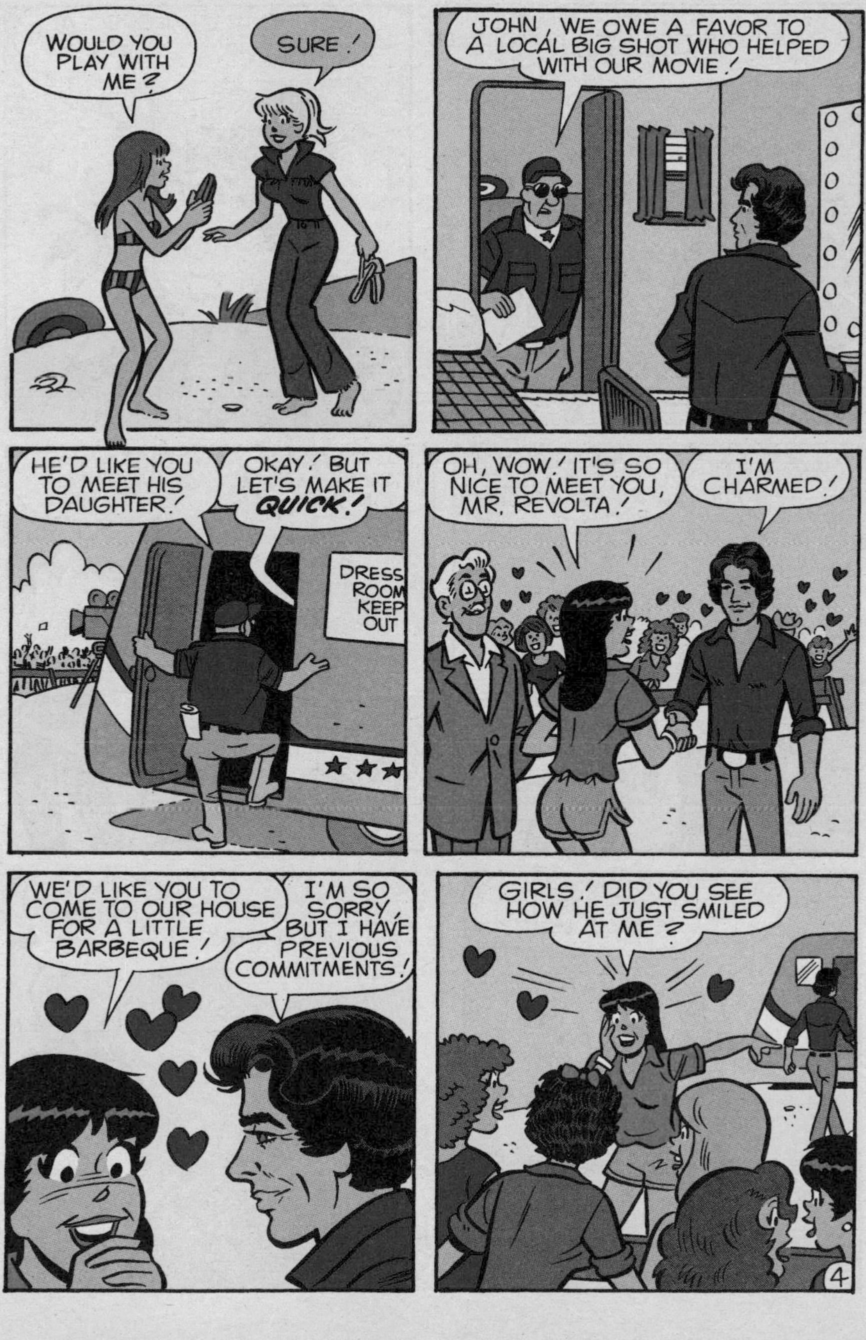
WOULD YOU PLAY WITH ME?
SURE!
JOHN, WE OWE A FAVOR TO A LOCAL BIG SHOT WHO HELPED WITH OUR MOVIE!
HE'D LIKE YOU TO MEET HIS DAUGHTER!
OKAY! BUT LET'S MAKE IT QUICK!
DRESS ROOM KEEP OUT
OH, WOW! IT'S SO NICE TO MEET YOU, MR. REVOLTA!
I'M CHARMED!
WE'D LIKE YOU TO COME TO OUR HOUSE FOR A LITTLE BARBEQUE!
I'M SO SORRY, BUT I HAVE PREVIOUS COMMITMENTS!
GIRLS! DID YOU SEE HOW HE JUST SMILED AT ME?
4

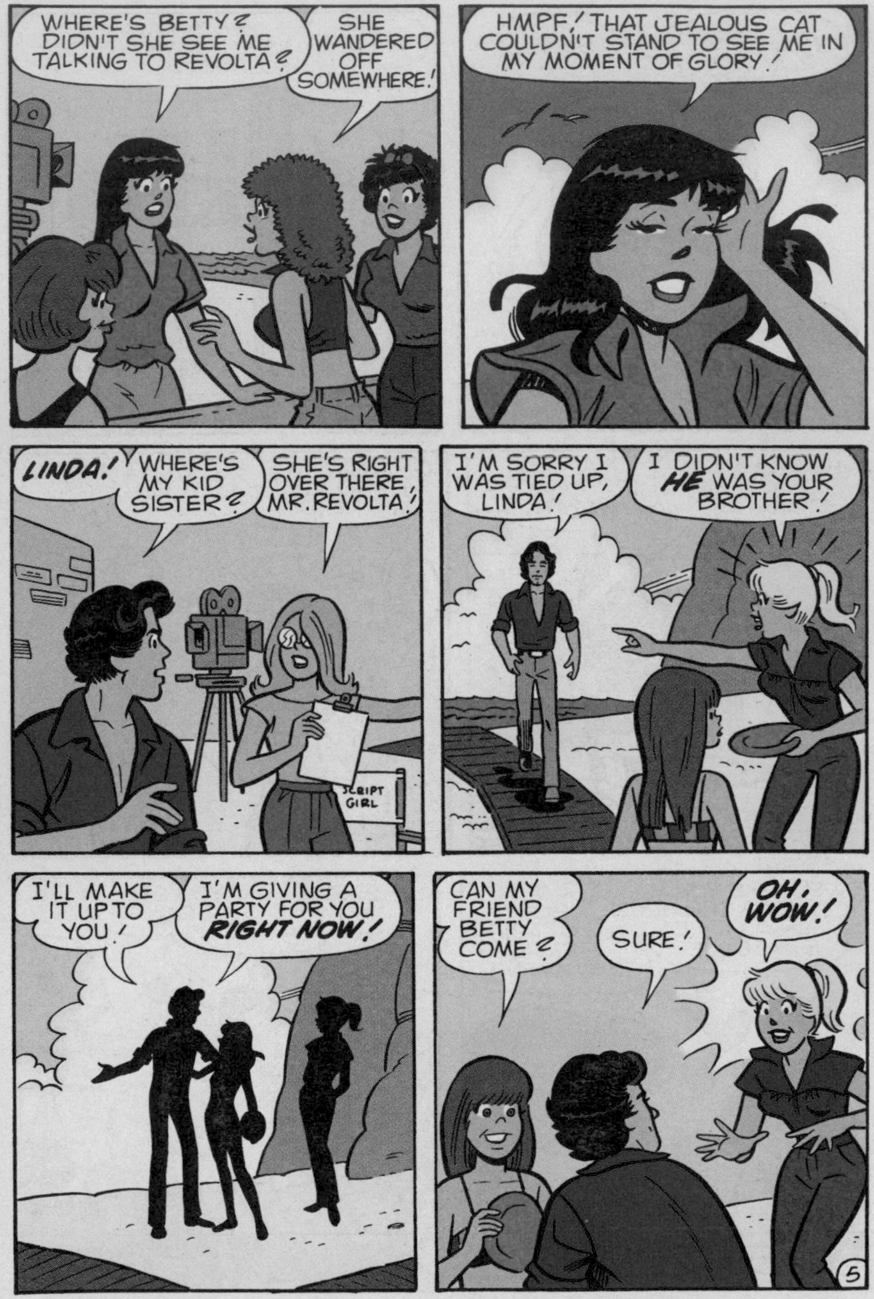
WHERE'S BETTY? DIDN'T SHE SEE ME TALKING TO REVOLTA?
SHE WANDERED OFF SOMEWHERE!
HMPF! THAT JEALOUS CAT COULDN'T STAND TO SEE ME IN MY MOMENT OF GLORY!
LINDA!
WHERE'S MY KID SISTER?
SHE'S RIGHT OVER THERE, MR. REVOLTA!
SCRIPT GIRL
I'M SORRY I WAS TIED UP, LINDA!
I DIDN'T KNOW HE WAS YOUR BROTHER!
I'LL MAKE IT UP TO YOU!
I'M GIVING A PARTY FOR YOU RIGHT NOW!
CAN MY FRIEND BETTY COME?
SURE!
OH, WOW!
5

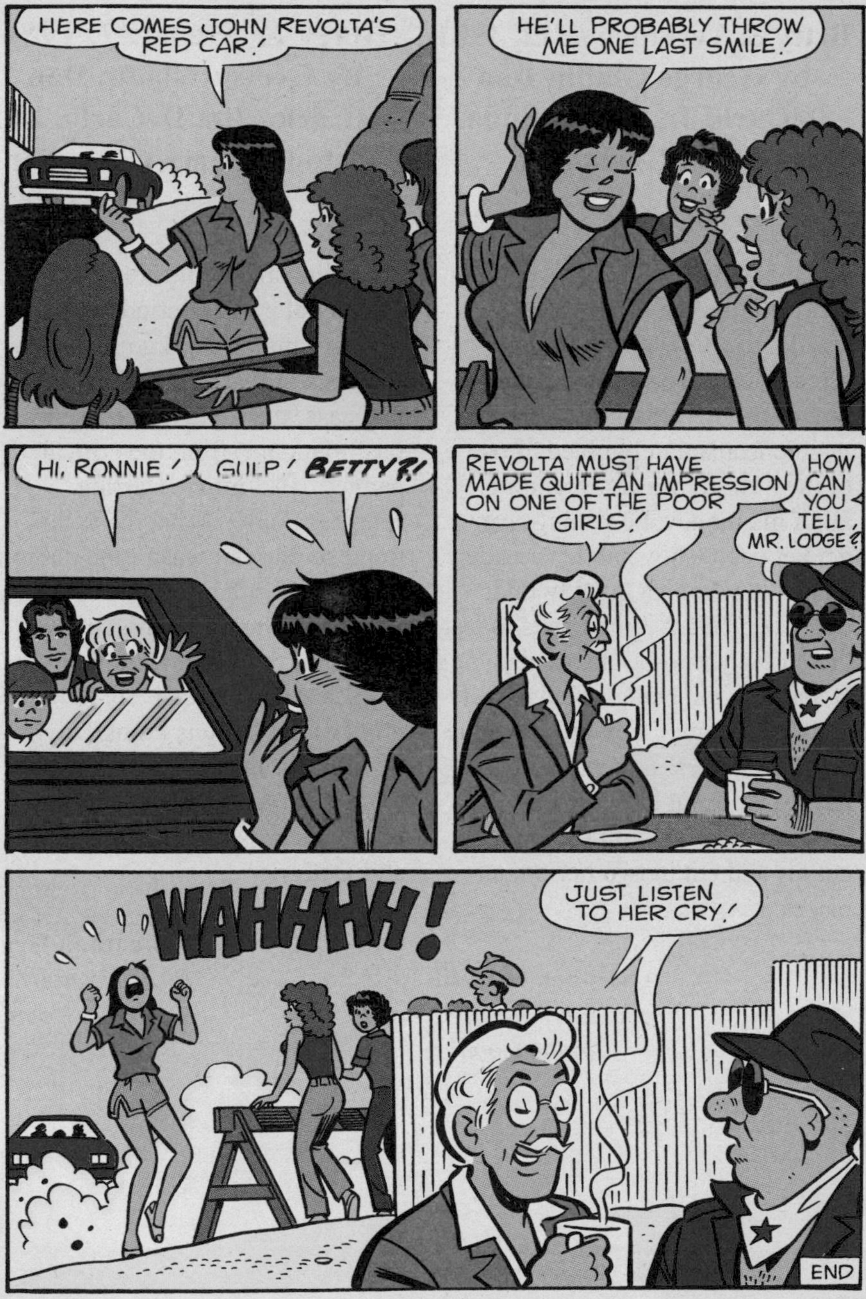
HERE COMES JOHN REVOLTA'S RED CAR!
HE'LL PROBABLY THROW ME ONE LAST SMILE!
HI, RONNIE!
GULP! BETTY?!
REVOLTA MUST HAVE MADE QUITE AN IMPRESSION ON ONE OF THE POOR GIRLS!
HOW CAN YOU TELL, MR. LODGE?
WAHHHH!
JUST LISTEN TO HER CRY!
END

Test Zest
**Betty & Veronica #312, 1981
by George Gladir, Dan
DeCarlo Jr., Bill Yoshida,
Barry Grossman**

Being a child of the '80s nothing beat hanging out at the local arcade, the draw of the flashing screens and awesome side art, the lure of the silverball. In "Test Zest" Archie is absolutely glued to one of the new games and spending all of his money. Few things can get between a boy and his arcade game, as Veronica quickly finds out. Even better, Archie gets to test out a new yet-to-be-released game! If that was me being asked to test out a new game I couldn't imagine anything better! Except maybe having a peanut butter (Skippy brand) sandwich with the crust cut off and cut in two horizontal pieces.

-- **Stephen Oswald**
*Production Manager,
Archie Comics*

Flash Dance
**Betty & Me #137, 1984
by George Gladir, Dan
DeCarlo, Jim DeCarlo, Bill
Yoshida, Barry Grossman**

Reading an Archie comic is like looking at a zany period-piece of every major trend going on in America at that date and time. In this case, the topic of the day was flash-dancing (from the critically panned 1983 movie starring Jennifer Beals). What made this trend so popular wasn't the dubious movie, but rather the launch of MTV, which was the first network to exploit the new medium of the "music video" effectively. The real point of the story is Frank Doyle giving Dan DeCarlo an excuse to do what he did best: drawing gorgeous girls. Cheers to Doyle and DeCarlo!

-- **Jonathan Gray**
*Production Artist,
Archie Comics*

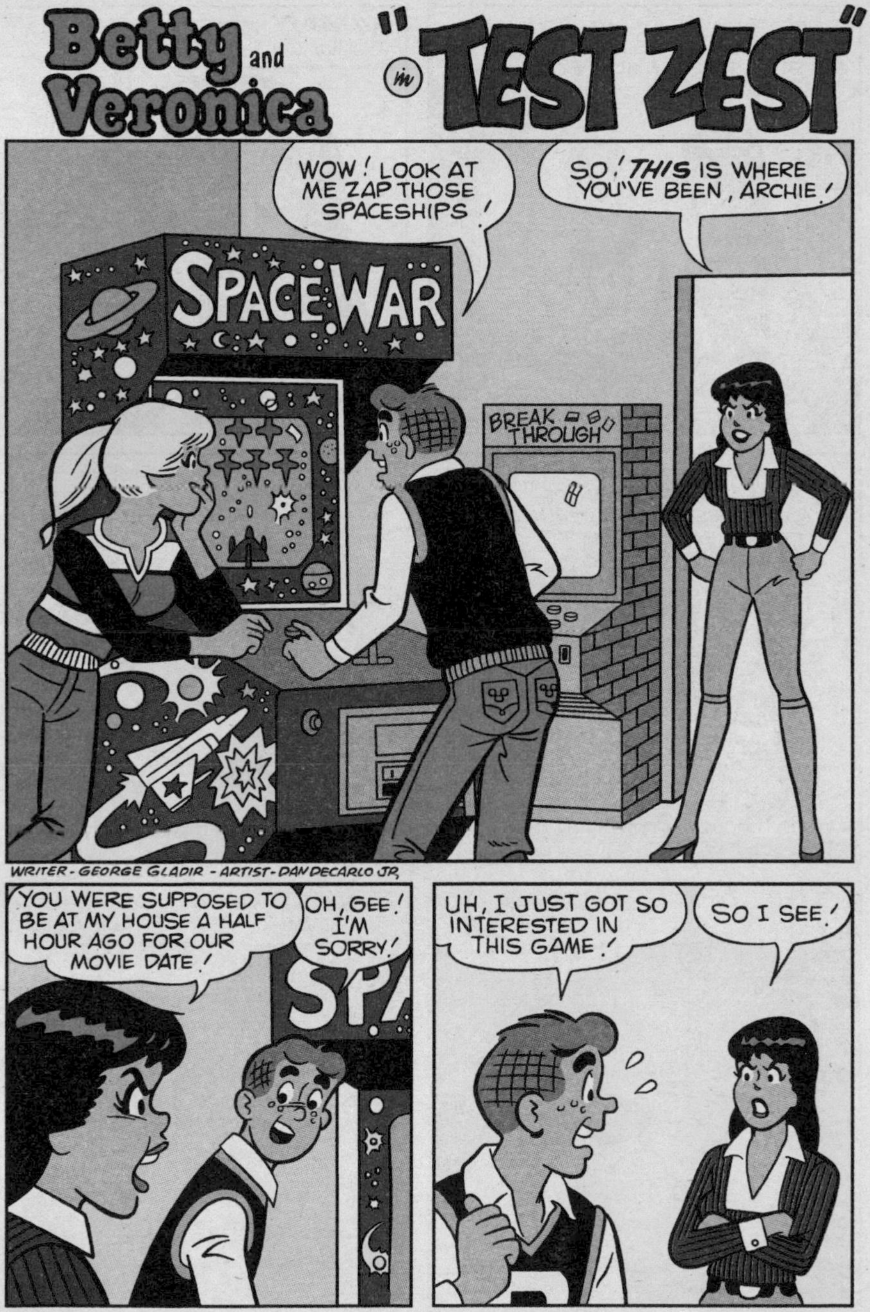
Betty and Veronica in "TEST ZEST"
WOW! LOOK AT ME ZAP THOSE SPACESHIPS!
SO! THIS IS WHERE YOU'VE BEEN, ARCHIE!
SPACE WAR
BREAK THROUGH
WRITER - GEORGE GLADIR - ARTIST - DAN DECARLO JR.
YOU WERE SUPPOSED TO BE AT MY HOUSE A HALF HOUR AGO FOR OUR MOVIE DATE!
OH, GEE! I'M SORRY!
UH, I JUST GOT SO INTERESTED IN THIS GAME!
SO I SEE!

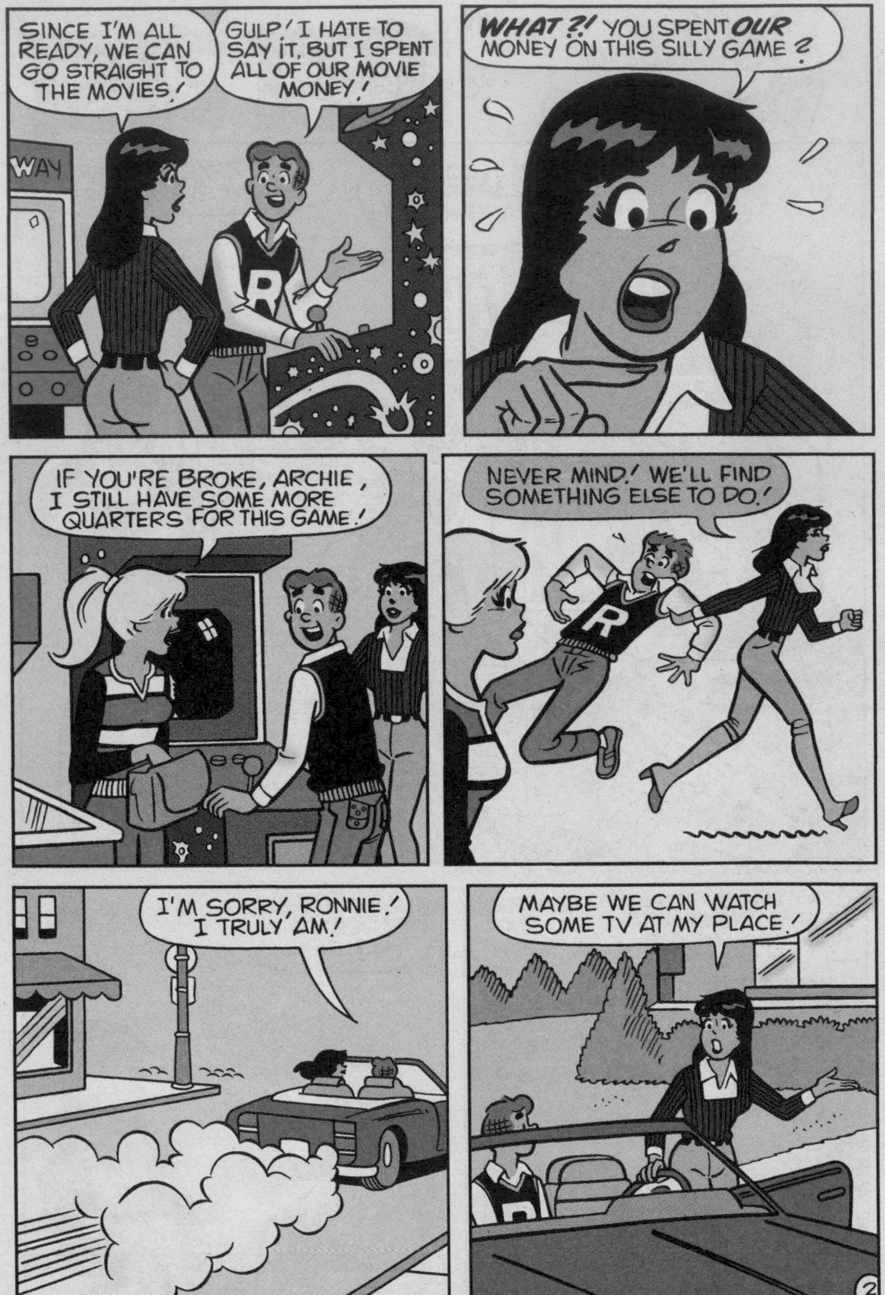
SINCE I'M ALL READY, WE CAN GO STRAIGHT TO THE MOVIES!
GULP! I HATE TO SAY IT, BUT I SPENT ALL OF OUR MOVIE MONEY!
WAY
WHAT?! YOU SPENT OUR MONEY ON THIS SILLY GAME?
IF YOU'RE BROKE, ARCHIE, I STILL HAVE SOME MORE QUARTERS FOR THIS GAME!
NEVER MIND! WE'LL FIND SOMETHING ELSE TO DO!
I'M SORRY, RONNIE! I TRULY AM!
MAYBE WE CAN WATCH SOME TV AT MY PLACE!
2

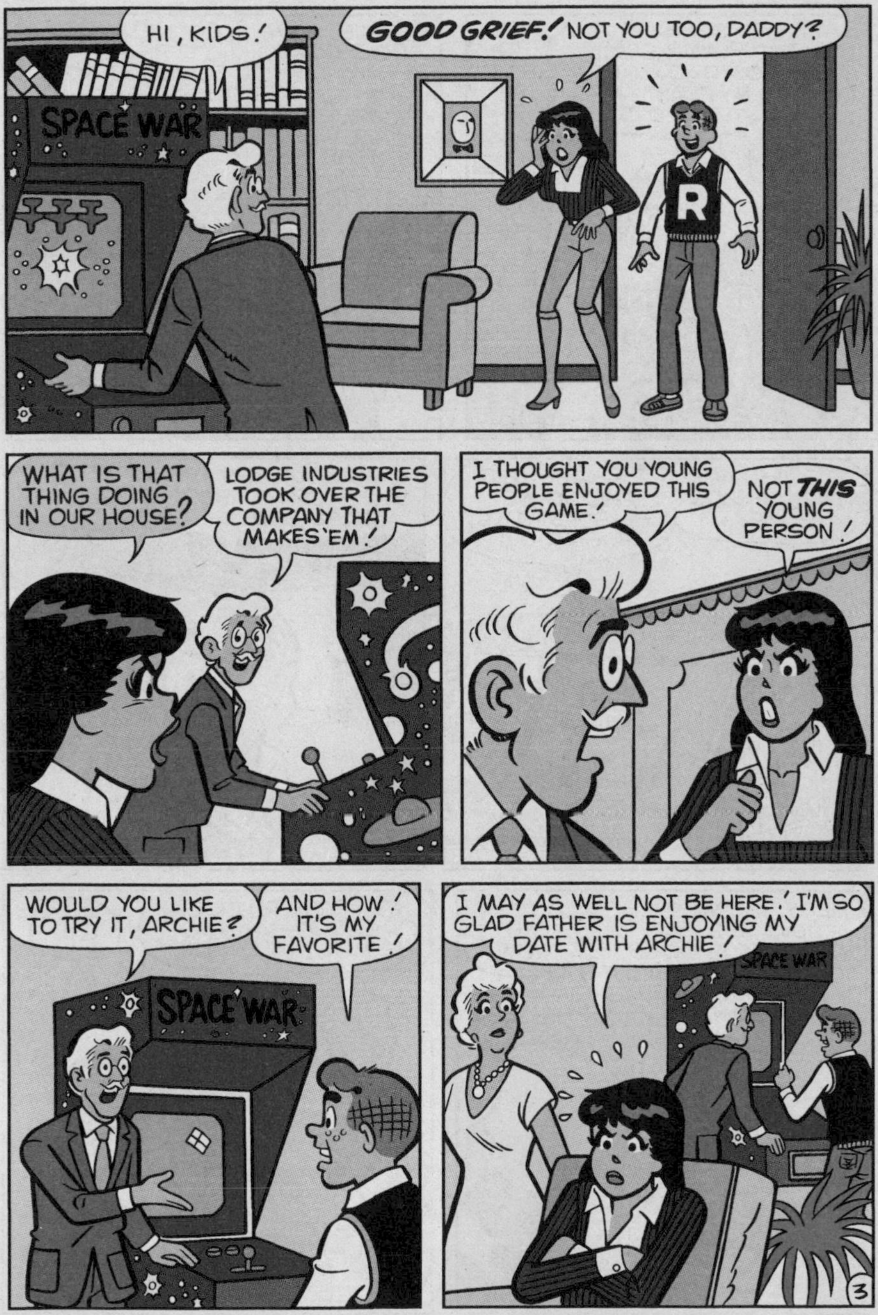

HI, KIDS!
GOOD GRIEF! NOT YOU TOO, DADDY?
SPACE WAR
WHAT IS THAT THING DOING IN OUR HOUSE?
LODGE INDUSTRIES TOOK OVER THE COMPANY THAT MAKES 'EM!
I THOUGHT YOU YOUNG PEOPLE ENJOYED THIS GAME!
NOT THIS YOUNG PERSON!
WOULD YOU LIKE TO TRY IT, ARCHIE?
AND HOW! IT'S MY FAVORITE!
SPACE WAR
I MAY AS WELL NOT BE HERE! I'M SO GLAD FATHER IS ENJOYING MY DATE WITH ARCHIE!
SPACE WAR
3

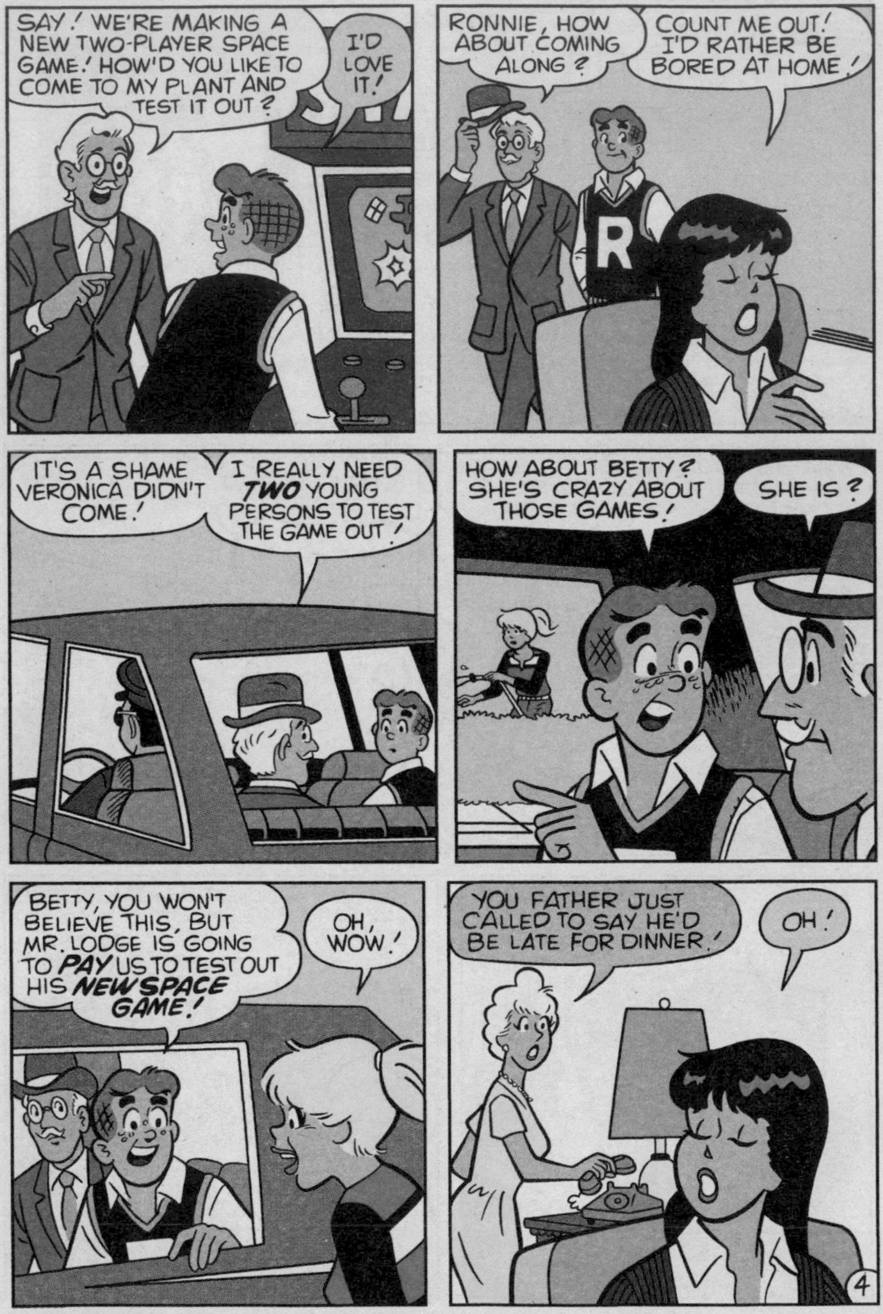
SAY! WE'RE MAKING A NEW TWO-PLAYER SPACE GAME! HOW'D YOU LIKE TO COME TO MY PLANT AND TEST IT OUT?
I'D LOVE IT!
RONNIE, HOW ABOUT COMING ALONG?
COUNT ME OUT! I'D RATHER BE BORED AT HOME!
IT'S A SHAME VERONICA DIDN'T COME!
I REALLY NEED TWO YOUNG PERSONS TO TEST THE GAME OUT!
HOW ABOUT BETTY? SHE'S CRAZY ABOUT THOSE GAMES!
SHE IS?
BETTY, YOU WON'T BELIEVE THIS, BUT MR. LODGE IS GOING TO PAY US TO TEST OUT HIS NEW SPACE GAME!
OH, WOW!
YOU FATHER JUST CALLED TO SAY HE'D BE LATE FOR DINNER!
OH!
4

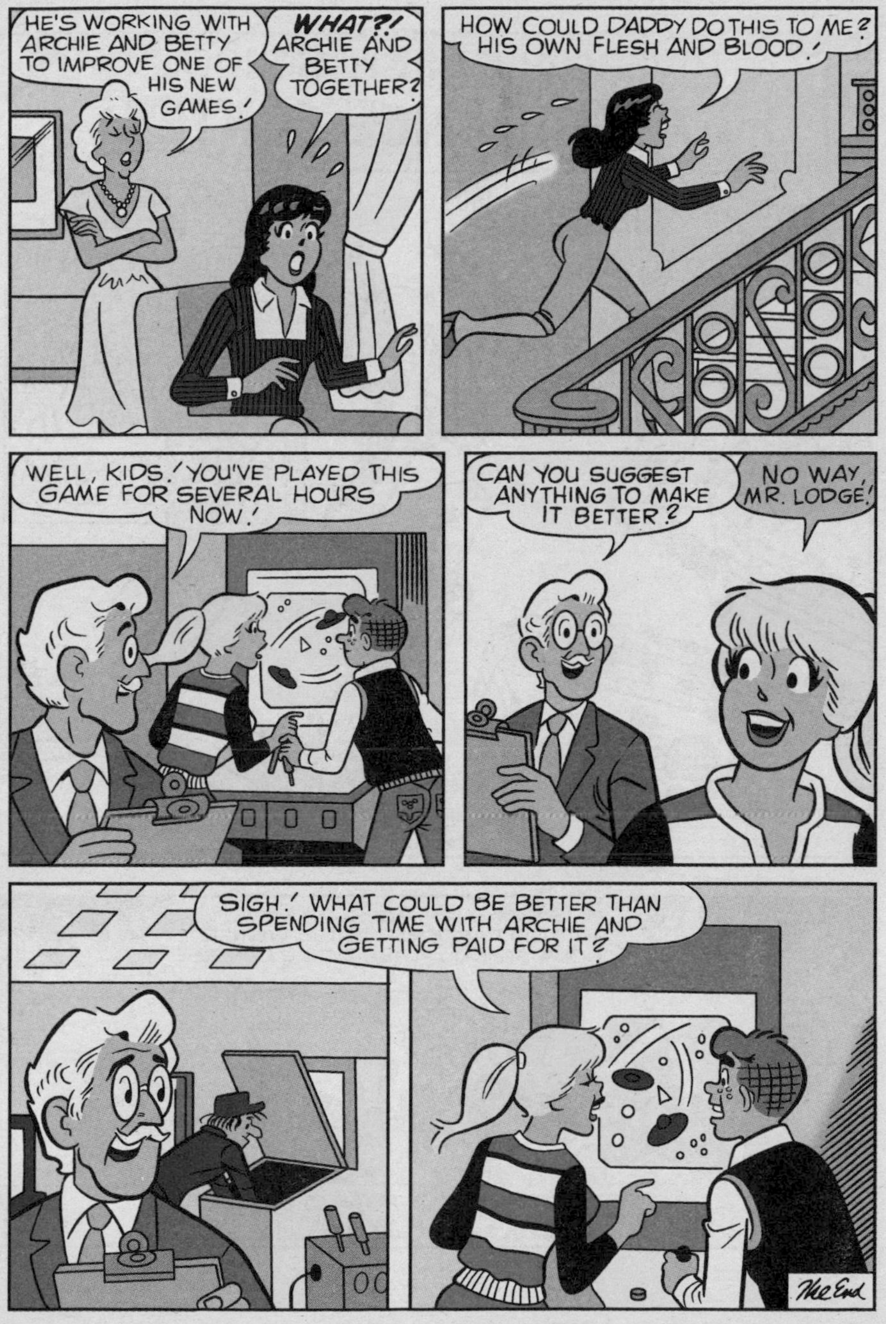
HE'S WORKING WITH ARCHIE AND BETTY TO IMPROVE ONE OF HIS NEW GAMES!
WHAT?! ARCHIE AND BETTY TOGETHER?
HOW COULD DADDY DO THIS TO ME? HIS OWN FLESH AND BLOOD!
WELL, KIDS! YOU'VE PLAYED THIS GAME FOR SEVERAL HOURS NOW!
CAN YOU SUGGEST ANYTHING TO MAKE IT BETTER?
NO WAY, MR. LODGE!
SIGH! WHAT COULD BE BETTER THAN SPENDING TIME WITH ARCHIE AND GETTING PAID FOR IT?
The End

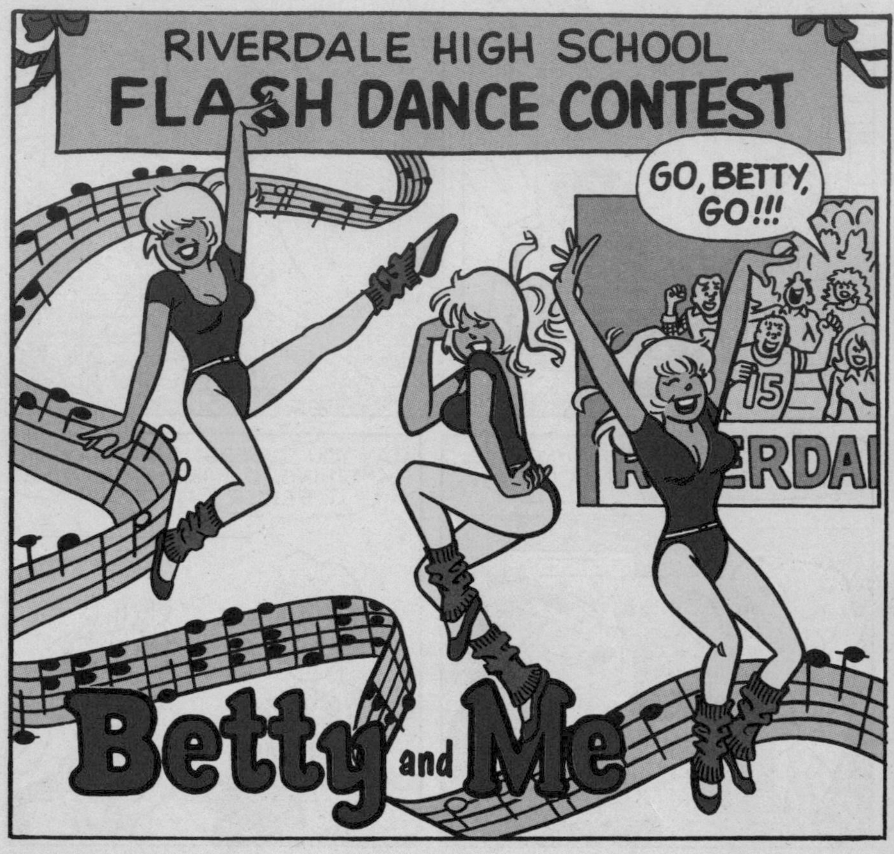
RIVERDALE HIGH SCHOOL
FLASH DANCE CONTEST
GO, BETTY, GO!!!
RIVERDAL
Betty and Me

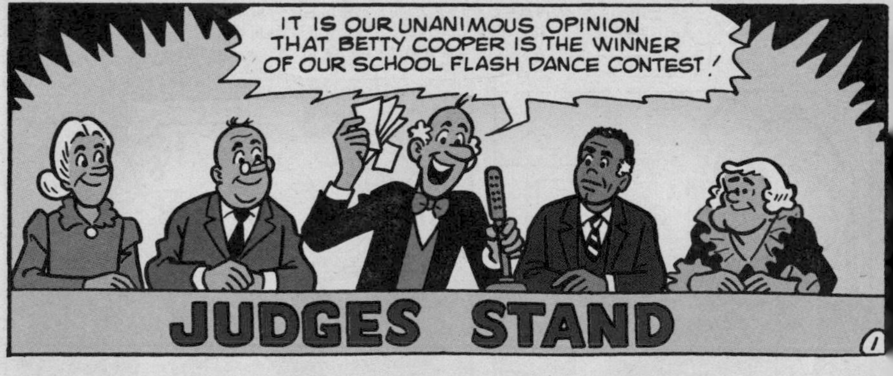
IT IS OUR UNANIMOUS OPINION THAT BETTY COOPER IS THE WINNER OF OUR SCHOOL FLASH DANCE CONTEST!
JUDGES STAND
1

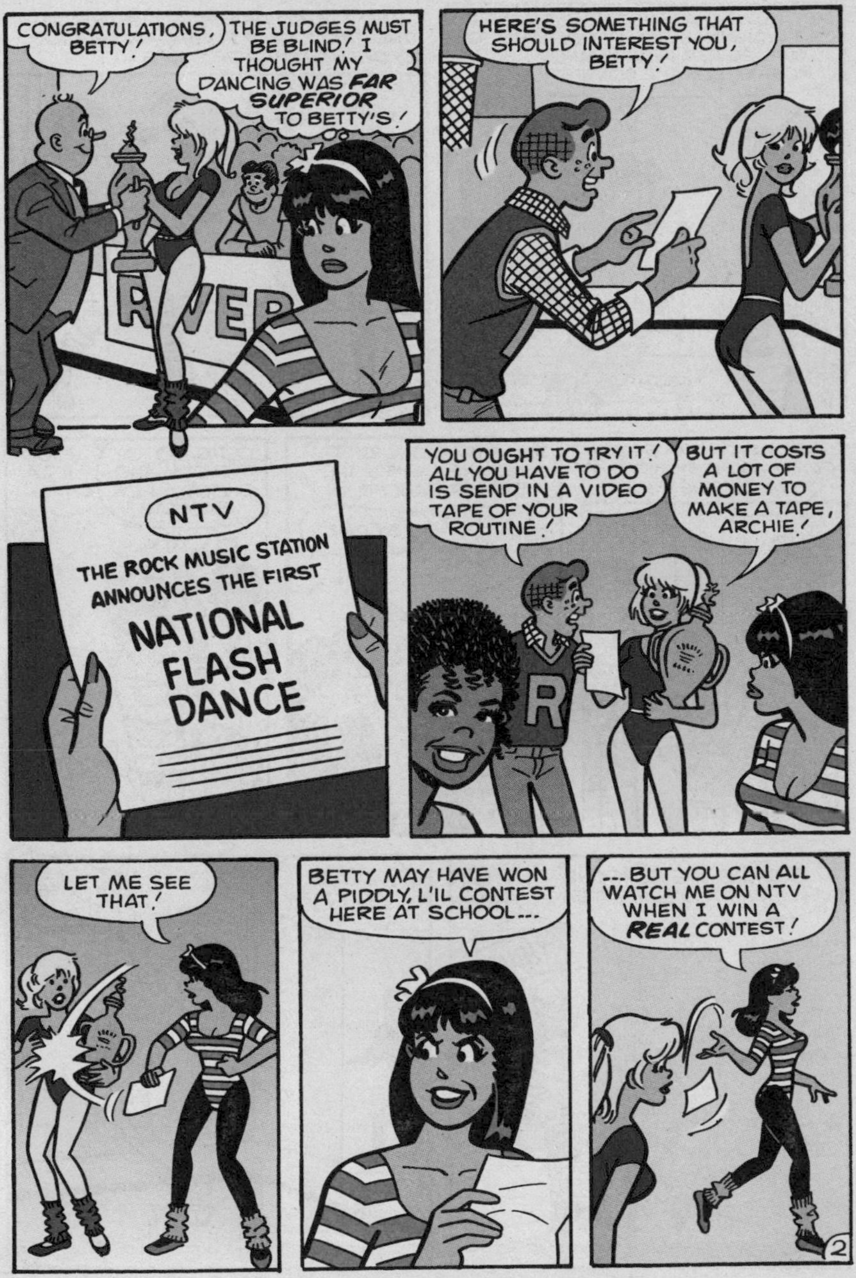
CONGRATULATIONS, BETTY!
THE JUDGES MUST BE BLIND! I THOUGHT MY DANCING WAS FAR SUPERIOR TO BETTY'S!
RIVER
HERE'S SOMETHING THAT SHOULD INTEREST YOU, BETTY!
NTV
THE ROCK MUSIC STATION ANNOUNCES THE FIRST
NATIONAL FLASH DANCE
YOU OUGHT TO TRY IT! ALL YOU HAVE TO DO IS SEND IN A VIDEO TAPE OF YOUR ROUTINE!
BUT IT COSTS A LOT OF MONEY TO MAKE A TAPE, ARCHIE!
R
LET ME SEE THAT!
BETTY MAY HAVE WON A PIDDLY, L'IL CONTEST HERE AT SCHOOL...
...BUT YOU CAN ALL WATCH ME ON NTV WHEN I WIN A REAL CONTEST!
2

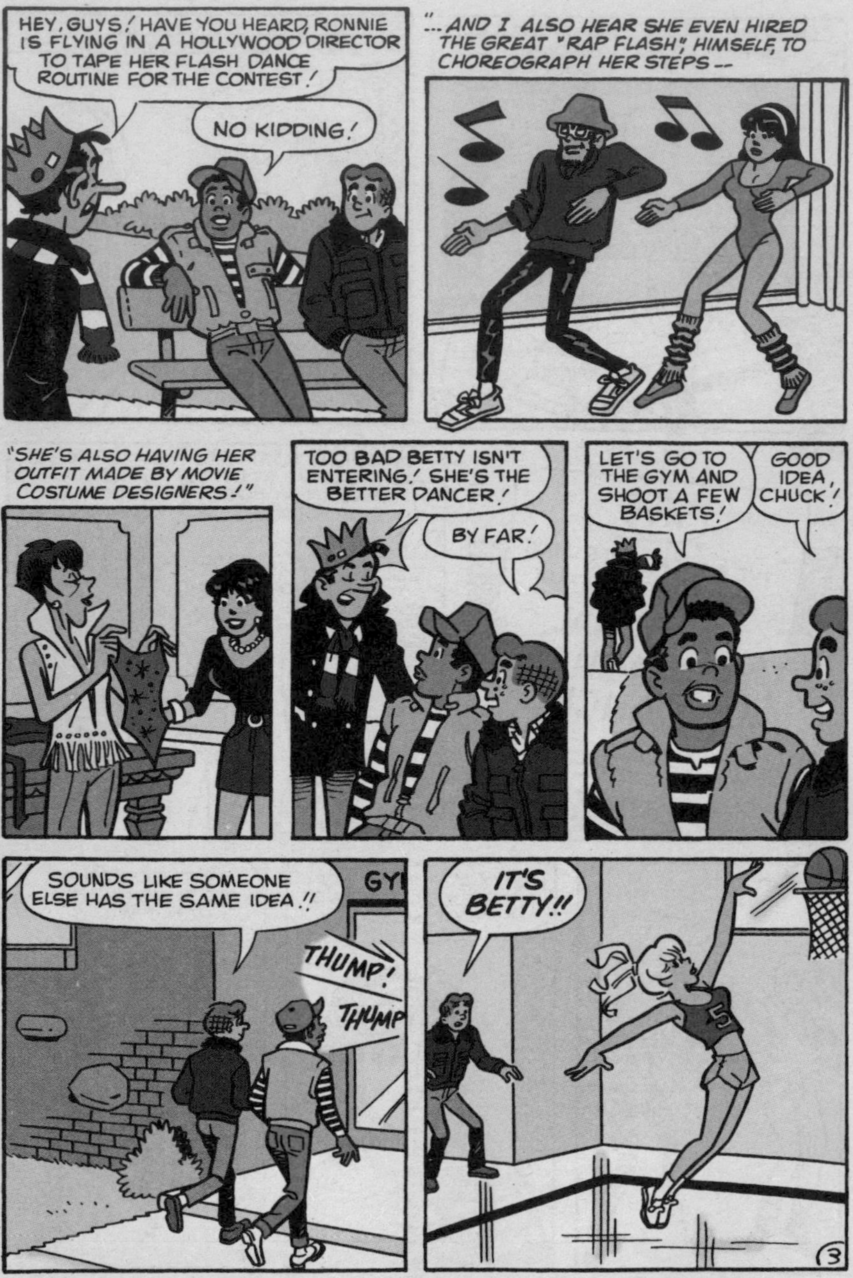
HEY, GUYS! HAVE YOU HEARD, RONNIE IS FLYING IN A HOLLYWOOD DIRECTOR TO TAPE HER FLASH DANCE ROUTINE FOR THE CONTEST!
NO KIDDING!
"...AND I ALSO HEAR SHE EVEN HIRED THE GREAT "RAP FLASH," HIMSELF, TO CHOREOGRAPH HER STEPS --
"SHE'S ALSO HAVING HER OUTFIT MADE BY MOVIE COSTUME DESIGNERS!"
TOO BAD BETTY ISN'T ENTERING! SHE'S THE BETTER DANCER!
BY FAR!
LET'S GO TO THE GYM AND SHOOT A FEW BASKETS!
GOOD IDEA, CHUCK!
SOUNDS LIKE SOMEONE ELSE HAS THE SAME IDEA!!
GY
THUMP!
THUMP
IT'S BETTY!!
3

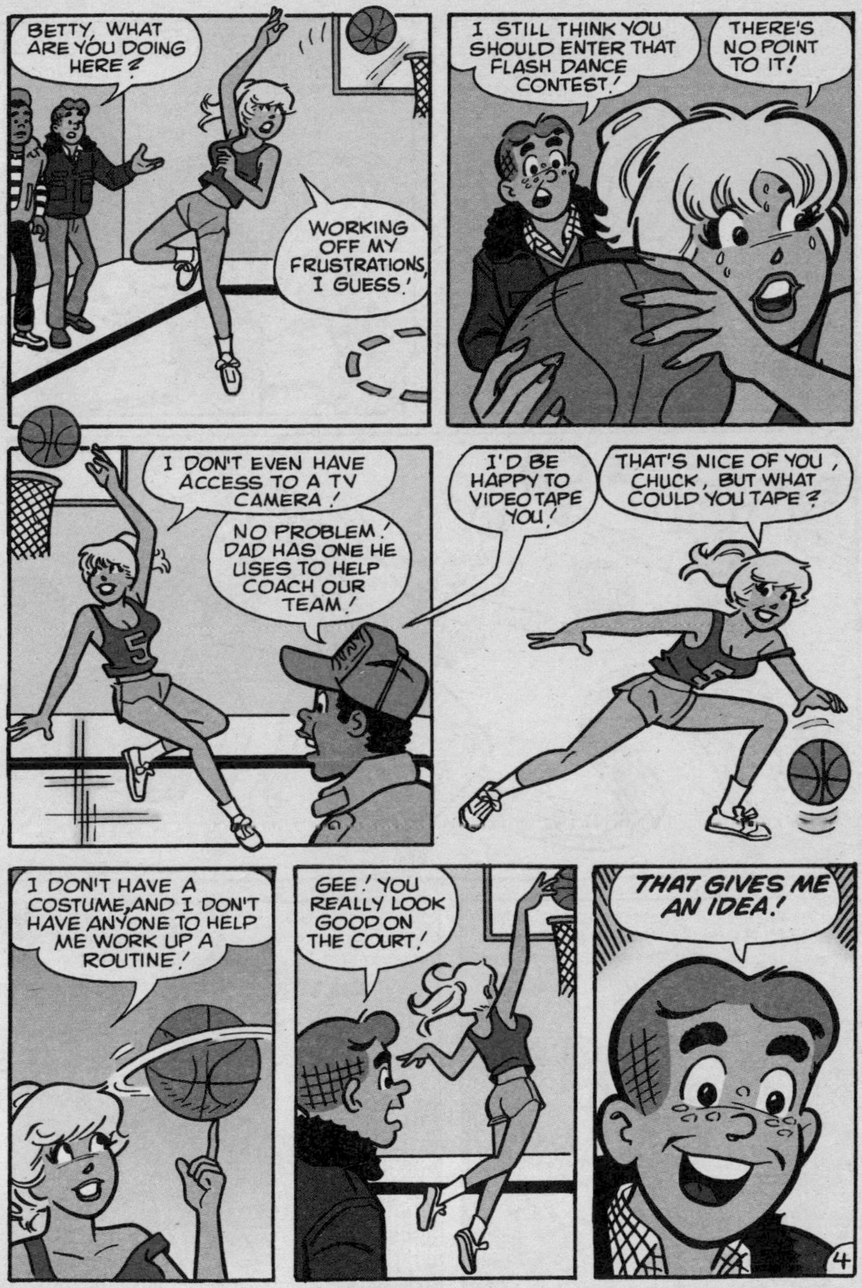
BETTY, WHAT ARE YOU DOING HERE?
WORKING OFF MY FRUSTRATIONS, I GUESS!
I STILL THINK YOU SHOULD ENTER THAT FLASH DANCE CONTEST!
THERE'S NO POINT TO IT!
I DON'T EVEN HAVE ACCESS TO A TV CAMERA!
NO PROBLEM! DAD HAS ONE HE USES TO HELP COACH OUR TEAM!
I'D BE HAPPY TO VIDEOTAPE YOU!
THAT'S NICE OF YOU, CHUCK, BUT WHAT COULD YOU TAPE?
I DON'T HAVE A COSTUME, AND I DON'T HAVE ANYONE TO HELP ME WORK UP A ROUTINE!
GEE! YOU REALLY LOOK GOOD ON THE COURT!
THAT GIVES ME AN IDEA!
4

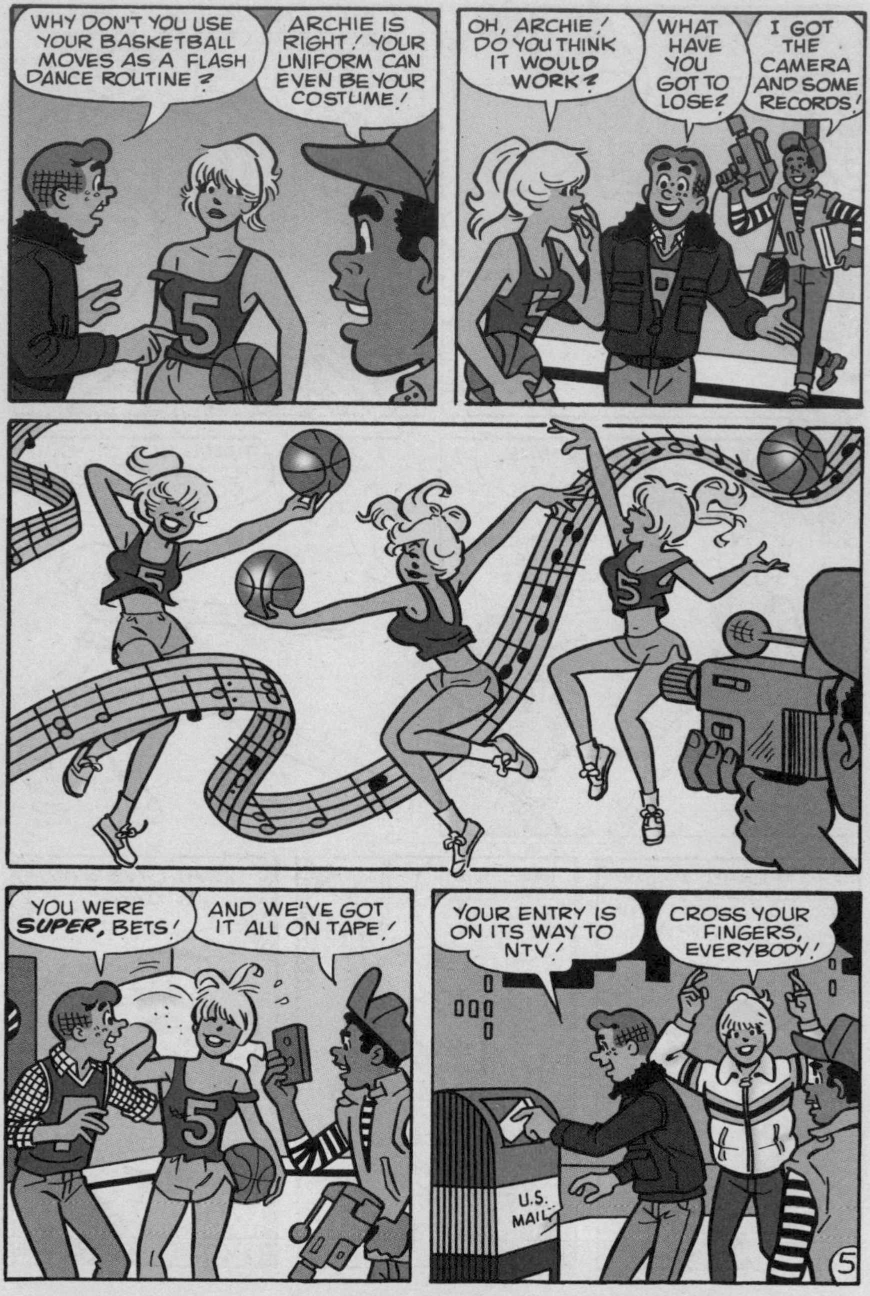
WHY DON'T YOU USE YOUR BASKETBALL MOVES AS A FLASH DANCE ROUTINE?
ARCHIE IS RIGHT! YOUR UNIFORM CAN EVEN BE YOUR COSTUME!
OH, ARCHIE! DO YOU THINK IT WOULD WORK?
WHAT HAVE YOU GOT TO LOSE?
I GOT THE CAMERA AND SOME RECORDS!
YOU WERE SUPER, BETS!
AND WE'VE GOT IT ALL ON TAPE!
YOUR ENTRY IS ON ITS WAY TO NTV!
CROSS YOUR FINGERS, EVERYBODY!
U.S. MAIL
5

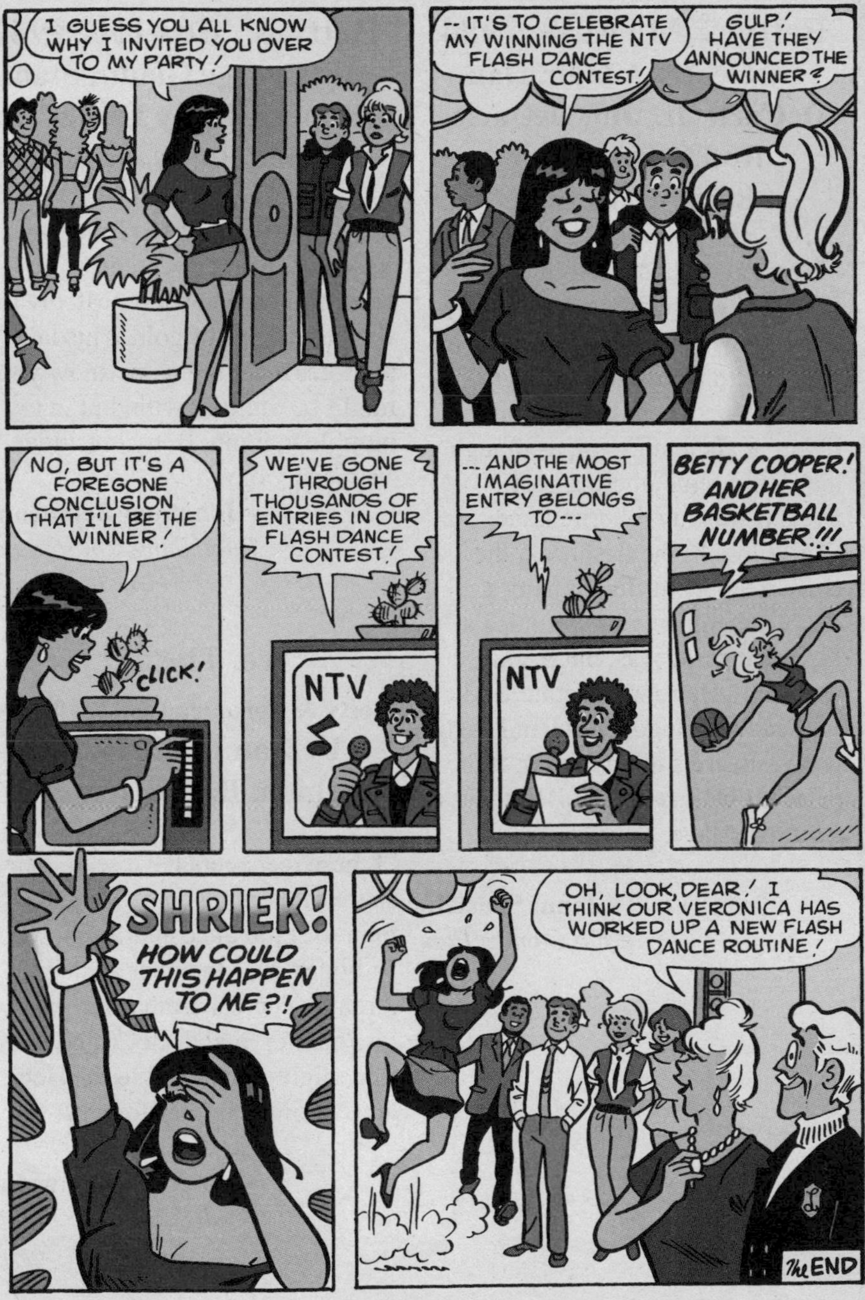
I GUESS YOU ALL KNOW WHY I INVITED YOU OVER TO MY PARTY!
-- IT'S TO CELEBRATE MY WINNING THE NTV FLASH DANCE CONTEST!
GULP! HAVE THEY ANNOUNCED THE WINNER?
NO, BUT IT'S A FOREGONE CONCLUSION THAT I'LL BE THE WINNER!
CLICK!
WE'VE GONE THROUGH THOUSANDS OF ENTRIES IN OUR FLASH DANCE CONTEST!
NTV
--- AND THE MOST IMAGINATIVE ENTRY BELONGS TO---
NTV
BETTY COOPER! AND HER BASKETBALL NUMBER!!!
SHRIEK!
HOW COULD THIS HAPPEN TO ME?!
OH, LOOK, DEAR! I THINK OUR VERONICA HAS WORKED UP A NEW FLASH DANCE ROUTINE!
The END

Nile Memories
Betty & Me #138, 1984
by George Gladir, Dan DeCarlo Jr., Jim DeCarlo, Rod Ollerenshaw, Barry Grossman

Years ago I had an Archie Digest in which the very last story was one where Archie and the gang are in a museum. It segues into a scene where the gang are living in ancient Egypt, as though they were remembering past lives. It was my favorite issue of all time. In the flashback, the characters had different names. I don't remember what Veronica's Egyptian name was, but Archie was Akhi, Betty was Bethte, and Jughead was Jugos. Akhi and Jugos were minstrels hired to play at the palace, I believe, while Bethte was a servant/slave.

--Jenni Sherriff
Archie Comics Fan

Wheel of Loot
Betty & Me #160, 1987
by George Gladir, Stan Goldberg, Rudy Lapick, Bill Yoshida, Barry Grossman

I've always preferred Betty over Veronica. She's sweet, down-to-earth and has shown repeatedly that she has a heart of gold. This tale parodies a certain game show you might be familiar with, but in my humble opinion, Betty outshines Vanna any day.

-- Jonathan Betancourt
Publishing Coordinator,
Archie Comics

We, The Jury
Betty & Veronica (vol.2) #9, 1988
by Dan DeCarlo, Bill Yoshida, Barry Grossman

These teenagers have seen their share of daytime court TV and plan to settle once and for all who truly deserves the over achieving Archie! There's drama, surprise testimonies, and a shocking verdict that might put an end to the Betty and Veronica rivalry forever!

-- Jonathan Betancourt
Publishing Coordinator,
Archie Comics

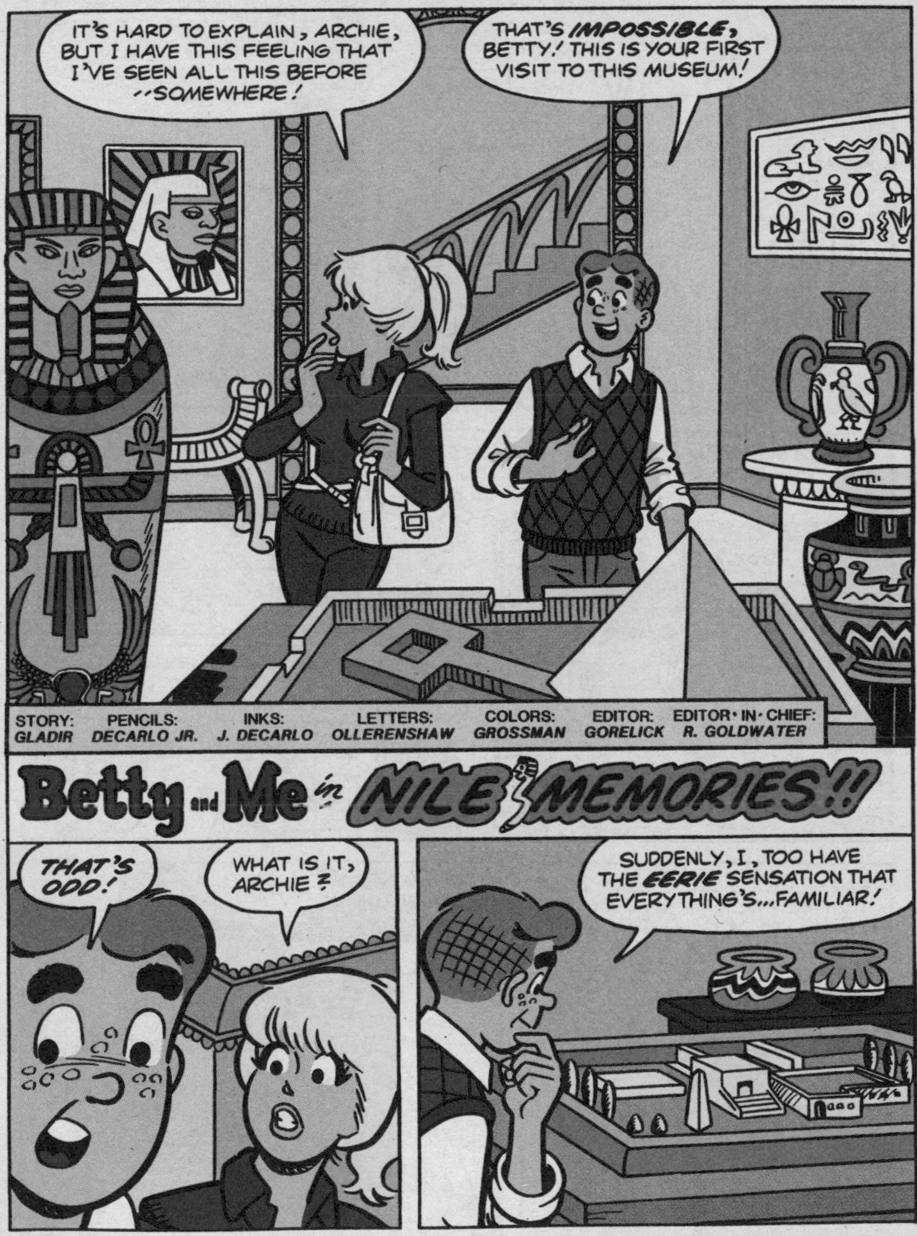
IT'S HARD TO EXPLAIN, ARCHIE, BUT I HAVE THIS FEELING THAT I'VE SEEN ALL THIS BEFORE --SOMEWHERE!
THAT'S IMPOSSIBLE, BETTY! THIS IS YOUR FIRST VISIT TO THIS MUSEUM!
STORY: GLADIR PENCILS: DECARLO JR. INKS: J. DECARLO LETTERS: OLLERENSHAW COLORS: GROSSMAN EDITOR: GORELICK EDITOR-IN-CHIEF: R. GOLDWATER
Betty and Me in NILE MEMORIES!!
THAT'S ODD!
WHAT IS IT, ARCHIE?
SUDDENLY, I, TOO HAVE THE EERIE SENSATION THAT EVERYTHING'S...FAMILIAR!

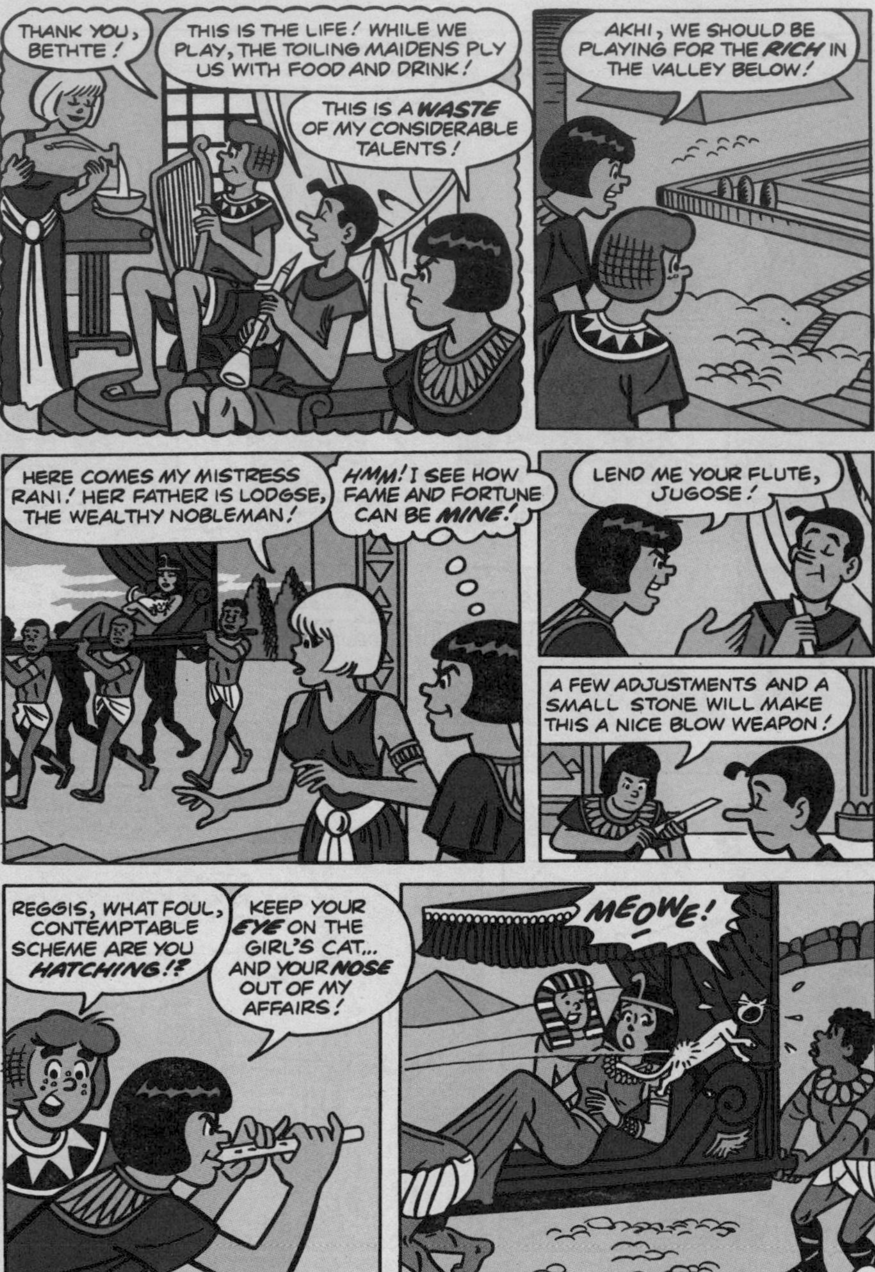
THANK YOU, BETHTE!
THIS IS THE LIFE! WHILE WE PLAY, THE TOILING MAIDENS PLY US WITH FOOD AND DRINK!
THIS IS A WASTE OF MY CONSIDERABLE TALENTS!
AKHI, WE SHOULD BE PLAYING FOR THE RICH IN THE VALLEY BELOW!
HERE COMES MY MISTRESS RANI! HER FATHER IS LODGSE, THE WEALTHY NOBLEMAN!
HMM! I SEE HOW FAME AND FORTUNE CAN BE MINE!
LEND ME YOUR FLUTE, JUGOSE!
A FEW ADJUSTMENTS AND A SMALL STONE WILL MAKE THIS A NICE BLOW WEAPON!
REGGIS, WHAT FOUL, CONTEMPTABLE SCHEME ARE YOU HATCHING!?
KEEP YOUR EYE ON THE GIRL'S CAT... AND YOUR NOSE OUT OF MY AFFAIRS!
MEOWE!
2

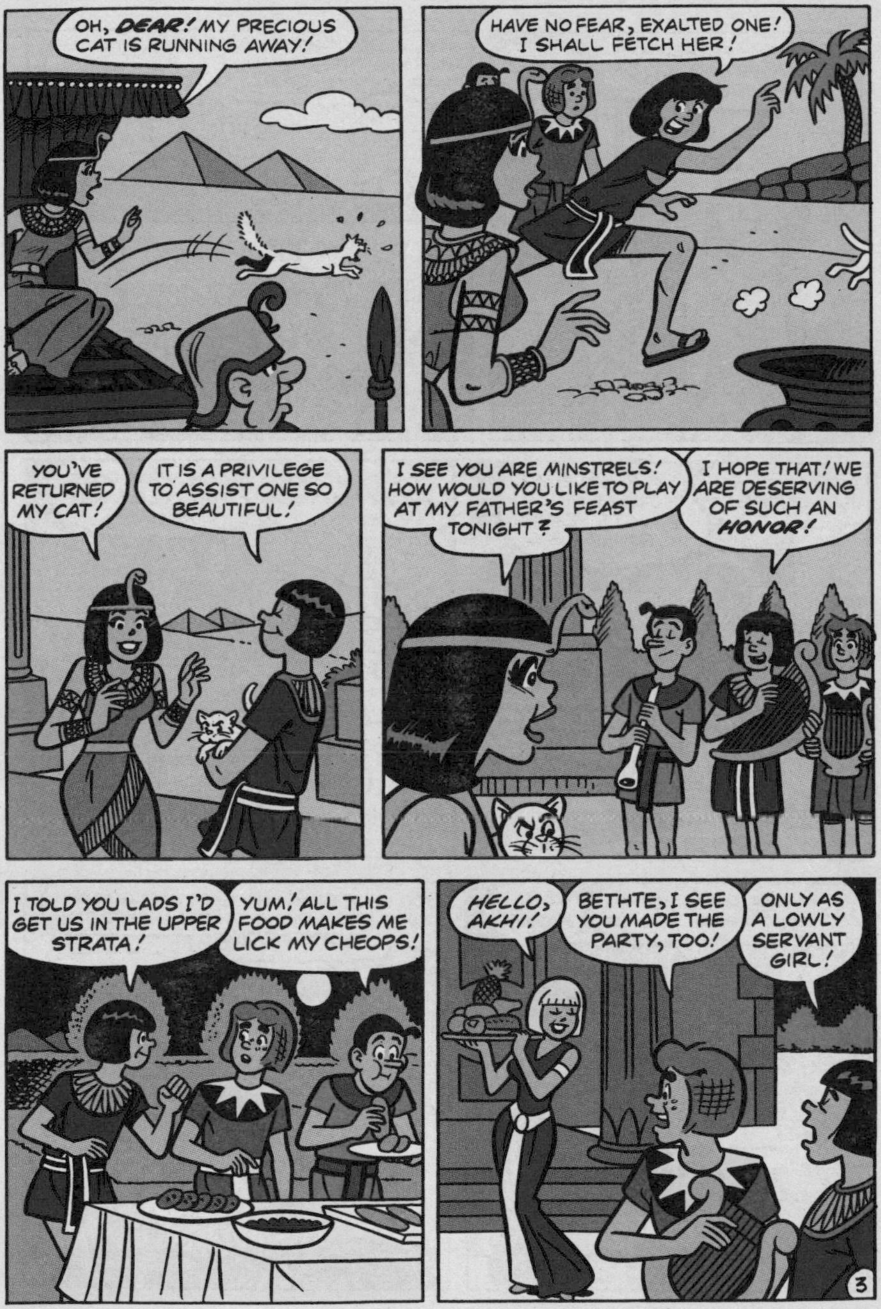
OH, DEAR! MY PRECIOUS CAT IS RUNNING AWAY!
HAVE NO FEAR, EXALTED ONE! I SHALL FETCH HER!
YOU'VE RETURNED MY CAT!
IT IS A PRIVILEGE TO ASSIST ONE SO BEAUTIFUL!
I SEE YOU ARE MINSTRELS! HOW WOULD YOU LIKE TO PLAY AT MY FATHER'S FEAST TONIGHT?
I HOPE THAT! WE ARE DESERVING OF SUCH AN HONOR!
I TOLD YOU LADS I'D GET US IN THE UPPER STRATA!
YUM! ALL THIS FOOD MAKES ME LICK MY CHEOPS!
HELLO, AKHI!
BETHTE, I SEE YOU MADE THE PARTY, TOO!
ONLY AS A LOWLY SERVANT GIRL!
3

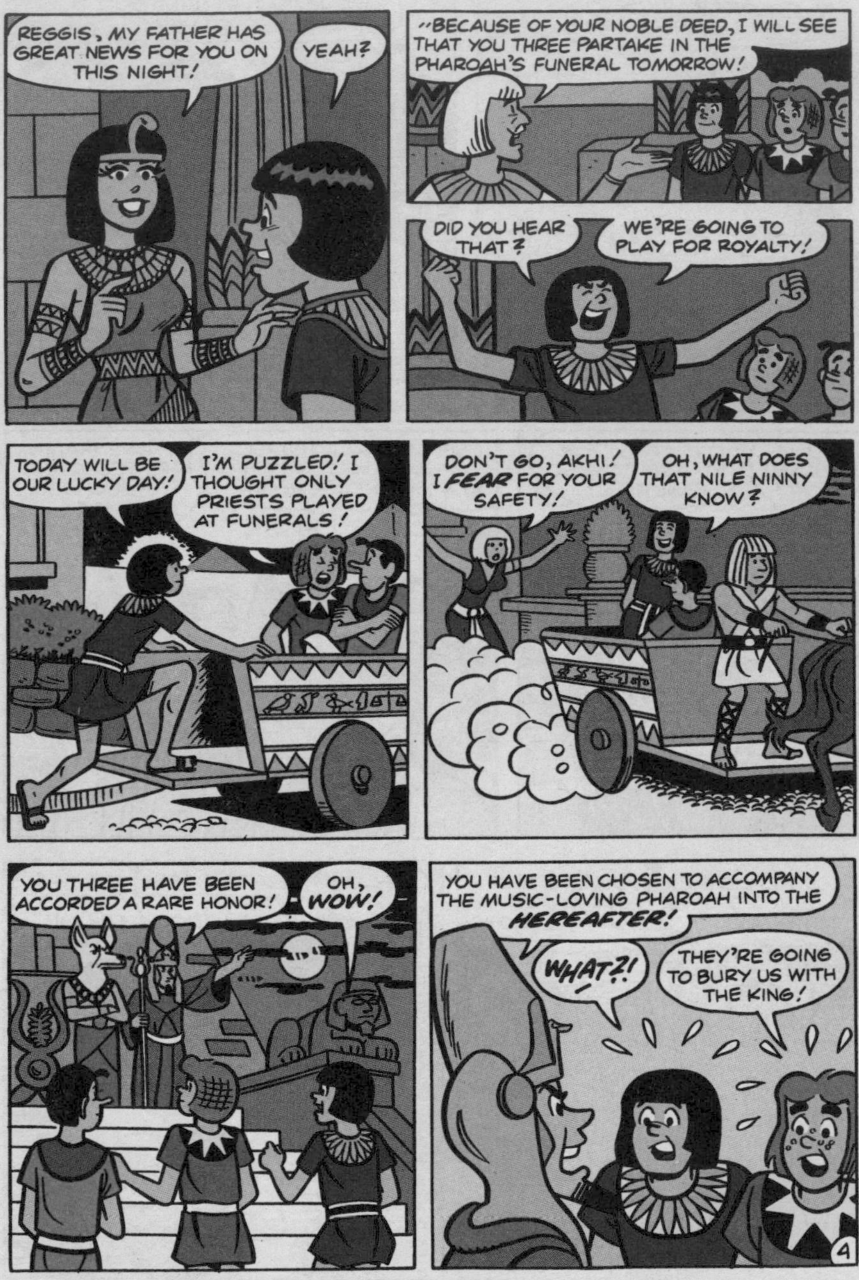
REGGIS, MY FATHER HAS GREAT NEWS FOR YOU ON THIS NIGHT!
YEAH?
..BECAUSE OF YOUR NOBLE DEED, I WILL SEE THAT YOU THREE PARTAKE IN THE PHAROAH'S FUNERAL TOMORROW!
DID YOU HEAR THAT?
WE'RE GOING TO PLAY FOR ROYALTY!
TODAY WILL BE OUR LUCKY DAY!
I'M PUZZLED! I THOUGHT ONLY PRIESTS PLAYED AT FUNERALS!
DON'T GO, AKHI! I FEAR FOR YOUR SAFETY!
OH, WHAT DOES THAT NILE NINNY KNOW?
YOU THREE HAVE BEEN ACCORDED A RARE HONOR!
OH, WOW!
YOU HAVE BEEN CHOSEN TO ACCOMPANY THE MUSIC-LOVING PHAROAH INTO THE HEREAFTER!
WHAT?!
THEY'RE GOING TO BURY US WITH THE KING!
4

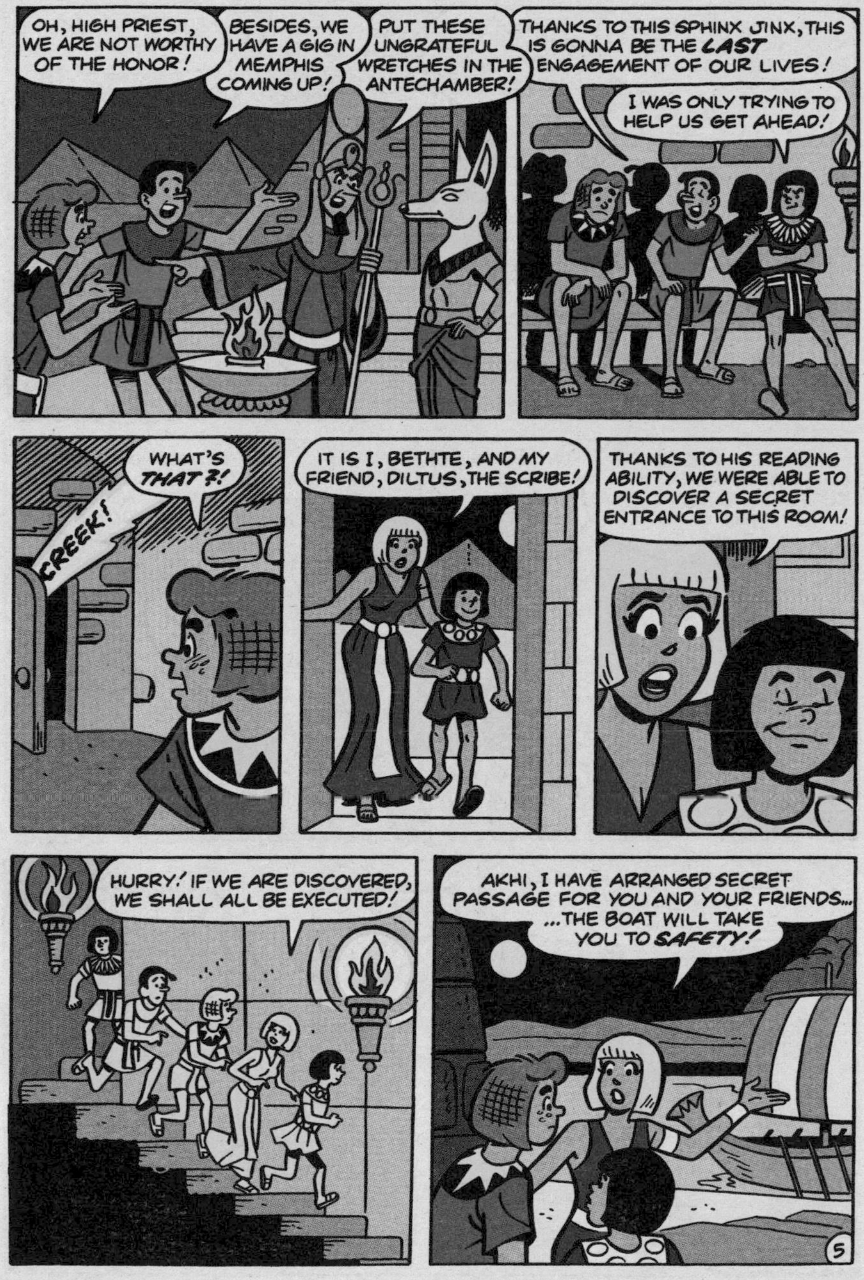
OH, HIGH PRIEST, WE ARE NOT WORTHY OF THE HONOR!
BESIDES, WE HAVE A GIG IN MEMPHIS COMING UP!
PUT THESE UNGRATEFUL WRETCHES IN THE ANTECHAMBER!
THANKS TO THIS SPHINX JINX, THIS IS GONNA BE THE LAST ENGAGEMENT OF OUR LIVES!
I WAS ONLY TRYING TO HELP US GET AHEAD!
CREEK!
WHAT'S THAT?!
IT IS I, BETHTE, AND MY FRIEND, DILTUS, THE SCRIBE!
THANKS TO HIS READING ABILITY, WE WERE ABLE TO DISCOVER A SECRET ENTRANCE TO THIS ROOM!
HURRY! IF WE ARE DISCOVERED, WE SHALL ALL BE EXECUTED!
AKHI, I HAVE ARRANGED SECRET PASSAGE FOR YOU AND YOUR FRIENDS...
...THE BOAT WILL TAKE YOU TO SAFETY!
5

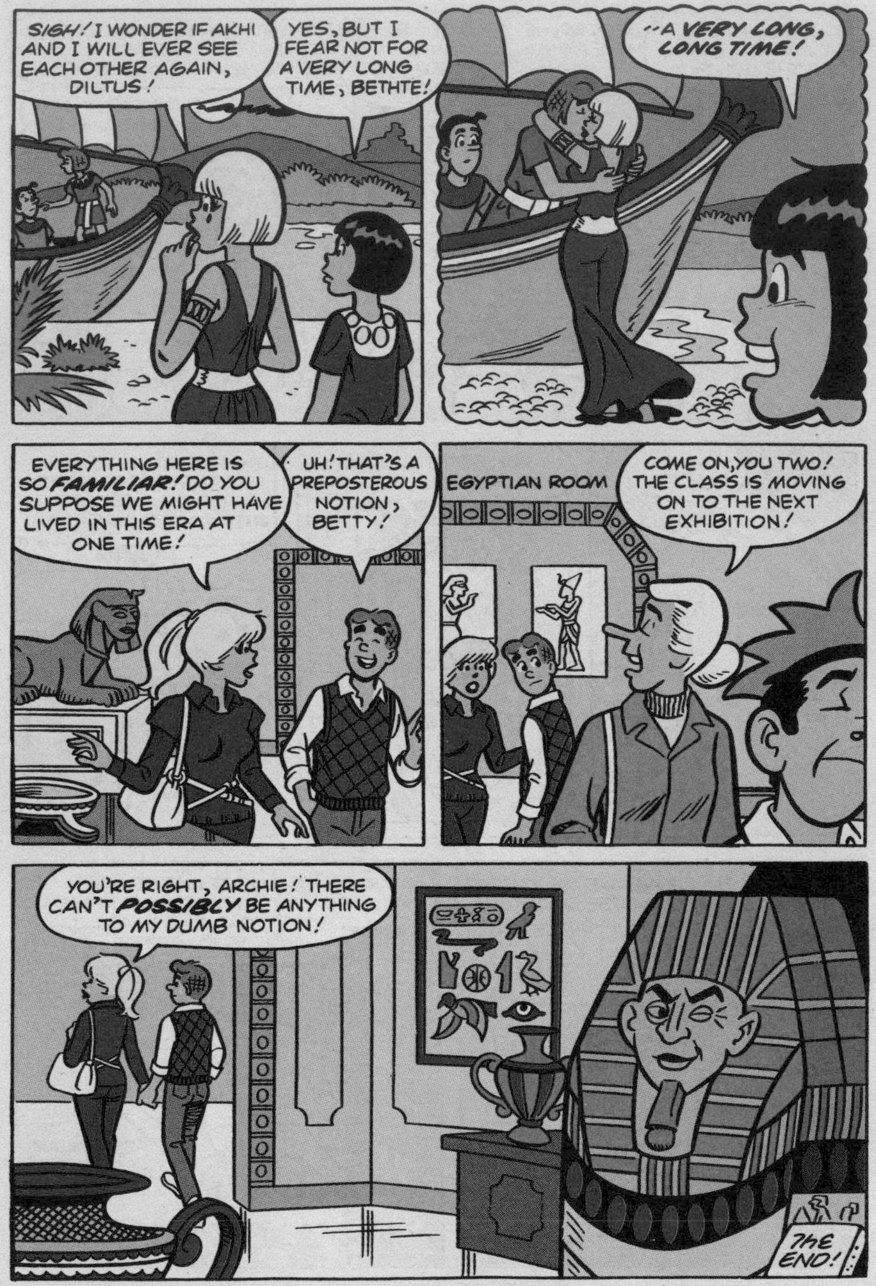
SIGH! I WONDER IF AKHI AND I WILL EVER SEE EACH OTHER AGAIN, DILTUS!
YES, BUT I FEAR NOT FOR A VERY LONG TIME, BETHTE!
--A VERY LONG, LONG TIME!
EVERYTHING HERE IS SO FAMILIAR! DO YOU SUPPOSE WE MIGHT HAVE LIVED IN THIS ERA AT ONE TIME!
UH! THAT'S A PREPOSTEROUS NOTION, BETTY!
EGYPTIAN ROOM
COME ON, YOU TWO! THE CLASS IS MOVING ON TO THE NEXT EXHIBITION!
YOU'RE RIGHT, ARCHIE! THERE CAN'T POSSIBLY BE ANYTHING TO MY DUMB NOTION!
THE END!

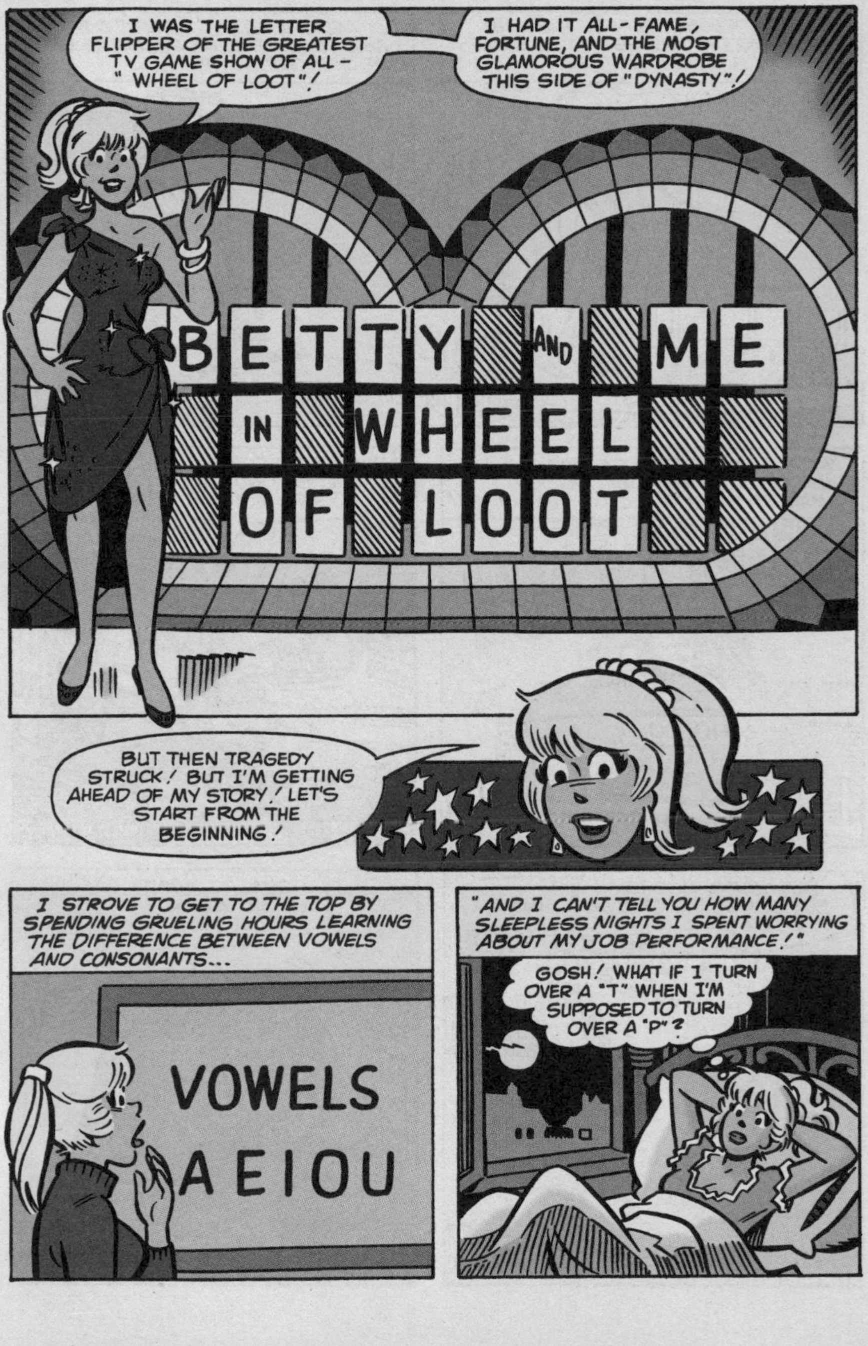
I WAS THE LETTER FLIPPER OF THE GREATEST TV GAME SHOW OF ALL - "WHEEL OF LOOT"!
I HAD IT ALL - FAME, FORTUNE, AND THE MOST GLAMOROUS WARDROBE THIS SIDE OF "DYNASTY"!
BETTY AND ME
IN WHEEL
OF LOOT
BUT THEN TRAGEDY STRUCK! BUT I'M GETTING AHEAD OF MY STORY! LET'S START FROM THE BEGINNING!
I STROVE TO GET TO THE TOP BY SPENDING GRUELING HOURS LEARNING THE DIFFERENCE BETWEEN VOWELS AND CONSONANTS...
VOWELS
A E I O U
"AND I CAN'T TELL YOU HOW MANY SLEEPLESS NIGHTS I SPENT WORRYING ABOUT MY JOB PERFORMANCE!"
GOSH! WHAT IF I TURN OVER A "T" WHEN I'M SUPPOSED TO TURN OVER A "P"?

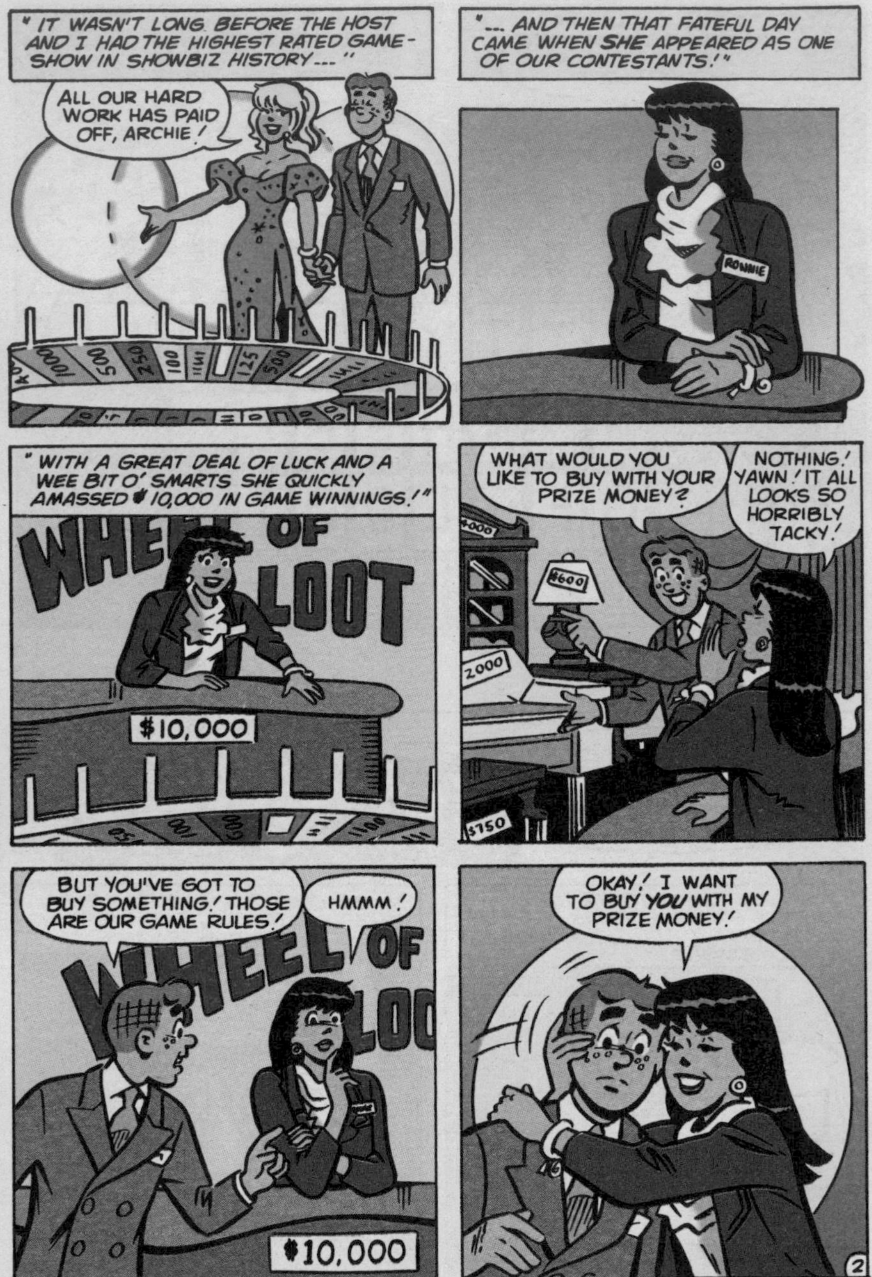
"IT WASN'T LONG BEFORE THE HOST AND I HAD THE HIGHEST RATED GAME-SHOW IN SHOWBIZ HISTORY--- "
ALL OUR HARD WORK HAS PAID OFF, ARCHIE!
"... AND THEN THAT FATEFUL DAY CAME WHEN SHE APPEARED AS ONE OF OUR CONTESTANTS!"
RONNIE
"WITH A GREAT DEAL OF LUCK AND A WEE BIT O' SMARTS SHE QUICKLY AMASSED $10,000 IN GAME WINNINGS!"
WHEEL OF LOOT
$10,000
WHAT WOULD YOU LIKE TO BUY WITH YOUR PRIZE MONEY?
NOTHING! YAWN! IT ALL LOOKS SO HORRIBLY TACKY!
$600
2000
$750
BUT YOU'VE GOT TO BUY SOMETHING! THOSE ARE OUR GAME RULES!
HMMM!
$10,000
OKAY! I WANT TO BUY YOU WITH MY PRIZE MONEY!
2

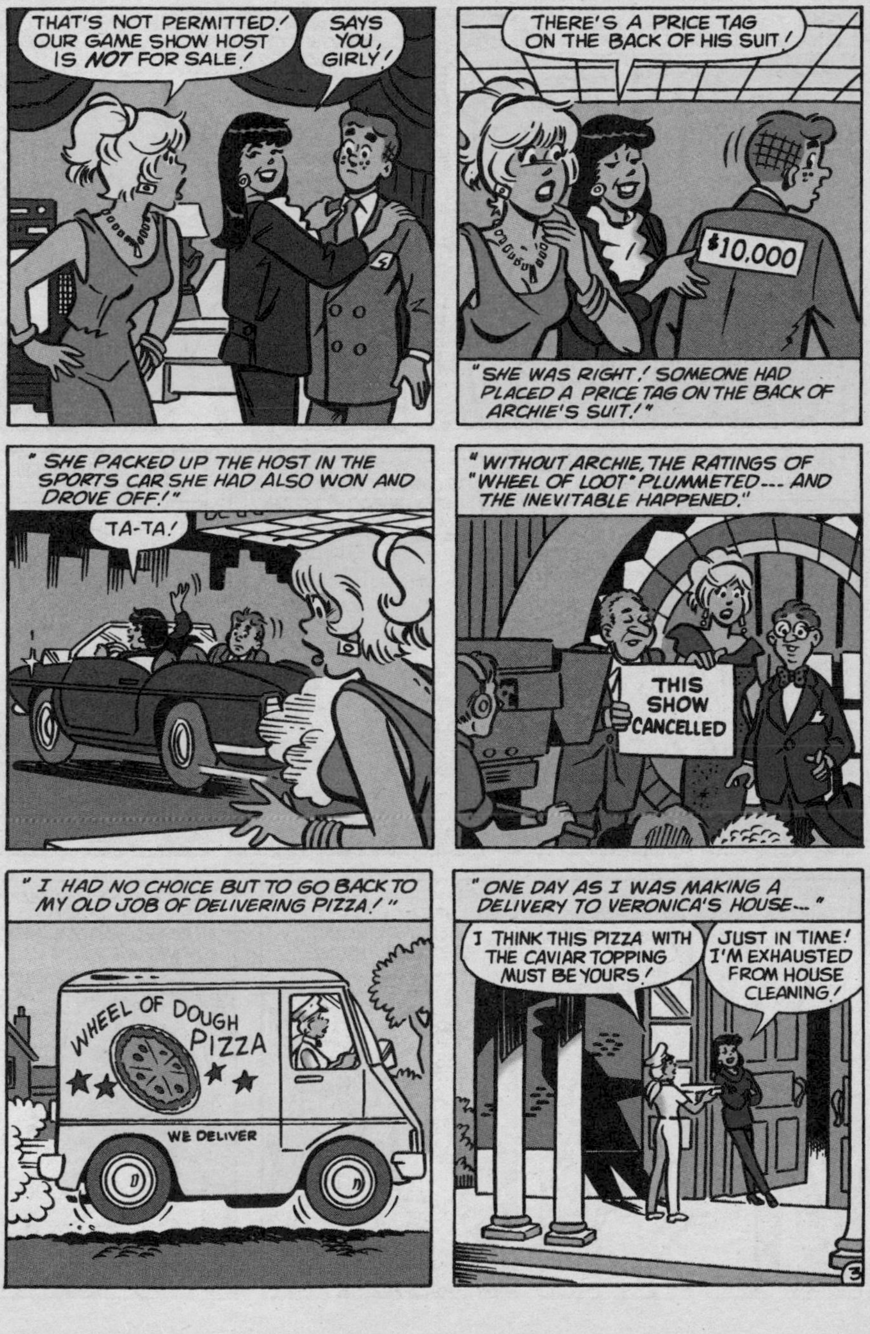
THAT'S NOT PERMITTED! OUR GAME SHOW HOST IS NOT FOR SALE!
SAYS YOU, GIRLY!
THERE'S A PRICE TAG ON THE BACK OF HIS SUIT!
$10,000
"SHE WAS RIGHT! SOMEONE HAD PLACED A PRICE TAG ON THE BACK OF ARCHIE'S SUIT!"
"SHE PACKED UP THE HOST IN THE SPORTS CAR SHE HAD ALSO WON AND DROVE OFF!"
TA-TA!
"WITHOUT ARCHIE, THE RATINGS OF "WHEEL OF LOOT" PLUMMETED--- AND THE INEVITABLE HAPPENED."
THIS SHOW CANCELLED
"I HAD NO CHOICE BUT TO GO BACK TO MY OLD JOB OF DELIVERING PIZZA!"
WHEEL OF DOUGH PIZZA
WE DELIVER
"ONE DAY AS I WAS MAKING A DELIVERY TO VERONICA'S HOUSE..."
I THINK THIS PIZZA WITH THE CAVIAR TOPPING MUST BE YOURS!
JUST IN TIME! I'M EXHAUSTED FROM HOUSE CLEANING!
3

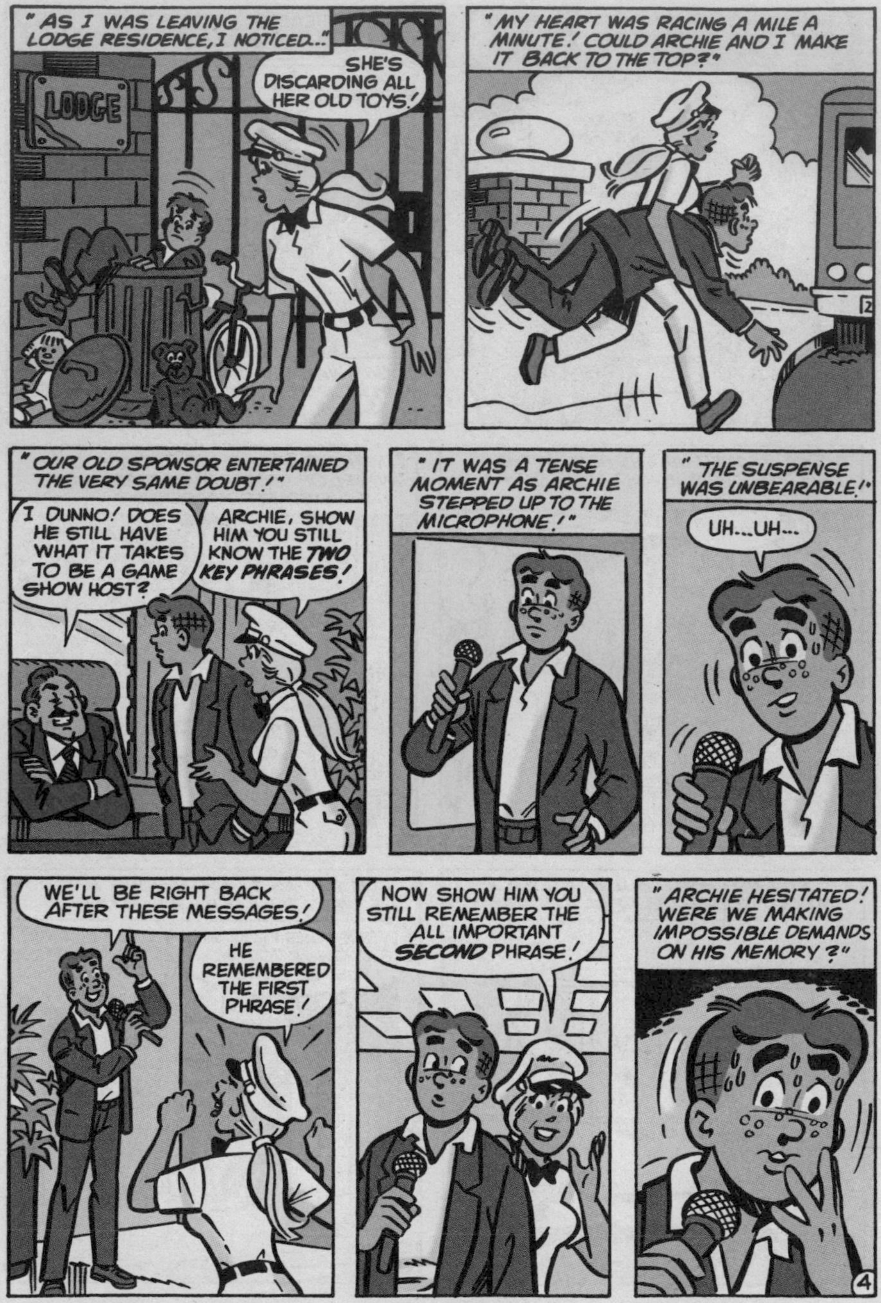
"AS I WAS LEAVING THE LODGE RESIDENCE, I NOTICED..."
LODGE
SHE'S DISCARDING ALL HER OLD TOYS!
"MY HEART WAS RACING A MILE A MINUTE! COULD ARCHIE AND I MAKE IT BACK TO THE TOP?"
"OUR OLD SPONSOR ENTERTAINED THE VERY SAME DOUBT!"
I DUNNO! DOES HE STILL HAVE WHAT IT TAKES TO BE A GAME SHOW HOST?
ARCHIE, SHOW HIM YOU STILL KNOW THE TWO KEY PHRASES!
"IT WAS A TENSE MOMENT AS ARCHIE STEPPED UP TO THE MICROPHONE!"
"THE SUSPENSE WAS UNBEARABLE!"
UH...UH...
WE'LL BE RIGHT BACK AFTER THESE MESSAGES!
HE REMEMBERED THE FIRST PHRASE!
NOW SHOW HIM YOU STILL REMEMBER THE ALL IMPORTANT SECOND PHRASE!
"ARCHIE HESITATED! WERE WE MAKING IMPOSSIBLE DEMANDS ON HIS MEMORY?"
4

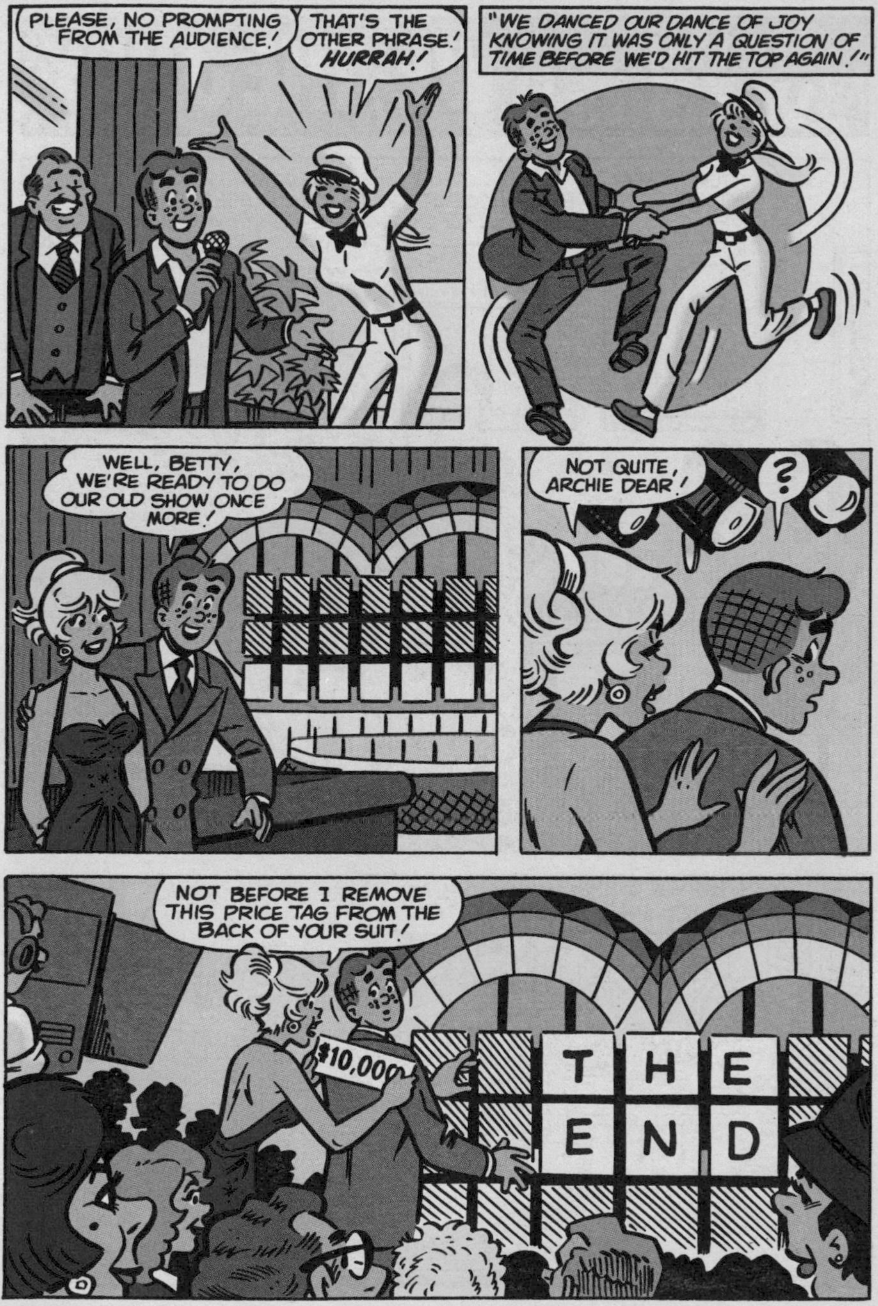
PLEASE, NO PROMPTING FROM THE AUDIENCE!
THAT'S THE OTHER PHRASE! HURRAH!
"WE DANCED OUR DANCE OF JOY KNOWING IT WAS ONLY A QUESTION OF TIME BEFORE WE'D HIT THE TOP AGAIN!"
WELL, BETTY, WE'RE READY TO DO OUR OLD SHOW ONCE MORE!
NOT QUITE, ARCHIE DEAR!
?
NOT BEFORE I REMOVE THIS PRICE TAG FROM THE BACK OF YOUR SUIT!
$10,000
THE
END

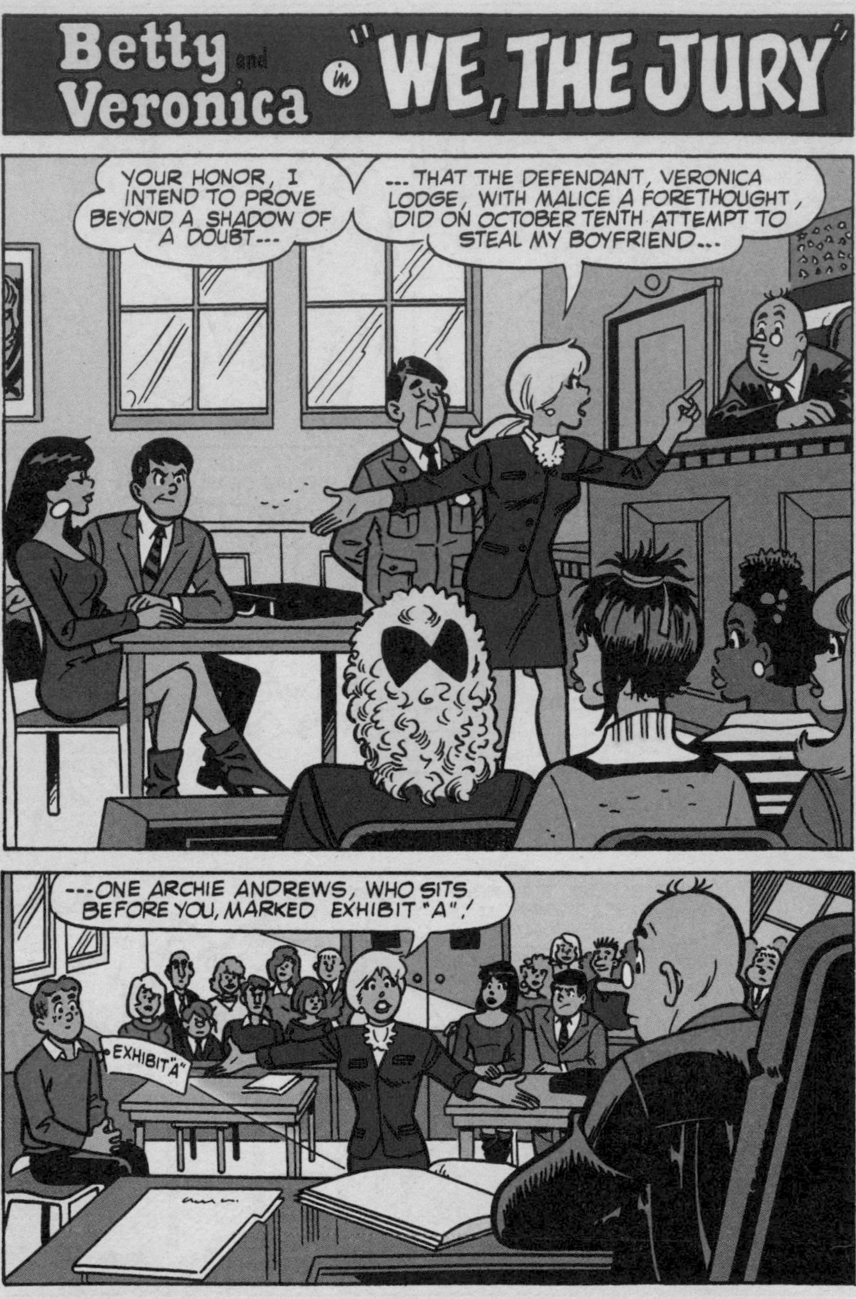
Betty and Veronica in "WE, THE JURY"
YOUR HONOR, I INTEND TO PROVE BEYOND A SHADOW OF A DOUBT---
--- THAT THE DEFENDANT, VERONICA LODGE, WITH MALICE A FORETHOUGHT, DID ON OCTOBER TENTH ATTEMPT TO STEAL MY BOYFRIEND---
---ONE ARCHIE ANDREWS, WHO SITS BEFORE YOU, MARKED EXHIBIT "A"!
EXHIBIT "A"

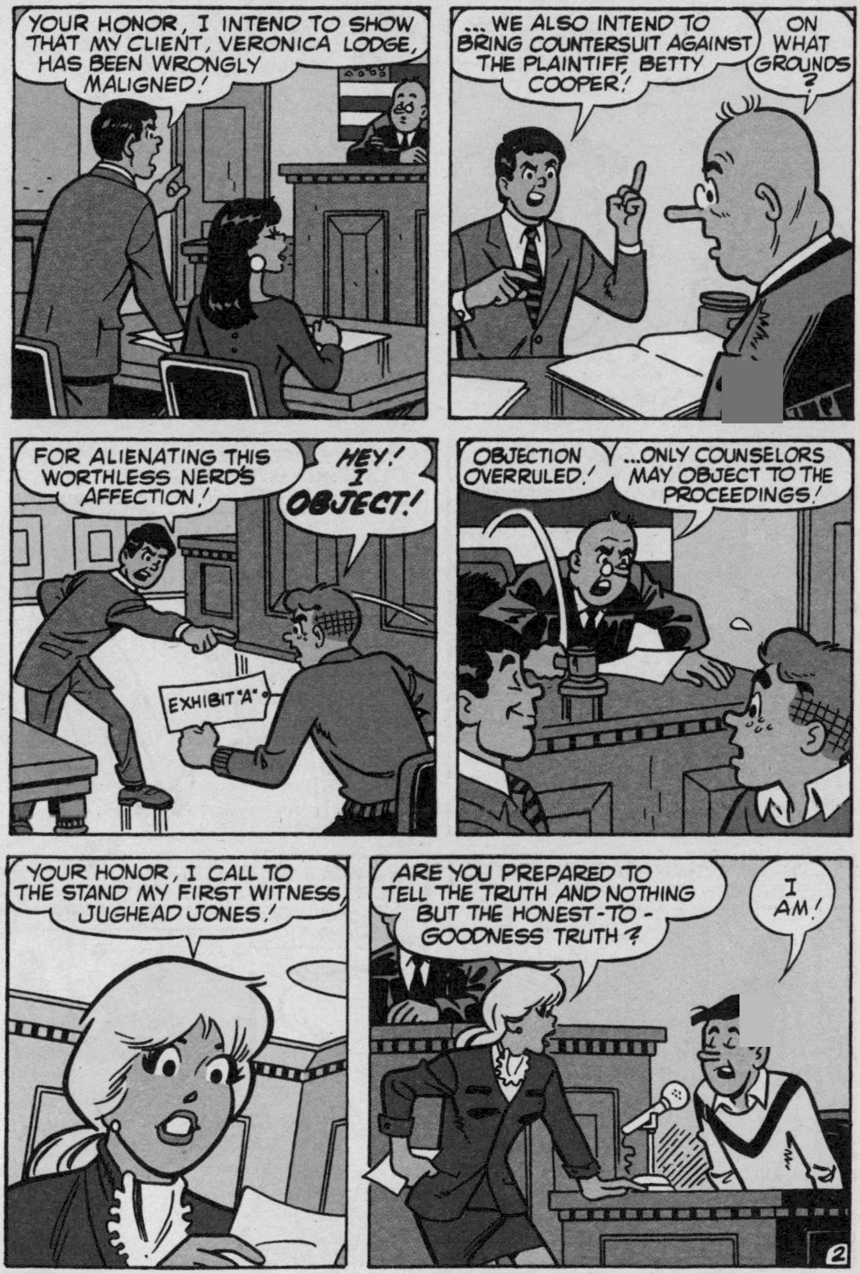
YOUR HONOR, I INTEND TO SHOW THAT MY CLIENT, VERONICA LODGE, HAS BEEN WRONGLY MALIGNED!
... WE ALSO INTEND TO BRING COUNTERSUIT AGAINST THE PLAINTIFF, BETTY COOPER!
ON WHAT GROUNDS?
FOR ALIENATING THIS WORTHLESS NERD'S AFFECTION!
HEY! I OBJECT!
EXHIBIT "A"
OBJECTION OVERRULED!
...ONLY COUNSELORS MAY OBJECT TO THE PROCEEDINGS!
YOUR HONOR, I CALL TO THE STAND MY FIRST WITNESS, JUGHEAD JONES!
ARE YOU PREPARED TO TELL THE TRUTH AND NOTHING BUT THE HONEST-TO-GOODNESS TRUTH?
I AM!
2

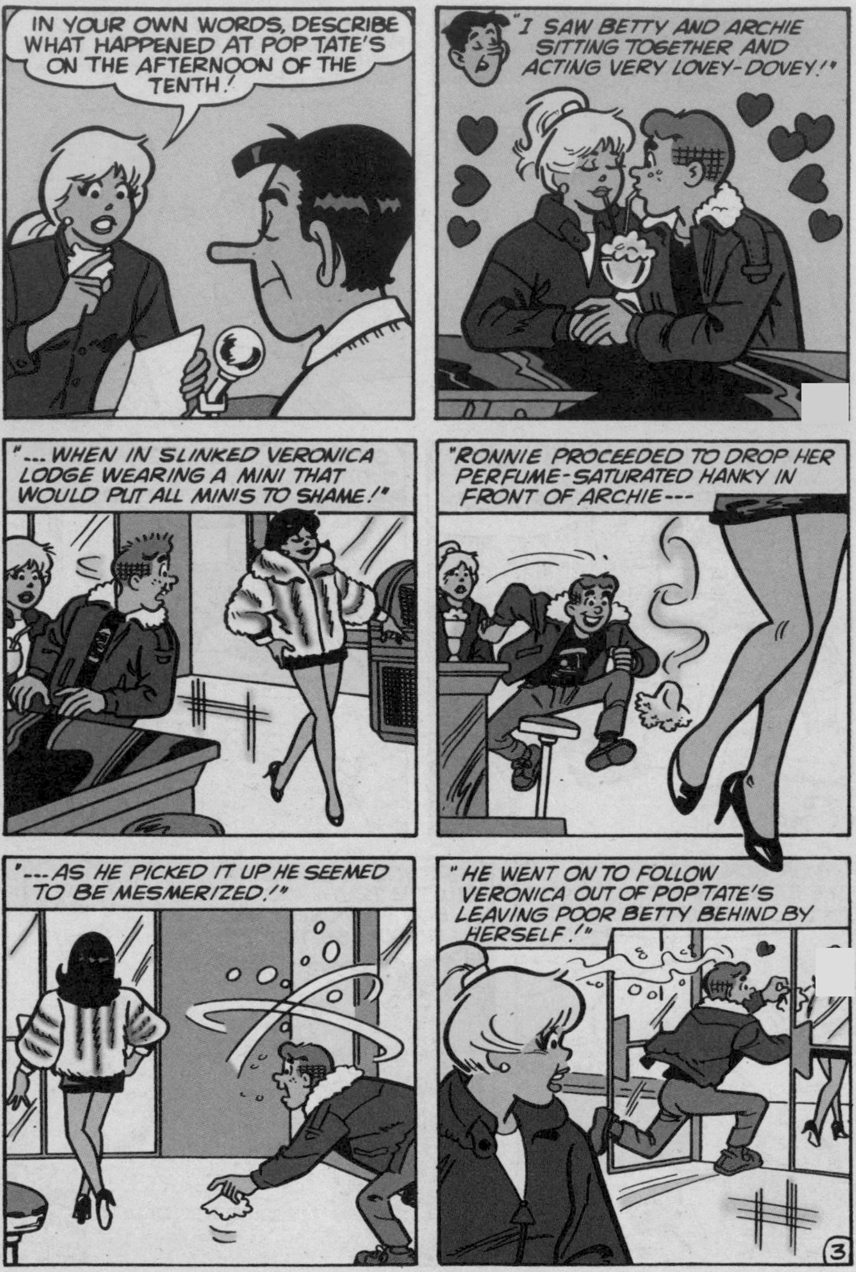
IN YOUR OWN WORDS, DESCRIBE WHAT HAPPENED AT POP TATE'S ON THE AFTERNOON OF THE TENTH!
"I SAW BETTY AND ARCHIE SITTING TOGETHER AND ACTING VERY LOVEY-DOVEY!"
"...WHEN IN SLINKED VERONICA LODGE WEARING A MINI THAT WOULD PUT ALL MINIS TO SHAME!"
"RONNIE PROCEEDED TO DROP HER PERFUME-SATURATED HANKY IN FRONT OF ARCHIE---
"---AS HE PICKED IT UP HE SEEMED TO BE MESMERIZED!"
"HE WENT ON TO FOLLOW VERONICA OUT OF POP TATE'S LEAVING POOR BETTY BEHIND BY HERSELF!"
3

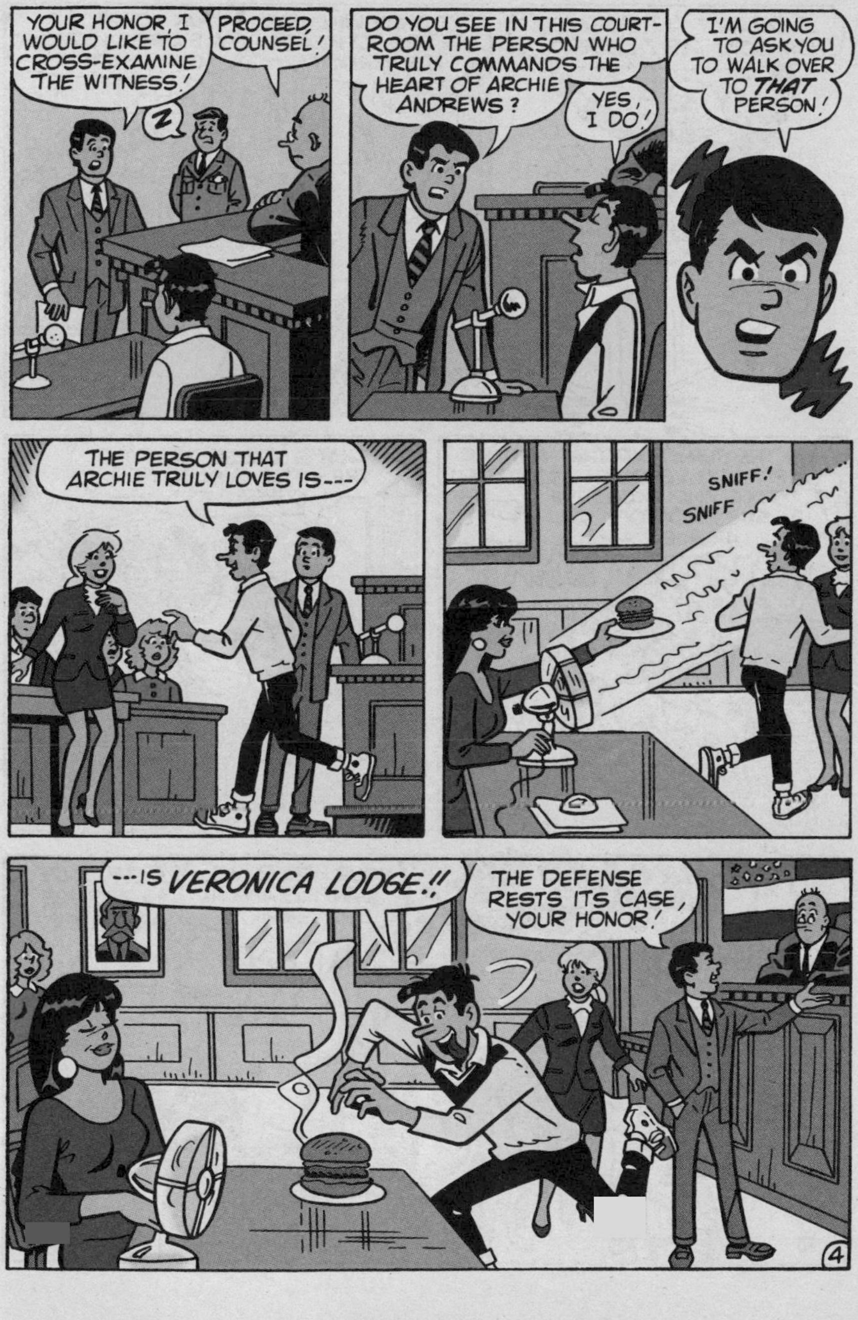
YOUR HONOR, I WOULD LIKE TO CROSS-EXAMINE THE WITNESS!
PROCEED, COUNSEL!
Z
DO YOU SEE IN THIS COURT-ROOM THE PERSON WHO TRULY COMMANDS THE HEART OF ARCHIE ANDREWS?
YES, I DO!
I'M GOING TO ASK YOU TO WALK OVER TO THAT PERSON!
THE PERSON THAT ARCHIE TRULY LOVES IS---
SNIFF!
SNIFF
---IS VERONICA LODGE!!
THE DEFENSE RESTS ITS CASE, YOUR HONOR!
4

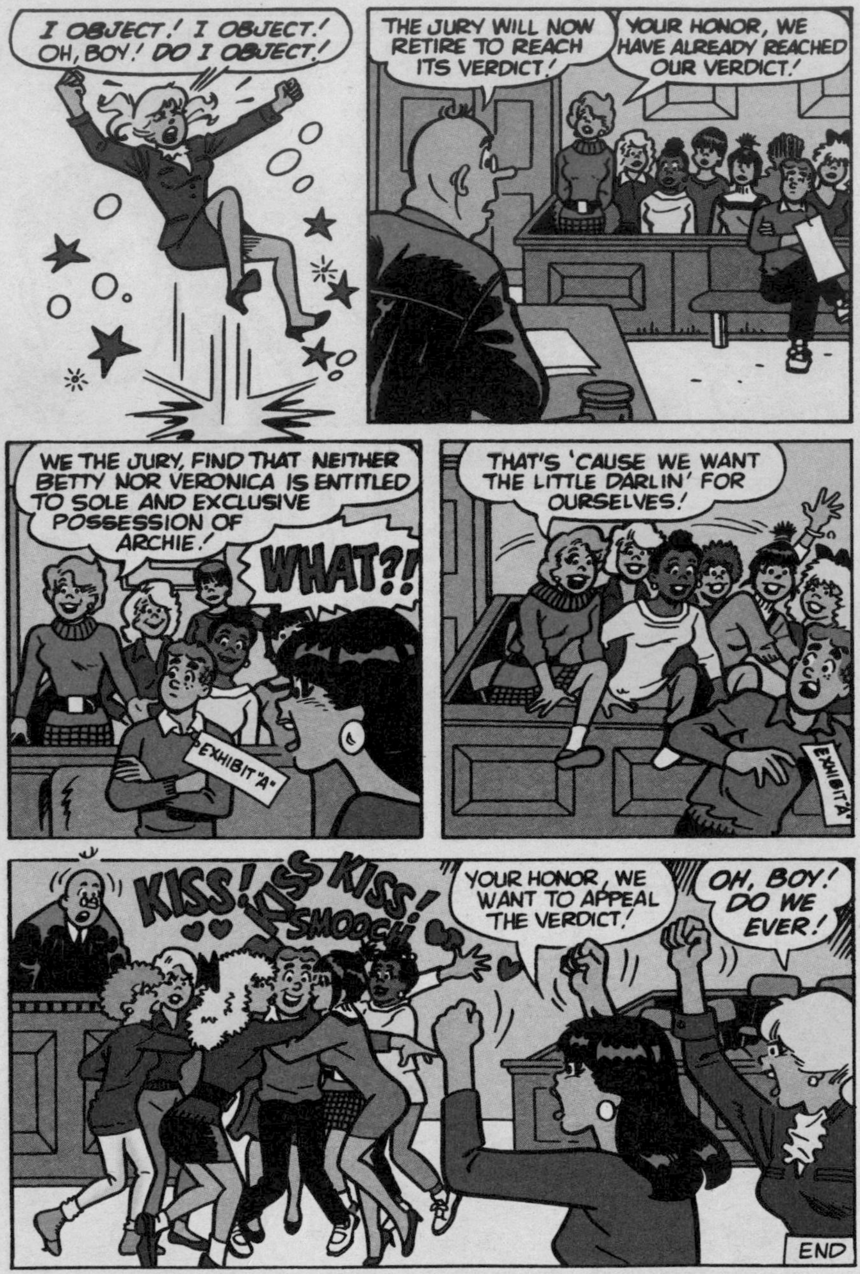
I OBJECT! I OBJECT! OH, BOY! DO I OBJECT!
THE JURY WILL NOW RETIRE TO REACH ITS VERDICT!
YOUR HONOR, WE HAVE ALREADY REACHED OUR VERDICT!
WE THE JURY, FIND THAT NEITHER BETTY NOR VERONICA IS ENTITLED TO SOLE AND EXCLUSIVE POSSESSION OF ARCHIE!
WHAT?!
EXHIBIT "A"
THAT'S 'CAUSE WE WANT THE LITTLE DARLIN' FOR OURSELVES!
EXHIBIT "A"
KISS!
KISS
KISS!
SMOOCH
YOUR HONOR, WE WANT TO APPEAL THE VERDICT!
OH, BOY! DO WE EVER!
END

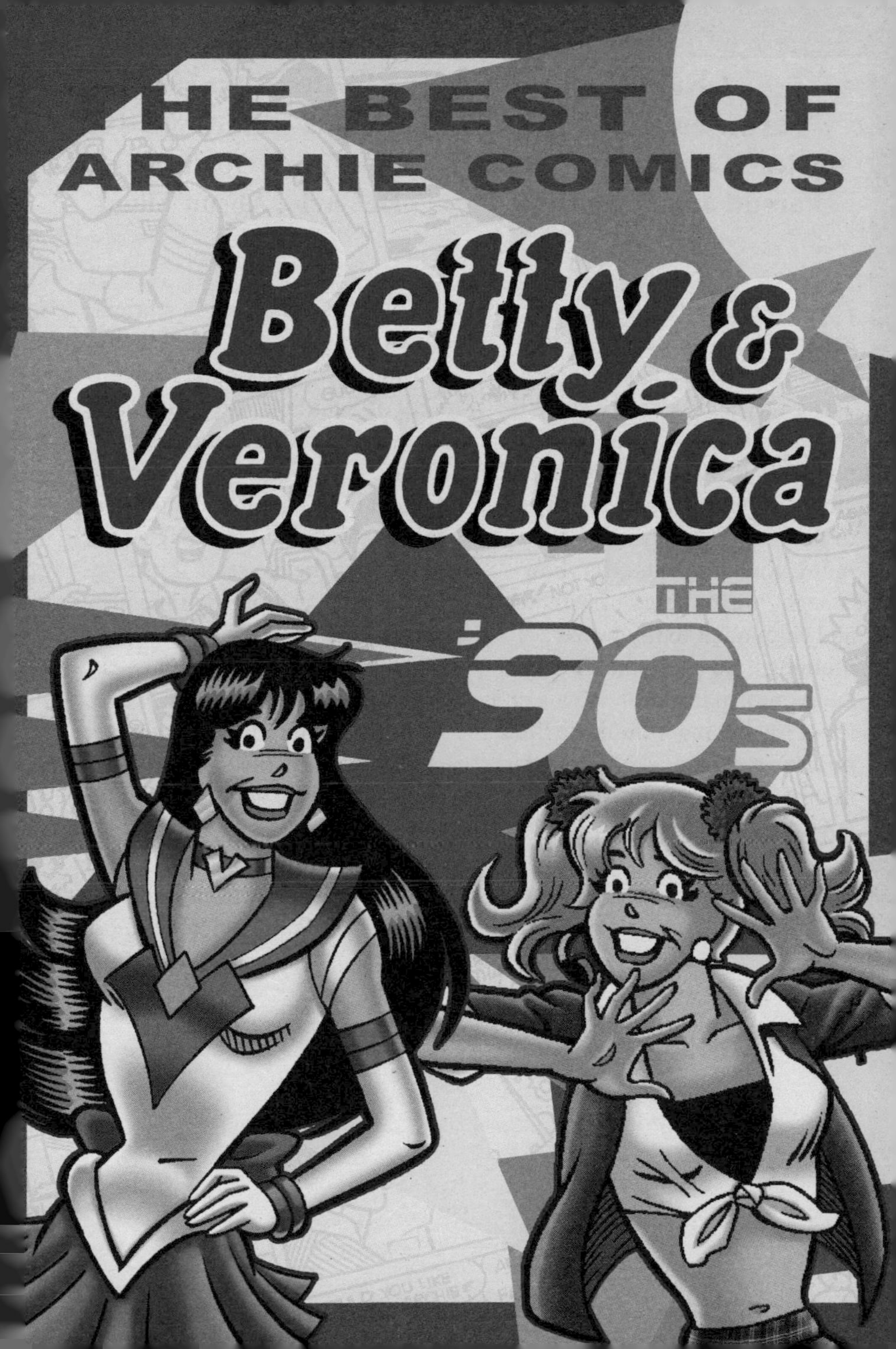
THE BEST OF
ARCHIE COMICS
Betty &
Veronica
THE
'90s

I Ratings
Veronica #20, 1992
by Rod Ollerenshaw, Dan Parent, Jon D'Agostino

Generation Gasp
Betty & Veronica #69 1993
by Frank Doyle, Dan DeCarlo, Alison Flood

As Digest Editor, I've come across many Archie stories that spoof pop culture icons. This Betty and Veronica story spoofs none other than the self-proclaimed "King of All Media," Howard Stern. I was a big fan of the Howard Stern radio show in my younger years. His show brought lots of hours of laughter and enjoyment to my weekday mornings. So enjoy this Betty and Veronica tale with Howie and his crew making Veronica's life miserable for a day. And, one last thing...

BABA BOOEY, BABA BOOEY!

Now, I could give you a brief history of grunge music. Maybe I could comment on the Emerald City of Seattle, or drop album and song titles in this introduction. Perhaps a listing of the finest flannel manufacturers would seal this as the definitive grunge write-up (minus the angst). I'll just say this: it was an amazing time in music when bands like Alice in Chains, Soundgarden—and yes—Nirvana, dominated the airwaves. With that in mind, let's not get too serious. Enjoy this tale that pokes some fun at the genre that defined the '90s.

-- **Carlos Antunes**
Digest Editor,
Archie Comics

-- **Jonathan Betancourt**
Publishing Coordinator,
Archie Comics

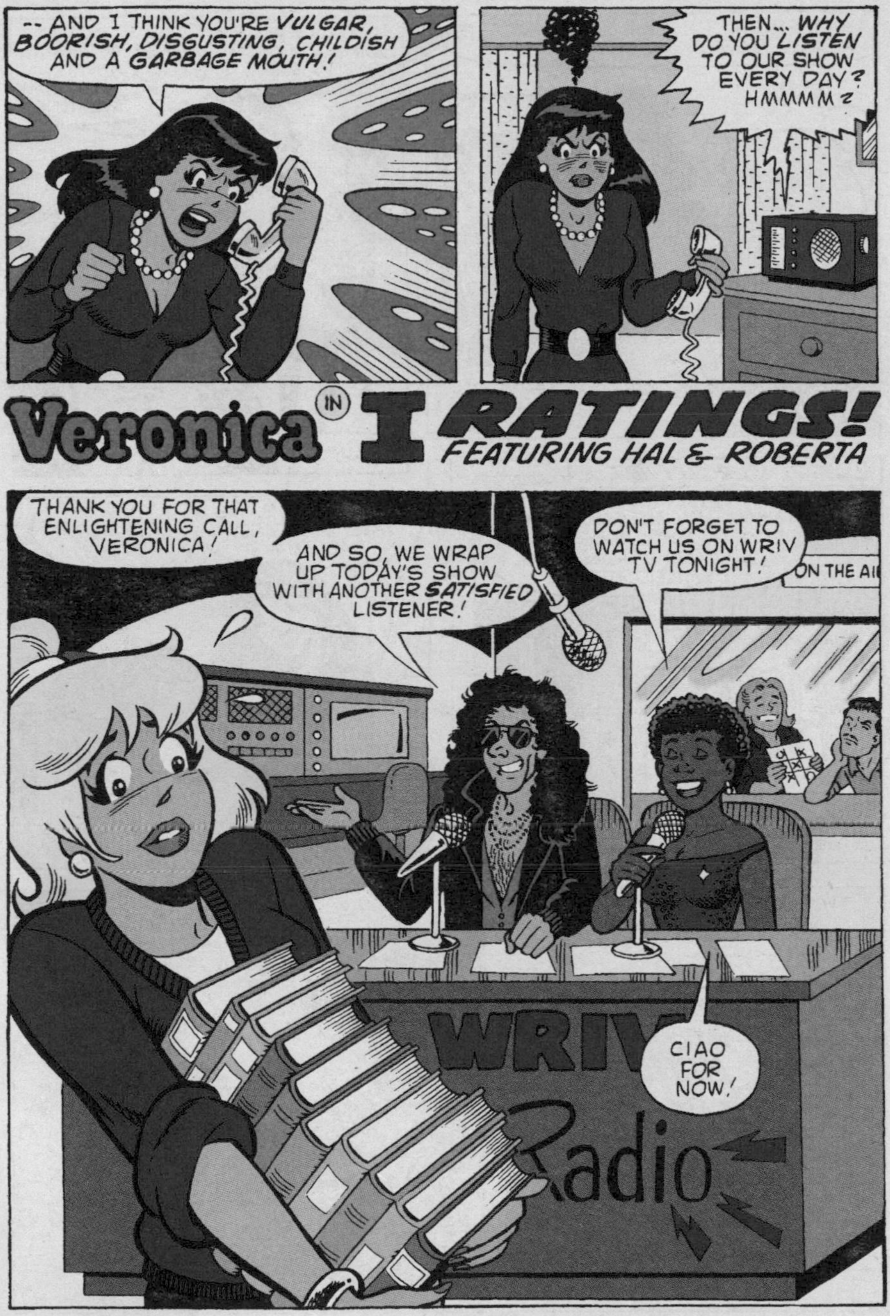
-- AND I THINK YOU'RE VULGAR, BOORISH, DISGUSTING, CHILDISH AND A GARBAGE MOUTH!
THEN... WHY DO YOU LISTEN TO OUR SHOW EVERY DAY? HMMMM?
Veronica IN I RATINGS! FEATURING HAL & ROBERTA
THANK YOU FOR THAT ENLIGHTENING CALL, VERONICA!
AND SO, WE WRAP UP TODAY'S SHOW WITH ANOTHER SATISFIED LISTENER!
DON'T FORGET TO WATCH US ON WRIV TV TONIGHT!
ON THE AI
CIAO FOR NOW!
WRIV
Radio

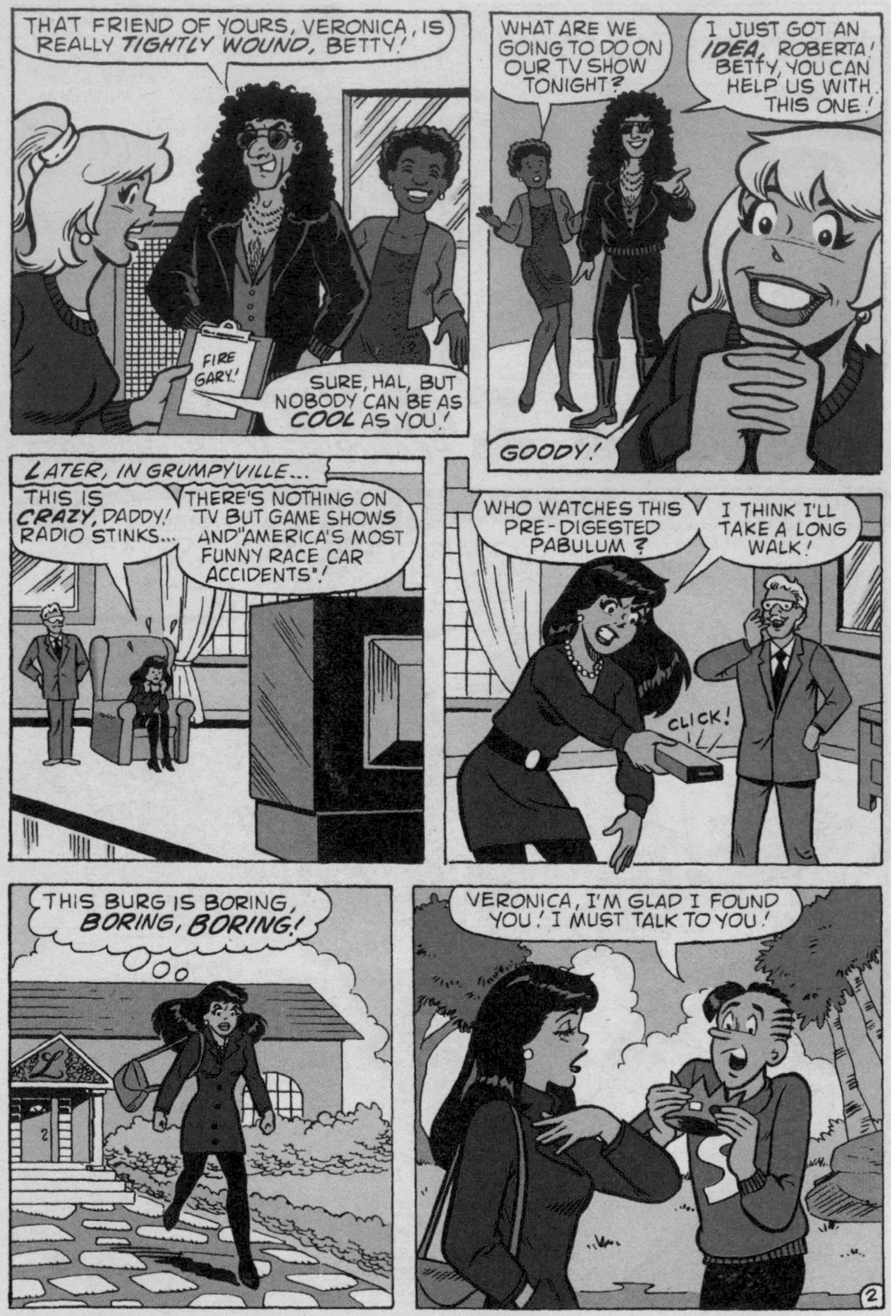
THAT FRIEND OF YOURS, VERONICA, IS REALLY TIGHTLY WOUND, BETTY!
FIRE GARY!
SURE, HAL, BUT NOBODY CAN BE AS COOL AS YOU!
WHAT ARE WE GOING TO DO ON OUR TV SHOW TONIGHT?
I JUST GOT AN IDEA, ROBERTA! BETTY, YOU CAN HELP US WITH THIS ONE!
GOODY!
LATER, IN GRUMPYVILLE...
THIS IS CRAZY, DADDY! RADIO STINKS...
THERE'S NOTHING ON TV BUT GAME SHOWS AND "AMERICA'S MOST FUNNY RACE CAR ACCIDENTS"!
WHO WATCHES THIS PRE-DIGESTED PABULUM?
I THINK I'LL TAKE A LONG WALK!
CLICK!
THIS BURG IS BORING, BORING, BORING!
VERONICA, I'M GLAD I FOUND YOU! I MUST TALK TO YOU!
2

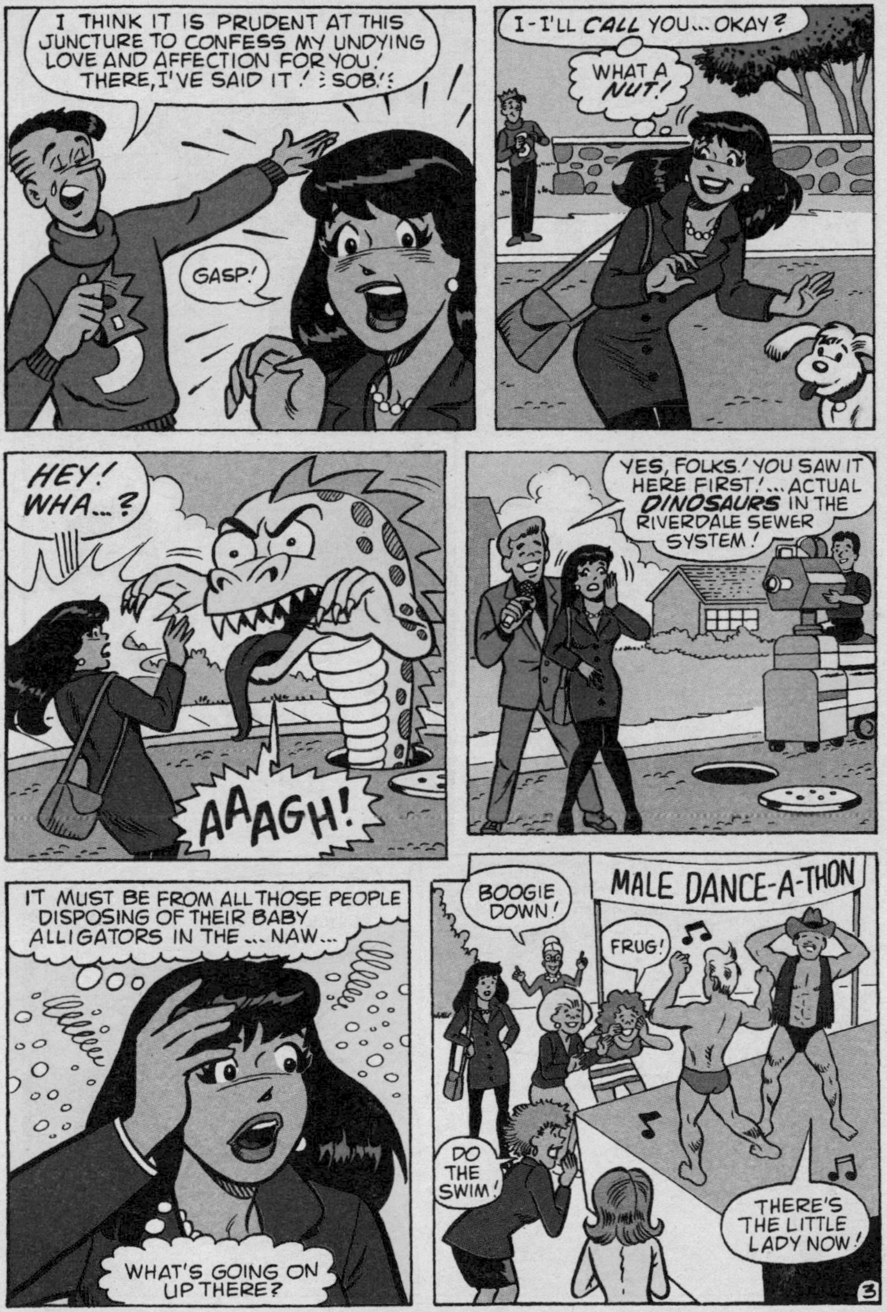
I THINK IT IS PRUDENT AT THIS JUNCTURE TO CONFESS MY UNDYING LOVE AND AFFECTION FOR YOU! THERE, I'VE SAID IT! :SOB!:
GASP!
I-I'LL CALL YOU... OKAY?
WHAT A NUT!
HEY! WHA...?
AAAGH!
YES, FOLKS! YOU SAW IT HERE FIRST! ...ACTUAL DINOSAURS IN THE RIVERDALE SEWER SYSTEM!
IT MUST BE FROM ALL THOSE PEOPLE DISPOSING OF THEIR BABY ALLIGATORS IN THE ... NAW...
WHAT'S GOING ON UP THERE?
MALE DANCE-A-THON
BOOGIE DOWN!
FRUG!
DO THE SWIM!
THERE'S THE LITTLE LADY NOW!
3

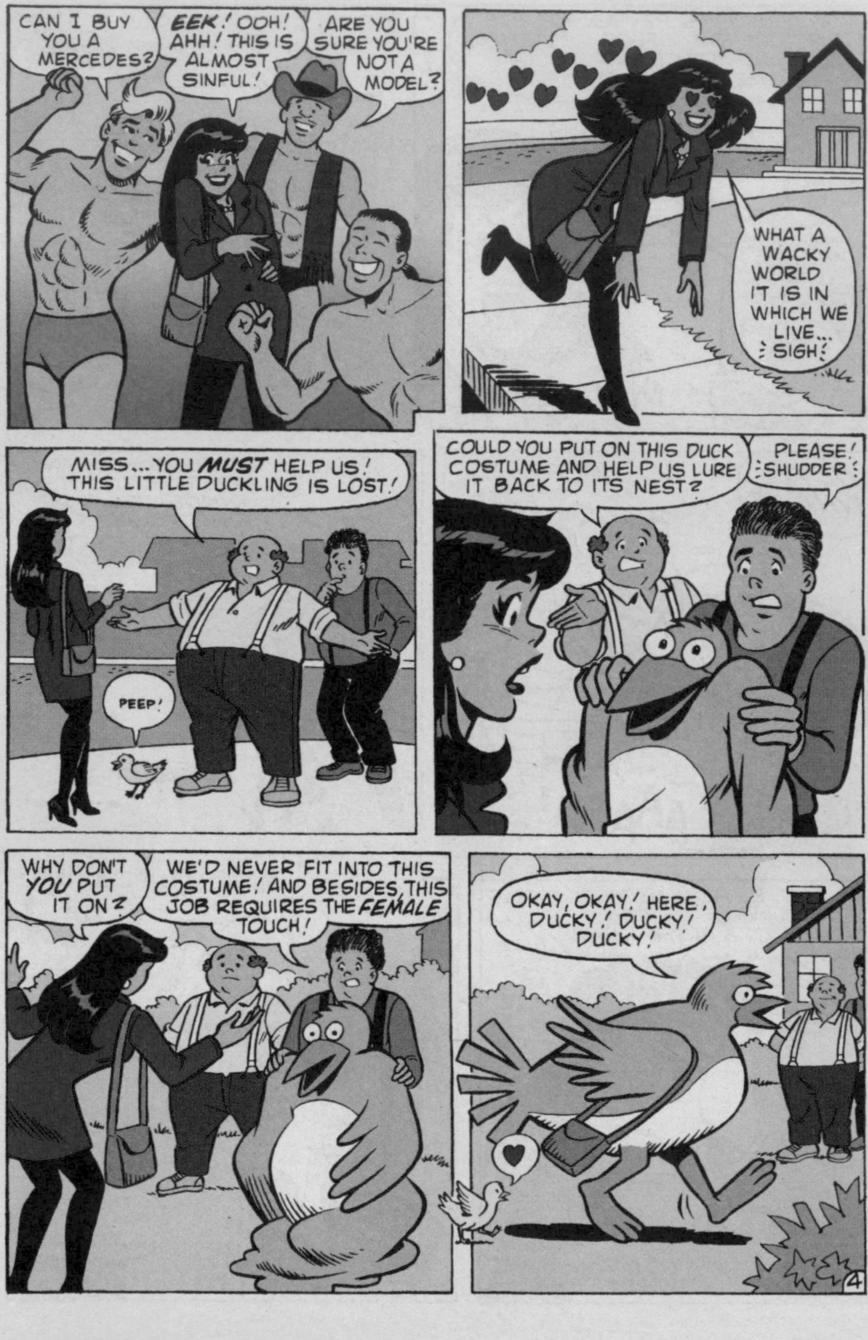
CAN I BUY YOU A MERCEDES?
EEK! OOH! AHH! THIS IS ALMOST SINFUL!
ARE YOU SURE YOU'RE NOT A MODEL?
WHAT A WACKY WORLD IT IS IN WHICH WE LIVE... SIGH
MISS... YOU MUST HELP US! THIS LITTLE DUCKLING IS LOST!
PEEP!
COULD YOU PUT ON THIS DUCK COSTUME AND HELP US LURE IT BACK TO ITS NEST?
PLEASE! SHUDDER
WHY DON'T YOU PUT IT ON?
WE'D NEVER FIT INTO THIS COSTUME! AND BESIDES, THIS JOB REQUIRES THE FEMALE TOUCH!
OKAY, OKAY! HERE, DUCKY! DUCKY! DUCKY!
4

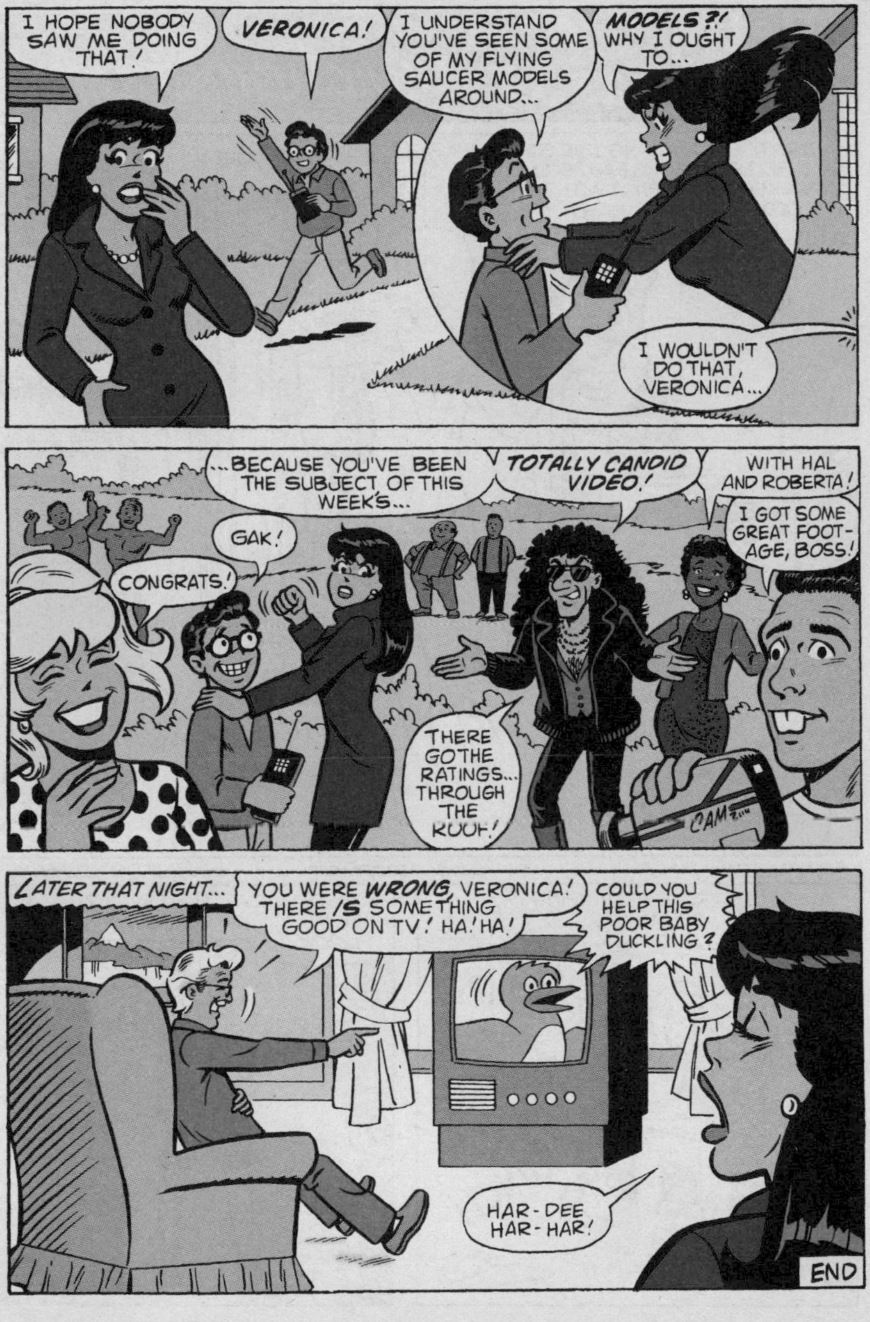
I HOPE NOBODY SAW ME DOING THAT!
VERONICA!
I UNDERSTAND YOU'VE SEEN SOME OF MY FLYING SAUCER MODELS AROUND...
MODELS?! WHY I OUGHT TO...
I WOULDN'T DO THAT, VERONICA...
...BECAUSE YOU'VE BEEN THE SUBJECT OF THIS WEEK'S...
TOTALLY CANDID VIDEO!
WITH HAL AND ROBERTA!
I GOT SOME GREAT FOOTAGE, BOSS!
GAK!
CONGRATS!
THERE GO THE RATINGS... THROUGH THE ROOF!
CAM
LATER THAT NIGHT...
YOU WERE WRONG, VERONICA! THERE IS SOMETHING GOOD ON TV! HA! HA!
COULD YOU HELP THIS POOR BABY DUCKLING?
HAR-DEE HAR-HAR!
END

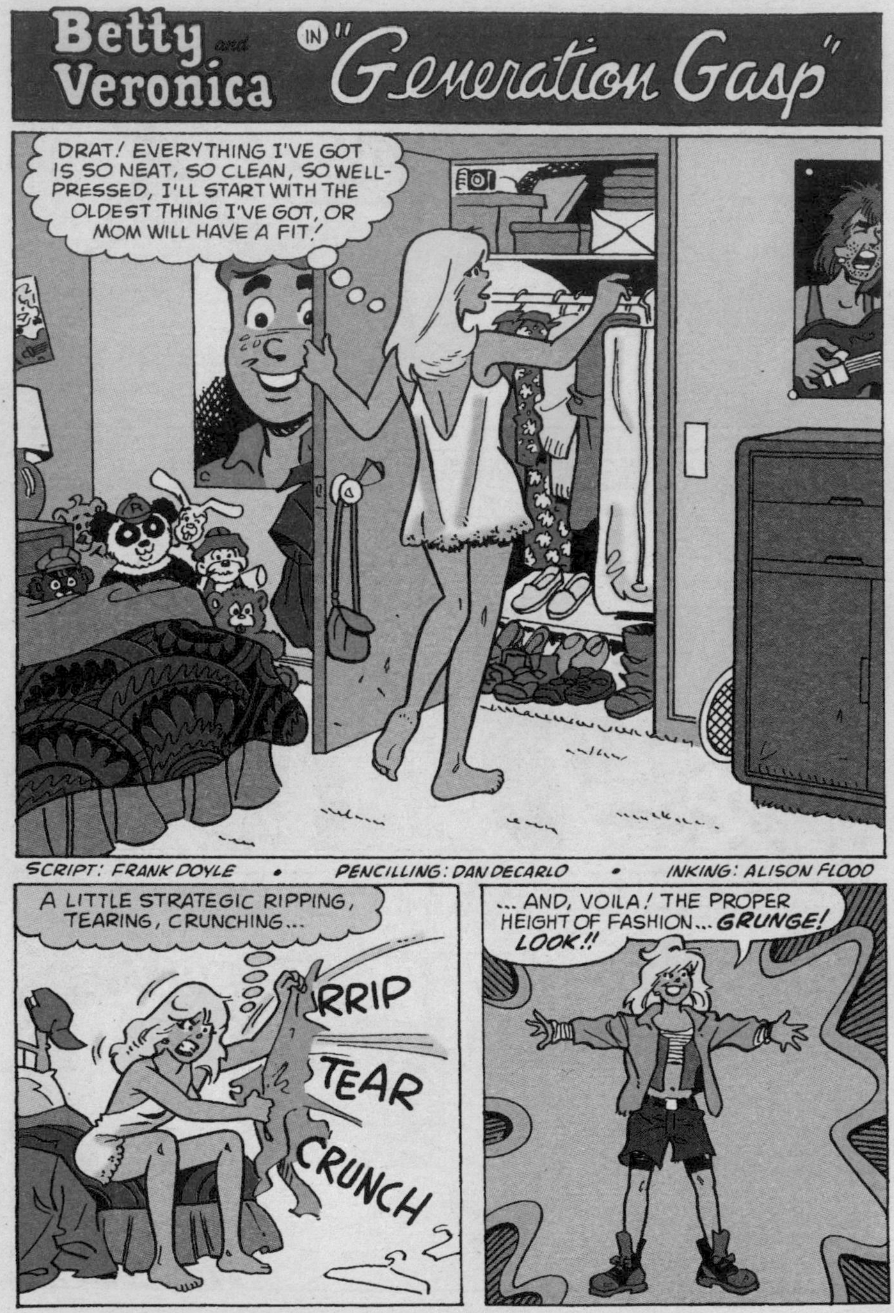
Betty and Veronica
IN "Generation Gasp"
DRAT! EVERYTHING I'VE GOT IS SO NEAT, SO CLEAN, SO WELL-PRESSED, I'LL START WITH THE OLDEST THING I'VE GOT, OR MOM WILL HAVE A FIT!
SCRIPT: FRANK DOYLE • PENCILLING: DAN DECARLO • INKING: ALISON FLOOD
A LITTLE STRATEGIC RIPPING, TEARING, CRUNCHING...
RRIP
TEAR
CRUNCH
... AND, VOILA! THE PROPER HEIGHT OF FASHION... GRUNGE! LOOK!!

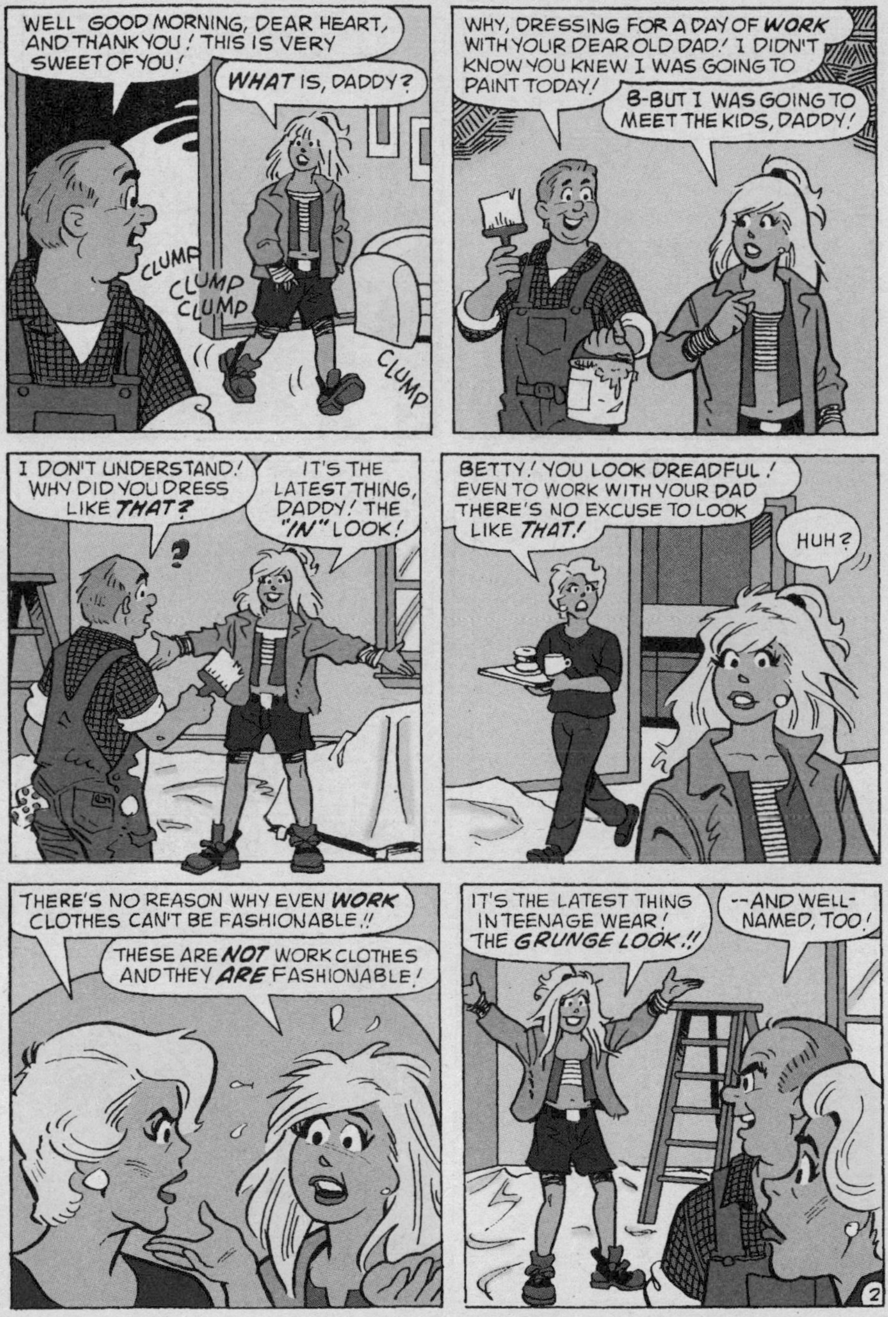
WELL GOOD MORNING, DEAR HEART, AND THANK YOU! THIS IS VERY SWEET OF YOU!
WHAT IS, DADDY?
CLUMP
CLUMP
CLUMP
CLUMP
WHY, DRESSING FOR A DAY OF WORK WITH YOUR DEAR OLD DAD! I DIDN'T KNOW YOU KNEW I WAS GOING TO PAINT TODAY!
B-BUT I WAS GOING TO MEET THE KIDS, DADDY!
I DON'T UNDERSTAND! WHY DID YOU DRESS LIKE THAT?
?
IT'S THE LATEST THING, DADDY! THE "IN" LOOK!
BETTY! YOU LOOK DREADFUL! EVEN TO WORK WITH YOUR DAD THERE'S NO EXCUSE TO LOOK LIKE THAT!
HUH?
THERE'S NO REASON WHY EVEN WORK CLOTHES CAN'T BE FASHIONABLE!!
THESE ARE NOT WORK CLOTHES AND THEY ARE FASHIONABLE!
IT'S THE LATEST THING IN TEENAGE WEAR! THE GRUNGE LOOK!!
--AND WELL-NAMED, TOO!
2

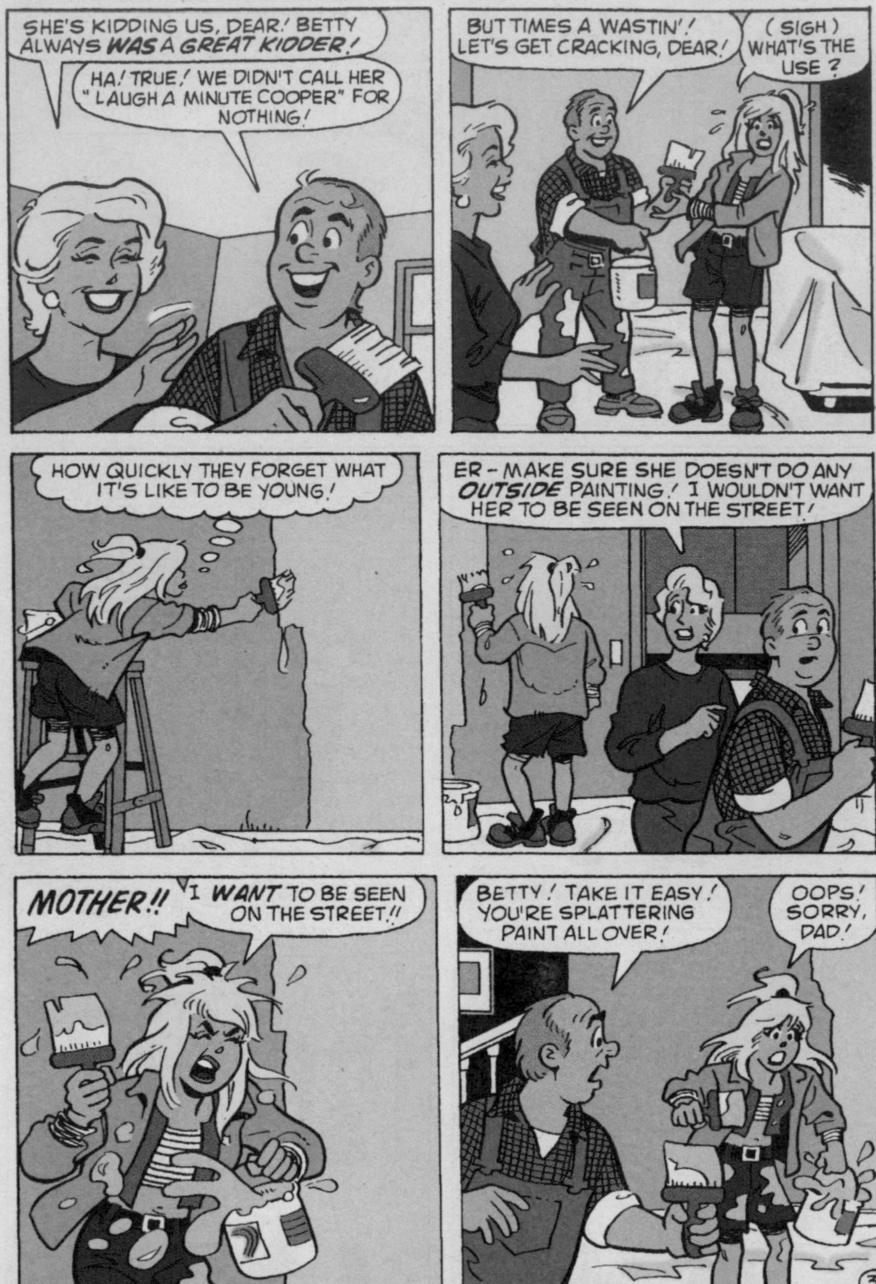
SHE'S KIDDING US, DEAR! BETTY ALWAYS WAS A GREAT KIDDER!
HA! TRUE! WE DIDN'T CALL HER "LAUGH A MINUTE COOPER" FOR NOTHING!
BUT TIMES A WASTIN'! LET'S GET CRACKING, DEAR!
(SIGH) WHAT'S THE USE ?
HOW QUICKLY THEY FORGET WHAT IT'S LIKE TO BE YOUNG!
ER - MAKE SURE SHE DOESN'T DO ANY OUTSIDE PAINTING! I WOULDN'T WANT HER TO BE SEEN ON THE STREET!
MOTHER!! I WANT TO BE SEEN ON THE STREET!!
BETTY! TAKE IT EASY! YOU'RE SPLATTERING PAINT ALL OVER!
OOPS! SORRY, DAD!
3

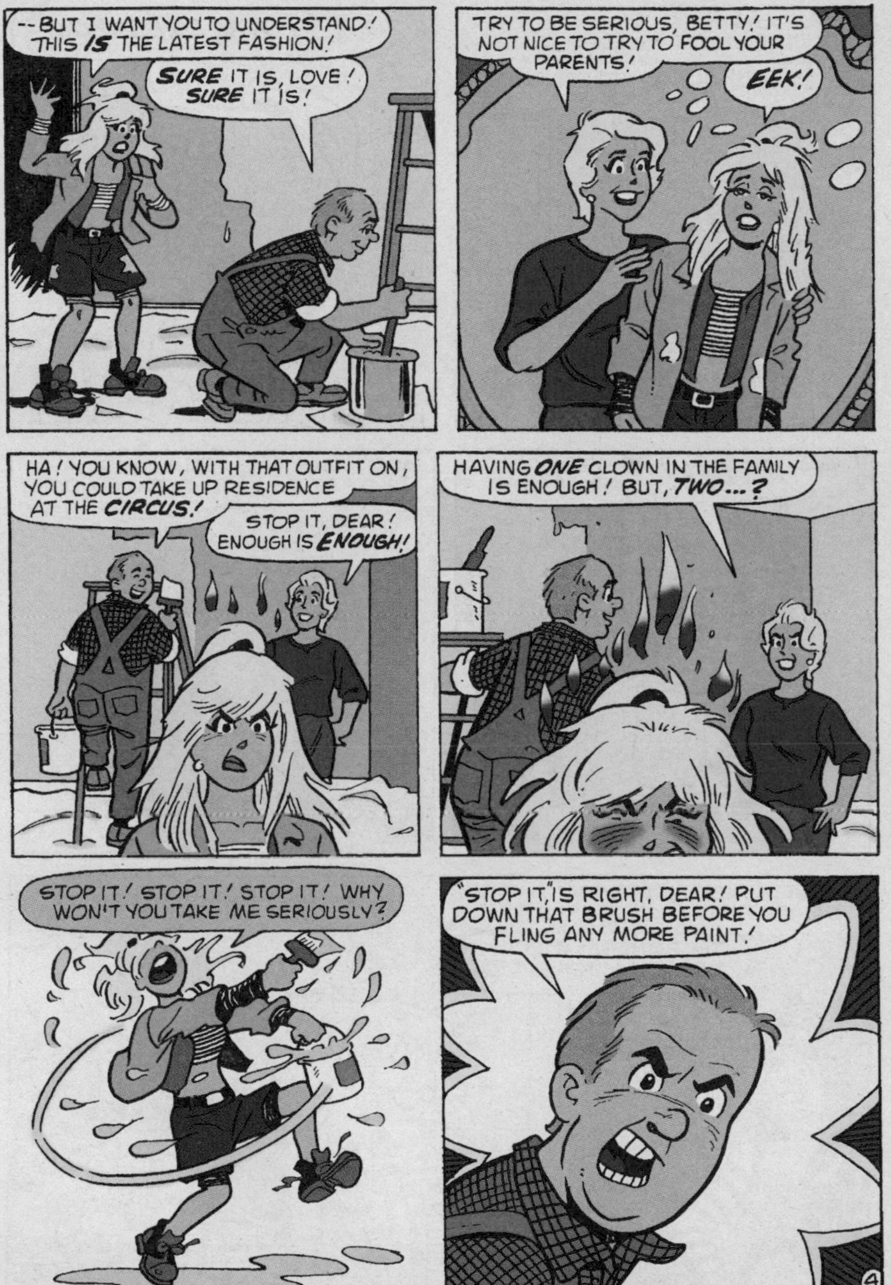
--BUT I WANT YOU TO UNDERSTAND! THIS IS THE LATEST FASHION!
SURE IT IS, LOVE! SURE IT IS!
TRY TO BE SERIOUS, BETTY! IT'S NOT NICE TO TRY TO FOOL YOUR PARENTS!
EEK!
HA! YOU KNOW, WITH THAT OUTFIT ON, YOU COULD TAKE UP RESIDENCE AT THE CIRCUS!
STOP IT, DEAR! ENOUGH IS ENOUGH!
HAVING ONE CLOWN IN THE FAMILY IS ENOUGH! BUT, TWO...?
STOP IT! STOP IT! STOP IT! WHY WON'T YOU TAKE ME SERIOUSLY?
"STOP IT," IS RIGHT, DEAR! PUT DOWN THAT BRUSH BEFORE YOU FLING ANY MORE PAINT!
4

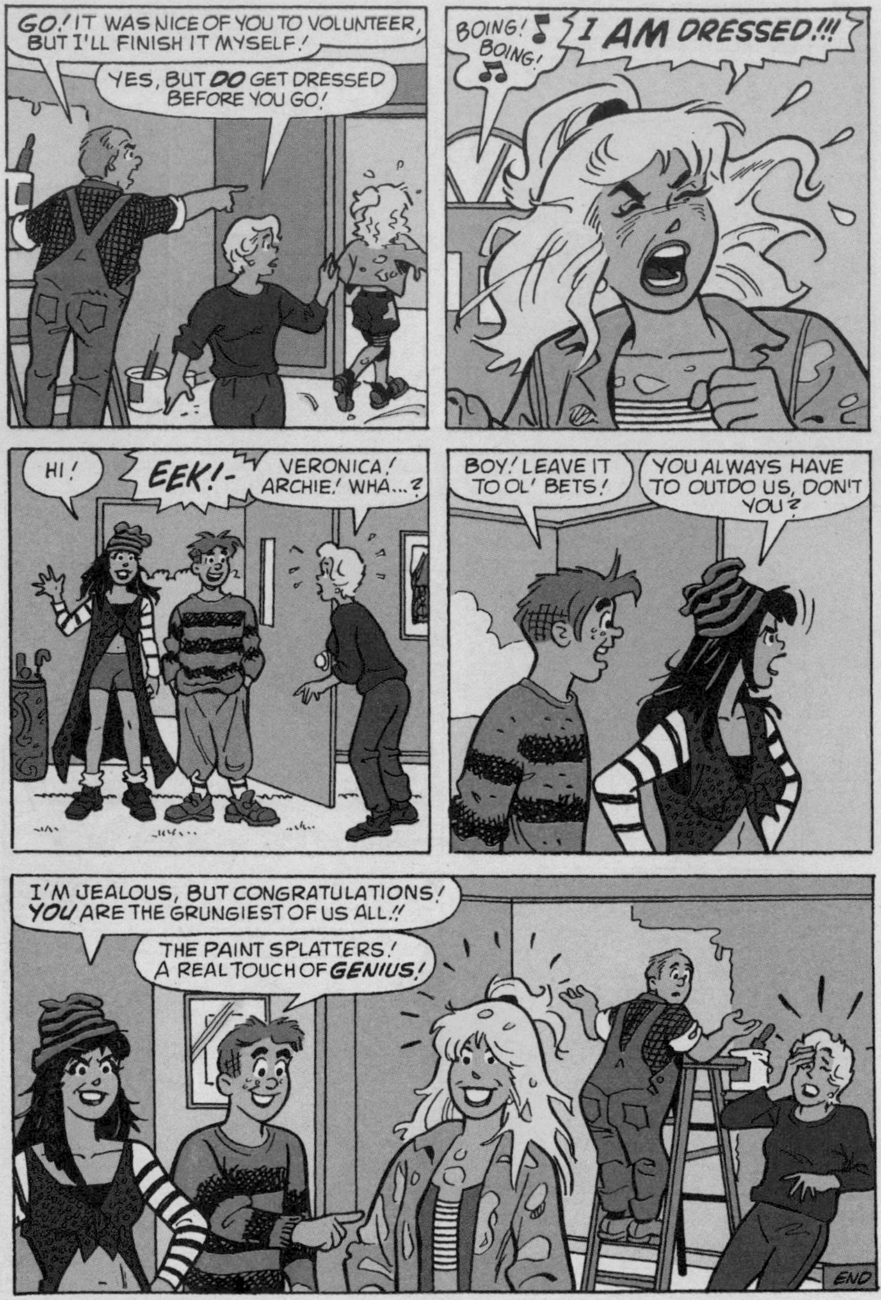
GO! IT WAS NICE OF YOU TO VOLUNTEER, BUT I'LL FINISH IT MYSELF!
YES, BUT DO GET DRESSED BEFORE YOU GO!
BOING! BOING!
I AM DRESSED!!!
HI!
EEK!-
VERONICA! ARCHIE! WHA...?
BOY! LEAVE IT TO OL' BETS!
YOU ALWAYS HAVE TO OUTDO US, DON'T YOU?
I'M JEALOUS, BUT CONGRATULATIONS! YOU ARE THE GRUNGIEST OF US ALL!!
THE PAINT SPLATTERS! A REAL TOUCH OF GENIUS!
END

Alternative Whirl
Betty #6, 1993
by Bob Bolling, Doug Crane, Rudy Lapick, Bill Yoshida, Barry Grossman

Once the mid-to-late 1970s had rolled around, "Crazy Betty" had gradually been phased out to "Girl-Next-Door Betty" which is who we find ourselves reading about in this '90s yarn as she tries to upstage a particularly nasty Veronica (with Jughead along representing the audience) at an alternative rock concert. "Girl-Next-Door Betty" might seem a little bland to most and not quite as fun, but in exchange for her zaniness her heart factor has been ramped up to eleven – and that's part of what makes her so lovable. Here she is willing to stand up for Archie even when he doesn't know he's being stood up for, all while being thoroughly outclassed and losing to Veronica. Betty is the underdog whom we root for. But what makes her relatable is that no matter how much charm she possesses, she doesn't always win.

-- **Jonathan Gray**
Production Artist,
Archie Comics

Trend Setters
Betty & Veronica (vol.2) #76, 1994
by George Gladir, Dan DeCarlo, Alison Flood, Bill Yoshida, Barry Grossman

I feel a particular kinship to this story. Perhaps it's because as I'm writing this, I too am wearing mismatched socks. Though, it is less as a conscious fashion effort and more of an "it's laundry day" issue. This story came out in the '90s, after the grunge "fad" was starting to taper out. Reading Betty & Veronica stories, I always admired and envied Veronica's confidence and keen sense of style, but I knew deep down that I was a truly a Betty—and this story is a perfect example of that. Betty unconsciously starts a fashion trend simply by being tired! (Though I was usually tired from staying up late and watching cartoons instead of hitting the books—I can't admit to being as noble as Betty!) It's funny re-reading the story now, as "grunge" fashion is making its way back around. Who knows—maybe my mismatched socks will be next week's fashion trend. And, like Betty, I'll be none the wiser!

-- **Jamie Lee Rotante**
Editorial Assistant/Proofreader,
Archie Comics

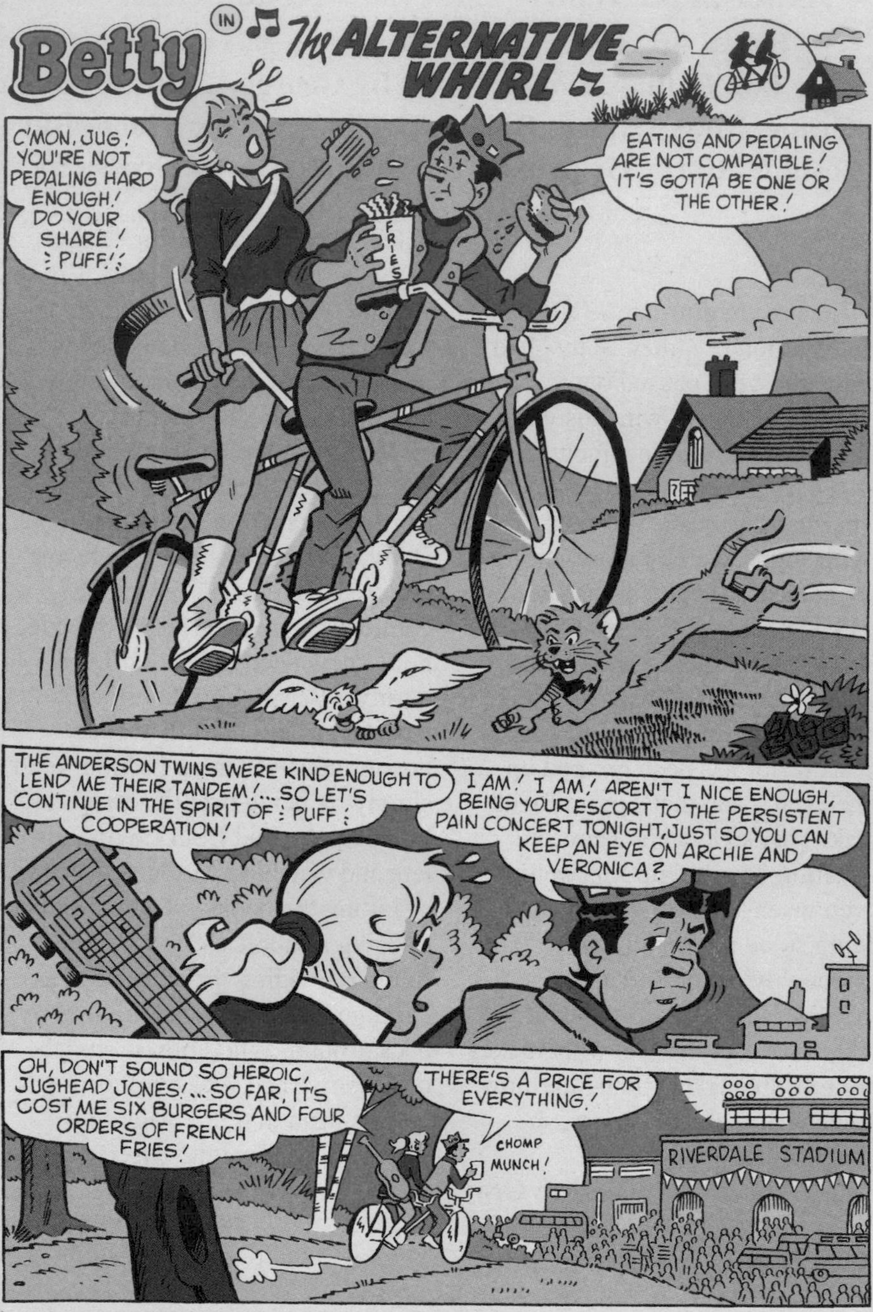
Betty
IN
The ALTERNATIVE WHIRL
C'MON, JUG! YOU'RE NOT PEDALING HARD ENOUGH! DO YOUR SHARE! PUFF!
EATING AND PEDALING ARE NOT COMPATIBLE! IT'S GOTTA BE ONE OR THE OTHER!
FRIES
THE ANDERSON TWINS WERE KIND ENOUGH TO LEND ME THEIR TANDEM!... SO LET'S CONTINUE IN THE SPIRIT OF PUFF COOPERATION!
I AM! I AM! AREN'T I NICE ENOUGH, BEING YOUR ESCORT TO THE PERSISTENT PAIN CONCERT TONIGHT, JUST SO YOU CAN KEEP AN EYE ON ARCHIE AND VERONICA?
OH, DON'T SOUND SO HEROIC, JUGHEAD JONES!... SO FAR, IT'S COST ME SIX BURGERS AND FOUR ORDERS OF FRENCH FRIES!
THERE'S A PRICE FOR EVERYTHING!
CHOMP MUNCH!
RIVERDALE STADIUM

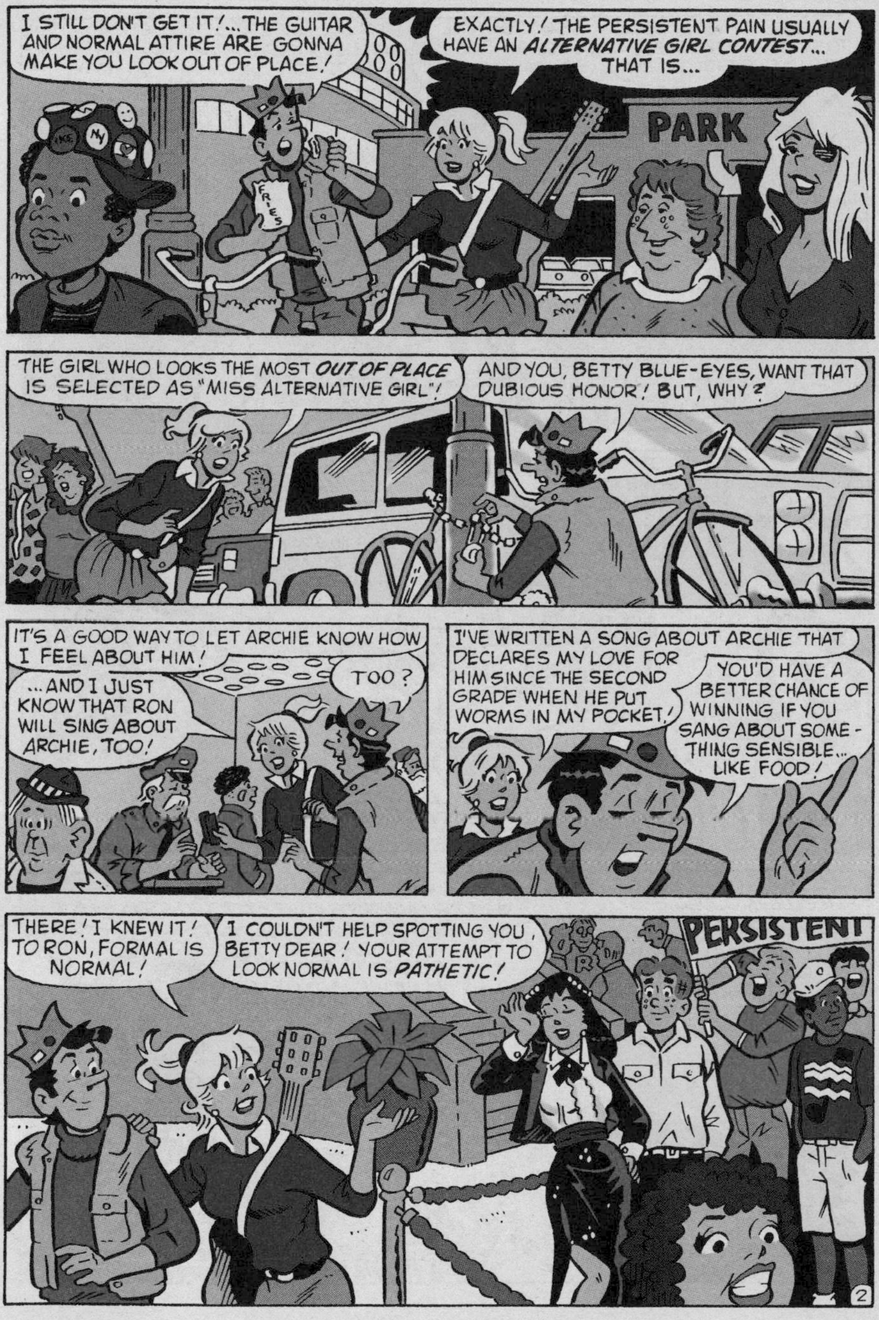
I STILL DON'T GET IT!... THE GUITAR AND NORMAL ATTIRE ARE GONNA MAKE YOU LOOK OUT OF PLACE!
EXACTLY! THE PERSISTENT PAIN USUALLY HAVE AN ALTERNATIVE GIRL CONTEST... THAT IS...
FRIES
PARK
THE GIRL WHO LOOKS THE MOST OUT OF PLACE IS SELECTED AS "MISS ALTERNATIVE GIRL"!
AND YOU, BETTY BLUE-EYES, WANT THAT DUBIOUS HONOR! BUT, WHY?
IT'S A GOOD WAY TO LET ARCHIE KNOW HOW I FEEL ABOUT HIM!
TOO?
...AND I JUST KNOW THAT RON WILL SING ABOUT ARCHIE, TOO!
I'VE WRITTEN A SONG ABOUT ARCHIE THAT DECLARES MY LOVE FOR HIM SINCE THE SECOND GRADE WHEN HE PUT WORMS IN MY POCKET!
YOU'D HAVE A BETTER CHANCE OF WINNING IF YOU SANG ABOUT SOMETHING SENSIBLE... LIKE FOOD!
THERE! I KNEW IT! TO RON, FORMAL IS NORMAL!
I COULDN'T HELP SPOTTING YOU, BETTY DEAR! YOUR ATTEMPT TO LOOK NORMAL IS PATHETIC!
PERSISTENT
2

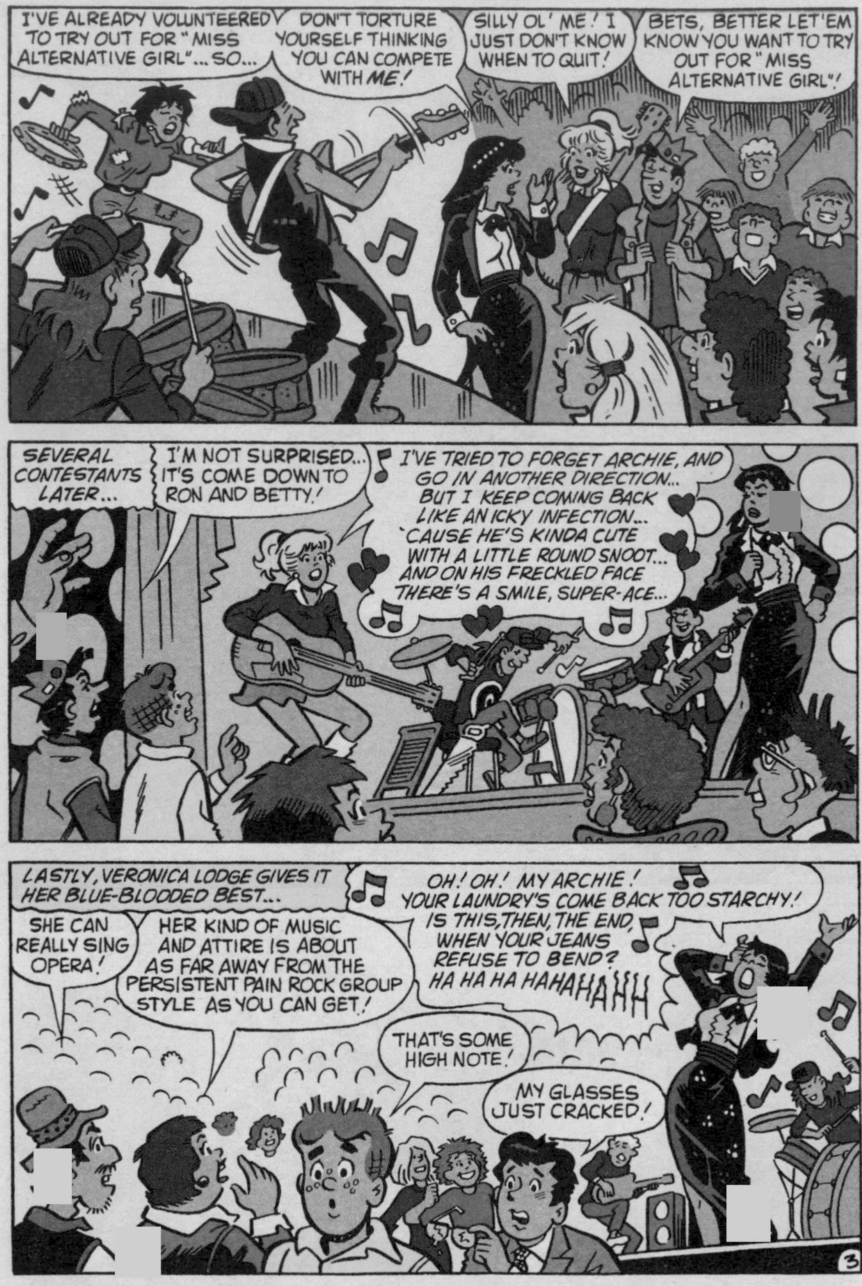
I'VE ALREADY VOLUNTEERED TO TRY OUT FOR "MISS ALTERNATIVE GIRL"... SO...
DON'T TORTURE YOURSELF THINKING YOU CAN COMPETE WITH ME!
SILLY OL' ME! I JUST DON'T KNOW WHEN TO QUIT!
BETS, BETTER LET'EM KNOW YOU WANT TO TRY OUT FOR "MISS ALTERNATIVE GIRL"!
SEVERAL CONTESTANTS LATER...
I'M NOT SURPRISED... IT'S COME DOWN TO RON AND BETTY!
I'VE TRIED TO FORGET ARCHIE, AND GO IN ANOTHER DIRECTION... BUT I KEEP COMING BACK LIKE AN ICKY INFECTION... 'CAUSE HE'S KINDA CUTE WITH A LITTLE ROUND SNOOT... AND ON HIS FRECKLED FACE THERE'S A SMILE, SUPER-ACE...
LASTLY, VERONICA LODGE GIVES IT HER BLUE-BLOODED BEST...
SHE CAN REALLY SING OPERA!
HER KIND OF MUSIC AND ATTIRE IS ABOUT AS FAR AWAY FROM THE PERSISTENT PAIN ROCK GROUP STYLE AS YOU CAN GET!
OH! OH! MY ARCHIE! YOUR LAUNDRY'S COME BACK TOO STARCHY! IS THIS, THEN, THE END, WHEN YOUR JEANS REFUSE TO BEND? HA HA HA HAHAHAHH
THAT'S SOME HIGH NOTE!
MY GLASSES JUST CRACKED!
3

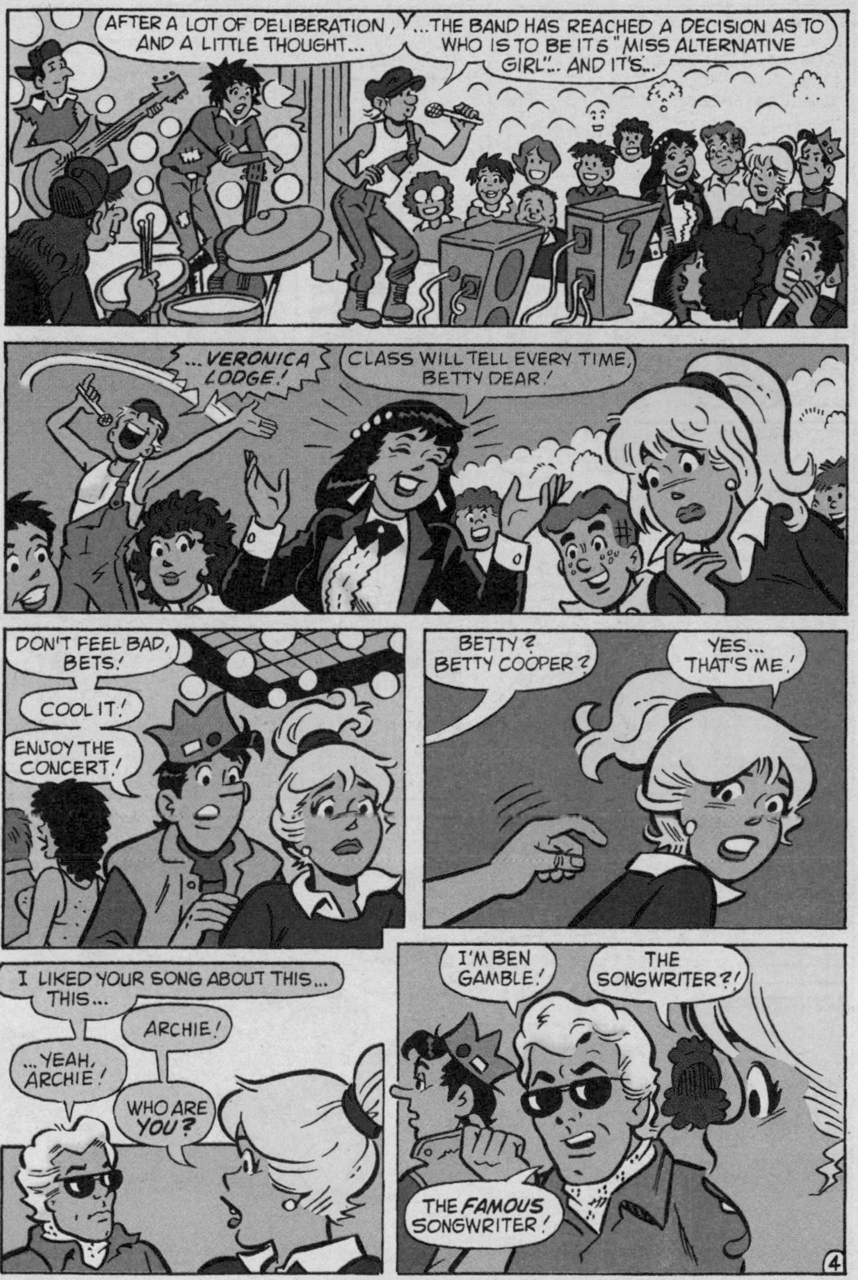
AFTER A LOT OF DELIBERATION, AND A LITTLE THOUGHT...
...THE BAND HAS REACHED A DECISION AS TO WHO IS TO BE ITS "MISS ALTERNATIVE GIRL"... AND IT'S...
...VERONICA LODGE!
CLASS WILL TELL EVERY TIME, BETTY DEAR!
DON'T FEEL BAD, BETS!
COOL IT!
ENJOY THE CONCERT!
BETTY? BETTY COOPER?
YES... THAT'S ME!
I LIKED YOUR SONG ABOUT THIS... THIS...
ARCHIE!
...YEAH, ARCHIE!
WHO ARE YOU?
I'M BEN GAMBLE!
THE SONGWRITER?!
THE FAMOUS SONGWRITER!
4

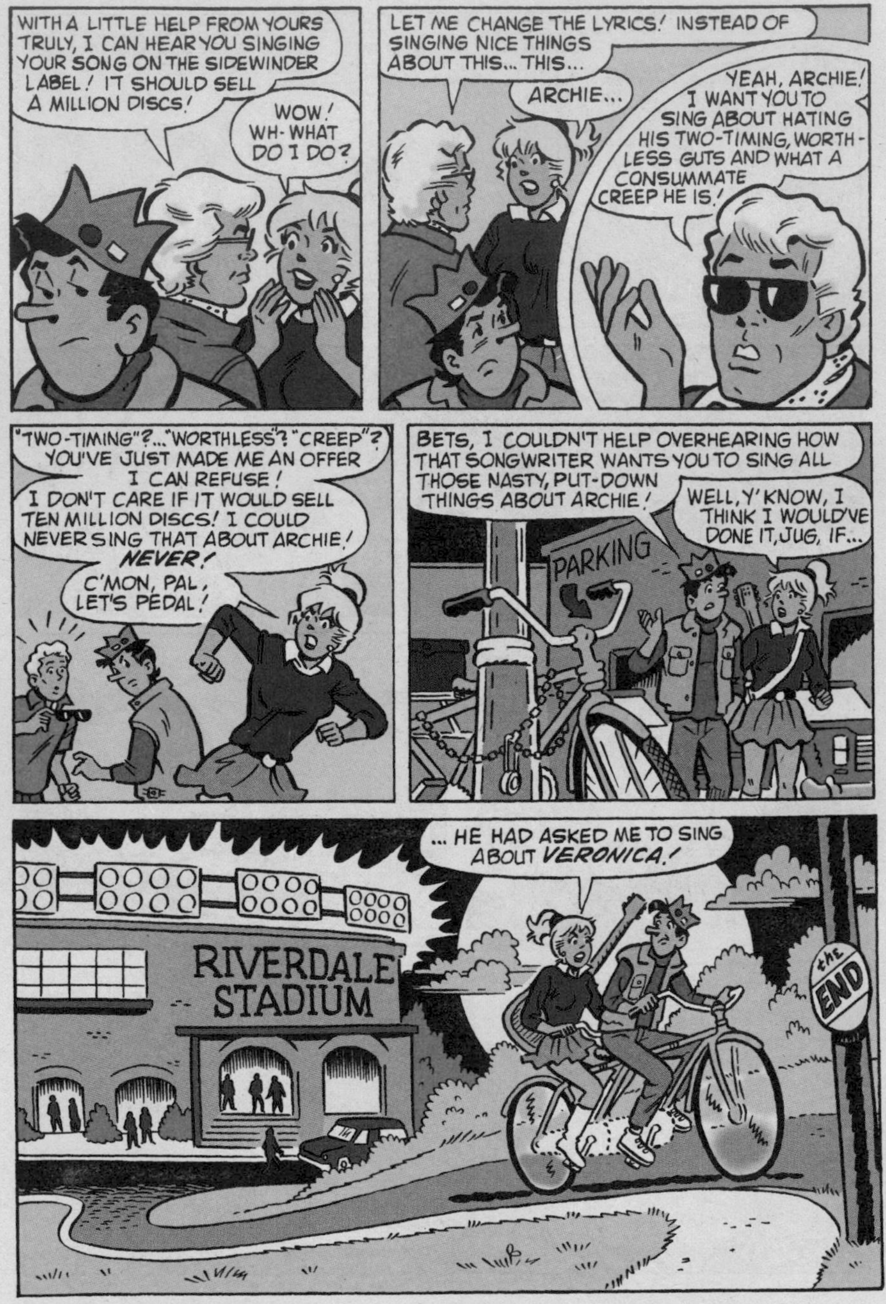
WITH A LITTLE HELP FROM YOURS TRULY, I CAN HEAR YOU SINGING YOUR SONG ON THE SIDEWINDER LABEL! IT SHOULD SELL A MILLION DISCS!
WOW! WH-WHAT DO I DO?
LET ME CHANGE THE LYRICS! INSTEAD OF SINGING NICE THINGS ABOUT THIS... THIS...
ARCHIE...
YEAH, ARCHIE! I WANT YOU TO SING ABOUT HATING HIS TWO-TIMING, WORTHLESS GUTS AND WHAT A CONSUMMATE CREEP HE IS!
"TWO-TIMING"?..."WORTHLESS"? "CREEP"? YOU'VE JUST MADE ME AN OFFER I CAN REFUSE! I DON'T CARE IF IT WOULD SELL TEN MILLION DISCS! I COULD NEVER SING THAT ABOUT ARCHIE! NEVER!
C'MON, PAL, LET'S PEDAL!
BETS, I COULDN'T HELP OVERHEARING HOW THAT SONGWRITER WANTS YOU TO SING ALL THOSE NASTY, PUT-DOWN THINGS ABOUT ARCHIE!
WELL, Y'KNOW, I THINK I WOULD'VE DONE IT, JUG, IF...
PARKING
...HE HAD ASKED ME TO SING ABOUT VERONICA!
RIVERDALE STADIUM
the END

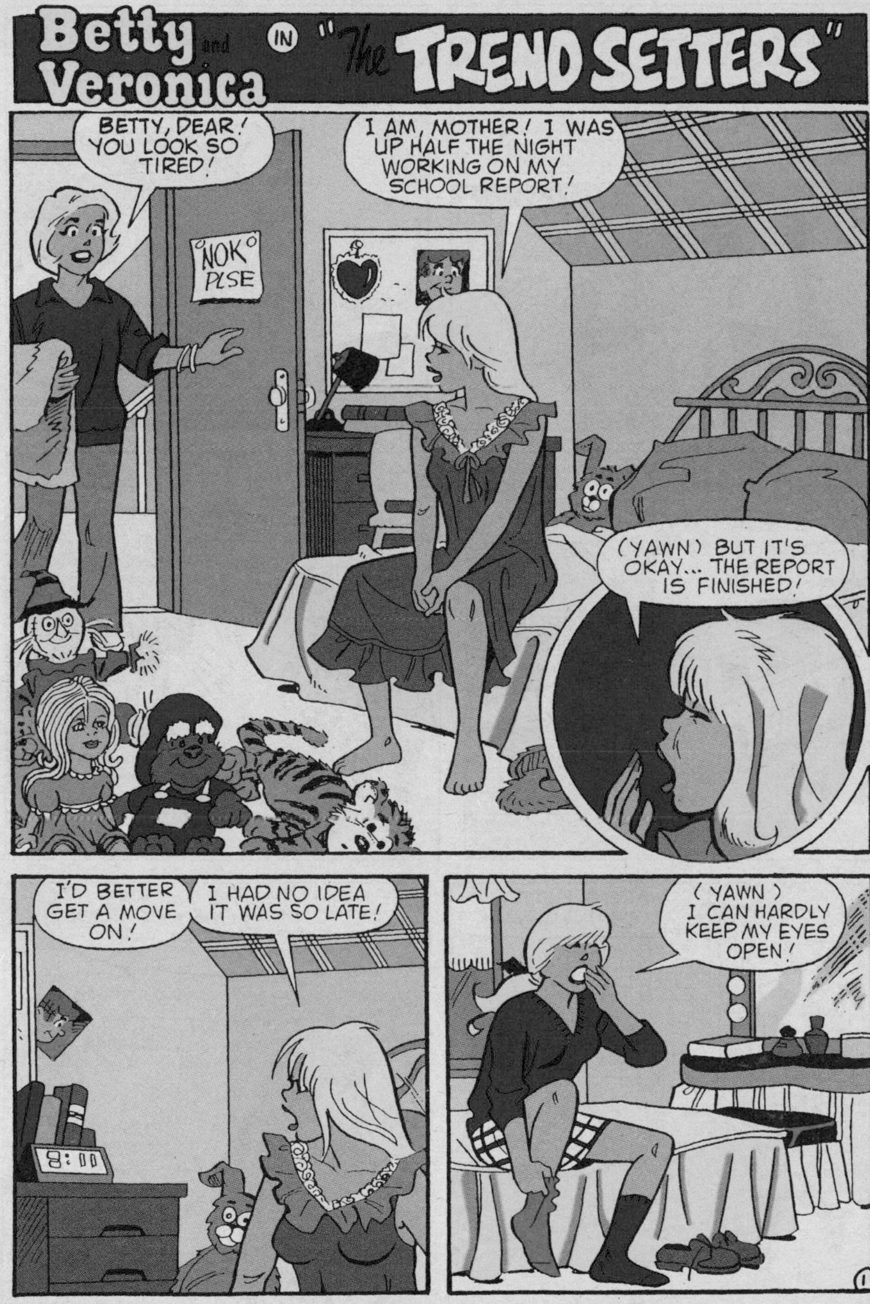
Betty and Veronica IN "The TREND SETTERS"
BETTY, DEAR! YOU LOOK SO TIRED!
I AM, MOTHER! I WAS UP HALF THE NIGHT WORKING ON MY SCHOOL REPORT!
NOK PLSE
(YAWN) BUT IT'S OKAY... THE REPORT IS FINISHED!
I'D BETTER GET A MOVE ON!
I HAD NO IDEA IT WAS SO LATE!
8:00
(YAWN) I CAN HARDLY KEEP MY EYES OPEN!
1

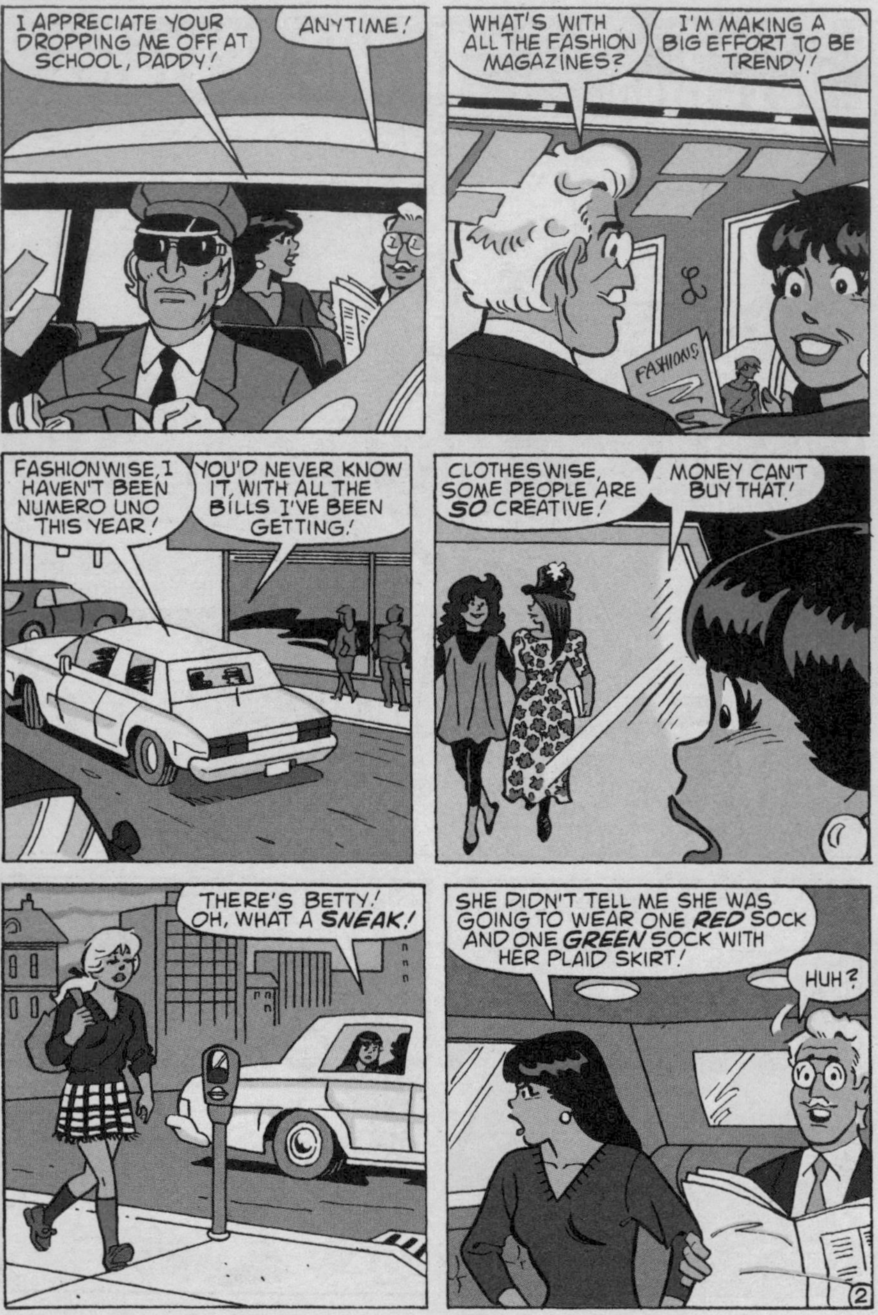
I APPRECIATE YOUR DROPPING ME OFF AT SCHOOL, DADDY!
ANYTIME!
WHAT'S WITH ALL THE FASHION MAGAZINES?
I'M MAKING A BIG EFFORT TO BE TRENDY!
FASHIONS
FASHIONWISE, I HAVEN'T BEEN NUMERO UNO THIS YEAR!
YOU'D NEVER KNOW IT, WITH ALL THE BILLS I'VE BEEN GETTING!
CLOTHESWISE, SOME PEOPLE ARE SO CREATIVE!
MONEY CAN'T BUY THAT!
THERE'S BETTY! OH, WHAT A SNEAK!
SHE DIDN'T TELL ME SHE WAS GOING TO WEAR ONE RED SOCK AND ONE GREEN SOCK WITH HER PLAID SKIRT!
HUH?
2

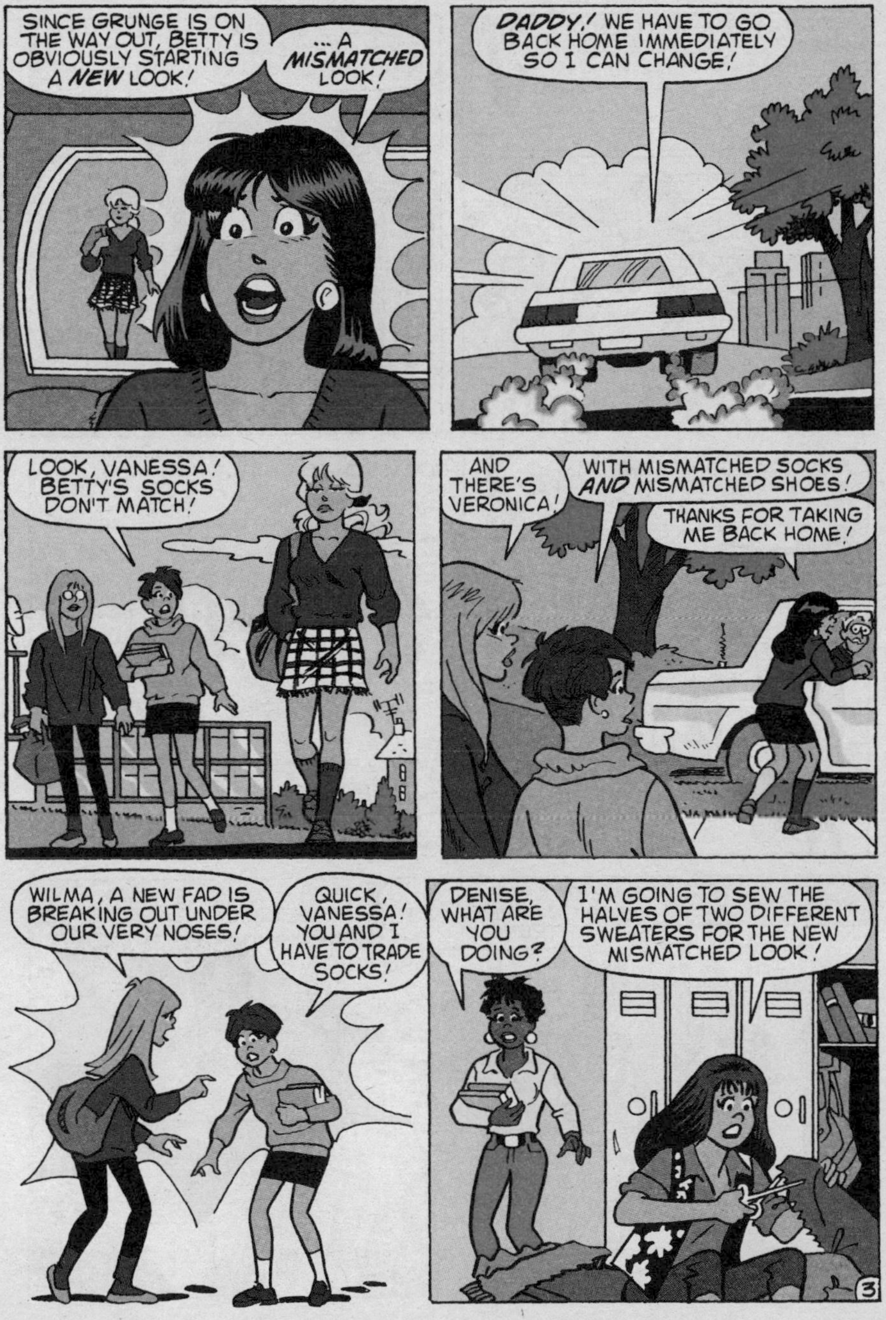
SINCE GRUNGE IS ON THE WAY OUT, BETTY IS OBVIOUSLY STARTING A NEW LOOK!
... A MISMATCHED LOOK!
DADDY! WE HAVE TO GO BACK HOME IMMEDIATELY SO I CAN CHANGE!
LOOK, VANESSA! BETTY'S SOCKS DON'T MATCH!
AND THERE'S VERONICA!
WITH MISMATCHED SOCKS AND MISMATCHED SHOES!
THANKS FOR TAKING ME BACK HOME!
WILMA, A NEW FAD IS BREAKING OUT UNDER OUR VERY NOSES!
QUICK, VANESSA! YOU AND I HAVE TO TRADE SOCKS!
DENISE, WHAT ARE YOU DOING?
I'M GOING TO SEW THE HALVES OF TWO DIFFERENT SWEATERS FOR THE NEW MISMATCHED LOOK!
3

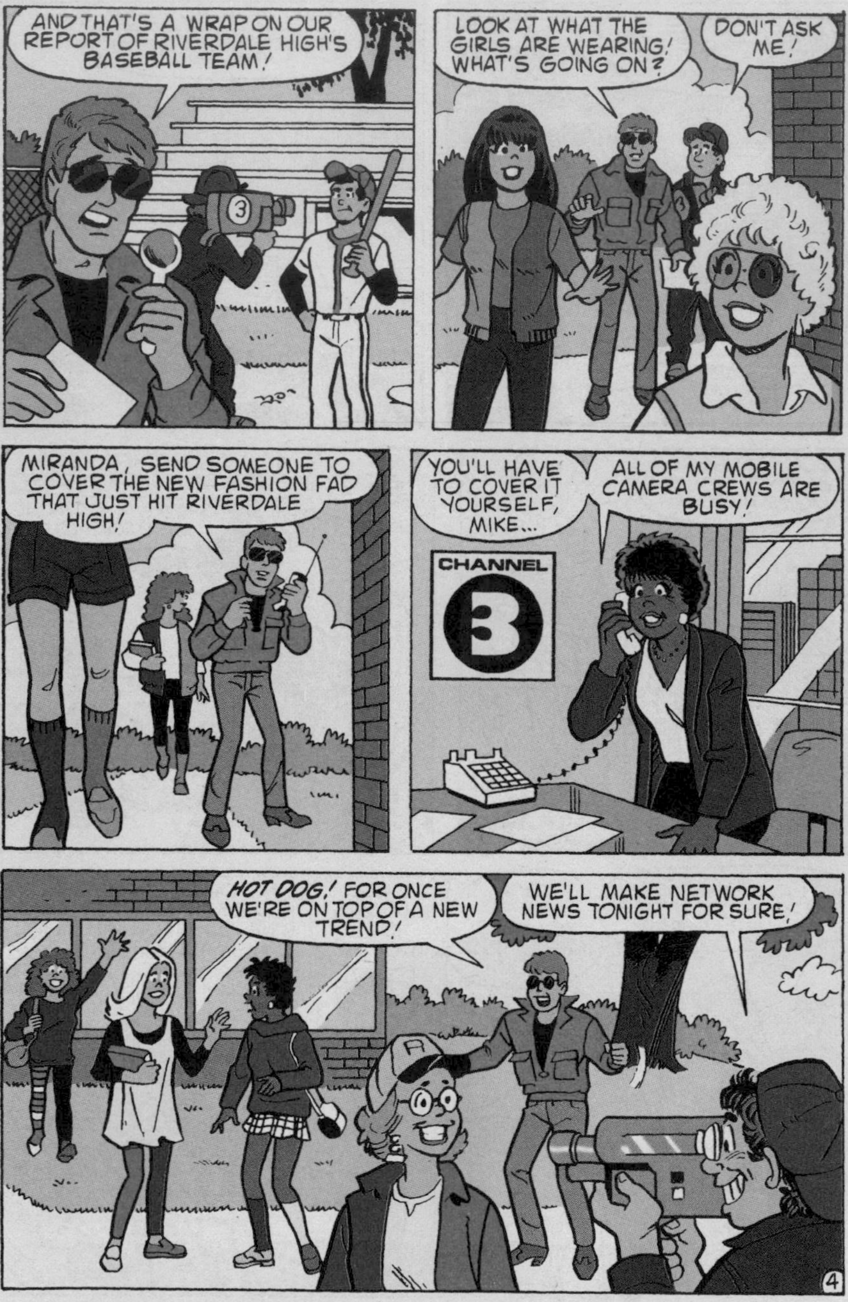
AND THAT'S A WRAP ON OUR REPORT OF RIVERDALE HIGH'S BASEBALL TEAM!
3
LOOK AT WHAT THE GIRLS ARE WEARING! WHAT'S GOING ON?
DON'T ASK ME!
MIRANDA, SEND SOMEONE TO COVER THE NEW FASHION FAD THAT JUST HIT RIVERDALE HIGH!
YOU'LL HAVE TO COVER IT YOURSELF, MIKE...
ALL OF MY MOBILE CAMERA CREWS ARE BUSY!
CHANNEL 3
HOT DOG! FOR ONCE WE'RE ON TOP OF A NEW TREND!
WE'LL MAKE NETWORK NEWS TONIGHT FOR SURE!
4

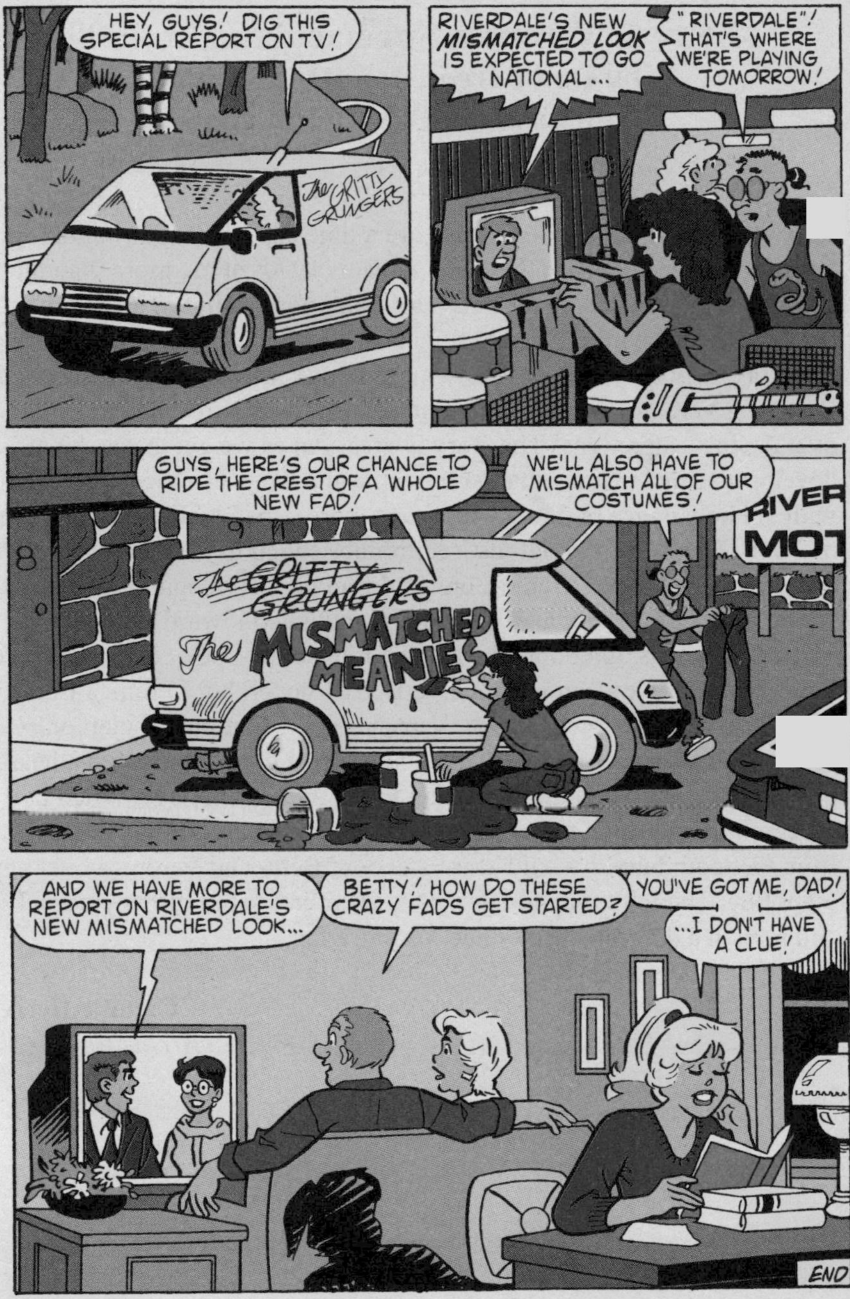
HEY, GUYS! DIG THIS SPECIAL REPORT ON TV!
The GRITTY GRUNGERS
RIVERDALE'S NEW MISMATCHED LOOK IS EXPECTED TO GO NATIONAL...
"RIVERDALE"! THAT'S WHERE WE'RE PLAYING TOMORROW!
GUYS, HERE'S OUR CHANCE TO RIDE THE CREST OF A WHOLE NEW FAD!
WE'LL ALSO HAVE TO MISMATCH ALL OF OUR COSTUMES!
The GRITTY GRUNGERS
The MISMATCHED MEANIES
AND WE HAVE MORE TO REPORT ON RIVERDALE'S NEW MISMATCHED LOOK...
BETTY! HOW DO THESE CRAZY FADS GET STARTED?
YOU'VE GOT ME, DAD!
...I DON'T HAVE A CLUE!
END

Swing Time
Betty & Veronica Spectacular #35, 1999
by Dan Parent, Jon D'Agostino,
Bill Yoshida, Barry Grossman

It is often said that Archie Comics are a time capsule, capturing the spirit and mood of each decade. Nothing screams 1990s at me more than the swing revival. "Swing Time" has a lot going for it. First of all, it features the 'Bee in a leopard print zoot suit. That should be enough to sell anyone this story. Secondly, and probably more importantly to some, it shows Betty and Veronica at their best: competitive, though for once it is not over Archie's affections! The story is great fun as we get to see the girls develop a shared interest that isn't Archie and we get to see them team up with unlikely dance partners who prove more dependable than our good ol' Arch. The 1990s did not just reintroduce swing to the masses but it also introduced me to Archie Comics. From the very beginning, I had a strong affinity for Betty and Veronica. I gravitated toward Veronica in particular, who is, undoubtedly, my favorite comic book character of all time. That doesn't mean I don't love Betty Cooper, but Veronica Lodge is in a league of her own. To me, Veronica is the epitome of glamor, sophistication, and confidence, but she is also a bratty snob with a heart of gold, creating much of the tension in the Archie universe. When I successfully managed to beg my dad for a comic book or had money from the tooth fairy, I would always choose Betty and Veronica over any other title. Though I may not get visits from the tooth fairy anymore, I still remain a dedicated Betty and Veronica fan.

-- **Camille Herrera**
Archie Comics Fan

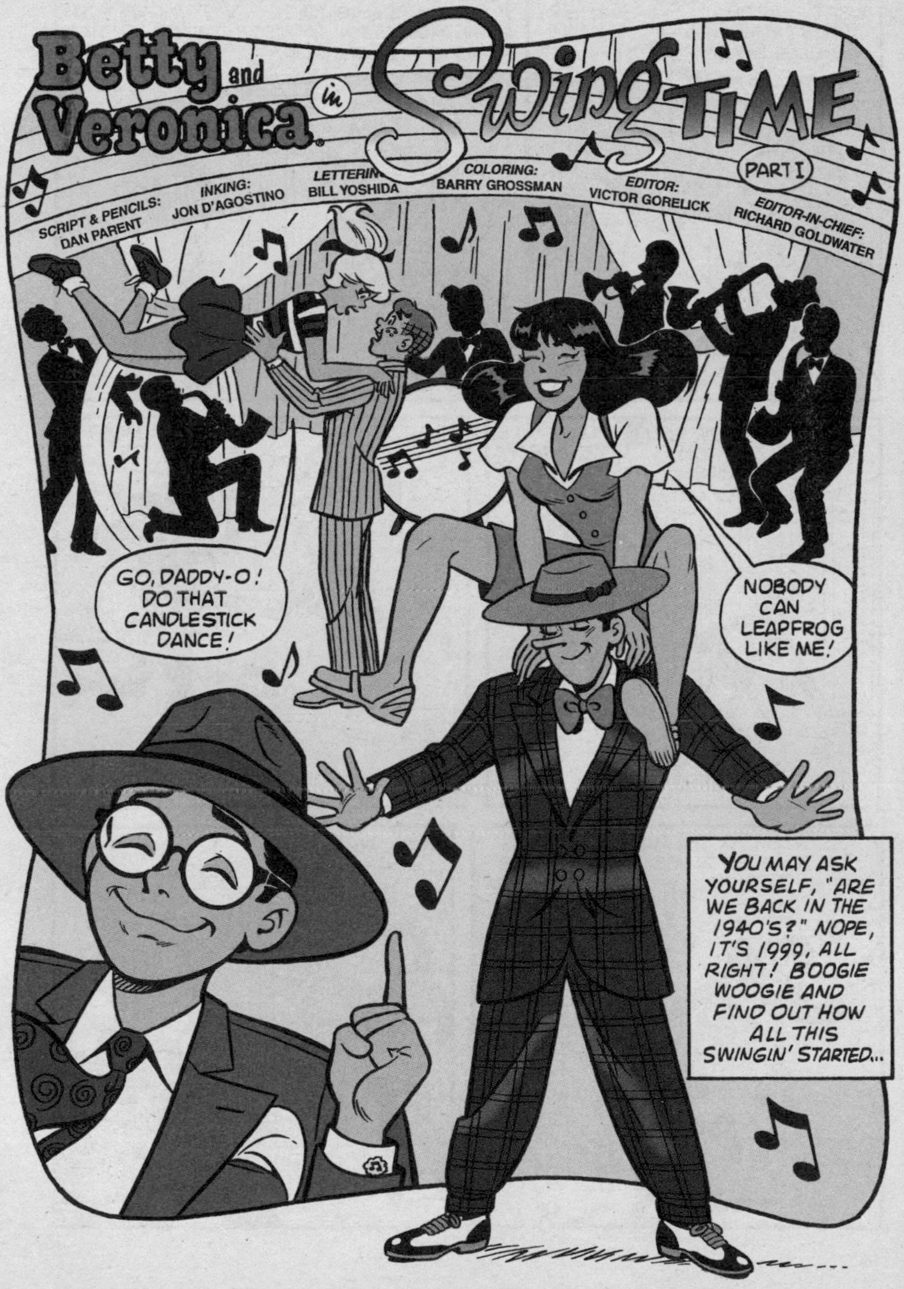
Betty and Veronica in Swing TIME
PART I
SCRIPT & PENCILS: DAN PARENT
INKING: JON D'AGOSTINO
LETTERING: BILL YOSHIDA
COLORING: BARRY GROSSMAN
EDITOR: VICTOR GORELICK
EDITOR-IN-CHIEF: RICHARD GOLDWATER
GO, DADDY-O! DO THAT CANDLESTICK DANCE!
NOBODY CAN LEAPFROG LIKE ME!
YOU MAY ASK YOURSELF, "ARE WE BACK IN THE 1940'S?" NOPE, IT'S 1999, ALL RIGHT! BOOGIE WOOGIE AND FIND OUT HOW ALL THIS SWINGIN' STARTED...

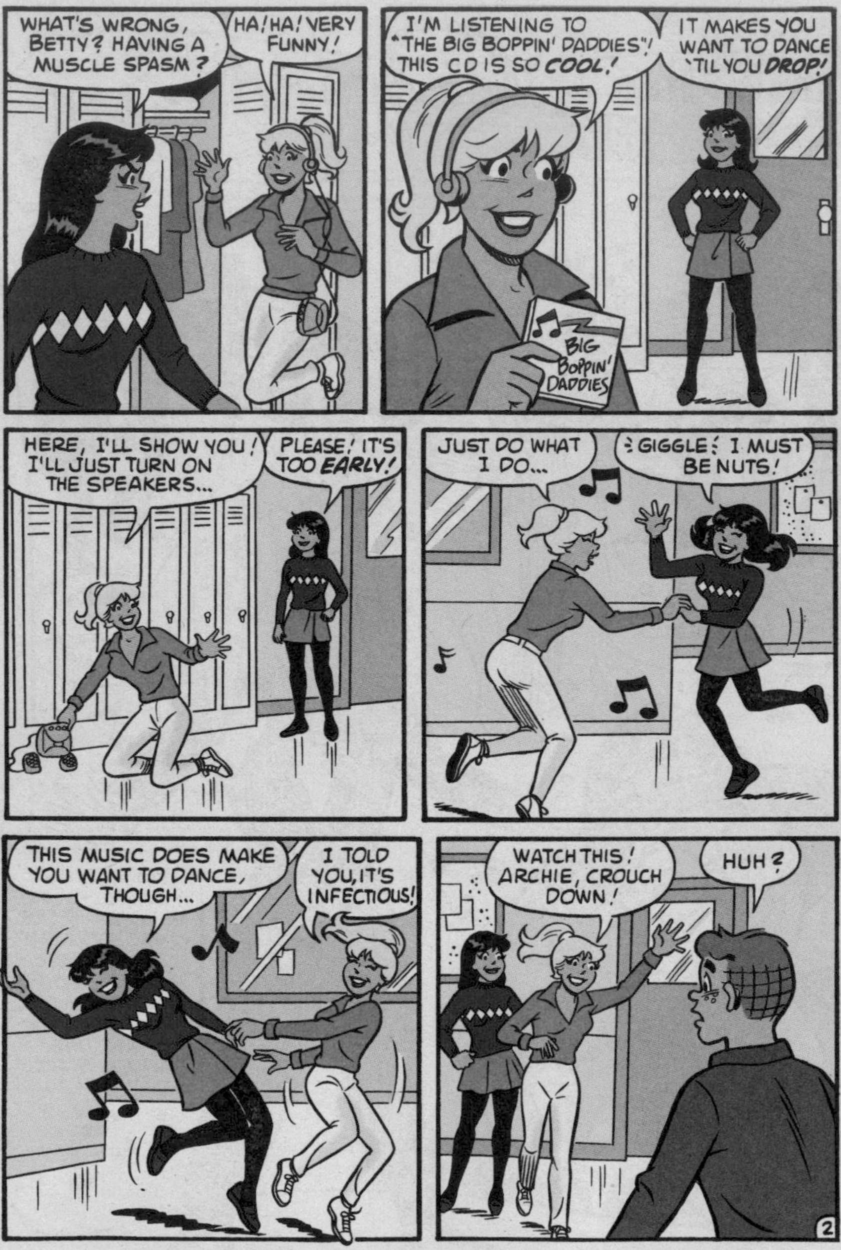
WHAT'S WRONG, BETTY? HAVING A MUSCLE SPASM?
HA! HA! VERY FUNNY!
I'M LISTENING TO "THE BIG BOPPIN' DADDIES"! THIS CD IS SO COOL!
IT MAKES YOU WANT TO DANCE 'TIL YOU DROP!
BIG BOPPIN' DADDIES
HERE, I'LL SHOW YOU! I'LL JUST TURN ON THE SPEAKERS...
PLEASE! IT'S TOO EARLY!
JUST DO WHAT I DO...
GIGGLE! I MUST BE NUTS!
THIS MUSIC DOES MAKE YOU WANT TO DANCE, THOUGH...
I TOLD YOU, IT'S INFECTIOUS!
WATCH THIS! ARCHIE, CROUCH DOWN!
HUH?
2

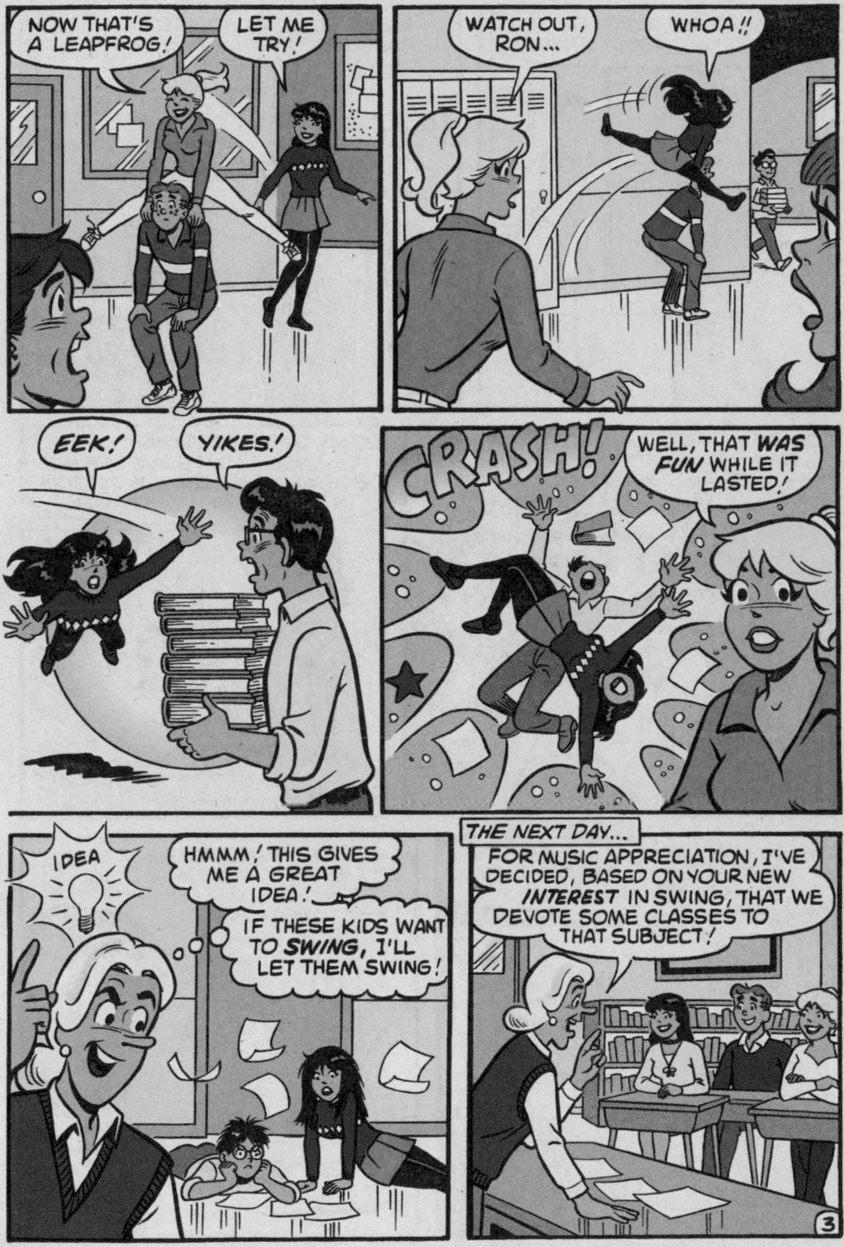
NOW THAT'S A LEAPFROG!
LET ME TRY!
WATCH OUT, RON...
WHOA!!
EEK!
YIKES!
CRASH!
WELL, THAT WAS FUN WHILE IT LASTED!
IDEA
HMMM! THIS GIVES ME A GREAT IDEA!
IF THESE KIDS WANT TO SWING, I'LL LET THEM SWING!
THE NEXT DAY...
FOR MUSIC APPRECIATION, I'VE DECIDED, BASED ON YOUR NEW INTEREST IN SWING, THAT WE DEVOTE SOME CLASSES TO THAT SUBJECT!
3

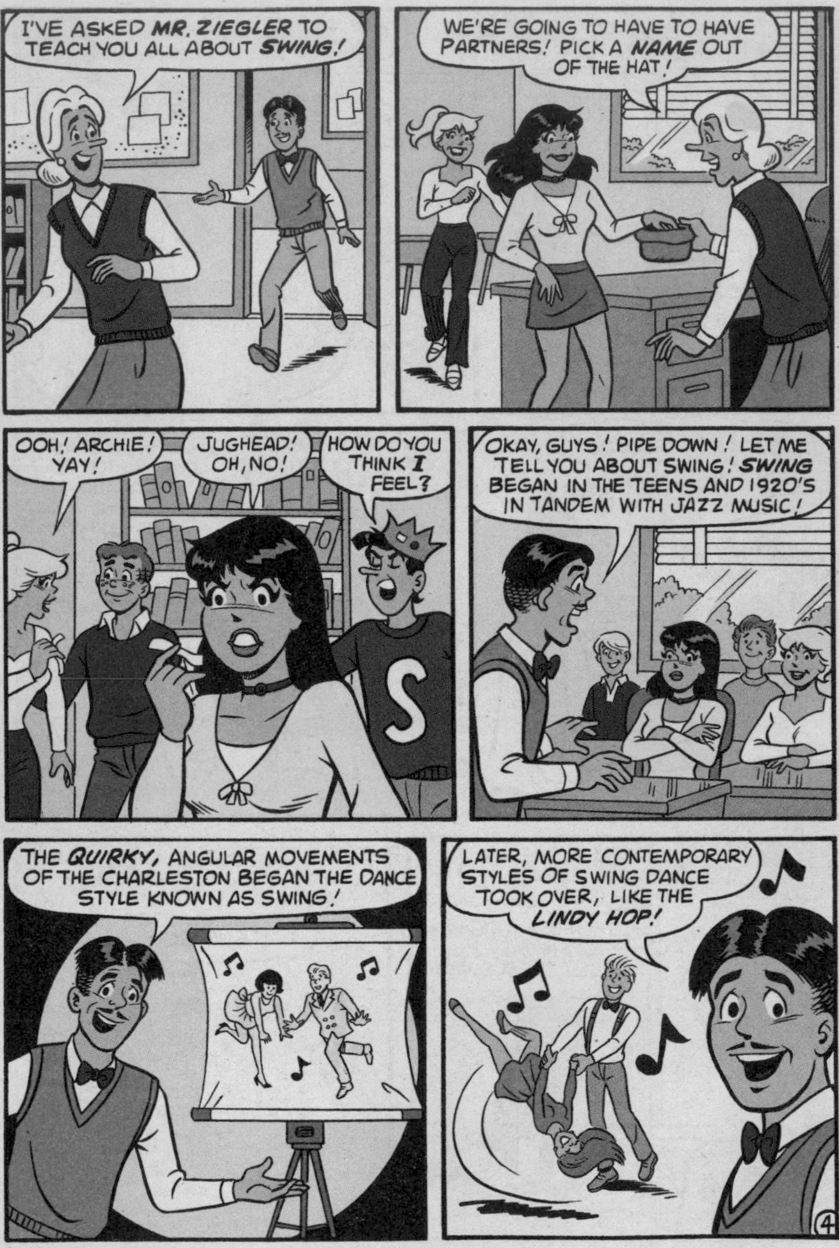
I'VE ASKED MR. ZIEGLER TO TEACH YOU ALL ABOUT SWING!
WE'RE GOING TO HAVE TO HAVE PARTNERS! PICK A NAME OUT OF THE HAT!
OOH! ARCHIE! YAY!
JUGHEAD! OH, NO!
HOW DO YOU THINK I FEEL?
OKAY, GUYS! PIPE DOWN! LET ME TELL YOU ABOUT SWING! SWING BEGAN IN THE TEENS AND 1920'S IN TANDEM WITH JAZZ MUSIC!
THE QUIRKY, ANGULAR MOVEMENTS OF THE CHARLESTON BEGAN THE DANCE STYLE KNOWN AS SWING!
LATER, MORE CONTEMPORARY STYLES OF SWING DANCE TOOK OVER, LIKE THE LINDY HOP!
4

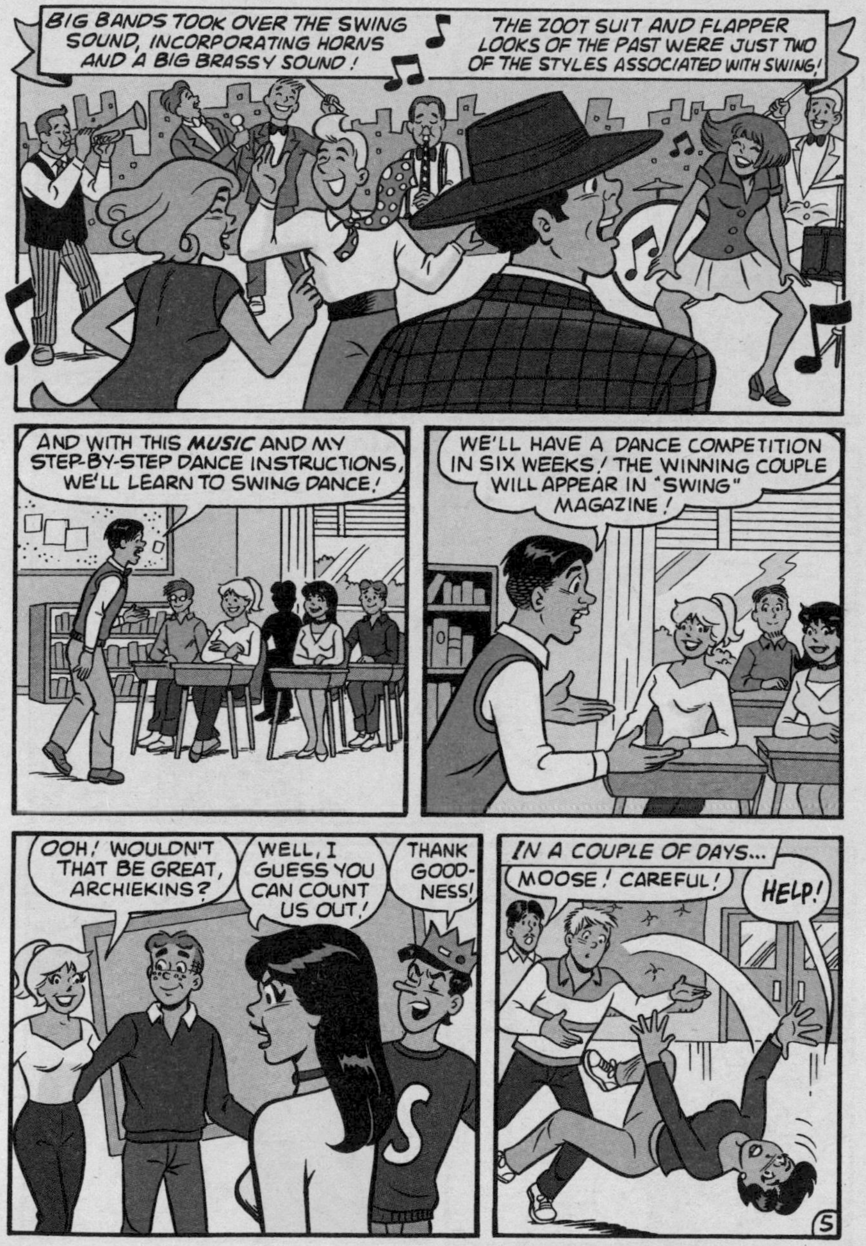
BIG BANDS TOOK OVER THE SWING SOUND, INCORPORATING HORNS AND A BIG BRASSY SOUND!
THE ZOOT SUIT AND FLAPPER LOOKS OF THE PAST WERE JUST TWO OF THE STYLES ASSOCIATED WITH SWING!
AND WITH THIS MUSIC AND MY STEP-BY-STEP DANCE INSTRUCTIONS, WE'LL LEARN TO SWING DANCE!
WE'LL HAVE A DANCE COMPETITION IN SIX WEEKS! THE WINNING COUPLE WILL APPEAR IN "SWING" MAGAZINE!
OOH! WOULDN'T THAT BE GREAT, ARCHIEKINS?
WELL, I GUESS YOU CAN COUNT US OUT!
THANK GOODNESS!
IN A COUPLE OF DAYS...
MOOSE! CAREFUL!
HELP!
5

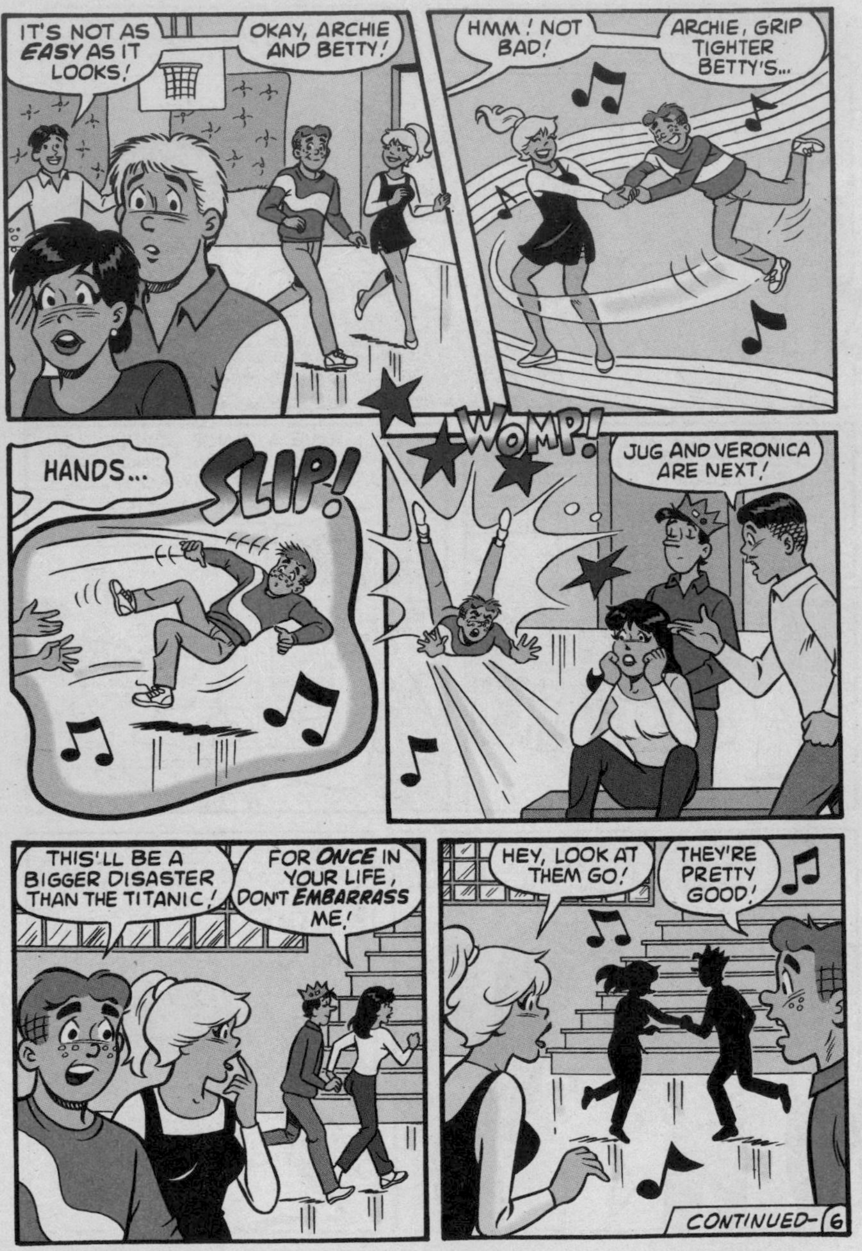
IT'S NOT AS EASY AS IT LOOKS!
OKAY, ARCHIE AND BETTY!
HMM! NOT BAD!
ARCHIE, GRIP TIGHTER BETTY'S...
HANDS...
SLIP!
WOMP!
JUG AND VERONICA ARE NEXT!
THIS'LL BE A BIGGER DISASTER THAN THE TITANIC!
FOR ONCE IN YOUR LIFE, DON'T EMBARRASS ME!
HEY, LOOK AT THEM GO!
THEY'RE PRETTY GOOD!
CONTINUED- 6

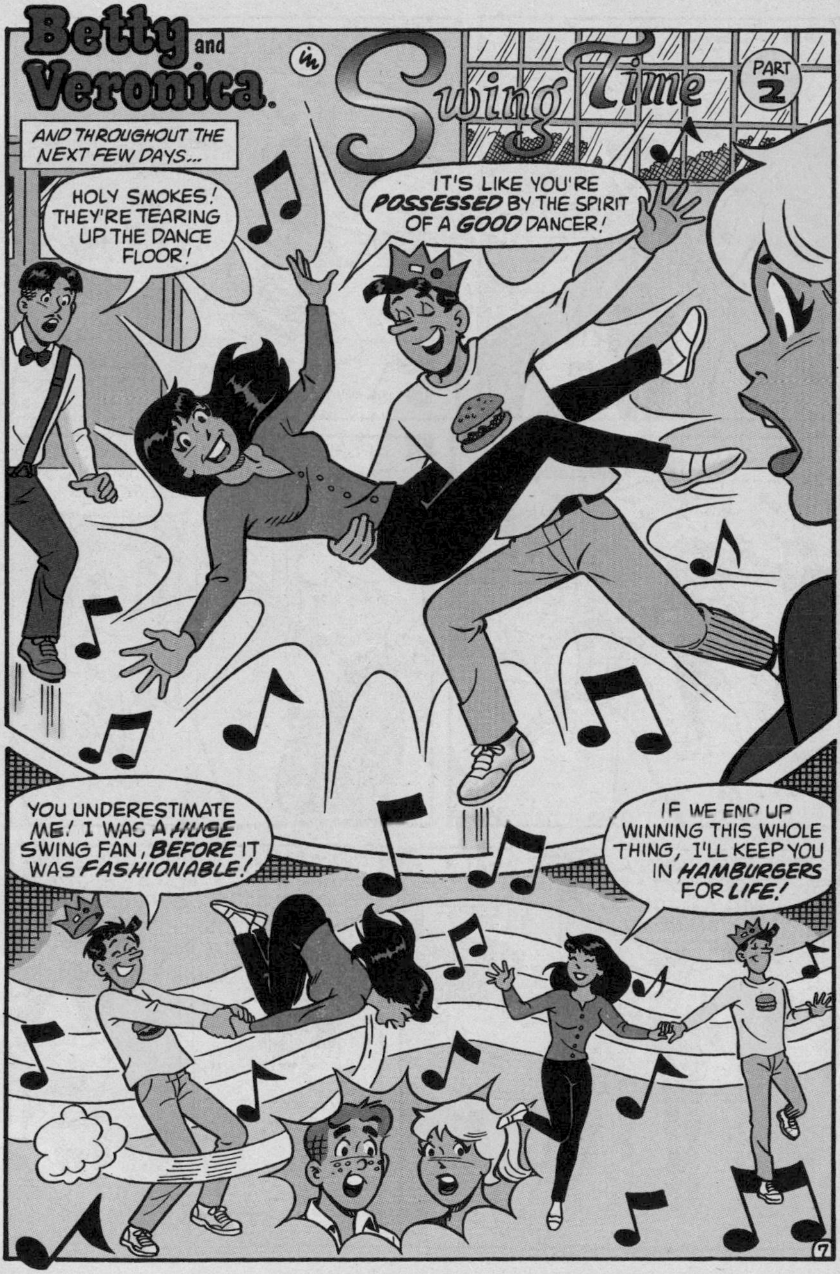
Betty and Veronica
in
Swing Time
PART 2
AND THROUGHOUT THE NEXT FEW DAYS...
HOLY SMOKES! THEY'RE TEARING UP THE DANCE FLOOR!
IT'S LIKE YOU'RE POSSESSED BY THE SPIRIT OF A GOOD DANCER!
YOU UNDERESTIMATE ME! I WAS A HUGE SWING FAN, BEFORE IT WAS FASHIONABLE!
IF WE END UP WINNING THIS WHOLE THING, I'LL KEEP YOU IN HAMBURGERS FOR LIFE!
7

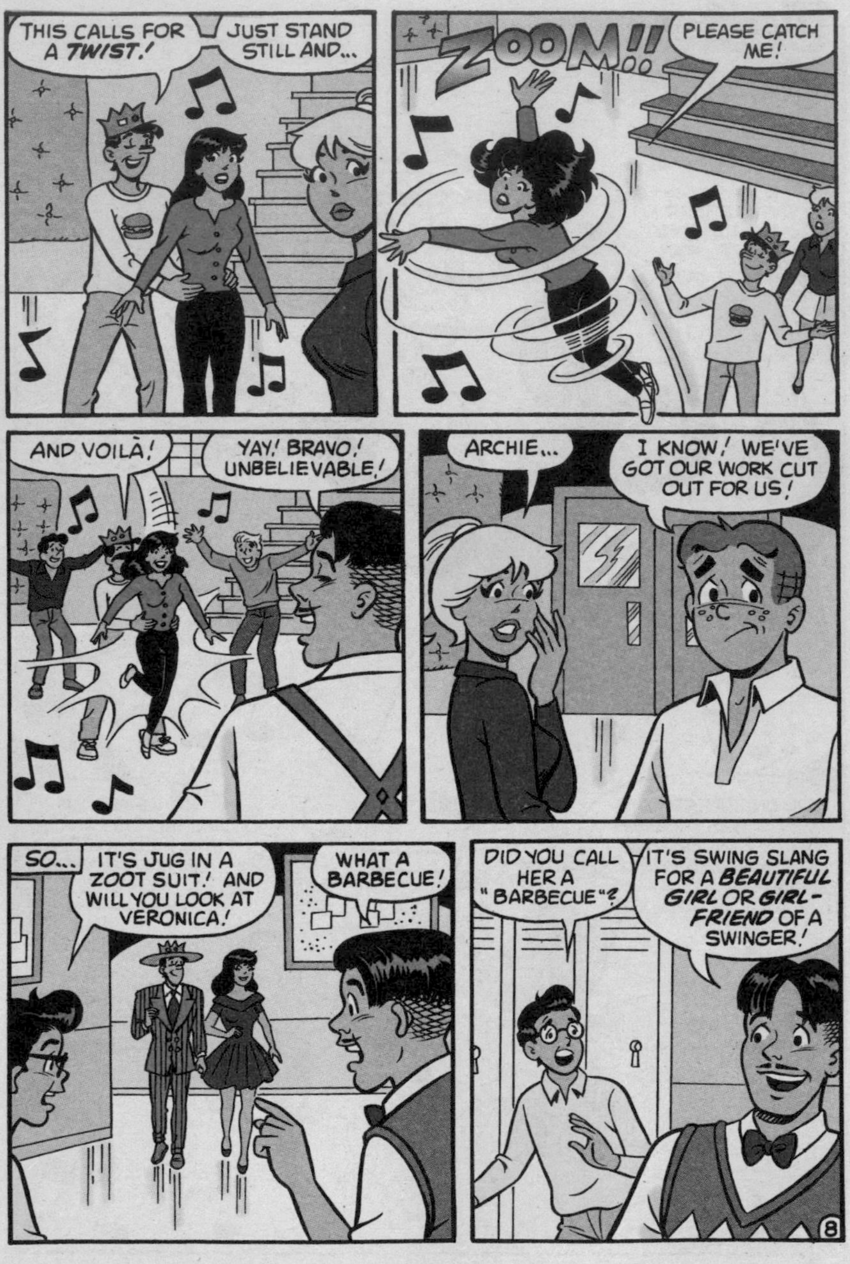
THIS CALLS FOR A TWIST!
JUST STAND STILL AND...
ZOOM!!
PLEASE CATCH ME!
AND VOILÀ!
YAY! BRAVO! UNBELIEVABLE!
ARCHIE...
I KNOW! WE'VE GOT OUR WORK CUT OUT FOR US!
SO...
IT'S JUG IN A ZOOT SUIT! AND WILL YOU LOOK AT VERONICA!
WHAT A BARBECUE!
DID YOU CALL HER A "BARBECUE"?
IT'S SWING SLANG FOR A BEAUTIFUL GIRL OR GIRL-FRIEND OF A SWINGER!
8

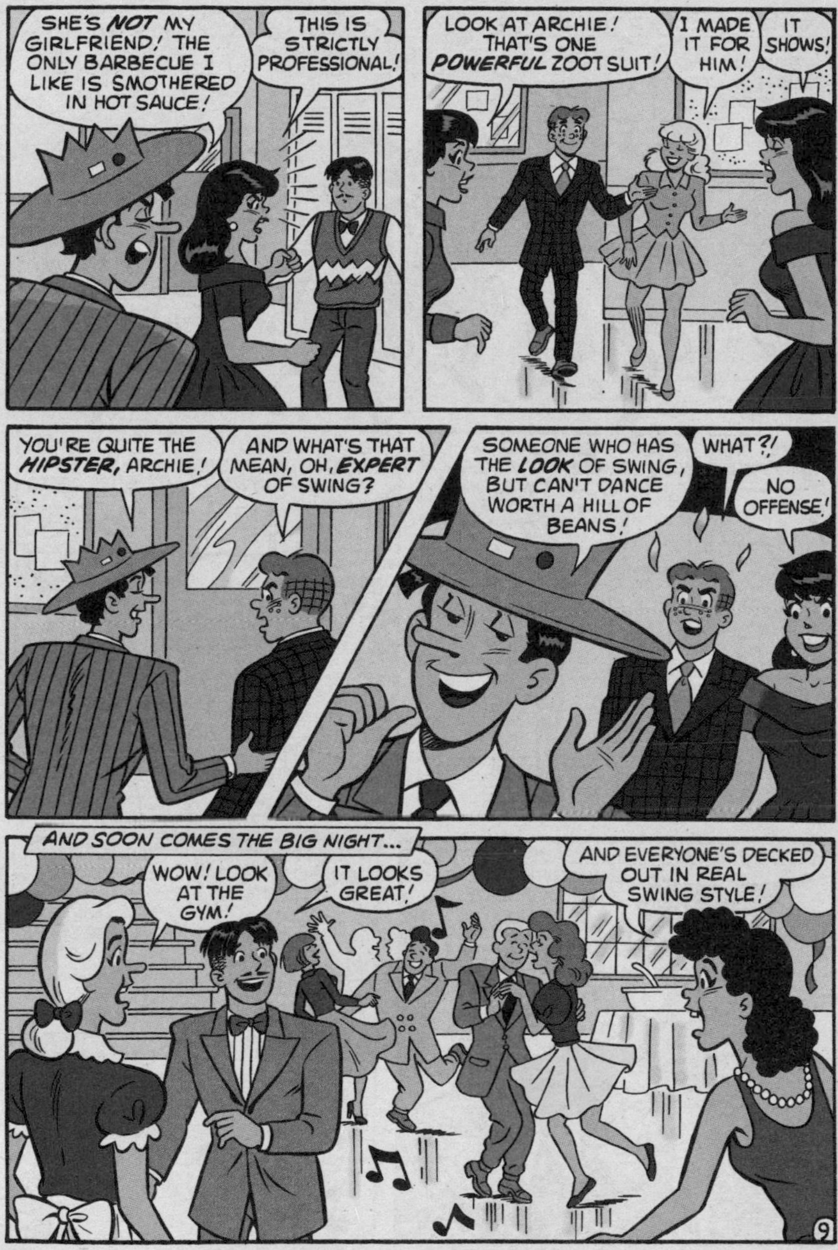
SHE'S NOT MY GIRLFRIEND! THE ONLY BARBECUE I LIKE IS SMOTHERED IN HOT SAUCE!
THIS IS STRICTLY PROFESSIONAL!
LOOK AT ARCHIE! THAT'S ONE POWERFUL ZOOT SUIT!
I MADE IT FOR HIM!
IT SHOWS!
YOU'RE QUITE THE HIPSTER, ARCHIE!
AND WHAT'S THAT MEAN, OH, EXPERT OF SWING?
SOMEONE WHO HAS THE LOOK OF SWING, BUT CAN'T DANCE WORTH A HILL OF BEANS!
WHAT?!
NO OFFENSE!
AND SOON COMES THE BIG NIGHT...
WOW! LOOK AT THE GYM!
IT LOOKS GREAT!
AND EVERYONE'S DECKED OUT IN REAL SWING STYLE!
9

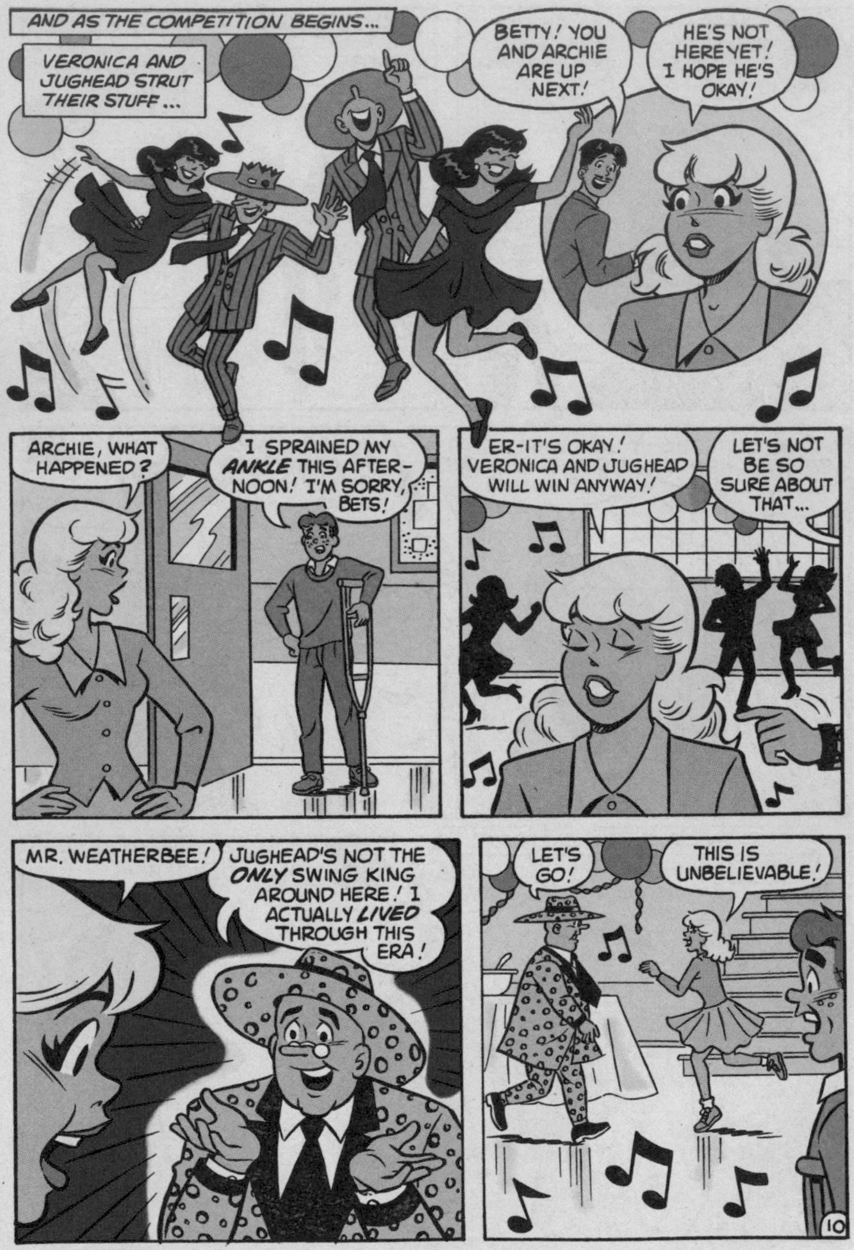
AND AS THE COMPETITION BEGINS...
VERONICA AND JUGHEAD STRUT THEIR STUFF...
BETTY! YOU AND ARCHIE ARE UP NEXT!
HE'S NOT HERE YET! I HOPE HE'S OKAY!
ARCHIE, WHAT HAPPENED?
I SPRAINED MY ANKLE THIS AFTERNOON! I'M SORRY, BETS!
ER-IT'S OKAY! VERONICA AND JUGHEAD WILL WIN ANYWAY!
LET'S NOT BE SO SURE ABOUT THAT...
MR. WEATHERBEE!
JUGHEAD'S NOT THE ONLY SWING KING AROUND HERE! I ACTUALLY LIVED THROUGH THIS ERA!
LET'S GO!
THIS IS UNBELIEVABLE!
10

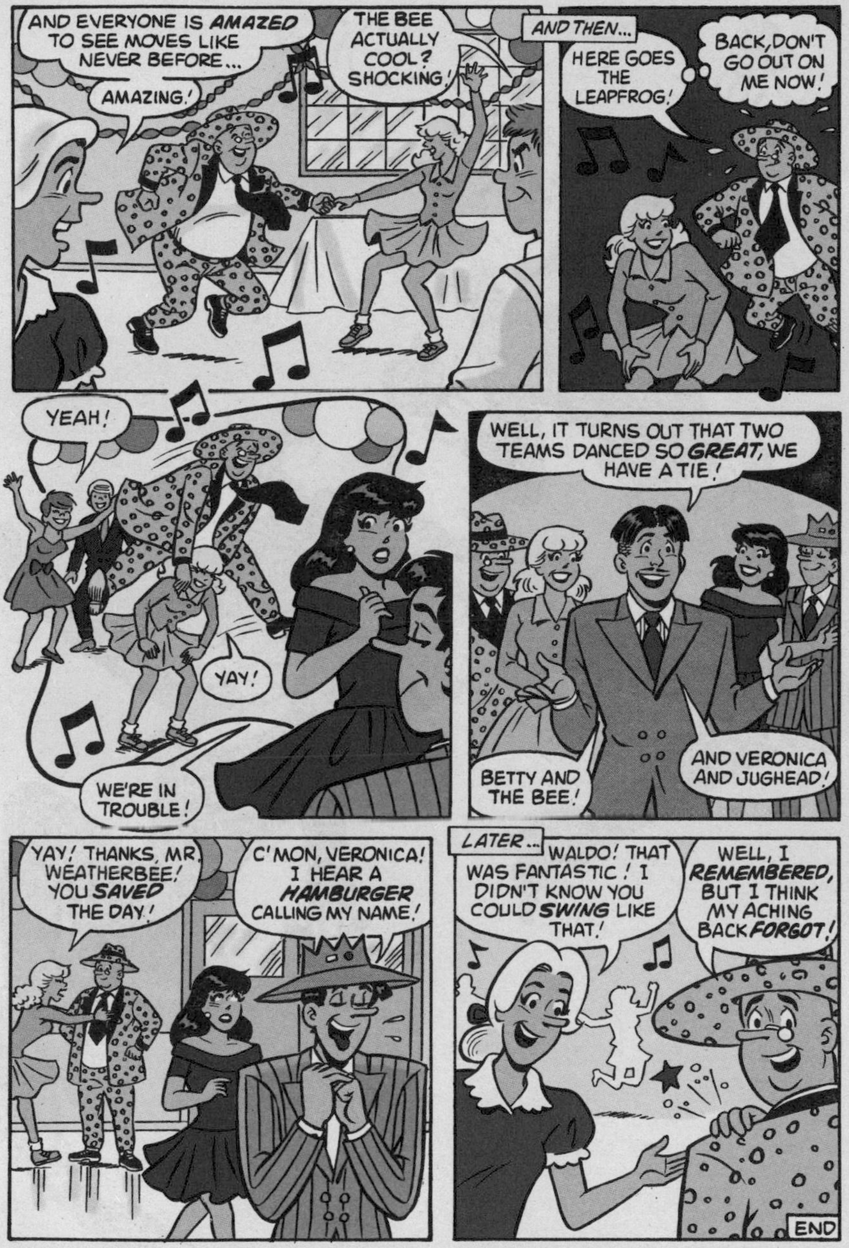
AND EVERYONE IS AMAZED TO SEE MOVES LIKE NEVER BEFORE...
AMAZING!
THE BEE ACTUALLY COOL? SHOCKING!
AND THEN...
HERE GOES THE LEAPFROG!
BACK, DON'T GO OUT ON ME NOW!
YEAH!
YAY!
WE'RE IN TROUBLE!
WELL, IT TURNS OUT THAT TWO TEAMS DANCED SO GREAT, WE HAVE A TIE!
BETTY AND THE BEE!
AND VERONICA AND JUGHEAD!
YAY! THANKS, MR. WEATHERBEE! YOU SAVED THE DAY!
C'MON, VERONICA! I HEAR A HAMBURGER CALLING MY NAME!
LATER...
WALDO! THAT WAS FANTASTIC! I DIDN'T KNOW YOU COULD SWING LIKE THAT!
WELL, I REMEMBERED, BUT I THINK MY ACHING BACK FORGOT!
END

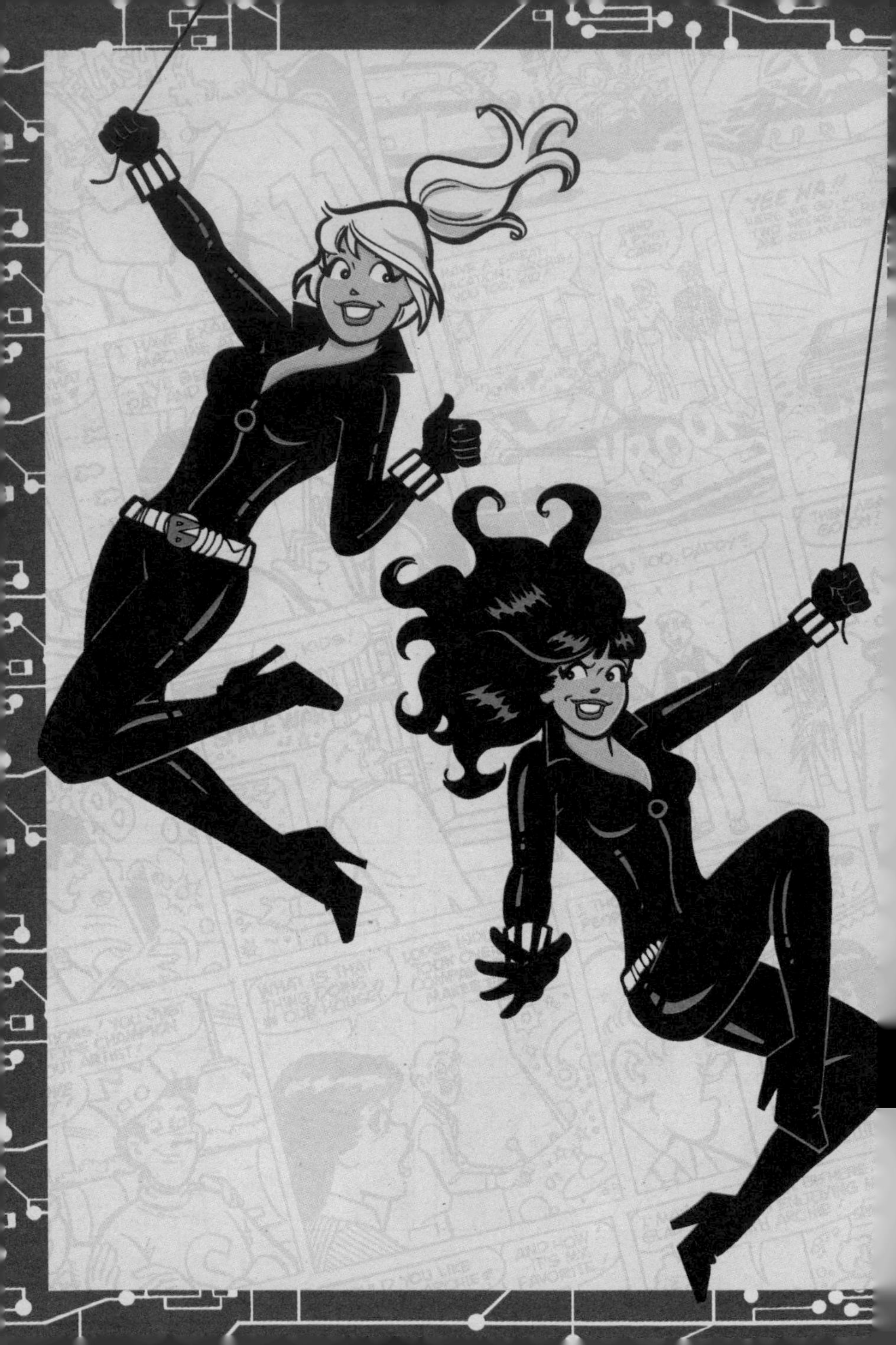
YOU TOO, DADDY!
WHAT IS THAT THING DOING IN OUR HOUSE?

THE BEST OF ARCHIE COMICS

Betty & Veronica®

the 2000s

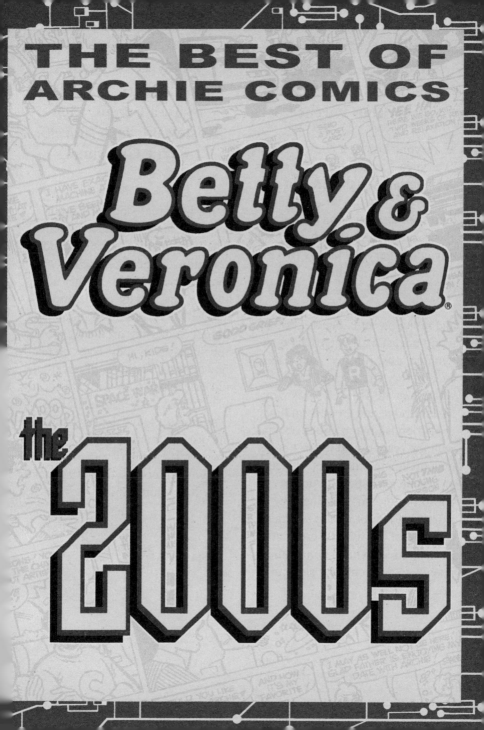

Ginger Adds Spice
Betty & Veronica
Spectacular #50, 2001
by Dan Parent

Everyone knows a "Betty" and a "Veronica", which I think explains their appeal. And the B&V in your life doesn't have to be a wealthy heiress or a small town school cheerleader... or even a blonde and brunette. Everyone knows two girls who are simpatico, despite that one is prone to being bossy and a bit of a diva while the other is easy-going and rather sweet natured. They might occasionally be rivals over a mutual goal (or guy!) that causes a temporary rift but, no matter what, they are BFFs. This is why Mses. Lodge and Cooper endure: their friendship and antics resonate with the reader. And it can't be underestimated that a lot of Betty & Veronica's appeal comes as a result of the girls having the extreme good fortune to be drawn by some of the world's greatest cartoonists who have helped them remain so darn cute for close to 75 years!

-- **Batton Lash**
Writer,
Archie Comics

Fashion Victims
Betty & Veronica
Spectacular #75, 2006
by Dan Parent, Rich Koslowski, Jack Morelli, Barry Grossman

This is a great story of a friend in need of a brilliant idea which is actually inspired by Betty and Veronica. Ginger Lopez can't come up with an idea for her next fashion line, but during a simple spat between Bets and Ronnie, Ginger thinks she hit the jackpot. She simply puts their faces on her new clothes. The girls of Riverdale and celebrities walk the catwalk in a Betty look or Veronica look. And Ginger can't leave the boys out so she dresses them as well.

P.S. Ginger, could you please make me a XXL Betty Shirt?

-- **Erin B.**
Archie Comics Fan

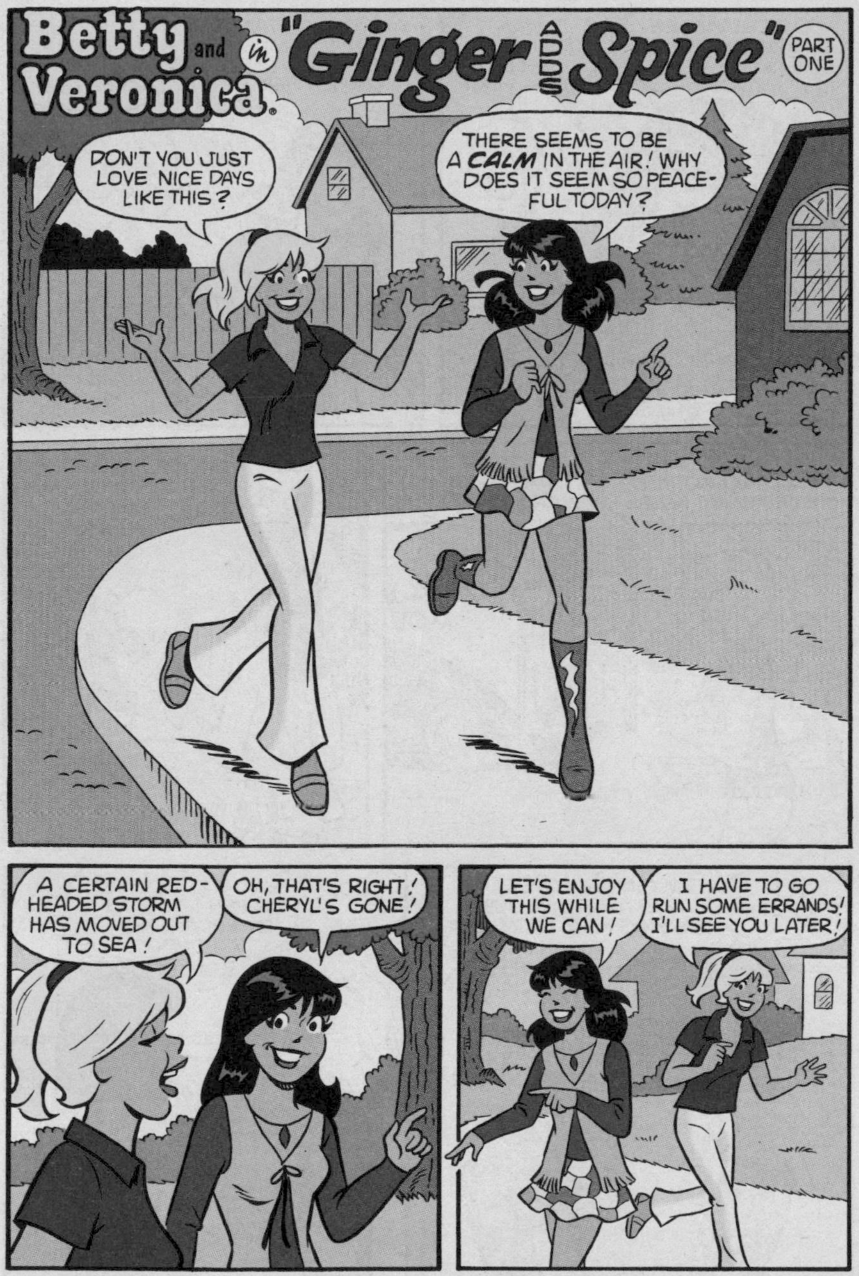
Betty and Veronica in "Ginger Adds Spice" PART ONE
DON'T YOU JUST LOVE NICE DAYS LIKE THIS?
THERE SEEMS TO BE A CALM IN THE AIR! WHY DOES IT SEEM SO PEACE-FUL TODAY?
A CERTAIN RED-HEADED STORM HAS MOVED OUT TO SEA!
OH, THAT'S RIGHT! CHERYL'S GONE!
LET'S ENJOY THIS WHILE WE CAN!
I HAVE TO GO RUN SOME ERRANDS! I'LL SEE YOU LATER!

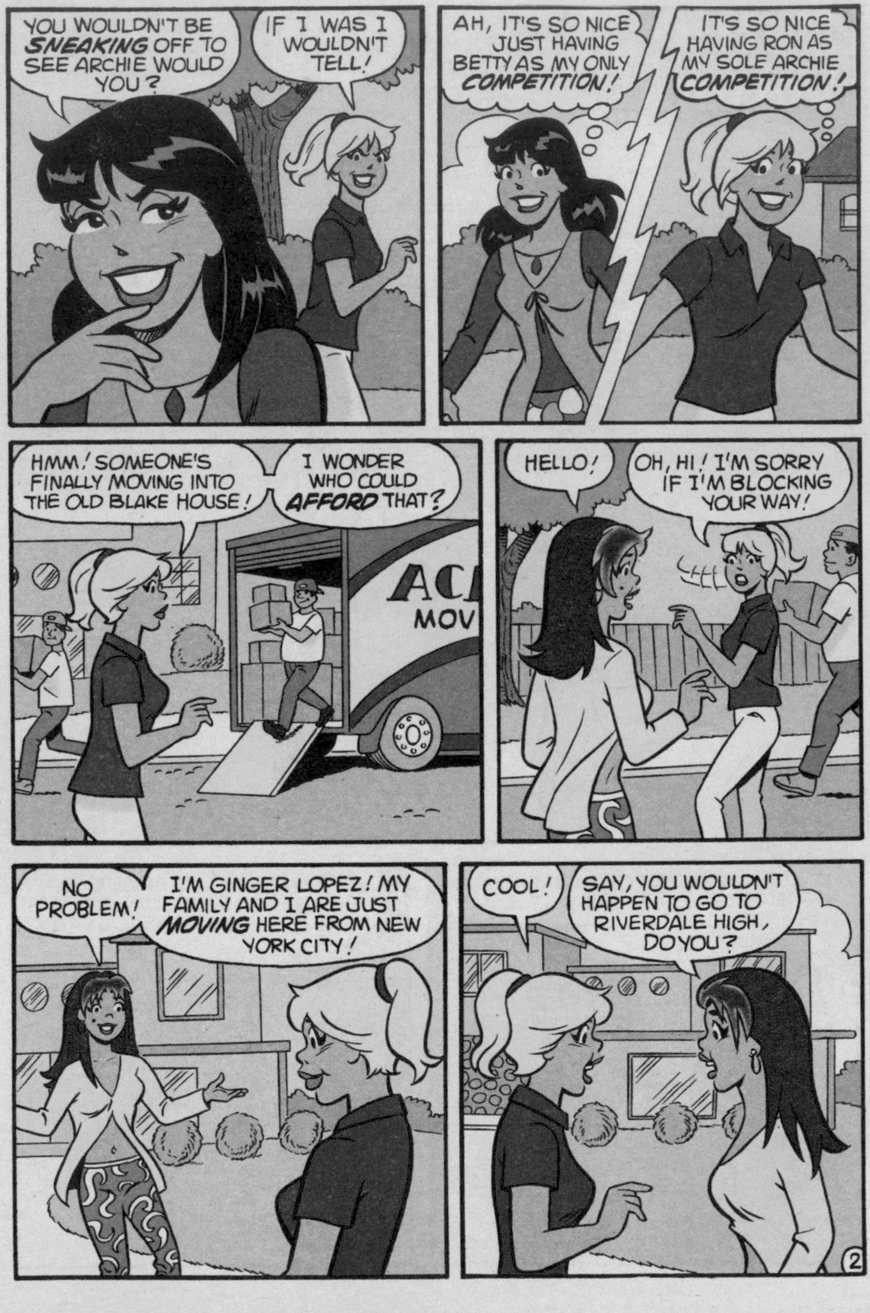
YOU WOULDN'T BE SNEAKING OFF TO SEE ARCHIE WOULD YOU?
IF I WAS I WOULDN'T TELL!
AH, IT'S SO NICE JUST HAVING BETTY AS MY ONLY COMPETITION!
IT'S SO NICE HAVING RON AS MY SOLE ARCHIE COMPETITION!
HMM! SOMEONE'S FINALLY MOVING INTO THE OLD BLAKE HOUSE!
I WONDER WHO COULD AFFORD THAT?
HELLO!
OH, HI! I'M SORRY IF I'M BLOCKING YOUR WAY!
NO PROBLEM!
I'M GINGER LOPEZ! MY FAMILY AND I ARE JUST MOVING HERE FROM NEW YORK CITY!
COOL!
SAY, YOU WOULDN'T HAPPEN TO GO TO RIVERDALE HIGH, DO YOU?
2

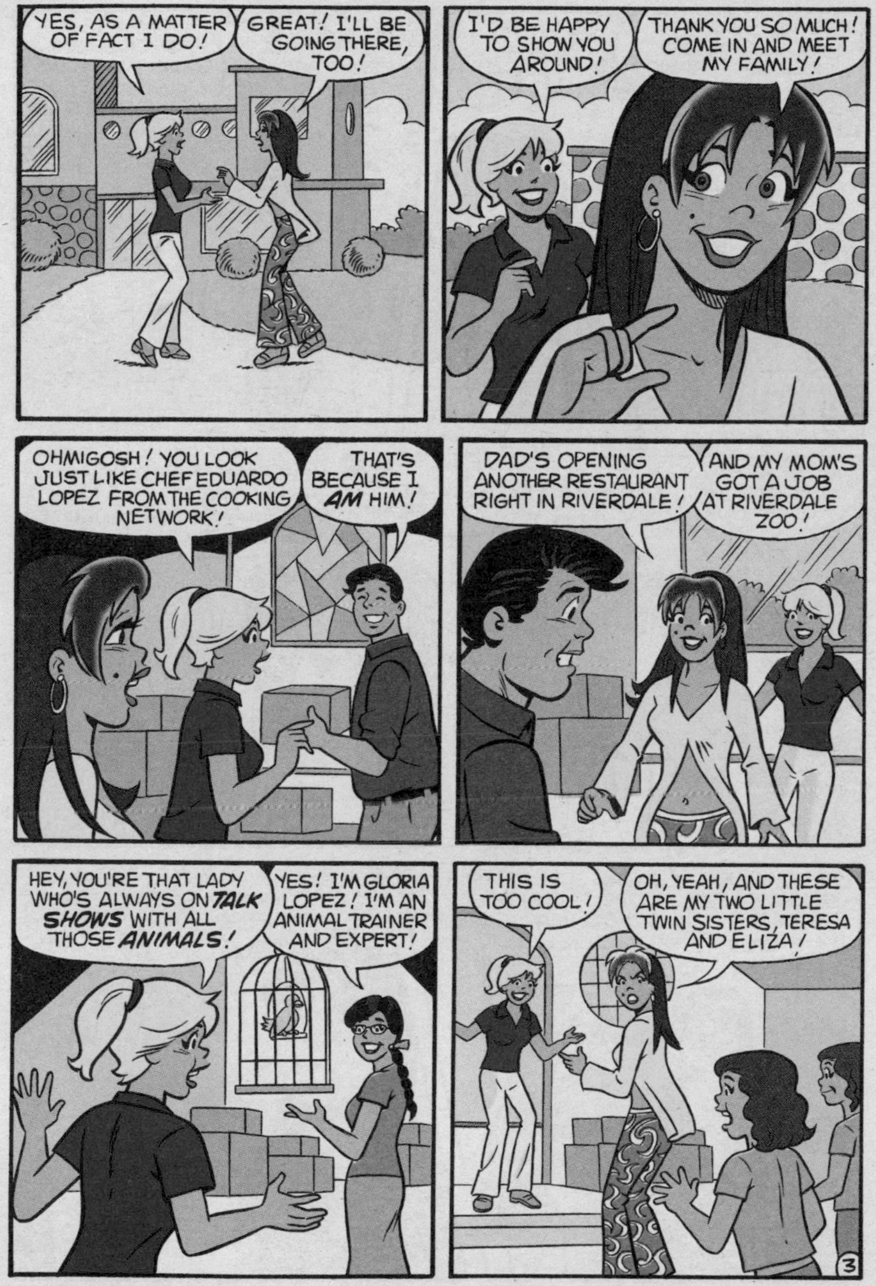
YES, AS A MATTER OF FACT I DO!
GREAT! I'LL BE GOING THERE, TOO!
I'D BE HAPPY TO SHOW YOU AROUND!
THANK YOU SO MUCH! COME IN AND MEET MY FAMILY!
OHMIGOSH! YOU LOOK JUST LIKE CHEF EDUARDO LOPEZ FROM THE COOKING NETWORK!
THAT'S BECAUSE I AM HIM!
DAD'S OPENING ANOTHER RESTAURANT RIGHT IN RIVERDALE!
AND MY MOM'S GOT A JOB AT RIVERDALE ZOO!
HEY, YOU'RE THAT LADY WHO'S ALWAYS ON TALK SHOWS WITH ALL THOSE ANIMALS!
YES! I'M GLORIA LOPEZ! I'M AN ANIMAL TRAINER AND EXPERT!
THIS IS TOO COOL!
OH, YEAH, AND THESE ARE MY TWO LITTLE TWIN SISTERS, TERESA AND ELIZA!
3

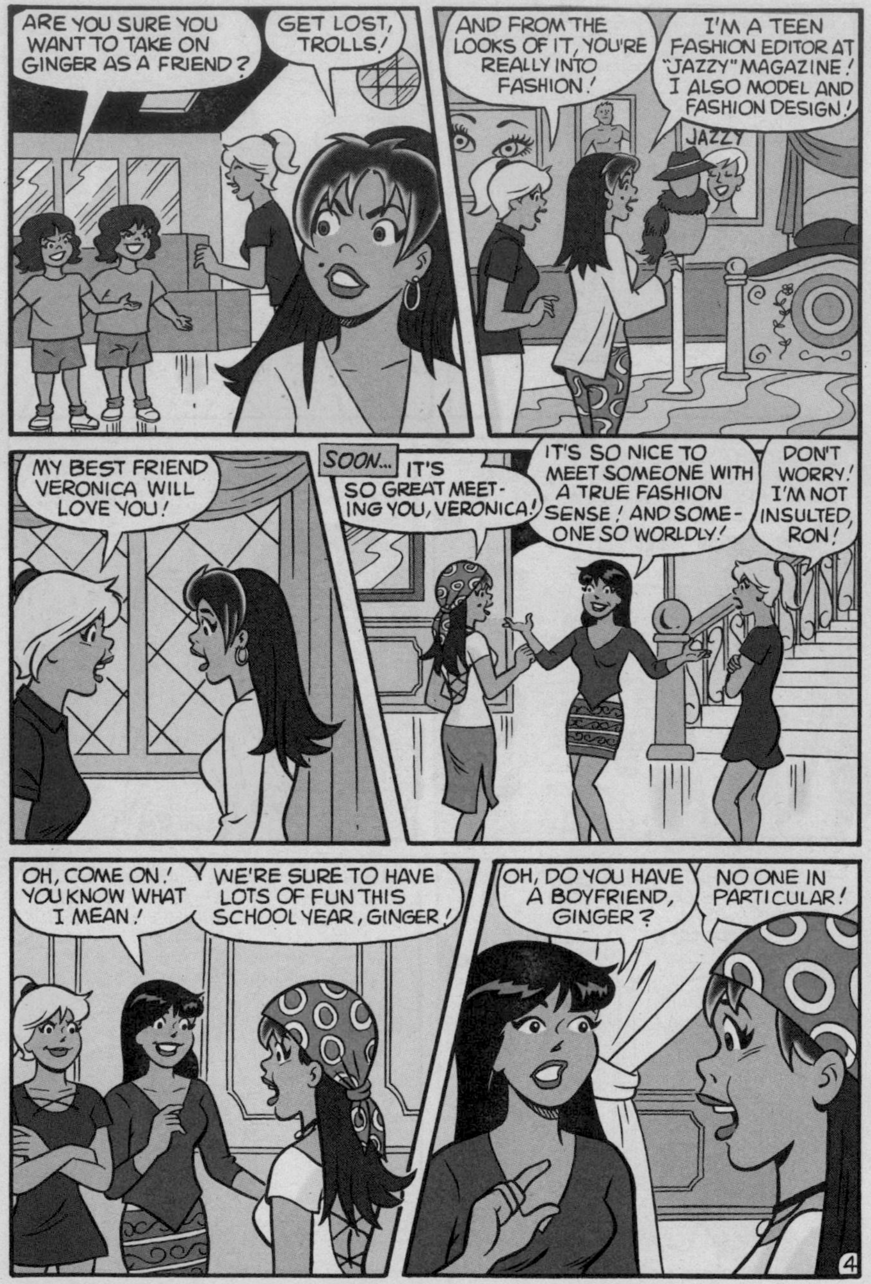
ARE YOU SURE YOU WANT TO TAKE ON GINGER AS A FRIEND?
GET LOST, TROLLS!
AND FROM THE LOOKS OF IT, YOU'RE REALLY INTO FASHION!
I'M A TEEN FASHION EDITOR AT "JAZZY" MAGAZINE! I ALSO MODEL AND FASHION DESIGN!
JAZZY
MY BEST FRIEND VERONICA WILL LOVE YOU!
SOON...
IT'S SO GREAT MEETING YOU, VERONICA!
IT'S SO NICE TO MEET SOMEONE WITH A TRUE FASHION SENSE! AND SOMEONE SO WORLDLY!
DON'T WORRY! I'M NOT INSULTED, RON!
OH, COME ON! YOU KNOW WHAT I MEAN!
WE'RE SURE TO HAVE LOTS OF FUN THIS SCHOOL YEAR, GINGER!
OH, DO YOU HAVE A BOYFRIEND, GINGER?
NO ONE IN PARTICULAR!
4

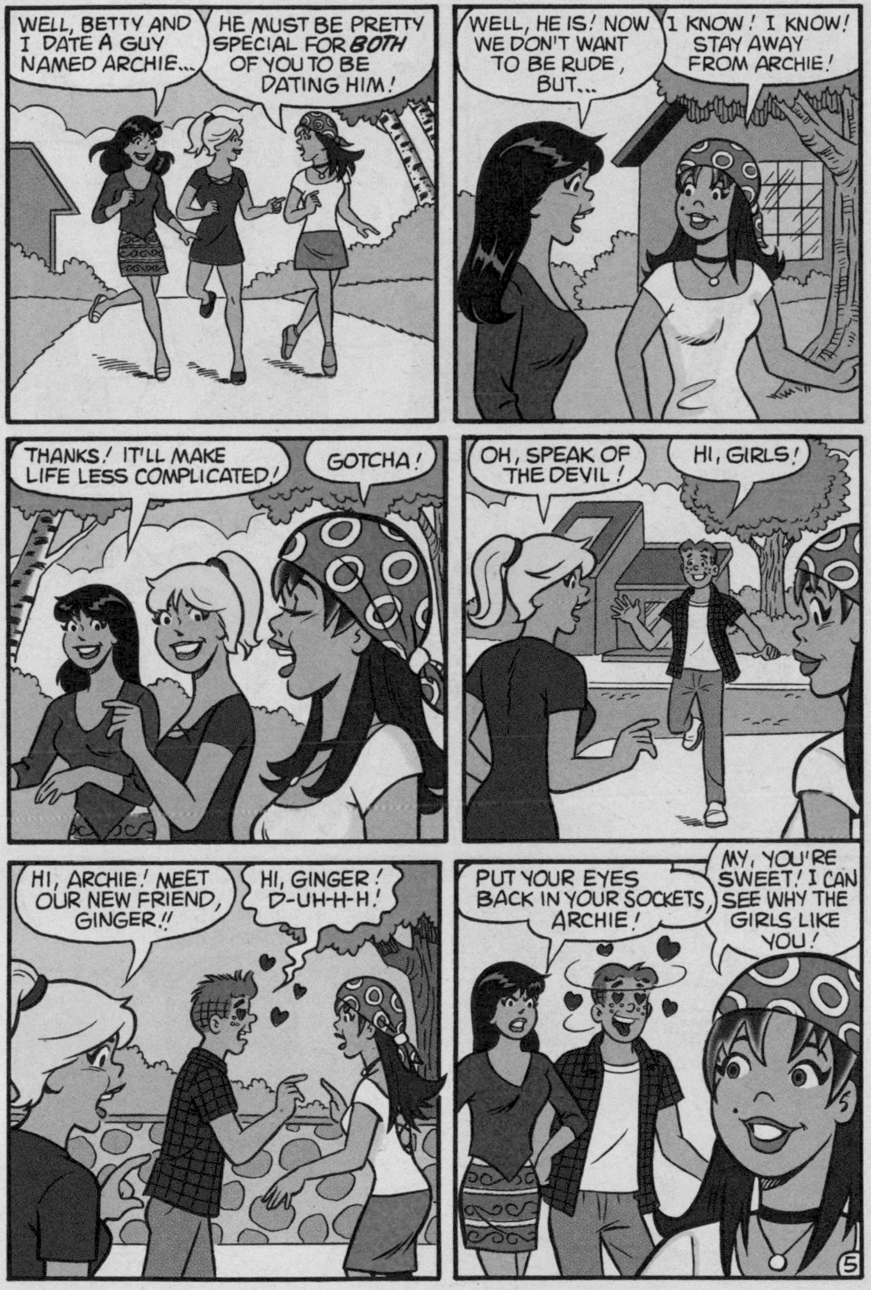
WELL, BETTY AND I DATE A GUY NAMED ARCHIE...
HE MUST BE PRETTY SPECIAL FOR BOTH OF YOU TO BE DATING HIM!
WELL, HE IS! NOW WE DON'T WANT TO BE RUDE, BUT...
I KNOW! I KNOW! STAY AWAY FROM ARCHIE!
THANKS! IT'LL MAKE LIFE LESS COMPLICATED!
GOTCHA!
OH, SPEAK OF THE DEVIL!
HI, GIRLS!
HI, ARCHIE! MEET OUR NEW FRIEND, GINGER!!
HI, GINGER! D-UH-H-H!
PUT YOUR EYES BACK IN YOUR SOCKETS, ARCHIE!
MY, YOU'RE SWEET! I CAN SEE WHY THE GIRLS LIKE YOU!
5

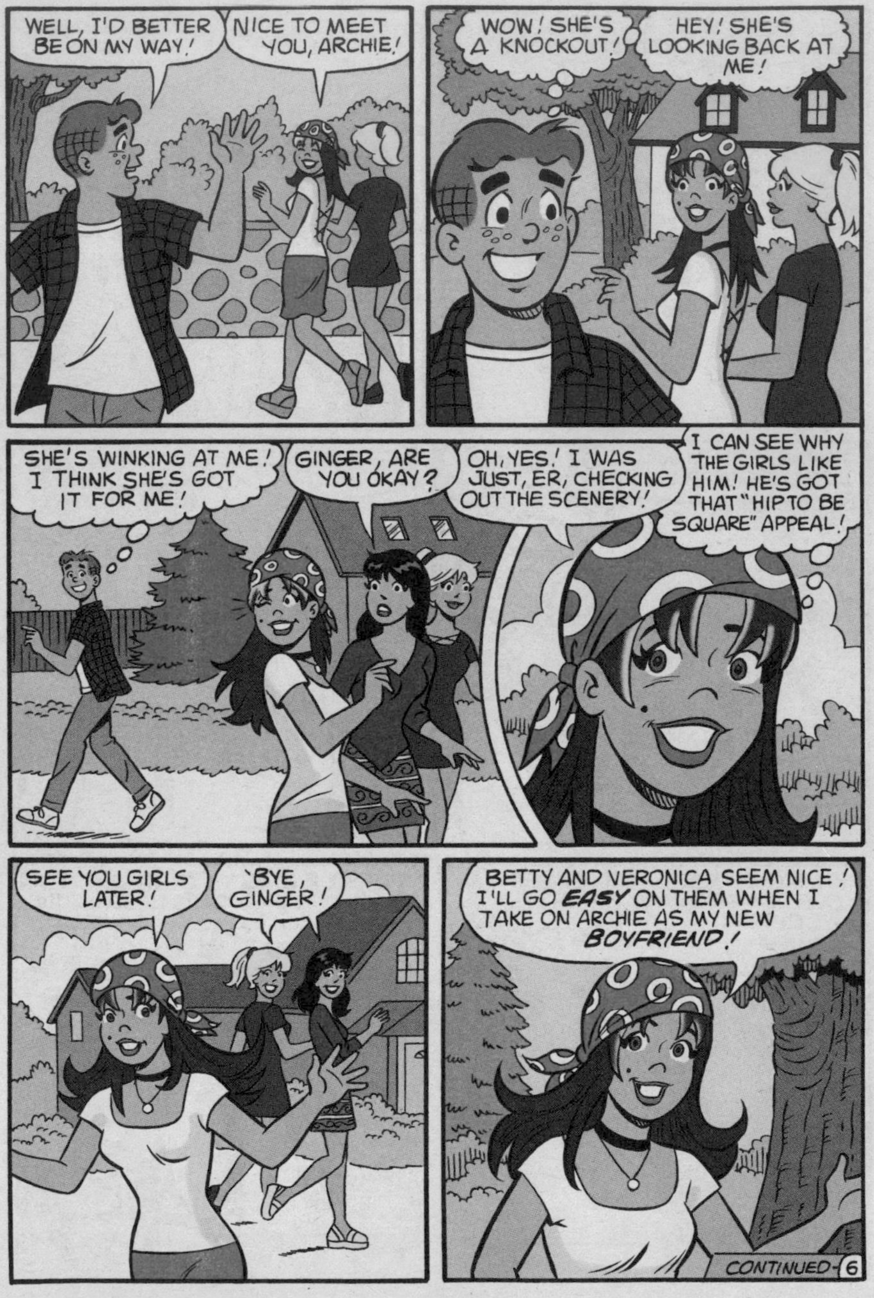
WELL, I'D BETTER BE ON MY WAY!
NICE TO MEET YOU, ARCHIE!
WOW! SHE'S A KNOCKOUT!
HEY! SHE'S LOOKING BACK AT ME!
SHE'S WINKING AT ME! I THINK SHE'S GOT IT FOR ME!
GINGER, ARE YOU OKAY?
OH, YES! I WAS JUST, ER, CHECKING OUT THE SCENERY!
I CAN SEE WHY THE GIRLS LIKE HIM! HE'S GOT THAT "HIP TO BE SQUARE" APPEAL!
SEE YOU GIRLS LATER!
'BYE, GINGER!
BETTY AND VERONICA SEEM NICE! I'LL GO EASY ON THEM WHEN I TAKE ON ARCHIE AS MY NEW BOYFRIEND!
CONTINUED-6

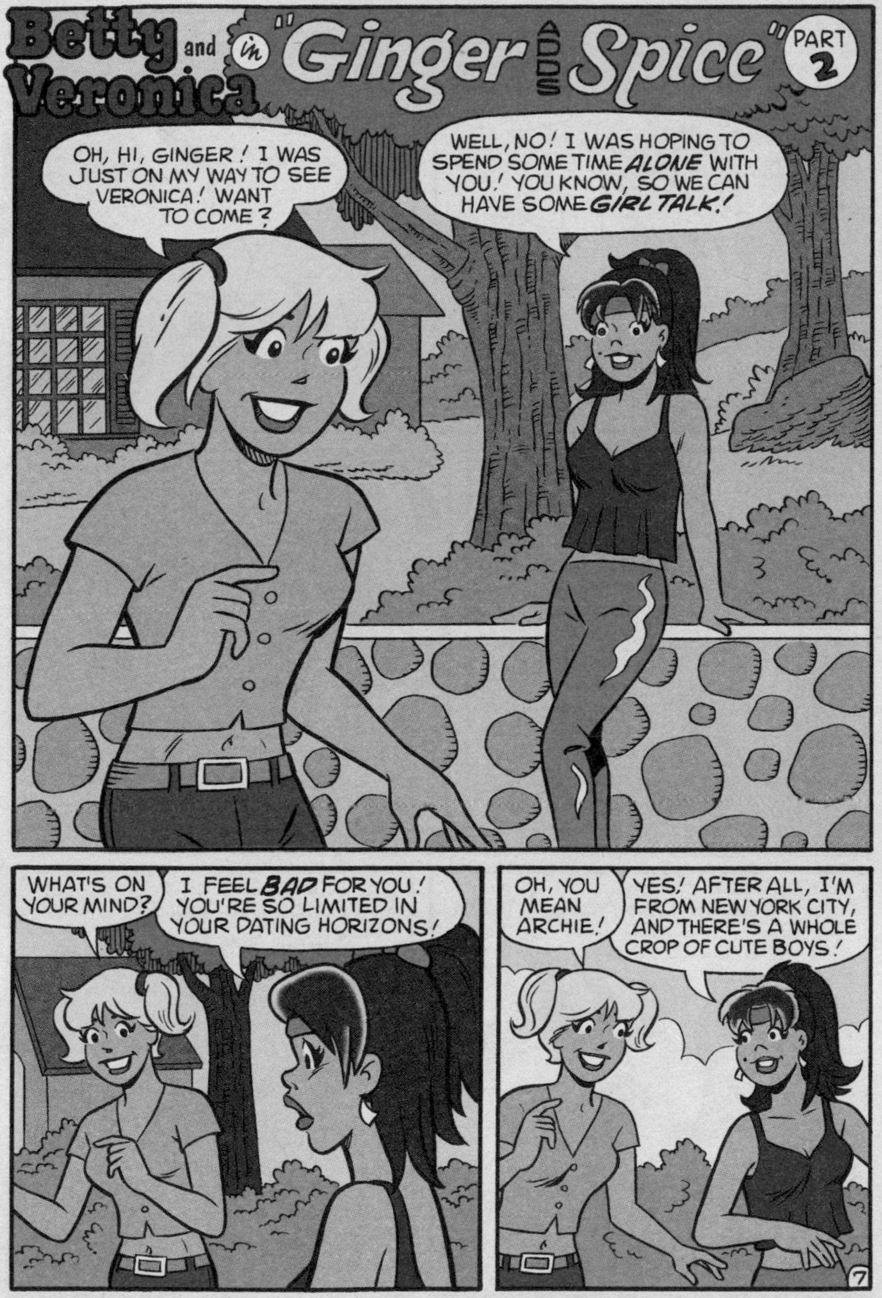
Betty and Veronica in "Ginger ADDS Spice" PART 2
OH, HI, GINGER! I WAS JUST ON MY WAY TO SEE VERONICA! WANT TO COME?
WELL, NO! I WAS HOPING TO SPEND SOME TIME ALONE WITH YOU! YOU KNOW, SO WE CAN HAVE SOME GIRL TALK!
WHAT'S ON YOUR MIND?
I FEEL BAD FOR YOU! YOU'RE SO LIMITED IN YOUR DATING HORIZONS!
OH, YOU MEAN ARCHIE!
YES! AFTER ALL, I'M FROM NEW YORK CITY, AND THERE'S A WHOLE CROP OF CUTE BOYS!
7

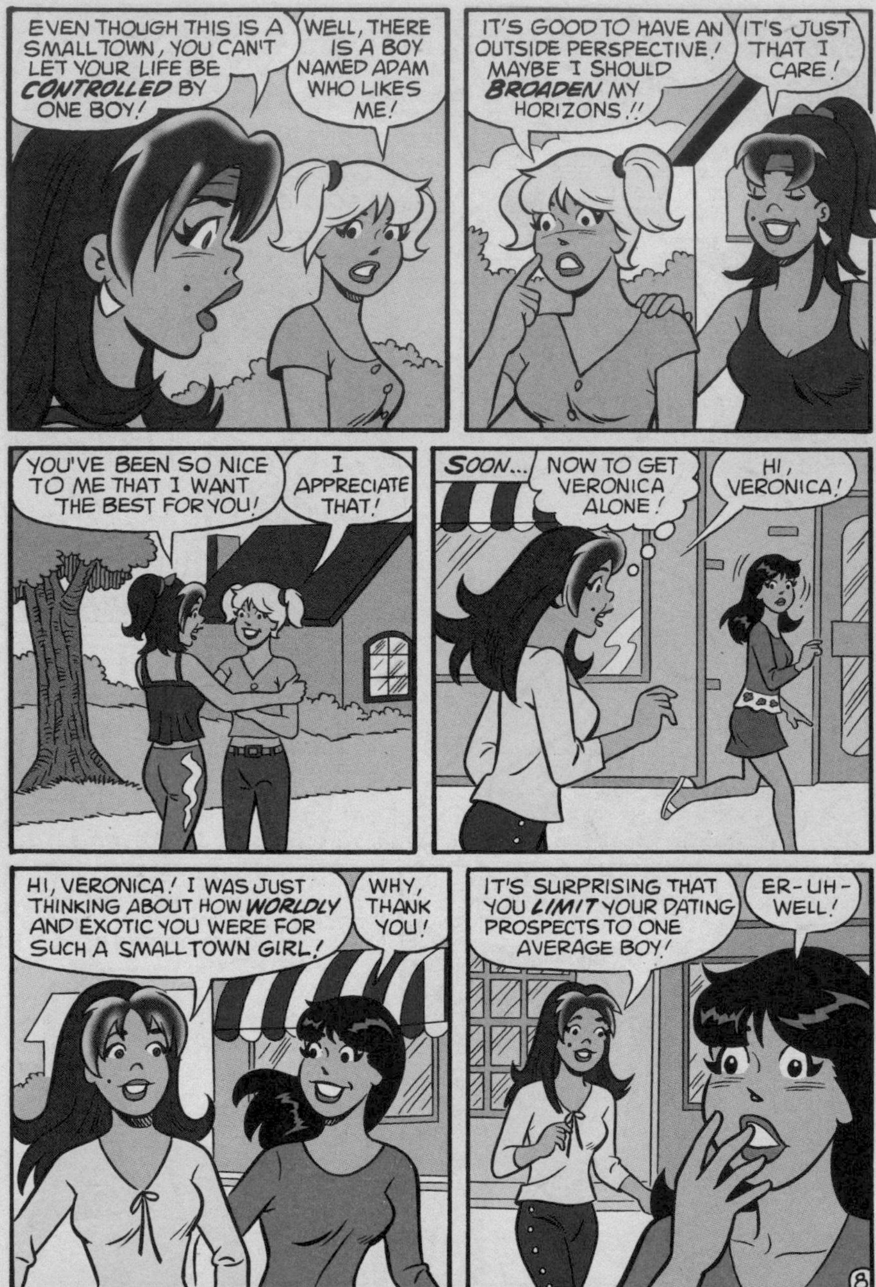
EVEN THOUGH THIS IS A SMALLTOWN, YOU CAN'T LET YOUR LIFE BE CONTROLLED BY ONE BOY!
WELL, THERE IS A BOY NAMED ADAM WHO LIKES ME!
IT'S GOOD TO HAVE AN OUTSIDE PERSPECTIVE! MAYBE I SHOULD BROADEN MY HORIZONS!!
IT'S JUST THAT I CARE!
YOU'VE BEEN SO NICE TO ME THAT I WANT THE BEST FOR YOU!
I APPRECIATE THAT!
SOON...
NOW TO GET VERONICA ALONE!
HI, VERONICA!
HI, VERONICA! I WAS JUST THINKING ABOUT HOW WORLDLY AND EXOTIC YOU WERE FOR SUCH A SMALLTOWN GIRL!
WHY, THANK YOU!
IT'S SURPRISING THAT YOU LIMIT YOUR DATING PROSPECTS TO ONE AVERAGE BOY!
ER-UH-WELL!
8

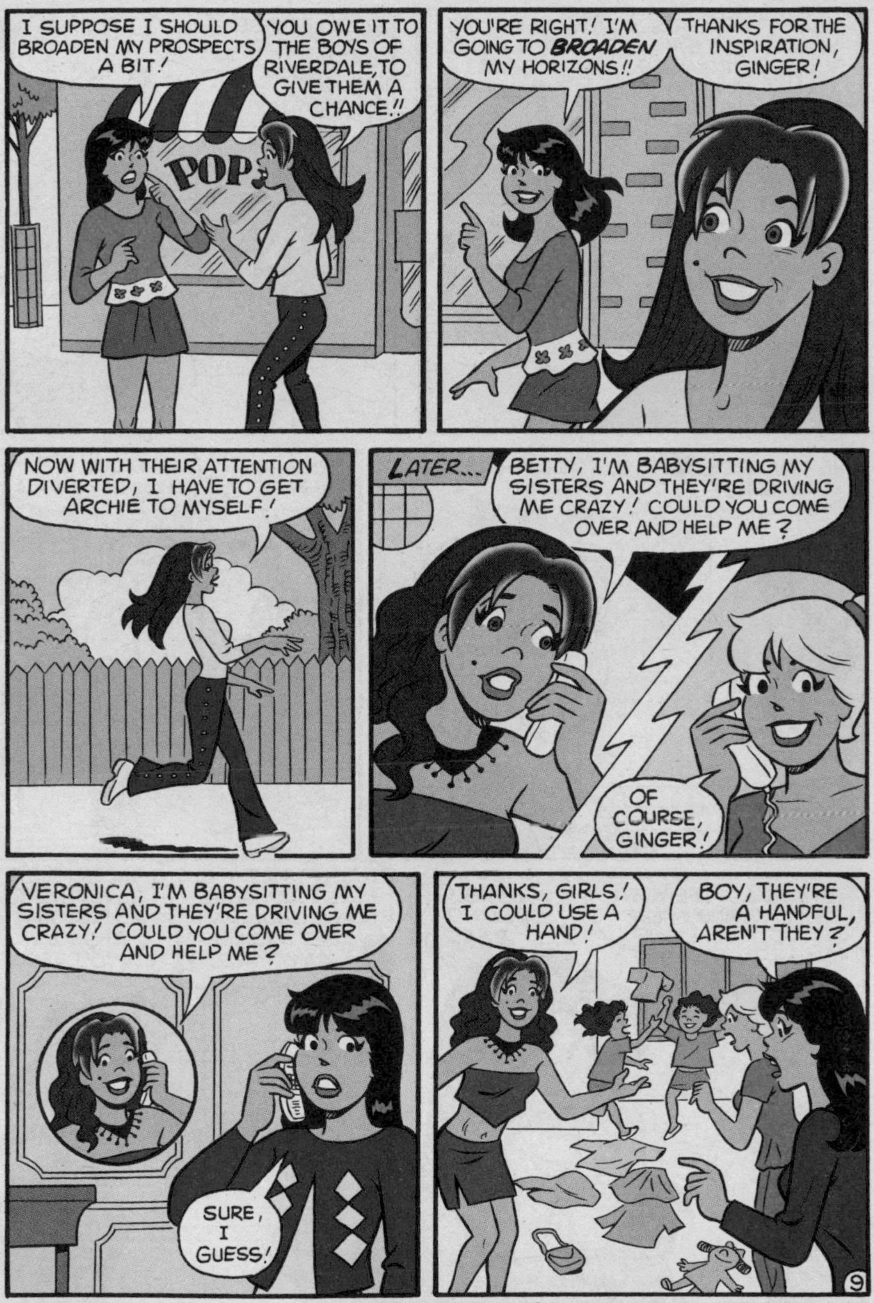
I SUPPOSE I SHOULD BROADEN MY PROSPECTS A BIT!
YOU OWE IT TO THE BOYS OF RIVERDALE, TO GIVE THEM A CHANCE!!
POP
YOU'RE RIGHT! I'M GOING TO BROADEN MY HORIZONS!!
THANKS FOR THE INSPIRATION, GINGER!
NOW WITH THEIR ATTENTION DIVERTED, I HAVE TO GET ARCHIE TO MYSELF!
LATER...
BETTY, I'M BABYSITTING MY SISTERS AND THEY'RE DRIVING ME CRAZY! COULD YOU COME OVER AND HELP ME?
OF COURSE, GINGER!
VERONICA, I'M BABYSITTING MY SISTERS AND THEY'RE DRIVING ME CRAZY! COULD YOU COME OVER AND HELP ME?
SURE, I GUESS!
THANKS, GIRLS! I COULD USE A HAND!
BOY, THEY'RE A HANDFUL, AREN'T THEY?
9

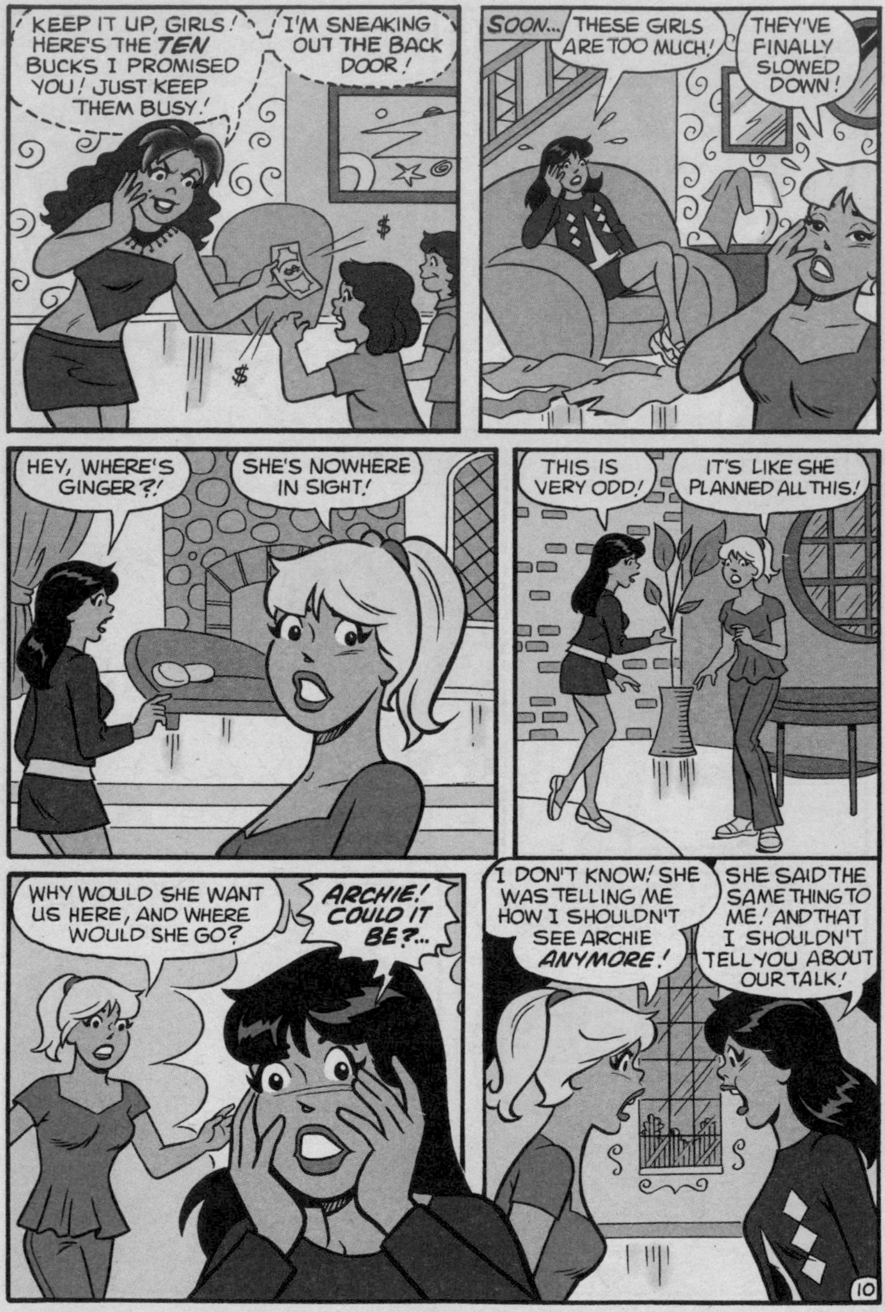
KEEP IT UP, GIRLS! HERE'S THE TEN BUCKS I PROMISED YOU! JUST KEEP THEM BUSY!
I'M SNEAKING OUT THE BACK DOOR!
SOON...
THESE GIRLS ARE TOO MUCH!
THEY'VE FINALLY SLOWED DOWN!
HEY, WHERE'S GINGER?!
SHE'S NOWHERE IN SIGHT!
THIS IS VERY ODD!
IT'S LIKE SHE PLANNED ALL THIS!
WHY WOULD SHE WANT US HERE, AND WHERE WOULD SHE GO?
ARCHIE! COULD IT BE?...
I DON'T KNOW! SHE WAS TELLING ME HOW I SHOULDN'T SEE ARCHIE ANYMORE!
SHE SAID THE SAME THING TO ME! AND THAT I SHOULDN'T TELL YOU ABOUT OUR TALK!
10

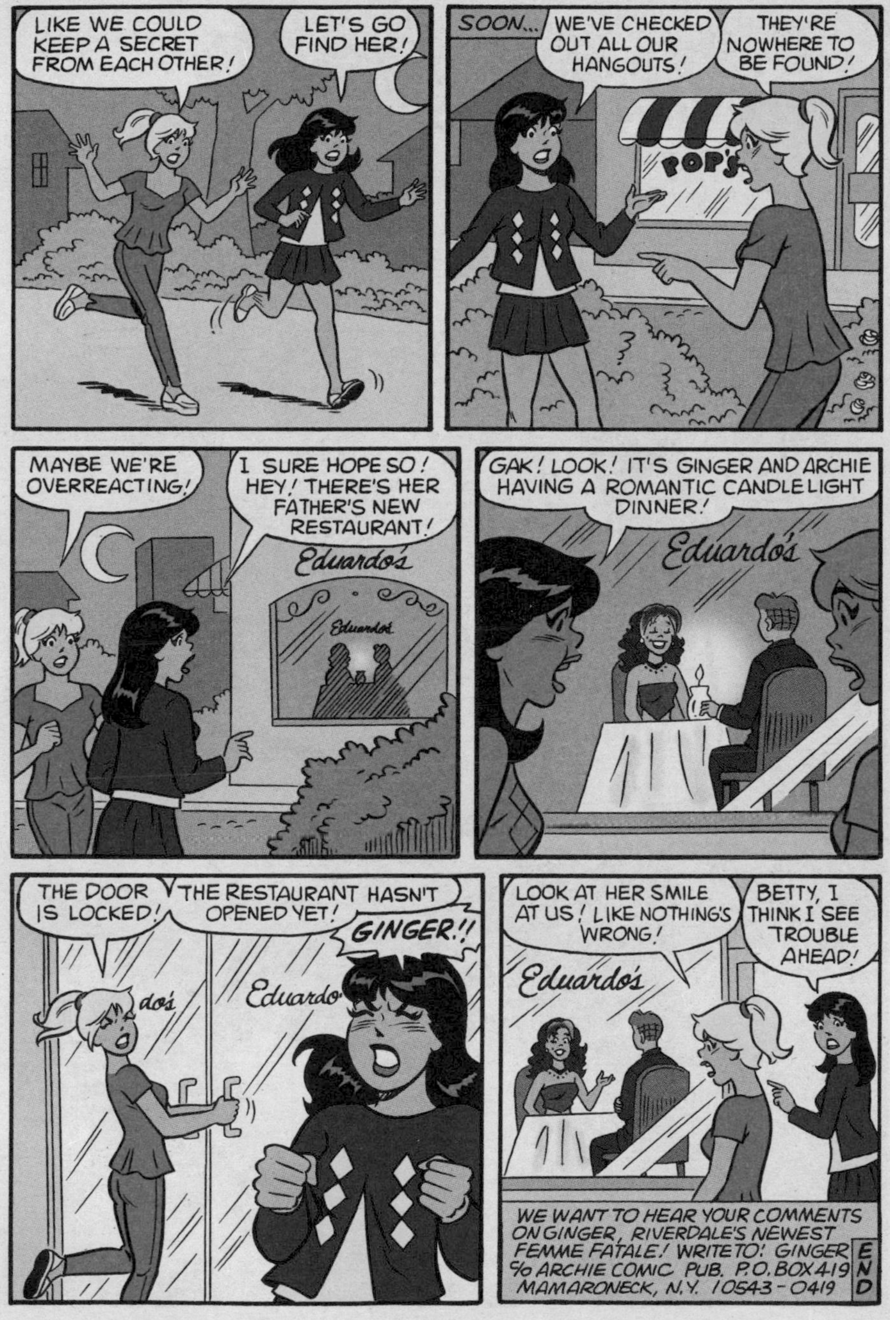
LIKE WE COULD KEEP A SECRET FROM EACH OTHER!
LET'S GO FIND HER!
SOON...
WE'VE CHECKED OUT ALL OUR HANGOUTS!
THEY'RE NOWHERE TO BE FOUND!
POP'S
MAYBE WE'RE OVERREACTING!
I SURE HOPE SO! HEY! THERE'S HER FATHER'S NEW RESTAURANT!
Eduardo's
GAK! LOOK! IT'S GINGER AND ARCHIE HAVING A ROMANTIC CANDLE LIGHT DINNER!
Eduardo's
THE DOOR IS LOCKED!
THE RESTAURANT HASN'T OPENED YET!
GINGER!!
LOOK AT HER SMILE AT US! LIKE NOTHING'S WRONG!
BETTY, I THINK I SEE TROUBLE AHEAD!
Eduardo's
WE WANT TO HEAR YOUR COMMENTS ON GINGER, RIVERDALE'S NEWEST FEMME FATALE! WRITE TO: GINGER % ARCHIE COMIC PUB. P.O. BOX 419 MAMARONECK, N.Y. 10543-0419
END

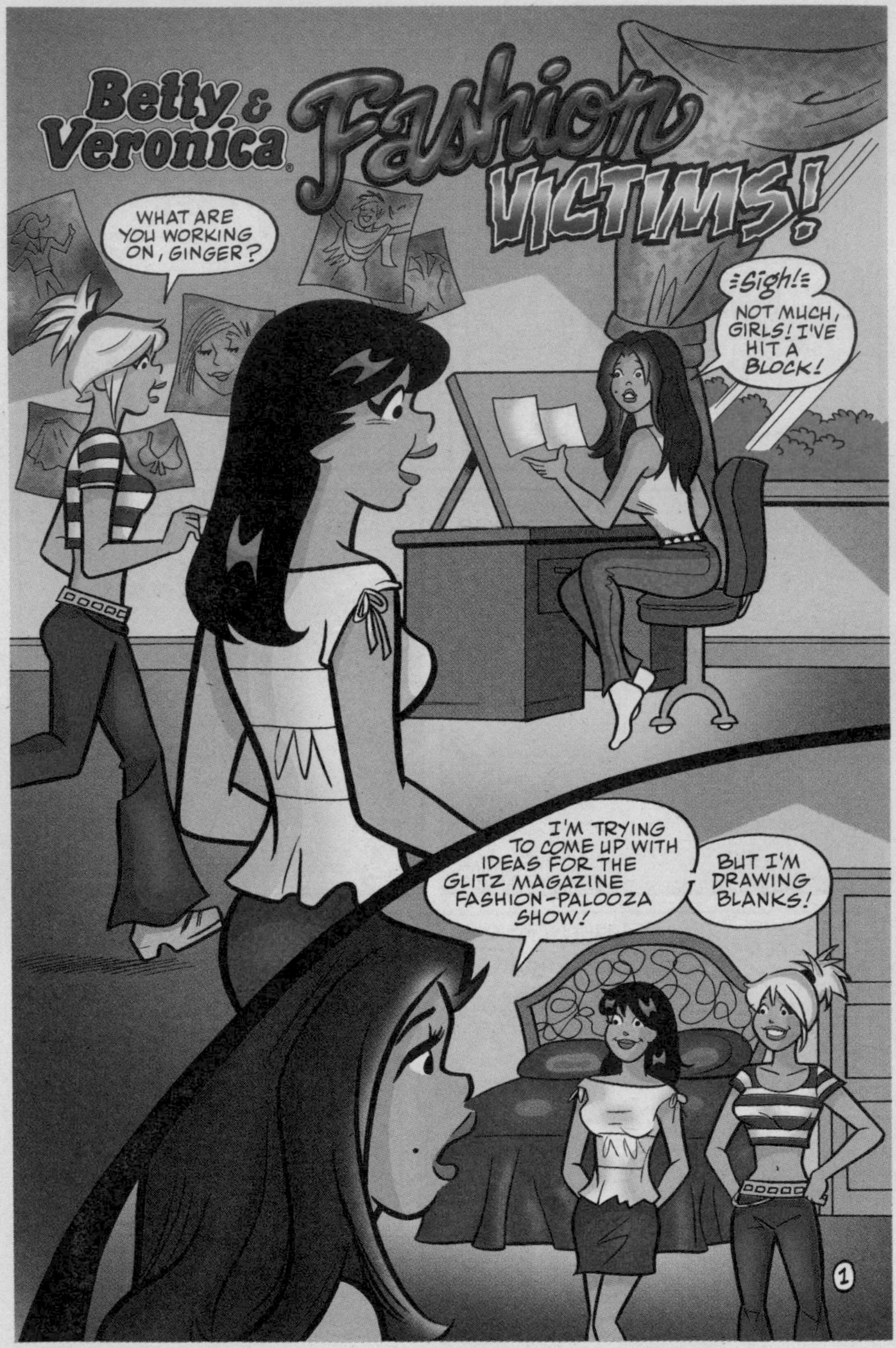

Betty & Veronica
Fashion VICTIMS!
WHAT ARE YOU WORKING ON, GINGER?
Sigh! NOT MUCH, GIRLS! I'VE HIT A BLOCK!
I'M TRYING TO COME UP WITH IDEAS FOR THE GLITZ MAGAZINE FASHION-PALOOZA SHOW!
BUT I'M DRAWING BLANKS!
1

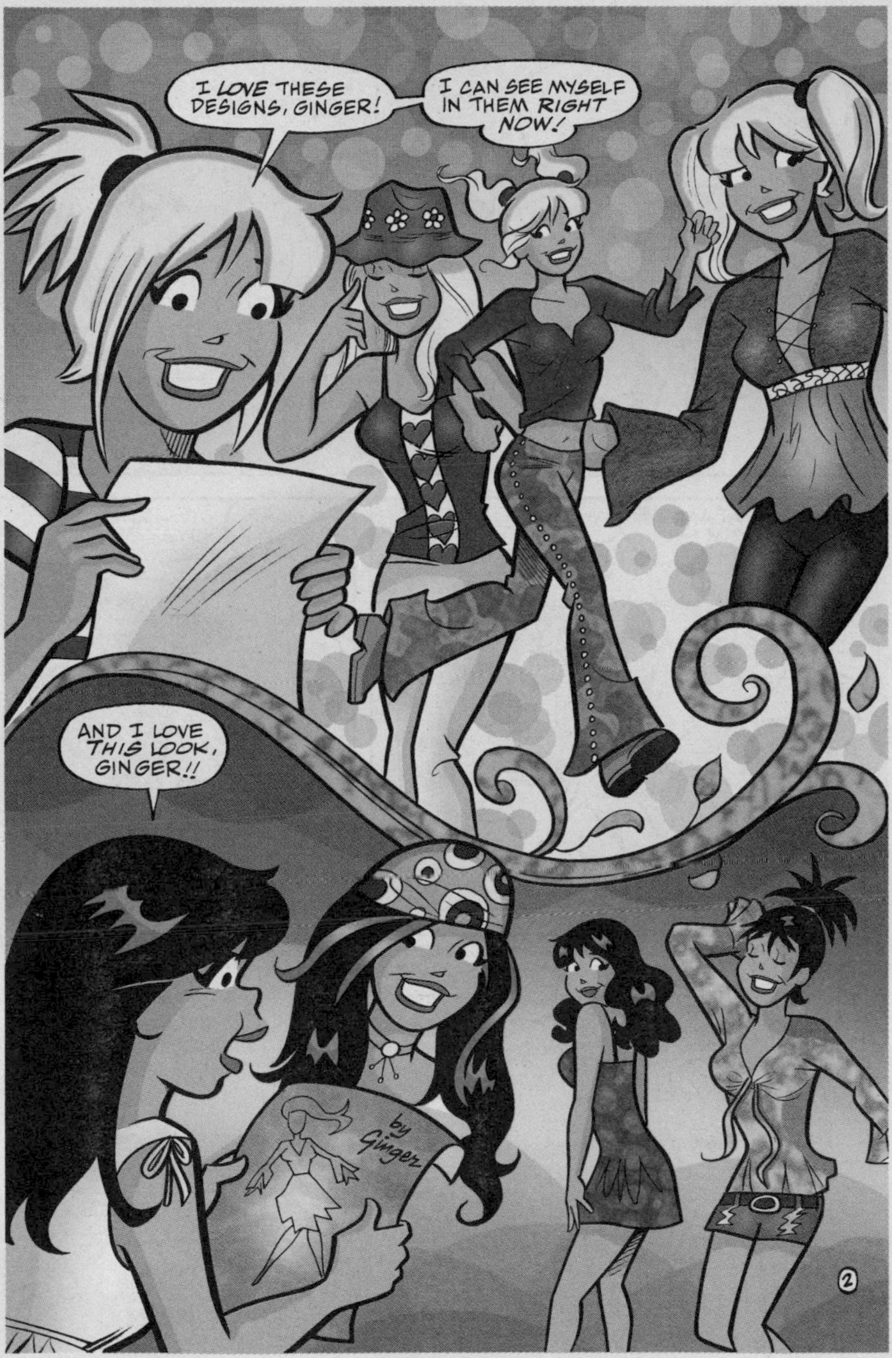
I LOVE THESE DESIGNS, GINGER!
I CAN SEE MYSELF IN THEM RIGHT NOW!
AND I LOVE THIS LOOK, GINGER!!
by Ginger
2

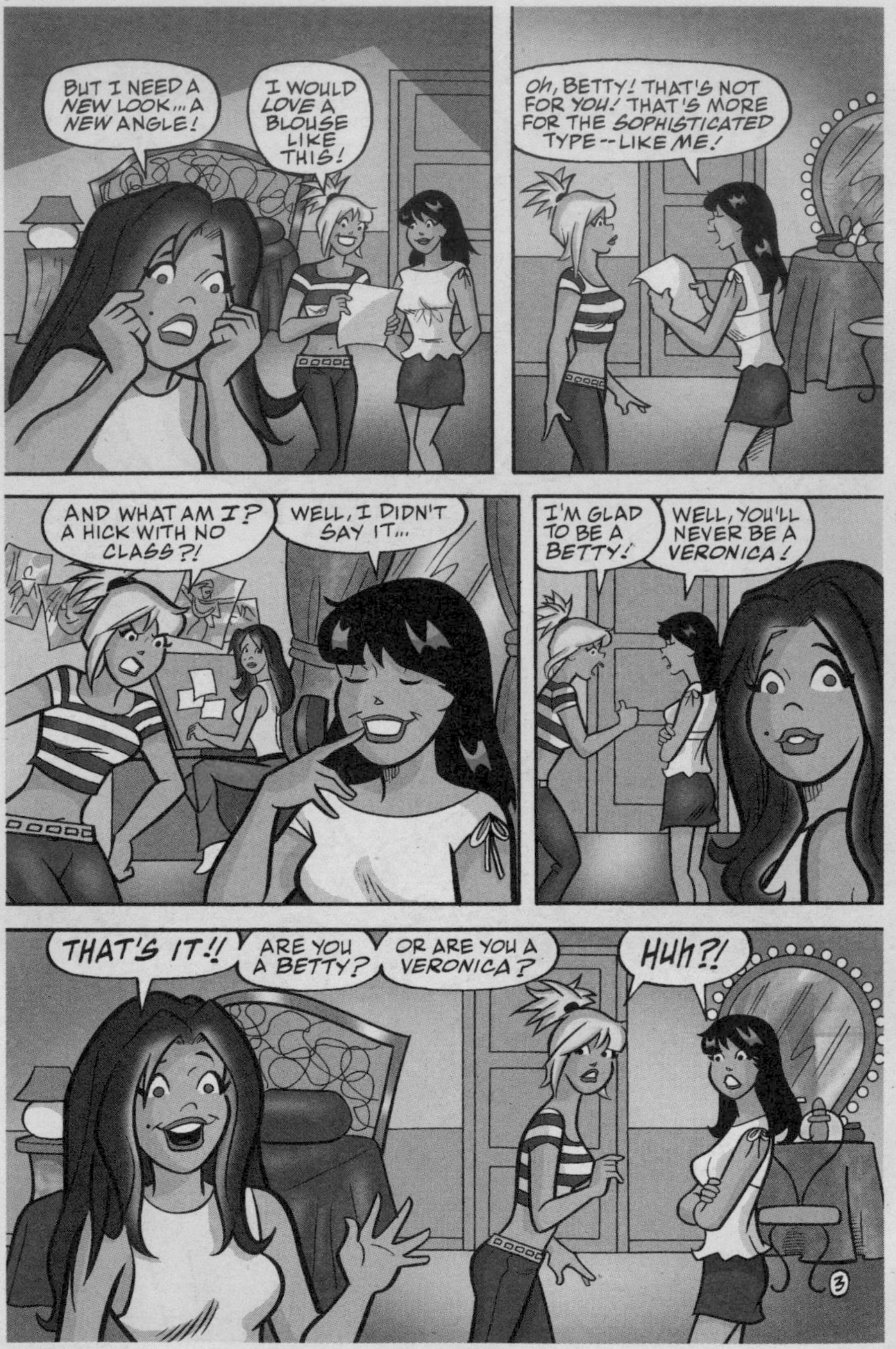
BUT I NEED A NEW LOOK... A NEW ANGLE!
I WOULD LOVE A BLOUSE LIKE THIS!
Oh, BETTY! THAT'S NOT FOR YOU! THAT'S MORE FOR THE SOPHISTICATED TYPE -- LIKE ME!
AND WHAT AM I? A HICK WITH NO CLASS?!
WELL, I DIDN'T SAY IT...
I'M GLAD TO BE A BETTY!
WELL, YOU'LL NEVER BE A VERONICA!
THAT'S IT!!
ARE YOU A BETTY?
OR ARE YOU A VERONICA?
Huh?!
3

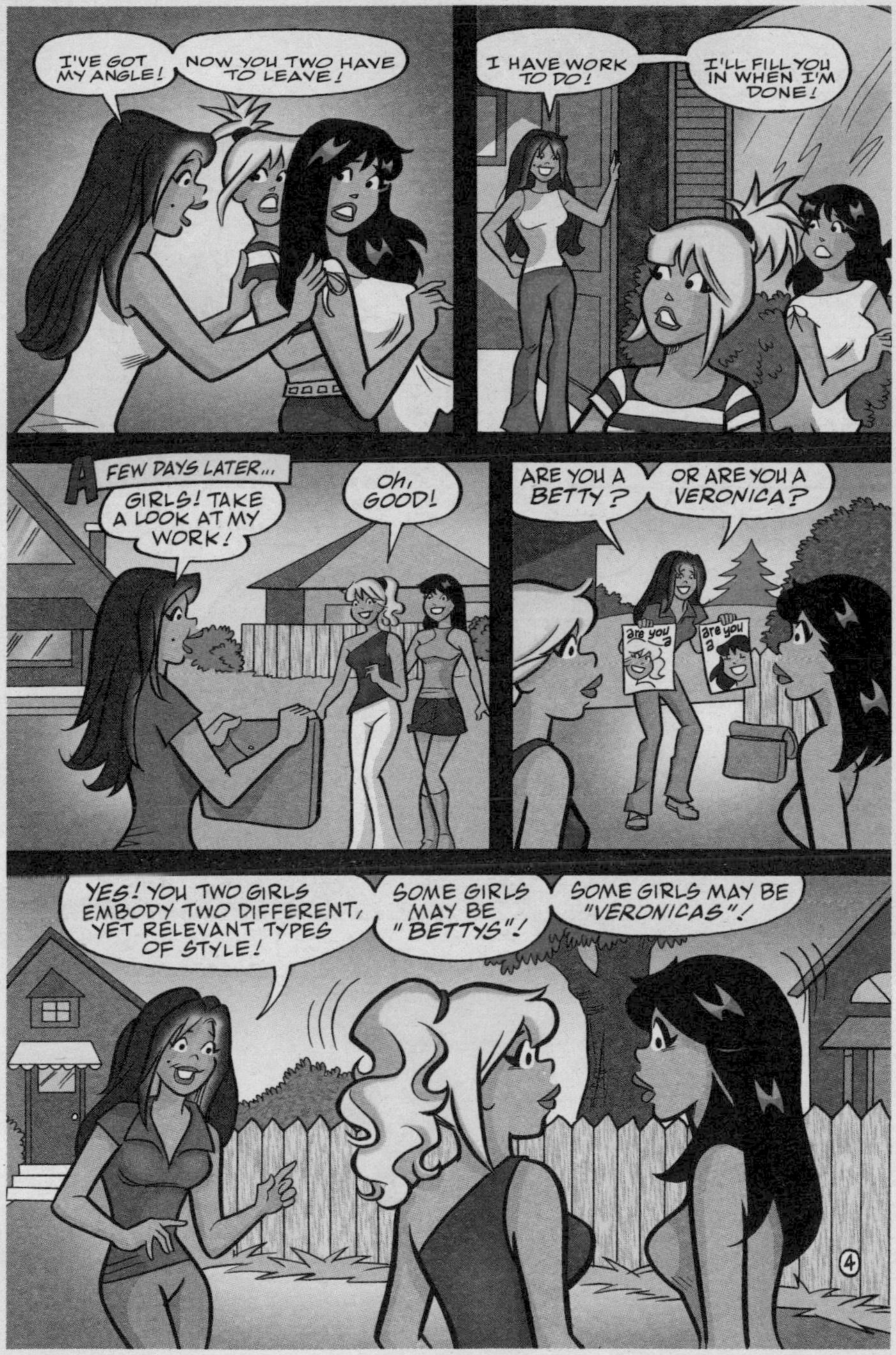
I'VE GOT MY ANGLE!
NOW YOU TWO HAVE TO LEAVE!
I HAVE WORK TO DO!
I'LL FILL YOU IN WHEN I'M DONE!
A FEW DAYS LATER...
GIRLS! TAKE A LOOK AT MY WORK!
Oh, GOOD!
ARE YOU A BETTY?
OR ARE YOU A VERONICA?
are you a
are you a
YES! YOU TWO GIRLS EMBODY TWO DIFFERENT, YET RELEVANT TYPES OF STYLE!
SOME GIRLS MAY BE "BETTYS"!
SOME GIRLS MAY BE "VERONICAS"!
4

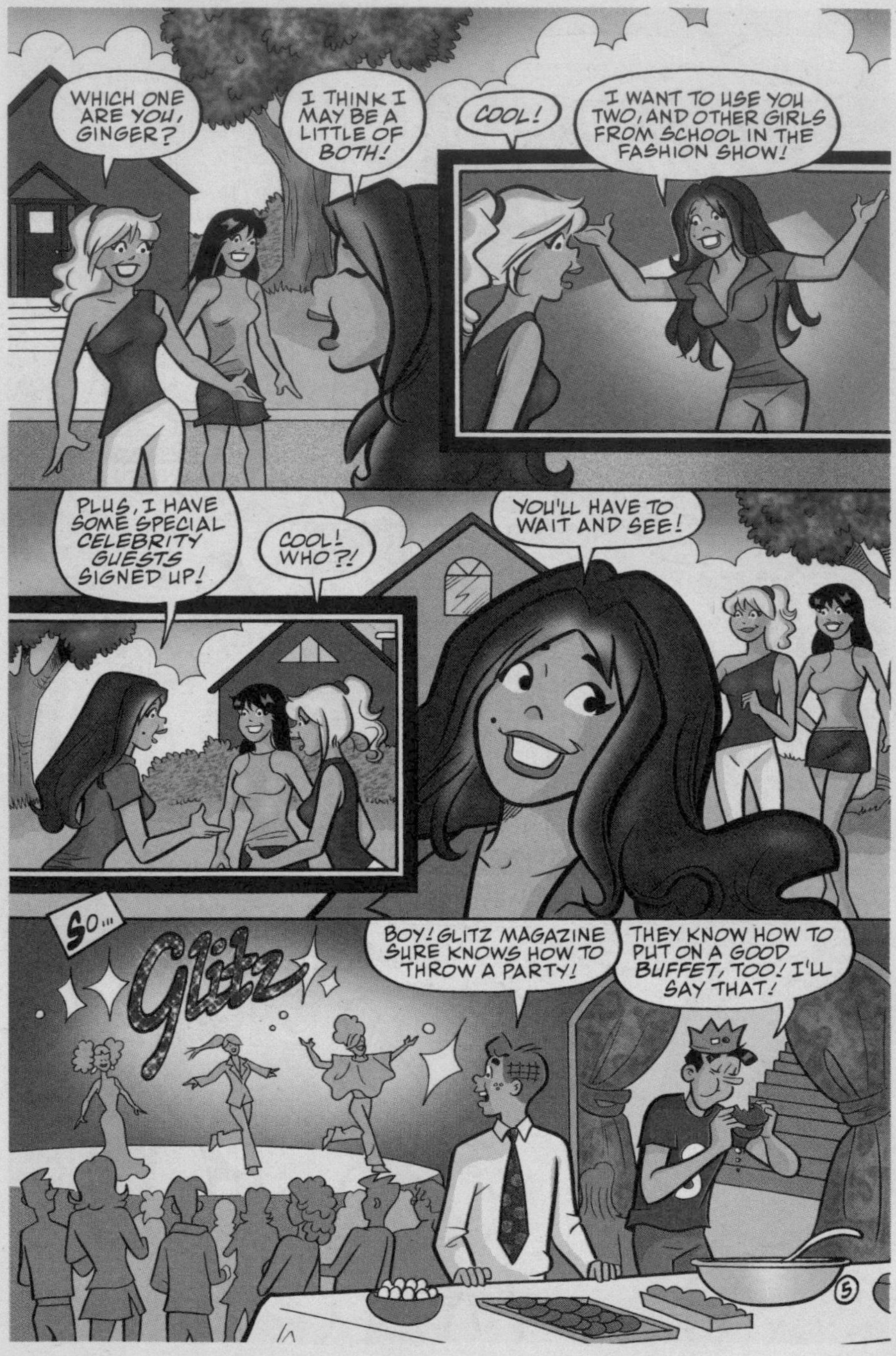
WHICH ONE ARE YOU, GINGER?
I THINK I MAY BE A LITTLE OF BOTH!
COOL!
I WANT TO USE YOU TWO, AND OTHER GIRLS FROM SCHOOL IN THE FASHION SHOW!
PLUS, I HAVE SOME SPECIAL CELEBRITY GUESTS SIGNED UP!
COOL! WHO?!
YOU'LL HAVE TO WAIT AND SEE!
SO...
Glitz
BOY! GLITZ MAGAZINE SURE KNOWS HOW TO THROW A PARTY!
THEY KNOW HOW TO PUT ON A GOOD BUFFET, TOO! I'LL SAY THAT!
5

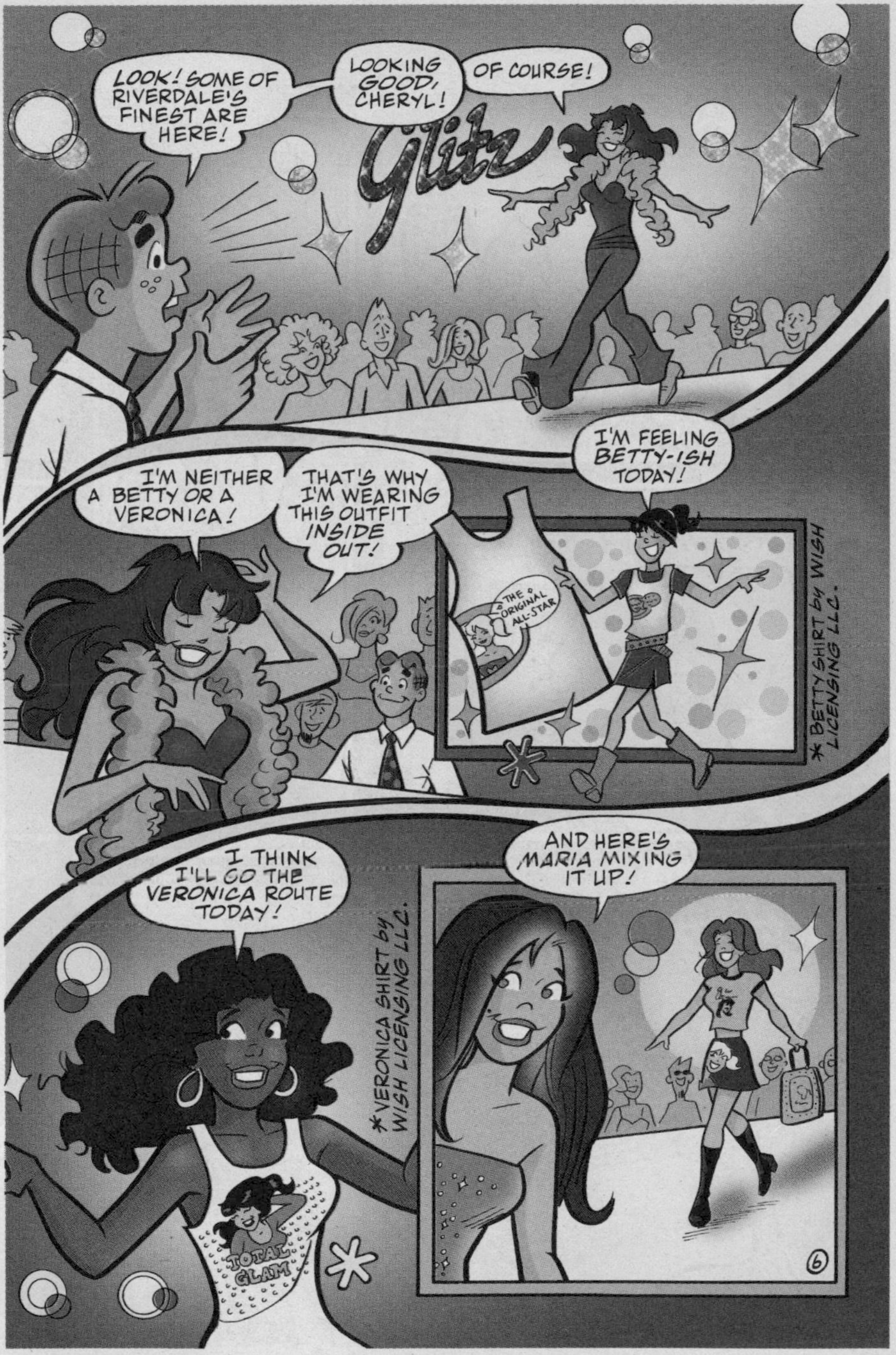
LOOK! SOME OF RIVERDALE'S FINEST ARE HERE!
LOOKING GOOD, CHERYL!
OF COURSE!
Glitz
I'M NEITHER A BETTY OR A VERONICA!
THAT'S WHY I'M WEARING THIS OUTFIT INSIDE OUT!
I'M FEELING BETTY-ISH TODAY!
THE ORIGINAL ALL-STAR
* BETTY SHIRT by WISH LICENSING LLC.
I THINK I'LL GO THE VERONICA ROUTE TODAY!
* VERONICA SHIRT by WISH LICENSING LLC.
TOTAL GLAM
AND HERE'S MARIA MIXING IT UP!
6

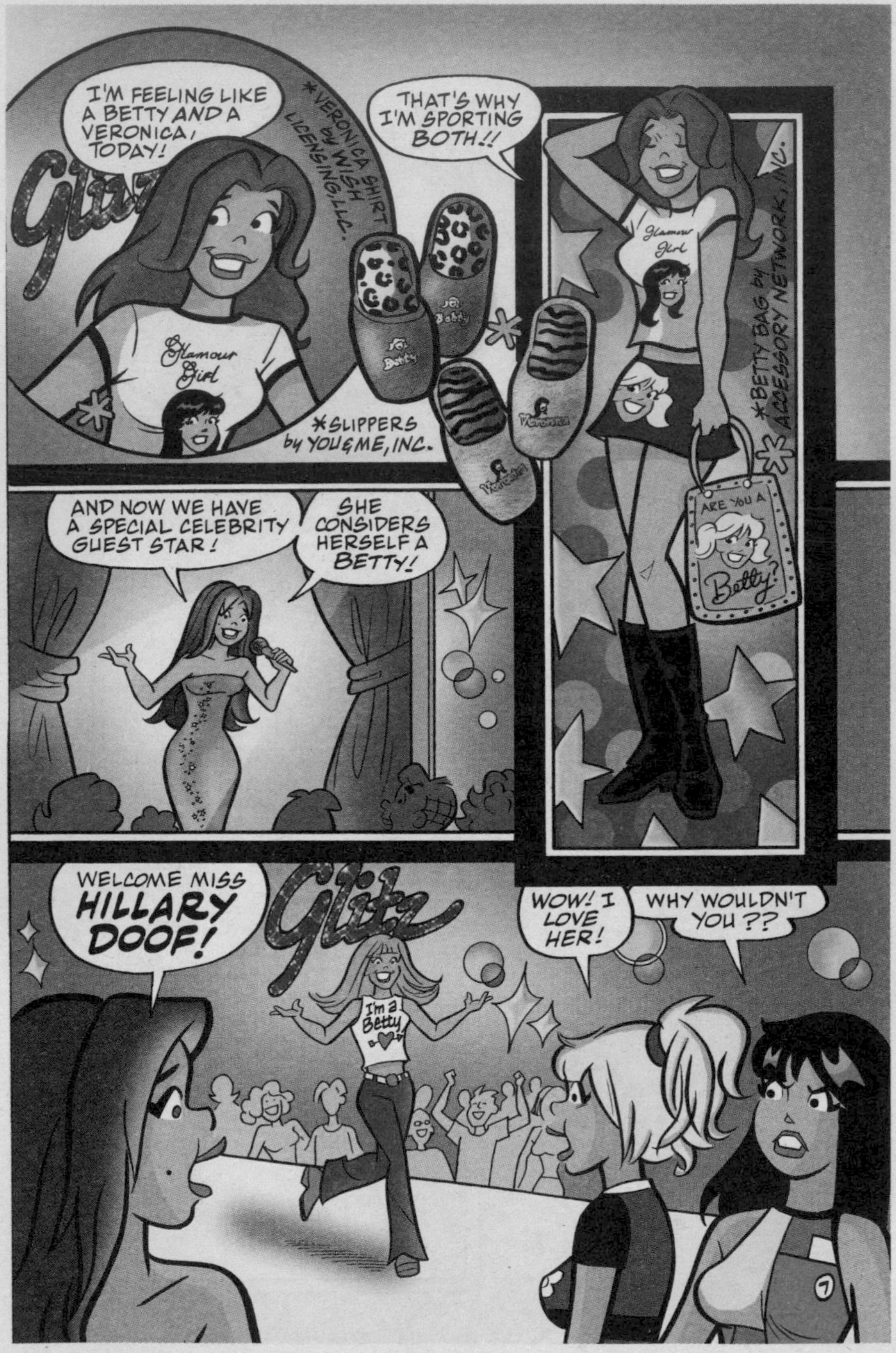
I'M FEELING LIKE A BETTY AND A VERONICA, TODAY!
*VERONICA SHIRT by WISH LICENSING, LLC.
THAT'S WHY I'M SPORTING BOTH!!
*SLIPPERS by YOU&ME, INC.
*BETTY BAG by ACCESSORY NETWORK, INC.
Glamour Girl
ARE YOU A Betty?
AND NOW WE HAVE A SPECIAL CELEBRITY GUEST STAR!
SHE CONSIDERS HERSELF A BETTY!
WELCOME MISS HILLARY DOOF!
Glitz
I'm a Betty
WOW! I LOVE HER!
WHY WOULDN'T YOU??

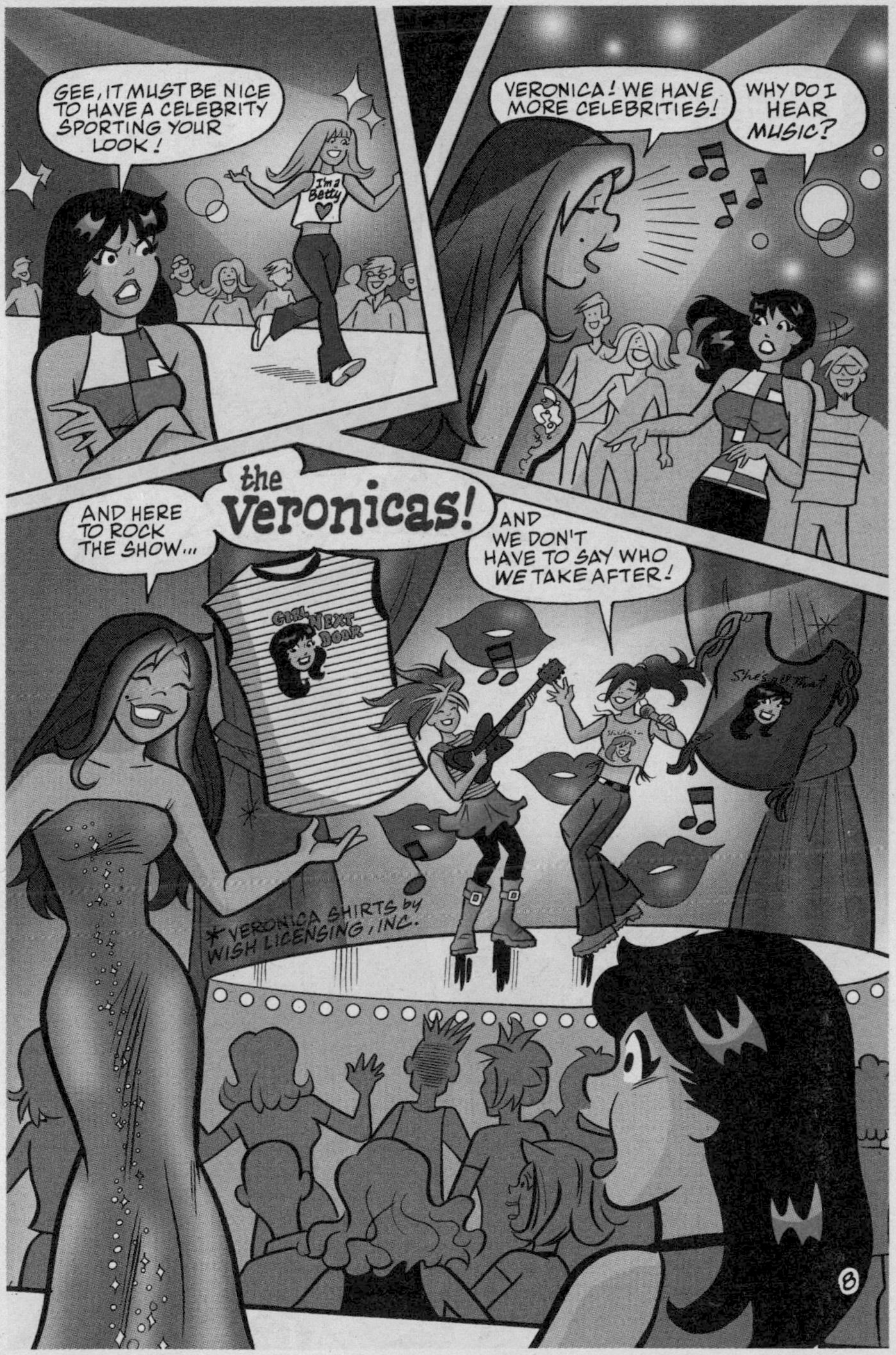
GEE, IT MUST BE NICE TO HAVE A CELEBRITY SPORTING YOUR LOOK!
I'm a Betty
VERONICA! WE HAVE MORE CELEBRITIES!
WHY DO I HEAR MUSIC?
AND HERE TO ROCK THE SHOW...
the Veronicas!
AND WE DON'T HAVE TO SAY WHO WE TAKE AFTER!
GIRL NEXT DOOR
* VERONICA SHIRTS by WISH LICENSING, INC.

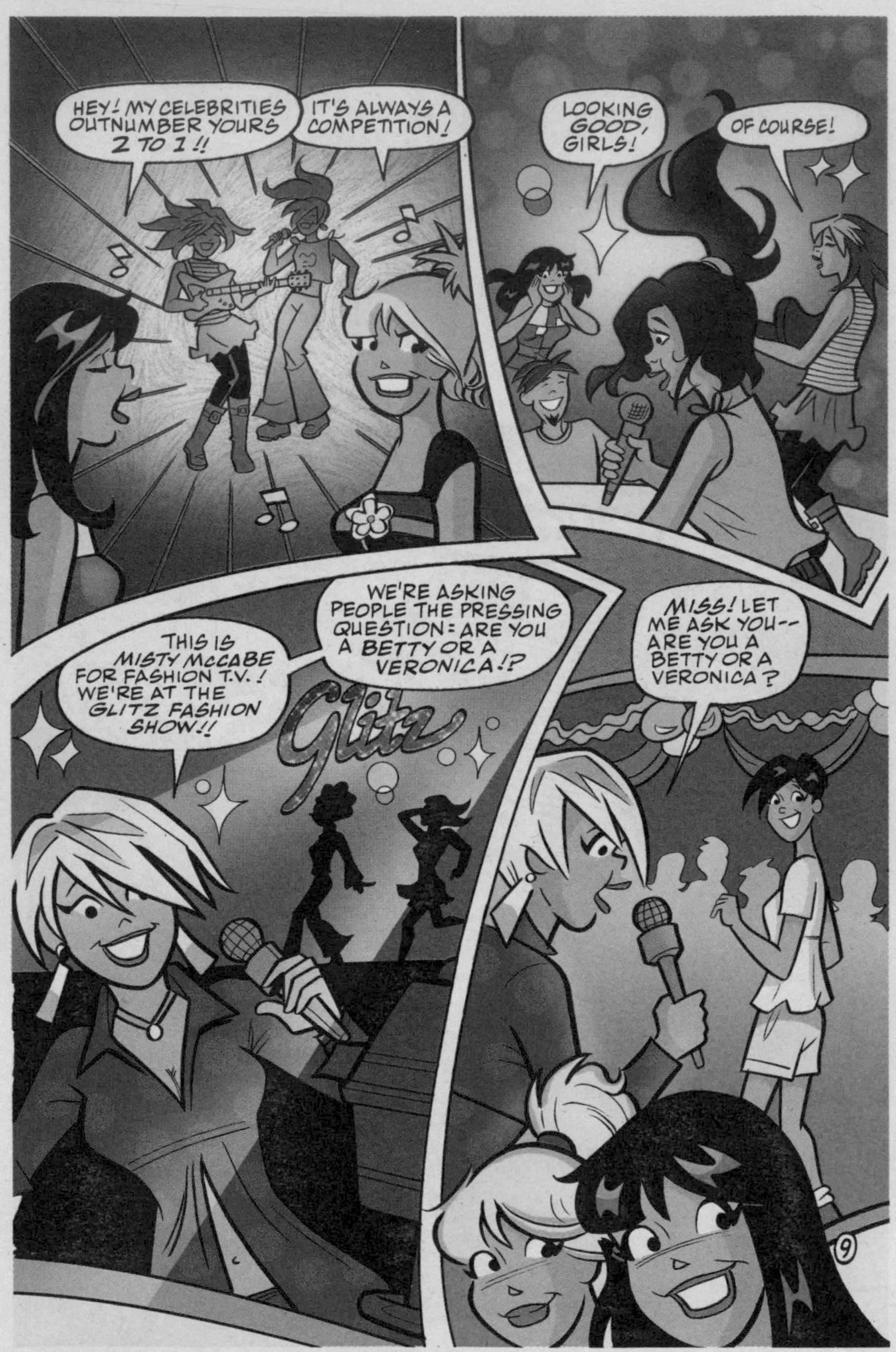
HEY! MY CELEBRITIES OUTNUMBER YOURS 2 TO 1!!
IT'S ALWAYS A COMPETITION!
LOOKING GOOD, GIRLS!
OF COURSE!
THIS IS MISTY McCABE FOR FASHION T.V.! WE'RE AT THE GLITZ FASHION SHOW!!
WE'RE ASKING PEOPLE THE PRESSING QUESTION: ARE YOU A BETTY OR A VERONICA!?
Glitz
MISS! LET ME ASK YOU-- ARE YOU A BETTY OR A VERONICA?

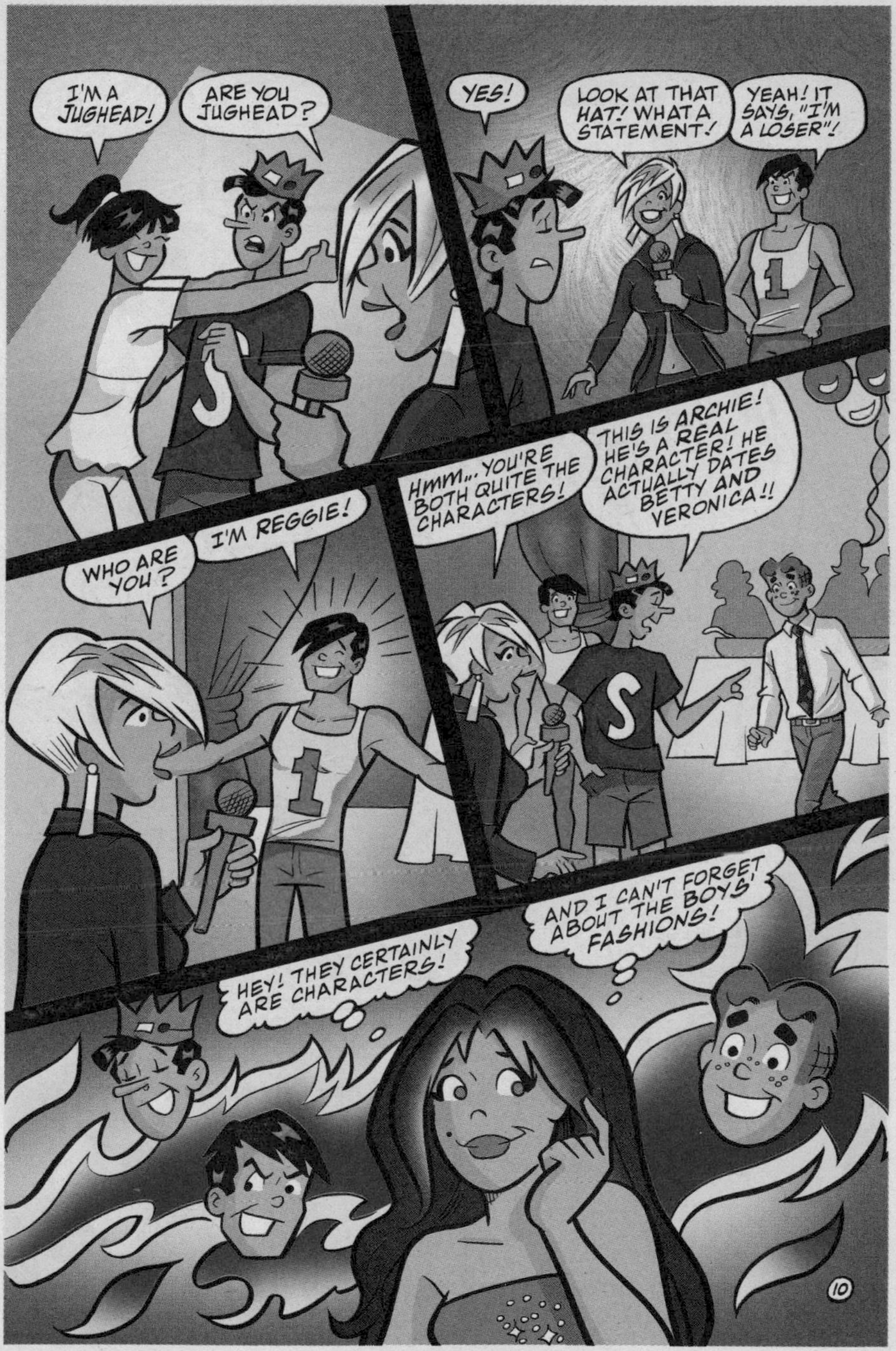
I'M A JUGHEAD!
ARE YOU JUGHEAD?
YES!
LOOK AT THAT HAT! WHAT A STATEMENT!
YEAH! IT SAYS, "I'M A LOSER"!
WHO ARE YOU?
I'M REGGIE!
Hmm... YOU'RE BOTH QUITE THE CHARACTERS!
THIS IS ARCHIE! HE'S A REAL CHARACTER! HE ACTUALLY DATES BETTY AND VERONICA!!
HEY! THEY CERTAINLY ARE CHARACTERS!
AND I CAN'T FORGET ABOUT THE BOYS' FASHIONS!
10

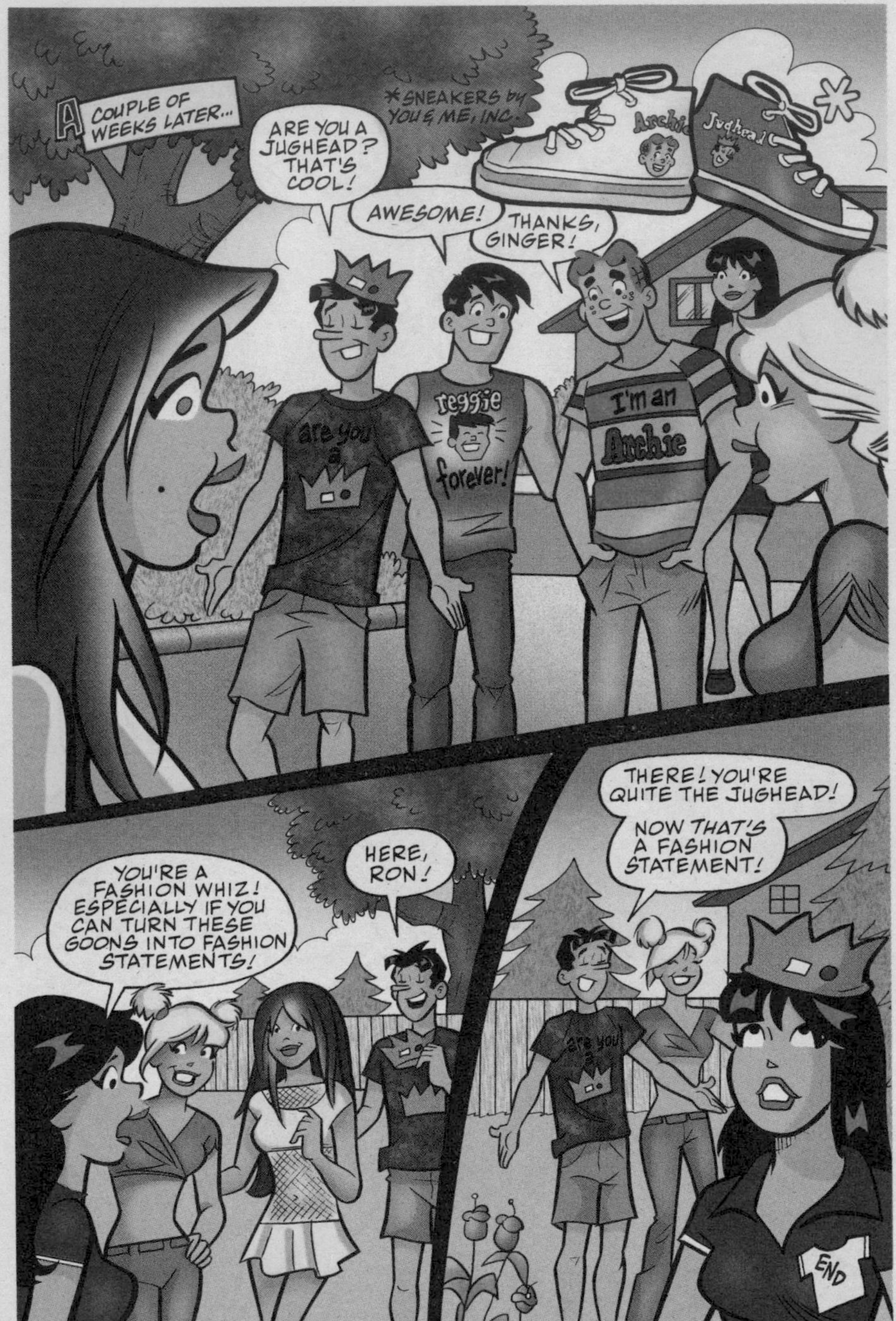
A COUPLE OF WEEKS LATER...
*SNEAKERS by YOU & ME, INC.
Archie
Jughead
ARE YOU A JUGHEAD? THAT'S COOL!
AWESOME!
THANKS, GINGER!
are you a
reggie forever!
I'm an Archie
YOU'RE A FASHION WHIZ! ESPECIALLY IF YOU CAN TURN THESE GOONS INTO FASHION STATEMENTS!
HERE, RON!
THERE! YOU'RE QUITE THE JUGHEAD!
NOW THAT'S A FASHION STATEMENT!
are you a
END

Double Take
Betty & Veronica
Digest #183, 2008
by Mike Pellowski, Jeff Shultz, Al Milgrom, Jack Morelli, Barry Grossman

The best Betty & Veronica stories are the ones where Betty asserts her dominance and doesn't let Veronica have the last word. "Double Take" is a perfect example of that. I mean, Betty calling Veronica a "Fashion Maven Misfit" might actually be my most favorite thing ever.

Also, now I really want to start a band called the "Fashion Maven Misfits," who's with me?

-- **Jamie Lee Rotante**
Editorial Assistant/Proofreader,
Archie Comics

Where The Action Is
Betty & Veronica
Spectacular #87, 2008
by Dan Parent, Rich Koslowski, Jack Morelli, Rosario "Tito" Peña

We all love spy-style action movies, another genre ripe for the picking when it comes to Betty and Veronica. Plus the girls look so cool in their slick spy outfits! It's always fun to do action-style stories, bringing in new characters... and some old. In this story we are revisited from a character from the past... way in the past: none other than Evelyn Evernever from the classic Little Archie comics. She returns with a vengeance, out to correct some wrongs from her past. The Archie universe is so big that it's fun to delve into the past and revisit old characters, and give them a new twist here and there! This was one of a few B&V spy girl-themed stories, and I'm already getting the feeling that we need to do more.

-- **Dan Parent**
Writer/Artist,
Archie Comics

Betty and Veronica in DOUBLE TAKE

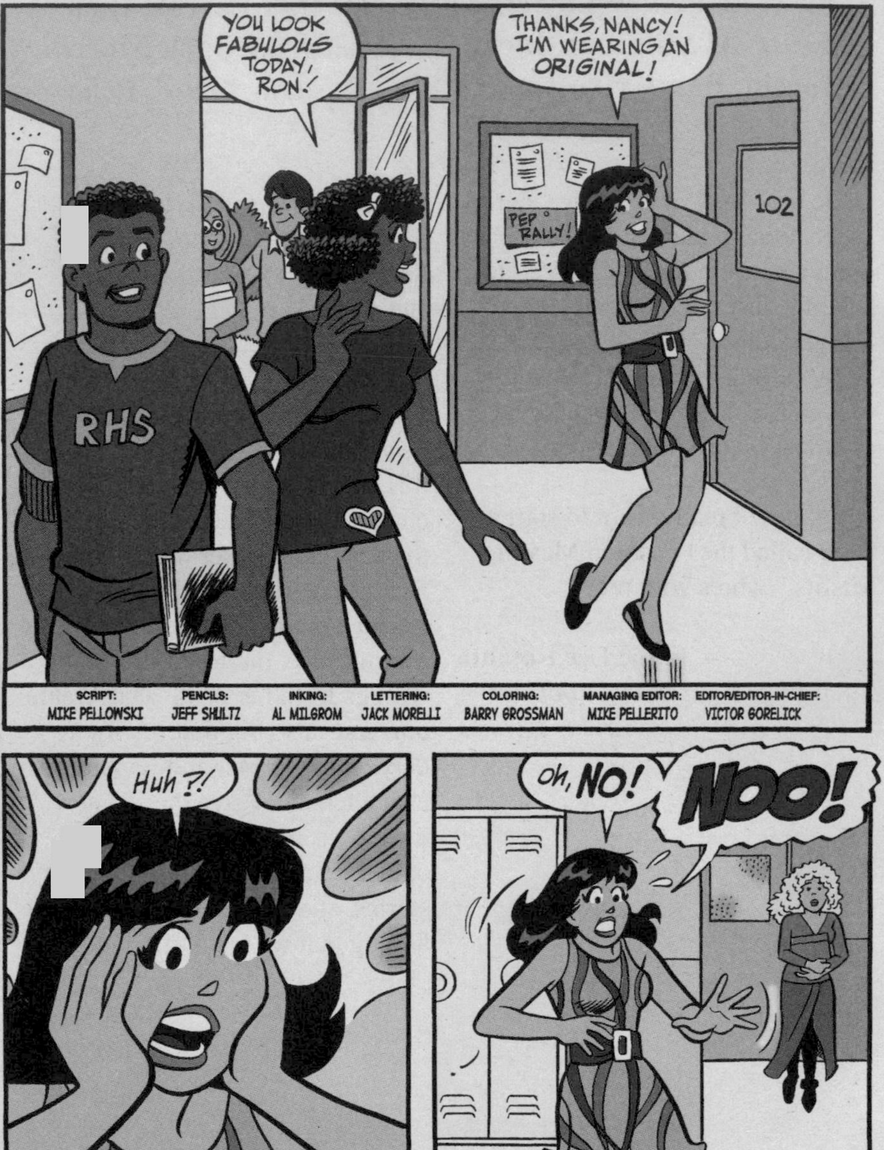
YOU LOOK FABULOUS TODAY, RON!
THANKS, NANCY! I'M WEARING AN ORIGINAL!
PEP RALLY!
102
RHS
SCRIPT: MIKE PELLOWSKI
PENCILS: JEFF SHULTZ
INKING: AL MILGROM
LETTERING: JACK MORELLI
COLORING: BARRY GROSSMAN
MANAGING EDITOR: MIKE PELLERITO
EDITOR/EDITOR-IN-CHIEF: VICTOR GORELICK
Huh?!
Oh, NO!
NOO!
1

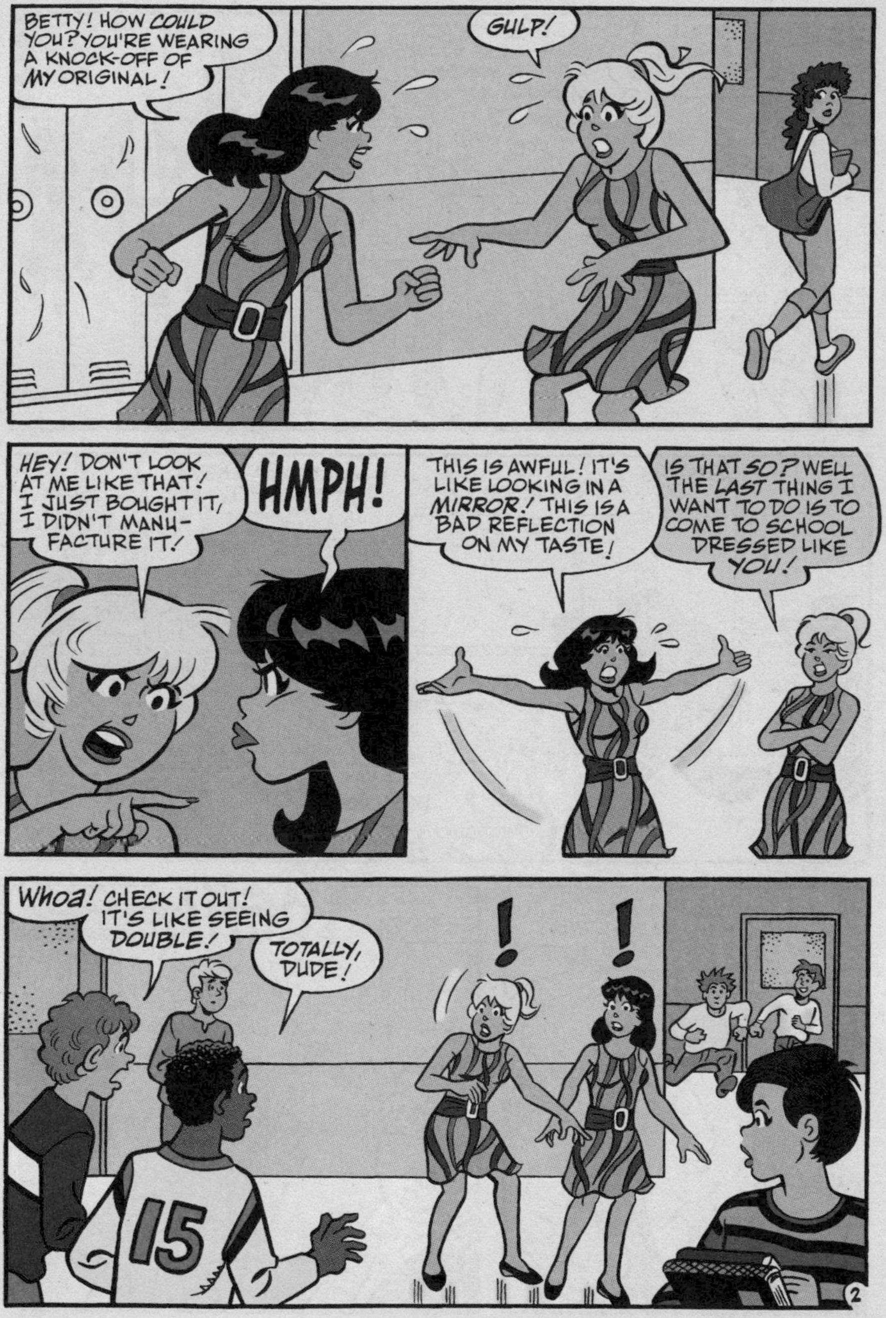
BETTY! HOW COULD YOU? YOU'RE WEARING A KNOCK-OFF OF MY ORIGINAL!
GULP!
HEY! DON'T LOOK AT ME LIKE THAT! I JUST BOUGHT IT, I DIDN'T MANU-FACTURE IT!
HMPH!
THIS IS AWFUL! IT'S LIKE LOOKING IN A MIRROR! THIS IS A BAD REFLECTION ON MY TASTE!
IS THAT SO? WELL THE LAST THING I WANT TO DO IS TO COME TO SCHOOL DRESSED LIKE YOU!
Whoa! CHECK IT OUT! IT'S LIKE SEEING DOUBLE!
TOTALLY, DUDE!
!
!
15
2

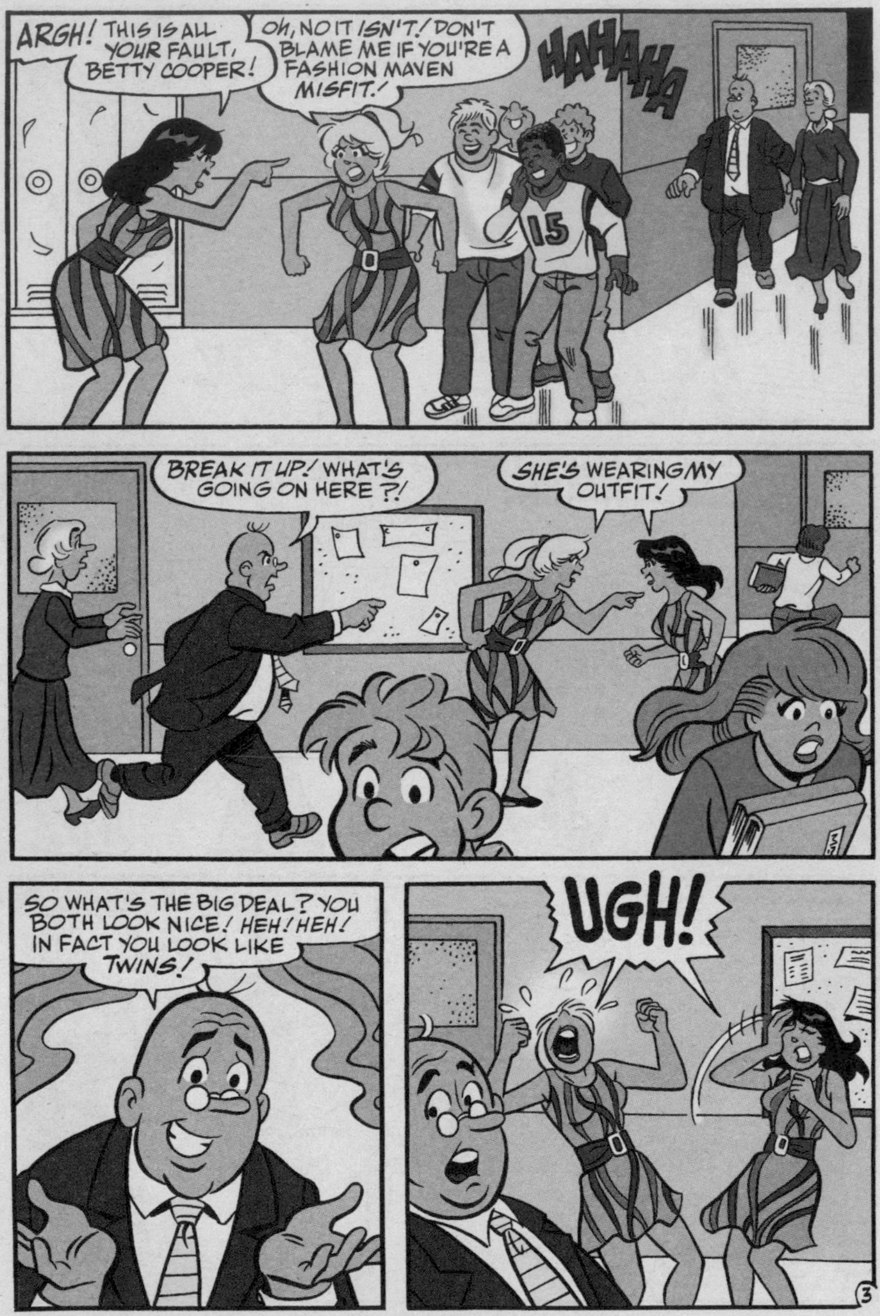
ARGH! THIS IS ALL YOUR FAULT, BETTY COOPER!
OH, NO IT ISN'T! DON'T BLAME ME IF YOU'RE A FASHION MAVEN MISFIT!
HAHAHA
15
BREAK IT UP! WHAT'S GOING ON HERE?!
SHE'S WEARING MY OUTFIT!
SO WHAT'S THE BIG DEAL? YOU BOTH LOOK NICE! HEH! HEH! IN FACT YOU LOOK LIKE TWINS!
UGH!
3

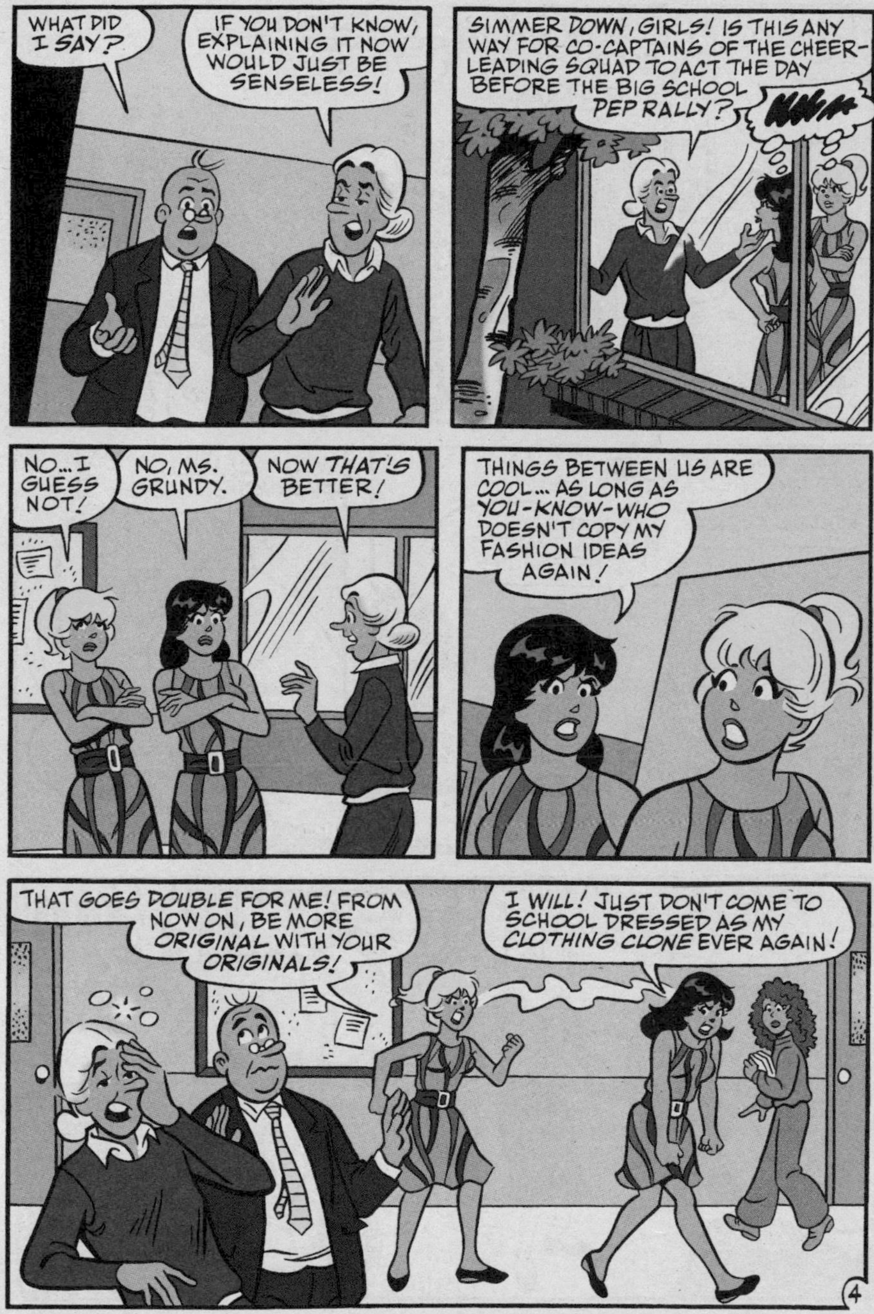
WHAT DID I SAY?
IF YOU DON'T KNOW, EXPLAINING IT NOW WOULD JUST BE SENSELESS!
SIMMER DOWN, GIRLS! IS THIS ANY WAY FOR CO-CAPTAINS OF THE CHEER-LEADING SQUAD TO ACT THE DAY BEFORE THE BIG SCHOOL PEP RALLY?
NO... I GUESS NOT!
NO, MS. GRUNDY.
NOW THAT'S BETTER!
THINGS BETWEEN US ARE COOL... AS LONG AS YOU-KNOW-WHO DOESN'T COPY MY FASHION IDEAS AGAIN!
THAT GOES DOUBLE FOR ME! FROM NOW ON, BE MORE ORIGINAL WITH YOUR ORIGINALS!
I WILL! JUST DON'T COME TO SCHOOL DRESSED AS MY CLOTHING CLONE EVER AGAIN!
4

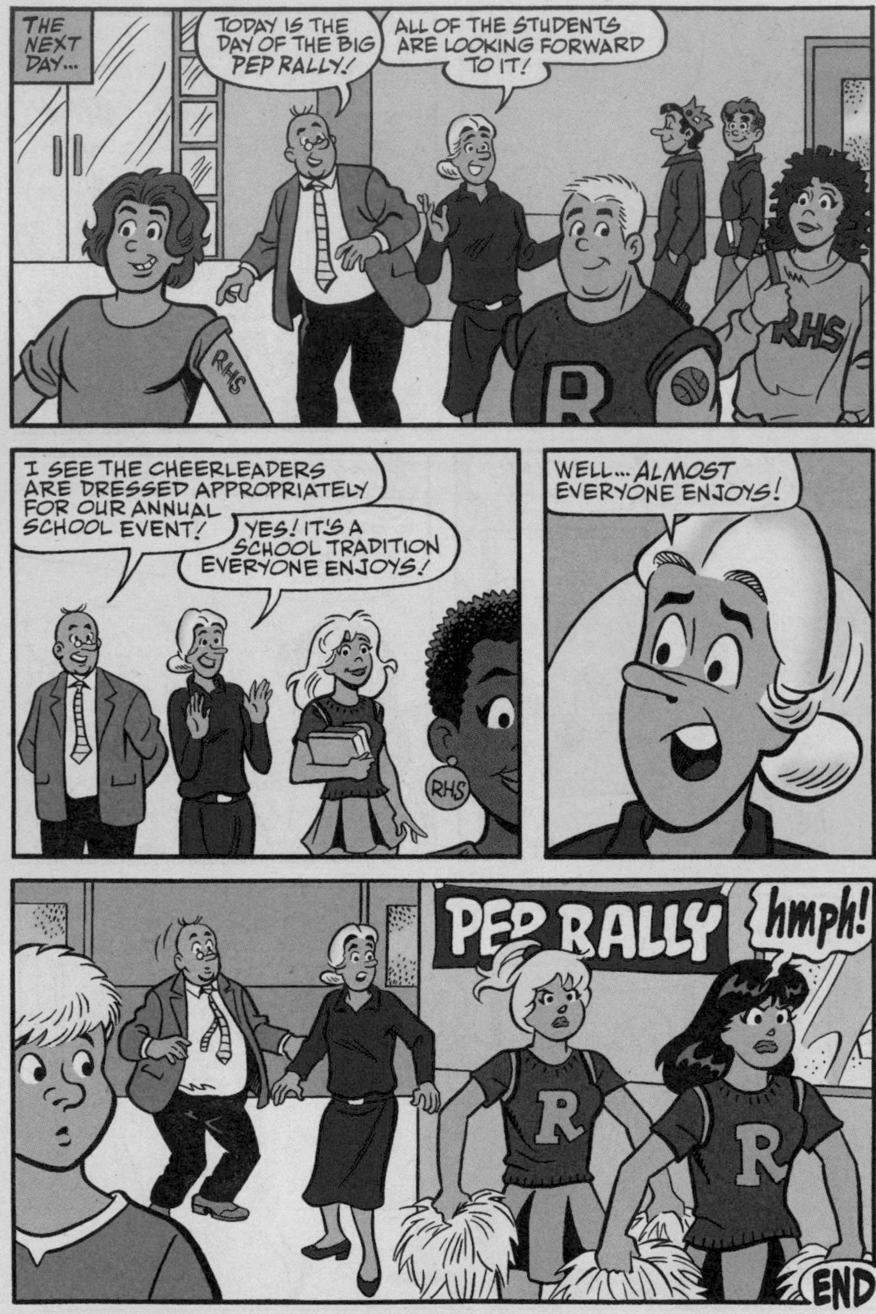
THE NEXT DAY...
TODAY IS THE DAY OF THE BIG PEP RALLY!
ALL OF THE STUDENTS ARE LOOKING FORWARD TO IT!
RHS
R
RHS
I SEE THE CHEERLEADERS ARE DRESSED APPROPRIATELY FOR OUR ANNUAL SCHOOL EVENT!
YES! IT'S A SCHOOL TRADITION EVERYONE ENJOYS!
RHS
WELL... ALMOST EVERYONE ENJOYS!
PEP RALLY
hmph!
R
R
END

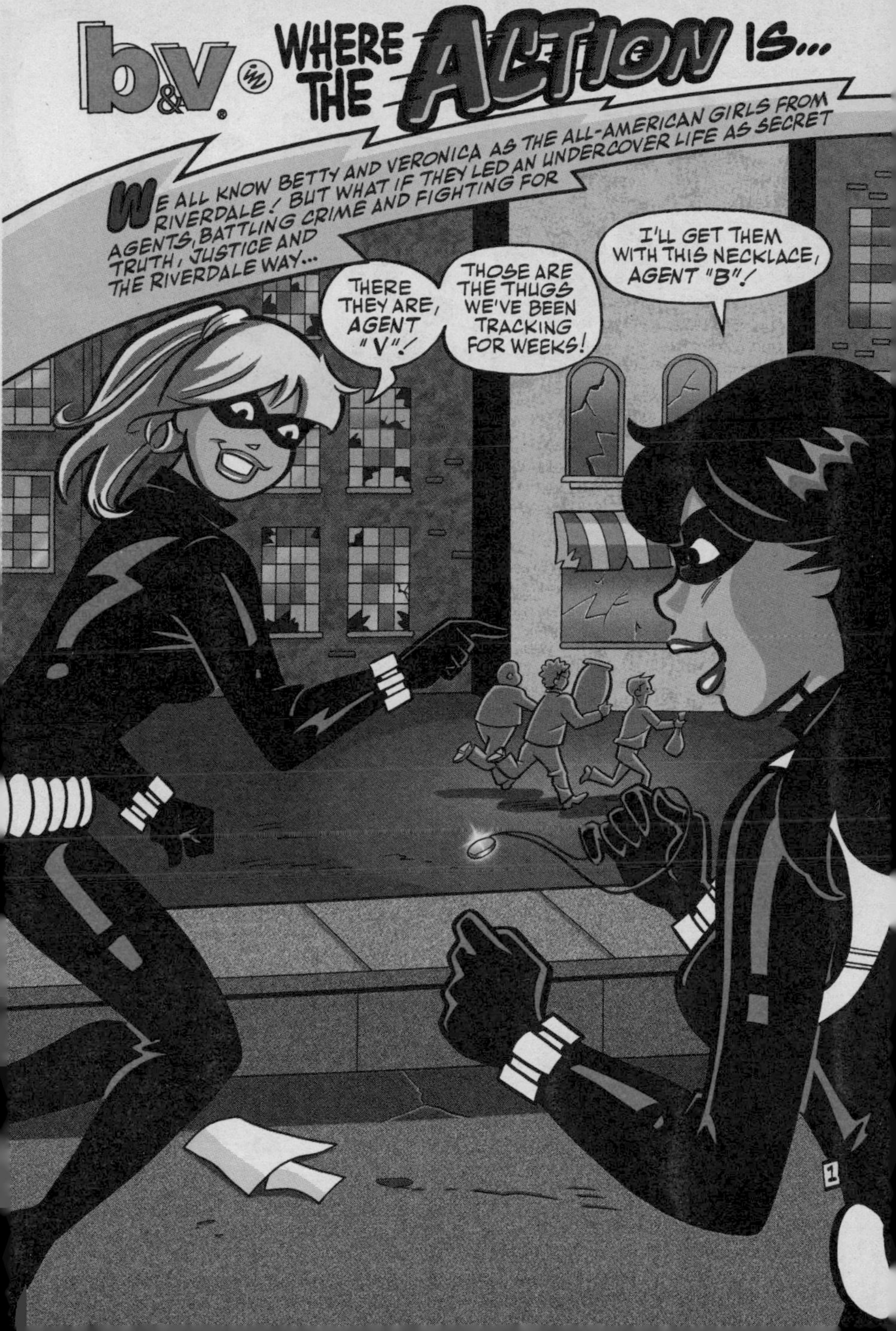

b&v
WHERE THE ACTION IS...
WE ALL KNOW BETTY AND VERONICA AS THE ALL-AMERICAN GIRLS FROM RIVERDALE! BUT WHAT IF THEY LED AN UNDERCOVER LIFE AS SECRET AGENTS, BATTLING CRIME AND FIGHTING FOR TRUTH, JUSTICE AND THE RIVERDALE WAY...
THERE THEY ARE, AGENT "V"!
THOSE ARE THE THUGS WE'VE BEEN TRACKING FOR WEEKS!
I'LL GET THEM WITH THIS NECKLACE, AGENT "B"!
1

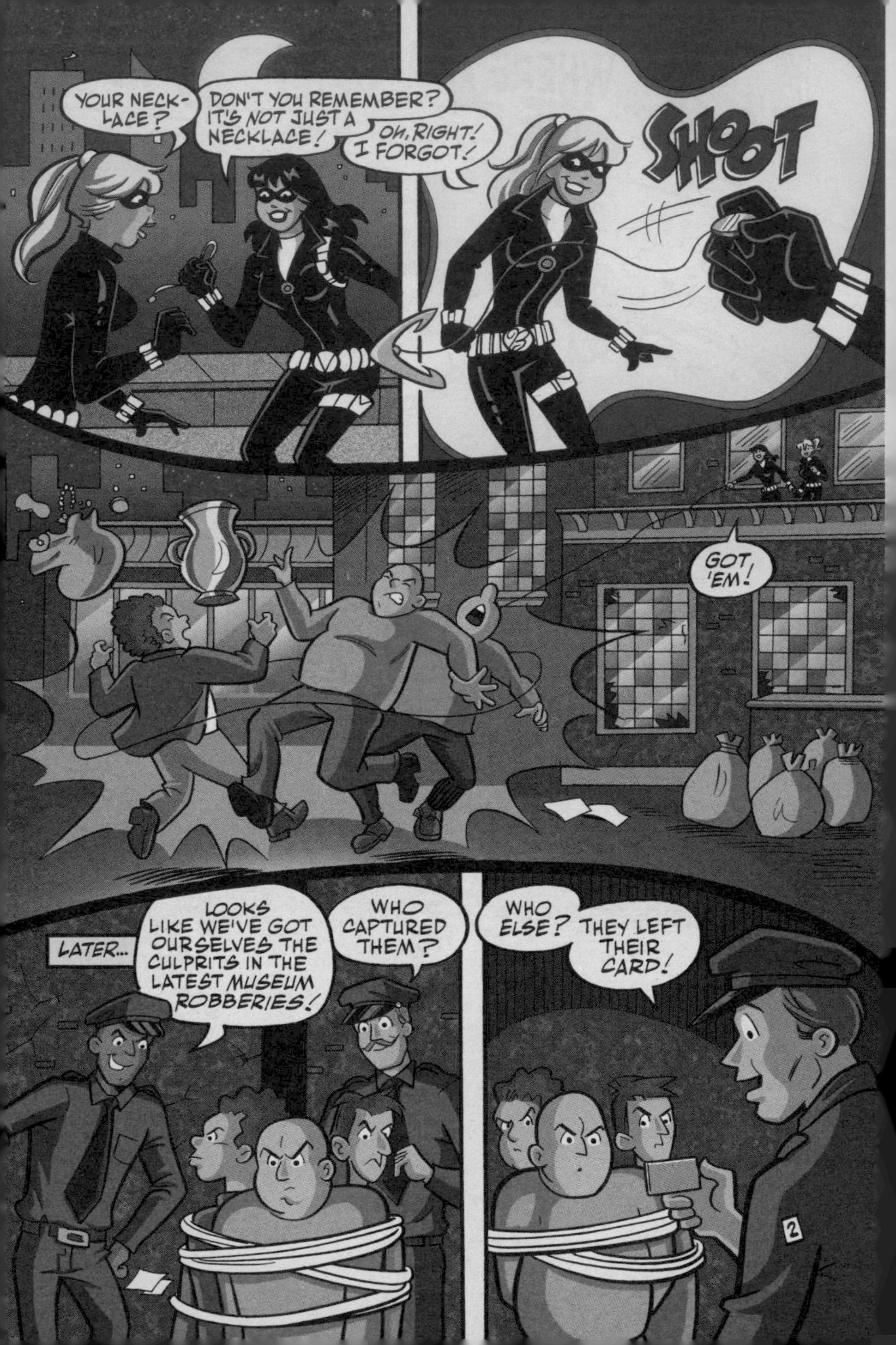

YOUR NECK-LACE?
DON'T YOU REMEMBER? IT'S NOT JUST A NECKLACE!
OH, RIGHT! I FORGOT!
SHOOT
GOT 'EM!
LATER...
LOOKS LIKE WE'VE GOT OURSELVES THE CULPRITS IN THE LATEST MUSEUM ROBBERIES!
WHO CAPTURED THEM?
WHO ELSE? THEY LEFT THEIR CARD!
2

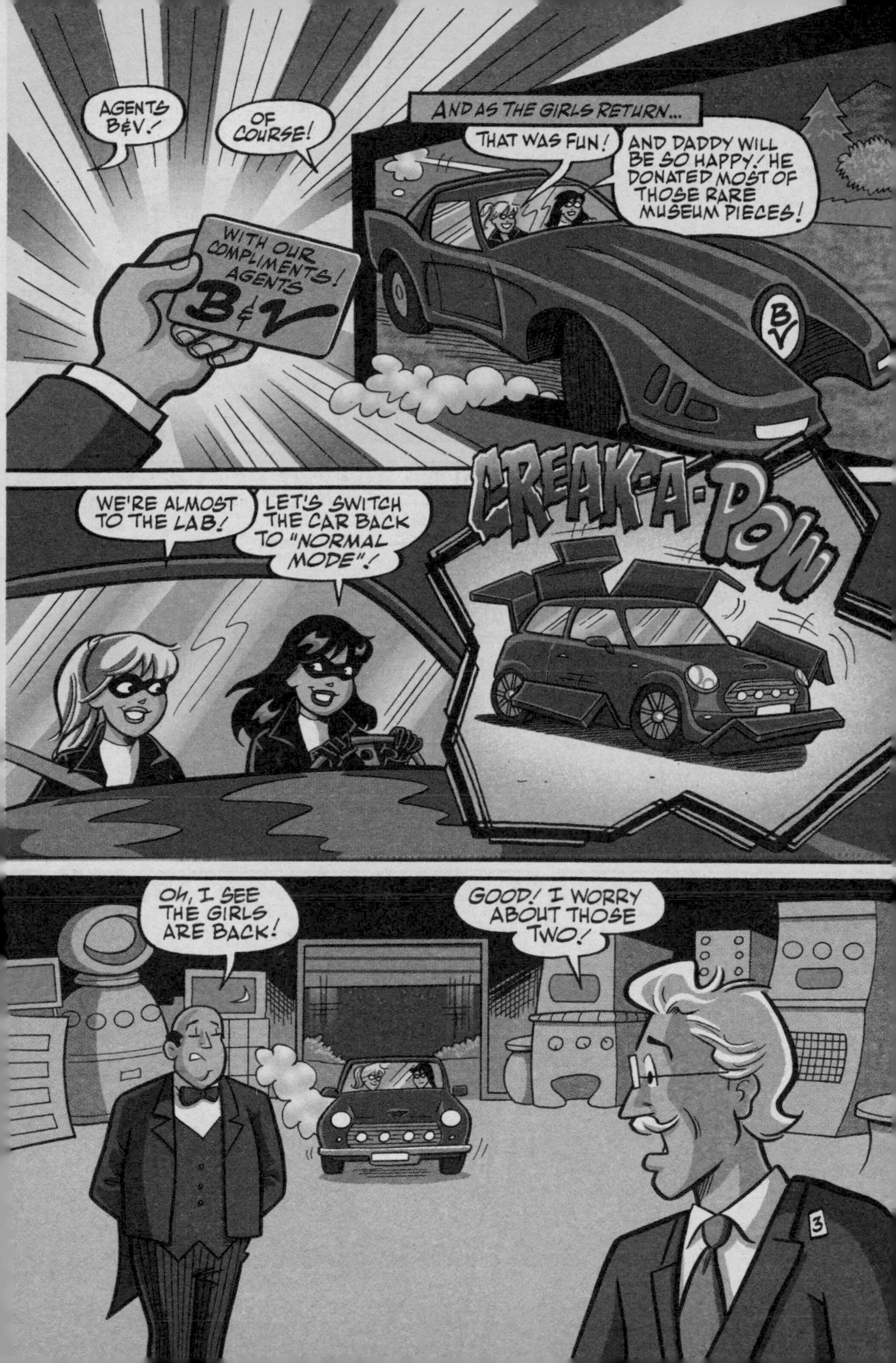
AGENTS B&V!
OF COURSE!
WITH OUR COMPLIMENTS! AGENTS B&V
AND AS THE GIRLS RETURN...
THAT WAS FUN!
AND DADDY WILL BE SO HAPPY! HE DONATED MOST OF THOSE RARE MUSEUM PIECES!
B/V
WE'RE ALMOST TO THE LAB!
LET'S SWITCH THE CAR BACK TO "NORMAL MODE"!
CREAK-A-POW
Oh, I SEE THE GIRLS ARE BACK!
GOOD! I WORRY ABOUT THOSE TWO!
3

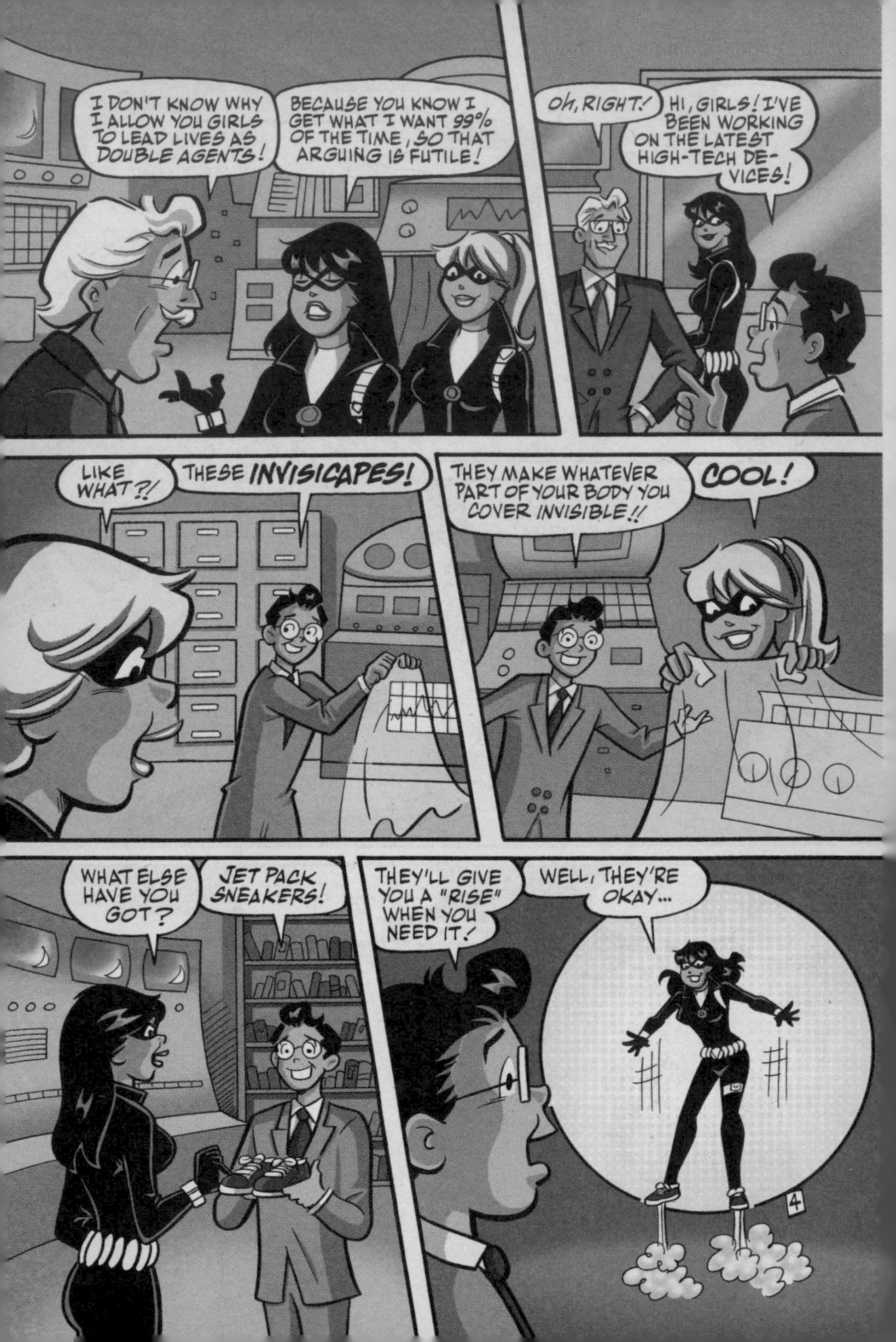
I DON'T KNOW WHY I ALLOW YOU GIRLS TO LEAD LIVES AS DOUBLE AGENTS!
BECAUSE YOU KNOW I GET WHAT I WANT 99% OF THE TIME, SO THAT ARGUING IS FUTILE!
Oh, RIGHT!
HI, GIRLS! I'VE BEEN WORKING ON THE LATEST HIGH-TECH DE-VICES!
LIKE WHAT?!
THESE INVISICAPES!
THEY MAKE WHATEVER PART OF YOUR BODY YOU COVER INVISIBLE!!
COOL!
WHAT ELSE HAVE YOU GOT?
JET PACK SNEAKERS!
THEY'LL GIVE YOU A "RISE" WHEN YOU NEED IT!
WELL, THEY'RE OKAY...
4

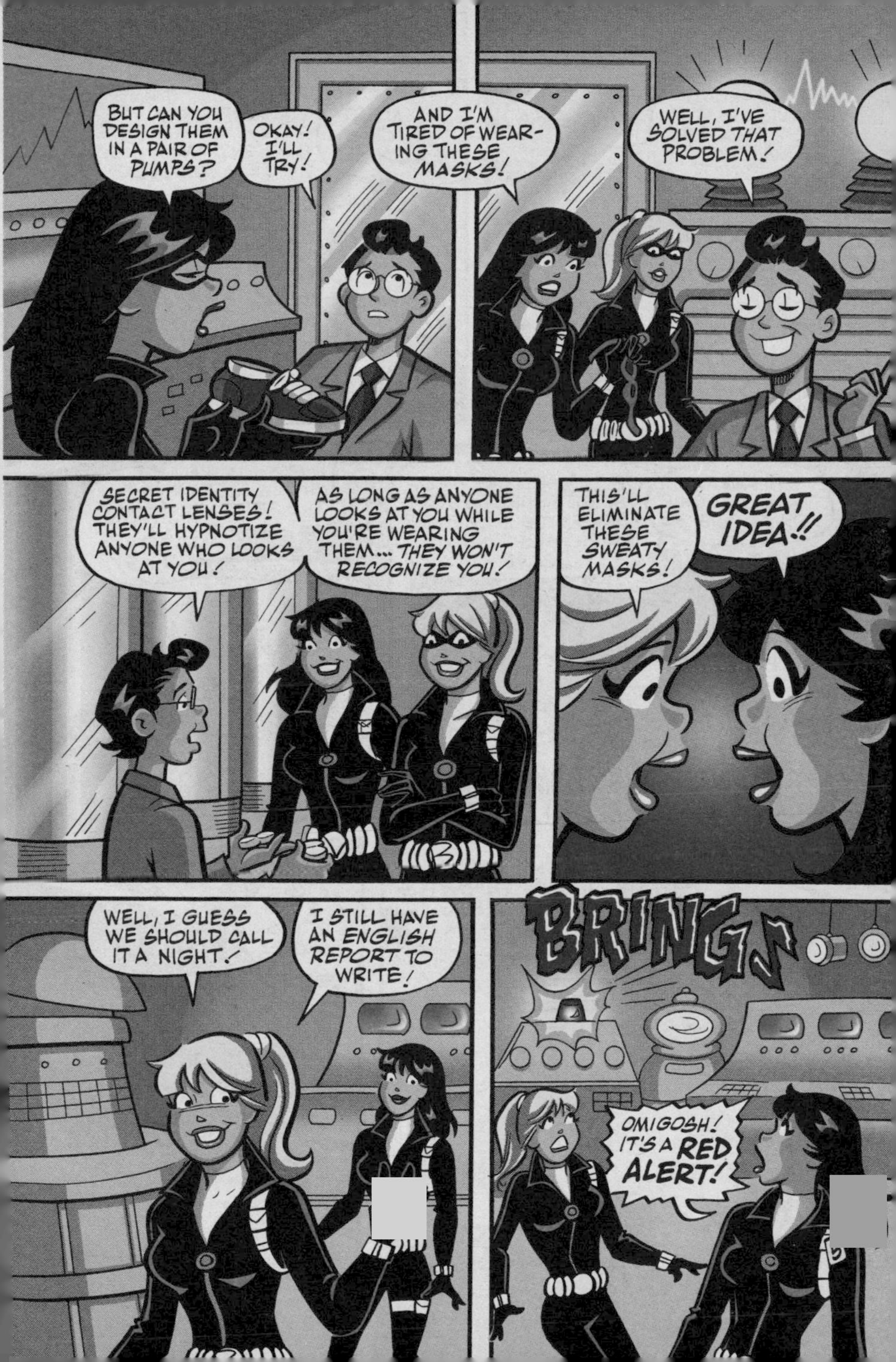
BUT CAN YOU DESIGN THEM IN A PAIR OF PUMPS?
OKAY! I'LL TRY!
AND I'M TIRED OF WEARING THESE MASKS!
WELL, I'VE SOLVED THAT PROBLEM!
SECRET IDENTITY CONTACT LENSES! THEY'LL HYPNOTIZE ANYONE WHO LOOKS AT YOU!
AS LONG AS ANYONE LOOKS AT YOU WHILE YOU'RE WEARING THEM... THEY WON'T RECOGNIZE YOU!
THIS'LL ELIMINATE THESE SWEATY MASKS!
GREAT IDEA!!
WELL, I GUESS WE SHOULD CALL IT A NIGHT!
I STILL HAVE AN ENGLISH REPORT TO WRITE!
BRINGG
OMIGOSH! IT'S A RED ALERT!

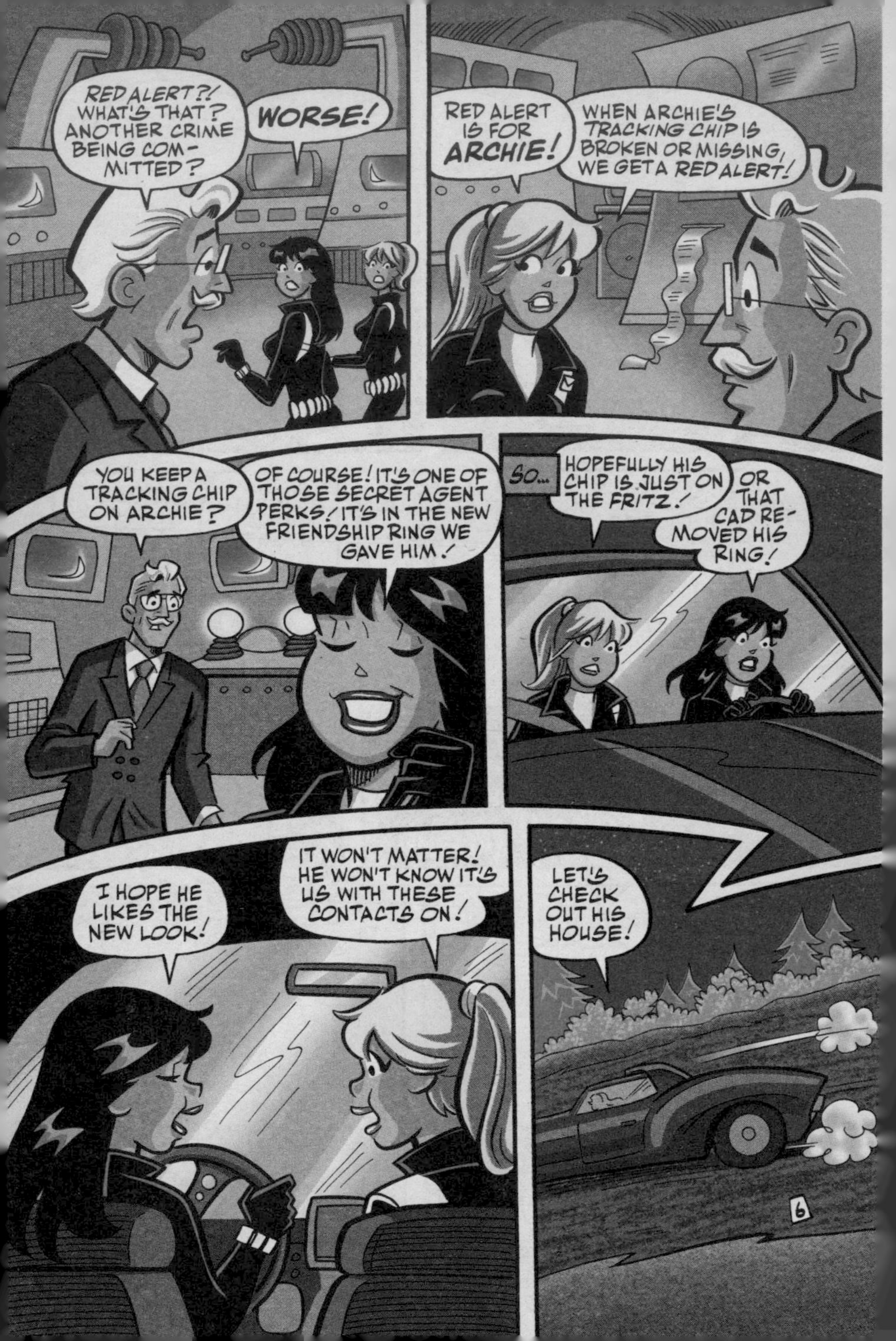
RED ALERT?! WHAT'S THAT? ANOTHER CRIME BEING COM-MITTED?
WORSE!
RED ALERT IS FOR ARCHIE!
WHEN ARCHIE'S TRACKING CHIP IS BROKEN OR MISSING, WE GET A RED ALERT!
YOU KEEP A TRACKING CHIP ON ARCHIE?
OF COURSE! IT'S ONE OF THOSE SECRET AGENT PERKS! IT'S IN THE NEW FRIENDSHIP RING WE GAVE HIM!
SO...
HOPEFULLY HIS CHIP IS JUST ON THE FRITZ!
OR THAT CAD RE-MOVED HIS RING!
I HOPE HE LIKES THE NEW LOOK!
IT WON'T MATTER! HE WON'T KNOW IT'S US WITH THESE CONTACTS ON!
LET'S CHECK OUT HIS HOUSE!
6

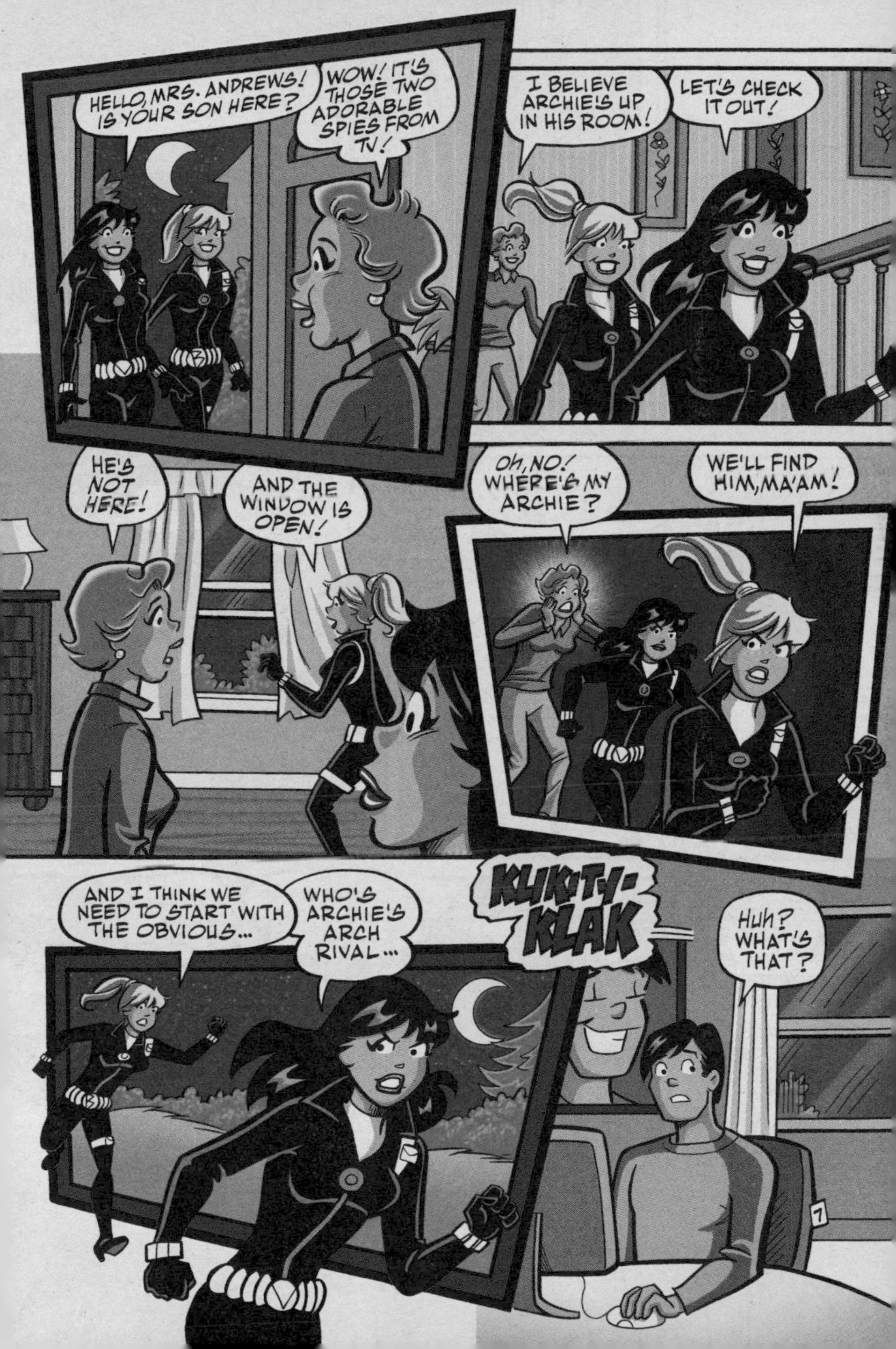
HELLO, MRS. ANDREWS! IS YOUR SON HERE?
WOW! IT'S THOSE TWO ADORABLE SPIES FROM TV!
I BELIEVE ARCHIE'S UP IN HIS ROOM!
LET'S CHECK IT OUT!
HE'S NOT HERE!
AND THE WINDOW IS OPEN!
Oh, NO! WHERE'S MY ARCHIE?
WE'LL FIND HIM, MA'AM!
AND I THINK WE NEED TO START WITH THE OBVIOUS...
WHO'S ARCHIE'S ARCH RIVAL...
KLIKITY-KLAK
Huh? WHAT'S THAT?
7

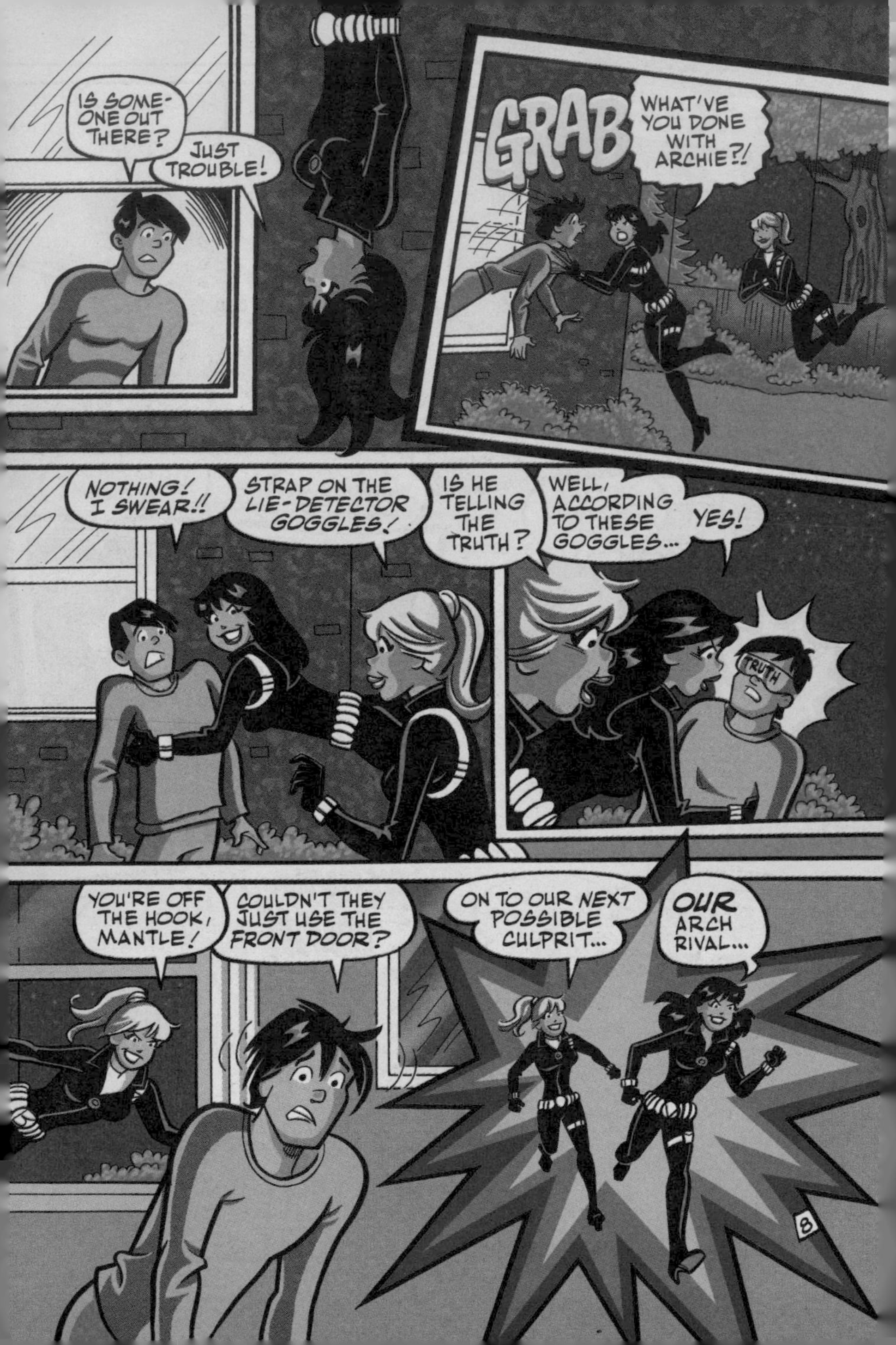
IS SOME-ONE OUT THERE?
JUST TROUBLE!
GRAB
WHAT'VE YOU DONE WITH ARCHIE?!
NOTHING! I SWEAR!!
STRAP ON THE LIE-DETECTOR GOGGLES!
IS HE TELLING THE TRUTH?
WELL, ACCORDING TO THESE GOGGLES...
YES!
TRUTH
YOU'RE OFF THE HOOK, MANTLE!
COULDN'T THEY JUST USE THE FRONT DOOR?
ON TO OUR NEXT POSSIBLE CULPRIT...
OUR ARCH RIVAL...
8

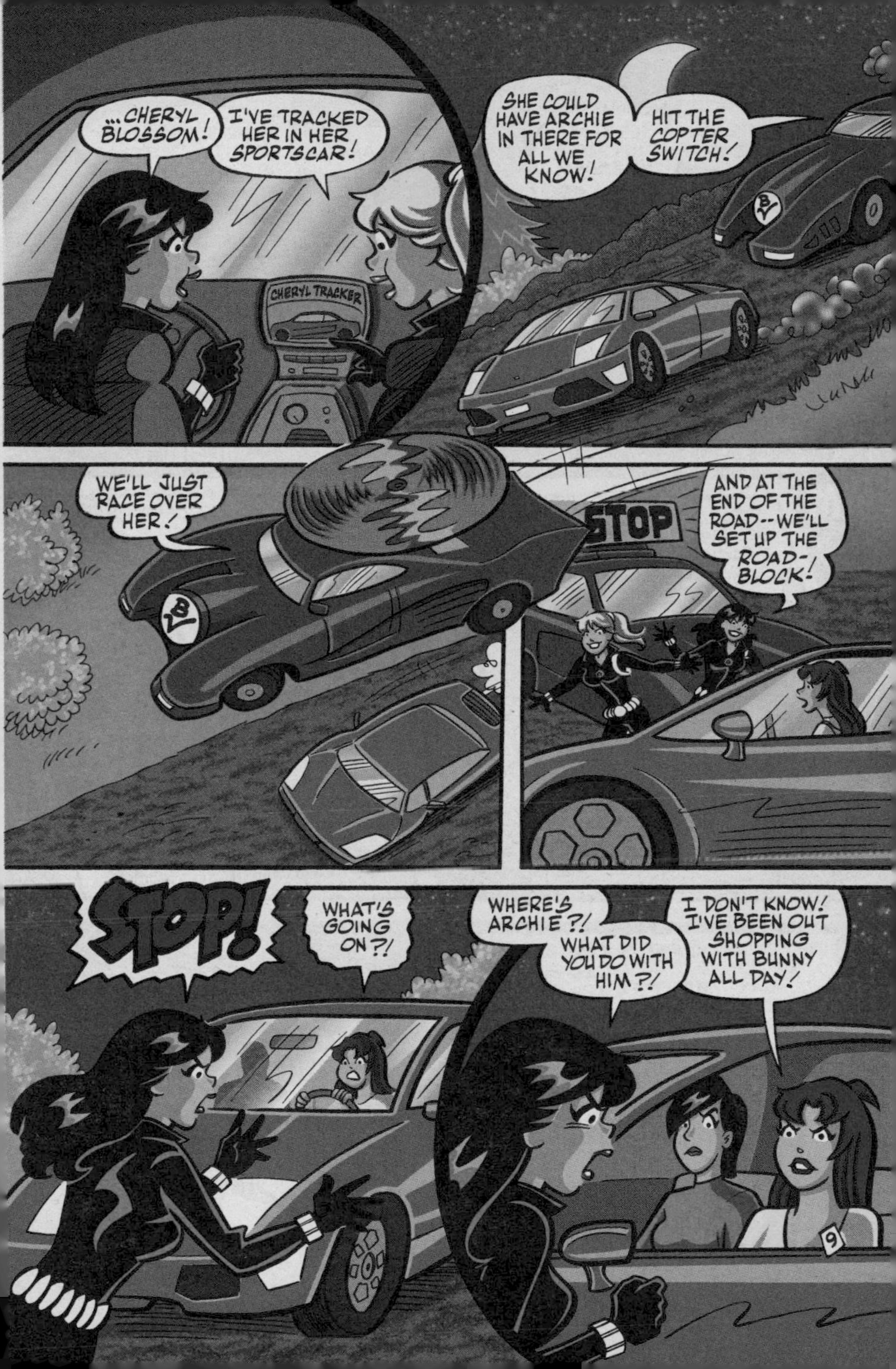
...CHERYL BLOSSOM!
I'VE TRACKED HER IN HER SPORTSCAR!
CHERYL TRACKER
SHE COULD HAVE ARCHIE IN THERE FOR ALL WE KNOW!
HIT THE COPTER SWITCH!
WE'LL JUST RACE OVER HER!
STOP
AND AT THE END OF THE ROAD--WE'LL SET UP THE ROAD-BLOCK!
STOP!
WHAT'S GOING ON?!
WHERE'S ARCHIE?! WHAT DID YOU DO WITH HIM?!
I DON'T KNOW! I'VE BEEN OUT SHOPPING WITH BUNNY ALL DAY!
9

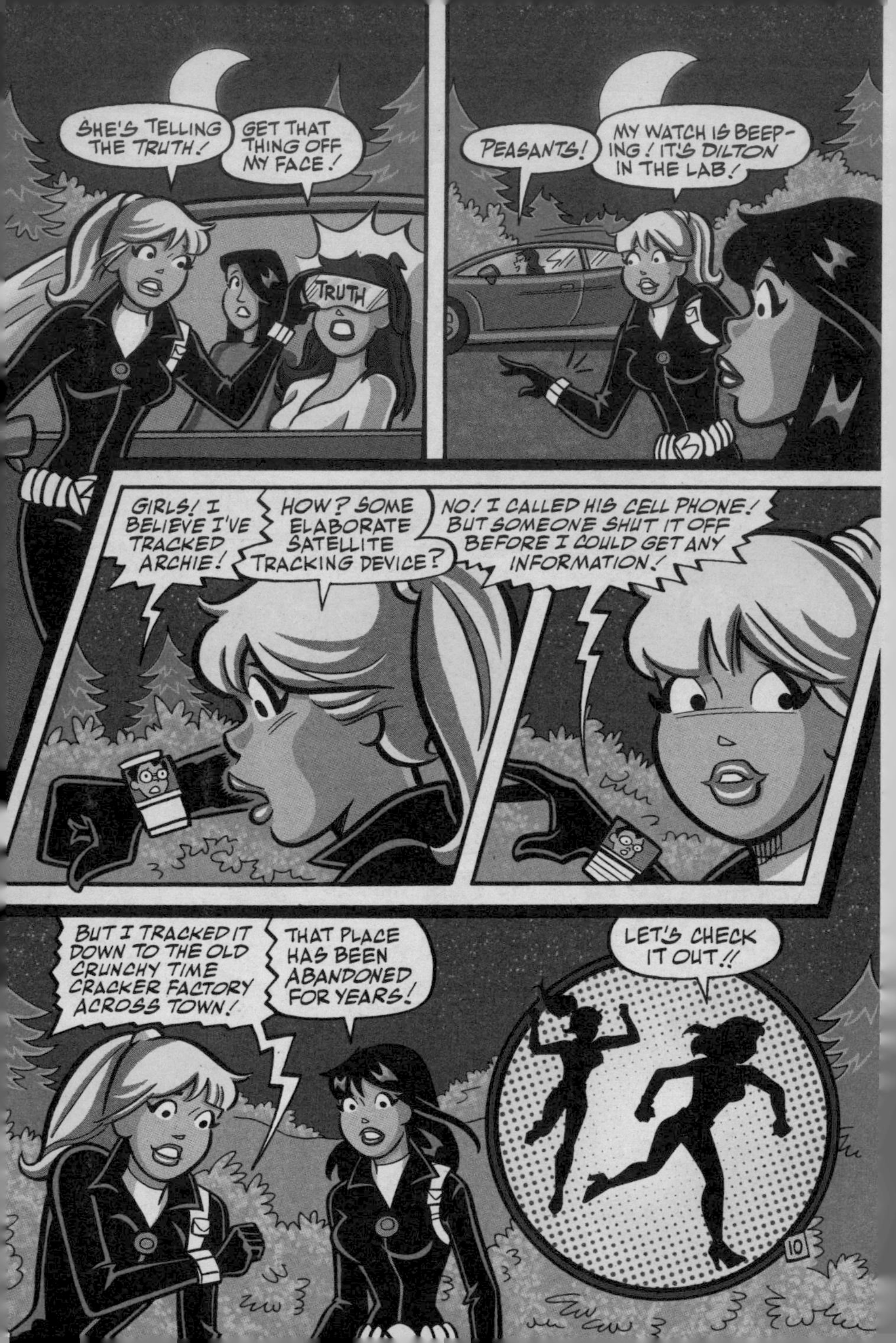
SHE'S TELLING THE TRUTH!
GET THAT THING OFF MY FACE!
TRUTH
PEASANTS!
MY WATCH IS BEEPING! IT'S DILTON IN THE LAB!
GIRLS! I BELIEVE I'VE TRACKED ARCHIE!
HOW? SOME ELABORATE SATELLITE TRACKING DEVICE?
NO! I CALLED HIS CELL PHONE! BUT SOMEONE SHUT IT OFF BEFORE I COULD GET ANY INFORMATION!
BUT I TRACKED IT DOWN TO THE OLD CRUNCHY TIME CRACKER FACTORY ACROSS TOWN!
THAT PLACE HAS BEEN ABANDONED FOR YEARS!
LET'S CHECK IT OUT!!
10

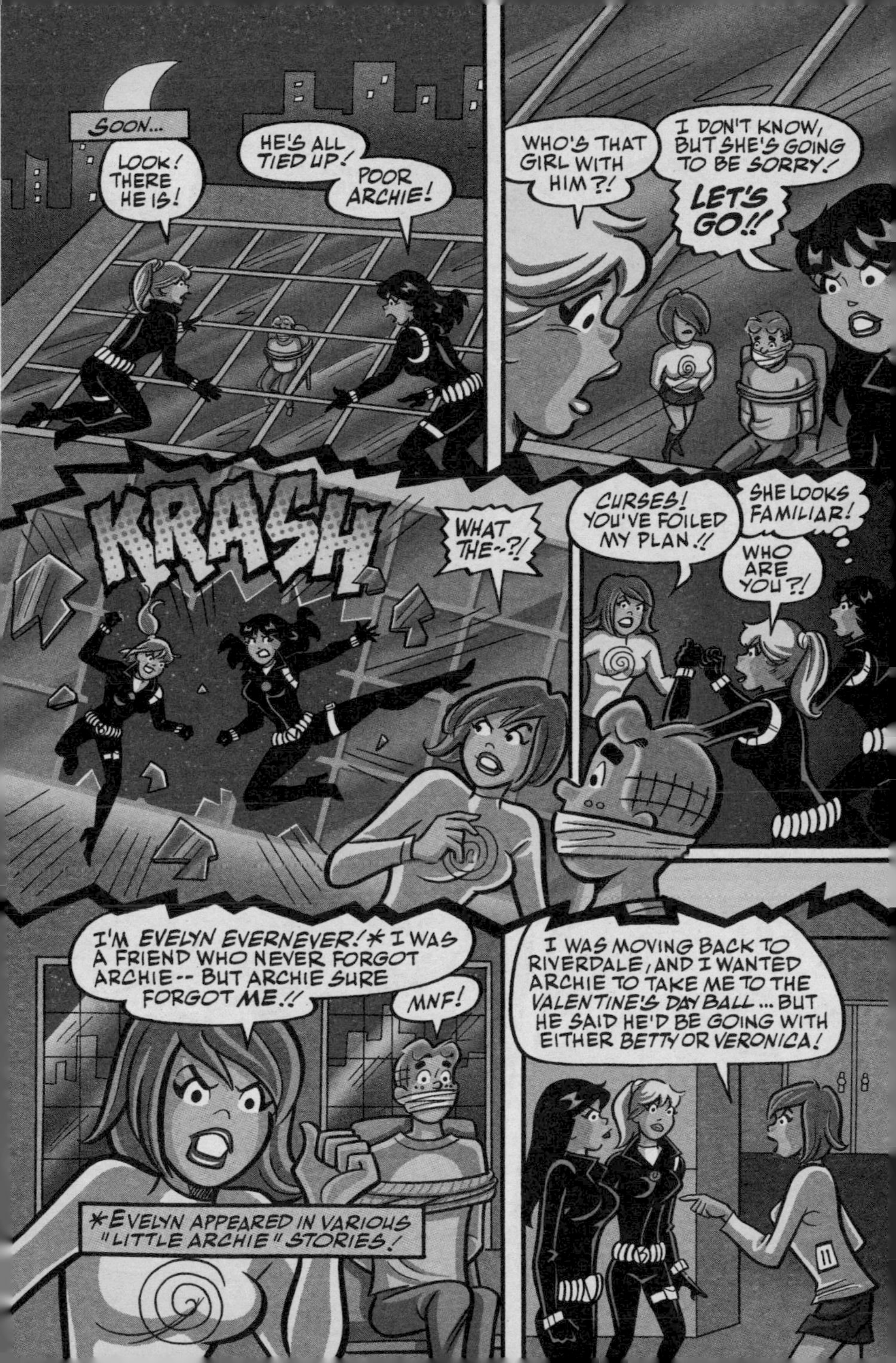
SOON...
LOOK! THERE HE IS!
HE'S ALL TIED UP!
POOR ARCHIE!
WHO'S THAT GIRL WITH HIM?!
I DON'T KNOW, BUT SHE'S GOING TO BE SORRY!
LET'S GO!!
KRASH
WHAT THE--?!
CURSES! YOU'VE FOILED MY PLAN!!
SHE LOOKS FAMILIAR!
WHO ARE YOU?!
I'M EVELYN EVERNEVER!* I WAS A FRIEND WHO NEVER FORGOT ARCHIE-- BUT ARCHIE SURE FORGOT ME!!
MNF!
*EVELYN APPEARED IN VARIOUS "LITTLE ARCHIE" STORIES!
I WAS MOVING BACK TO RIVERDALE, AND I WANTED ARCHIE TO TAKE ME TO THE VALENTINE'S DAY BALL ... BUT HE SAID HE'D BE GOING WITH EITHER BETTY OR VERONICA!

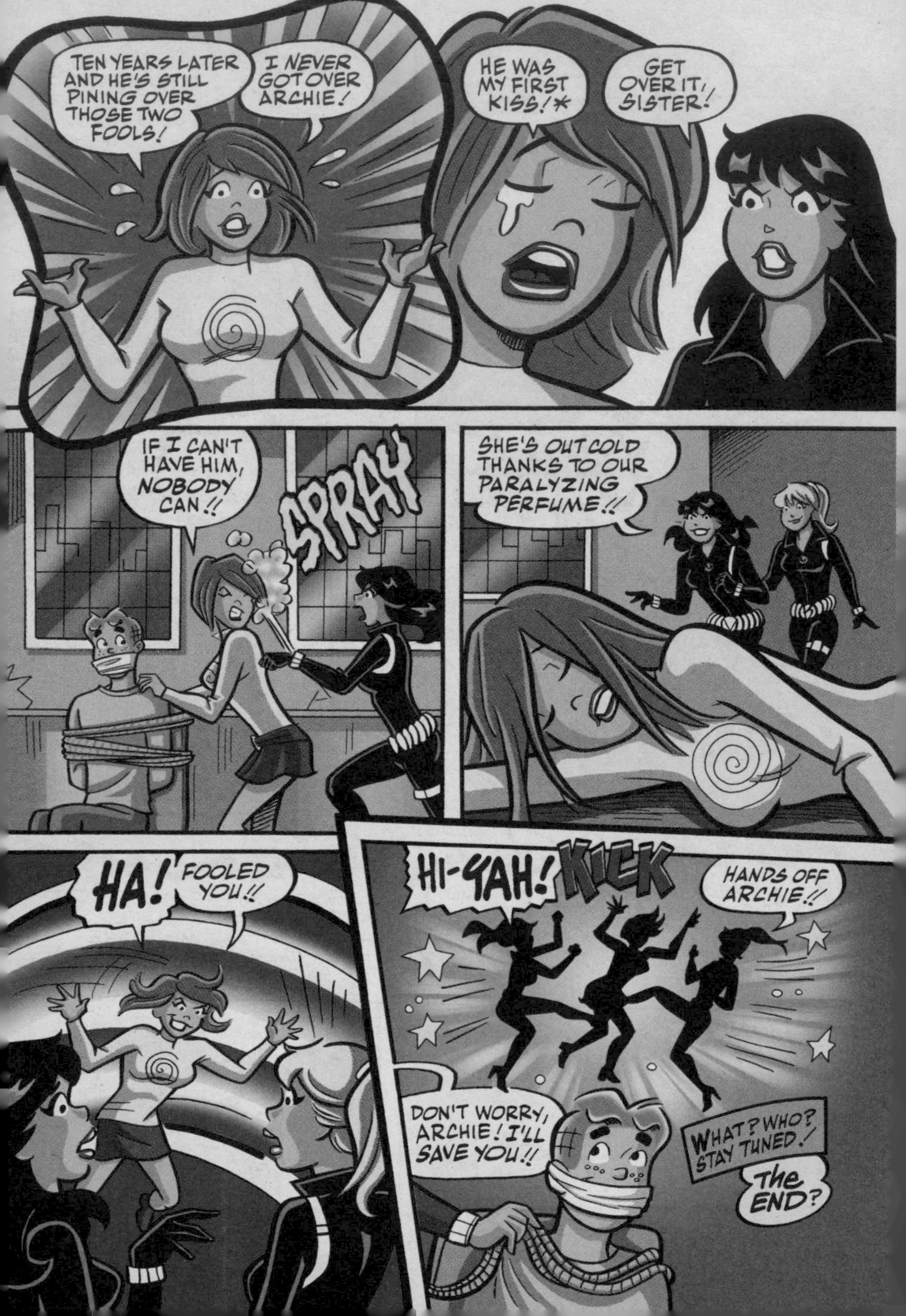
TEN YEARS LATER AND HE'S STILL PINING OVER THOSE TWO FOOLS!
I NEVER GOT OVER ARCHIE!
HE WAS MY FIRST KISS!*
GET OVER IT, SISTER!
IF I CAN'T HAVE HIM, NOBODY CAN!!
SPRAY
SHE'S OUT COLD THANKS TO OUR PARALYZING PERFUME!!
HA!
FOOLED YOU!!
HI-YAH!
KICK
HANDS OFF ARCHIE!!
DON'T WORRY, ARCHIE! I'LL SAVE YOU!!
WHAT? WHO? STAY TUNED!
The END?

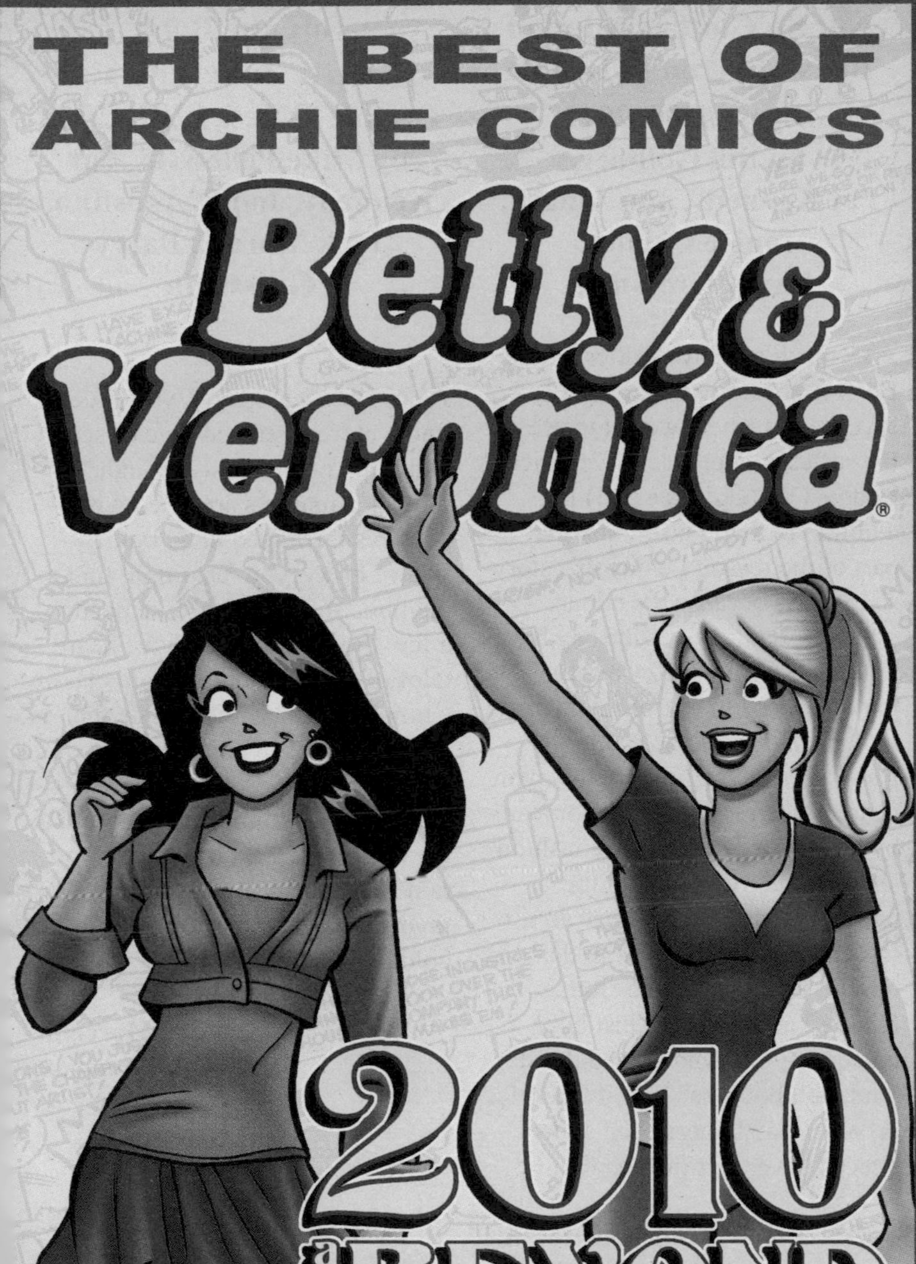
THE BEST OF
ARCHIE COMICS
Betty & Veronica®
2010
and BEYOND

Not So Clothes Minded
Betty & Veronica Double Digest #200, 2012
by Bill Golliher,
Pat Kennedy, Jim Amash,
Janice Chiang,
Barry Grossman

As much as I love stories where Betty is strong-willed, I equally love stories where we get to see the softer, kinder side of Veronica Lodge. (Yes, it does exist!) In addition to that, I also think that part of the reason I enjoy this story so much is because the climax where Veronica saves the day by holding a fashion show reminds me of a scene in one of my favorite movies, *Don't Tell Mom the Babysitter's Dead*, where the main character saves a uniform company by holding a revolutionary fashion show. Actually—some of the outfits featured in this story aren't too far off from the ones in that movie! Speaking of the clothes featured in the story, I just have one question—who owned the star burst bell bottoms? Was it Cheryl or Veronica? I guess even style queens have their fashion don'ts!

-- Jamie Lee Rotante
Editorial Assistant/Proofreader,
Archie Comics

Buy the Book
Betty & Veronica Double Digest #201, 2012
by Mike Pellowski, Pat Kennedy, Jon D'Agostino, Jack Morelli, Barry Grossman

Ahh, the flea market, you'll never find a more wretched hive of scum and villainy. Seriously though, most flea markets are filled with people's unwanted junk, but if you're lucky, you just might find a diamond in the rough. I've been to a few flea markets and have heard tales of amazing finds. From classic gaming consoles mint inside the original boxes to complete sets of vintage Star Wars action figures, it seems like anything can be found at the flea market. So it should come to no surprise that everybody's favorite girl-next-door would strike gold on this outing.

-- Joe Morciglio
Project Coordinator,
Archie Comics

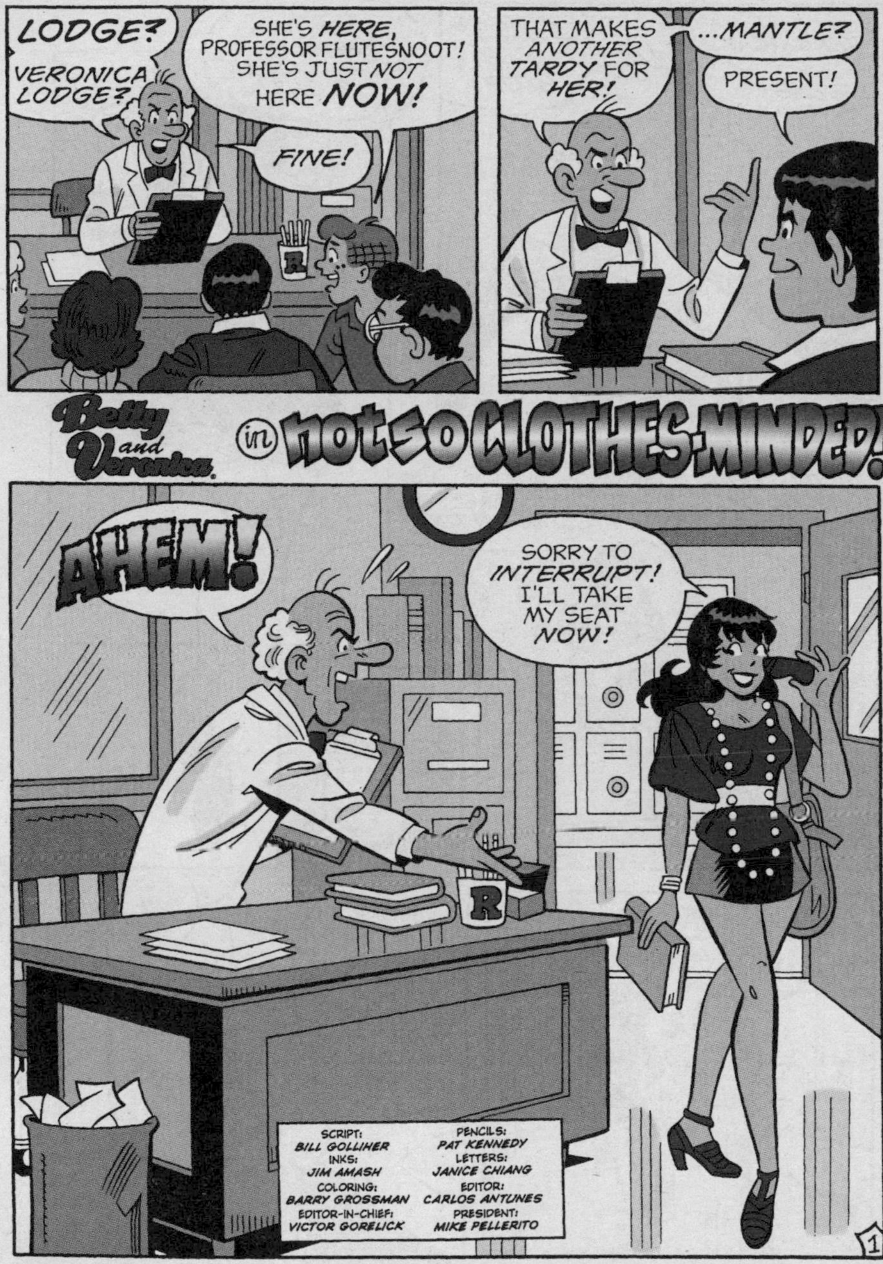
LODGE?
VERONICA LODGE?
SHE'S HERE, PROFESSOR FLUTESNOOT! SHE'S JUST NOT HERE NOW!
FINE!
THAT MAKES ANOTHER TARDY FOR HER!
...MANTLE?
PRESENT!
Betty and Veronica
in not so CLOTHES-MINDED!
AHEM!
SORRY TO INTERRUPT! I'LL TAKE MY SEAT NOW!
SCRIPT: BILL GOLLIHER
PENCILS: PAT KENNEDY
INKS: JIM AMASH
LETTERS: JANICE CHIANG
COLORING: BARRY GROSSMAN
EDITOR: CARLOS ANTUNES
EDITOR-IN-CHIEF: VICTOR GORELICK
PRESIDENT: MIKE PELLERITO
1

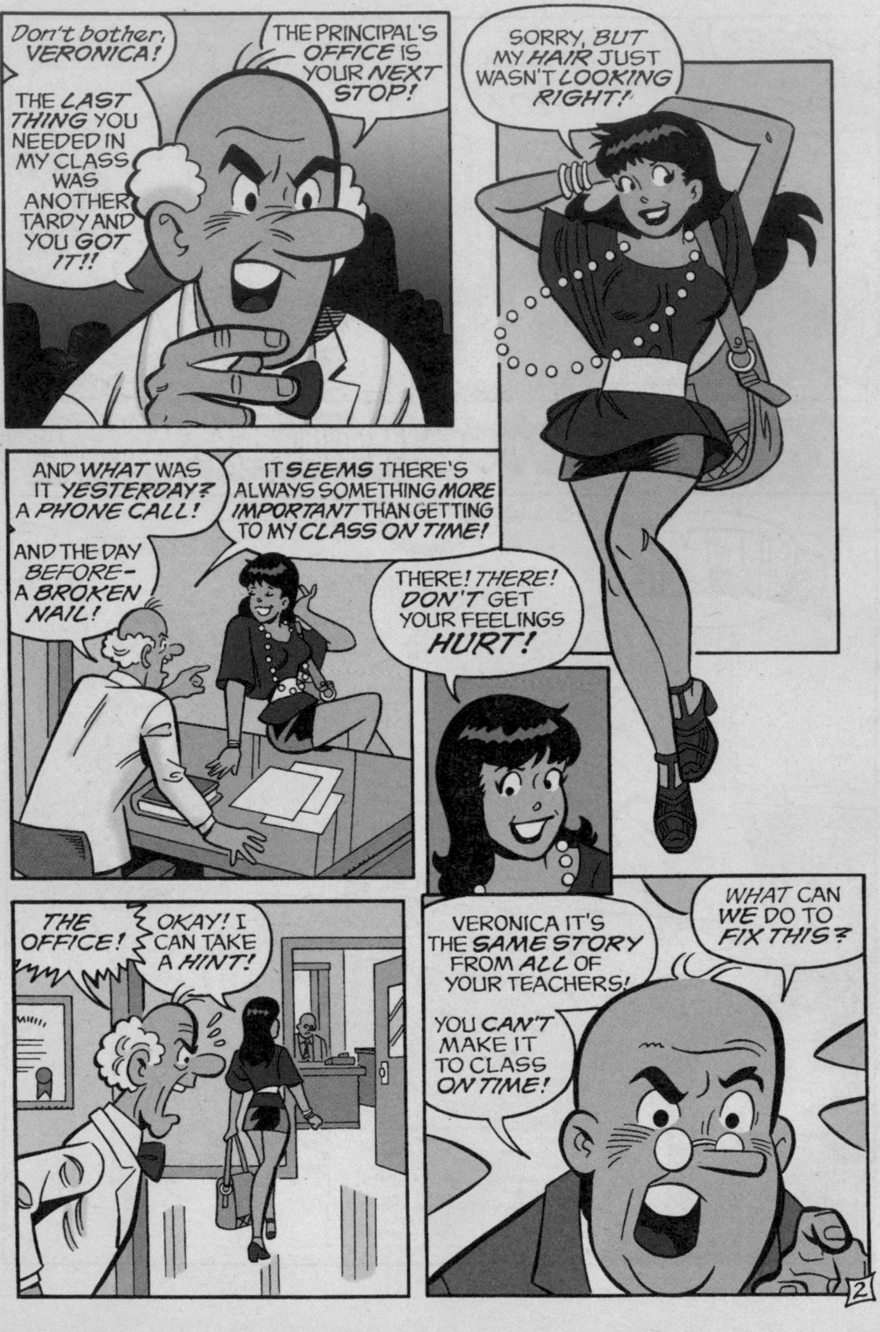
Don't bother, VERONICA!
THE LAST THING YOU NEEDED IN MY CLASS WAS ANOTHER TARDY AND YOU GOT IT!!
THE PRINCIPAL'S OFFICE IS YOUR NEXT STOP!
SORRY, BUT MY HAIR JUST WASN'T LOOKING RIGHT!
AND WHAT WAS IT YESTERDAY? A PHONE CALL!
AND THE DAY BEFORE- A BROKEN NAIL!
IT SEEMS THERE'S ALWAYS SOMETHING MORE IMPORTANT THAN GETTING TO MY CLASS ON TIME!
THERE! THERE! DON'T GET YOUR FEELINGS HURT!
THE OFFICE!
OKAY! I CAN TAKE A HINT!
VERONICA IT'S THE SAME STORY FROM ALL OF YOUR TEACHERS!
YOU CAN'T MAKE IT TO CLASS ON TIME!
WHAT CAN WE DO TO FIX THIS?
2

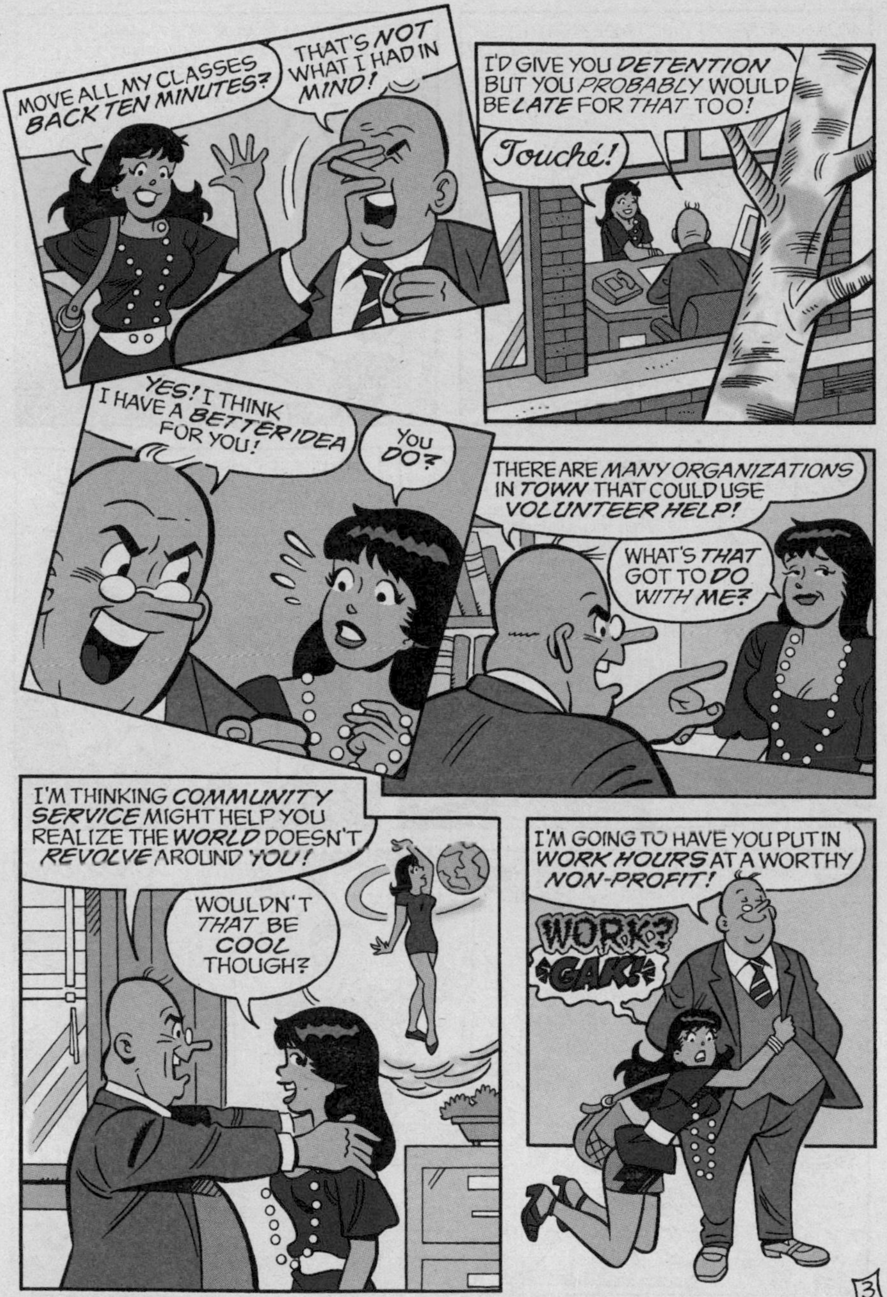
MOVE ALL MY CLASSES BACK TEN MINUTES?
THAT'S NOT WHAT I HAD IN MIND!
I'D GIVE YOU DETENTION BUT YOU PROBABLY WOULD BE LATE FOR THAT TOO!
Touché!
YES! I THINK I HAVE A BETTER IDEA FOR YOU!
You DO?
THERE ARE MANY ORGANIZATIONS IN TOWN THAT COULD USE VOLUNTEER HELP!
WHAT'S THAT GOT TO DO WITH ME?
I'M THINKING COMMUNITY SERVICE MIGHT HELP YOU REALIZE THE WORLD DOESN'T REVOLVE AROUND YOU!
WOULDN'T THAT BE COOL THOUGH?
I'M GOING TO HAVE YOU PUT IN WORK HOURS AT A WORTHY NON-PROFIT!
WORK?
GAK!
3

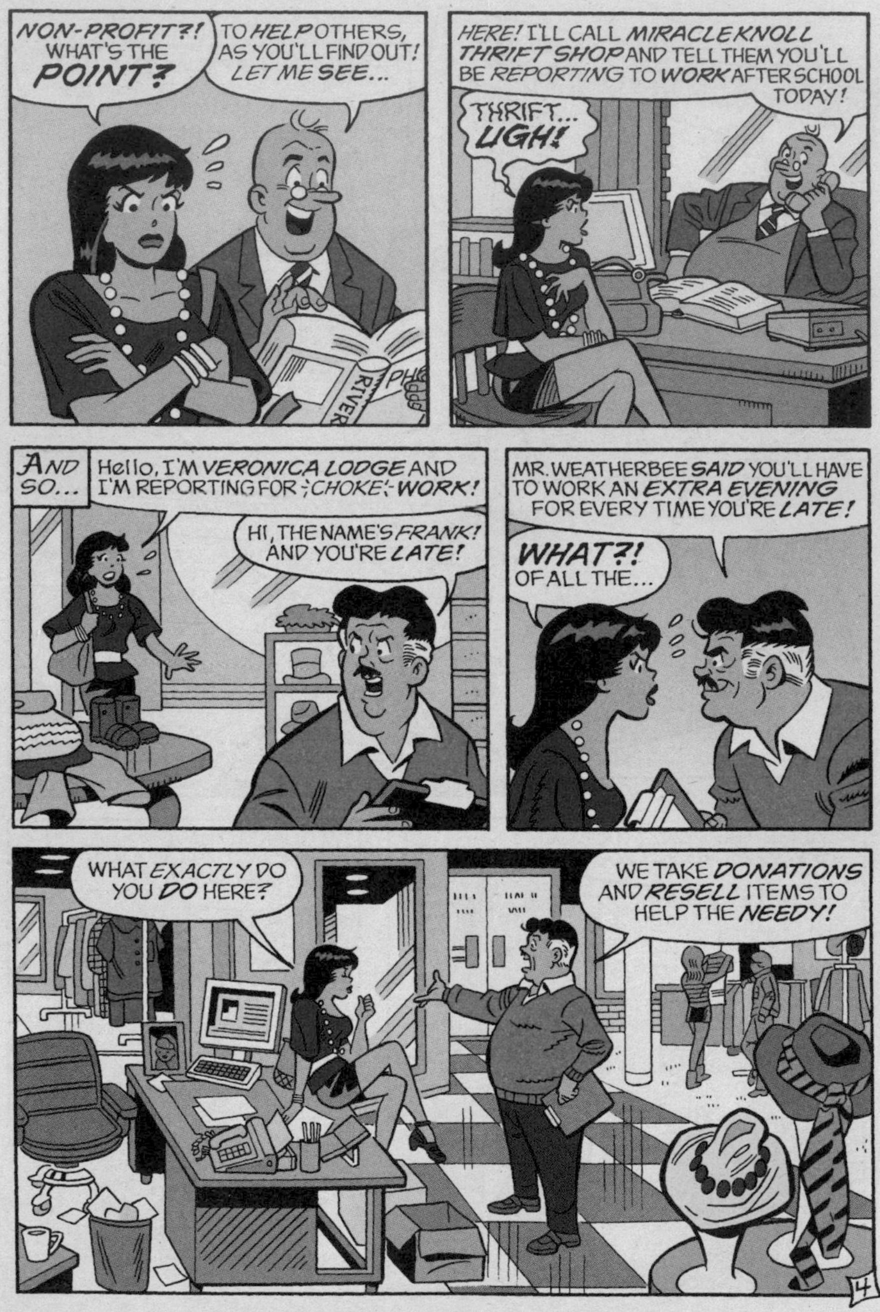
NON-PROFIT?! WHAT'S THE POINT?
TO HELP OTHERS, AS YOU'LL FIND OUT! LET ME SEE...
HERE! I'LL CALL MIRACLEKNOLL THRIFT SHOP AND TELL THEM YOU'LL BE REPORTING TO WORK AFTER SCHOOL TODAY!
THRIFT... UGH!
AND SO...
Hello, I'M VERONICA LODGE AND I'M REPORTING FOR -CHOKE- WORK!
HI, THE NAME'S FRANK! AND YOU'RE LATE!
MR. WEATHERBEE SAID YOU'LL HAVE TO WORK AN EXTRA EVENING FOR EVERY TIME YOU'RE LATE!
WHAT?! OF ALL THE...
WHAT EXACTLY DO YOU DO HERE?
WE TAKE DONATIONS AND RESELL ITEMS TO HELP THE NEEDY!
4

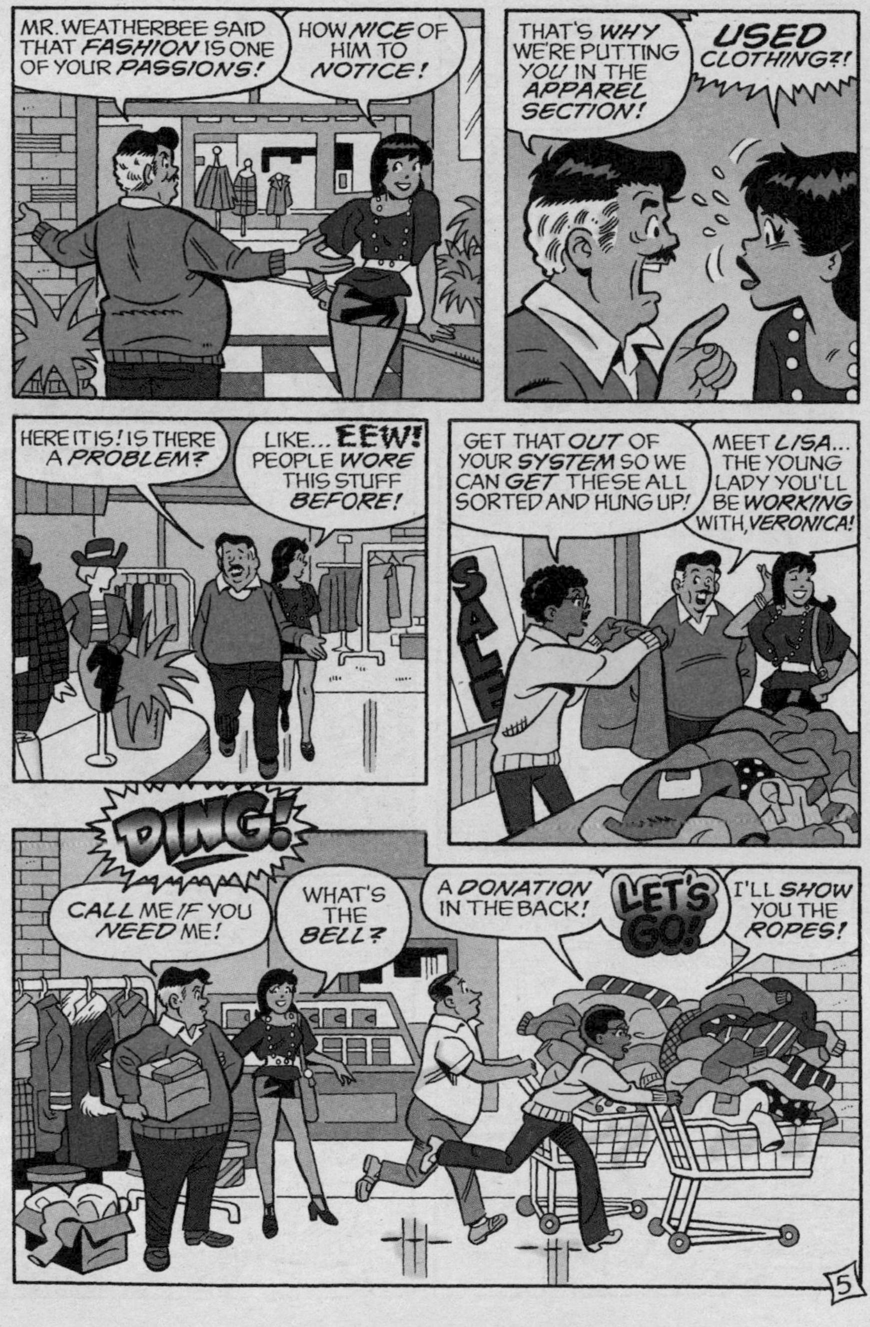
MR. WEATHERBEE SAID THAT FASHION IS ONE OF YOUR PASSIONS!
HOW NICE OF HIM TO NOTICE!
THAT'S WHY WE'RE PUTTING YOU IN THE APPAREL SECTION!
USED CLOTHING?!
HERE IT IS! IS THERE A PROBLEM?
LIKE... EEW! PEOPLE WORE THIS STUFF BEFORE!
GET THAT OUT OF YOUR SYSTEM SO WE CAN GET THESE ALL SORTED AND HUNG UP!
MEET LISA... THE YOUNG LADY YOU'LL BE WORKING WITH, VERONICA!
SALE
DING!
CALL ME IF YOU NEED ME!
WHAT'S THE BELL?
A DONATION IN THE BACK!
LET'S GO!
I'LL SHOW YOU THE ROPES!
5

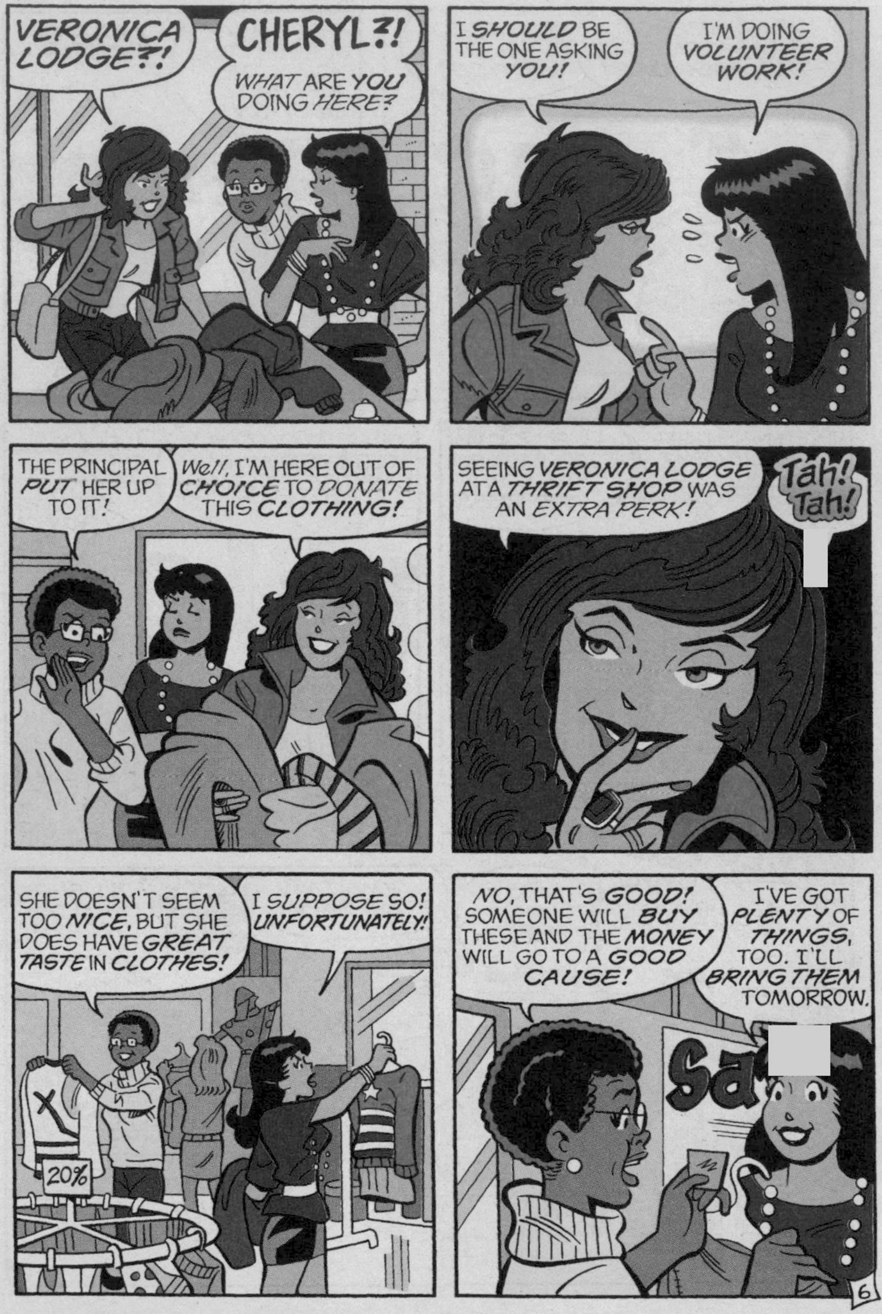
VERONICA LODGE?!
CHERYL?!
WHAT ARE YOU DOING HERE?
I SHOULD BE THE ONE ASKING YOU!
I'M DOING VOLUNTEER WORK!
THE PRINCIPAL PUT HER UP TO IT!
Well, I'M HERE OUT OF CHOICE TO DONATE THIS CLOTHING!
SEEING VERONICA LODGE AT A THRIFT SHOP WAS AN EXTRA PERK!
Tah! Tah!
SHE DOESN'T SEEM TOO NICE, BUT SHE DOES HAVE GREAT TASTE IN CLOTHES!
I SUPPOSE SO! UNFORTUNATELY!
20%
NO, THAT'S GOOD! SOMEONE WILL BUY THESE AND THE MONEY WILL GO TO A GOOD CAUSE!
I'VE GOT PLENTY OF THINGS, TOO. I'LL BRING THEM TOMORROW.
6

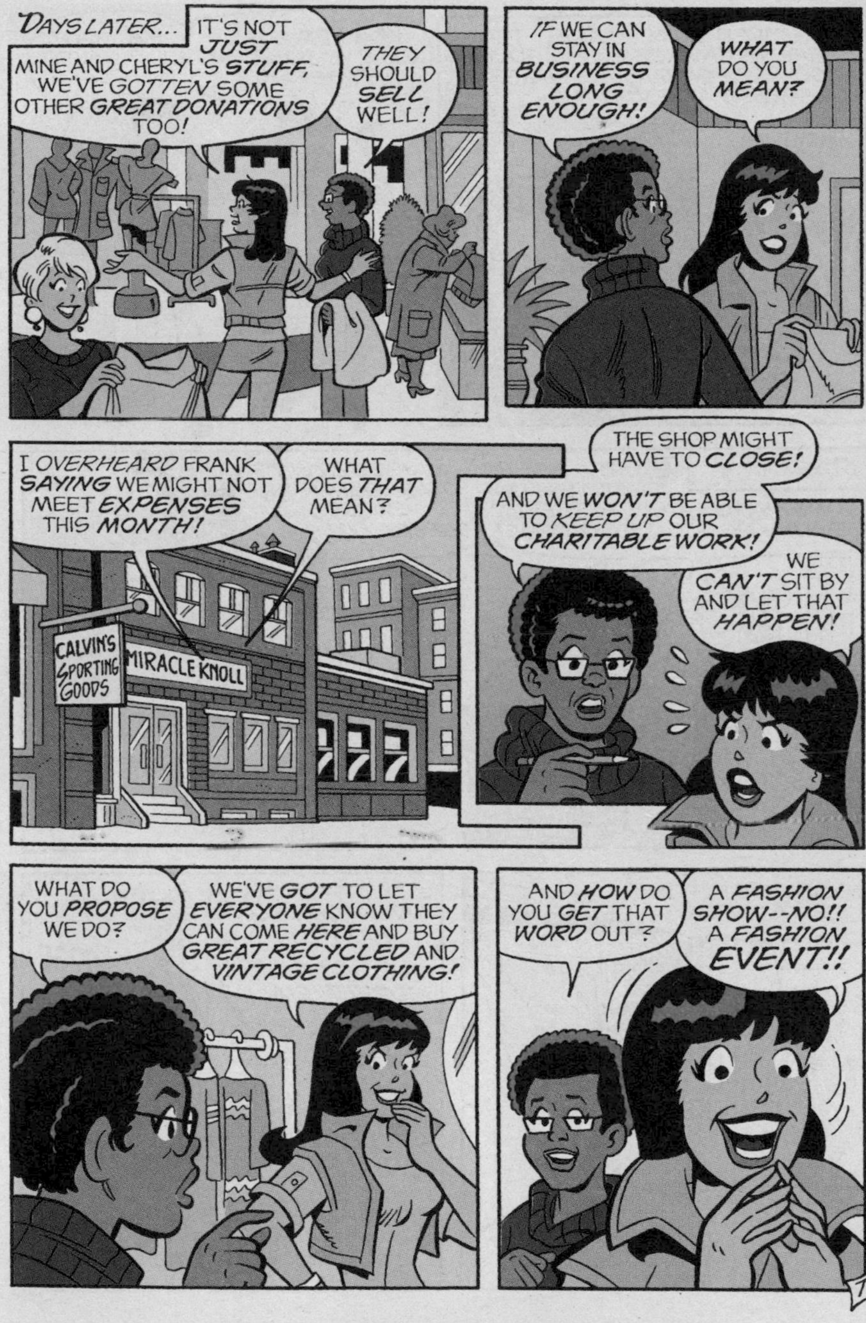
DAYS LATER...
IT'S NOT JUST MINE AND CHERYL'S STUFF, WE'VE GOTTEN SOME OTHER GREAT DONATIONS TOO!
THEY SHOULD SELL WELL!
IF WE CAN STAY IN BUSINESS LONG ENOUGH!
WHAT DO YOU MEAN?
I OVERHEARD FRANK SAYING WE MIGHT NOT MEET EXPENSES THIS MONTH!
WHAT DOES THAT MEAN?
CALVIN'S SPORTING GOODS
MIRACLE KNOLL
THE SHOP MIGHT HAVE TO CLOSE!
AND WE WON'T BE ABLE TO KEEP UP OUR CHARITABLE WORK!
WE CAN'T SIT BY AND LET THAT HAPPEN!
WHAT DO YOU PROPOSE WE DO?
WE'VE GOT TO LET EVERYONE KNOW THEY CAN COME HERE AND BUY GREAT RECYCLED AND VINTAGE CLOTHING!
AND HOW DO YOU GET THAT WORD OUT?
A FASHION SHOW--NO!! A FASHION EVENT!!
7

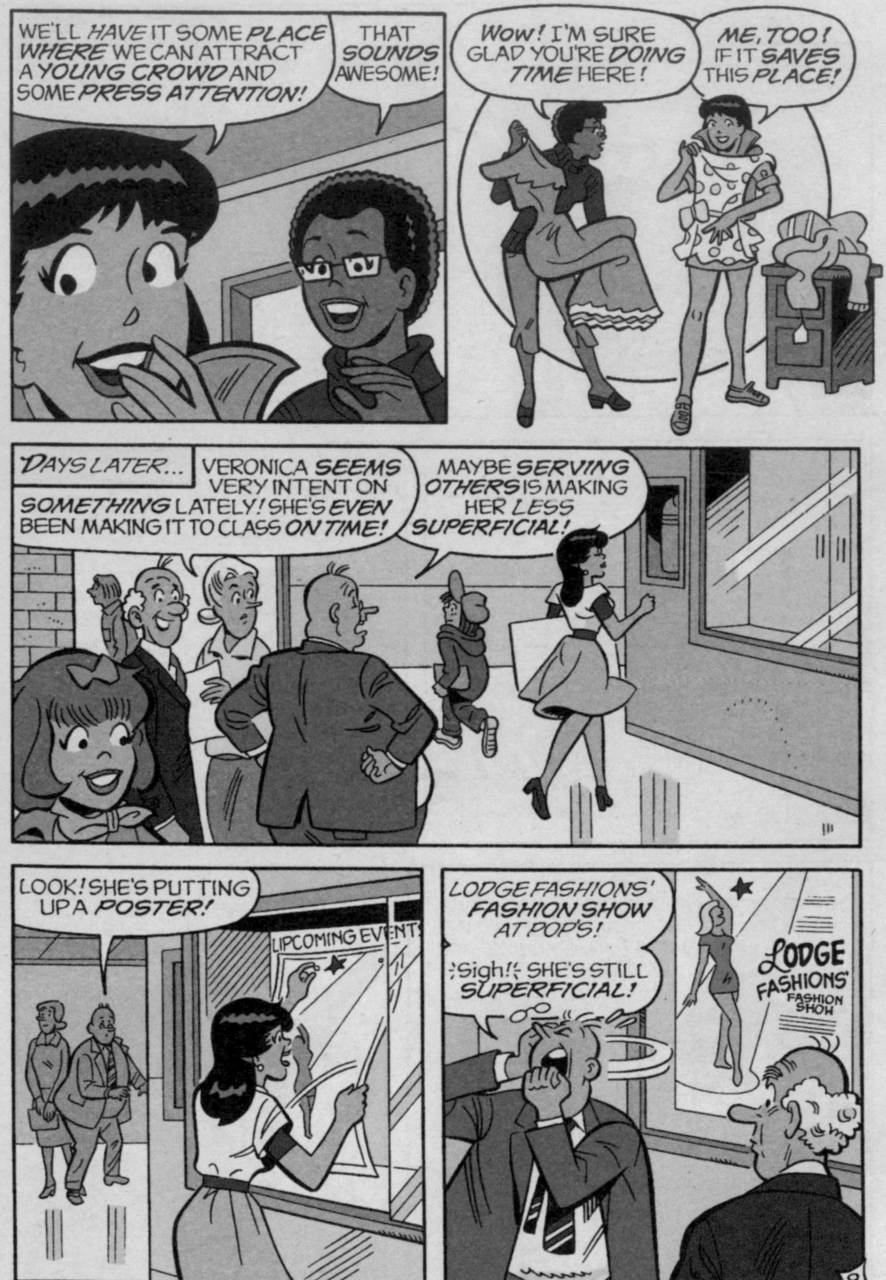
WE'LL HAVE IT SOME PLACE WHERE WE CAN ATTRACT A YOUNG CROWD AND SOME PRESS ATTENTION!
THAT SOUNDS AWESOME!
Wow! I'M SURE GLAD YOU'RE DOING TIME HERE!
ME, TOO! IF IT SAVES THIS PLACE!
DAYS LATER...
VERONICA SEEMS VERY INTENT ON SOMETHING LATELY! SHE'S EVEN BEEN MAKING IT TO CLASS ON TIME!
MAYBE SERVING OTHERS IS MAKING HER LESS SUPERFICIAL!
LOOK! SHE'S PUTTING UP A POSTER!
UPCOMING EVENTS
LODGE FASHIONS' FASHION SHOW AT POP'S!
-Sigh!- SHE'S STILL SUPERFICIAL!
LODGE FASHIONS' FASHION SHOW
8

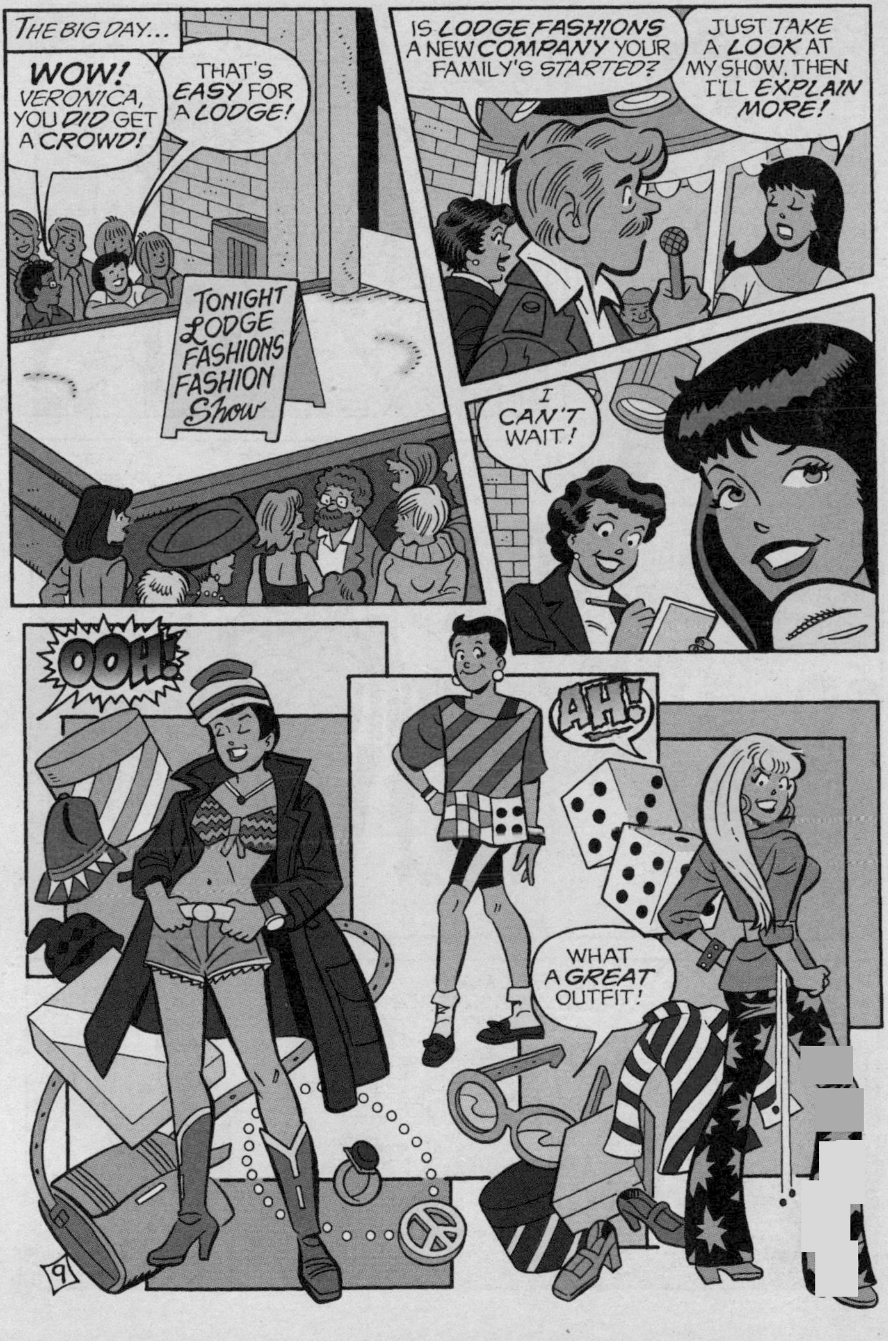
THE BIG DAY...
WOW! VERONICA, YOU DID GET A CROWD!
THAT'S EASY FOR A LODGE!
TONIGHT LODGE FASHIONS FASHION Show
IS LODGE FASHIONS A NEW COMPANY YOUR FAMILY'S STARTED?
JUST TAKE A LOOK AT MY SHOW. THEN I'LL EXPLAIN MORE!
I CAN'T WAIT!
OOH!
AH!
WHAT A GREAT OUTFIT!
9

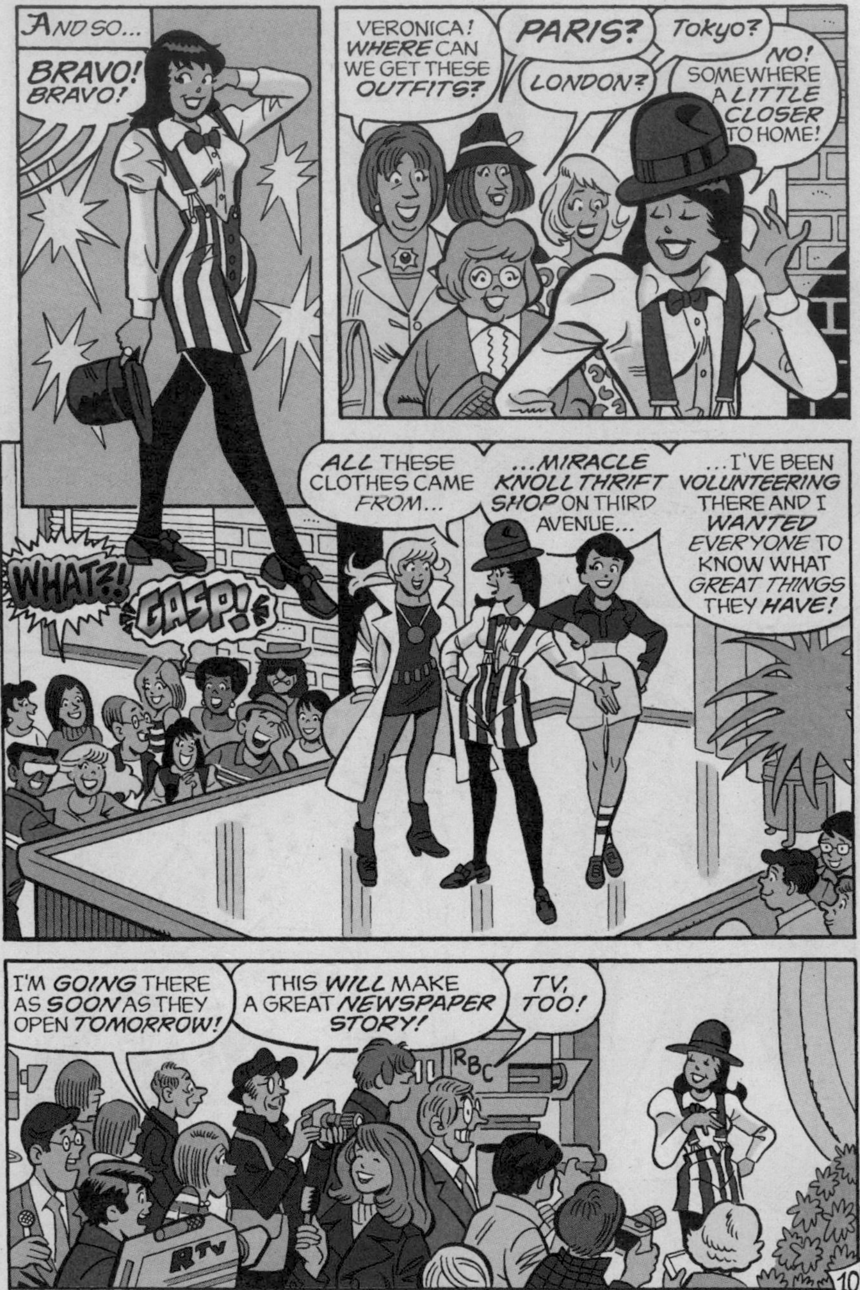
AND SO...
BRAVO! BRAVO!
VERONICA! WHERE CAN WE GET THESE OUTFITS?
PARIS?
LONDON?
Tokyo?
NO! SOMEWHERE A LITTLE CLOSER TO HOME!
WHAT?!
GASP!
ALL THESE CLOTHES CAME FROM...
...MIRACLE KNOLL THRIFT SHOP ON THIRD AVENUE...
...I'VE BEEN VOLUNTEERING THERE AND I WANTED EVERYONE TO KNOW WHAT GREAT THINGS THEY HAVE!
I'M GOING THERE AS SOON AS THEY OPEN TOMORROW!
THIS WILL MAKE A GREAT NEWSPAPER STORY!
TV, TOO!
RBC
RTV
10

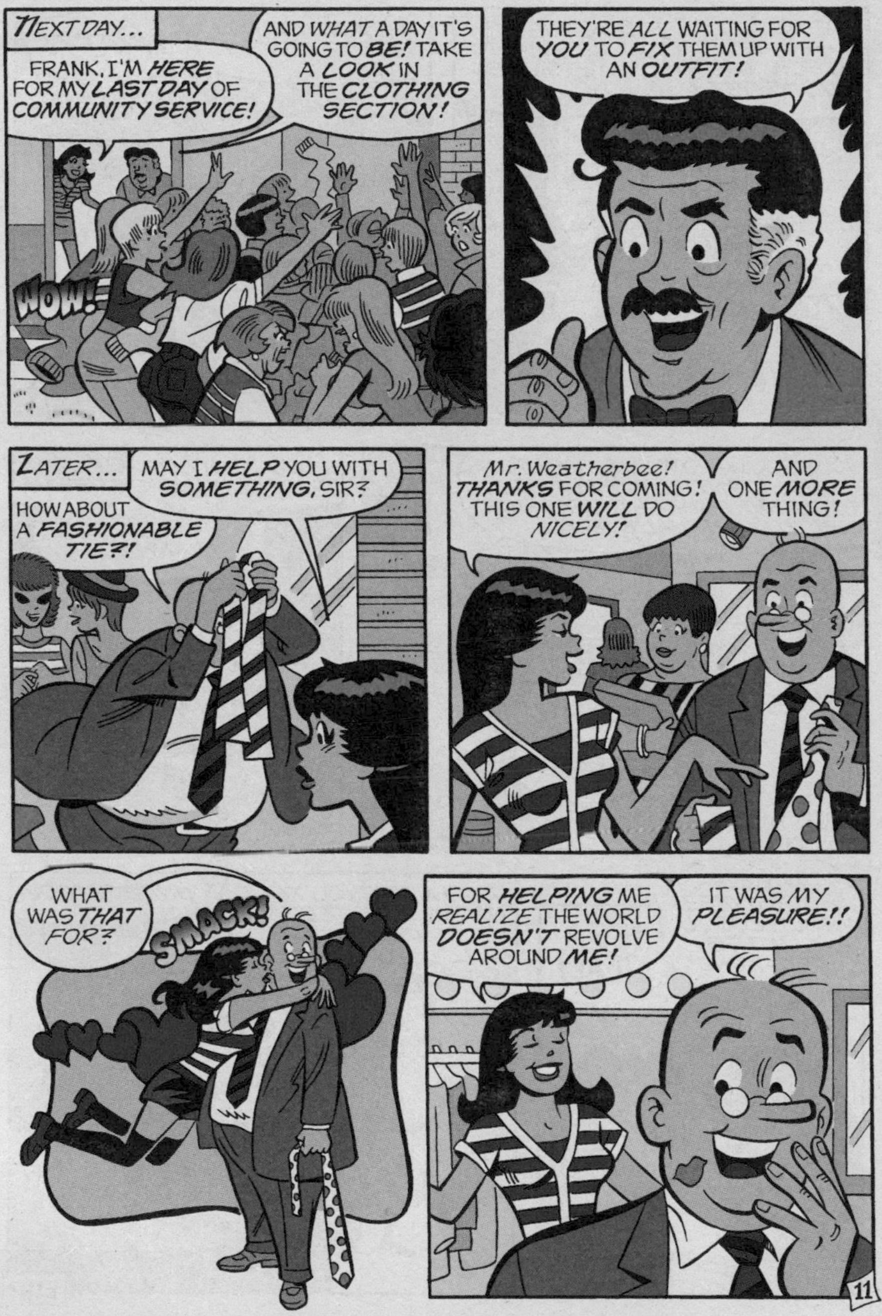
NEXT DAY...
FRANK, I'M HERE FOR MY LAST DAY OF COMMUNITY SERVICE!
AND WHAT A DAY IT'S GOING TO BE! TAKE A LOOK IN THE CLOTHING SECTION!
WOW!
THEY'RE ALL WAITING FOR YOU TO FIX THEM UP WITH AN OUTFIT!
LATER...
MAY I HELP YOU WITH SOMETHING, SIR?
HOW ABOUT A FASHIONABLE TIE?!
Mr. Weatherbee! THANKS FOR COMING! THIS ONE WILL DO NICELY!
AND ONE MORE THING!
WHAT WAS THAT FOR?
SMACK!
FOR HELPING ME REALIZE THE WORLD DOESN'T REVOLVE AROUND ME!
IT WAS MY PLEASURE!!
11

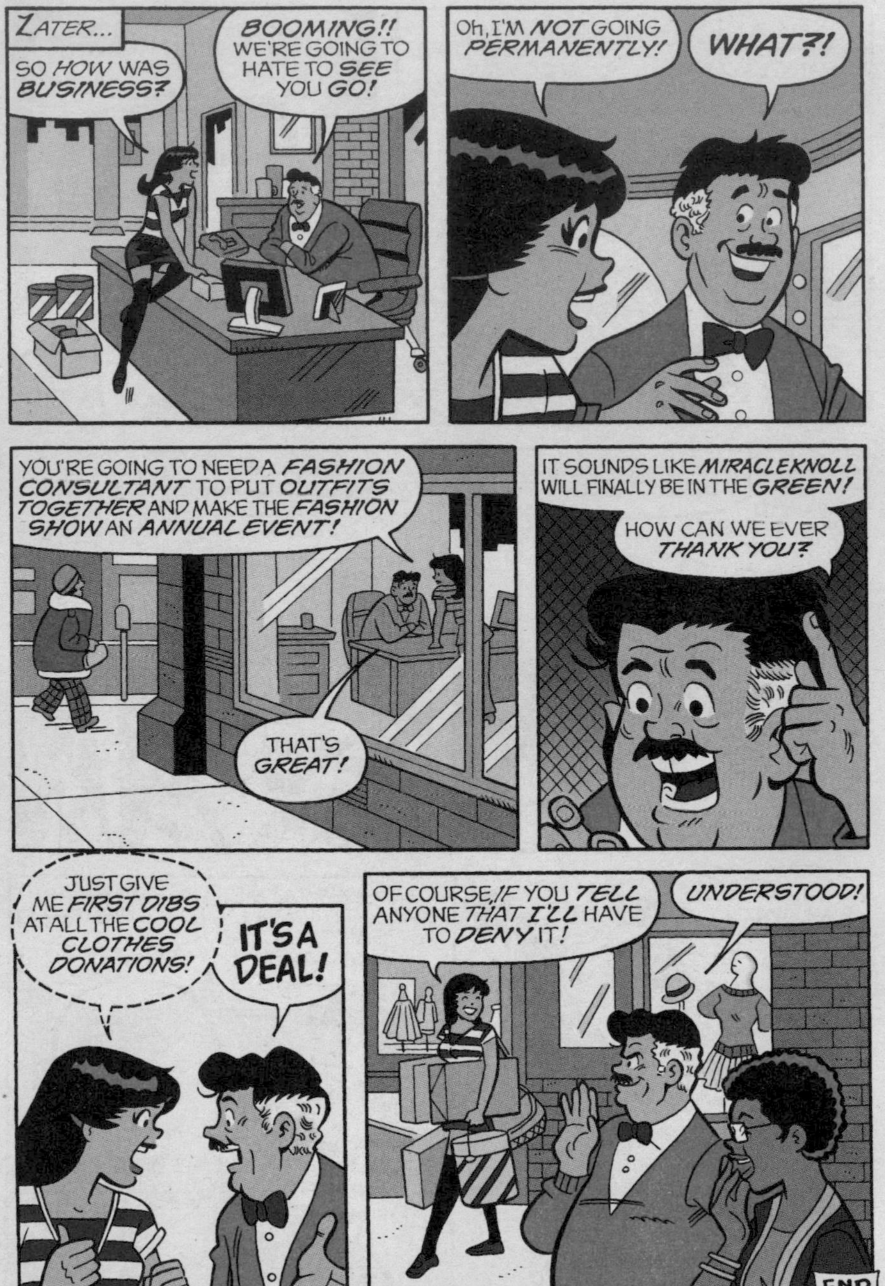
LATER...
SO HOW WAS BUSINESS?
BOOMING!! WE'RE GOING TO HATE TO SEE YOU GO!
Oh, I'M NOT GOING PERMANENTLY!
WHAT?!
YOU'RE GOING TO NEED A FASHION CONSULTANT TO PUT OUTFITS TOGETHER AND MAKE THE FASHION SHOW AN ANNUAL EVENT!
THAT'S GREAT!
IT SOUNDS LIKE MIRACLEKNOLL WILL FINALLY BE IN THE GREEN!
HOW CAN WE EVER THANK YOU?
JUST GIVE ME FIRST DIBS AT ALL THE COOL CLOTHES DONATIONS!
IT'S A DEAL!
OF COURSE, IF YOU TELL ANYONE THAT I'LL HAVE TO DENY IT!
UNDERSTOOD!
END.

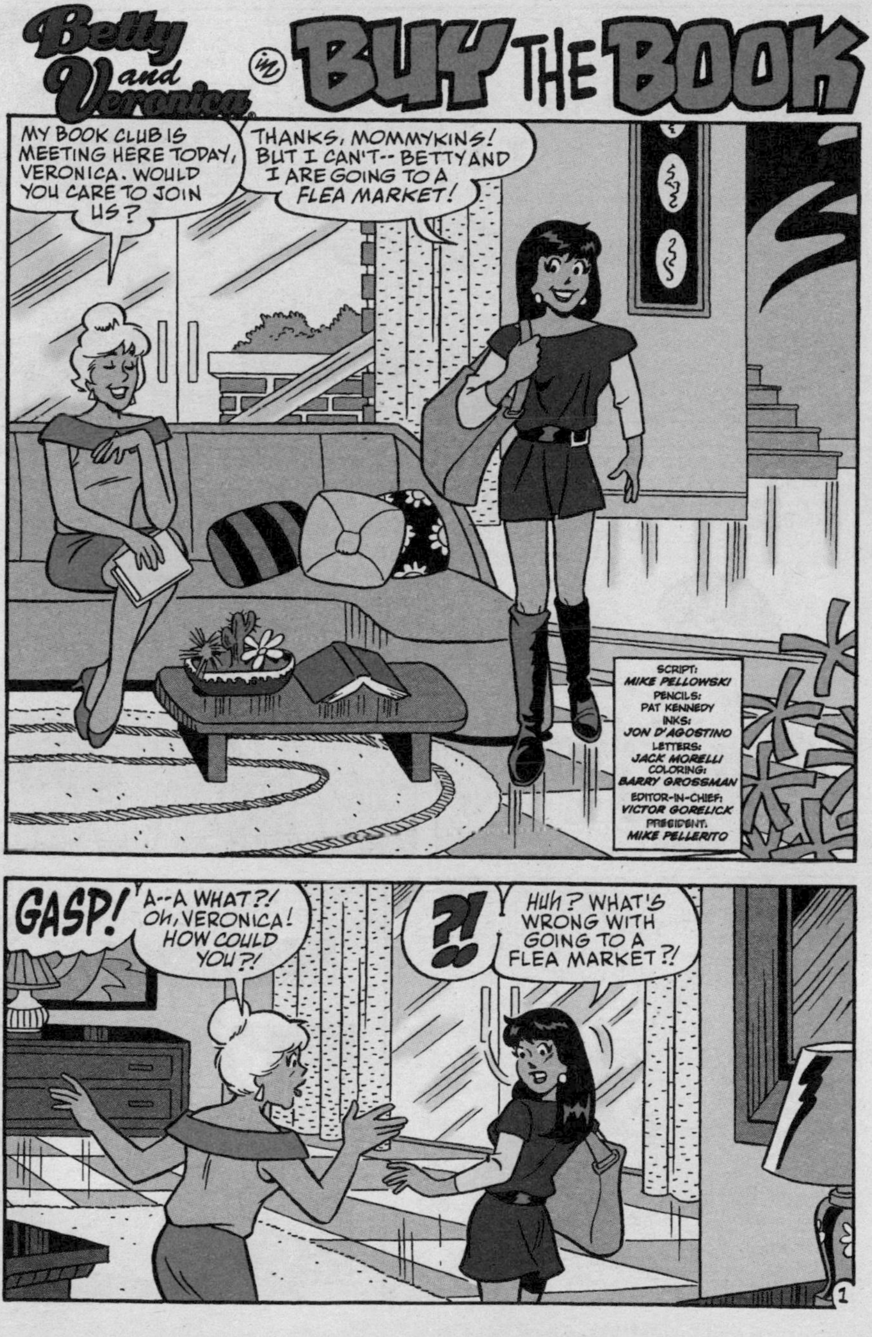
Betty and Veronica in
BUY THE BOOK
MY BOOK CLUB IS MEETING HERE TODAY, VERONICA. WOULD YOU CARE TO JOIN US?
THANKS, MOMMYKINS! BUT I CAN'T-- BETTY AND I ARE GOING TO A FLEA MARKET!
SCRIPT: MIKE PELLOWSKI PENCILS: PAT KENNEDY INKS: JON D'AGOSTINO LETTERS: JACK MORELLI COLORING: BARRY GROSSMAN EDITOR-IN-CHIEF: VICTOR GORELICK PRESIDENT: MIKE PELLERITO
GASP!
A--A WHAT?! OH, VERONICA! HOW COULD YOU?!
?!
HUH? WHAT'S WRONG WITH GOING TO A FLEA MARKET?!
1

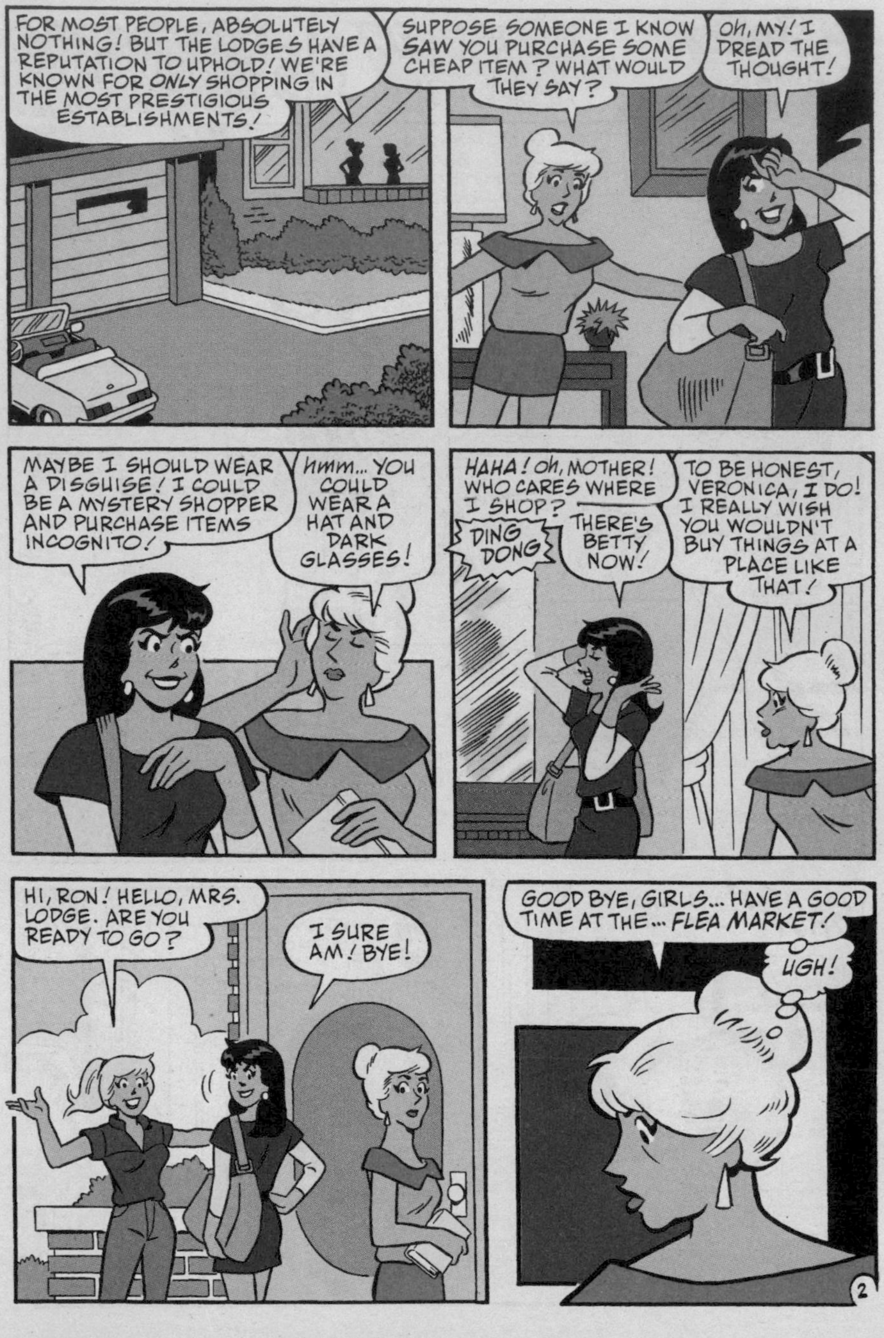
FOR MOST PEOPLE, ABSOLUTELY NOTHING! BUT THE LODGES HAVE A REPUTATION TO UPHOLD! WE'RE KNOWN FOR ONLY SHOPPING IN THE MOST PRESTIGIOUS ESTABLISHMENTS!
SUPPOSE SOMEONE I KNOW SAW YOU PURCHASE SOME CHEAP ITEM? WHAT WOULD THEY SAY?
OH, MY! I DREAD THE THOUGHT!
MAYBE I SHOULD WEAR A DISGUISE! I COULD BE A MYSTERY SHOPPER AND PURCHASE ITEMS INCOGNITO!
HMM... YOU COULD WEAR A HAT AND DARK GLASSES!
HAHA! OH, MOTHER! WHO CARES WHERE I SHOP?
DING DONG
THERE'S BETTY NOW!
TO BE HONEST, VERONICA, I DO! I REALLY WISH YOU WOULDN'T BUY THINGS AT A PLACE LIKE THAT!
HI, RON! HELLO, MRS. LODGE. ARE YOU READY TO GO?
I SURE AM! BYE!
GOOD BYE, GIRLS... HAVE A GOOD TIME AT THE... FLEA MARKET!
UGH!
2

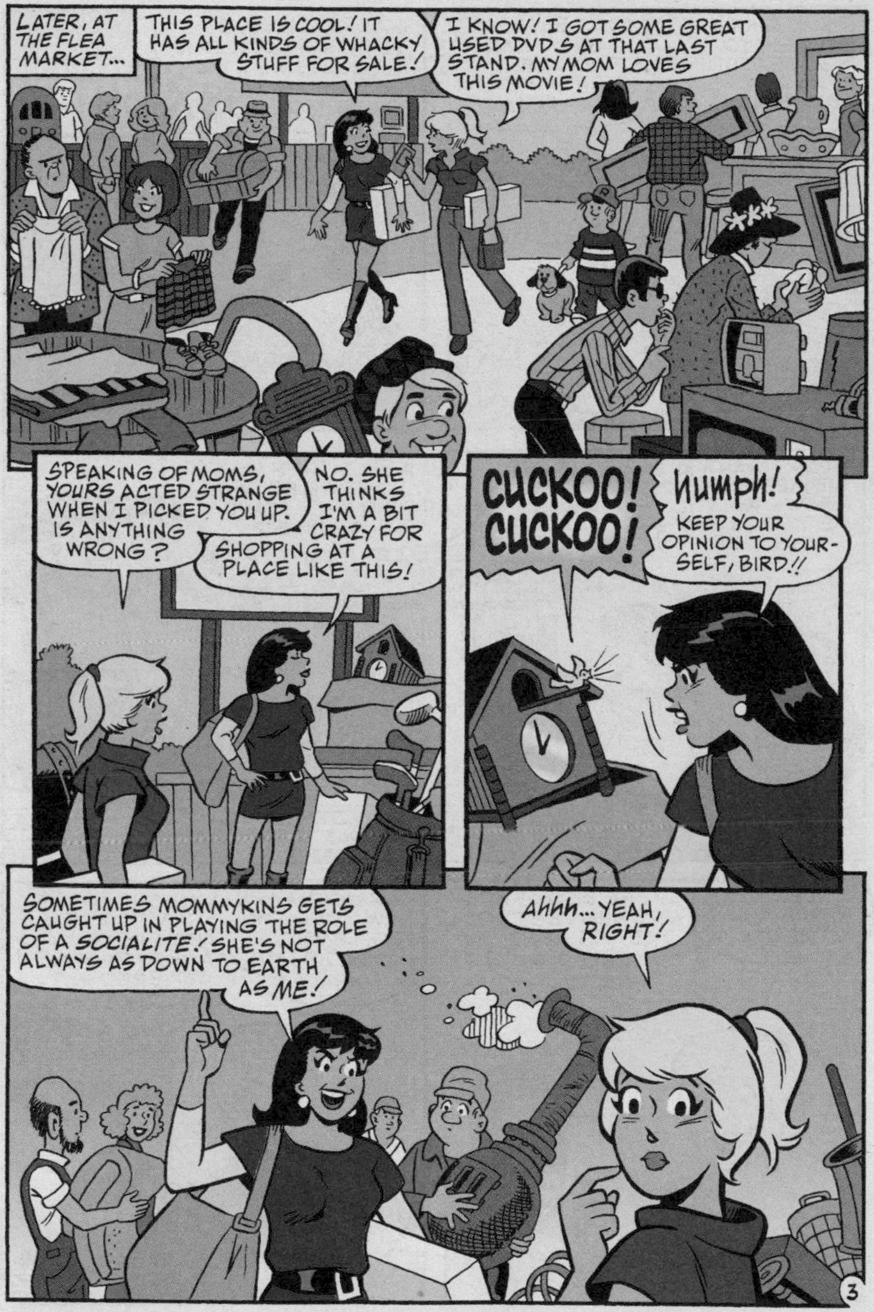
LATER, AT THE FLEA MARKET...
THIS PLACE IS COOL! IT HAS ALL KINDS OF WHACKY STUFF FOR SALE!
I KNOW! I GOT SOME GREAT USED DVDS AT THAT LAST STAND. MY MOM LOVES THIS MOVIE!
SPEAKING OF MOMS, YOURS ACTED STRANGE WHEN I PICKED YOU UP. IS ANYTHING WRONG?
NO. SHE THINKS I'M A BIT CRAZY FOR SHOPPING AT A PLACE LIKE THIS!
CUCKOO! CUCKOO!
humph! KEEP YOUR OPINION TO YOURSELF, BIRD!!
SOMETIMES MOMMYKINS GETS CAUGHT UP IN PLAYING THE ROLE OF A SOCIALITE! SHE'S NOT ALWAYS AS DOWN TO EARTH AS ME!
Ahhh... YEAH, RIGHT!
3

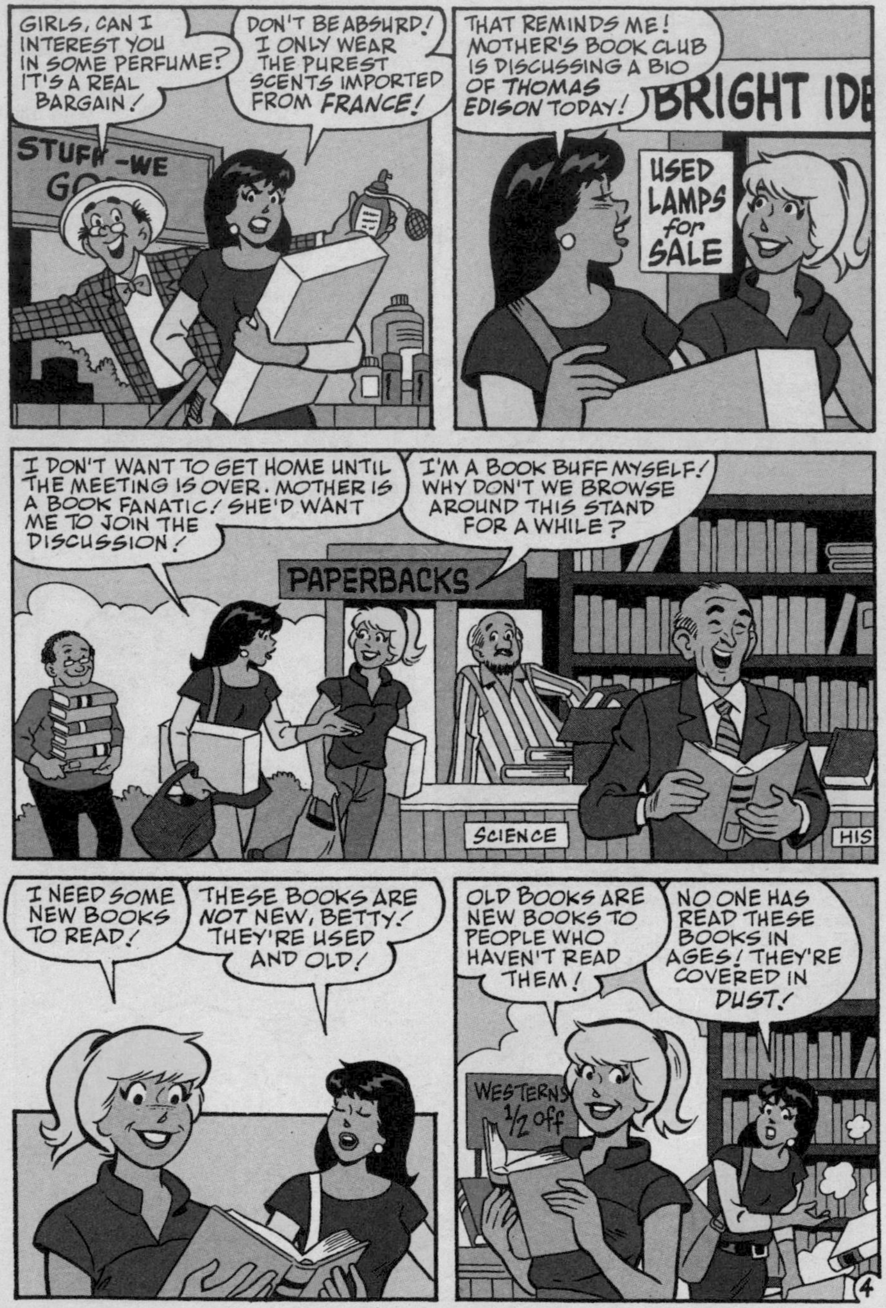
GIRLS, CAN I INTEREST YOU IN SOME PERFUME? IT'S A REAL BARGAIN!
DON'T BE ABSURD! I ONLY WEAR THE PUREST SCENTS IMPORTED FROM FRANCE!
STUFF -WE GO
THAT REMINDS ME! MOTHER'S BOOK CLUB IS DISCUSSING A BIO OF THOMAS EDISON TODAY!
BRIGHT IDE
USED LAMPS for SALE
I DON'T WANT TO GET HOME UNTIL THE MEETING IS OVER. MOTHER IS A BOOK FANATIC! SHE'D WANT ME TO JOIN THE DISCUSSION!
I'M A BOOK BUFF MYSELF! WHY DON'T WE BROWSE AROUND THIS STAND FOR A WHILE?
PAPERBACKS
SCIENCE
HIS
I NEED SOME NEW BOOKS TO READ!
THESE BOOKS ARE NOT NEW, BETTY! THEY'RE USED AND OLD!
OLD BOOKS ARE NEW BOOKS TO PEOPLE WHO HAVEN'T READ THEM!
NO ONE HAS READ THESE BOOKS IN AGES! THEY'RE COVERED IN DUST!
WESTERNS 1/2 off
4

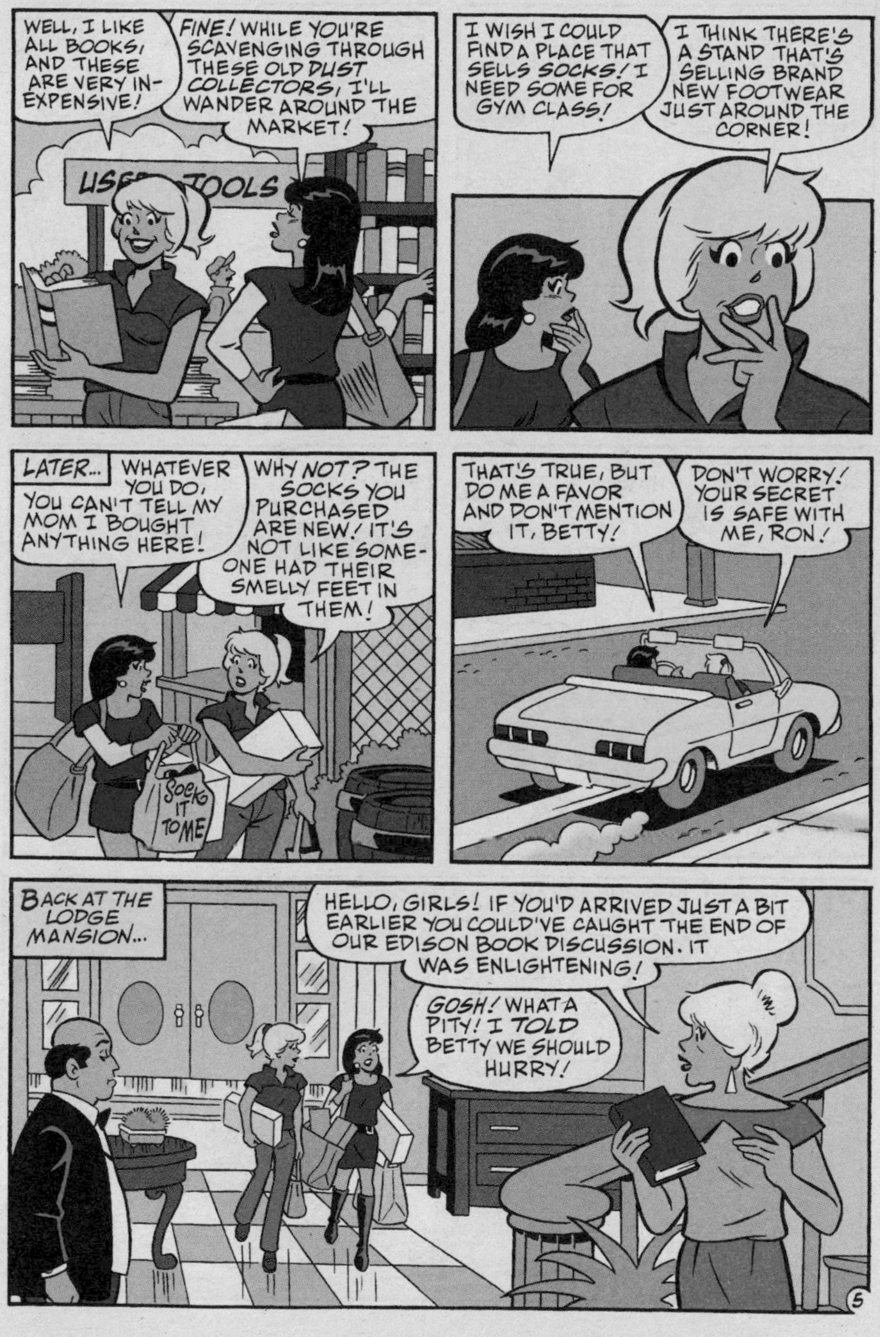
WELL, I LIKE ALL BOOKS, AND THESE ARE VERY IN-EXPENSIVE!
FINE! WHILE YOU'RE SCAVENGING THROUGH THESE OLD DUST COLLECTORS, I'LL WANDER AROUND THE MARKET!
I WISH I COULD FIND A PLACE THAT SELLS SOCKS! I NEED SOME FOR GYM CLASS!
I THINK THERE'S A STAND THAT'S SELLING BRAND NEW FOOTWEAR JUST AROUND THE CORNER!
LATER...
WHATEVER YOU DO, YOU CAN'T TELL MY MOM I BOUGHT ANYTHING HERE!
WHY NOT? THE SOCKS YOU PURCHASED ARE NEW! IT'S NOT LIKE SOME-ONE HAD THEIR SMELLY FEET IN THEM!
SOCK IT TO ME
THAT'S TRUE, BUT DO ME A FAVOR AND DON'T MENTION IT, BETTY!
DON'T WORRY! YOUR SECRET IS SAFE WITH ME, RON!
BACK AT THE LODGE MANSION...
HELLO, GIRLS! IF YOU'D ARRIVED JUST A BIT EARLIER YOU COULD'VE CAUGHT THE END OF OUR EDISON BOOK DISCUSSION. IT WAS ENLIGHTENING!
GOSH! WHAT A PITY! I TOLD BETTY WE SHOULD HURRY!
5

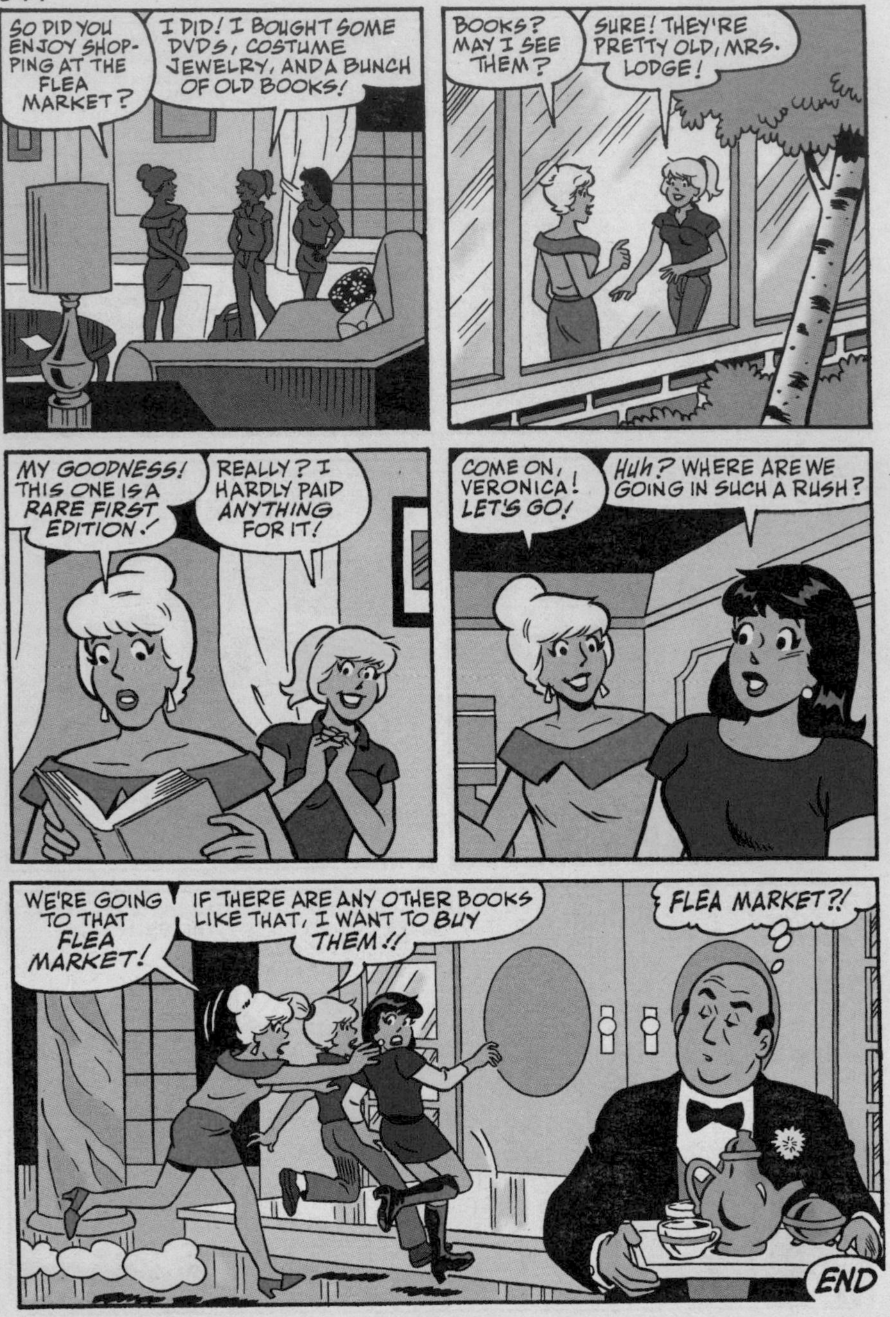
SO DID YOU ENJOY SHOPPING AT THE FLEA MARKET?
I DID! I BOUGHT SOME DVDS, COSTUME JEWELRY, AND A BUNCH OF OLD BOOKS!
BOOKS? MAY I SEE THEM?
SURE! THEY'RE PRETTY OLD, MRS. LODGE!
MY GOODNESS! THIS ONE IS A RARE FIRST EDITION!
REALLY? I HARDLY PAID ANYTHING FOR IT!
COME ON, VERONICA! LET'S GO!
Huh? WHERE ARE WE GOING IN SUCH A RUSH?
WE'RE GOING TO THAT FLEA MARKET!
IF THERE ARE ANY OTHER BOOKS LIKE THAT, I WANT TO BUY THEM!!
FLEA MARKET?!
END

Vamp It Up
Betty & Veronica #261, 2012
by Dan Parent,
Rich Koslowski,
Jack Morelli, Tom Chu

This story was so much fun, because drawing the summery beach-type stories are always the best. And this story was twice the fun because I borrowed from the very popular genre of vampires, which we know permeates in pop culture today with everything from *Twilight* to *True Blood*. For those of us comic geeks, Vampirella was another popular vampire character. So with a few tweaks, we have Vampironica! And we all know Buffy the Vampire Slayer, so why not make the plunge and go for Betty the Vampire Slayer? This was another one of those fun stories that just sort of writes itself. Because when you have vampire teen beach parties, vampire slayers and mad vampire scientists, what else do you need?

-- **Dan Parent**
Writer/Artist,
Archie Comics

Taking Care of Business
Betty & Veronica #257, 2012
by Paul Kupperberg,
Jeff Shultz, Jim Amash,
Jack Morelli, DigiKore
Studios

Betty and Veronica are like most teenage girls — they have boy trouble, lots of homework and big dreams! But what makes the story "Taking Care of Business" unique is that it deals with a very serious threat to all teenagers: getting into a car accident. And despite being an all ages comic this story doesn't sugarcoat the situation, putting Betty and Veronica in genuine danger. That really impressed me when I first read it, plus it incorporates actual business techniques as Veronica applies them to the business of survival! And while even today it's nice to have a cute boy like Archie or a caring father like Mr. Lodge do things for you, it's important for girls to be able to handle themselves in an emergency... or just in life! Yes, Betty and Veronica are heroes because they save themselves. Enjoy!

-- **Grace Randolph**
Host/Writer,
Think About the Ink/ Supurbia

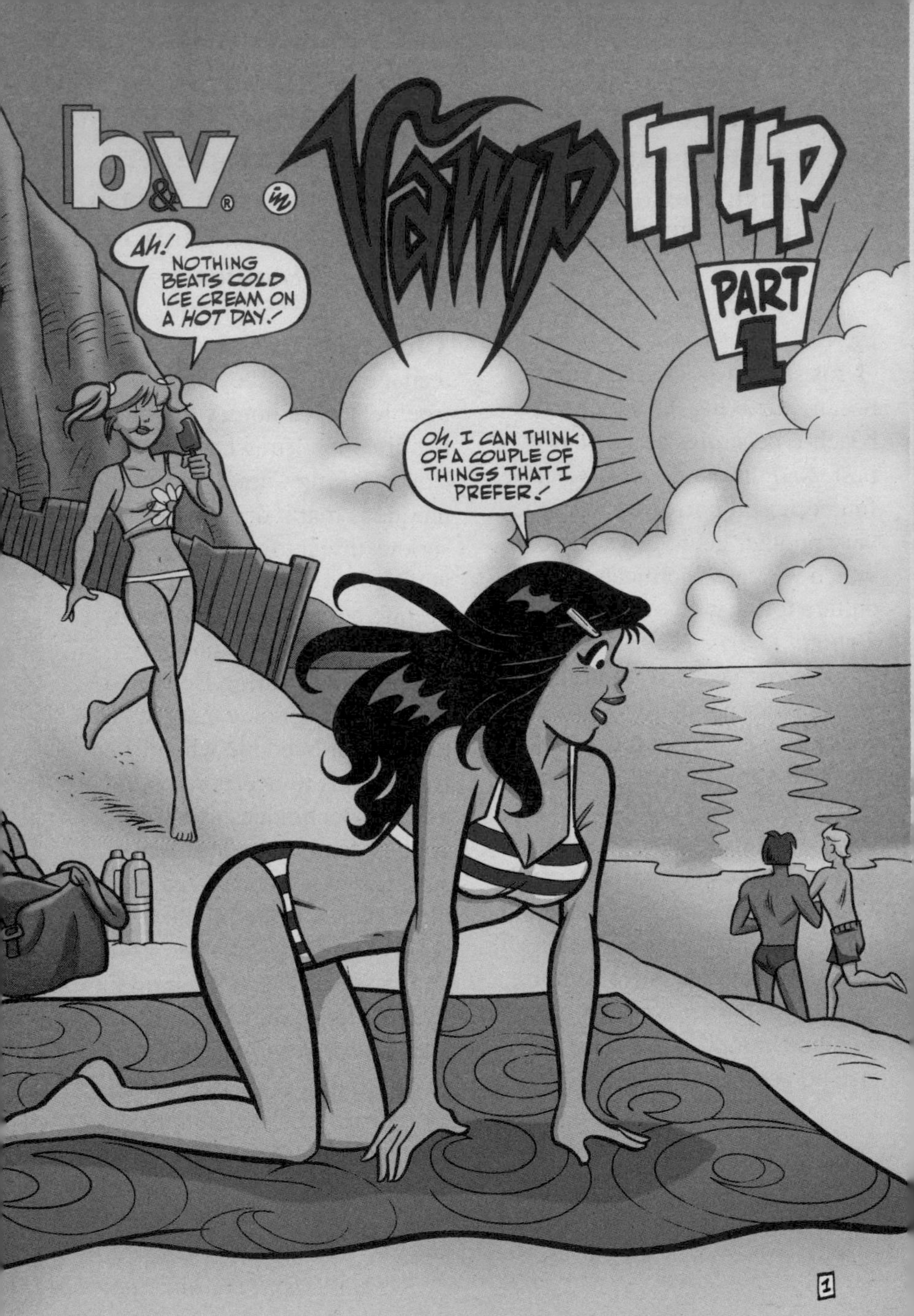
b&v® in Vamp IT UP
PART 1
Ah! NOTHING BEATS COLD ICE CREAM ON A HOT DAY!
Oh, I CAN THINK OF A COUPLE OF THINGS THAT I PREFER!
1

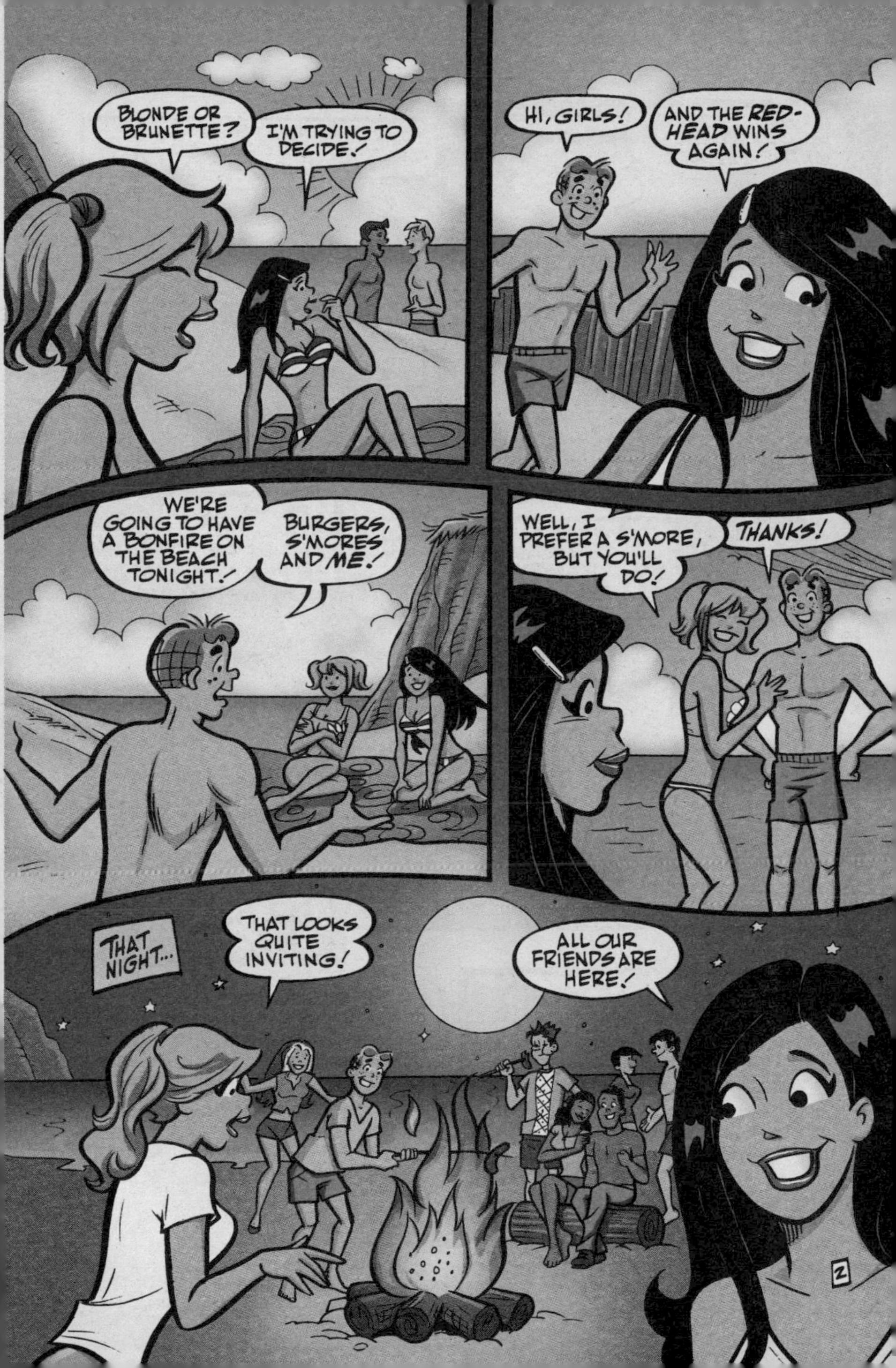
BLONDE OR BRUNETTE?
I'M TRYING TO DECIDE!
HI, GIRLS!
AND THE RED-HEAD WINS AGAIN!
WE'RE GOING TO HAVE A BONFIRE ON THE BEACH TONIGHT!
BURGERS, S'MORES AND ME!
WELL, I PREFER A S'MORE, BUT YOU'LL DO!
THANKS!
THAT NIGHT...
THAT LOOKS QUITE INVITING!
ALL OUR FRIENDS ARE HERE!
2

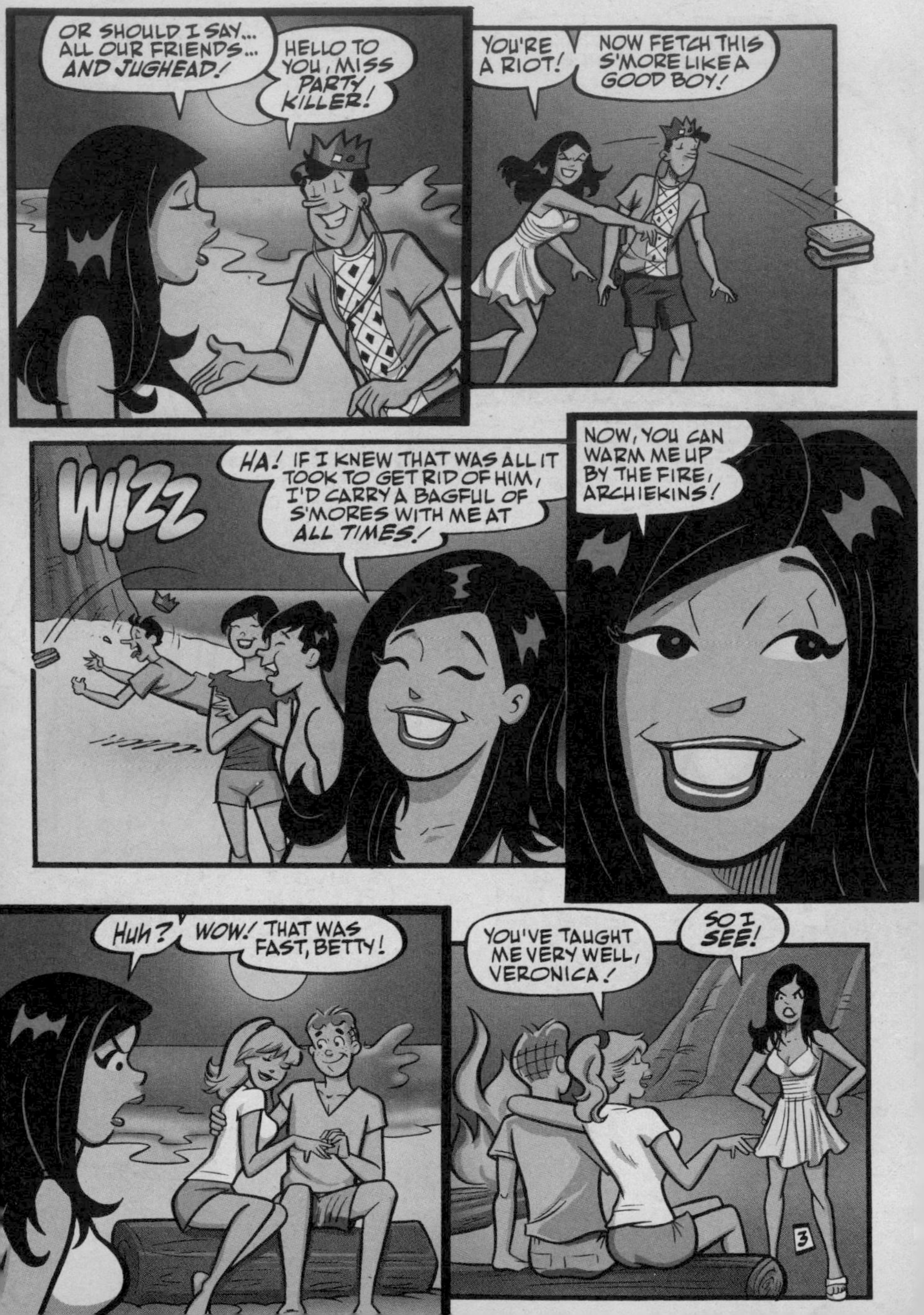
OR SHOULD I SAY... ALL OUR FRIENDS... AND JUGHEAD!
HELLO TO YOU, MISS PARTY KILLER!
YOU'RE A RIOT!
NOW FETCH THIS S'MORE LIKE A GOOD BOY!
WIZZ
HA! IF I KNEW THAT WAS ALL IT TOOK TO GET RID OF HIM, I'D CARRY A BAGFUL OF S'MORES WITH ME AT ALL TIMES!
NOW, YOU CAN WARM ME UP BY THE FIRE, ARCHIEKINS!
HUH?
WOW! THAT WAS FAST, BETTY!
YOU'VE TAUGHT ME VERY WELL, VERONICA!
SO I SEE!
3

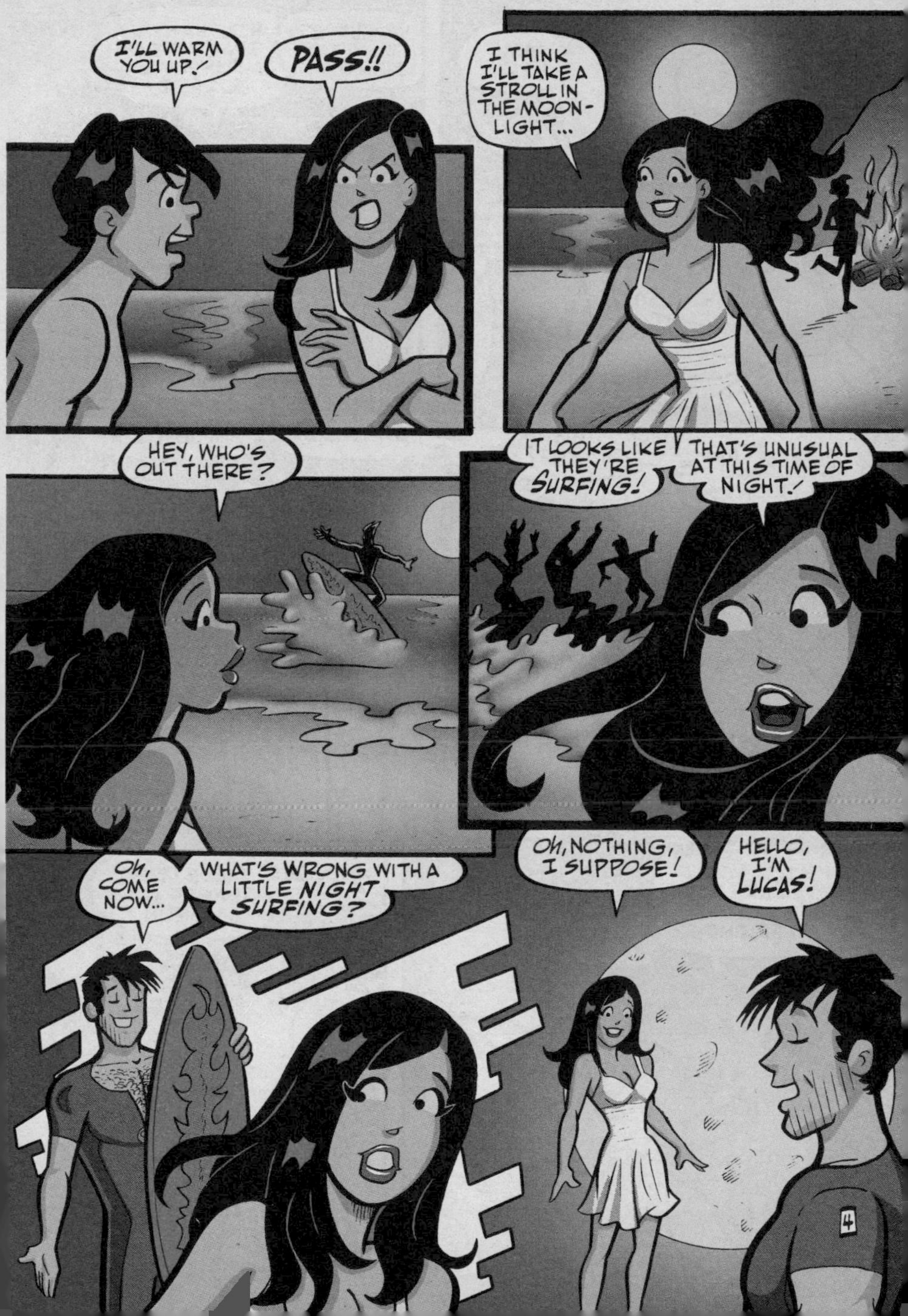
I'LL WARM YOU UP!
PASS!!
I THINK I'LL TAKE A STROLL IN THE MOON-LIGHT...
HEY, WHO'S OUT THERE?
IT LOOKS LIKE THEY'RE SURFING!
THAT'S UNUSUAL AT THIS TIME OF NIGHT!
Oh, COME NOW...
WHAT'S WRONG WITH A LITTLE NIGHT SURFING?
Oh, NOTHING, I SUPPOSE!
HELLO, I'M LUCAS!

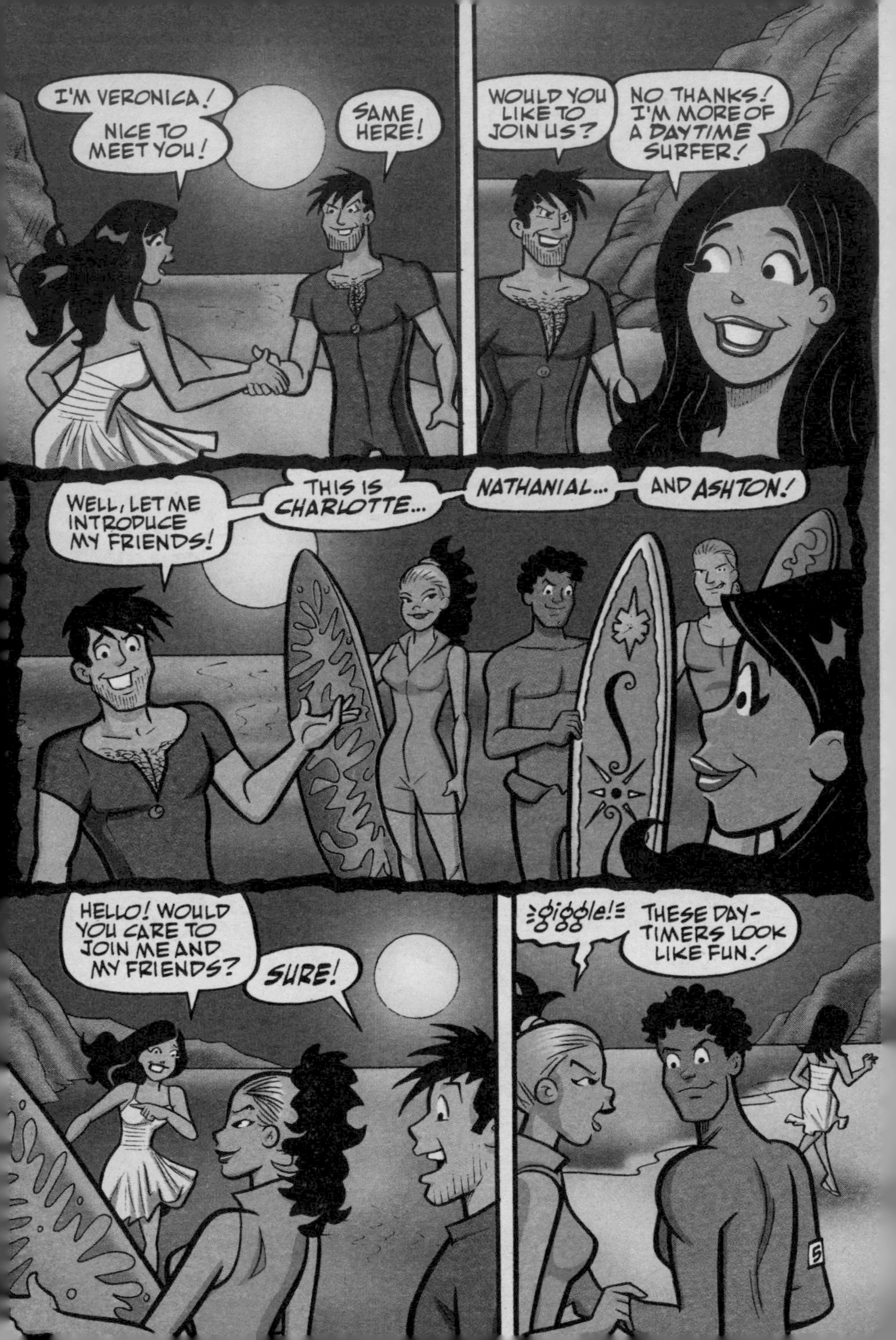
I'M VERONICA! NICE TO MEET YOU!
SAME HERE!
WOULD YOU LIKE TO JOIN US?
NO THANKS! I'M MORE OF A DAYTIME SURFER!
WELL, LET ME INTRODUCE MY FRIENDS!
THIS IS CHARLOTTE...
NATHANIAL...
AND ASHTON!
HELLO! WOULD YOU CARE TO JOIN ME AND MY FRIENDS?
SURE!
giggle!
THESE DAY-TIMERS LOOK LIKE FUN!

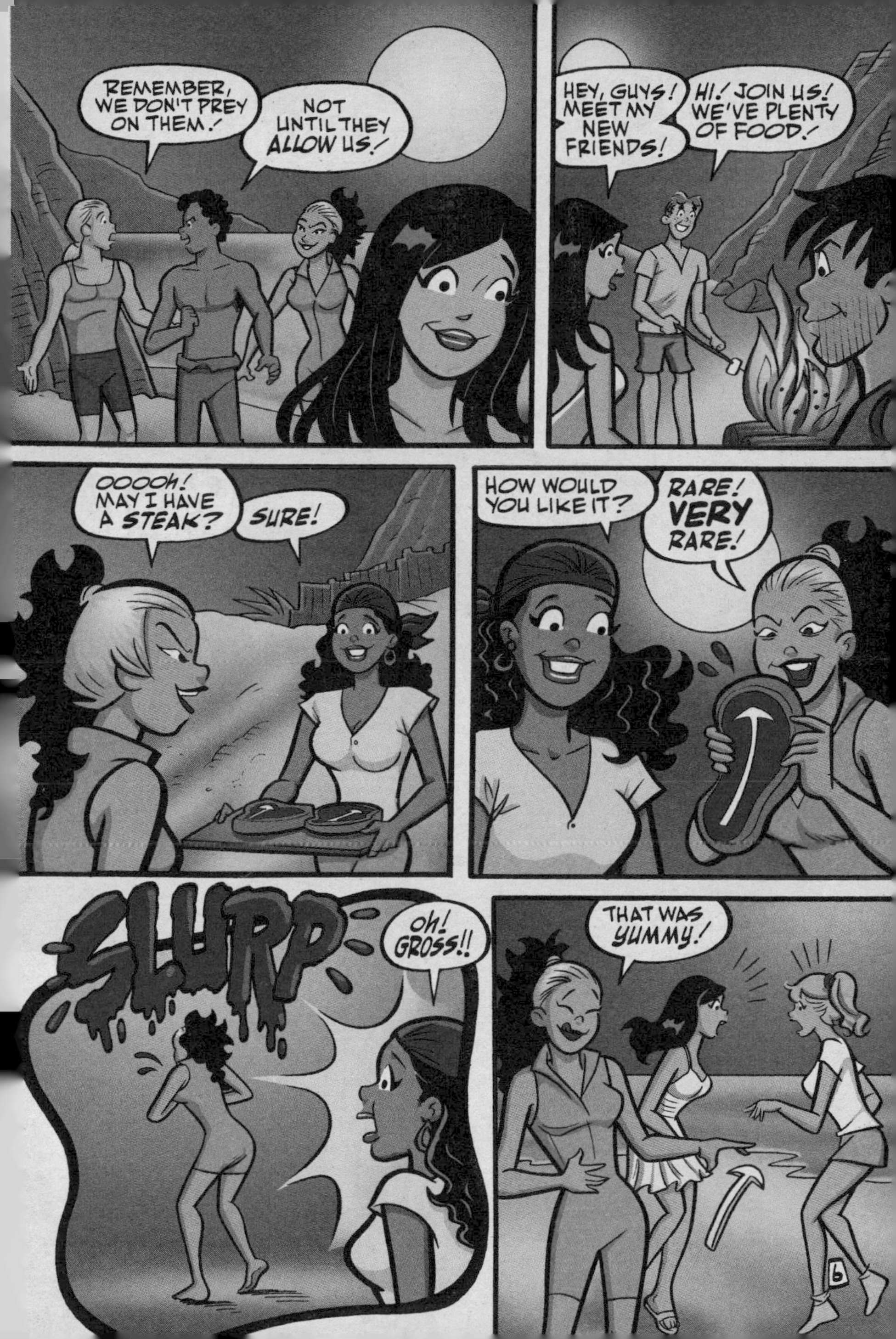
REMEMBER, WE DON'T PREY ON THEM.!
NOT UNTIL THEY ALLOW US!
HEY, GUYS! MEET MY NEW FRIENDS!
HI! JOIN US! WE'VE PLENTY OF FOOD!
OOOOh! MAY I HAVE A STEAK?
SURE!
HOW WOULD YOU LIKE IT?
RARE! VERY RARE!
SLURP
oh! GROSS!!
THAT WAS YUMMY!
6

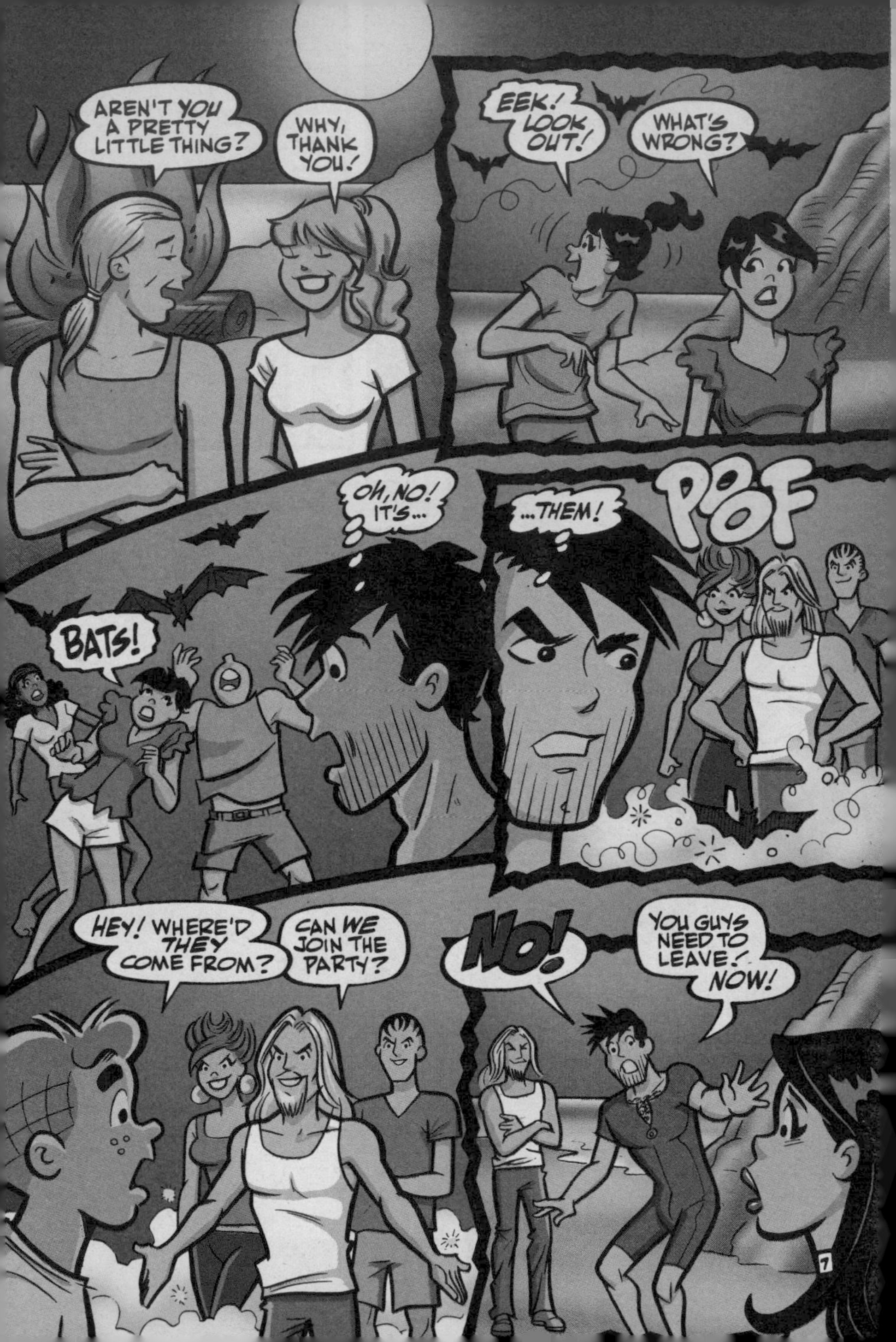

AREN'T YOU A PRETTY LITTLE THING?
WHY, THANK YOU!
EEK! LOOK OUT!
WHAT'S WRONG?
BATS!
OH, NO! IT'S...
...THEM!
POOF
HEY! WHERE'D THEY COME FROM?
CAN WE JOIN THE PARTY?
NO!
YOU GUYS NEED TO LEAVE! NOW!

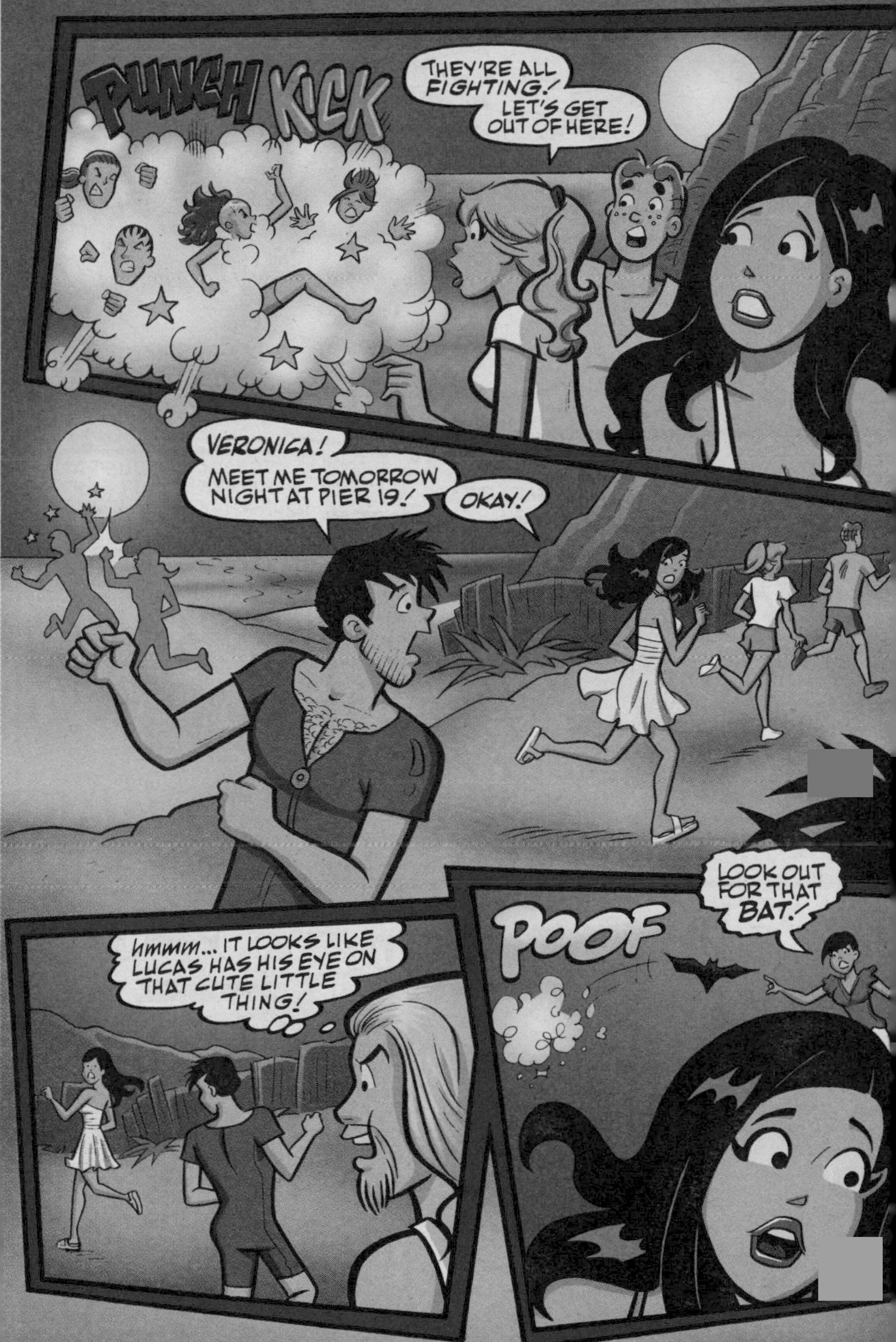
PUNCH
KICK
THEY'RE ALL FIGHTING! LET'S GET OUT OF HERE!
VERONICA!
MEET ME TOMORROW NIGHT AT PIER 19!
OKAY!
hmmm... IT LOOKS LIKE LUCAS HAS HIS EYE ON THAT CUTE LITTLE THING!
LOOK OUT FOR THAT BAT!
POOF

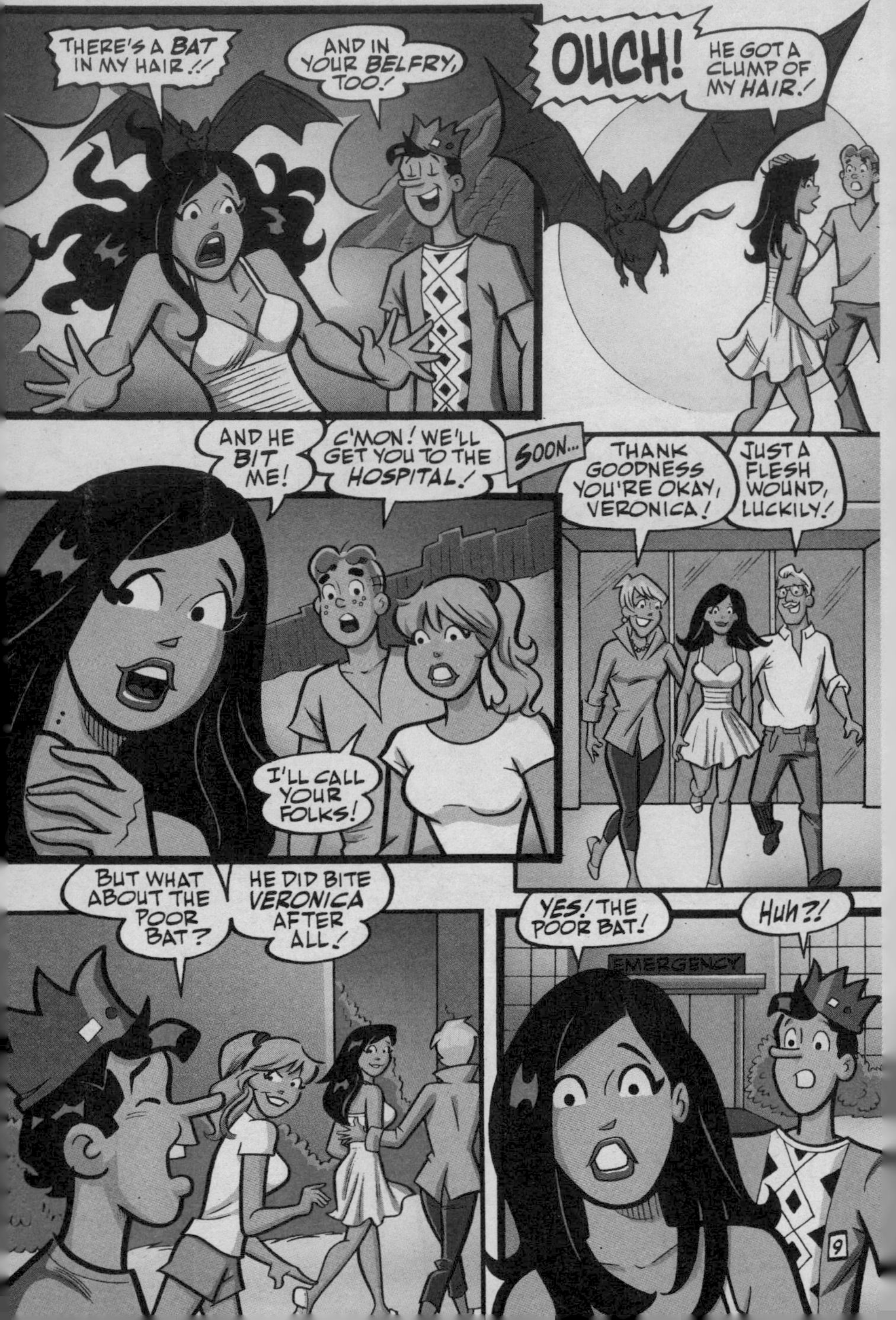

THERE'S A BAT IN MY HAIR!!
AND IN YOUR BELFRY, TOO!
OUCH!
HE GOT A CLUMP OF MY HAIR!
AND HE BIT ME!
C'MON! WE'LL GET YOU TO THE HOSPITAL!
I'LL CALL YOUR FOLKS!
SOON...
THANK GOODNESS YOU'RE OKAY, VERONICA!
JUST A FLESH WOUND, LUCKILY!
BUT WHAT ABOUT THE POOR BAT?
HE DID BITE VERONICA AFTER ALL!
YES! THE POOR BAT!
Huh?!
EMERGENCY
9

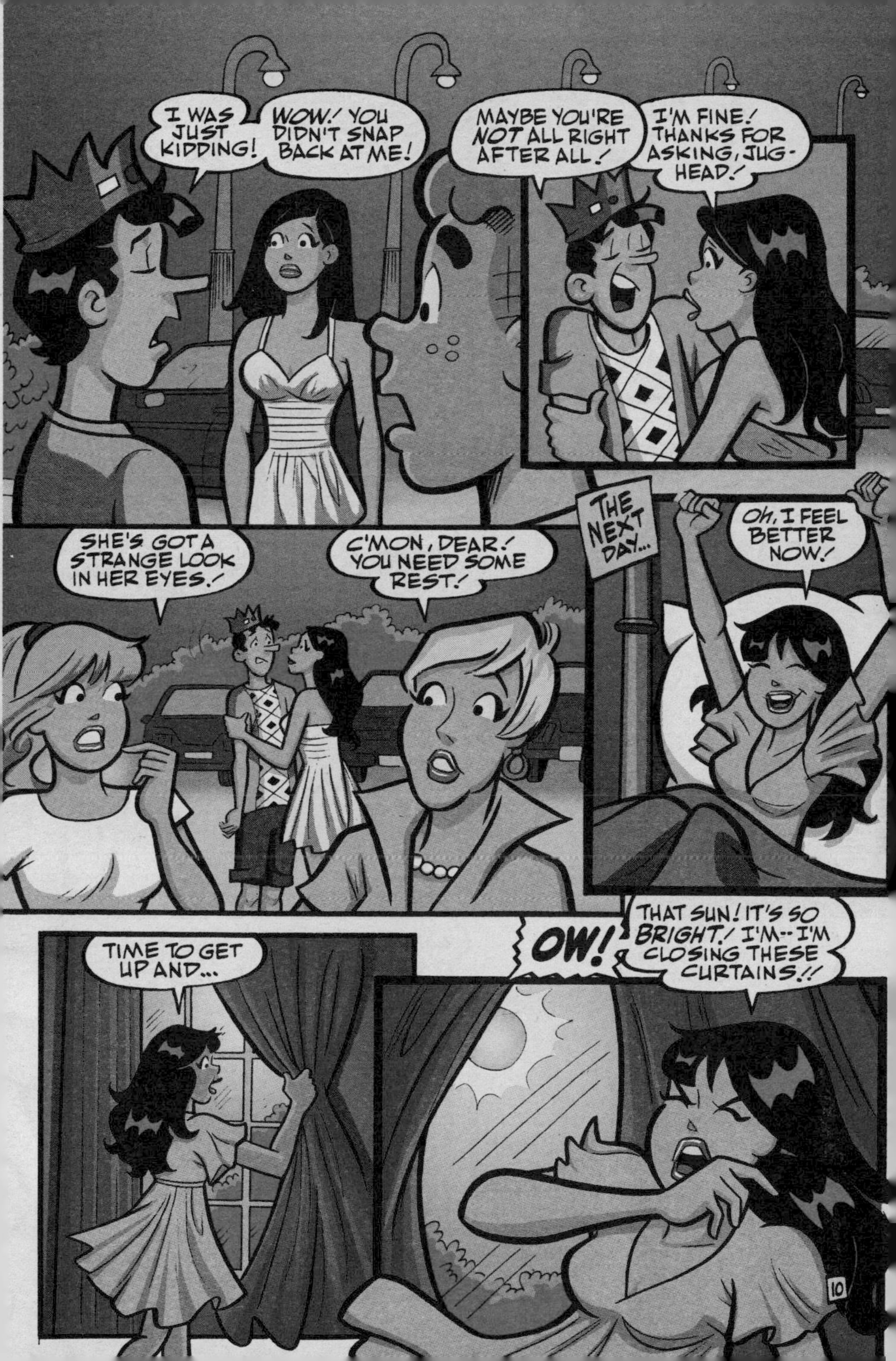
I WAS JUST KIDDING!
WOW! YOU DIDN'T SNAP BACK AT ME!
MAYBE YOU'RE NOT ALL RIGHT AFTER ALL!
I'M FINE! THANKS FOR ASKING, JUG-HEAD!
SHE'S GOT A STRANGE LOOK IN HER EYES!
C'MON, DEAR! YOU NEED SOME REST!
THE NEXT DAY...
Oh, I FEEL BETTER NOW!
TIME TO GET UP AND...
OW!
THAT SUN! IT'S SO BRIGHT! I'M-- I'M CLOSING THESE CURTAINS!!
10

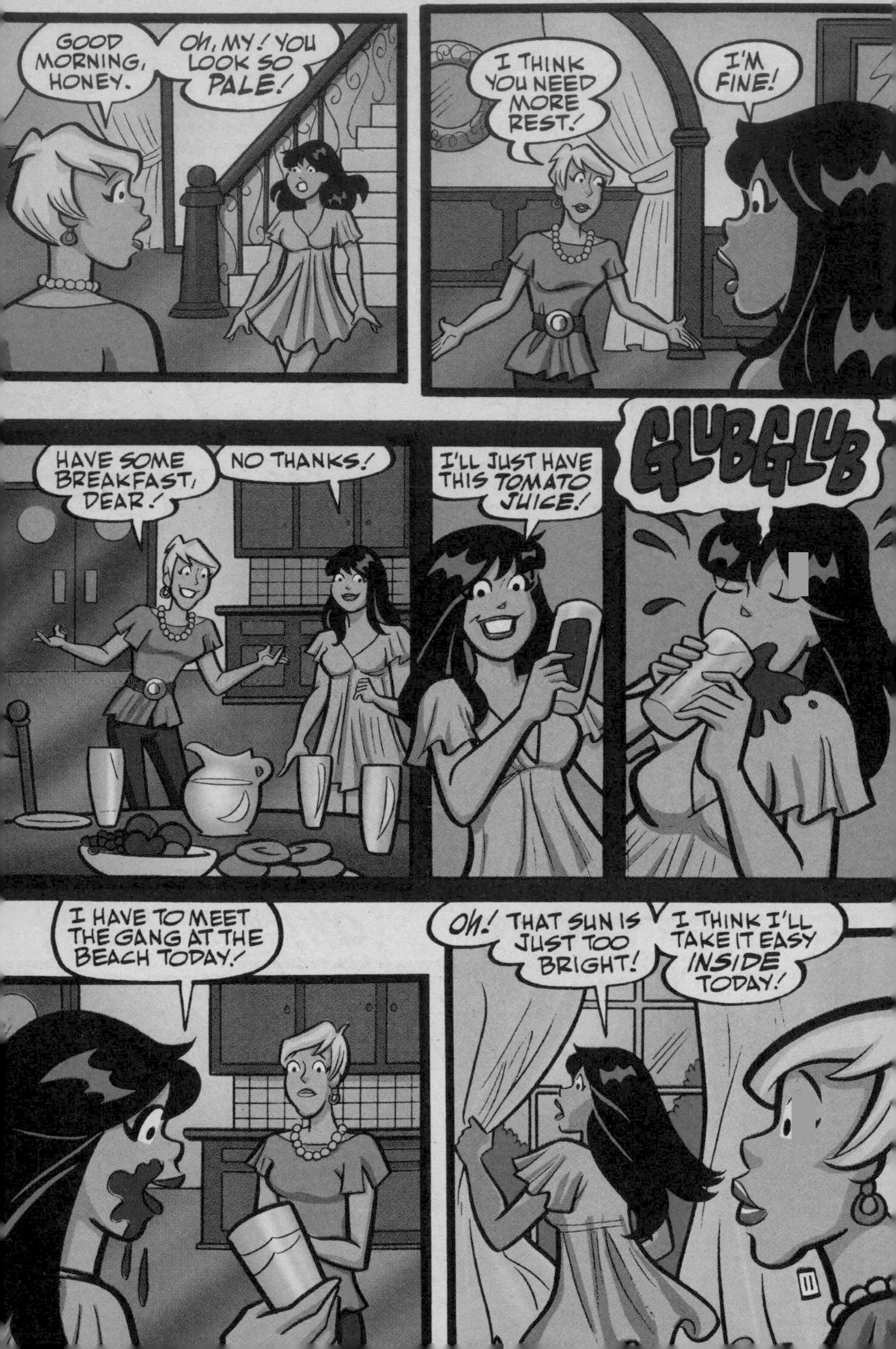

GOOD MORNING, HONEY.
Oh, MY! YOU LOOK SO PALE!
I THINK YOU NEED MORE REST!
I'M FINE!
HAVE SOME BREAKFAST, DEAR!
NO THANKS!
I'LL JUST HAVE THIS TOMATO JUICE!
GLUBGLUB
I HAVE TO MEET THE GANG AT THE BEACH TODAY!
Oh! THAT SUN IS JUST TOO BRIGHT!
I THINK I'LL TAKE IT EASY INSIDE TODAY!

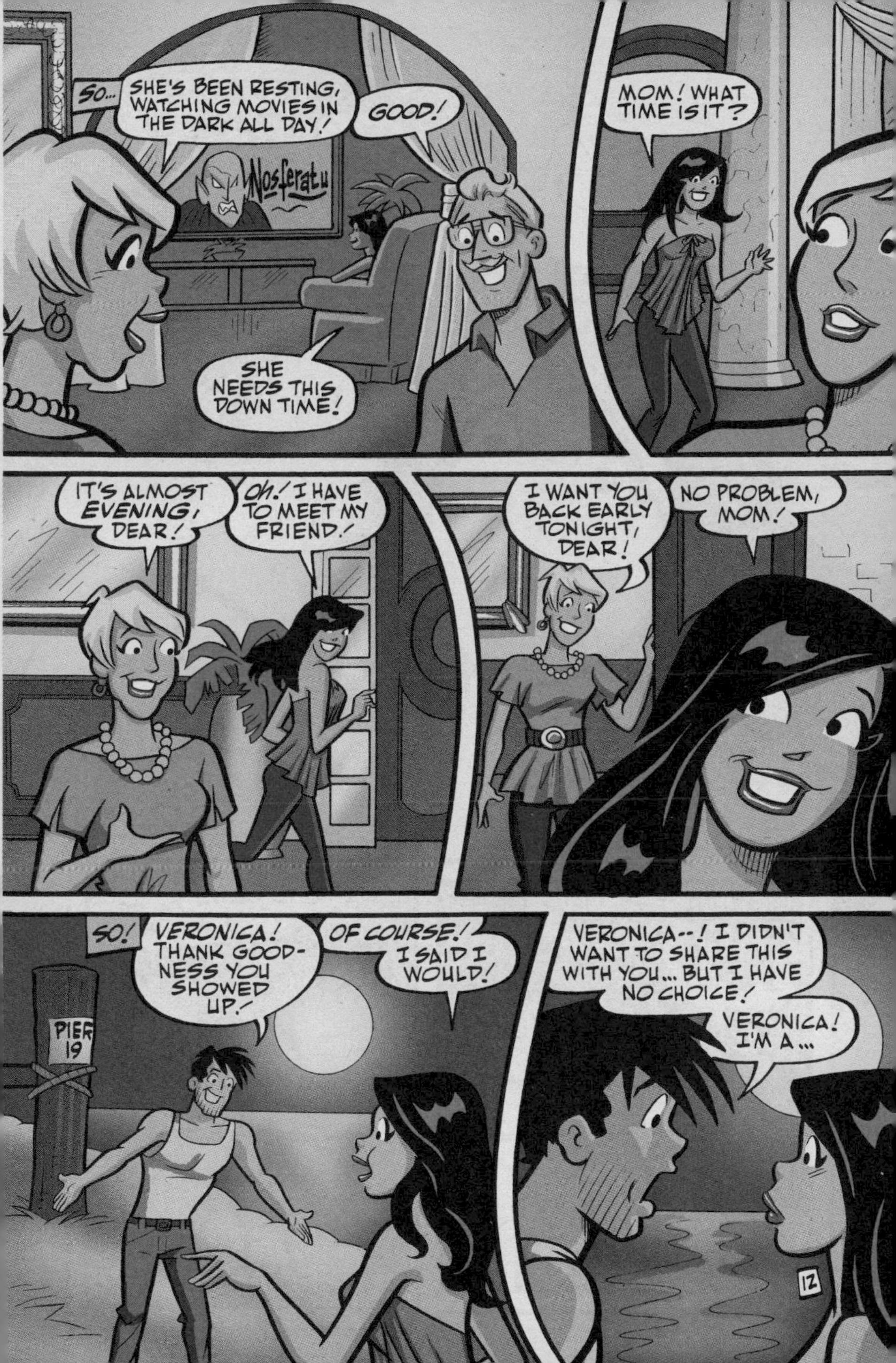

SO...
SHE'S BEEN RESTING, WATCHING MOVIES IN THE DARK ALL DAY!
GOOD!
Nosferatu
SHE NEEDS THIS DOWN TIME!
MOM! WHAT TIME IS IT?
IT'S ALMOST EVENING, DEAR!
Oh! I HAVE TO MEET MY FRIEND!
I WANT YOU BACK EARLY TONIGHT, DEAR!
NO PROBLEM, MOM!
SO!
VERONICA! THANK GOODNESS YOU SHOWED UP!
OF COURSE! I SAID I WOULD!
PIER 19
VERONICA--! I DIDN'T WANT TO SHARE THIS WITH YOU... BUT I HAVE NO CHOICE!
VERONICA! I'M A...
12

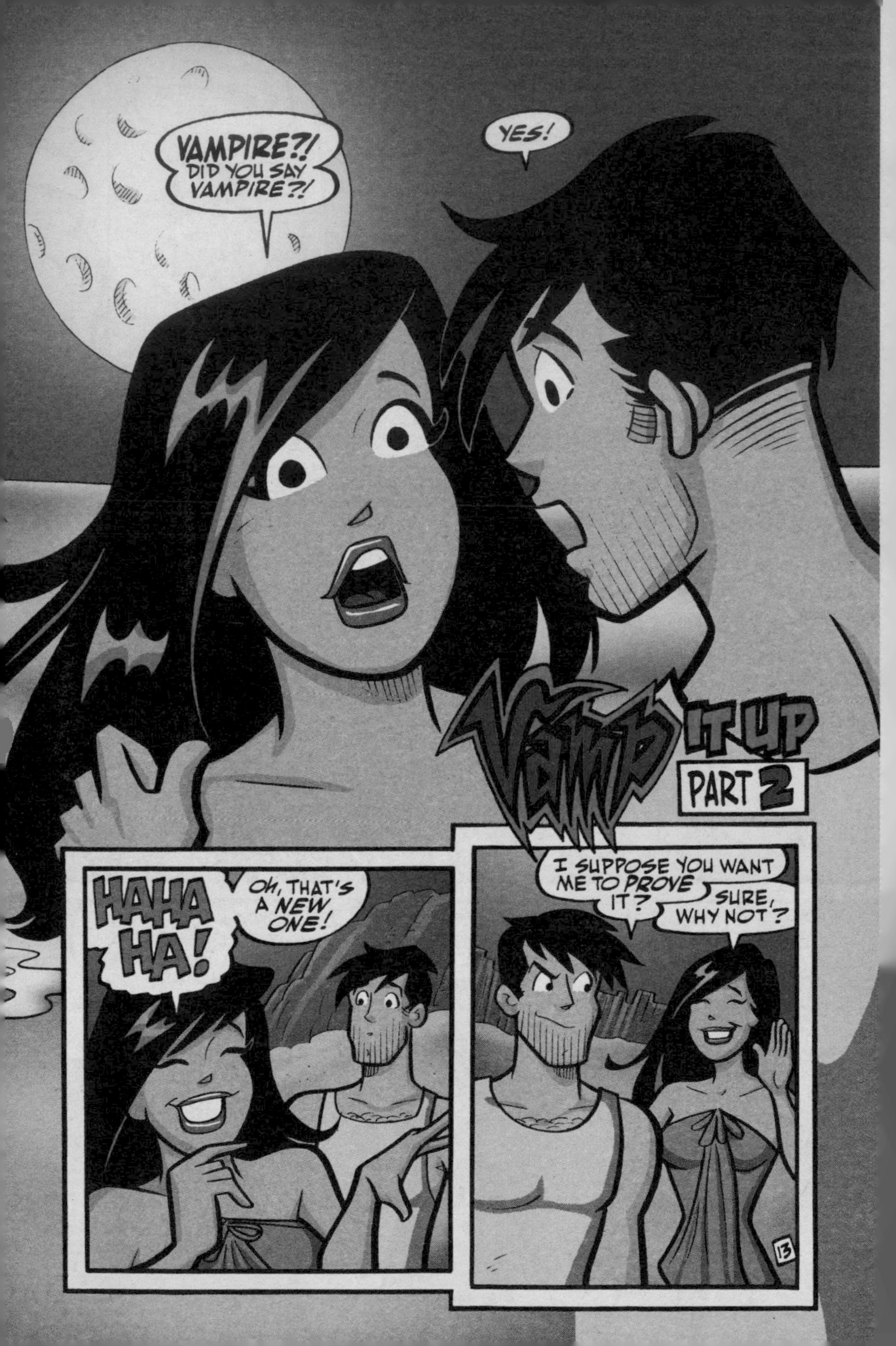
VAMPIRE?! DID YOU SAY VAMPIRE?!
YES!
VAMP IT UP
PART 2
HAHA HA!
Oh, THAT'S A NEW ONE!
I SUPPOSE YOU WANT ME TO PROVE IT?
SURE, WHY NOT?
13

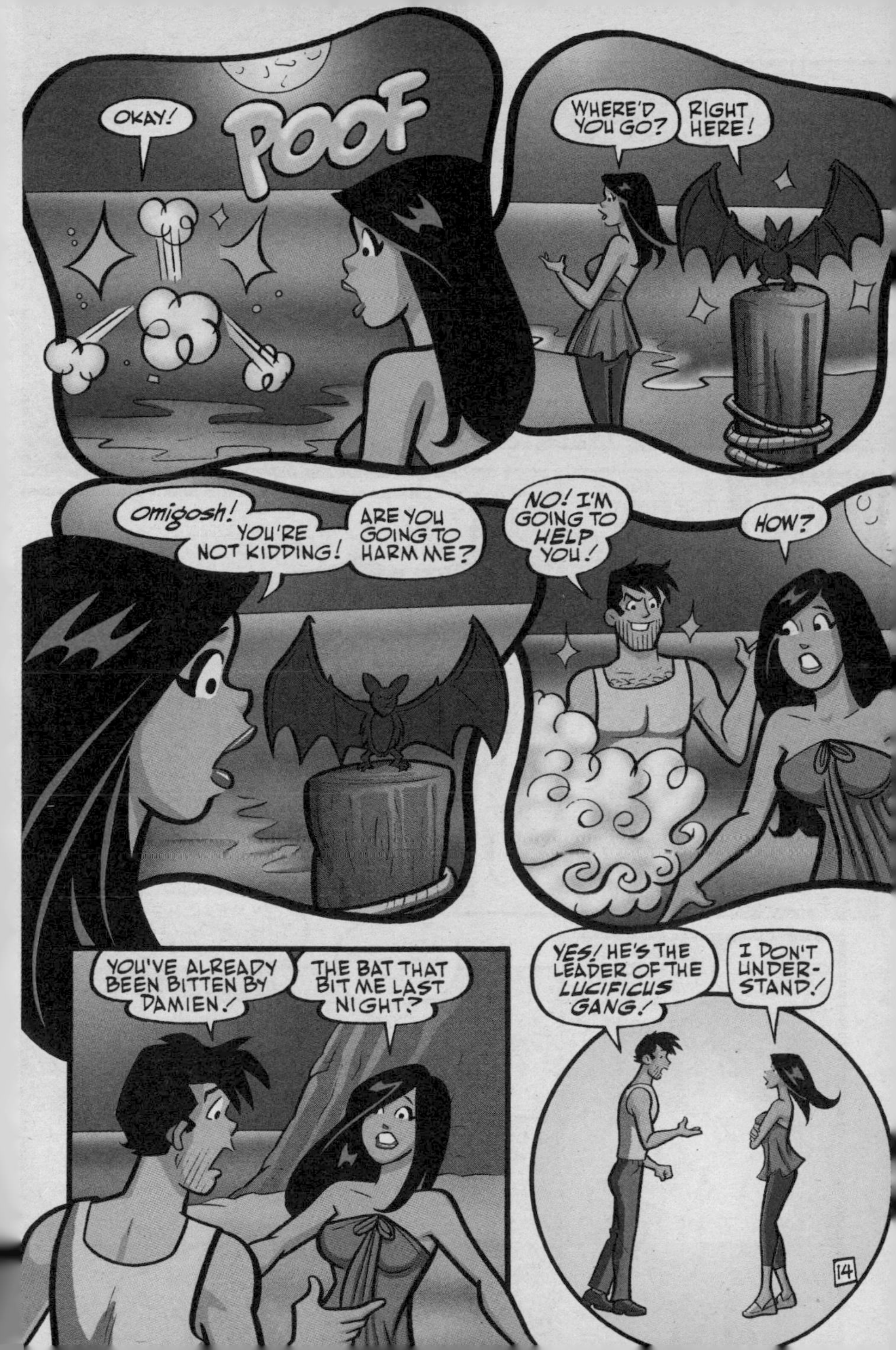
OKAY!
POOF
WHERE'D YOU GO?
RIGHT HERE!
Omigosh! YOU'RE NOT KIDDING!
ARE YOU GOING TO HARM ME?
NO! I'M GOING TO HELP YOU!
HOW?
YOU'VE ALREADY BEEN BITTEN BY DAMIEN!
THE BAT THAT BIT ME LAST NIGHT?
YES! HE'S THE LEADER OF THE LUCIFICUS GANG!
I DON'T UNDER-STAND!
14

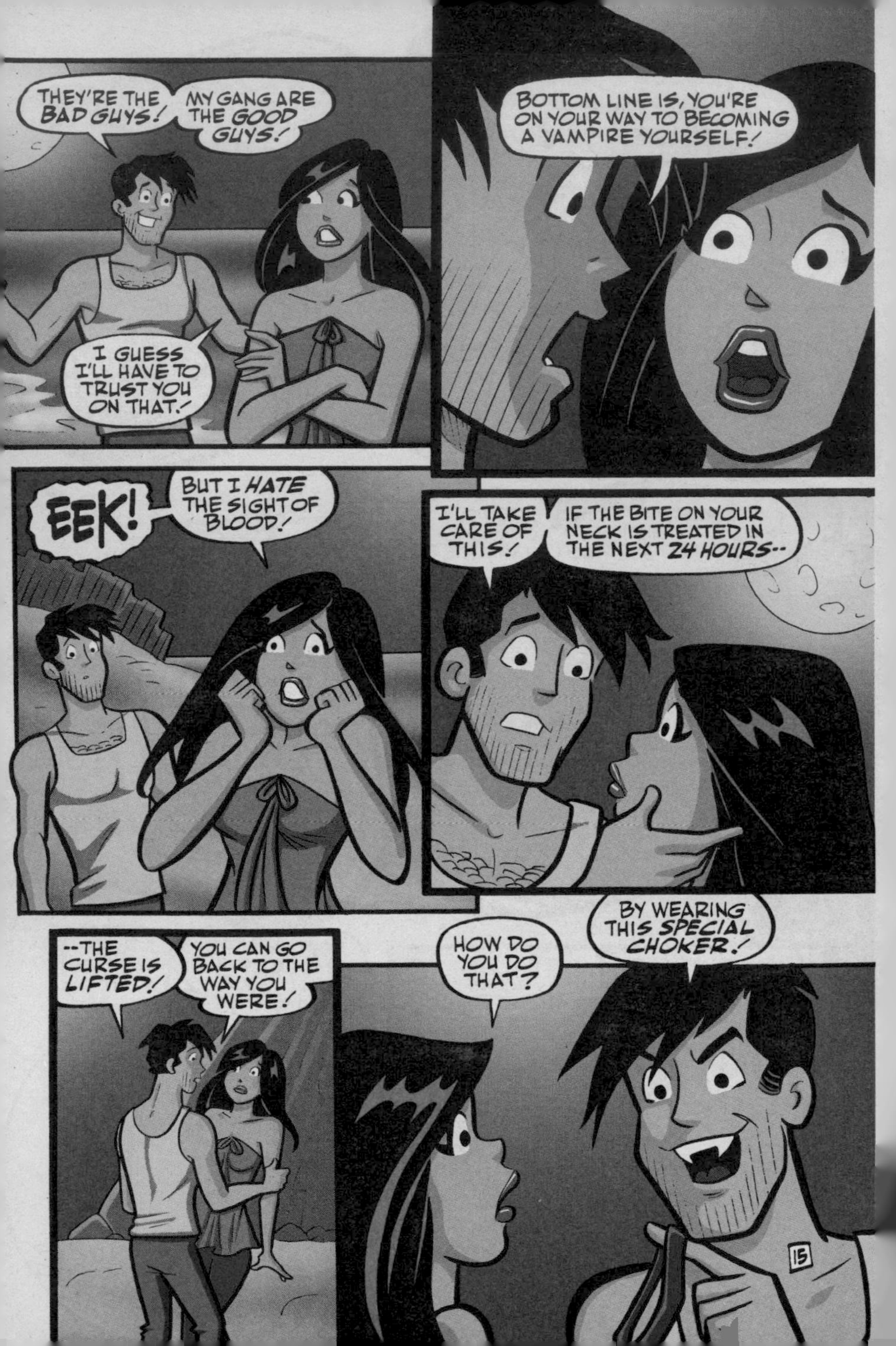
THEY'RE THE BAD GUYS!
MY GANG ARE THE GOOD GUYS!
I GUESS I'LL HAVE TO TRUST YOU ON THAT!
BOTTOM LINE IS, YOU'RE ON YOUR WAY TO BECOMING A VAMPIRE YOURSELF!
EEK!
BUT I HATE THE SIGHT OF BLOOD!
I'LL TAKE CARE OF THIS!
IF THE BITE ON YOUR NECK IS TREATED IN THE NEXT 24 HOURS--
--THE CURSE IS LIFTED!
YOU CAN GO BACK TO THE WAY YOU WERE!
HOW DO YOU DO THAT?
BY WEARING THIS SPECIAL CHOKER!
15

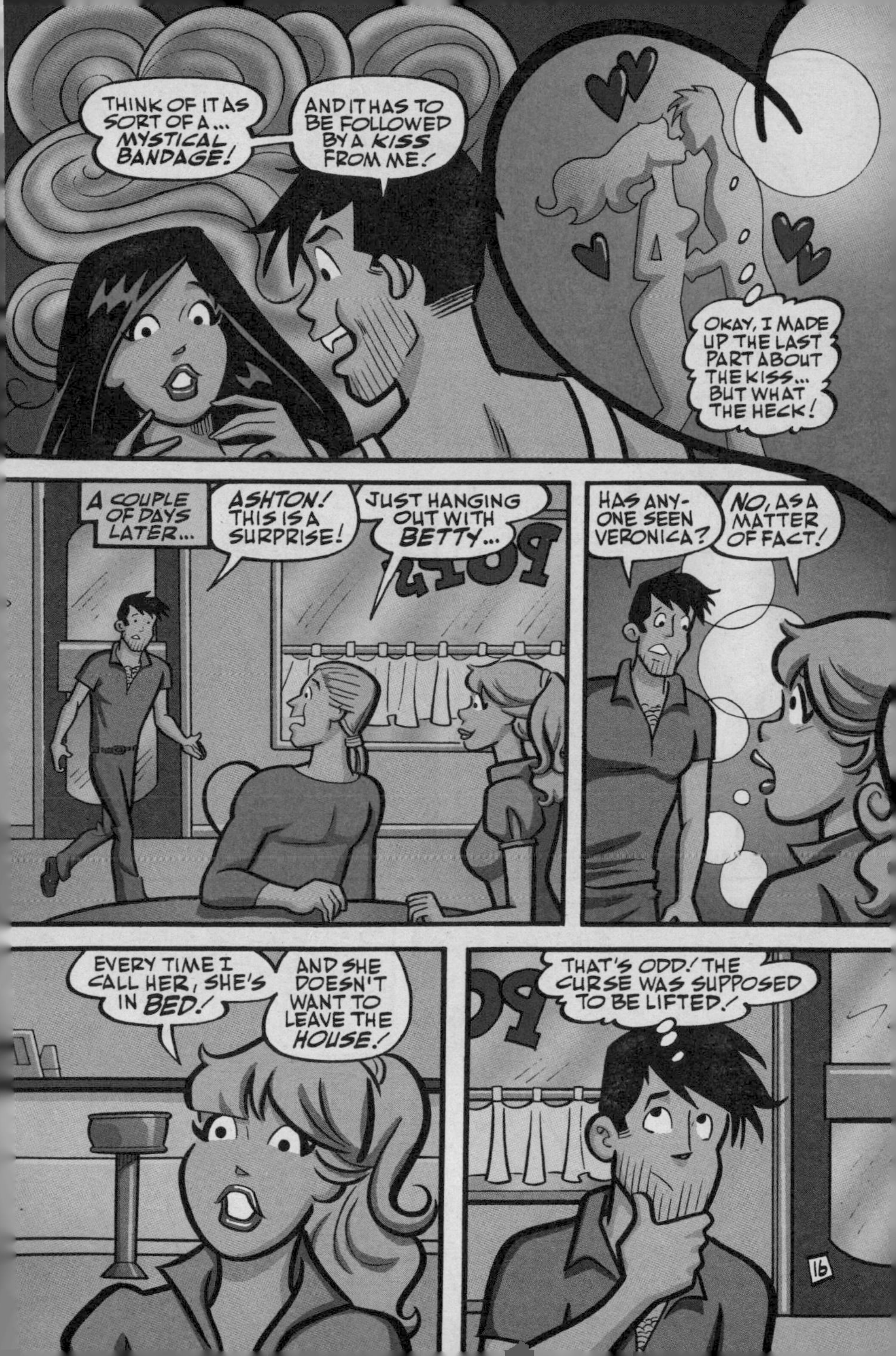
THINK OF IT AS SORT OF A... MYSTICAL BANDAGE!
AND IT HAS TO BE FOLLOWED BY A KISS FROM ME!
OKAY, I MADE UP THE LAST PART ABOUT THE KISS... BUT WHAT THE HECK!
A COUPLE OF DAYS LATER...
ASHTON! THIS IS A SURPRISE!
JUST HANGING OUT WITH BETTY...
POPS
HAS ANYONE SEEN VERONICA?
NO, AS A MATTER OF FACT!
EVERY TIME I CALL HER, SHE'S IN BED!
AND SHE DOESN'T WANT TO LEAVE THE HOUSE!
POP
THAT'S ODD! THE CURSE WAS SUPPOSED TO BE LIFTED!
16

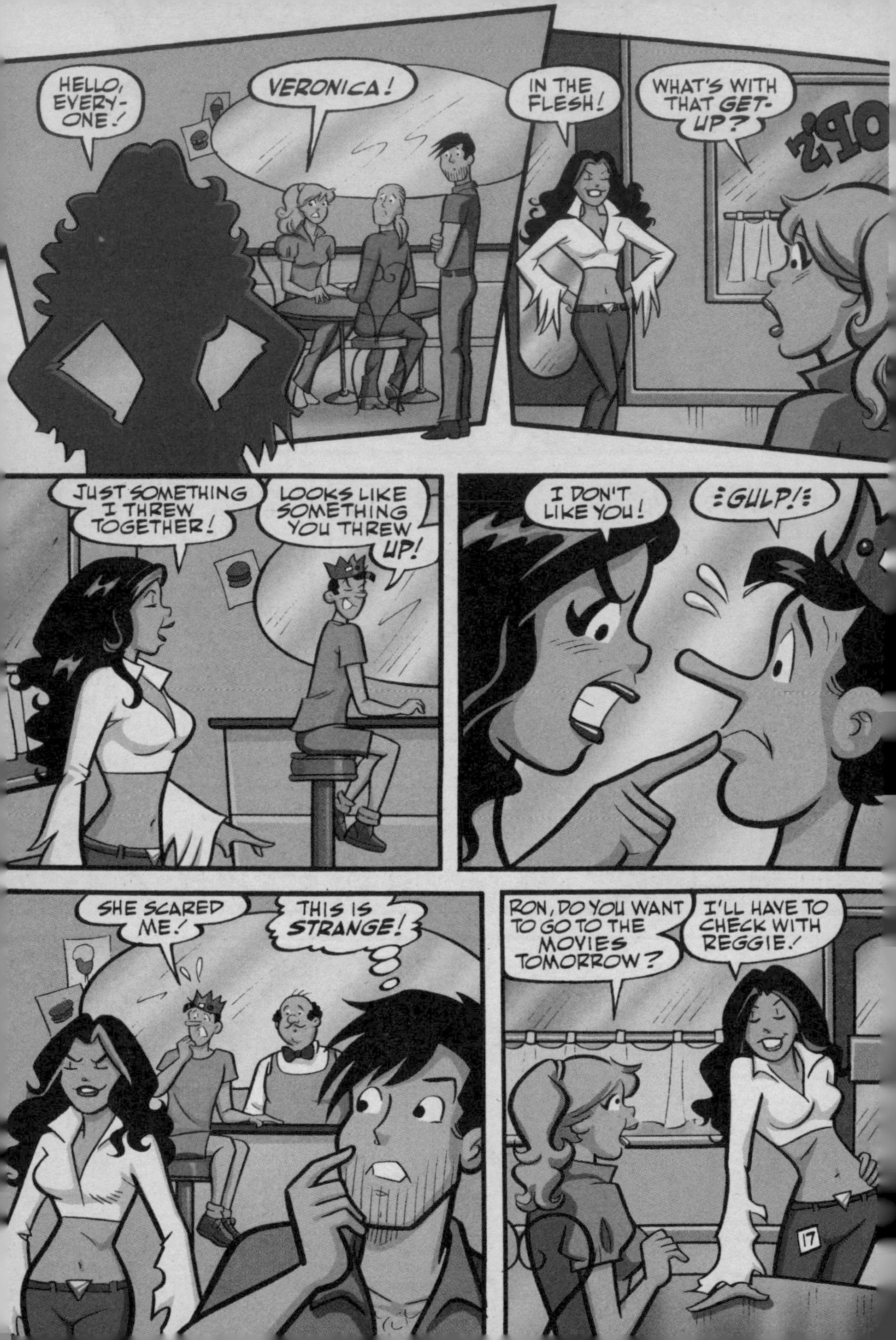
HELLO, EVERY-ONE!
VERONICA!
IN THE FLESH!
WHAT'S WITH THAT GET-UP?
JUST SOMETHING I THREW TOGETHER!
LOOKS LIKE SOMETHING YOU THREW UP!
I DON'T LIKE YOU!
GULP!
SHE SCARED ME!
THIS IS STRANGE!
RON, DO YOU WANT TO GO TO THE MOVIES TOMORROW?
I'LL HAVE TO CHECK WITH REGGIE!

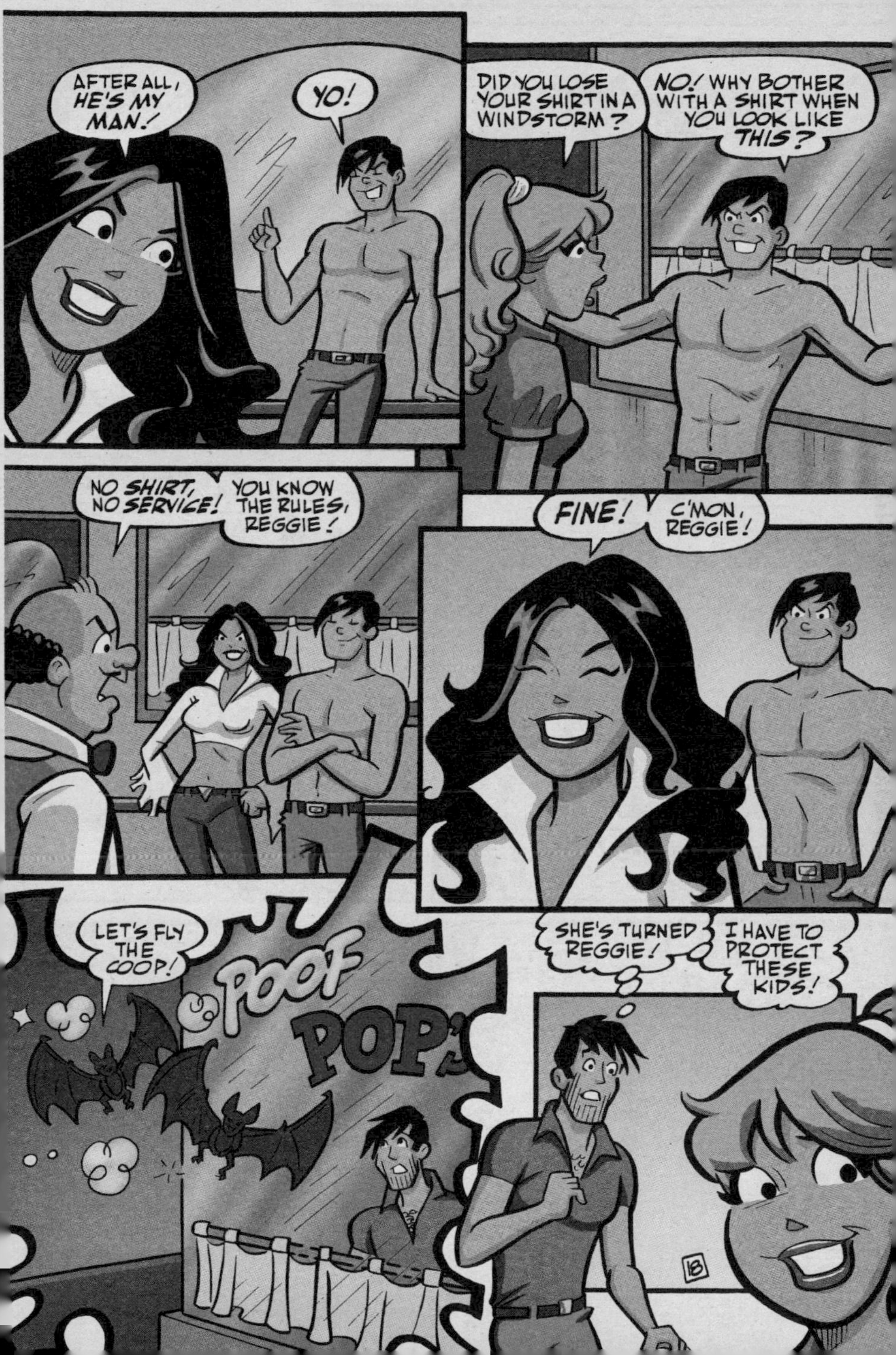
AFTER ALL, HE'S MY MAN!
YO!
DID YOU LOSE YOUR SHIRT IN A WINDSTORM?
NO! WHY BOTHER WITH A SHIRT WHEN YOU LOOK LIKE THIS?
NO SHIRT, NO SERVICE!
YOU KNOW THE RULES, REGGIE!
FINE!
C'MON, REGGIE!
LET'S FLY THE COOP!
POOF
POP'S
SHE'S TURNED REGGIE!
I HAVE TO PROTECT THESE KIDS!

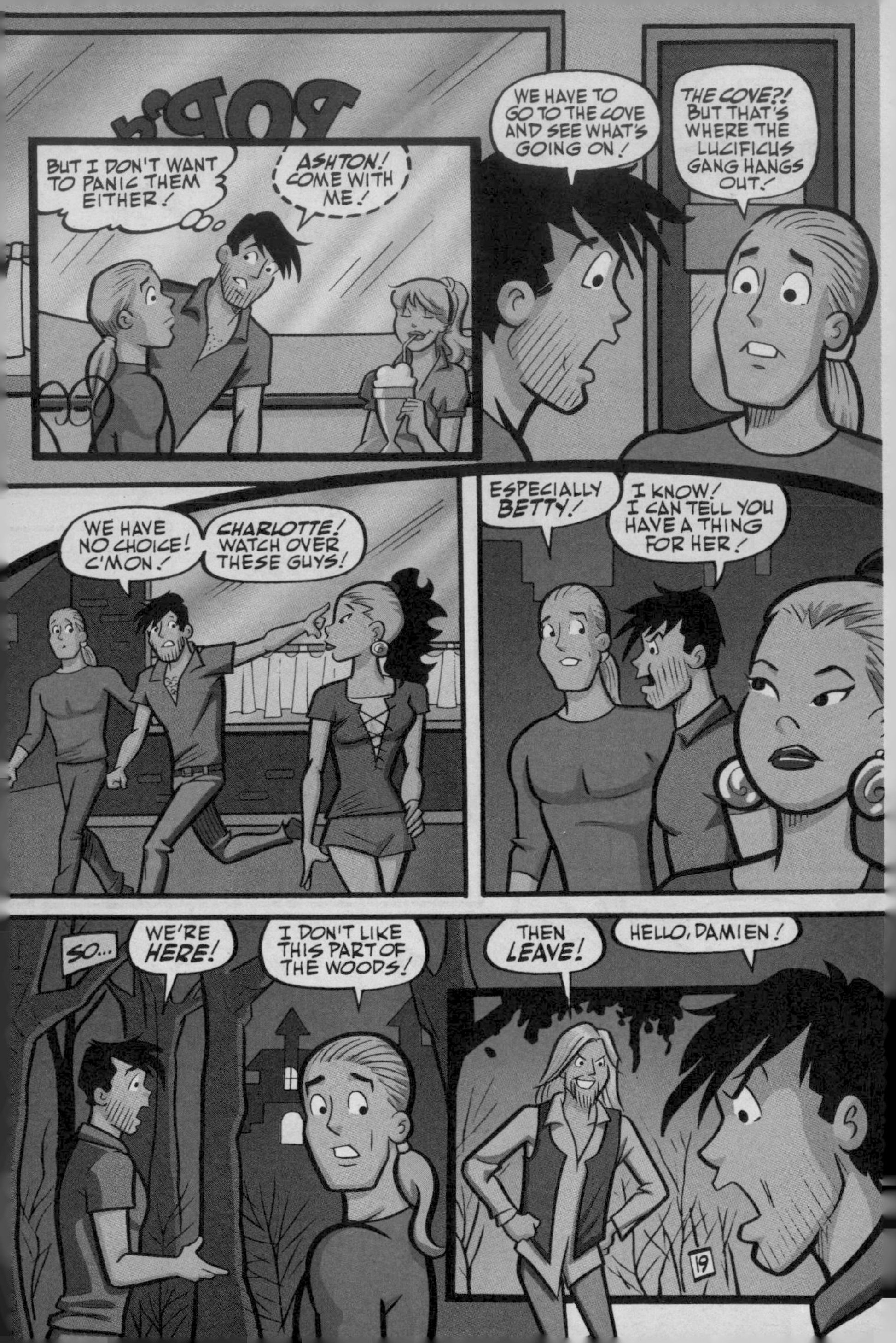
POP'S
BUT I DON'T WANT TO PANIC THEM EITHER!
ASHTON! COME WITH ME!
WE HAVE TO GO TO THE COVE AND SEE WHAT'S GOING ON!
THE COVE?! BUT THAT'S WHERE THE LUCIFICUS GANG HANGS OUT!
WE HAVE NO CHOICE! C'MON!
CHARLOTTE! WATCH OVER THESE GUYS!
ESPECIALLY BETTY!
I KNOW! I CAN TELL YOU HAVE A THING FOR HER!
SO...
WE'RE HERE!
I DON'T LIKE THIS PART OF THE WOODS!
THEN LEAVE!
HELLO, DAMIEN!
19

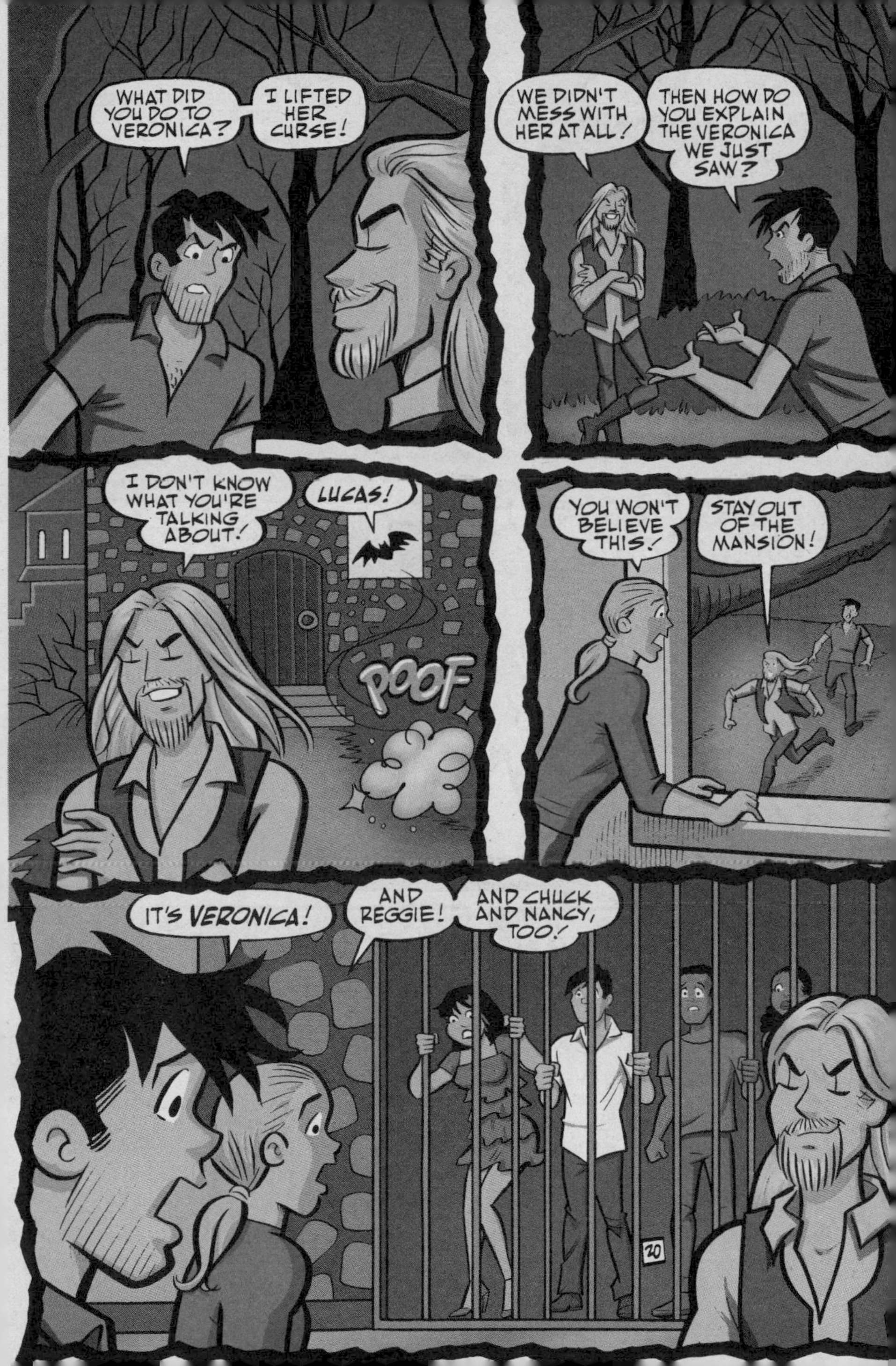
WHAT DID YOU DO TO VERONICA?
I LIFTED HER CURSE!
WE DIDN'T MESS WITH HER AT ALL!
THEN HOW DO YOU EXPLAIN THE VERONICA WE JUST SAW?
I DON'T KNOW WHAT YOU'RE TALKING ABOUT!
LUCAS!
POOF
YOU WON'T BELIEVE THIS!
STAY OUT OF THE MANSION!
IT'S VERONICA!
AND REGGIE!
AND CHUCK AND NANCY, TOO!
20

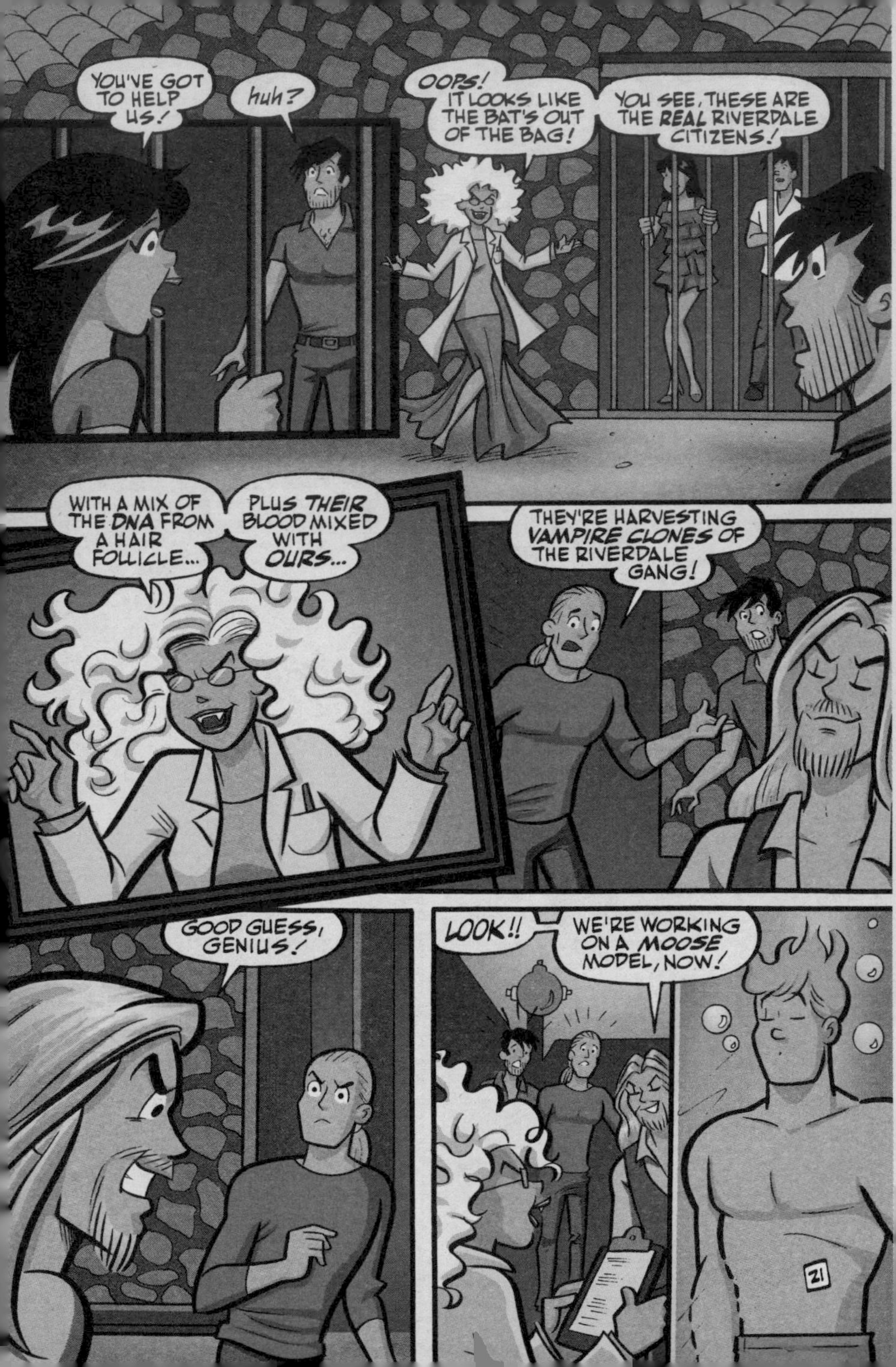
YOU'VE GOT TO HELP US!
huh?
OOPS! IT LOOKS LIKE THE BAT'S OUT OF THE BAG!
YOU SEE, THESE ARE THE REAL RIVERDALE CITIZENS!
WITH A MIX OF THE DNA FROM A HAIR FOLLICLE...
PLUS THEIR BLOOD MIXED WITH OURS...
THEY'RE HARVESTING VAMPIRE CLONES OF THE RIVERDALE GANG!
GOOD GUESS, GENIUS!
LOOK!!
WE'RE WORKING ON A MOOSE MODEL, NOW!
21

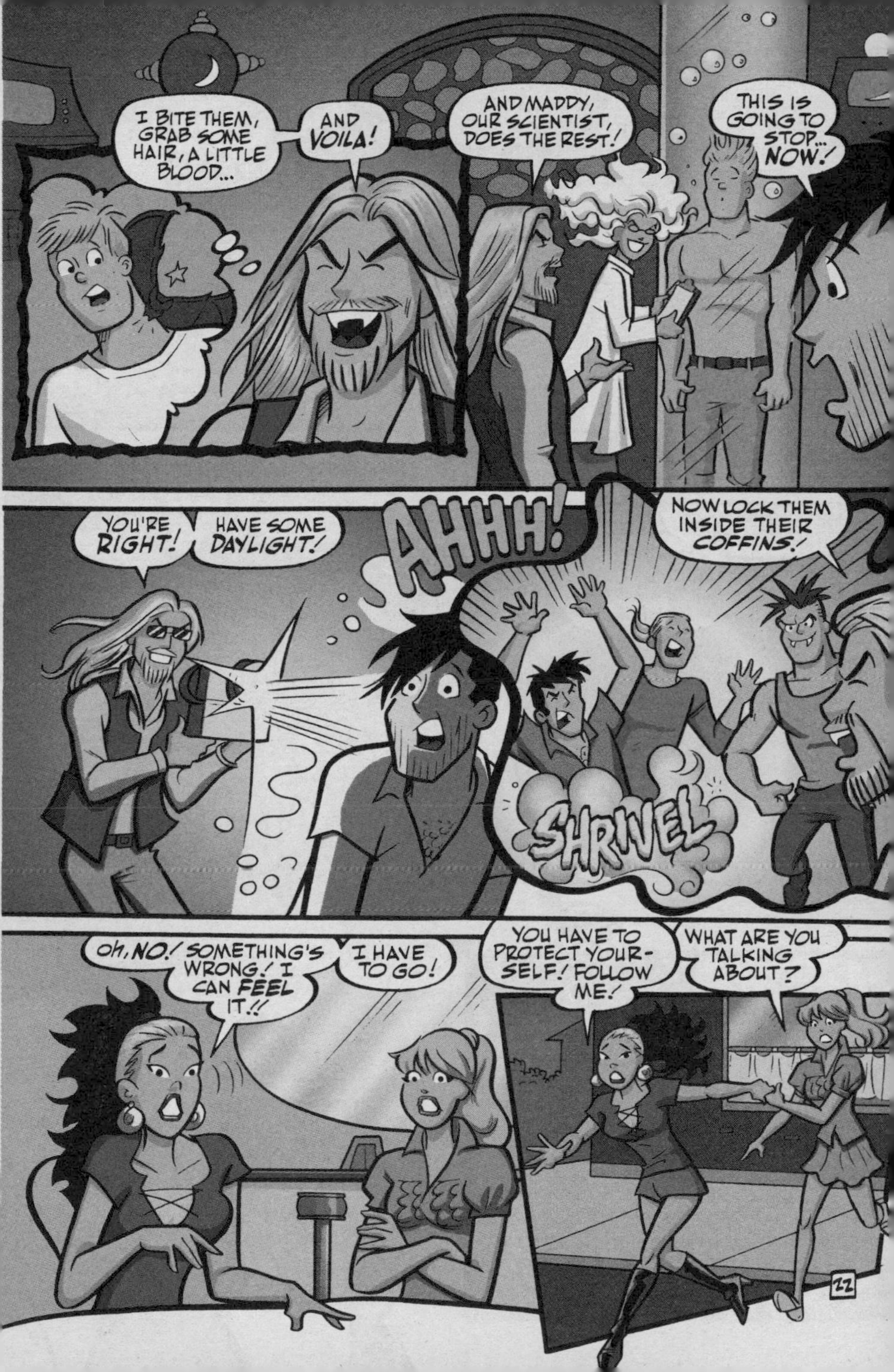
I BITE THEM, GRAB SOME HAIR, A LITTLE BLOOD...
AND VOILA!
AND MADDY, OUR SCIENTIST, DOES THE REST!
THIS IS GOING TO STOP... NOW!
YOU'RE RIGHT!
HAVE SOME DAYLIGHT!
AHHH!
NOW LOCK THEM INSIDE THEIR COFFINS!
SHRIVEL
OH, NO! SOMETHING'S WRONG! I CAN FEEL IT!!
I HAVE TO GO!
YOU HAVE TO PROTECT YOURSELF! FOLLOW ME!
WHAT ARE YOU TALKING ABOUT?
22

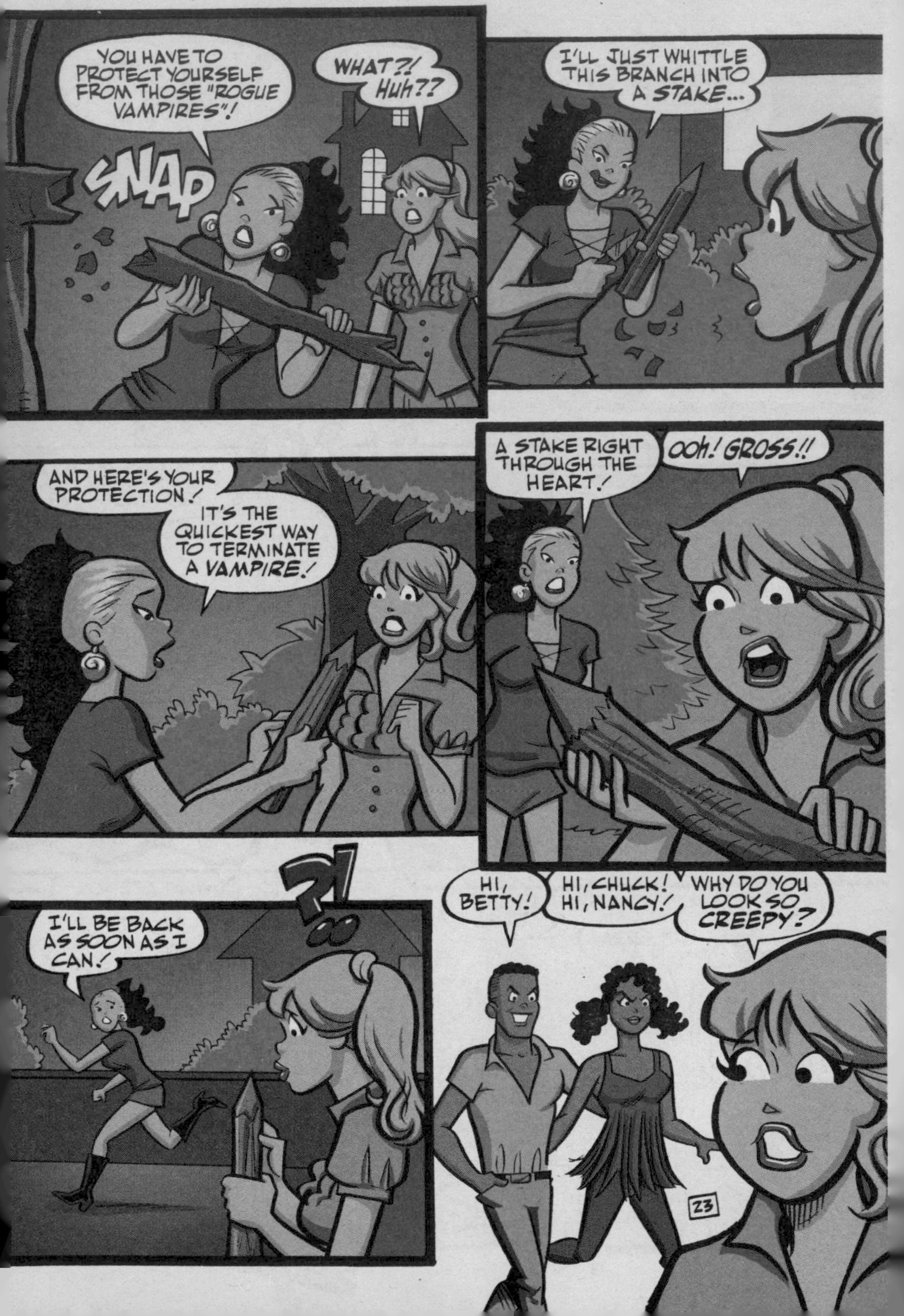
YOU HAVE TO PROTECT YOURSELF FROM THOSE "ROGUE VAMPIRES"!
WHAT?! Huh??
SNAP
I'LL JUST WHITTLE THIS BRANCH INTO A STAKE...
AND HERE'S YOUR PROTECTION!
IT'S THE QUICKEST WAY TO TERMINATE A VAMPIRE!
A STAKE RIGHT THROUGH THE HEART!
OOh! GROSS!!
I'LL BE BACK AS SOON AS I CAN!
?!
HI, BETTY!
HI, CHUCK! HI, NANCY!
WHY DO YOU LOOK SO CREEPY?
23

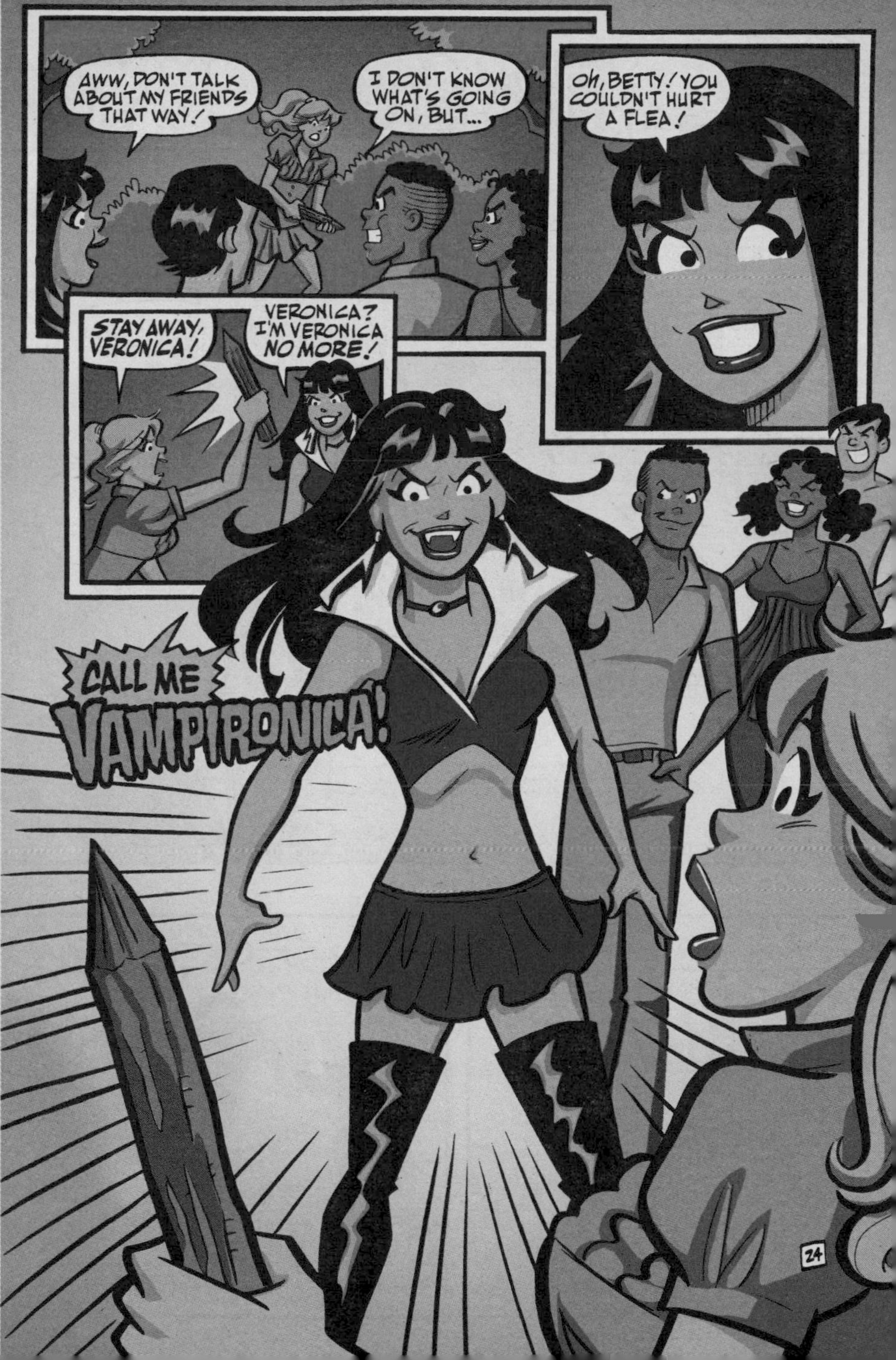

AWW, DON'T TALK ABOUT MY FRIENDS THAT WAY!
I DON'T KNOW WHAT'S GOING ON, BUT...
OH, BETTY! YOU COULDN'T HURT A FLEA!
STAY AWAY, VERONICA!
VERONICA? I'M VERONICA NO MORE!
CALL ME VAMPIRONICA!
24

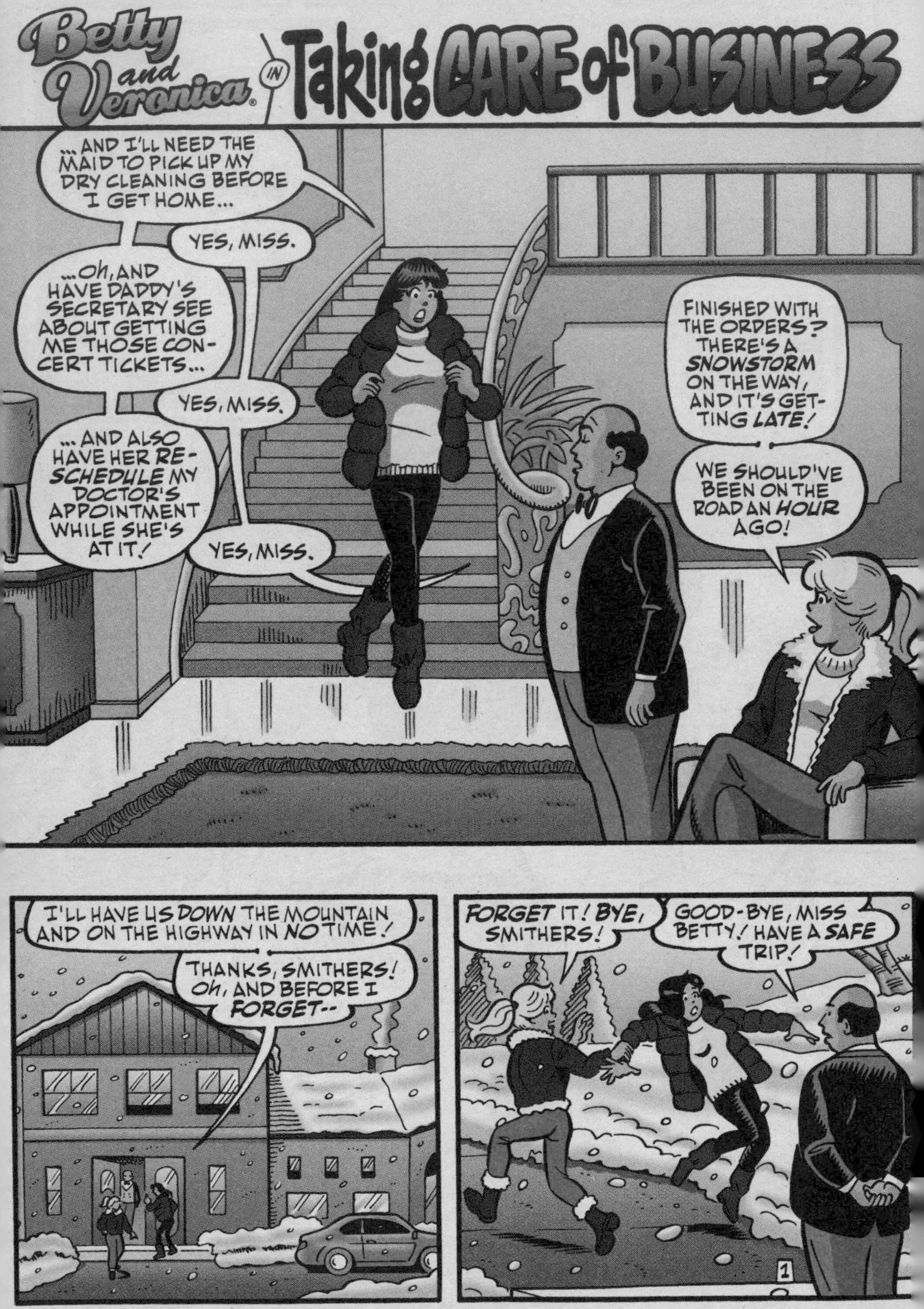
Betty and Veronica in Taking CARE of BUSINESS
...AND I'LL NEED THE MAID TO PICK UP MY DRY CLEANING BEFORE I GET HOME...
YES, MISS.
...Oh, AND HAVE DADDY'S SECRETARY SEE ABOUT GETTING ME THOSE CONCERT TICKETS...
YES, MISS.
...AND ALSO HAVE HER RESCHEDULE MY DOCTOR'S APPOINTMENT WHILE SHE'S AT IT!
YES, MISS.
FINISHED WITH THE ORDERS? THERE'S A SNOWSTORM ON THE WAY, AND IT'S GETTING LATE!
WE SHOULD'VE BEEN ON THE ROAD AN HOUR AGO!
I'LL HAVE US DOWN THE MOUNTAIN AND ON THE HIGHWAY IN NO TIME!
THANKS, SMITHERS! Oh, AND BEFORE I FORGET--
FORGET IT! BYE, SMITHERS!
GOOD-BYE, MISS BETTY! HAVE A SAFE TRIP!
1

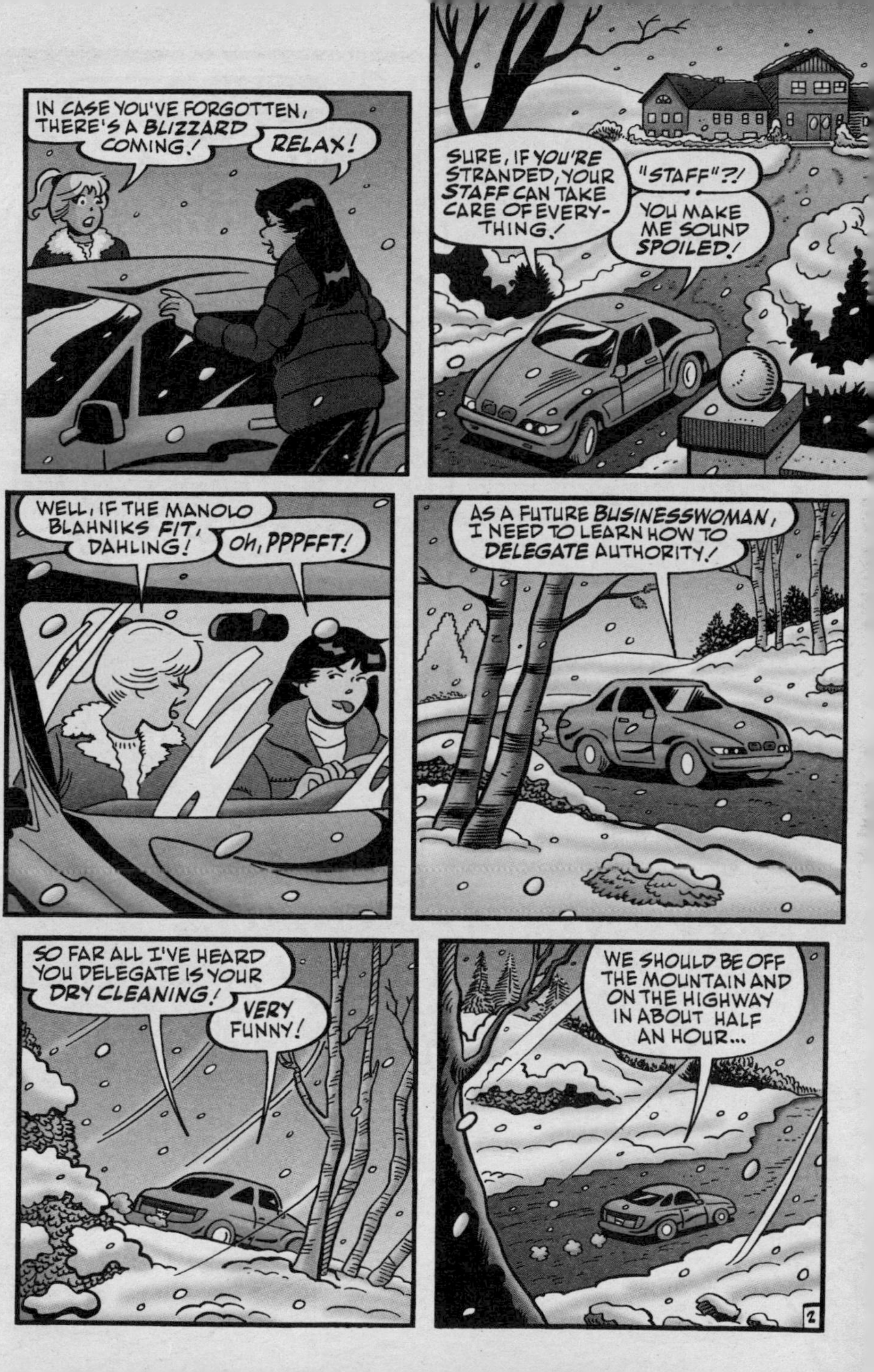
IN CASE YOU'VE FORGOTTEN, THERE'S A BLIZZARD COMING!
RELAX!
SURE, IF YOU'RE STRANDED, YOUR STAFF CAN TAKE CARE OF EVERY-THING!
"STAFF"?!
YOU MAKE ME SOUND SPOILED!
WELL, IF THE MANOLO BLAHNIKS FIT, DAHLING!
Oh, PPPFFT!
AS A FUTURE BUSINESSWOMAN, I NEED TO LEARN HOW TO DELEGATE AUTHORITY!
SO FAR ALL I'VE HEARD YOU DELEGATE IS YOUR DRY CLEANING!
VERY FUNNY!
WE SHOULD BE OFF THE MOUNTAIN AND ON THE HIGHWAY IN ABOUT HALF AN HOUR...
2

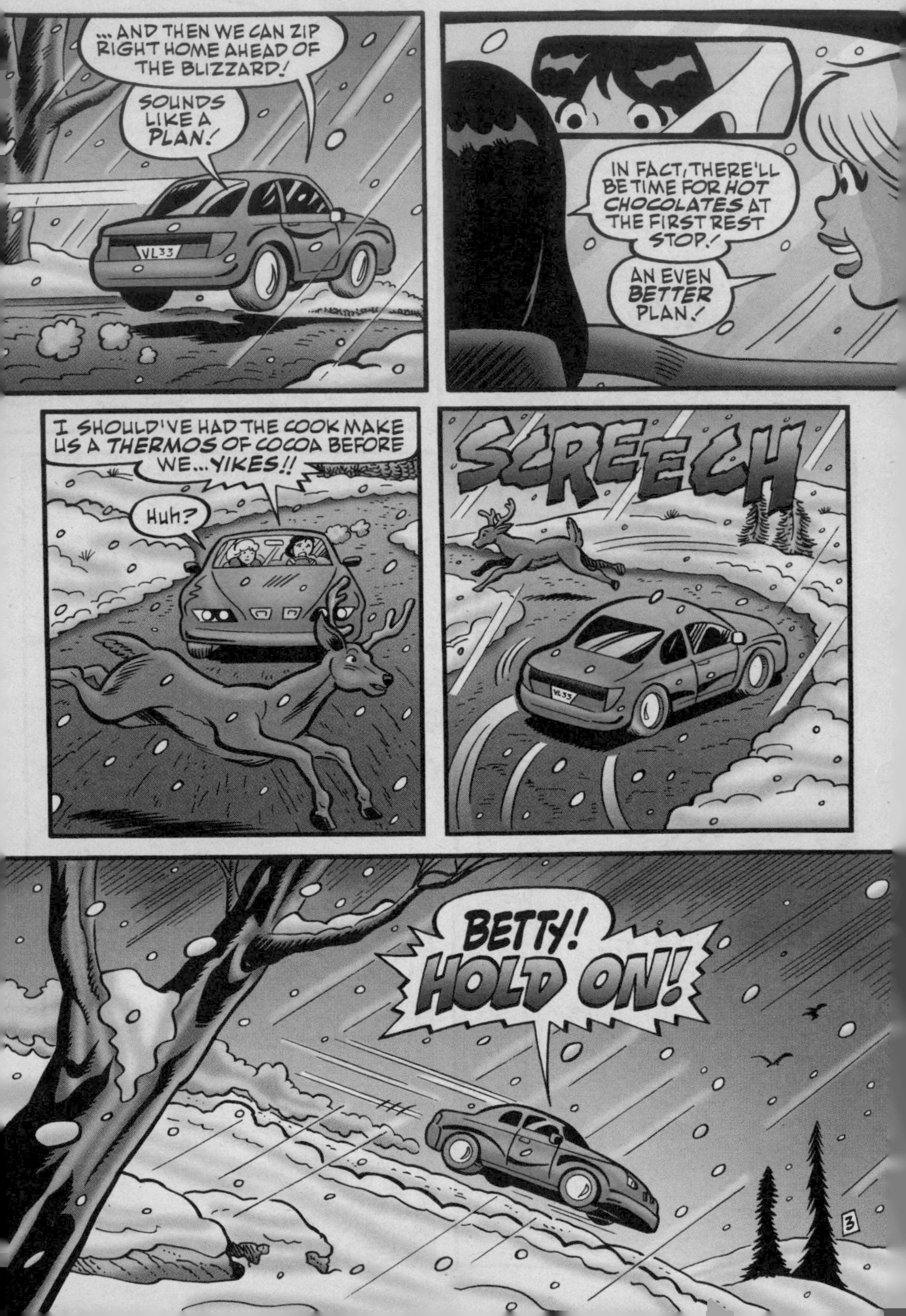
...AND THEN WE CAN ZIP RIGHT HOME AHEAD OF THE BLIZZARD!
SOUNDS LIKE A PLAN!
VL33
IN FACT, THERE'LL BE TIME FOR HOT CHOCOLATES AT THE FIRST REST STOP!
AN EVEN BETTER PLAN!
I SHOULD'VE HAD THE COOK MAKE US A THERMOS OF COCOA BEFORE WE...YIKES!!
Huh?
SCREECH
VL33
BETTY! HOLD ON!
3

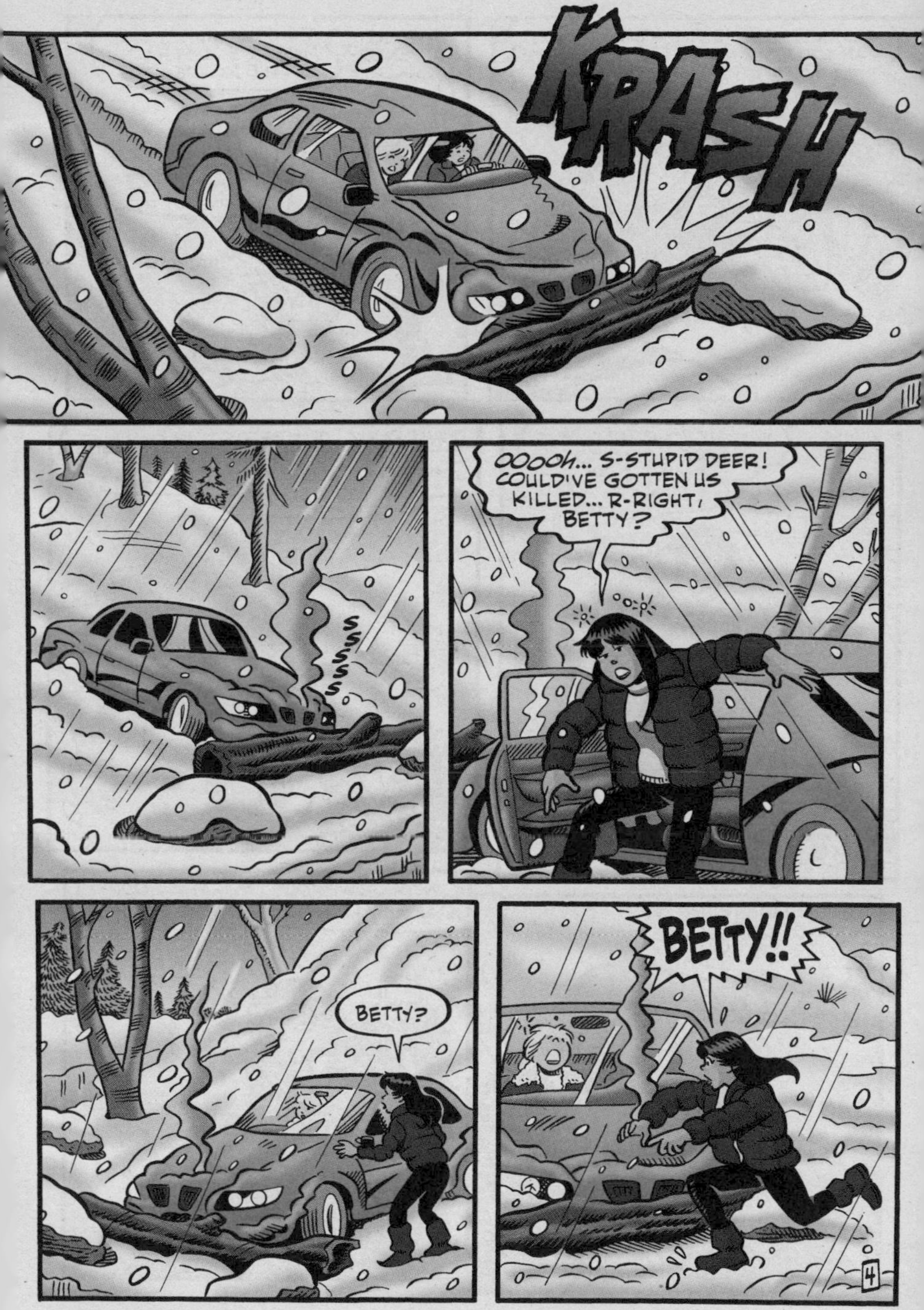
KRASH
SSSSSS
OOOOH... S-STUPID DEER! COULD'VE GOTTEN US KILLED... R-RIGHT, BETTY?
BETTY?
BETTY!!
4

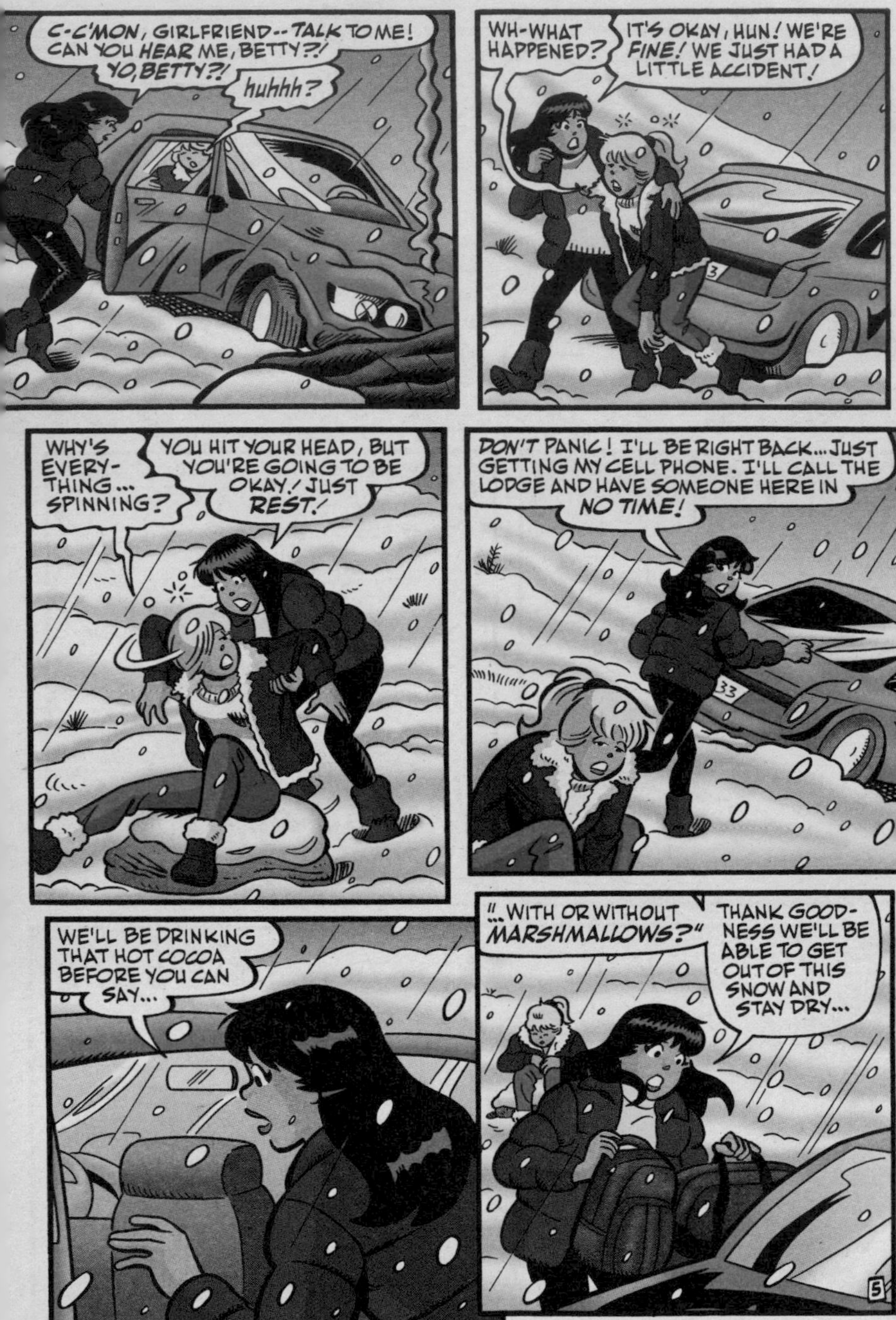

C-C'MON, GIRLFRIEND--TALK TO ME! CAN YOU HEAR ME, BETTY?! YO, BETTY?!
huhhh?
WH-WHAT HAPPENED?
IT'S OKAY, HUN! WE'RE FINE! WE JUST HAD A LITTLE ACCIDENT!
WHY'S EVERY-THING... SPINNING?
YOU HIT YOUR HEAD, BUT YOU'RE GOING TO BE OKAY! JUST REST!
DON'T PANIC! I'LL BE RIGHT BACK... JUST GETTING MY CELL PHONE. I'LL CALL THE LODGE AND HAVE SOMEONE HERE IN NO TIME!
33
WE'LL BE DRINKING THAT HOT COCOA BEFORE YOU CAN SAY...
"...WITH OR WITHOUT MARSHMALLOWS?"
THANK GOOD-NESS WE'LL BE ABLE TO GET OUT OF THIS SNOW AND STAY DRY...
5

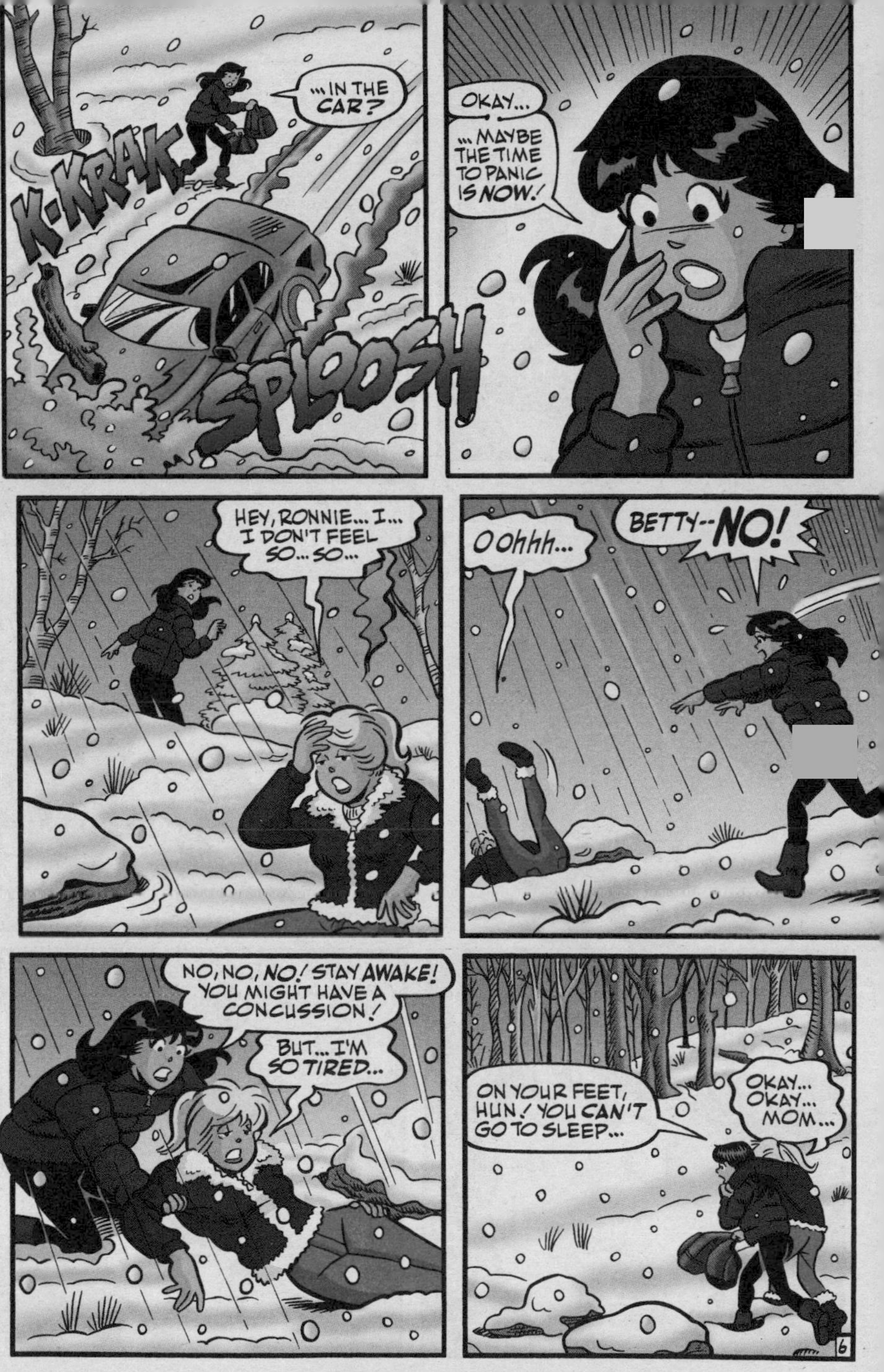
...IN THE CAR?
K-KRAK
SPLOOSH
OKAY...
...MAYBE THE TIME TO PANIC IS NOW!
HEY, RONNIE... I... I DON'T FEEL SO... SO...
Oohhh...
BETTY--NO!
NO, NO, NO! STAY AWAKE! YOU MIGHT HAVE A CONCUSSION!
BUT... I'M SO TIRED...
ON YOUR FEET, HUN! YOU CAN'T GO TO SLEEP...
OKAY... OKAY... MOM...
6

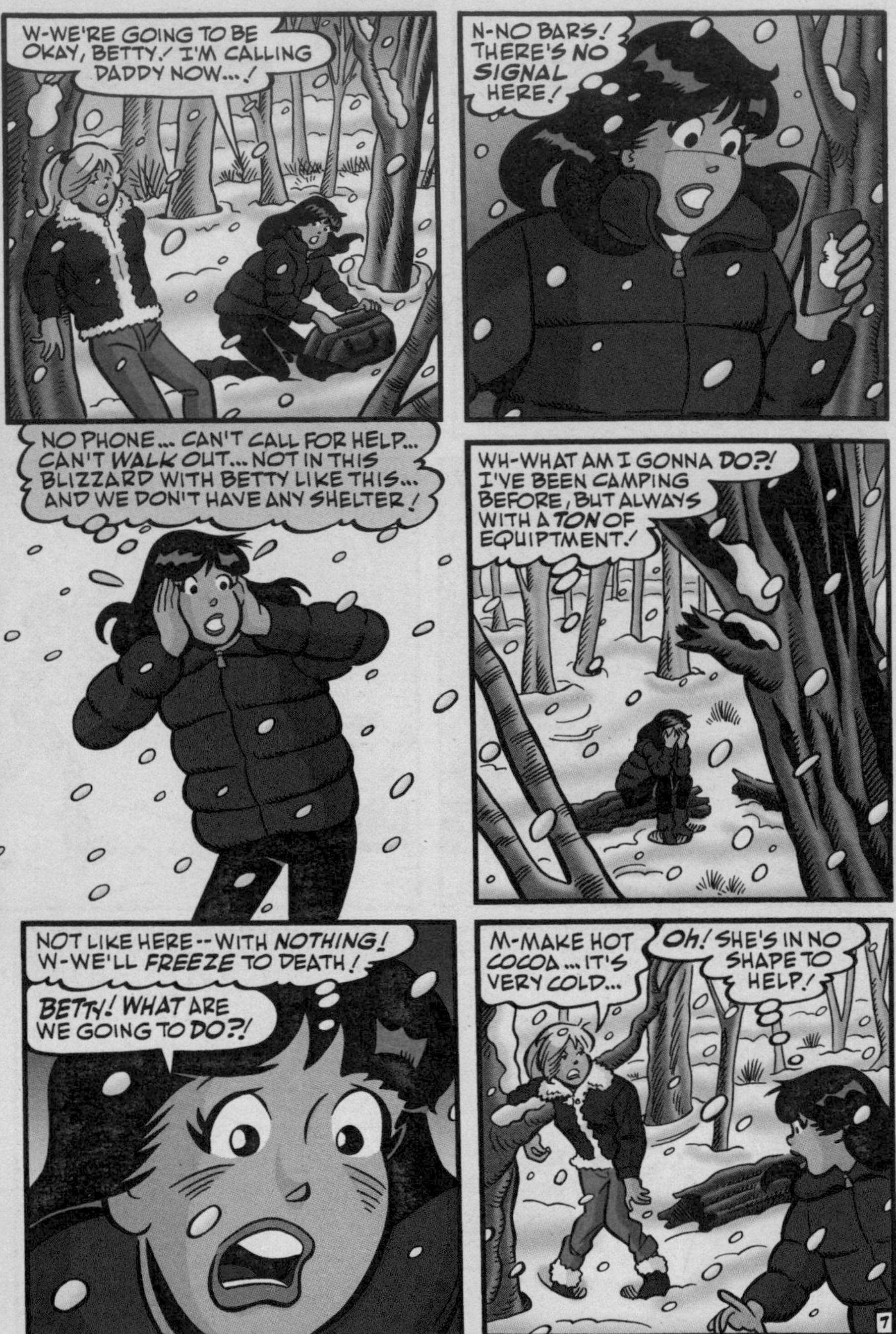
W-WE'RE GOING TO BE OKAY, BETTY! I'M CALLING DADDY NOW...!
N-NO BARS! THERE'S NO SIGNAL HERE!
NO PHONE... CAN'T CALL FOR HELP... CAN'T WALK OUT... NOT IN THIS BLIZZARD WITH BETTY LIKE THIS... AND WE DON'T HAVE ANY SHELTER!
WH-WHAT AM I GONNA DO?! I'VE BEEN CAMPING BEFORE, BUT ALWAYS WITH A TON OF EQUIPTMENT!
NOT LIKE HERE--WITH NOTHING! W-WE'LL FREEZE TO DEATH!
BETTY! WHAT ARE WE GOING TO DO?!
M-MAKE HOT COCOA... IT'S VERY COLD...
Oh! SHE'S IN NO SHAPE TO HELP!
7

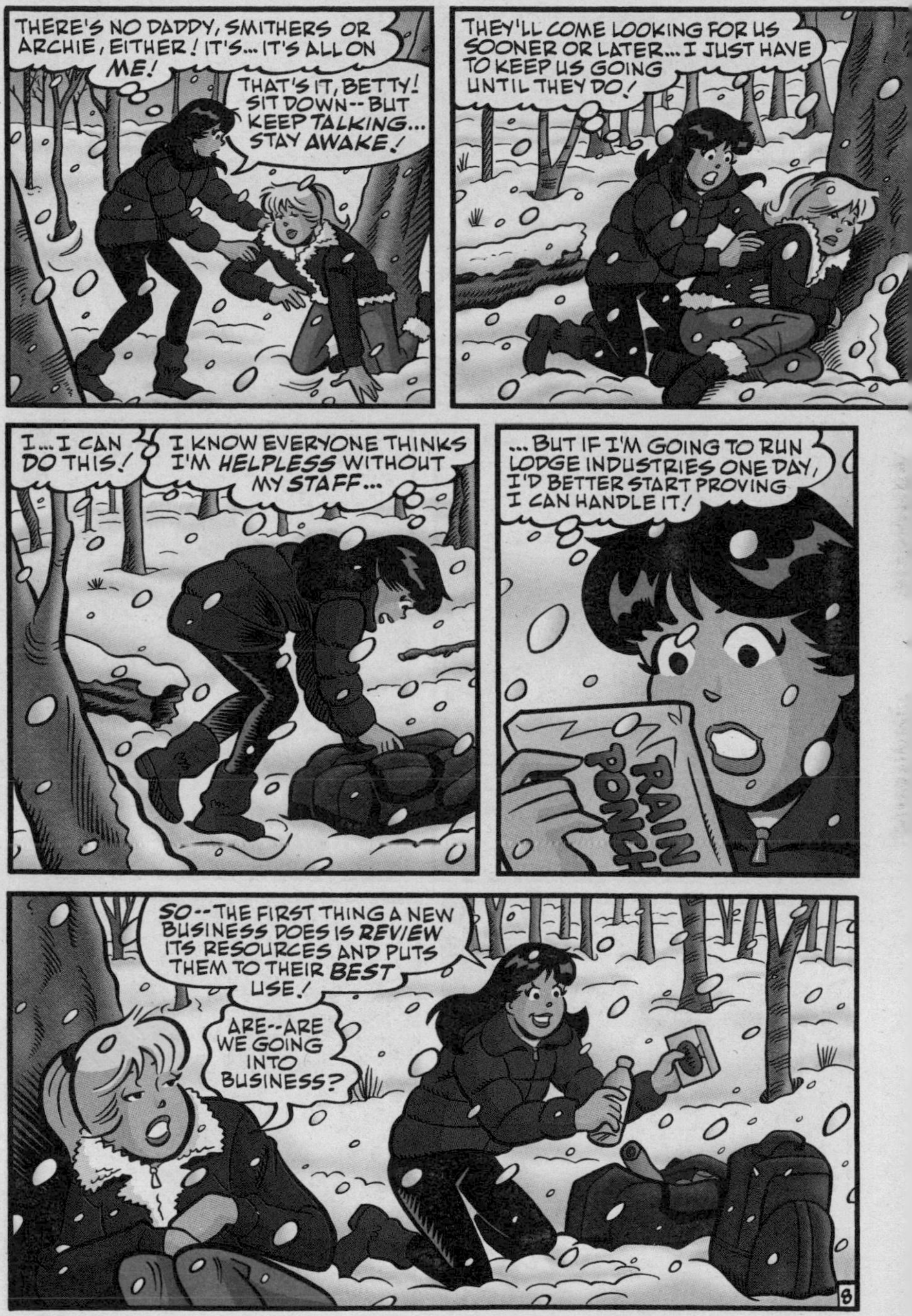
THERE'S NO DADDY, SMITHERS OR ARCHIE, EITHER! IT'S... IT'S ALL ON ME!
THAT'S IT, BETTY! SIT DOWN-- BUT KEEP TALKING... STAY AWAKE!
THEY'LL COME LOOKING FOR US SOONER OR LATER... I JUST HAVE TO KEEP US GOING UNTIL THEY DO!
I... I CAN DO THIS!
I KNOW EVERYONE THINKS I'M HELPLESS WITHOUT MY STAFF...
... BUT IF I'M GOING TO RUN LODGE INDUSTRIES ONE DAY, I'D BETTER START PROVING I CAN HANDLE IT!
RAIN PONCH
SO-- THE FIRST THING A NEW BUSINESS DOES IS REVIEW ITS RESOURCES AND PUTS THEM TO THEIR BEST USE!
ARE--ARE WE GOING INTO BUSINESS?
8

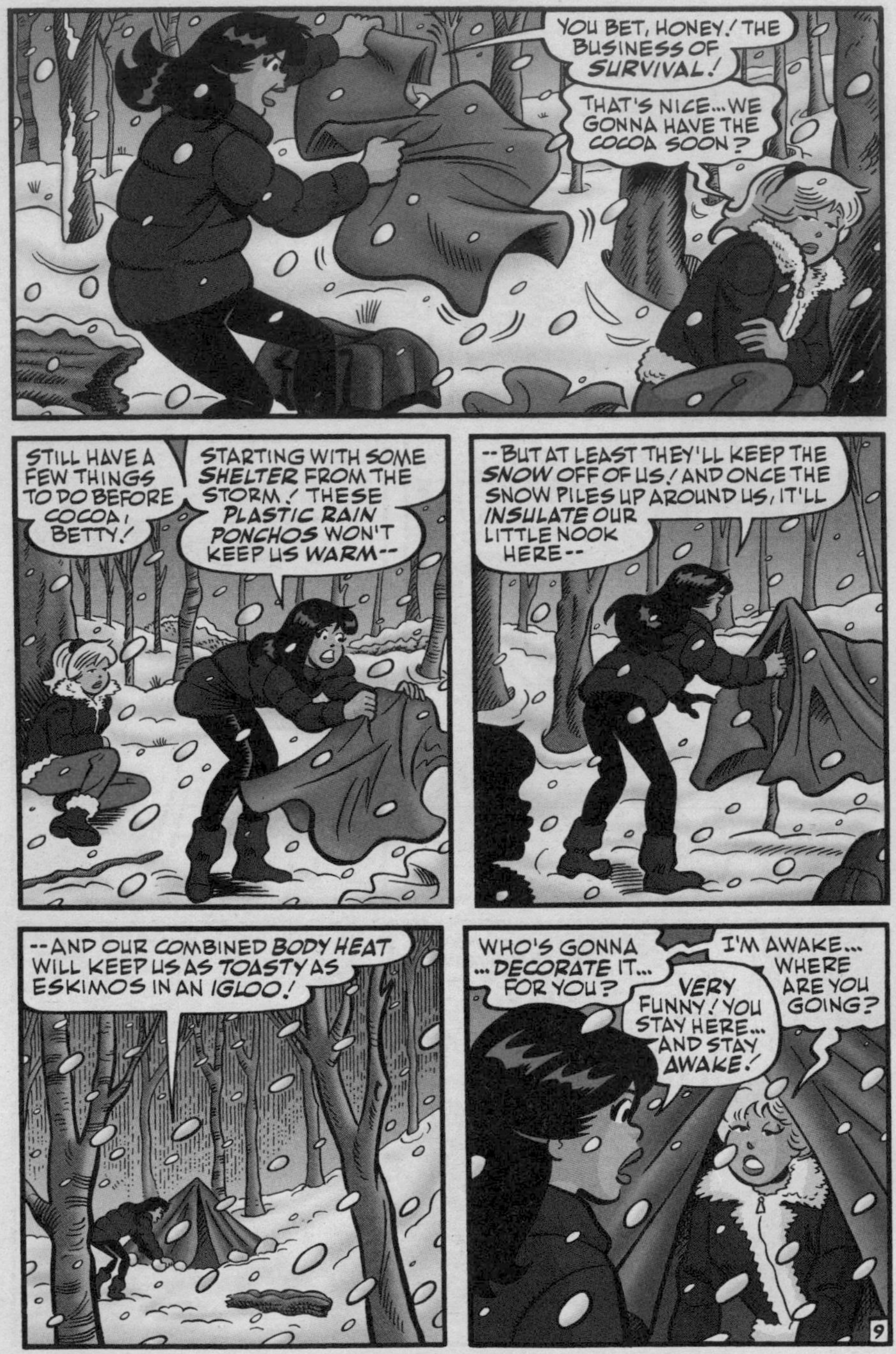
YOU BET, HONEY! THE BUSINESS OF SURVIVAL!
THAT'S NICE...WE GONNA HAVE THE COCOA SOON?
STILL HAVE A FEW THINGS TO DO BEFORE COCOA, BETTY!
STARTING WITH SOME SHELTER FROM THE STORM! THESE PLASTIC RAIN PONCHOS WON'T KEEP US WARM--
--BUT AT LEAST THEY'LL KEEP THE SNOW OFF OF US! AND ONCE THE SNOW PILES UP AROUND US, IT'LL INSULATE OUR LITTLE NOOK HERE--
--AND OUR COMBINED BODY HEAT WILL KEEP US AS TOASTY AS ESKIMOS IN AN IGLOO!
WHO'S GONNA ...DECORATE IT... FOR YOU?
I'M AWAKE... WHERE ARE YOU GOING?
VERY FUNNY! YOU STAY HERE... AND STAY AWAKE!
9

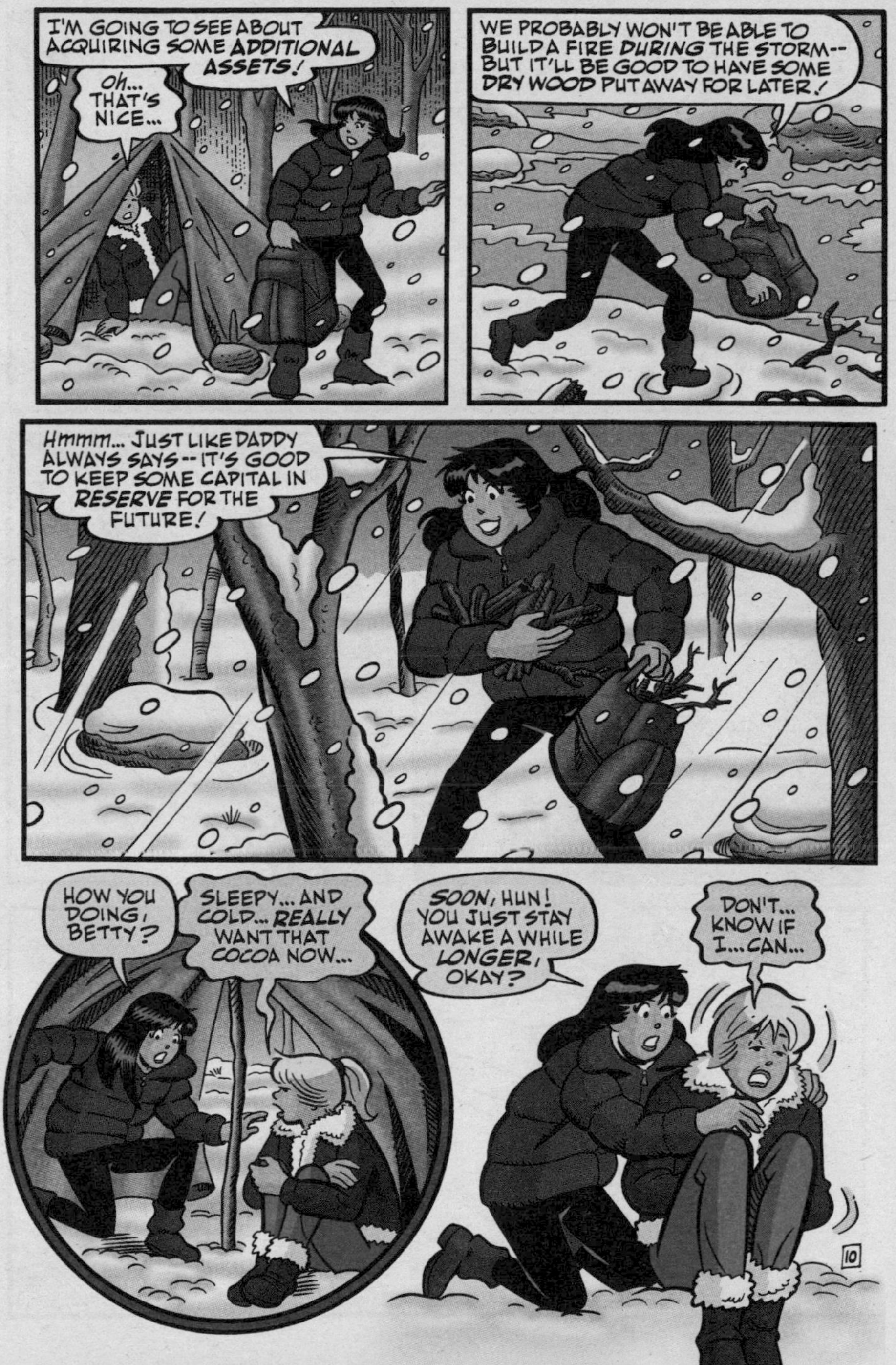
I'M GOING TO SEE ABOUT ACQUIRING SOME ADDITIONAL ASSETS!
Oh... THAT'S NICE...
WE PROBABLY WON'T BE ABLE TO BUILD A FIRE DURING THE STORM-- BUT IT'LL BE GOOD TO HAVE SOME DRY WOOD PUT AWAY FOR LATER!
Hmmm... JUST LIKE DADDY ALWAYS SAYS-- IT'S GOOD TO KEEP SOME CAPITAL IN RESERVE FOR THE FUTURE!
HOW YOU DOING, BETTY?
SLEEPY... AND COLD... REALLY WANT THAT COCOA NOW...
SOON, HUN! YOU JUST STAY AWAKE A WHILE LONGER, OKAY?
DON'T... KNOW IF I... CAN...
10

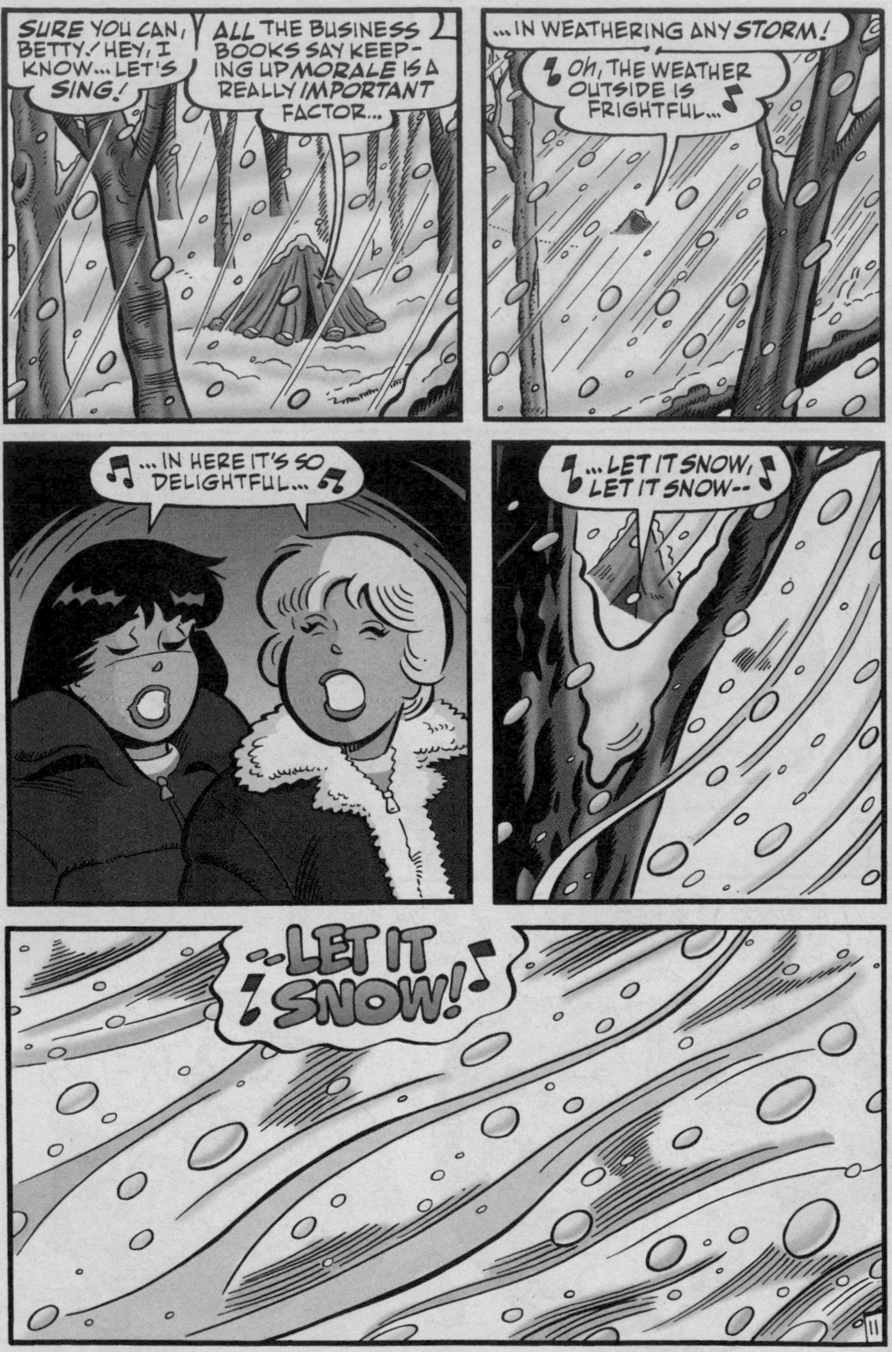
SURE YOU CAN, BETTY! HEY, I KNOW... LET'S SING!
ALL THE BUSINESS BOOKS SAY KEEPING UP MORALE IS A REALLY IMPORTANT FACTOR...
...IN WEATHERING ANY STORM!
OH, THE WEATHER OUTSIDE IS FRIGHTFUL...
...IN HERE IT'S SO DELIGHTFUL...
...LET IT SNOW, LET IT SNOW--
--LET IT SNOW!

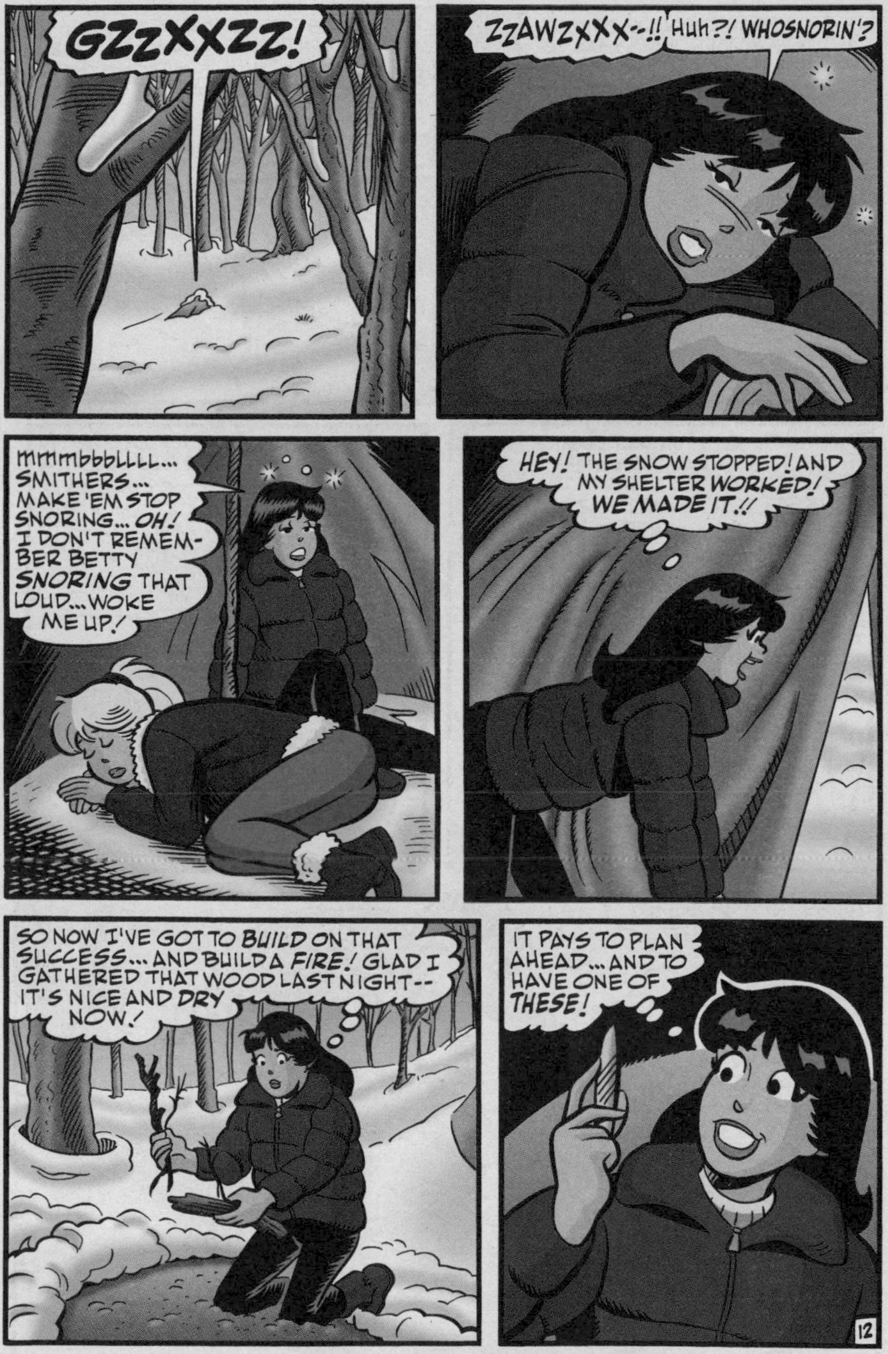
GZzXXZZ!
ZZAWZXXX--!! Huh?! WHOSNORIN'?
mmmbbbLLLL... SMITHERS... MAKE 'EM STOP SNORING... OH! I DON'T REMEMBER BETTY SNORING THAT LOUD... WOKE ME UP!
HEY! THE SNOW STOPPED! AND MY SHELTER WORKED! WE MADE IT!!
SO NOW I'VE GOT TO BUILD ON THAT SUCCESS... AND BUILD A FIRE! GLAD I GATHERED THAT WOOD LAST NIGHT-- IT'S NICE AND DRY NOW!
IT PAYS TO PLAN AHEAD... AND TO HAVE ONE OF THESE!
12

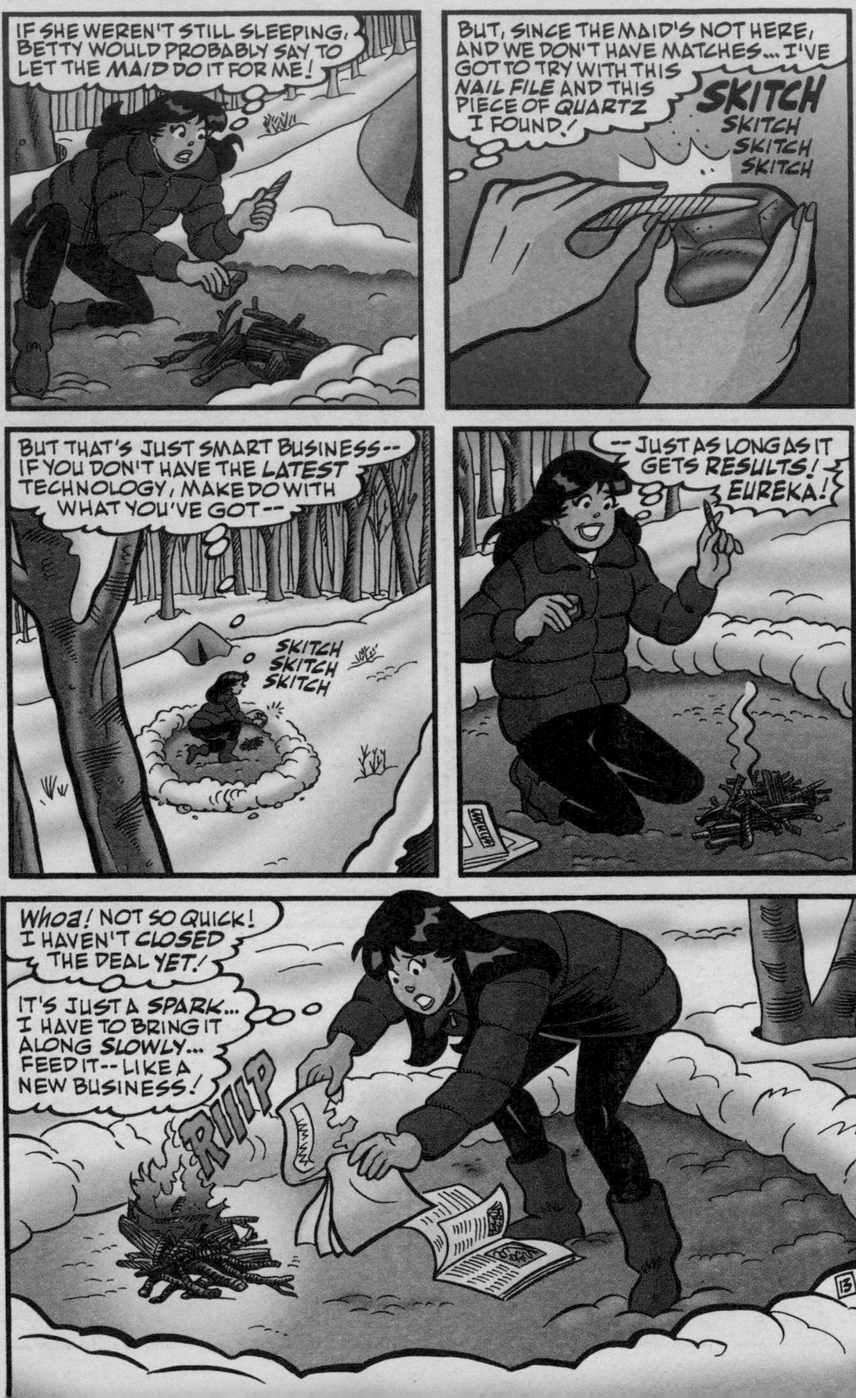
IF SHE WEREN'T STILL SLEEPING, BETTY WOULD PROBABLY SAY TO LET THE MAID DO IT FOR ME!
BUT, SINCE THE MAID'S NOT HERE, AND WE DON'T HAVE MATCHES... I'VE GOT TO TRY WITH THIS NAIL FILE AND THIS PIECE OF QUARTZ I FOUND!
SKITCH
SKITCH
SKITCH
SKITCH
BUT THAT'S JUST SMART BUSINESS-- IF YOU DON'T HAVE THE LATEST TECHNOLOGY, MAKE DO WITH WHAT YOU'VE GOT--
SKITCH
SKITCH
SKITCH
-- JUST AS LONG AS IT GETS RESULTS! EUREKA!
Whoa! NOT SO QUICK! I HAVEN'T CLOSED THE DEAL YET!
IT'S JUST A SPARK... I HAVE TO BRING IT ALONG SLOWLY... FEED IT-- LIKE A NEW BUSINESS!
RIIIP
13

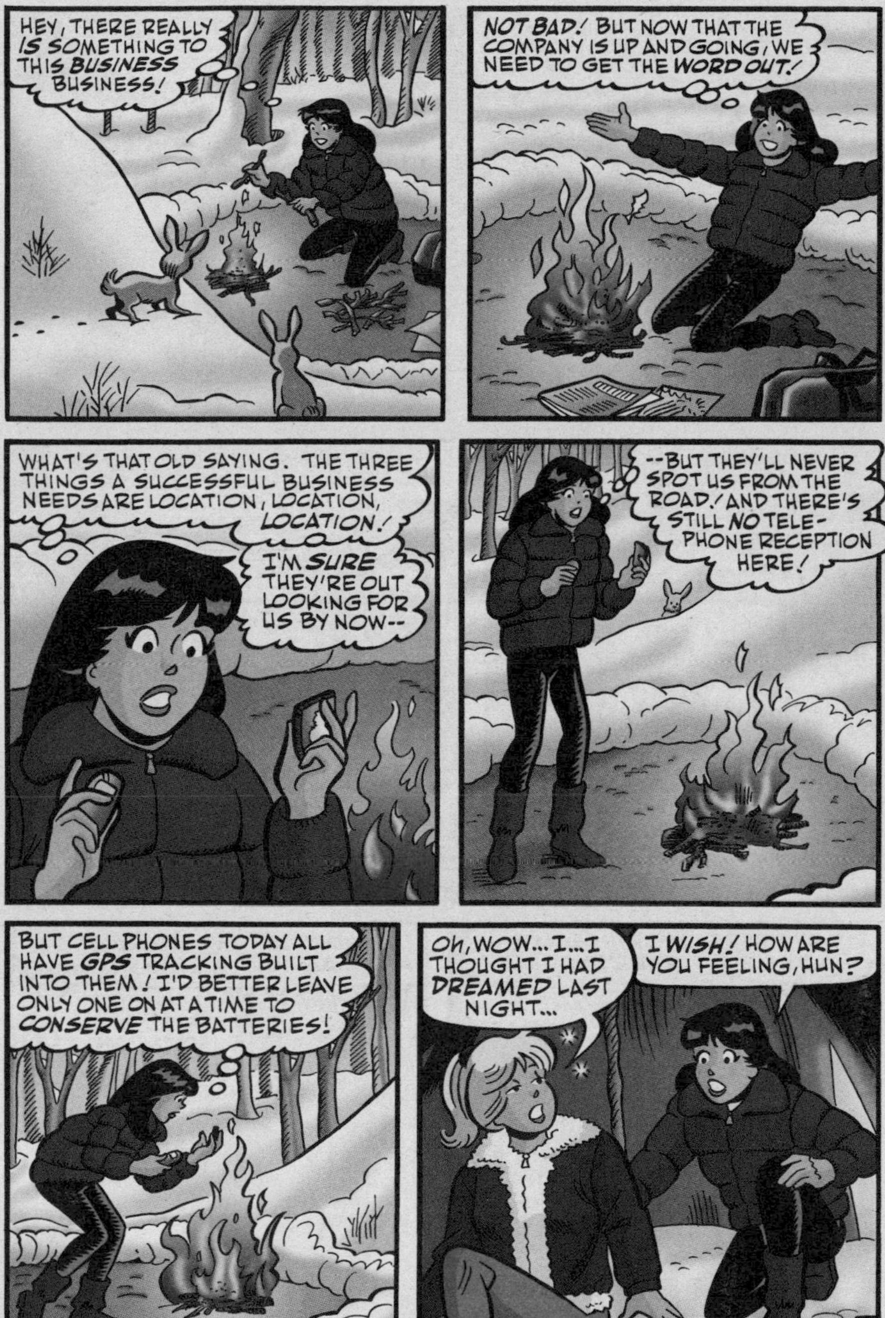

HEY, THERE REALLY IS SOMETHING TO THIS BUSINESS BUSINESS!
NOT BAD! BUT NOW THAT THE COMPANY IS UP AND GOING, WE NEED TO GET THE WORD OUT!
WHAT'S THAT OLD SAYING. THE THREE THINGS A SUCCESSFUL BUSINESS NEEDS ARE LOCATION, LOCATION, LOCATION!
I'M SURE THEY'RE OUT LOOKING FOR US BY NOW--
--BUT THEY'LL NEVER SPOT US FROM THE ROAD! AND THERE'S STILL NO TELEPHONE RECEPTION HERE!
BUT CELL PHONES TODAY ALL HAVE GPS TRACKING BUILT INTO THEM! I'D BETTER LEAVE ONLY ONE ON AT A TIME TO CONSERVE THE BATTERIES!
Oh, WOW... I... I THOUGHT I HAD DREAMED LAST NIGHT...
I WISH! HOW ARE YOU FEELING, HUN?
14

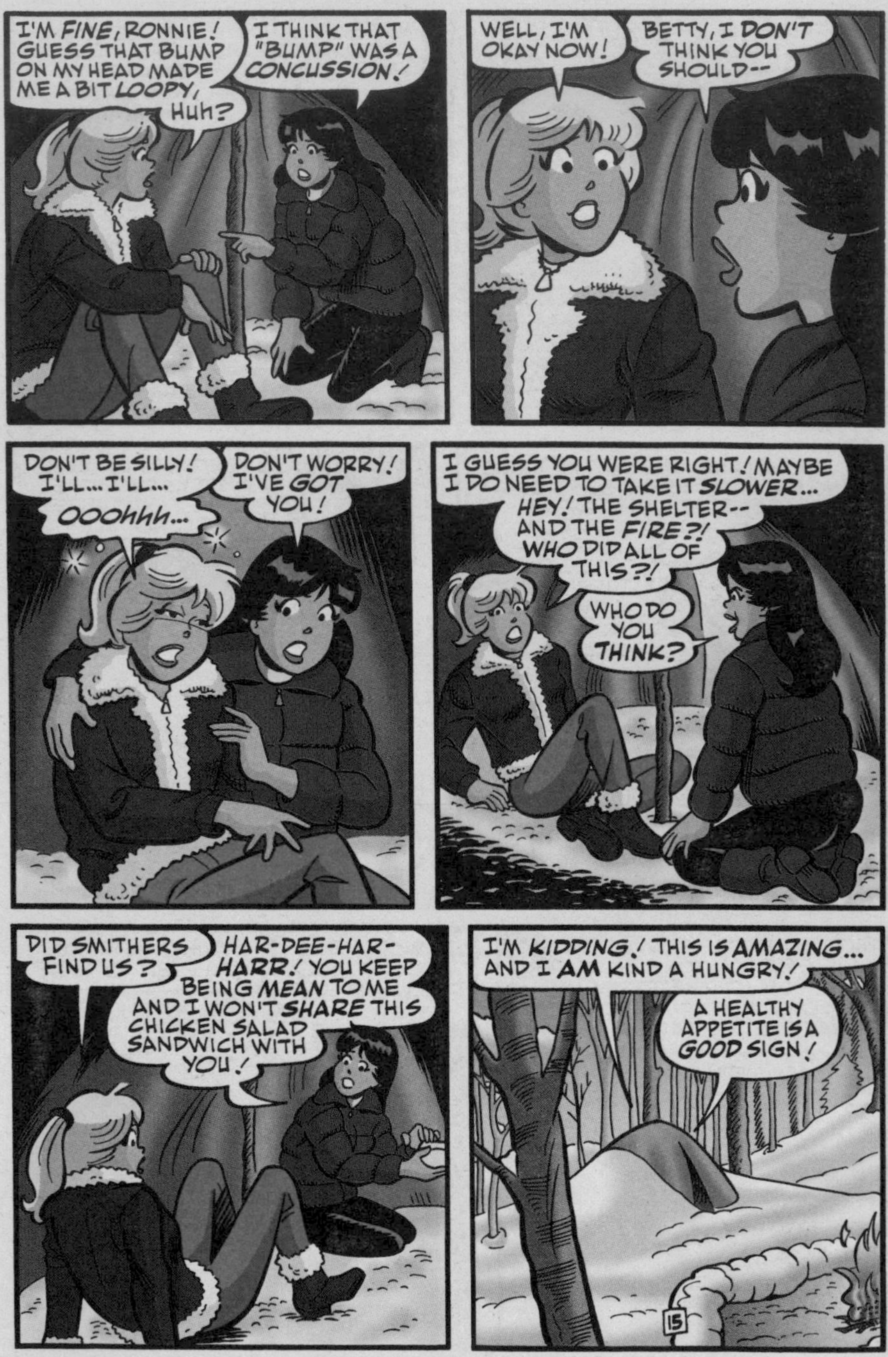

I'M FINE, RONNIE! GUESS THAT BUMP ON MY HEAD MADE ME A BIT LOOPY, HUH?
I THINK THAT "BUMP" WAS A CONCUSSION!
WELL, I'M OKAY NOW!
BETTY, I DON'T THINK YOU SHOULD--
DON'T BE SILLY! I'LL... I'LL... OOOhhh...
DON'T WORRY! I'VE GOT YOU!
I GUESS YOU WERE RIGHT! MAYBE I DO NEED TO TAKE IT SLOWER... HEY! THE SHELTER-- AND THE FIRE?! WHO DID ALL OF THIS?!
WHO DO YOU THINK?
DID SMITHERS FIND US?
HAR-DEE-HAR-HARR! YOU KEEP BEING MEAN TO ME AND I WON'T SHARE THIS CHICKEN SALAD SANDWICH WITH YOU!
I'M KIDDING! THIS IS AMAZING... AND I AM KIND A HUNGRY!
A HEALTHY APPETITE IS A GOOD SIGN!
15

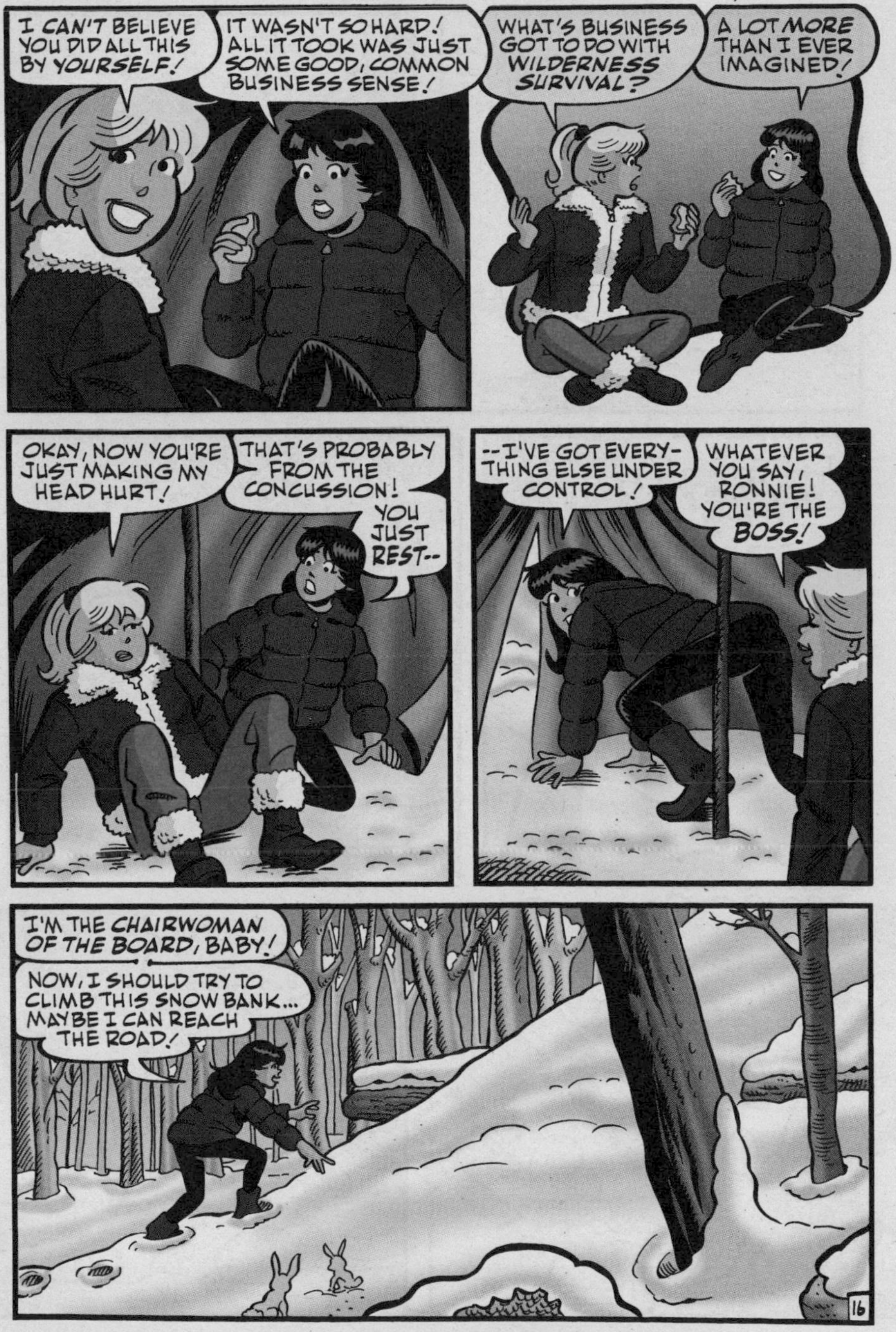
I CAN'T BELIEVE YOU DID ALL THIS BY YOURSELF!
IT WASN'T SO HARD! ALL IT TOOK WAS JUST SOME GOOD, COMMON BUSINESS SENSE!
WHAT'S BUSINESS GOT TO DO WITH WILDERNESS SURVIVAL?
A LOT MORE THAN I EVER IMAGINED!
OKAY, NOW YOU'RE JUST MAKING MY HEAD HURT!
THAT'S PROBABLY FROM THE CONCUSSION!
YOU JUST REST--
--I'VE GOT EVERY-THING ELSE UNDER CONTROL!
WHATEVER YOU SAY, RONNIE! YOU'RE THE BOSS!
I'M THE CHAIRWOMAN OF THE BOARD, BABY!
NOW, I SHOULD TRY TO CLIMB THIS SNOW BANK... MAYBE I CAN REACH THE ROAD!
16

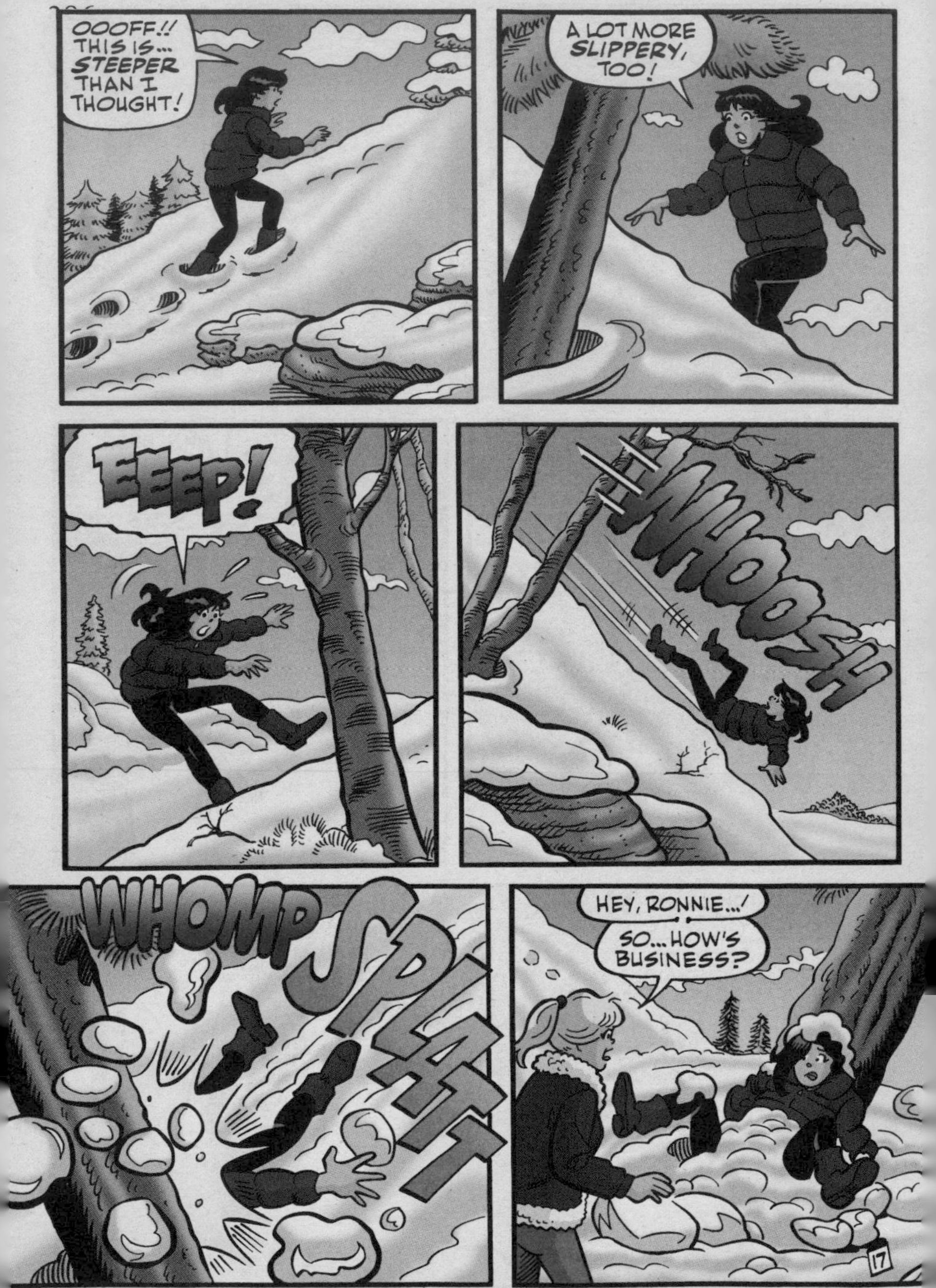
OOOFF!! THIS IS... STEEPER THAN I THOUGHT!
A LOT MORE SLIPPERY, TOO!
EEEP!
WHOOSH
WHOMP
SPLAT
HEY, RONNIE...!
SO... HOW'S BUSINESS?
17

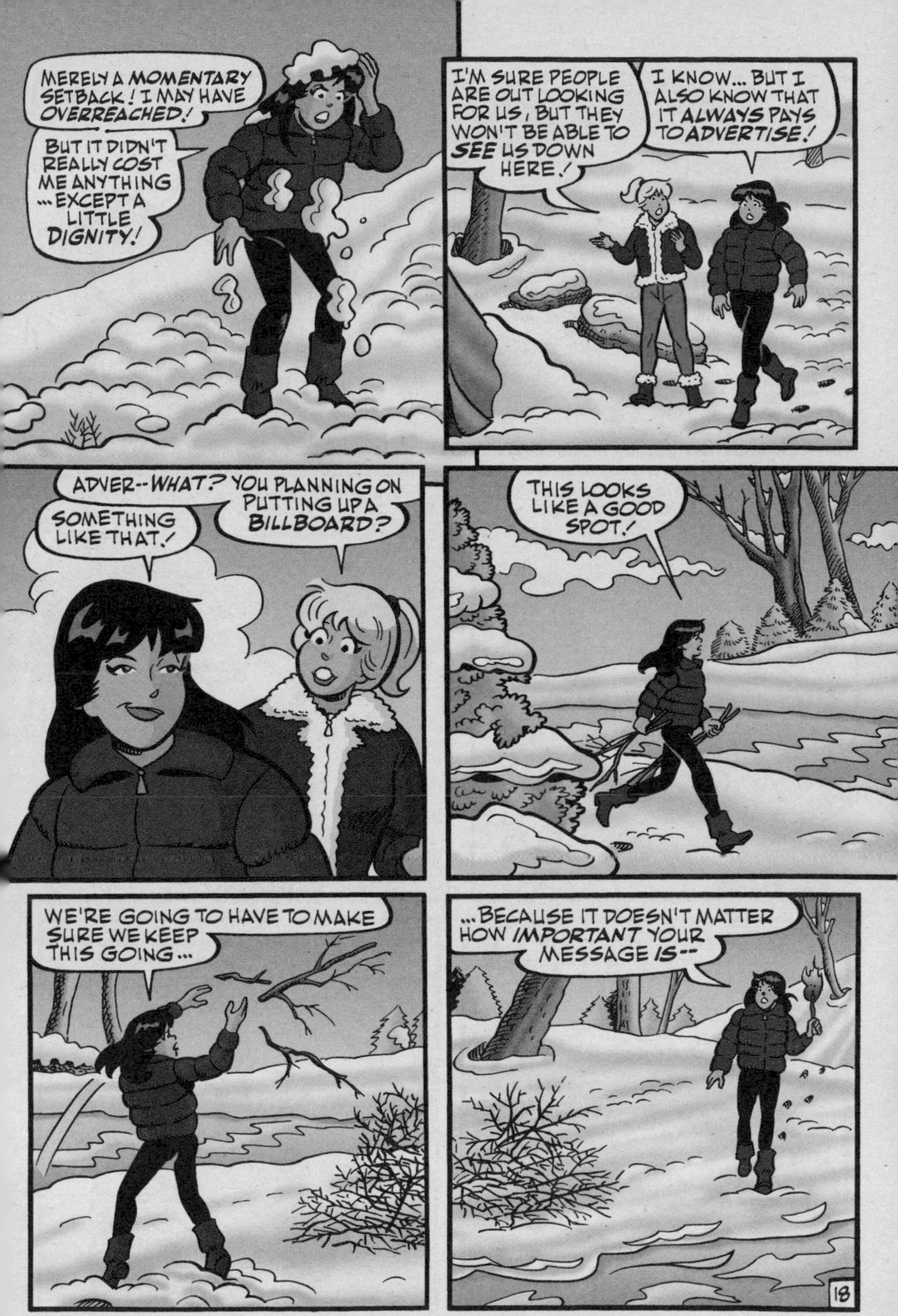
MERELY A MOMENTARY SETBACK! I MAY HAVE OVERREACHED!
BUT IT DIDN'T REALLY COST ME ANYTHING ...EXCEPT A LITTLE DIGNITY!
I'M SURE PEOPLE ARE OUT LOOKING FOR US, BUT THEY WON'T BE ABLE TO SEE US DOWN HERE!
I KNOW... BUT I ALSO KNOW THAT IT ALWAYS PAYS TO ADVERTISE!
ADVER--WHAT? YOU PLANNING ON PUTTING UP A BILLBOARD?
SOMETHING LIKE THAT!
THIS LOOKS LIKE A GOOD SPOT!
WE'RE GOING TO HAVE TO MAKE SURE WE KEEP THIS GOING...
...BECAUSE IT DOESN'T MATTER HOW IMPORTANT YOUR MESSAGE IS--
18

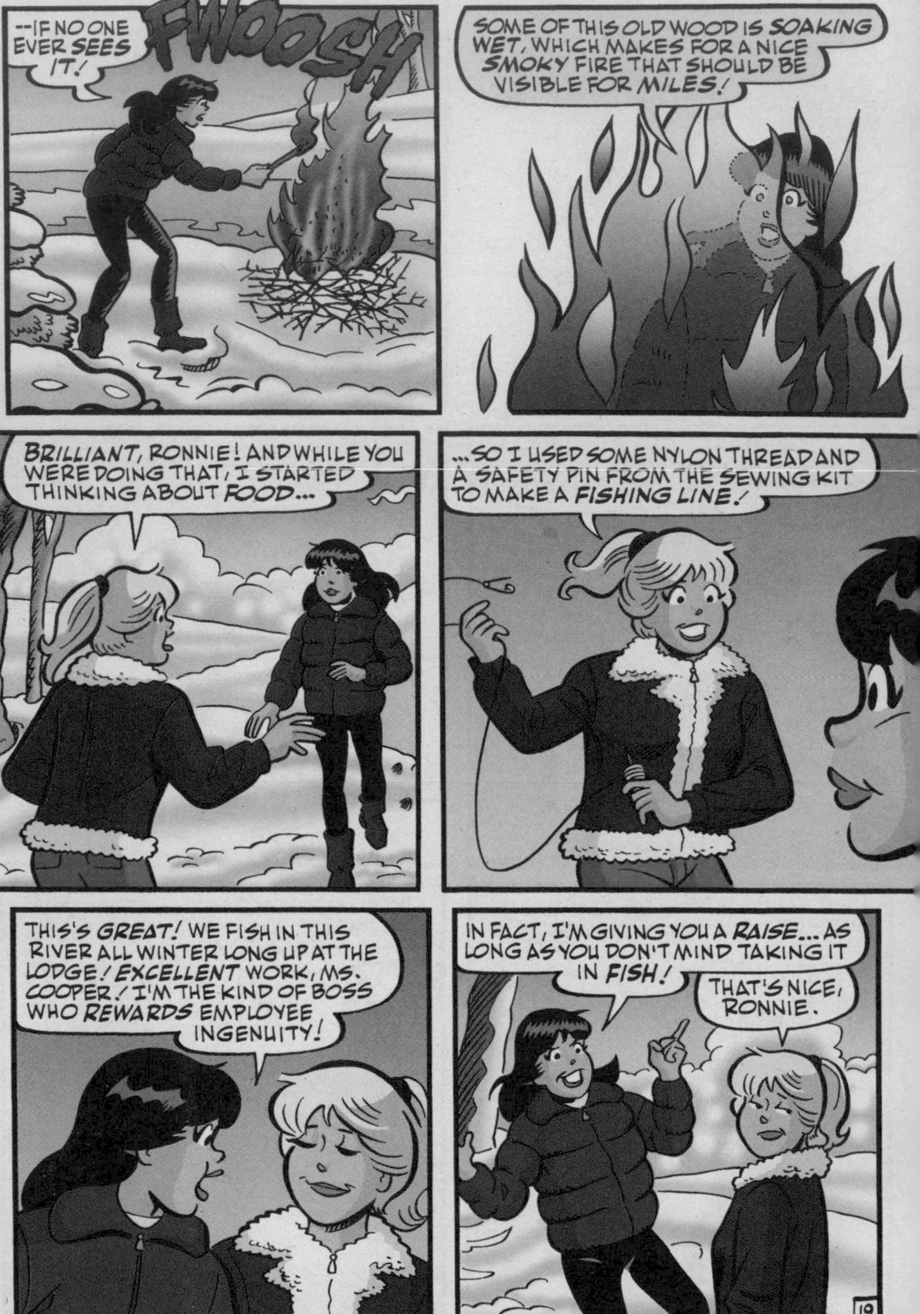
--IF NO ONE EVER SEES IT!
FWOOSH
SOME OF THIS OLD WOOD IS SOAKING WET, WHICH MAKES FOR A NICE SMOKY FIRE THAT SHOULD BE VISIBLE FOR MILES!
BRILLIANT, RONNIE! AND WHILE YOU WERE DOING THAT, I STARTED THINKING ABOUT FOOD...
...SO I USED SOME NYLON THREAD AND A SAFETY PIN FROM THE SEWING KIT TO MAKE A FISHING LINE!
THIS'S GREAT! WE FISH IN THIS RIVER ALL WINTER LONG UP AT THE LODGE! EXCELLENT WORK, MS. COOPER! I'M THE KIND OF BOSS WHO REWARDS EMPLOYEE INGENUITY!
IN FACT, I'M GIVING YOU A RAISE... AS LONG AS YOU DON'T MIND TAKING IT IN FISH!
THAT'S NICE, RONNIE.
19

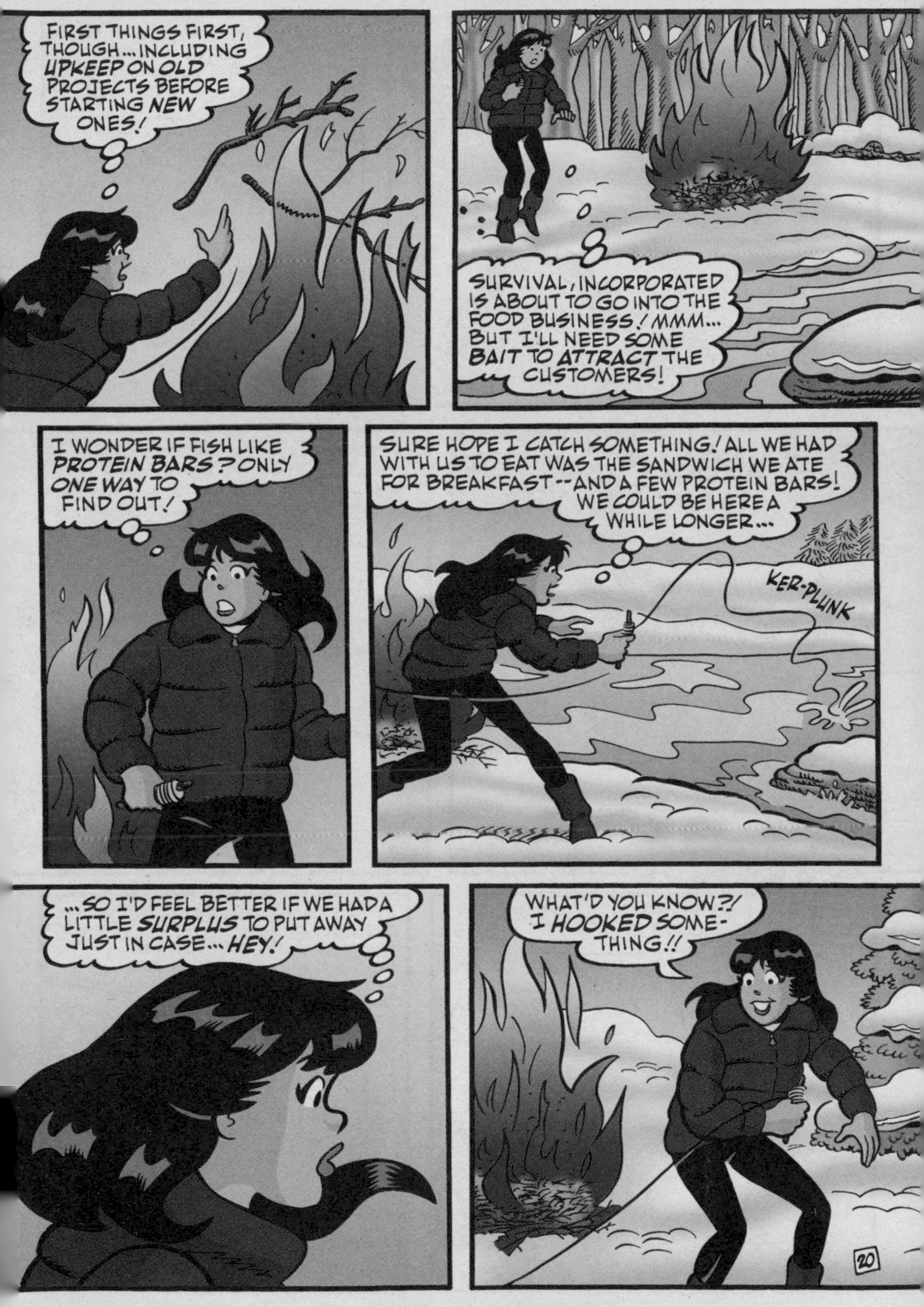
FIRST THINGS FIRST, THOUGH... INCLUDING UPKEEP ON OLD PROJECTS BEFORE STARTING NEW ONES!
SURVIVAL, INCORPORATED IS ABOUT TO GO INTO THE FOOD BUSINESS! MMM... BUT I'LL NEED SOME BAIT TO ATTRACT THE CUSTOMERS!
I WONDER IF FISH LIKE PROTEIN BARS? ONLY ONE WAY TO FIND OUT!
SURE HOPE I CATCH SOMETHING! ALL WE HAD WITH US TO EAT WAS THE SANDWICH WE ATE FOR BREAKFAST--AND A FEW PROTEIN BARS! WE COULD BE HERE A WHILE LONGER...
KER-PLUNK
...SO I'D FEEL BETTER IF WE HAD A LITTLE SURPLUS TO PUT AWAY JUST IN CASE... HEY!
WHAT'D YOU KNOW?! I HOOKED SOME-THING!!
20

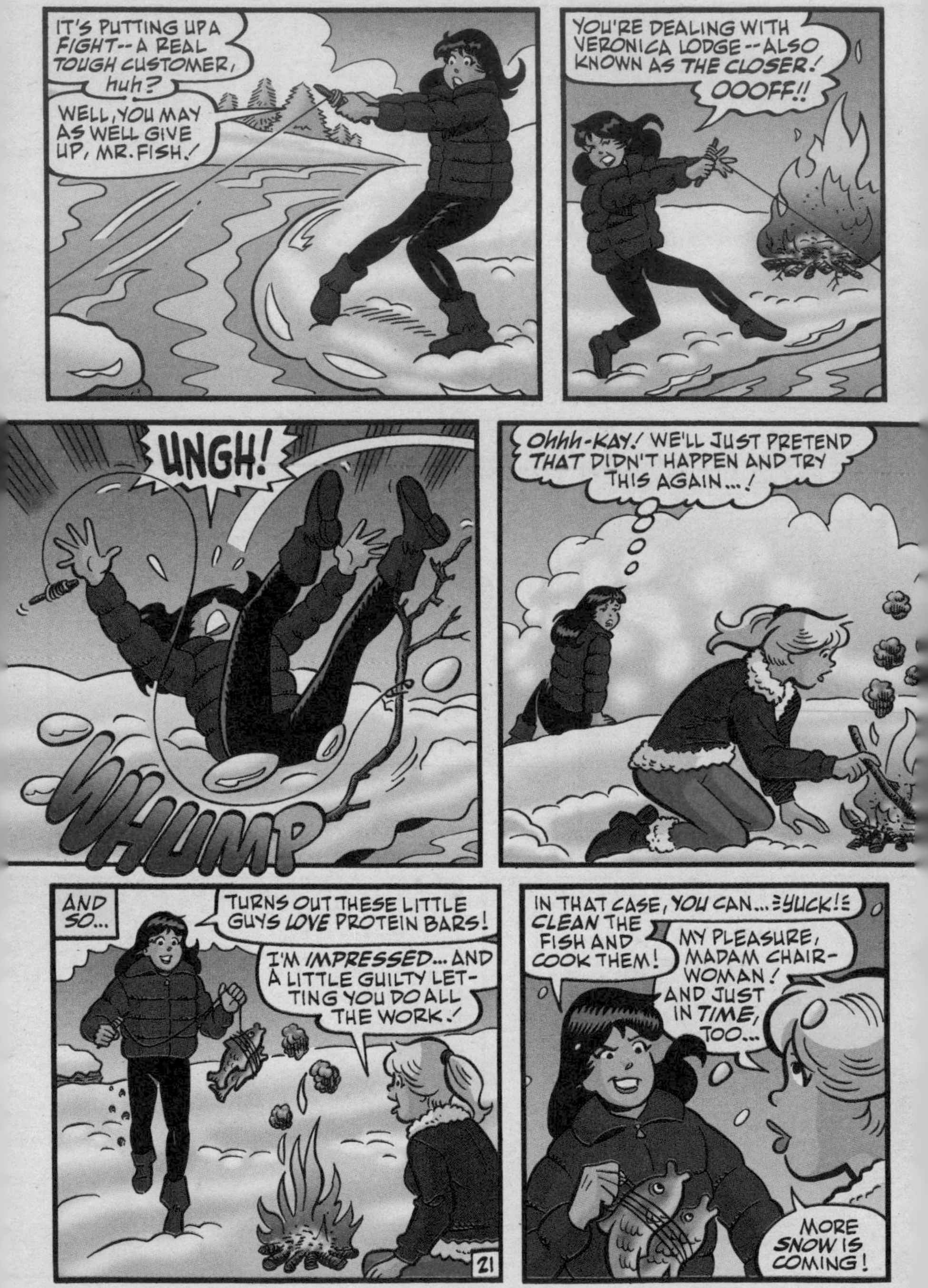
IT'S PUTTING UP A FIGHT-- A REAL TOUGH CUSTOMER, huh?
WELL, YOU MAY AS WELL GIVE UP, MR. FISH!
YOU'RE DEALING WITH VERONICA LODGE -- ALSO KNOWN AS THE CLOSER!
OOOFF!!
UNGH!
WHUMP
Ohhh-KAY! WE'LL JUST PRETEND THAT DIDN'T HAPPEN AND TRY THIS AGAIN...!
AND SO...
TURNS OUT THESE LITTLE GUYS LOVE PROTEIN BARS!
I'M IMPRESSED... AND A LITTLE GUILTY LETTING YOU DO ALL THE WORK!
IN THAT CASE, YOU CAN... YUCK! CLEAN THE FISH AND COOK THEM!
MY PLEASURE, MADAM CHAIRWOMAN! AND JUST IN TIME, TOO...
MORE SNOW IS COMING!

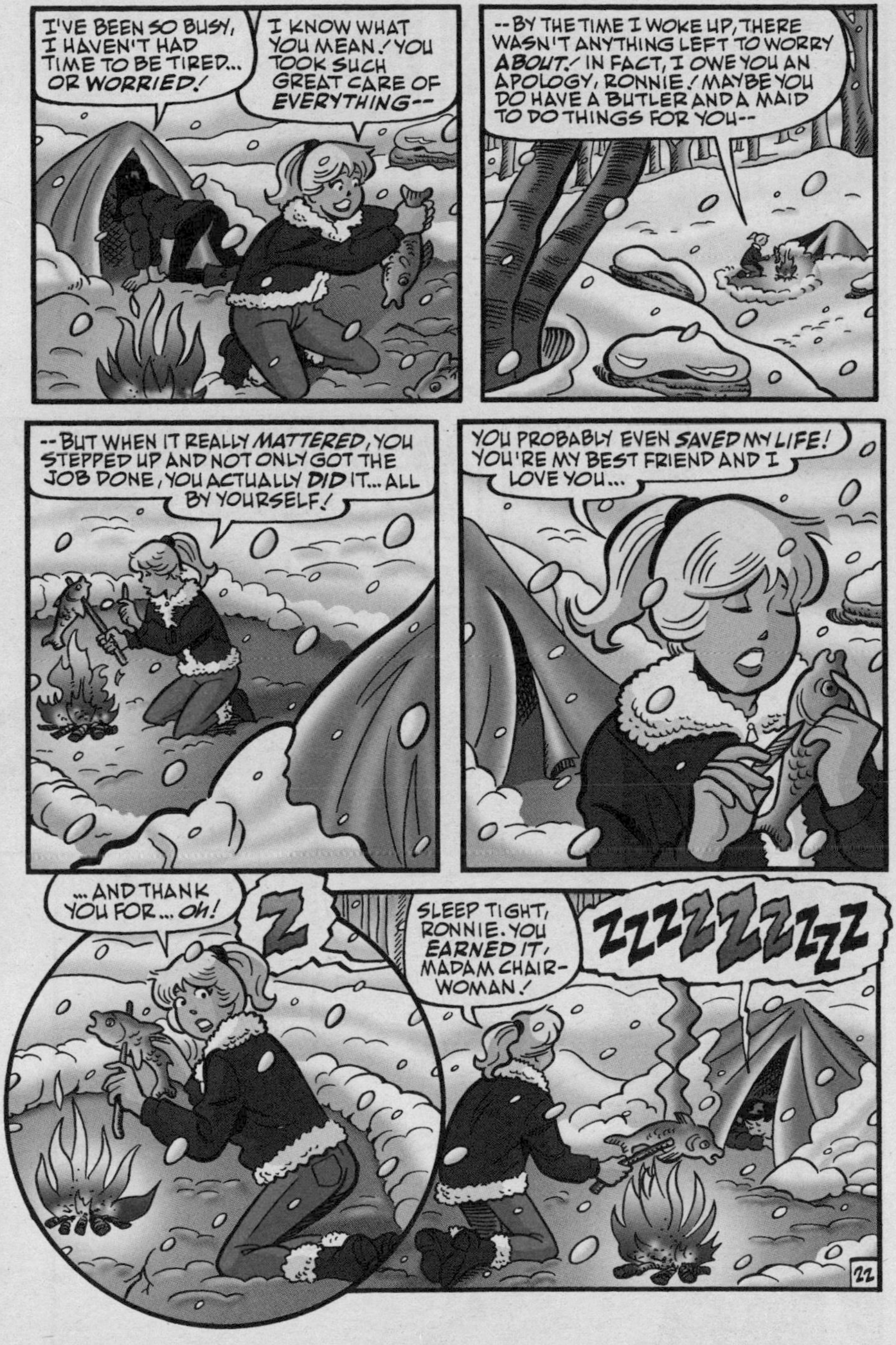

I'VE BEEN SO BUSY, I HAVEN'T HAD TIME TO BE TIRED... OR WORRIED!
I KNOW WHAT YOU MEAN! YOU TOOK SUCH GREAT CARE OF EVERYTHING--
--BY THE TIME I WOKE UP, THERE WASN'T ANYTHING LEFT TO WORRY ABOUT! IN FACT, I OWE YOU AN APOLOGY, RONNIE! MAYBE YOU DO HAVE A BUTLER AND A MAID TO DO THINGS FOR YOU--
--BUT WHEN IT REALLY MATTERED, YOU STEPPED UP AND NOT ONLY GOT THE JOB DONE, YOU ACTUALLY DID IT... ALL BY YOURSELF!
YOU PROBABLY EVEN SAVED MY LIFE! YOU'RE MY BEST FRIEND AND I LOVE YOU...
...AND THANK YOU FOR... OH!
Z
SLEEP TIGHT, RONNIE. YOU EARNED IT, MADAM CHAIR-WOMAN!
ZZZZZZZZZZ
22

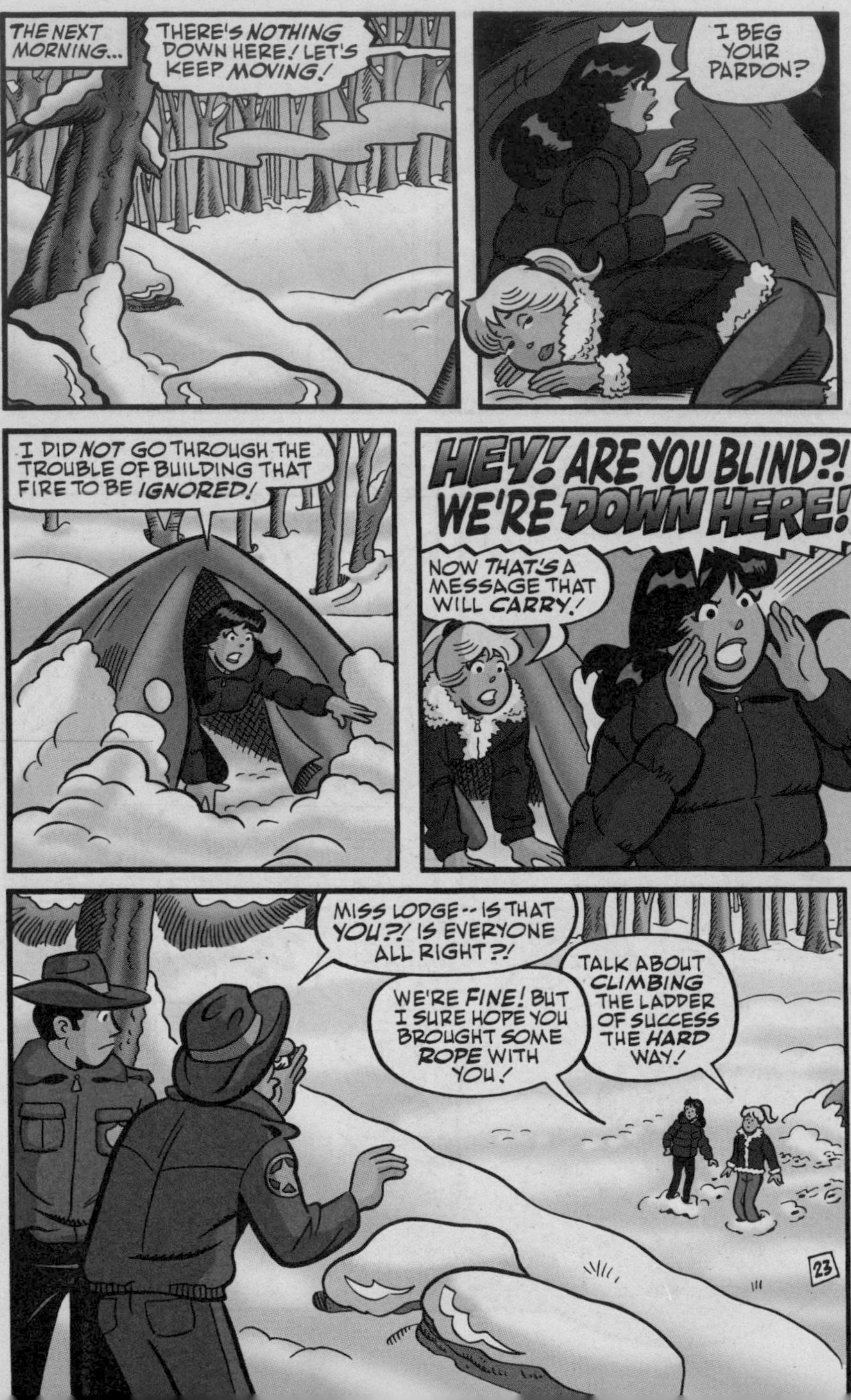

THE NEXT MORNING...
THERE'S NOTHING DOWN HERE! LET'S KEEP MOVING!
I BEG YOUR PARDON?
I DID NOT GO THROUGH THE TROUBLE OF BUILDING THAT FIRE TO BE IGNORED!
HEY! ARE YOU BLIND?! WE'RE DOWN HERE!
NOW THAT'S A MESSAGE THAT WILL CARRY!
MISS LODGE -- IS THAT YOU?! IS EVERYONE ALL RIGHT?!
WE'RE FINE! BUT I SURE HOPE YOU BROUGHT SOME ROPE WITH YOU!
TALK ABOUT CLIMBING THE LADDER OF SUCCESS THE HARD WAY!
23

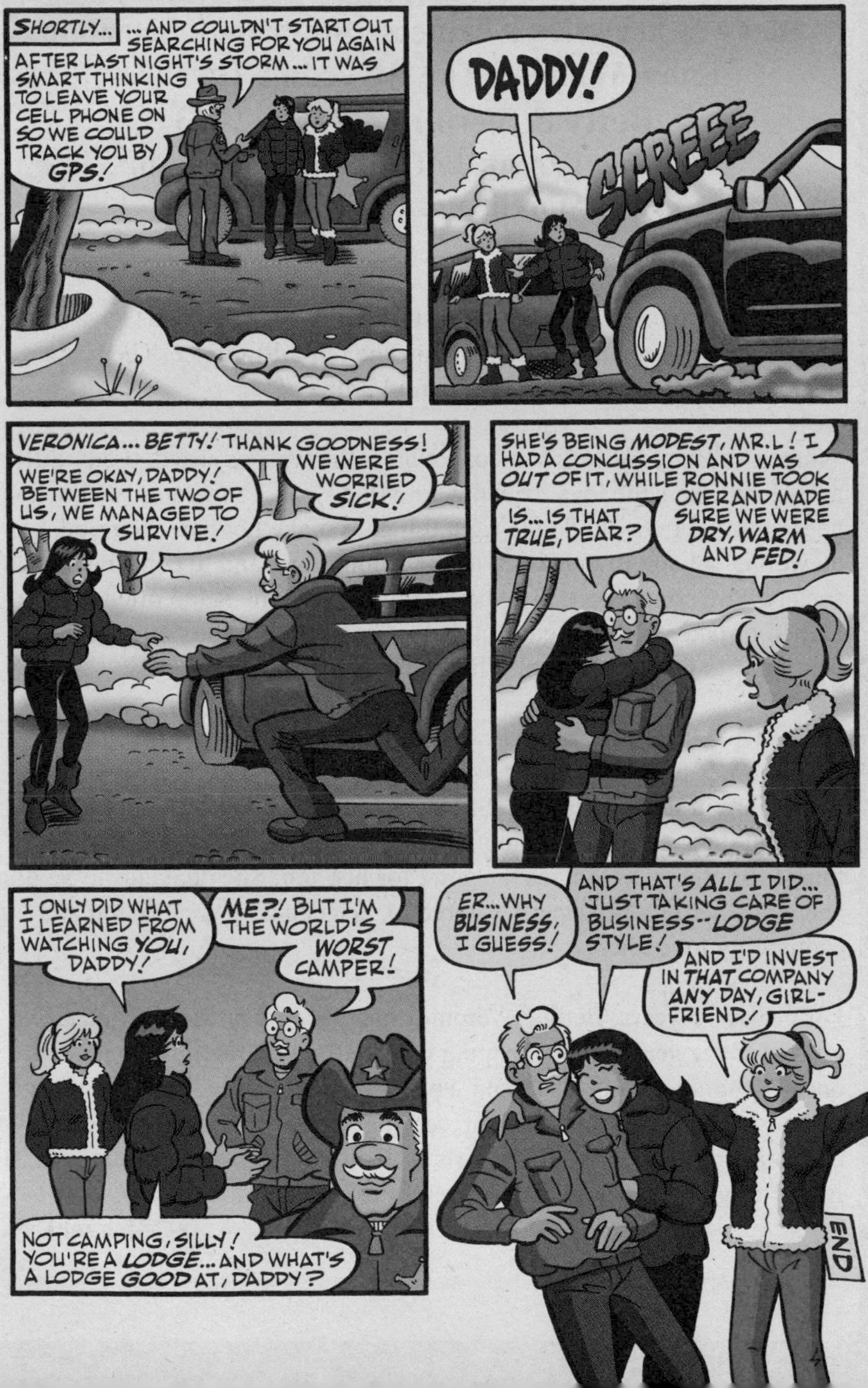
SHORTLY...
... AND COULDN'T START OUT SEARCHING FOR YOU AGAIN AFTER LAST NIGHT'S STORM... IT WAS SMART THINKING TO LEAVE YOUR CELL PHONE ON SO WE COULD TRACK YOU BY GPS!
DADDY!
SCREEE
VERONICA... BETTY! THANK GOODNESS! WE WERE WORRIED SICK!
WE'RE OKAY, DADDY! BETWEEN THE TWO OF US, WE MANAGED TO SURVIVE!
SHE'S BEING MODEST, MR. L! I HAD A CONCUSSION AND WAS OUT OF IT, WHILE RONNIE TOOK OVER AND MADE SURE WE WERE DRY, WARM AND FED!
IS... IS THAT TRUE, DEAR?
I ONLY DID WHAT I LEARNED FROM WATCHING YOU, DADDY!
ME?! BUT I'M THE WORLD'S WORST CAMPER!
NOT CAMPING, SILLY! YOU'RE A LODGE... AND WHAT'S A LODGE GOOD AT, DADDY?
ER... WHY BUSINESS, I GUESS!
AND THAT'S ALL I DID... JUST TAKING CARE OF BUSINESS--LODGE STYLE!
AND I'D INVEST IN THAT COMPANY ANY DAY, GIRL-FRIEND!
END

Betty & Veronica's Princess Storybook Selection:
Snow White & The Riverdale Dwarves
Betty & Veronica #266, 2013
by Dan Parent, Jeff Shultz, Bob Smith,
Jack Morelli and Digikore Studios

They are two teenage girls who historically have the same face and body, with different hair. But hair isn't the only difference. There is a world of difference between Betty and Veronica!

What is "a Betty?" She's someone who is the well-adjusted, pretty girl-next-door. She's the loyal friend who will always be there for you, who goes out of her way to do the right thing, to make her parents proud, to do well in school, to give back to her community, and to contribute to society with compassion. Maybe, unfortunately, she is too often over-looked or taken for granted. But that's okay for her. She nurtures and continues to put everyone else first.

What is a "Veronica?" She's beautiful, exotic, worldly, and comes from money. She's born with a silver spoon in her mouth. As a result, everything in life comes easy. She's flamboyant, talkative, and thrives on being the center of attention. She will go out of her way to do nice things for others, as long as it's good for her, too. She demands to be first and when her ego is properly catered to, she can be a great friend and captivating love interest.

For nearly 75 years, Betty & Veronica have been the icons for teenage girls of every generation, changing constantly with the times but never once changing who they are and what makes them tick. Thus, they have always been current and relevant, serving as the role models for each type of teenager over the decades... girls who either think of themselves as "a Betty" or girls who think of themselves as "a Veronica."

-- **Michael Uslan**
Writer

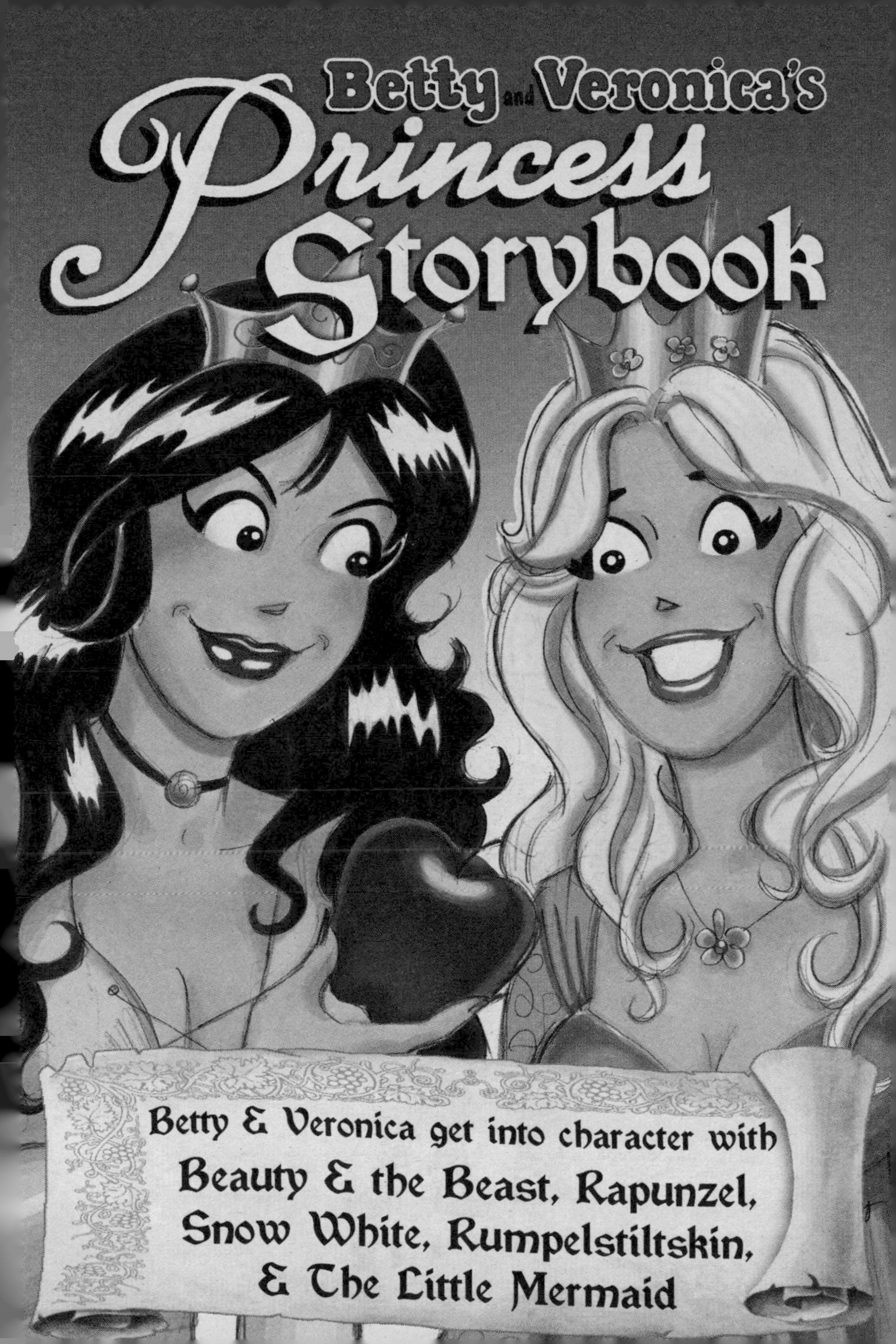
Betty and Veronica's
Princess Storybook
Betty & Veronica get into character with
Beauty & the Beast, Rapunzel,
Snow White, Rumpelstiltskin,
& The Little Mermaid

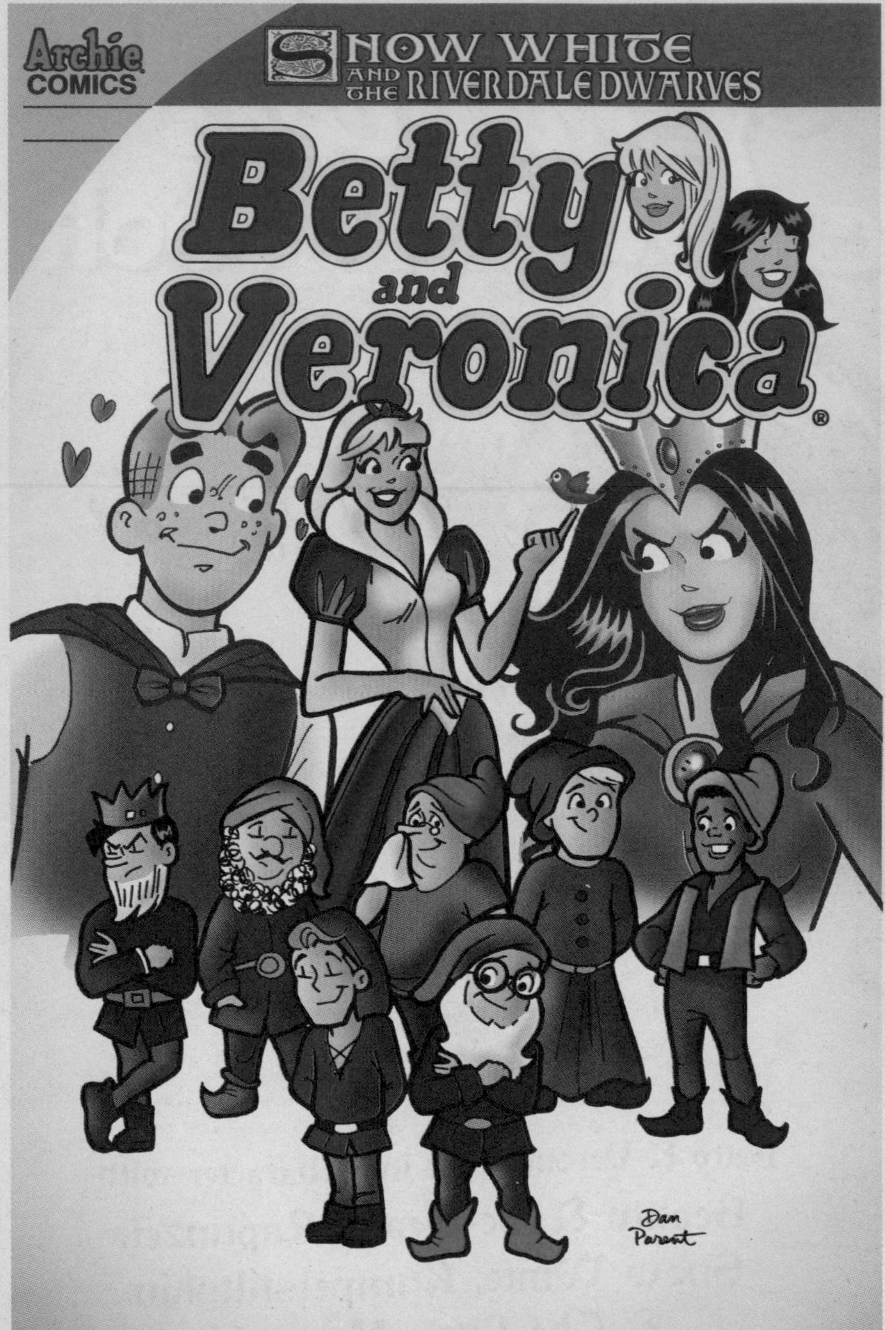

Archie COMICS
SNOW WHITE AND THE RIVERDALE DWARVES
Betty and Veronica
Dan Parent

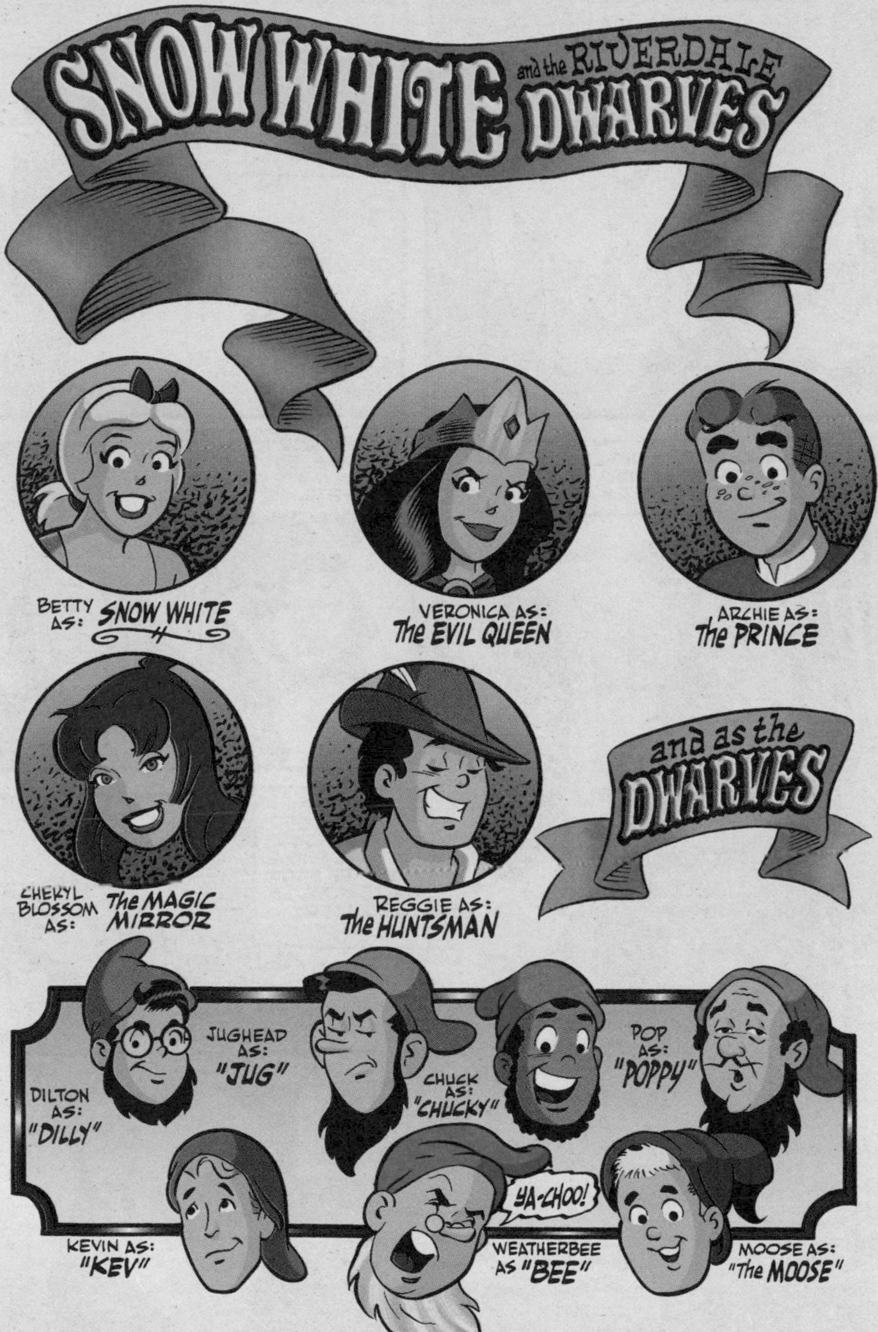

SNOW WHITE and the RIVERDALE DWARVES
BETTY AS: SNOW WHITE
VERONICA AS: The EVIL QUEEN
ARCHIE AS: The PRINCE
CHERYL BLOSSOM AS: The MAGIC MIRROR
REGGIE AS: The HUNTSMAN
and as the DWARVES
DILTON AS: "DILLY"
JUGHEAD AS: "JUG"
CHUCK AS: "CHUCKY"
POP AS: "POPPY"
KEVIN AS: "KEV"
YA-CHOO!
WEATHERBEE AS "BEE"
MOOSE AS: "The MOOSE"

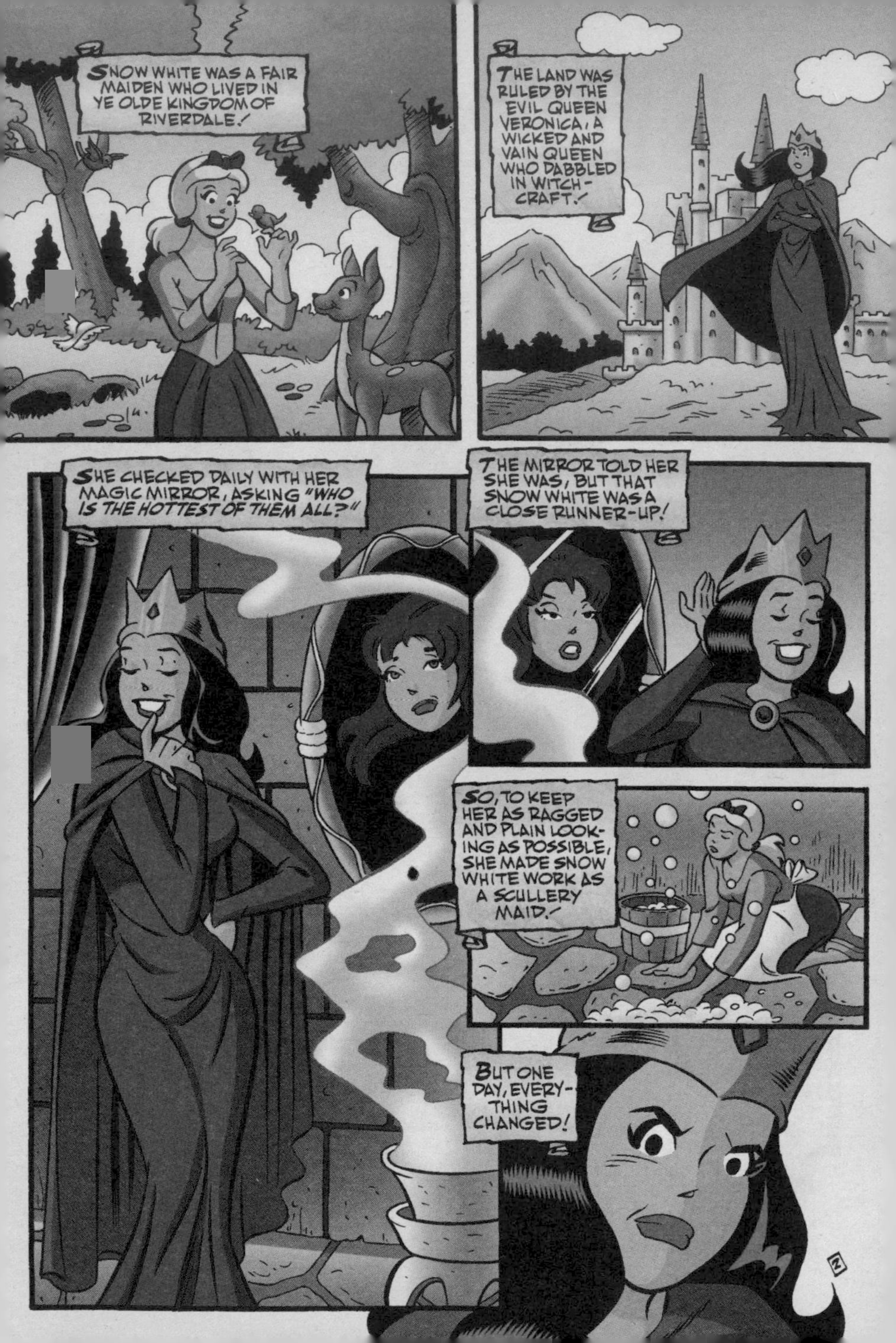
SNOW WHITE WAS A FAIR MAIDEN WHO LIVED IN YE OLDE KINGDOM OF RIVERDALE!
THE LAND WAS RULED BY THE EVIL QUEEN VERONICA, A WICKED AND VAIN QUEEN WHO DABBLED IN WITCH-CRAFT!
SHE CHECKED DAILY WITH HER MAGIC MIRROR, ASKING "WHO IS THE HOTTEST OF THEM ALL?"
THE MIRROR TOLD HER SHE WAS, BUT THAT SNOW WHITE WAS A CLOSE RUNNER-UP!
SO, TO KEEP HER AS RAGGED AND PLAIN LOOK-ING AS POSSIBLE, SHE MADE SNOW WHITE WORK AS A SCULLERY MAID!
BUT ONE DAY, EVERY-THING CHANGED!
2

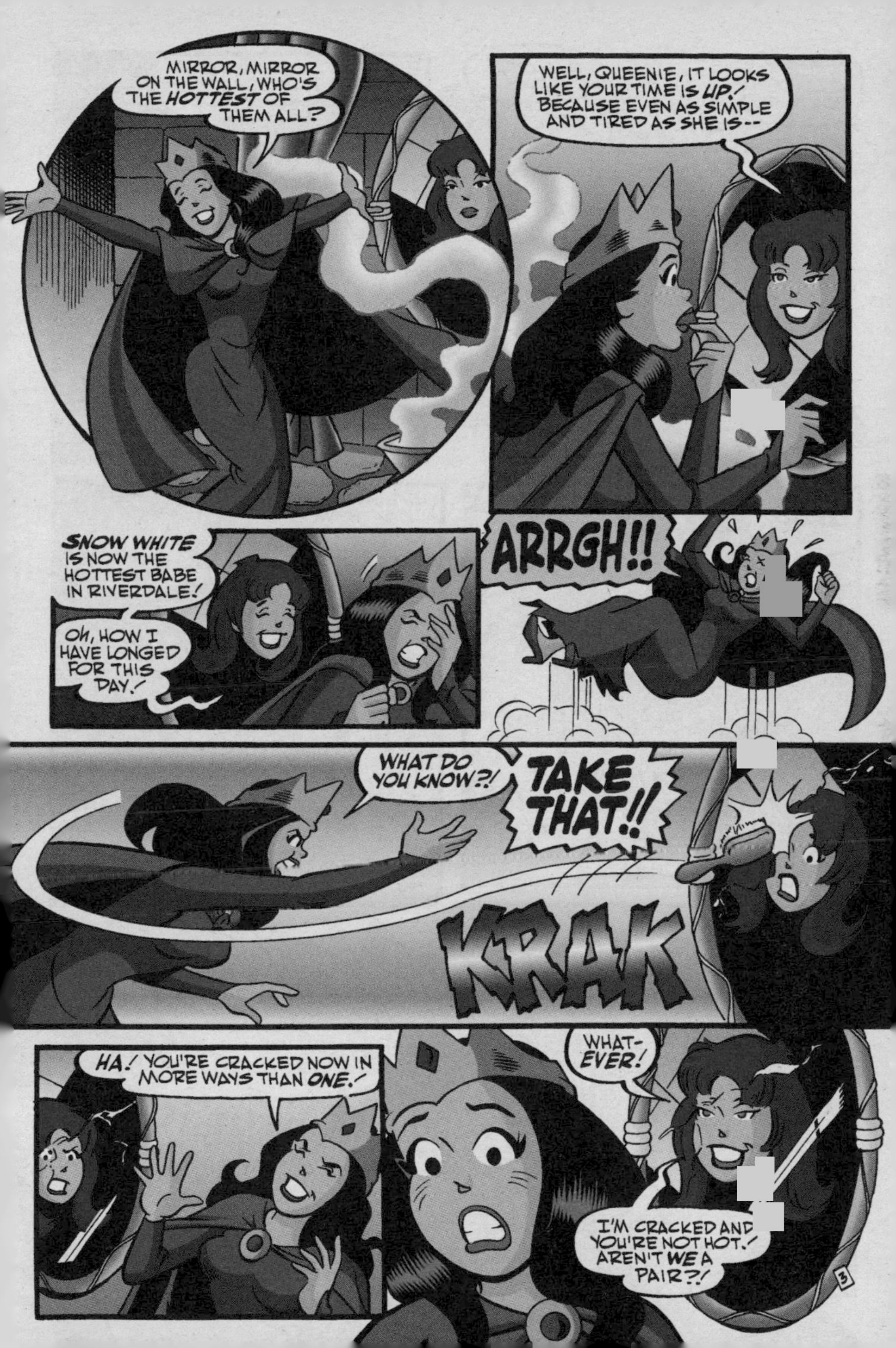
MIRROR, MIRROR ON THE WALL, WHO'S THE HOTTEST OF THEM ALL?
WELL, QUEENIE, IT LOOKS LIKE YOUR TIME IS UP! BECAUSE EVEN AS SIMPLE AND TIRED AS SHE IS--
SNOW WHITE IS NOW THE HOTTEST BABE IN RIVERDALE!
OH, HOW I HAVE LONGED FOR THIS DAY!
ARRGH!!
WHAT DO YOU KNOW?!
TAKE THAT!!
KRAK
HA! YOU'RE CRACKED NOW IN MORE WAYS THAN ONE!
WHAT-EVER!
I'M CRACKED AND YOU'RE NOT HOT! AREN'T WE A PAIR?!
3

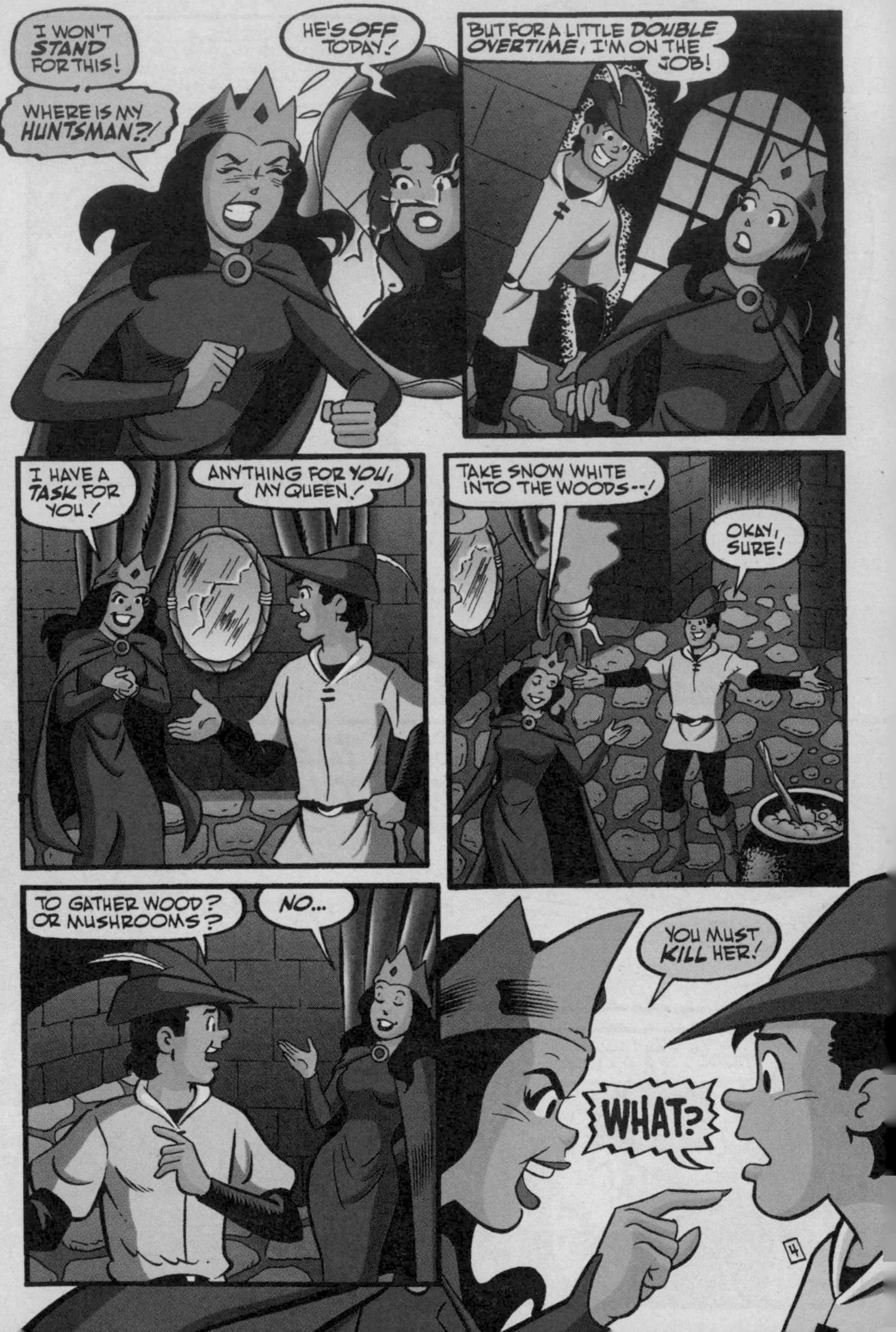
I WON'T STAND FOR THIS!
WHERE IS MY HUNTSMAN?!
HE'S OFF TODAY!
BUT FOR A LITTLE DOUBLE OVERTIME, I'M ON THE JOB!
I HAVE A TASK FOR YOU!
ANYTHING FOR YOU, MY QUEEN!
TAKE SNOW WHITE INTO THE WOODS--!
OKAY, SURE!
TO GATHER WOOD? OR MUSHROOMS?
NO...
YOU MUST KILL HER!
WHAT?

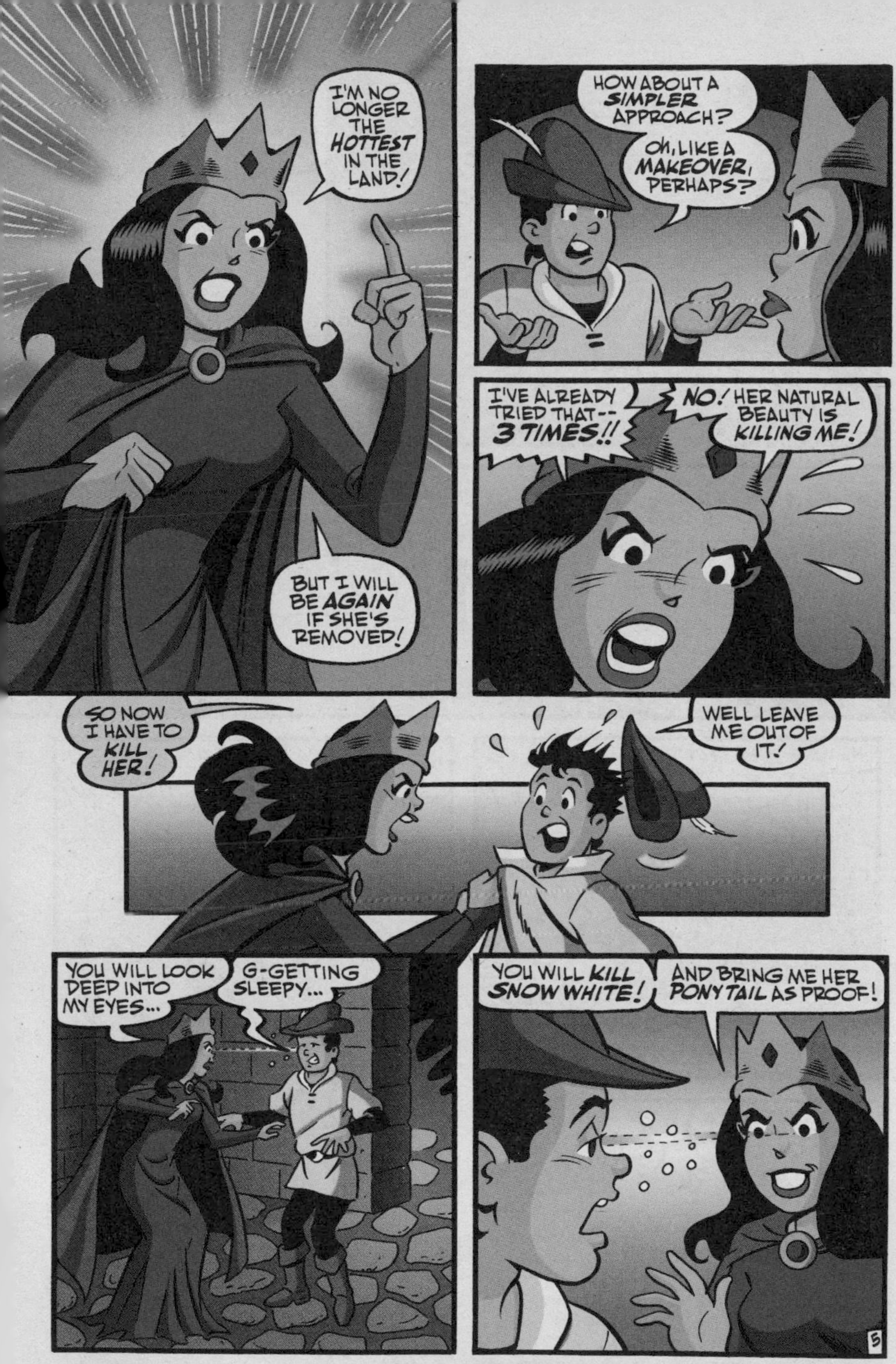
I'M NO LONGER THE HOTTEST IN THE LAND!
BUT I WILL BE AGAIN IF SHE'S REMOVED!
HOW ABOUT A SIMPLER APPROACH?
OH, LIKE A MAKEOVER, PERHAPS?
I'VE ALREADY TRIED THAT-- 3 TIMES!!
NO! HER NATURAL BEAUTY IS KILLING ME!
SO NOW I HAVE TO KILL HER!
WELL LEAVE ME OUT OF IT!
YOU WILL LOOK DEEP INTO MY EYES...
G-GETTING SLEEPY...
YOU WILL KILL SNOW WHITE!
AND BRING ME HER PONY TAIL AS PROOF!
5

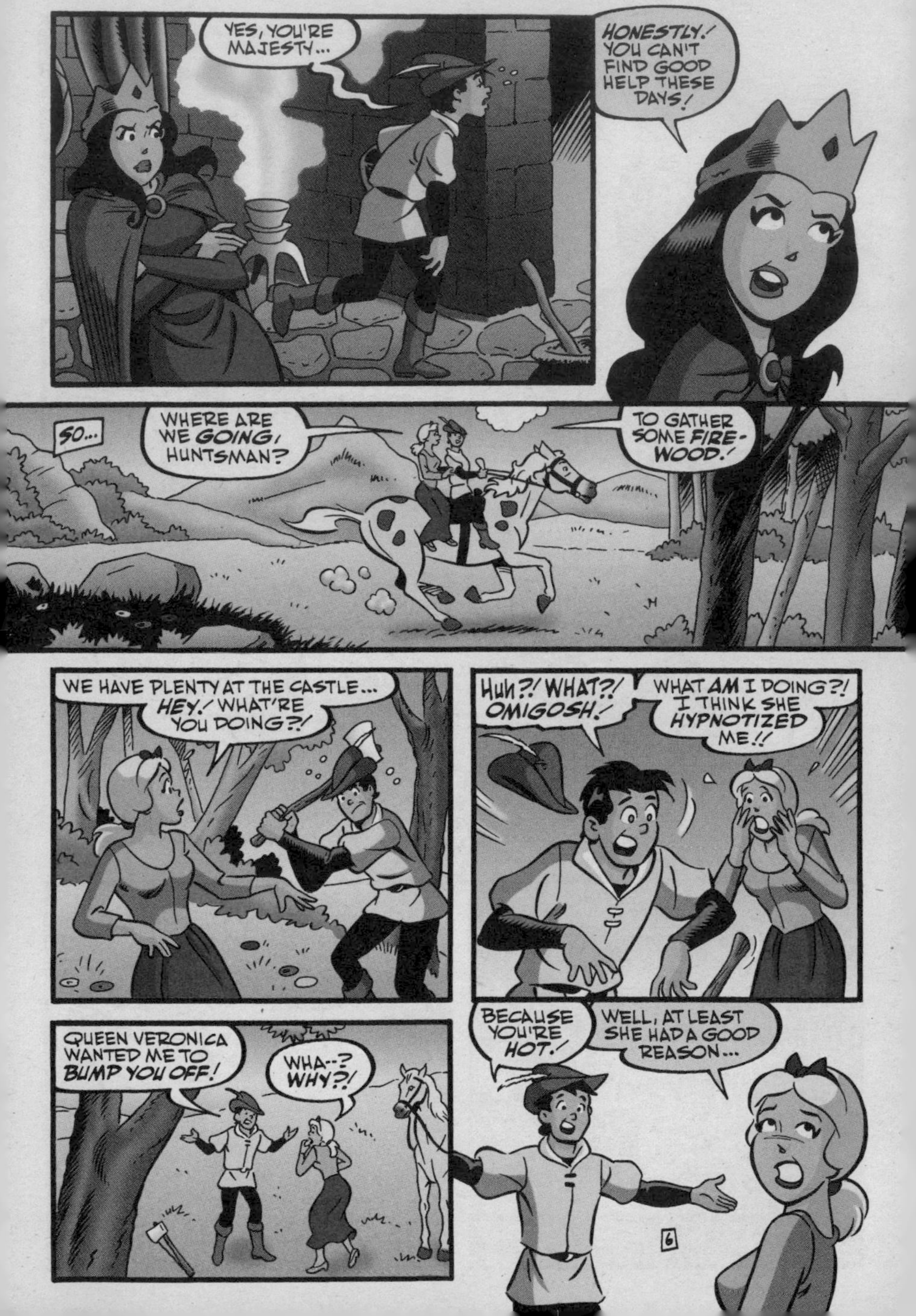
YES, YOU'RE MAJESTY...
HONESTLY! YOU CAN'T FIND GOOD HELP THESE DAYS!
SO...
WHERE ARE WE GOING, HUNTSMAN?
TO GATHER SOME FIRE-WOOD!
WE HAVE PLENTY AT THE CASTLE... HEY! WHAT'RE YOU DOING?!
HUH?! WHAT?! OMIGOSH!
WHAT AM I DOING?! I THINK SHE HYPNOTIZED ME!!
QUEEN VERONICA WANTED ME TO BUMP YOU OFF!
WHA--? WHY?!
BECAUSE YOU'RE HOT!
WELL, AT LEAST SHE HAD A GOOD REASON...
6

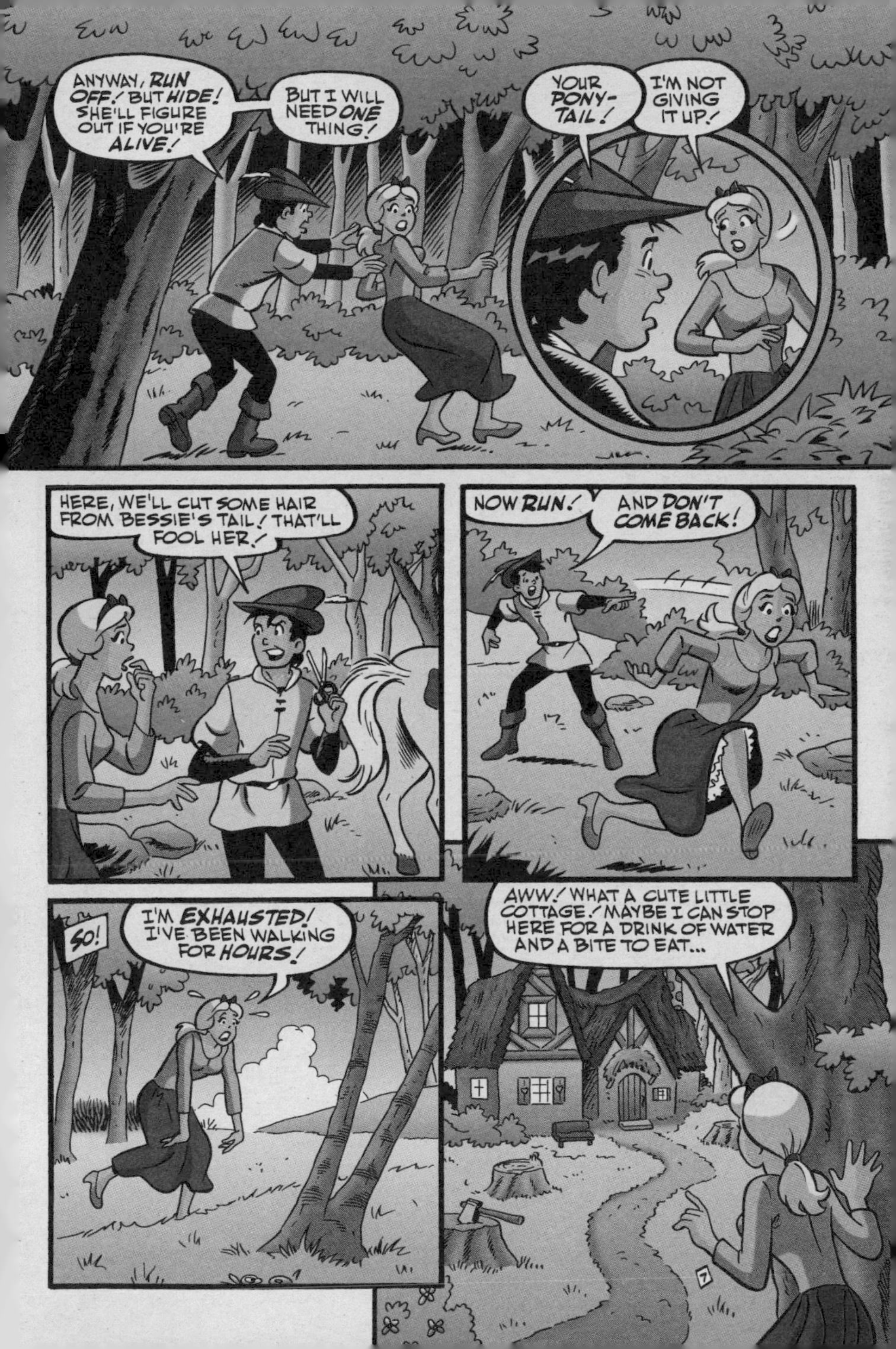

ANYWAY, RUN OFF! BUT HIDE! SHE'LL FIGURE OUT IF YOU'RE ALIVE!
BUT I WILL NEED ONE THING!
YOUR PONY-TAIL!
I'M NOT GIVING IT UP!
HERE, WE'LL CUT SOME HAIR FROM BESSIE'S TAIL! THAT'LL FOOL HER!
NOW RUN!
AND DON'T COME BACK!
SO!
I'M EXHAUSTED! I'VE BEEN WALKING FOR HOURS!
AWW! WHAT A CUTE LITTLE COTTAGE! MAYBE I CAN STOP HERE FOR A DRINK OF WATER AND A BITE TO EAT...

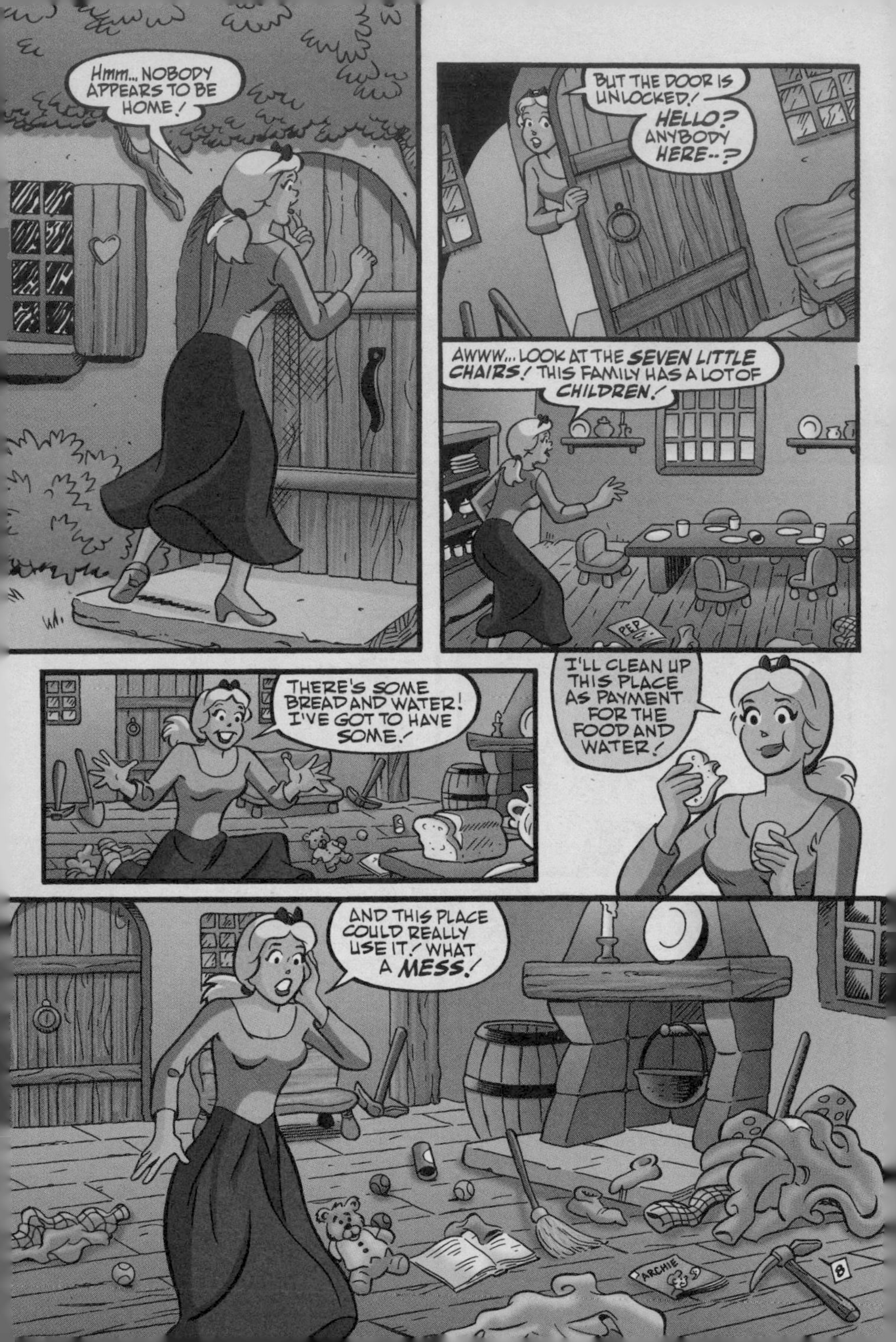

Hmm... NOBODY APPEARS TO BE HOME!
BUT THE DOOR IS UNLOCKED!
HELLO? ANYBODY HERE--?
AWWW... LOOK AT THE SEVEN LITTLE CHAIRS! THIS FAMILY HAS A LOT OF CHILDREN!
PEP
THERE'S SOME BREAD AND WATER! I'VE GOT TO HAVE SOME!
I'LL CLEAN UP THIS PLACE AS PAYMENT FOR THE FOOD AND WATER!
AND THIS PLACE COULD REALLY USE IT! WHAT A MESS!
ARCHIE
8

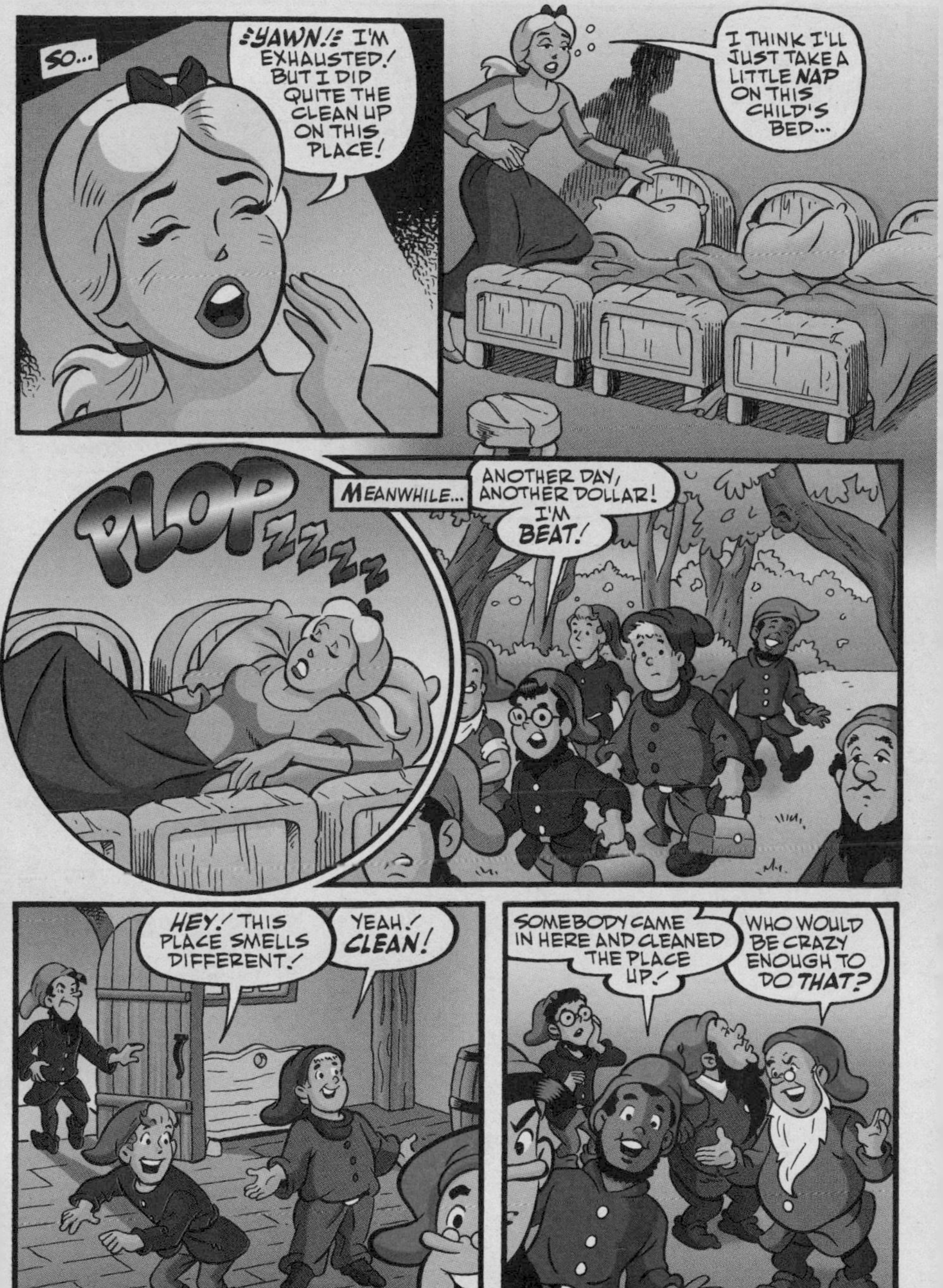
SO...
:YAWN!: I'M EXHAUSTED! BUT I DID QUITE THE CLEAN UP ON THIS PLACE!
I THINK I'LL JUST TAKE A LITTLE NAP ON THIS CHILD'S BED...
PLOP ZZZZ
MEANWHILE...
ANOTHER DAY, ANOTHER DOLLAR! I'M BEAT!
HEY! THIS PLACE SMELLS DIFFERENT!
YEAH! CLEAN!
SOMEBODY CAME IN HERE AND CLEANED THE PLACE UP!
WHO WOULD BE CRAZY ENOUGH TO DO THAT?
9

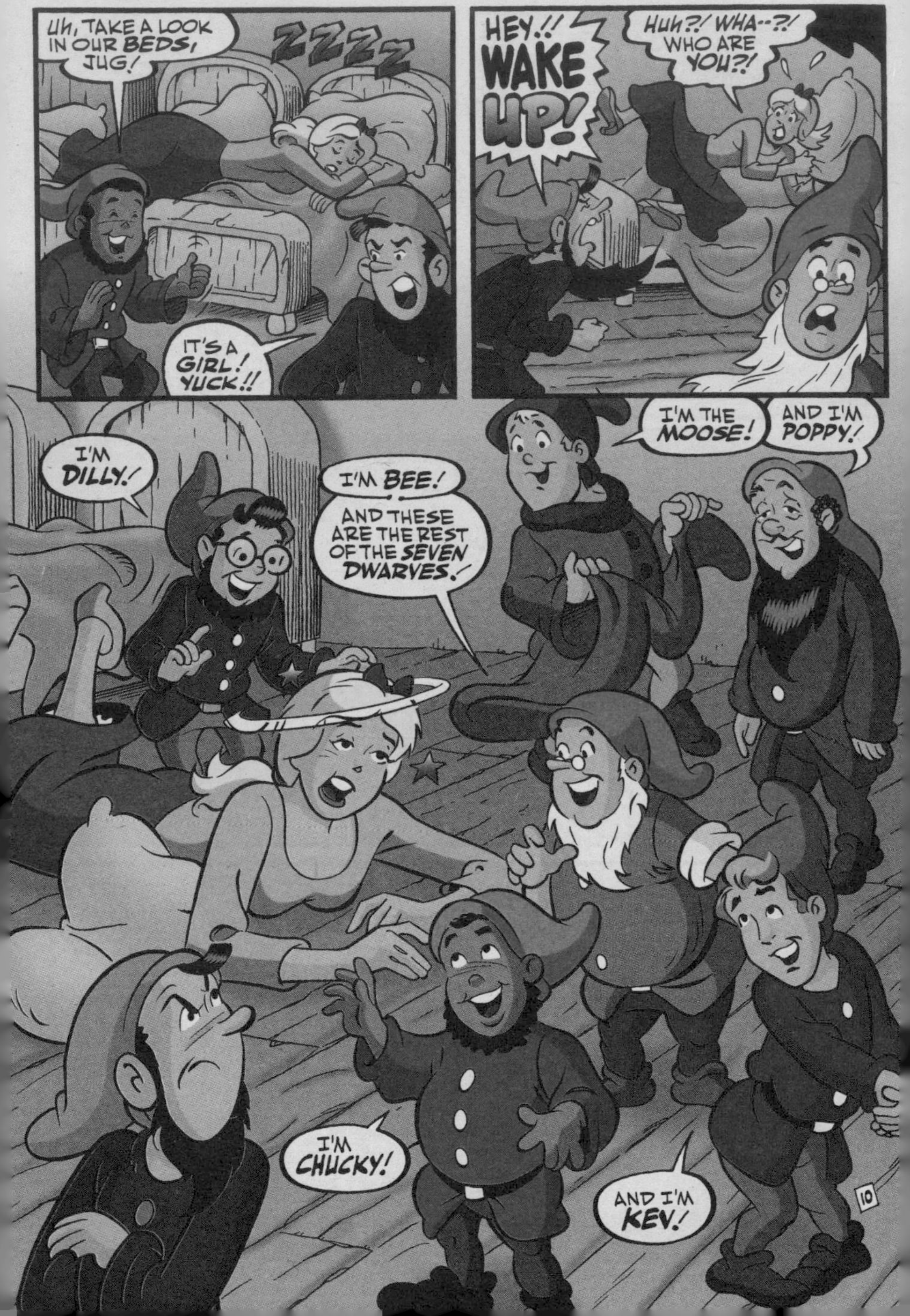
UH, TAKE A LOOK IN OUR BEDS, JUG!
ZZZZZ
IT'S A GIRL! YUCK!!
HEY!! WAKE UP!
HUH?! WHA--?! WHO ARE YOU?!
I'M DILLY!
I'M BEE!
AND THESE ARE THE REST OF THE SEVEN DWARVES!
I'M THE MOOSE!
AND I'M POPPY!
I'M CHUCKY!
AND I'M KEV!
10

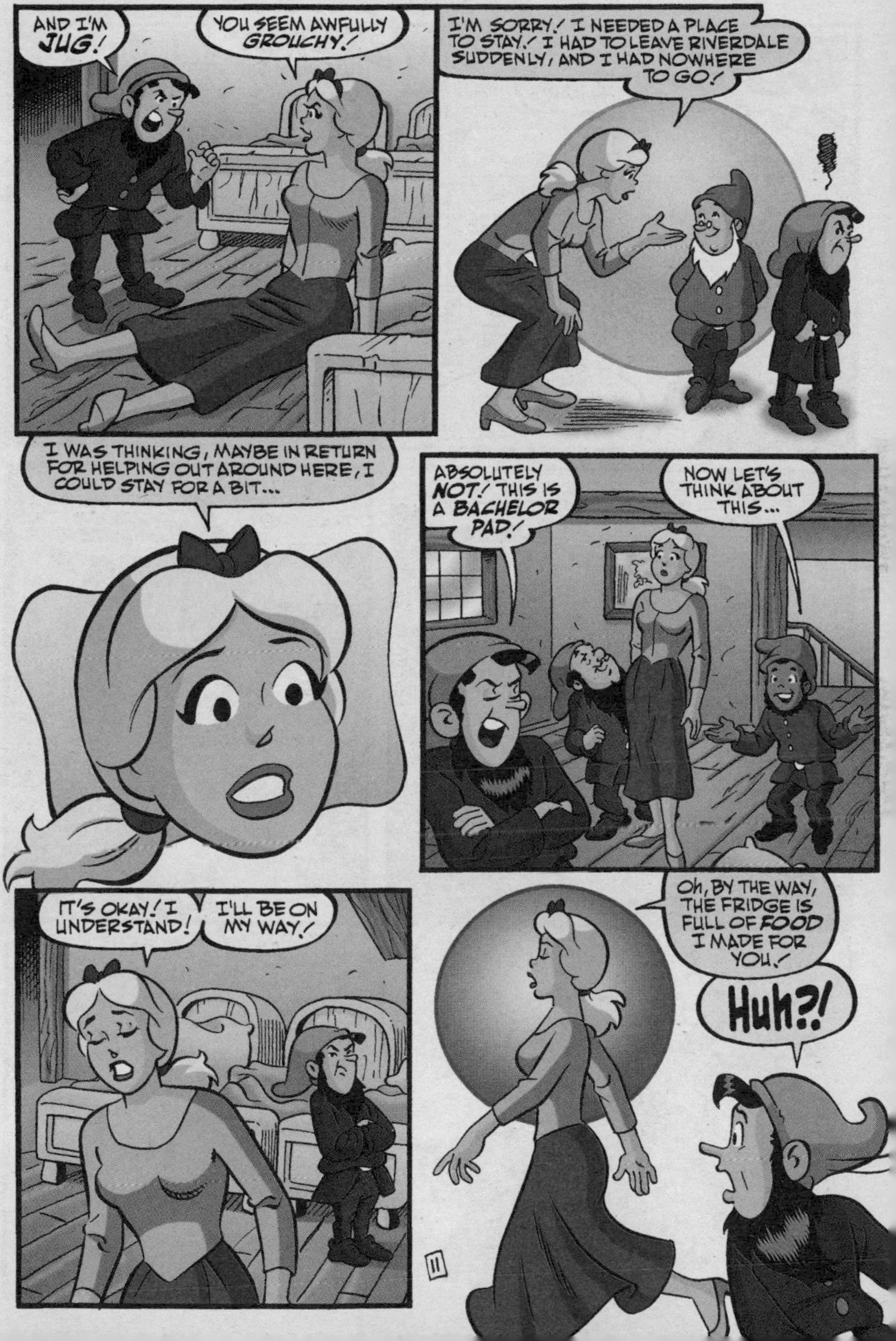

AND I'M JUG!
YOU SEEM AWFULLY GROUCHY!
I'M SORRY! I NEEDED A PLACE TO STAY! I HAD TO LEAVE RIVERDALE SUDDENLY, AND I HAD NOWHERE TO GO!
I WAS THINKING, MAYBE IN RETURN FOR HELPING OUT AROUND HERE, I COULD STAY FOR A BIT...
ABSOLUTELY NOT! THIS IS A BACHELOR PAD!
NOW LET'S THINK ABOUT THIS...
IT'S OKAY! I UNDERSTAND!
I'LL BE ON MY WAY!
Oh, BY THE WAY, THE FRIDGE IS FULL OF FOOD I MADE FOR YOU!
Huh?!
11

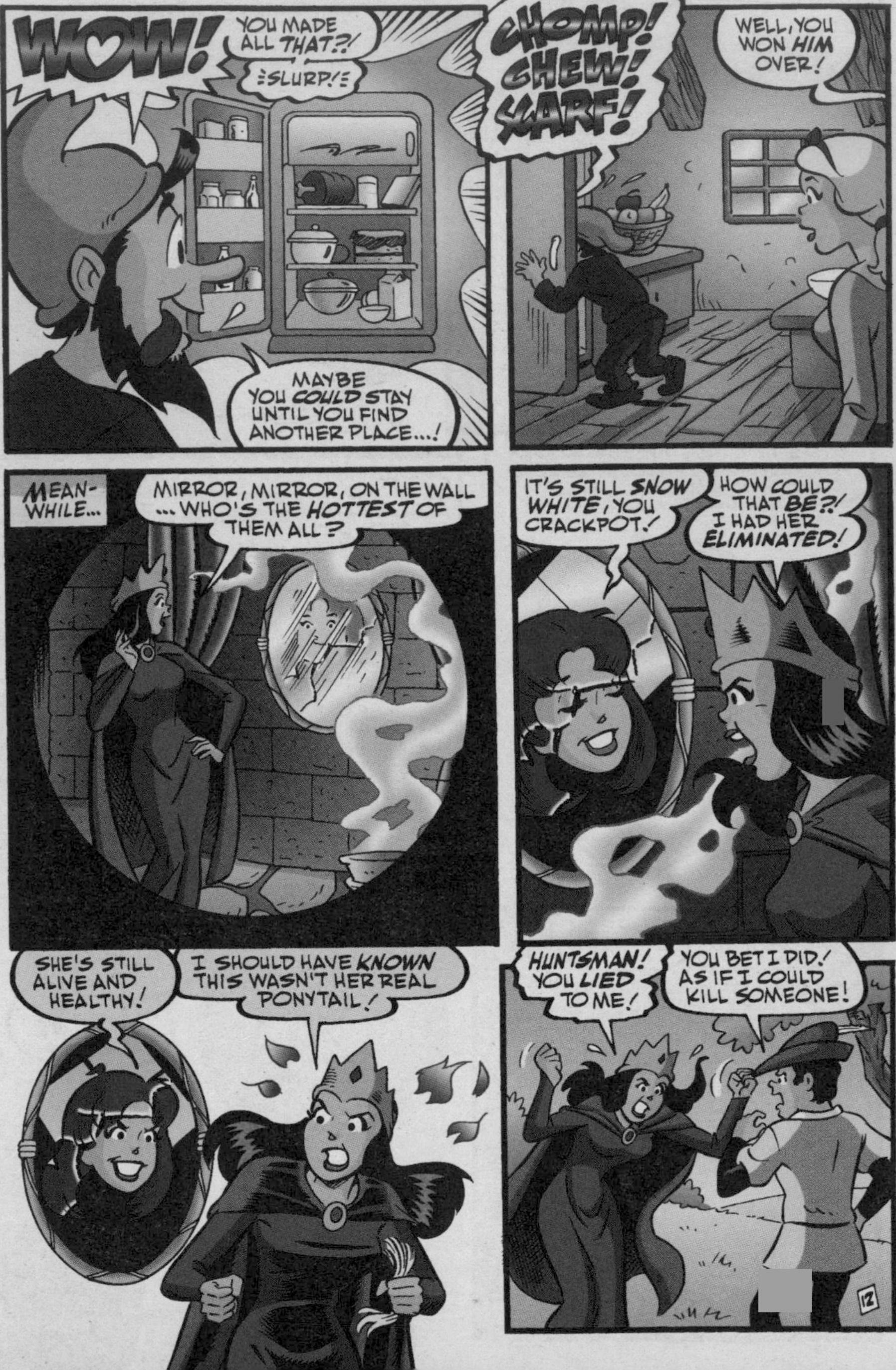
WOW!
YOU MADE ALL THAT?!
SLURP!
MAYBE YOU COULD STAY UNTIL YOU FIND ANOTHER PLACE...!
CHOMP! CHEW! SCARF!
WELL, YOU WON HIM OVER!
MEANWHILE...
MIRROR, MIRROR, ON THE WALL ... WHO'S THE HOTTEST OF THEM ALL?
IT'S STILL SNOW WHITE, YOU CRACKPOT!
HOW COULD THAT BE?! I HAD HER ELIMINATED!
SHE'S STILL ALIVE AND HEALTHY!
I SHOULD HAVE KNOWN THIS WASN'T HER REAL PONYTAIL!
HUNTSMAN! YOU LIED TO ME!
YOU BET I DID! AS IF I COULD KILL SOMEONE!
12

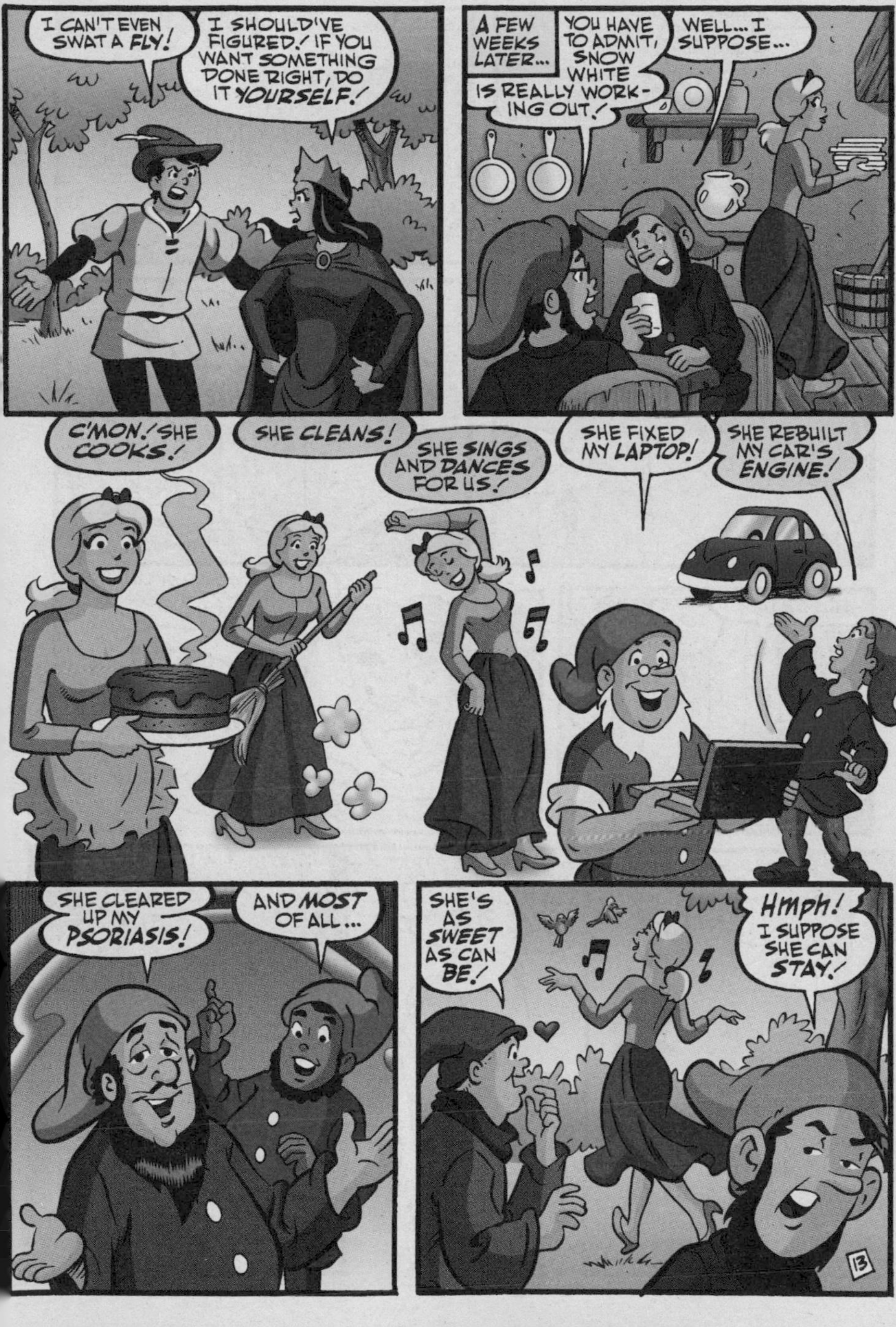

I CAN'T EVEN SWAT A FLY!
I SHOULD'VE FIGURED! IF YOU WANT SOMETHING DONE RIGHT, DO IT YOURSELF!
A FEW WEEKS LATER...
YOU HAVE TO ADMIT, SNOW WHITE IS REALLY WORKING OUT!
WELL... I SUPPOSE...
C'MON! SHE COOKS!
SHE CLEANS!
SHE SINGS AND DANCES FOR US!
SHE FIXED MY LAPTOP!
SHE REBUILT MY CAR'S ENGINE!
SHE CLEARED UP MY PSORIASIS!
AND MOST OF ALL...
SHE'S AS SWEET AS CAN BE!
Hmph! I SUPPOSE SHE CAN STAY!

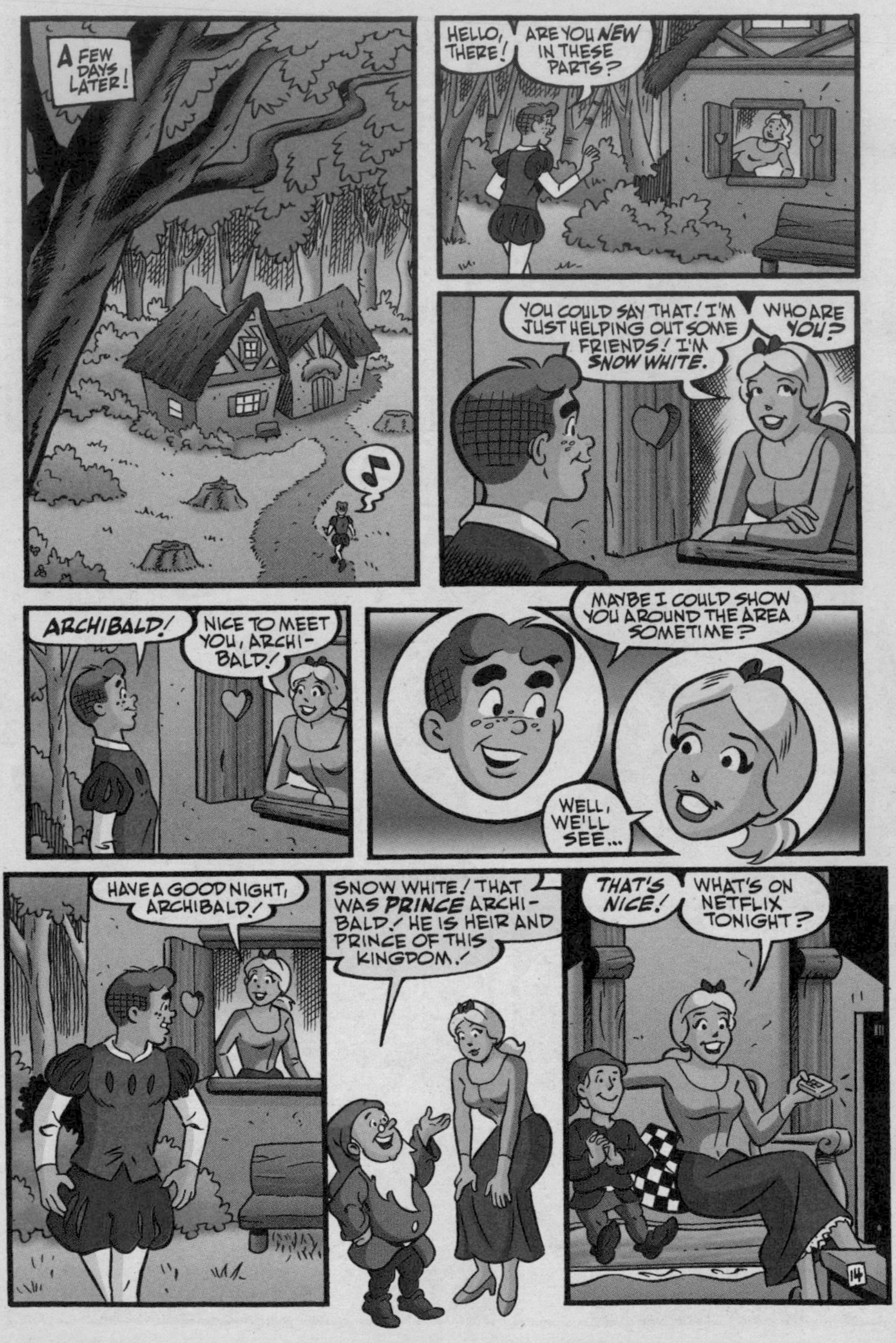

A FEW DAYS LATER!
HELLO, THERE!
ARE YOU NEW IN THESE PARTS?
YOU COULD SAY THAT! I'M JUST HELPING OUT SOME FRIENDS! I'M SNOW WHITE.
WHO ARE YOU?
ARCHIBALD!
NICE TO MEET YOU, ARCHI-BALD!
MAYBE I COULD SHOW YOU AROUND THE AREA SOMETIME?
WELL, WE'LL SEE...
HAVE A GOOD NIGHT, ARCHIBALD!
SNOW WHITE! THAT WAS PRINCE ARCHI-BALD! HE IS HEIR AND PRINCE OF THIS KINGDOM!
THAT'S NICE!
WHAT'S ON NETFLIX TONIGHT?
14

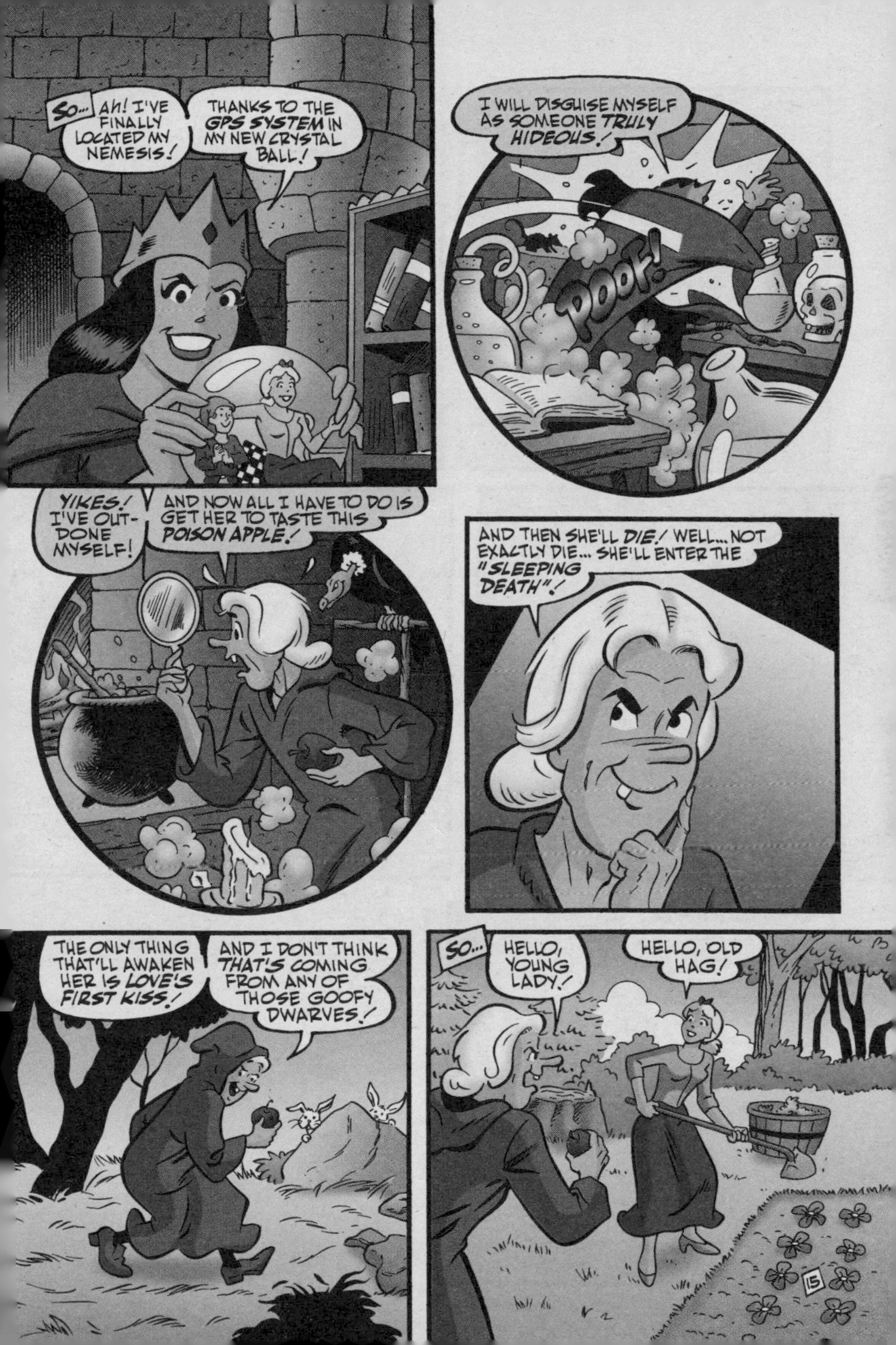

SO...
AH! I'VE FINALLY LOCATED MY NEMESIS!
THANKS TO THE GPS SYSTEM IN MY NEW CRYSTAL BALL!
I WILL DISGUISE MYSELF AS SOMEONE TRULY HIDEOUS!
POOF!
YIKES! I'VE OUT-DONE MYSELF!
AND NOW ALL I HAVE TO DO IS GET HER TO TASTE THIS POISON APPLE!
AND THEN SHE'LL DIE! WELL... NOT EXACTLY DIE... SHE'LL ENTER THE "SLEEPING DEATH"!
THE ONLY THING THAT'LL AWAKEN HER IS LOVE'S FIRST KISS!
AND I DON'T THINK THAT'S COMING FROM ANY OF THOSE GOOFY DWARVES!
SO...
HELLO, YOUNG LADY!
HELLO, OLD HAG!
15

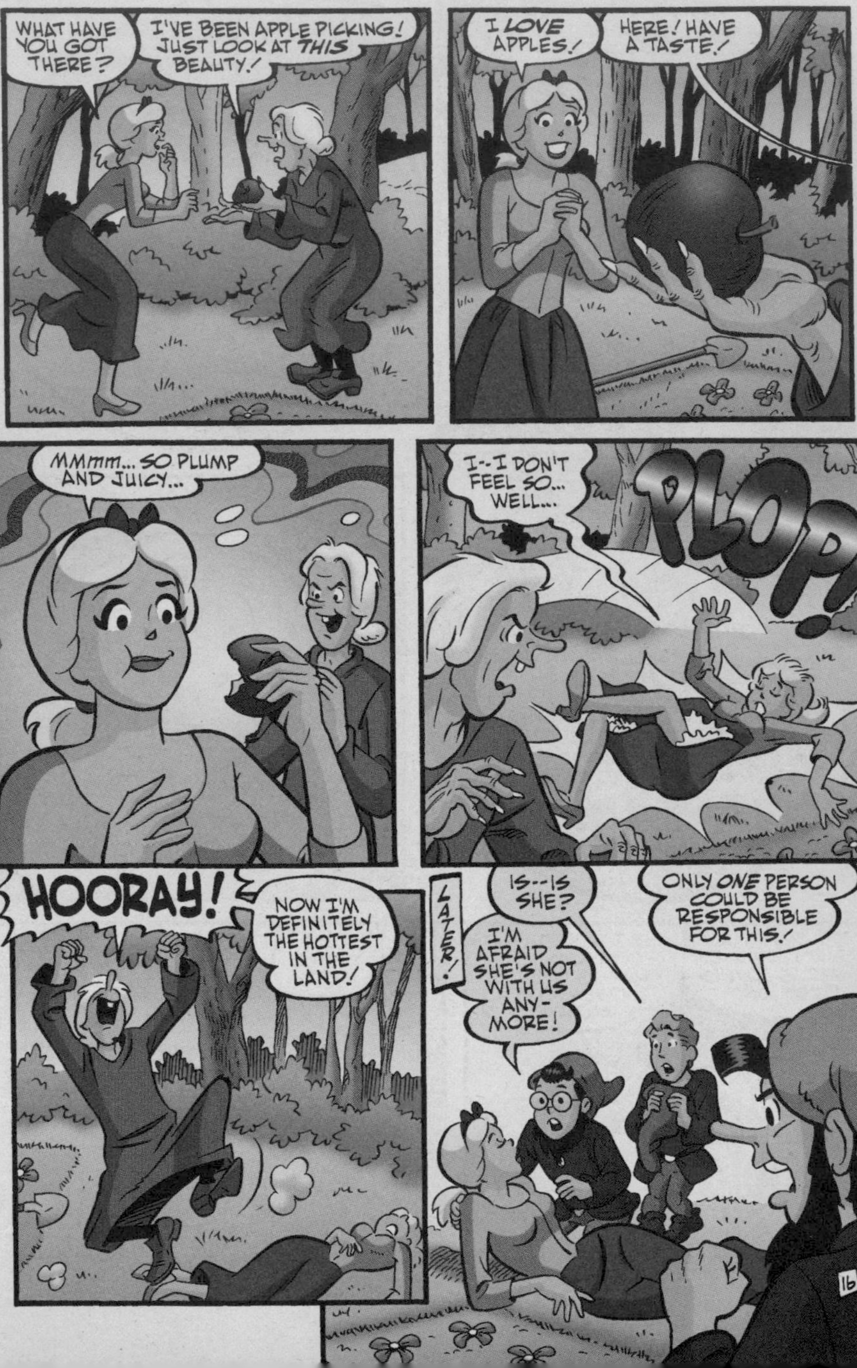
WHAT HAVE YOU GOT THERE?
I'VE BEEN APPLE PICKING! JUST LOOK AT THIS BEAUTY!
I LOVE APPLES!
HERE! HAVE A TASTE!
MMmm... SO PLUMP AND JUICY...
I--I DON'T FEEL SO... WELL...
PLOP!
HOORAY!
NOW I'M DEFINITELY THE HOTTEST IN THE LAND!
LATER!
IS--IS SHE?
I'M AFRAID SHE'S NOT WITH US ANY-MORE!
ONLY ONE PERSON COULD BE RESPONSIBLE FOR THIS!
16

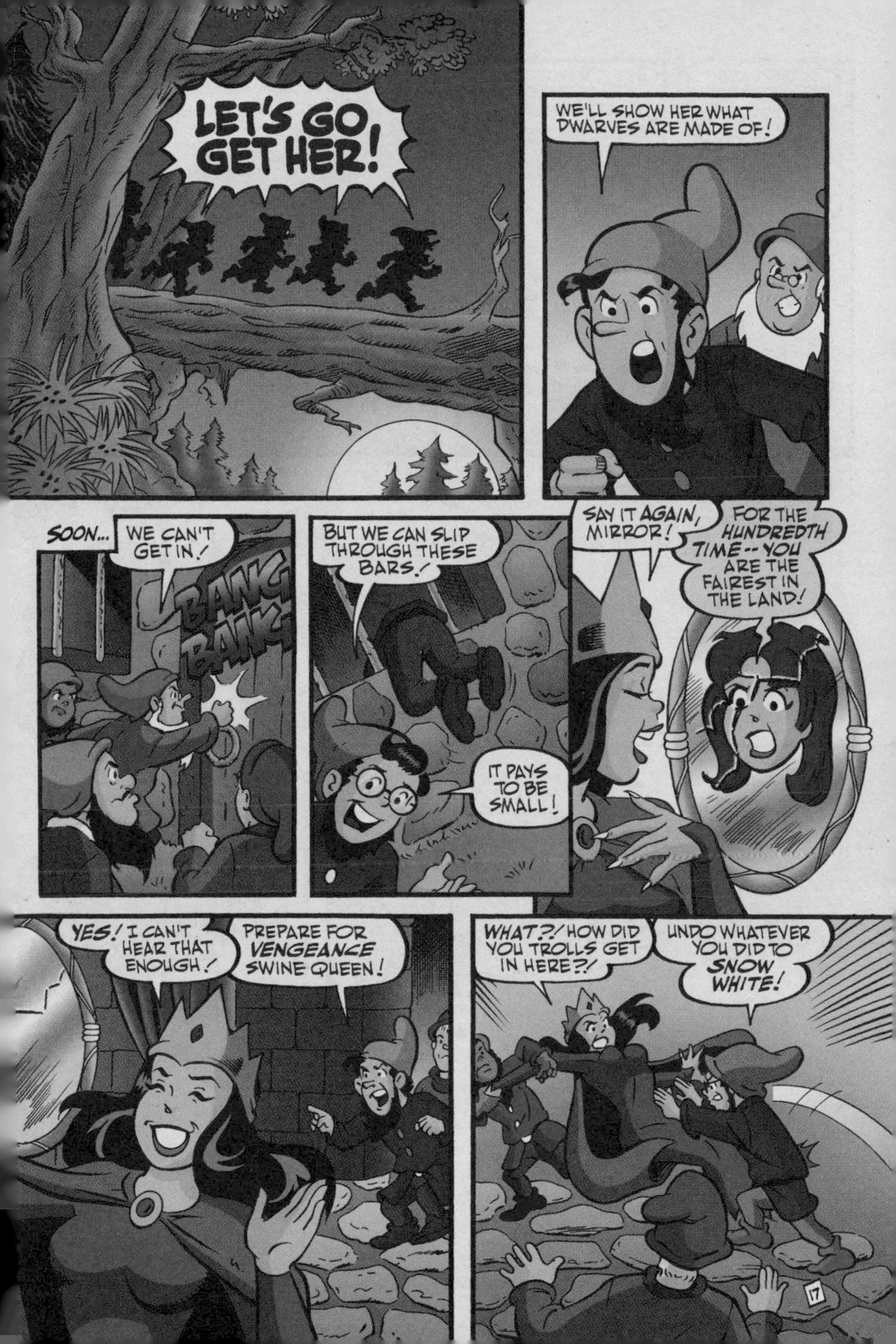

LET'S GO GET HER!
WE'LL SHOW HER WHAT DWARVES ARE MADE OF!
SOON...
WE CAN'T GET IN!
BANG BANG
BUT WE CAN SLIP THROUGH THESE BARS!
IT PAYS TO BE SMALL!
SAY IT AGAIN, MIRROR!
FOR THE HUNDREDTH TIME -- YOU ARE THE FAIREST IN THE LAND!
YES! I CAN'T HEAR THAT ENOUGH!
PREPARE FOR VENGEANCE SWINE QUEEN!
WHAT?! HOW DID YOU TROLLS GET IN HERE?!
UNDO WHATEVER YOU DID TO SNOW WHITE!

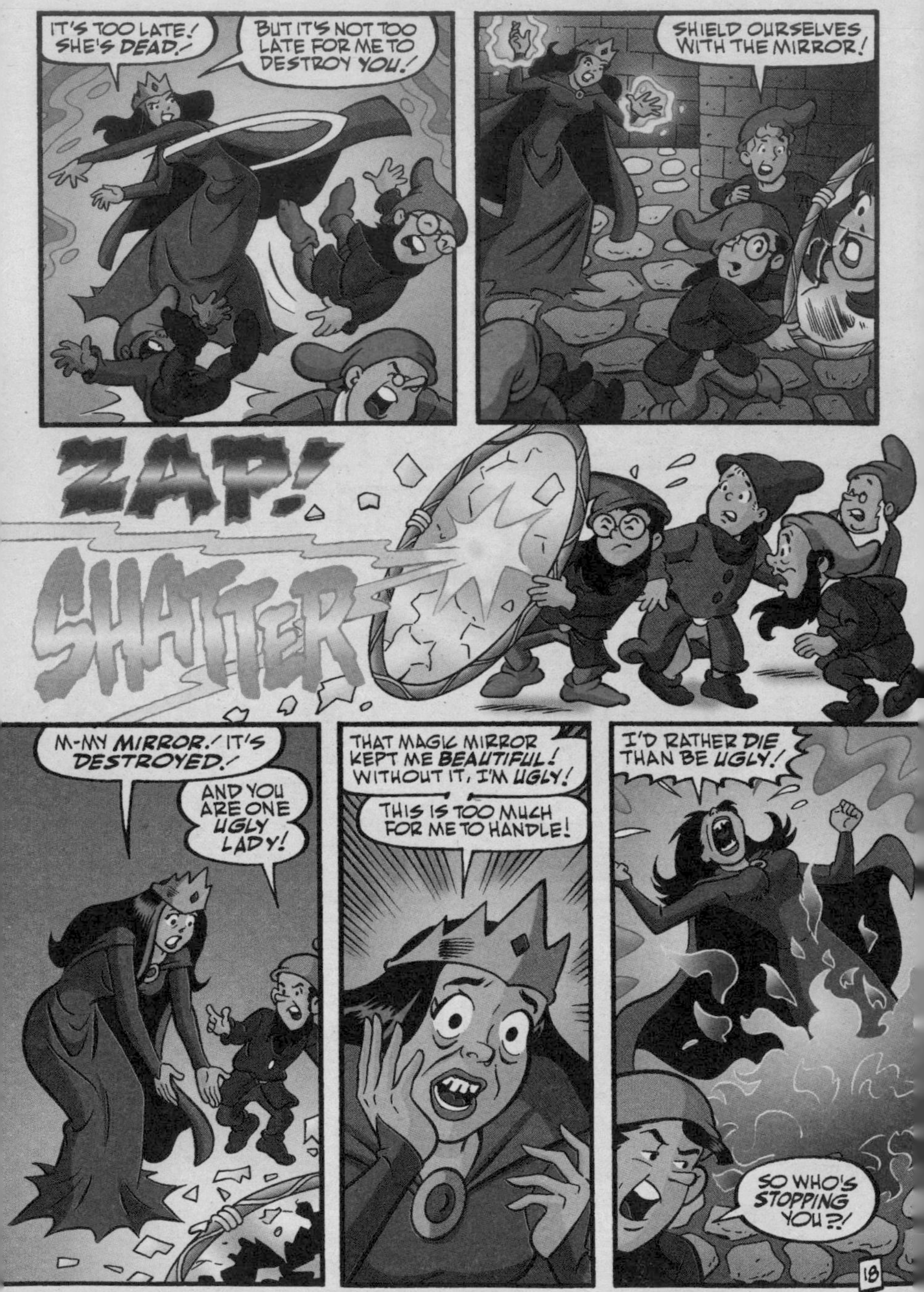
IT'S TOO LATE! SHE'S DEAD!
BUT IT'S NOT TOO LATE FOR ME TO DESTROY YOU!
SHIELD OURSELVES WITH THE MIRROR!
ZAP!
SHATTER
M-MY MIRROR! IT'S DESTROYED!
AND YOU ARE ONE UGLY LADY!
THAT MAGIC MIRROR KEPT ME BEAUTIFUL! WITHOUT IT, I'M UGLY!
THIS IS TOO MUCH FOR ME TO HANDLE!
I'D RATHER DIE THAN BE UGLY!
SO WHO'S STOPPING YOU?!

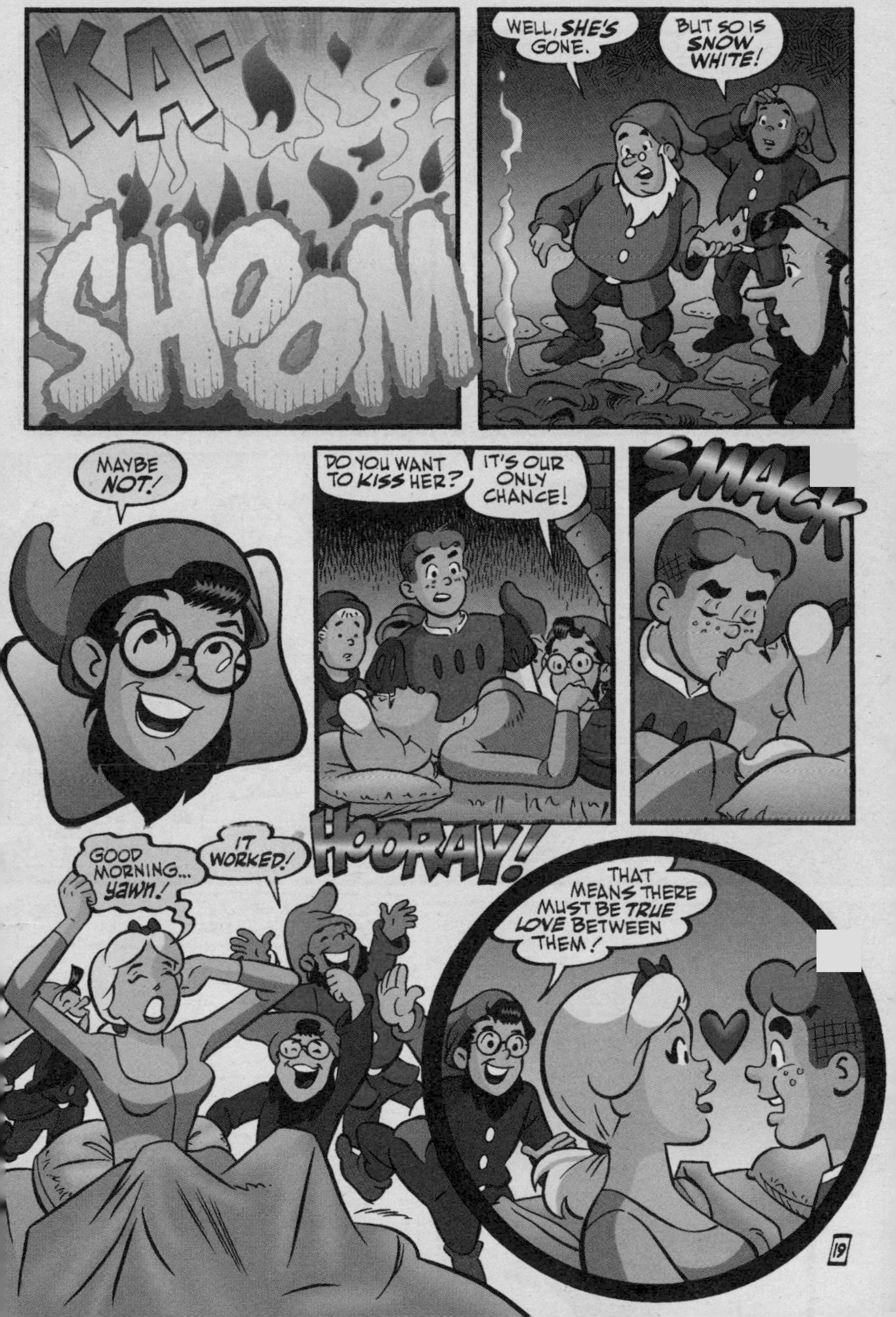
KA-SHOOM
WELL, SHE'S GONE.
BUT SO IS SNOW WHITE!
MAYBE NOT!
DO YOU WANT TO KISS HER?
IT'S OUR ONLY CHANCE!
SMACK
GOOD MORNING... yawn!
IT WORKED!
HOORAY!
THAT MEANS THERE MUST BE TRUE LOVE BETWEEN THEM!

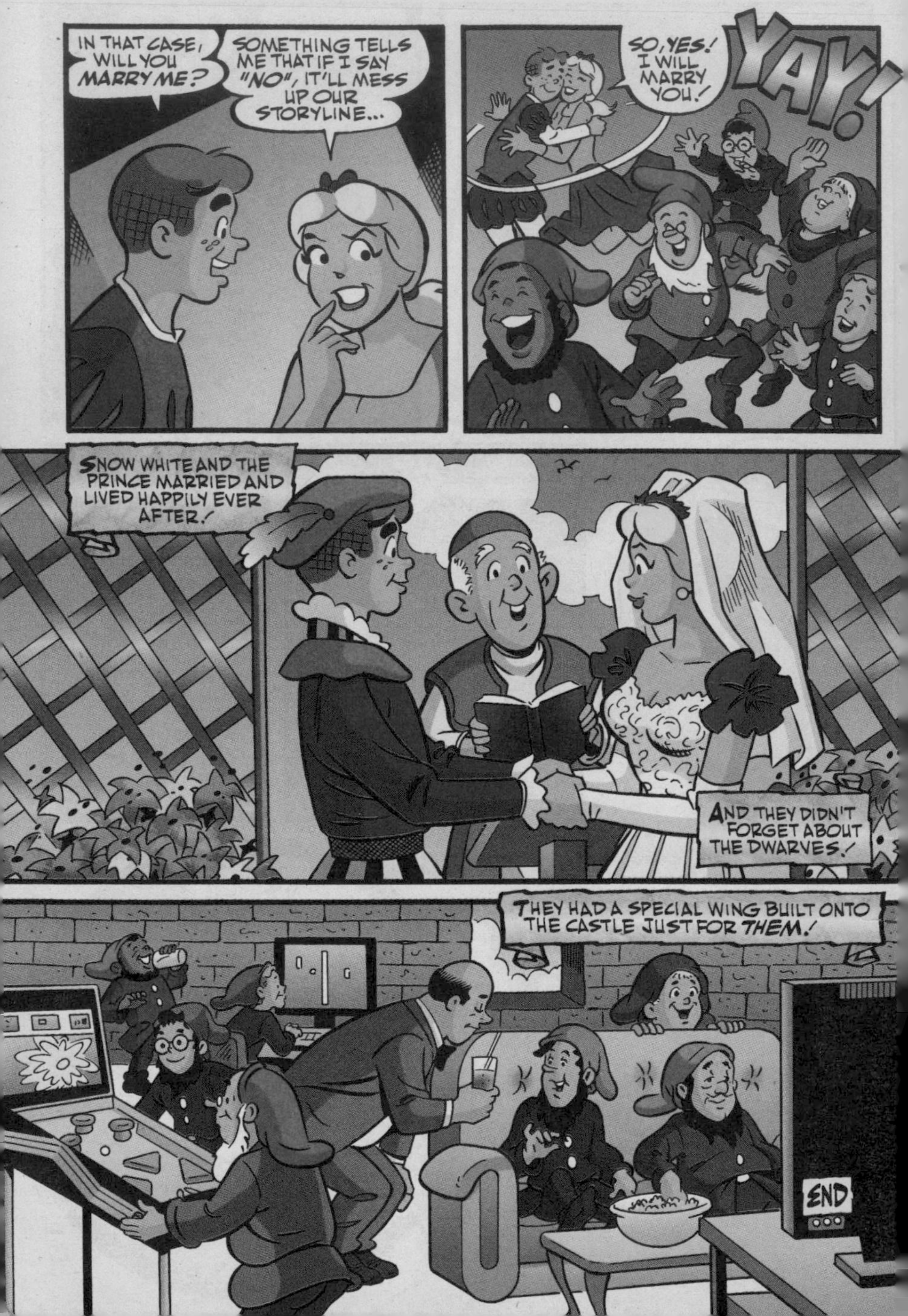
IN THAT CASE, WILL YOU MARRY ME?
SOMETHING TELLS ME THAT IF I SAY "NO", IT'LL MESS UP OUR STORYLINE...
SO, YES! I WILL MARRY YOU!
YAY!
SNOW WHITE AND THE PRINCE MARRIED AND LIVED HAPPILY EVER AFTER!
AND THEY DIDN'T FORGET ABOUT THE DWARVES!
THEY HAD A SPECIAL WING BUILT ONTO THE CASTLE JUST FOR THEM!
END